Charlotte's Wedding

Charlotte's Wedding

A single dad, teacher, brother's friend, instalove, alpha male, romantic suspense book.

Heart's Destiny Book 5

Leah Mae Wright

Copyright

Contents

Dedication

To Uncle Ray. Though I know you'll never share your stories of your time undercover with the DEA, I want to thank you for your selfless service to our country, both then and during your time in the military. It's my memories of how your appearance changed so much every time we visited you, to the point that I didn't always recognize you at first, that inspired me to write about an undercover agent going through a similar transformation. Hopefully, if you ever read this book to see the character you inspired me to have go by his middle name, you'll appreciate that being a former undercover agent and going by his middle name are the only traits I based on you. And maybe skip reading the sex scenes, so neither one of us have to be embarrassed next time we see each other. Love you!

Introduction

Former DEA agent Michael Ian Campbell struggled with civilian life after leaving the agency when his wife, Mari, was killed after blowing his cover with the Rodriguez Cartel. He'd gone in with the alias of Michael Smith, trying to get the intel needed to bring down the infamous drug ring. He'd worked his way up to only a couple of levels down from the ringleader, Roberto "Rojo" Rodriguez, when Mari posted a picture of him with their son, Brody, on social media, identifying him as her husband. He barely made it out alive the day he and his family were ambushed in a drive-by ordered by Rojo to take him out.

With his cover blown and Brody now motherless, he retired from the DEA and scrubbed all records of Michael Campbell from existence, so he could safely raise his son with the help of his sister, Cait. As a parting gift, the agency created a new identity for him, using only his middle and last name. In exchange for the anonymity, Ian used his new job as a high school English teacher to funnel information back to his former partner on the lower-level drug dealers in and around the San Diego schools. Until the day he got word that Rojo Rodriguez had escaped, when the rest of the major players in his cartel were captured in a raid in South Texas, that is. With limited resources keeping the DEA and local law enforcement from having someone in Heart's Destiny, Texas, actively looking for the cartel kingpin, Ian moved there with his family to capture the man responsible for his wife's death.

Charlotte Burleson didn't know the new English teacher she had to work with was actually a friend of her brother, Jake, and a former undercover DEA agent. She only knew him as a one-night stand she thought she'd never see again, and the most infuriating man she'd ever met.

After the most intense sexual experience of her life, Charlotte woke up to an empty bed with no information on how to contact the mysterious Ian for another round. Two weeks later, he showed up at her family's late Christmas celebration and acted as if they'd never met. He continued the charade of not knowing her when he started working in the classroom next door to hers at the beginning of January.

Ian wasn't sure how to deal with finding out the hot-as-hell one-night stand he had on the night he interviewed for his new job was with the sister of a man he'd worked with on a joint task force a few years back and considered a friend. He had to keep his cover and not let on to anyone in town that he knew Jake Burleson before moving there. Not to mention the fact that he couldn't tell his friend Jake that he'd slept with his sister. So, when the owner of the bed and breakfast, where he and his family were staying until their rental was available for them to move, insisted on taking them to a late Christmas celebration, Ian pretended he'd never met Jake or Charlotte.

When he started work and realized he was supposed to coordinate the seventh-grade lesson plans with her, Ian couldn't resist pushing her buttons to get a glimpse of the fiery passion he'd seen on their one night together. But even as hot as his time with Charlotte was, he couldn't risk getting burned if Rojo Rodriguez caught wind of his presence in town and went after her, the way he had Mari.

As danger loomed, the couple fought their instant attraction and growing connection, not realizing that standing together was the only way they could win in the end.

DISCLAIMER: This single dad, teacher, brother's friend, instalove, alpha male, romantic suspense book contains references to past gun violence and child abuse, as well as the kidnapping and rescue of a main character, profanity, and graphic sex scenes. It is intended for adult readers (18+) who are not easily offended.

Saturday, October 20, 2018

Charlotte Burleson had just finished grading the seventh-grade spelling tests she'd given her afternoon classes the day before when her cell phone rang on the desk beside her. She was surprised to see her youngest brother's name on the screen when she picked it up. Since he was off flying the GWA plane across the country for the next few days, after spending the last week in Heart's Destiny getting engaged and moving his new family into the house on the ranch beside their parents, she didn't expect to talk to him again until he came home to the ranch for his time off in a few days.

"Yo, Bro, what's up?" Charlotte wasn't sure why he'd called from wherever he was working, but she knew he'd be in a good mood since his fiancée and stepdaughters had wiped away the depression he'd been in since leaving the Navy.

"Calling to pick your brain," Anthony joked, his smile evident in his tone, even though she couldn't see him through the phone. "I have you on speaker, so Kay, Tia, and Dan, the company education coordinator, can all hear you. Do you know anything about the acceleration process for gifted students in Heart's Destiny?"

"Yeah, we give the tests four times a year," Charlotte replied automatically. "With the outdated school board still insisting that kids have to be six to start kindergarten, so they can keep them in school until they're nineteen or twenty, as if they were still needed to work the farms and ranches in the area, we have a lot of kids that try to accelerate, so they can graduate at eighteen like the rest of the country. Why do you need to know about those tests?"

"Tia tested above the twelfth-grade level when we administered her placement tests for our online modules last week," explained a voice that Charlotte assumed was Dan. "In order to prevent her from being bored with assignments that are way below her level, I suggested we accelerate her, so she can start college classes next semester."

"Can you schedule Tia to test with your other eighth-grade students the next time you administer the test?" Anthony sounded hopeful as he made the request.

"I'll have to get permission from the principal since she's not enrolled here." Charlotte was pretty sure Lisa Walker wouldn't have a problem with Tia coming to school for a week to test, but she wasn't sure if they might have to convince the school board to allow it since Tia wasn't actually enrolled in their school, or even an official resident of their town yet. "But I'm pretty sure we can do that. The next round of testing is scheduled for the week of December tenth. Are ya'll home that week?"

"Um, let me check." Charlotte heard the clacking of keys and knew her brother was checking his schedule on his computer. "No, we'll be in Maine, New Hampshire, Vermont, New York, and Massachusetts that week."

"Seriously?" Charlotte couldn't fathom how anyone could handle the GWA schedule. The thought of that much travel made her skin crawl. "Your schedule is insane. But no worries, Tia can stay here in Heart's Destiny with me that week, so she doesn't have to miss the testing."

"Thanks, Aunt Charlotte!" Tia squealed in excitement. "We have to wait until after that week to convince her to come be our language arts tutor."

"What was that?" Charlotte wasn't sure she really wanted Tia to repeat herself, but her voice had gotten quieter, so she could have possibly heard her wrong. *Geez, I hope I heard her wrong. There's no way I'd go to work with the GWA.*

"We're looking for a couple of teachers to join us, so we can cover all the different subjects and grade levels, and Tia suggested you for one of the open positions," Dan replied.

"Sorry, kiddo," Charlotte nervously chuckled. "Ya'll can keep flying off all over the world, but I'll keep my feet firmly planted on the ground here in Heart's Destiny."

"Yeah, I didn't think you'd be interested." Anthony's tone was placating, letting Charlotte know he wouldn't try to push her, no matter what his stepdaughters wanted.

"But if you know of any teachers looking to travel, they're looking for both language arts and history," Kay interjected, giving her an option for helping them without having to leave her comfort zone of home.

Yeah, I can probably pass the opportunity on to a couple of people I know who might be interested, Charlotte thought, grateful her brother had gotten so lucky as to find his Kay. Even barely knowing her, Charlotte already knew she fit in their family as if she'd always been a Burleson.

"And we'd all prefer it if they wouldn't flirt with our husbands all the time," a strange female voice chimed in.

"I take it that's been a problem before today?" Kay sounded like she was questioning her friend, so Charlotte didn't say a word in response.

"Oh, yeah, why do you think Matt and Jeff don't ever come to the classroom?" another strange female voice asked.

"They don't have to spend those three hours rehearsing every day," the first strange voice explained. "But they still go to the ring to spar, even when they aren't booked to wrestle that night, so they can avoid Stacy. Same with most of the guys."

"But with two dozen kids, spanning the grades from kindergarten to eighth grade, and Dan and Ivy specializing in science and math, we can't get rid of her until we find a replacement," the second strange voice continued.

"Sounds like ya'll have a definite need for some good teachers." Charlotte shook her head, glad she didn't have the drama going on at her school that they seemed to have in the GWA. "So, even though I don't know who all of ya'll are, I'll keep my ears open for anyone who might be interested in teaching and flying all over the world."

"Sorry, Sis," Anthony apologized. "I should have introduced you to Jana and Emily, since they're sitting at the table with us."

"Nice to meet you, Jana and Emily," Charlotte chuckled at her brother's nonchalant response. "Now, Bro, I'm going to let you go, so I can call my principal and make sure Tia's testing won't be an issue. I'll see ya'll next week when you get home."

They said their goodbyes and Charlotte called Lisa Walker to get the ball rolling on the arrangements for Tia to test with her students in December. After that, she put away her things for school on Monday and made her way out to the stables to spend some time with her favorite horse, Westley.

Riding Westley was all the adventure Charlotte could handle in her life. She was exceptionally careful whenever she rode him, since the accident she'd had when she was thirteen, when she was knocked off his back by a low-hanging branch that she didn't see from running him too fast on the trail.

She didn't remember actually hitting her head on the branch, or how she hung upside down from the stirrup until Westley made enough noise to attract the ranch manager to rescue her, since she was unconscious. But she did remember the lessons about avoiding dangerous situations her mother and Memmaw Judy drilled into her while she was recovering from the concussion and stuck in the house with them while her siblings and cousins were off running around the ranch.

She had taken those lessons to heart. And not just when riding the horse she'd had since he was a foal, who saved her life that day by stopping on a dime and neighing for help.

She mostly stayed in the small town where she grew up, not wanting to venture out to larger cities, where there was more crime and reckless drivers, if she could avoid it. She had to move to Austin for college, but she stayed on campus the whole time. Instead of going out with friends on the weekends, she drove home to Heart's Destiny to stay safe.

There were times when she had to go into San Antonio, which was the nearest major city to her small hometown. But she made sure to only go in daylight hours when she had to go alone and only went out there at night with a friend or family member. Even when she went looking for a one-night stand to satisfy her feminine needs, she started the evening with a girlfriend, and she didn't go off with her guy for the night until she felt comfortable enough with them to know she'd be safe. Needless to say, those encounters were few and far between.

She knew her more adventurous family members didn't understand her lack of desire to travel, especially her younger siblings. But she hoped the way Kay had offered her suggestion earlier, for Charlotte to pass the word along about the teacher jobs with the GWA to other teachers she knew, instead of pushing for her to apply, meant she would at least help Anthony understand her homebody ways a little more.

As she and Westley meandered along her favorite trail through the middle of the ten-thousand-acre ranch where she was raised, Charlotte cleared her mind of any residual anxiety that had been brought up by the suggestion of her working in a traveling job. Instead, she focused on how happy she was for her youngest brother as he embarked on the next phase of life. He had suffered through some tragic losses in his life and deserved all the love and happiness he'd recently found with Kay and her daughters.

While she was out away from the watchful eyes of her family, though, she could also admit to herself that she was a little jealous that he'd found the love of his life already. She was three-and-a-half years older than him and had absolutely no prospects on the horizon for her happily ever after.

She'd had a plan for her life since she was in high school, complete with a timeline for meeting the man of her dreams while she was in college, getting married by the age of twenty-five, and having babies by the time she turned thirty. Her plan had been so detailed, she even included the timeline for each event in the wedding planning book she did as a project in her home economics class in ninth grade.

She still had the notebook in her closet with pictures of all the flowers, decorations, and other items she wanted for her wedding. She hoped to one day be able to use all those ideas from when she was fifteen to have her dream wedding, especially the strapless wedding dress she envisioned wearing when she married the man of her dreams.

She was less than three months away from her twenty-ninth birthday and hadn't hit a single one of her personal life goals. She hadn't had nearly as much of a plan for her professional goals until the end of her sophomore year of college, and she'd hit every single one of those. So, Charlotte was starting to wonder if she should have reevaluated her romantic and family planning goals at least once in the ten years since her senior year of high school, when she set them in stone in her mind after refining them throughout the rest of her high school years.

"Oh, Memmaw Judy, I wish you were still here to offer your words of wisdom," Charlotte whispered to the winds rustling through the trees she was riding Westley through.

Charlotte was sixteen when she lost her paternal grandmother. As the first Burleson granddaughter of her generation, Charlotte always felt a special connection to her grandma that none of her siblings or cousins seemed to share. Even as a baby, she spent more time with Memmaw Judy than the other kids.

Anytime Memmaw Judy wasn't busy with cooking for the ranch hands and the family, she'd take Charlotte off somewhere on the land and tell her stories about growing up in Oklahoma. While she also taught Charlotte to cook alongside her mother and Aunt Susan, Memmaw Judy always seemed to delve deeper into the stories she told whenever she and Char were alone.

She shared the wisdom of life passed down from her Native American ancestors, along with more than a few fanciful stories to keep Charlotte's creative mind occupied. Charlotte wished she'd thought to record her stories to share with future generations. Or, at least, to have to listen to when she missed her memmaw.

"I guess I'll have to try to imagine what you'd say to me instead," Charlotte sighed. "It'd probably be something about not trying to do God's job for him by planning out my life. Maybe something about being patient and waiting for His plan to reveal itself to me."

Westley curved around the pond that signaled the turn back toward the stables without Charlotte having to do anything to guide him. They'd taken this ride so many times over the years that Westley could probably walk this trail blindfolded.

"I know you always said I couldn't plan to fall in love, Memmaw. That it'll happen when it's meant to happen, and probably when I'll least expect it. But if you wouldn't mind putting in a good word for me with the Great Spirit to let Him know I'm ready, I'd appreciate it. And if you could also ask Him to get Mom to stop pushing me toward dating the same guys she's tried to get me to date since I was a teenager, that'd be awesome."

As she made her way back to the stable to take care of her equine best friend, Charlotte imagined her memmaw smiling down from Heaven and laughing at her mom's misguided attempts at matchmaking. And maybe even searching the world to hand-pick Charlotte's future groom.

With Memmaw Judy working on finding my Mr. Right from Heaven, maybe I'll get to break out that book of wedding plans to plan my dream wedding before I turn thirty. Charlotte chuckled at her whimsical wish, knowing it wasn't realistically possible.

~~~

Thursday, November 29, 2018

Ian Campbell bolted upright in bed as an alert went off on his secure satellite phone, awakening him at one in the morning. He looked down at his phone in shock at the text message he saw from his former partner in the DEA.

Jones: #2 captured. Cartel crumbling. Rojo in the wind.

Rojo, the masculine form of the word red in Spanish. The code name given to Roberto Rodriguez for the amount of blood on his hands as the head of the Rodriguez Cartel. The man that Ian and his former partner, Trent Jones, had been trying to capture for the last eight years. The man responsible for the untimely death of Ian's wife, Mari.

It was four days before the two-year anniversary of her death and Ian still struggled with the loss. He'd left the DEA immediately after, needing to be home to raise their son, Brody, without worrying about his safety constantly while working to hunt down the most dangerous drug dealers in the country.

Now he taught high school English Literature in one of the more impoverished schools in San Diego, so he could stay relatively safe while feeding info to his former partner about the lower-level dealers that would, hopefully, lead the DEA to the higher-ups.

Needing more information, Ian quickly typed out a message to his former partner.

Campbell: When? Where? Last sighting?
~~~

**Jones: Late last night. Bust in a small Texas town. Rojo
was last seen here but escaped the raid.**

Campbell: Leaving agents there to watch for him?

**Jones: No can do. Resources too thin & agents would
stick out like a sore thumb in this town.**

Campbell: Local LEO notified?

**Jones: Yes, but HDPD is too small to put a man on it full-
time. They're keeping watch. Will call me if Rojo
spotted.**

Campbell: How small is too small?

**Jones: So small the chief had to be the one to stay with us
for the stakeout.**

Jones: 8 total 6 cops + receptionist & dispatcher.

**Campbell: Damn, that is small. How'd they ever get
looped in on the investigation?**

**Jones: Chief spotted suspicious activity. Called his bro in
Naval Intelligence. His bro called me. Remember Jake
Burleson from that joint task force 3 years back?**

Campbell: The computer whiz?

Ian remembered Jake Burleson as an affable guy that he'd become
fast friends with while on a task force to bring down a drug ring that
was targeting naval officers at the base in San Diego to find partners to
move their products into the US without having to go through customs.
They'd had a few common interests, especially their favorite video

game. Ian hated that he'd lost contact with Jake when he'd left the
DEA after Mari died.

Jones: Yep. Rojo set up in his hometown.

Campbell: Any chance Jake will be heading home to keep
watch?

Jones: Just left from being here for another brother's
wedding. Plans to be back at Christmas, but he's
working on a major case in DC and can't stay.

Campbell: Fuck, we need someone who can be there full
time to watch for Rojo.

Jones: WE? You planning on putting a badge back on &
just haven't told me yet?

Campbell: You know I can't do that. I have to be here for
Brody. It's bad enough I'm having to leave him with
Cait during the day to work. I can't ask her to raise him
while I'm working 24/7 in a job I might not come home
from.

Jones: No, but maybe you could move to TX to keep an
eye out while teaching like you are now.

Campbell: Jake's hometown is big enough for a school?

Jones: 3 of 'em. Elementary, Middle, and High School.

Campbell: Check for openings in the English departments
while you're there & send me the info to apply. Look
in the surrounding cities too, if no openings there.

Jones: Will do.

"I must be fucking crazy to think moving my sister and son to Podunk Ville, Texas is a good plan for catching Rodriguez," Ian swore, tossing his phone back on his bedside table before rolling over to try to get a few more hours of sleep. He needed as much sleep as possible before going to teach a bunch of rowdy tenth graders all about Shakespeare, when they'd rather read comic books.

On his way home from school that evening, Ian's phone rang with a call from an unknown number. Knowing how few people actually had his secure phone number, he answered, assuming it was someone who got his number from his former partner or boss at the DEA.

"Campbell." Ian barked out the generic greeting.

"Dude, you're gonna have to relax a little, and go with a more normal greeting of hello, if you wanna fit in when you move to Heart's Destiny," the deep voice with a strong Texas drawl chuckled through the phone.

"Heart's Destiny?" Ian questioned, not recognizing the name of what he assumed was a town.

"Yeah, my hometown. The one Trent called and said you wanted to move to." Ian finally recognized the voice on the phone as Jake Burleson, when his middle-of-the-night text conversation with Trent came back to him.

"Sorry, Jake, didn't recognize your voice at first." Ian relaxed a little while silently berating himself for not immediately linking his text conversation in the wee hours of the morning with the unknown caller. *Damn, I'm getting sloppy in my mental connections since leaving the DEA.* "I didn't actually get the town name from Jones when he texted me at one a.m., so you mentioning it threw me off for a second."

"Yeah, I was confused when he told me you were looking for a job as an English teacher there, too." Jake roared with laughter. "But once he explained you leaving the DEA while still wanting to help out with the Rojo case, it made a lot more sense. And it just so happens, I know of an opening for an English teacher you might be interested in."

"Seriously?" Ian shook his head, slightly taken aback that there was actually an opening in the area where Rodriguez was probably still hiding out.

"Yeah, one of my sisters teaches English at the middle school." Jake's voice sounded a little more serious than his earlier jovial tone. "My baby brother told her about a job opening teaching with the wrestling company he works with, but she has no interest in flying around the world, so she passed the info on to the other middle school English teacher. Now Fiona is leaving for a new job after Christmas break, and Heart's Destiny Middle School needs an English teacher who can start when school resumes in January. Seemed like perfect timing for what you need. And it'll put my mind at ease to know you're in the classroom right next door to my sister, with Rojo possibly still being in town. Not that I expect him to try to make a move on the middle school, but with my oldest brother, Bobby, being the police chief that spotted his organization and led the feds to his door, I worry about my family being targeted to get revenge on Bobby."

"You know I wouldn't be going there to babysit your sister." Ian already had a hard enough time keeping his own sister safe. He didn't need to add babysitting Jake's sister to his overly full plate.

"Oh, yeah, I know that." Jake almost sounded like he was backtracking on his earlier statements. "Neither one of my sisters would ever allow anyone to babysit them. But it never hurts to have an extra set of eyes watching out for guys like Rojo when they aren't on the ranch."

"Let me guess, you have cameras on them when they're on the ranch?" Ian imagined Jake was as protective of a brother with his sisters as Ian was with Caitir.

"Not as many as I'd like," Jake laughed. "Naw, I know they're safe when they're on the ranch because they have access to their own weapons, in addition to having the rest of my family and all the ranch hands to watch out for trespassers. My sisters might look like sweet southern belles, but they were raised with four brothers, so they're more than equipped to defend themselves. The same goes for my female cousins, even though they only have two brothers. All of us guys tried to make sure the girls were tough enough to defend themselves before they went off to college. Well, with maybe the exception of my baby brother, Anthony, but that's only because the girls were all older than him and treated him more like a baby doll when he was a baby than a brother or cousin, so they wouldn't really listen to him as teenagers."

"So, if I move down there and things get sticky…" Ian's voice trailed off as he pondered the possibilities of the potential danger if he decided to move with his sister and son in tow. "I could send my sister and son to the Burleson Ranch to keep them safe?"

"Absolutely!" Jake's tone turned serious once again. "In fact, I can probably call my folks and arrange for ya'll to have a place to stay there on the ranch if you want."

"No, that's not necessary." Ian didn't want to impose on the other man's family any more than he wanted to babysit them. "In fact, it's probably best if you don't tell anyone you know me if we run into each other in town. I want to try to stay under the radar as much as possible, which means avoiding any questions about how we know each other that could lead to my former status as an agent coming out and spooking Rojo."

"You don't think he'll recognize your name?" Jake sounded suspicious. "Or are you coming in with an alias?"

"He only knew me under the alias Mike Smith. He might have figured out my last name, but Campbell is a relatively common surname." Ian fought off the flashbacks of his family being targeted after Mari posted a picture of him on social media. Even though his name wasn't listed in any way, real or alias, she used her married name on the site. Since his family was targeted at a local park that Mari had tagged in one of her check-ins on the social site, Ian didn't believe Rojo, or his underlings, had completely figured out his true identity. They probably just staked out the park for the next time he went there and got lucky enough to find the whole family gathered for Brody's second birthday. "And when I left the agency, I quit using my first name and had everything about Michael Campbell erased from existence. I doubt he'll figure out Ian Campbell is the same person, even if he figured out my real last name from Mari being online as Mari Campbell."

"Let's hope for the sake of your family, and mine, you're right," Jake replied somberly.

"I'm right." Ian smirked, even though his friend wouldn't see it through the phone. "So, who do I have to contact to apply for this job?"

"I'll send you an email with all the details." Jake's jovial mood returned. "Along with contact information for my brother, the police chief, and the local real estate office, so you can find a house when you come for the interview. Anything else you need from me?"

"Just any details about the bust you can pass along." Ian's mind was whirling with tasks he needed to complete to get everything set up. "Maybe site maps of the area, and the drug hot spots in the closest major city. Oh, and options for a TOC that isn't at my house with my sister and son."

"You got it."

They signed off the call, and Ian braced himself for how to break the news of their move to his little sister.

Fuck! I hope this move doesn't cause any setbacks for Caitir. As much as Ian worried about his sister, he knew catching Rojo Rodriguez was the only thing he could do to truly put her mind at ease. *But even if she has a setback or two at first, knowing he's finally behind bars, or dead, will ultimately set her free from the fear she lives with every day.*

Chapter One

After dropping her niece, Tia, off at the small airport where Anthony kept his plane, Charlotte Burleson ran late for what would probably be her last girls' night out with her best friend, Fiona Harrison. *Well, unless we sneak one in when she's home for the holidays after she starts her new job.*

Growing up in the small town of Heart's Destiny, Texas, Charlotte had known Fiona Harrison for as long as she could remember. But with Fiona being a year younger than Charlotte, they didn't become close until Fiona started teaching at the same school as Charlotte four-and-a-half years before.

Now, they not only worked together daily and coached the middle school softball team together every spring, but they also hung out quite often outside of their time at school. Every month, they spent at least one or two Friday nights together between their monthly book club meetings and their once-every-month-or-two girls' nights, when they each rented a hotel room in San Antonio, so they could drink in the hotel bar and not have to drive home. Then they'd spend their Saturdays volunteering at the shelter in San Antonio that the Heart's Destiny Community Church sponsored.

Since Fiona was leaving town to travel with her new job at the beginning of the new year, Charlotte was going to miss her best friend. Life wasn't going to be the same without Fiona around to push Char into interacting with the world outside her family ranch.

She wasn't fond of stepping outside her comfort zone to go out often, so if it wasn't for Fiona being her wing woman, Charlotte wouldn't have had much of a romantic life in the last few years. It wasn't that she was a prude. In fact, she was quite the opposite, enjoying a healthy sex life, even if it was mostly through self-pleasure and the books she read.

Since dating in Heart's Destiny was an impossibility for her, Charlotte had enjoyed more than one hot hookup after girls' night over the last few years. It wasn't that Charlotte didn't want more than random one-night stands to satisfy her feminine needs. But the guys she met at the hotel bar, generally, weren't in town long enough for there to ever be more.

Not that she was as desperate for a long-term relationship as her mother was to marry her off, either. Oh, she wanted to get married, and preferably before she turned thirty, but only when she met her soulmate. She didn't want to settle for anything less than the great love she'd always heard about from everyone in her family. And she definitely didn't want to marry someone she could only see as a friend, which was what would happen if she went along with one of her mom's matchmaking schemes.

Her mother's constant matchmaking was actually starting to grate on Charlotte's nerves. She tried not to mind all that much when her mom sat her next to one of the local guys she'd grown up with at every church potluck and town gathering. Those she could typically handle because her brothers had told all the local guys that she was off-limits before she was even in high school. So, hanging out with them was more like adopting a dozen other brothers. It was her mother's recent attempts to pair her up with the GWA wrestlers that really irritated Charlotte. *Like I really want to date a guy I can only see when he comes to town for holidays five times a year.*

When she really thought about it, though, she didn't have very many other prospects for finding her future husband. Unless she suddenly decided to become a buckle bunny and chase the rodeo that came through town regularly, she was pretty much stuck with hoping to find him while out on girls' night with Fiona in San Antonio.

I guess asking Memmaw to help find my Mr. Right a couple of months ago was a bust. I'm sure that's even harder for her to do than curtailing Mom's matchmaking. And she hasn't exactly done a stellar job of that from Heaven. Ah, if only my loved ones in Heaven could actually act as my guardian angels and help a girl out.

Resigned to probably never finding true love the way her youngest brother had recently, Charlotte settled for scratching the itch once in a while with a random guy that would never know anything about her peaceful life on the ranch. She was too much of a homebody to maintain the outgoing persona men seemed to like best for more than a night every couple of months, anyway.

And I'm not even going to look for a one-time guy tonight, Charlotte thought as she parked at the hotel on the RiverWalk where she and Fiona were meeting. *Tonight's about celebrating my bestie's new job, not hooking up with a hottie.*

After checking in at the front desk, Charlotte dropped her bags in her room and didn't even bother freshening up before rushing back down to the bar to find her friend. *It's not like I got my clothes messed up while taking Tia to the airport after school. Had we messed around with the horses in between, yeah, I'd have needed to clean up and change, but I'm fine in my typical teacher wear.*

When she got to the bar, she noticed Fiona had a faraway look in her eyes. *I wonder if she's nervous about starting her new job? Or daydreaming about one of the wrestling hotties she's about to start working with?*

"You look deep in thought." Charlotte sat down at the bar beside Fiona, flagged down the bartender, and ordered a chardonnay to go along with the appetizers they were having for their dinner.

"Yeah, just trying to picture how I'm going to fit in on this new job." Fiona took a sip from her own glass.

"You'll fit in wonderfully." Char tried to reassure Fiona, knowing her outgoing friend was worried about nothing. "Just like you instantly fit in at the middle school."

"Yeah, but I already knew everyone at the middle school." Fiona shook her head, her expression pensive. "The only people with the GWA that I've had more than a brief interaction with are your brother and the Hunters. And with them being a couple of years younger than me, I'm not exactly friends with them."

"I'm sure you'll make friends quickly." Charlotte hoped to reassure her bestie. "You met Kay and her sister the week of the wedding. They're both super sweet and will introduce you to the ladies they've made friends with so far and will point out the ones to avoid. Although, I think the only one I've heard anything negative about from Kay is the woman you're replacing, so I'm sure you'll get along fine with everyone else. Though you might have your hands full with some of the wrestlers I met that week."

"What do you mean?" Fiona looked at Charlotte with a quizzical expression on her face.

"Some of the single guys can be over-the-top flirts." Charlotte shrugged before shaking her head to try and shake out the memories of the guys who'd low-key hit on her at Anthony and Kay's wedding events. "Much to my mother's delight in the way she was trying to fix Becky, Jen, Julie, and me up with them."

"Yeah, I did notice you seemed to be seated with them at every event I attended that week," Fiona giggled. "I was half surprised my mom wasn't teaming up with her to throw me in there with you. Well, until she and Dad gave my new boss the third degree about my safety while traveling with them."

"Girl, if we weren't a year apart in age, I'd wonder if we were switched at birth." Char chuckled at the confused look Fiona gave her. "My mom would gladly send me flying off with the GWA in the hopes I'd fall in love with one of the guys, when I'd rather stay in Heart's Destiny. And your folks would rather keep you safe at home, when you're the one wanting to fly off on an adventure."

"I guess it does seem like we got the wrong set of parents when you put it like that." Fiona grinned.

"So, having met a few of the guys already, were there any that you might be interested in breaking your dry spell with?" Charlotte knew her friend hadn't had sex since graduating college four-and-a-half years before, and really hoped she would find her Mr. Right in her new job.

"There were certainly a few who were attractive," Fiona admitted as Charlotte took a sip of her wine. "But you know me. It'll take a lot more than good looks to get me to break the dry spell."

"Yeah, I know." Charlotte knew Fiona was a lot more averse to one-night stands than she was. "But you're going to be traveling the world with them, so surely you'll get to know at least one or two of the guys well enough to go on a date or two, maybe more. I'm just wondering if any of them caught your eye to possibly be candidate number one."

Fiona took a large gulp of her wine, finishing off her glass. The flush of her cheeks seemed to be from more than just the wine. Her almost guilty expression told Charlotte a whole lot more than her non-answer.

"Oh, shit, girl!" Charlotte shouted. "Someone did pique your interest!"

"Not so loud." Fiona whisper-shouted, motioning for Charlotte to not speak so loudly. "I don't want to announce it to all of San Antonio."

"Sorry." Char lowered her voice to a more typical tone for a conversation in a noisy bar. "But I need the details."

"Fine, if you must know," Fiona whisper-shouted, shaking her head like she wasn't sure she should admit who she was attracted to or not. "My new boss, Rick."

"Seriously?" Charlotte shouted once again. "The DILF my mom kept trying to get me to talk to?"

"Don't call him that!" Fiona's blush deepened.

"Why not? If ever there was a man that description was made for, it's Rick Robertson. Just because I don't want to marry him and fly around the world with him like my mom wants, doesn't mean I'd kick him out of bed for a night or two." Charlotte raised an eyebrow, challenging Fiona to disagree with her statement. "You can't tell me he's the one guy you're attracted to and then not agree that he's a DILF."

"Fine!" Fiona threw up her hands in defeat. "I agree it's an apt description, but it's still too crass for me to say."

"Whatever." Charlotte chuckled at Fiona not even being willing to use the acronym for *Dad I'd Like to Fuck*. "Hanging around all that testosterone daily, I bet you'll be saying that and a whole lot worse by the time you come home for your first holiday break."

"I'll mostly be hanging around with children daily, so I'm sure I'll keep my language clean." Fiona disagreed, but chuckled along.

"So, what are the chances you'll say yes if Daddy Rick asks you out?" Charlotte flagged down the bartender for another round of chardonnay, just as the nachos and quesadillas they'd ordered to counteract the effects of the alcohol arrived.

"Oh, geez, Char." Fiona shook her head, but she was still smiling. "Don't call him that either. That sounds like something out of one of those books Kay recommended when you first brought her to book club."

"Of course it does." Char grinned as she lifted a cheese-covered chip from the plate of nachos. "Where do you think I got it from?" She wagged her eyebrows at Fiona as she popped the chip into her mouth.

Fiona shook her head, but she giggled once again as she lifted a triangle of her quesadilla to take a bite.

"But seriously, quit deflecting and answer the question." Charlotte pointed at Fiona with her newly filled wine glass. "Would you go out with him and give him a shot at breaking your dry spell?"

Charlotte watched as Fiona took another drink and appeared to be gathering her thoughts before speaking. She allowed Fiona the time to think while she took another bite of her nachos.

"Maybe," she finally shrugged, drawing the word out to multiple syllables as she went back to her meal. "But I don't think I can really call it a dry spell when just thinking about him makes my panties wet."

Charlotte choked on the drink of wine she'd just taken to wash down her food, accidentally spewing it on the bar from being so surprised at Fiona's words. "Well, I guess that's my answer," Char noted once she'd regained her composure from the shock of Fiona talking about her wet panties. She held up her glass to toast her friend's lowered inhibitions. "Here's to my beautiful friend, Fiona, taking Daddy Rick the DILF off the market in the new year!"

Fiona barked out a laugh, but she still clinked her glass with Charlotte's before they each finished off their second glass of wine and their dinners. They ordered a third round before Fiona turned the conversation to Charlotte's lack of a love life.

"So, what are the chances you'll finally find Mr. Right in the new year?" Fiona looked around the bar, as if Mr. Right could be somewhere in the room, just waiting for Charlotte to find him.

"Oh, I'm probably just going to stick with book boyfriends for another year." Charlotte waved off the thought of meeting Mr. Right, shaking her head. "Maybe I'll get Cassidy, Lexi, or Kayla to come out for a girls' night when I want to look for a one-off, but I'm not about to give Mom the satisfaction of marrying me off anytime soon." *At least, not to anyone she'd pick out for me.*

"You seriously weren't interested in any of the GWA guys?" Fiona took another sip of her chardonnay.

"Don't get me wrong, they were nice eye candy when they were in town." Char wagged her eyebrows suggestively as she flashed back to the hotties that had come to town for her brother's wedding. She'd have probably been up for a night with one of them in different circumstances, but not with her mom pushing for romance and her brother being friends with them. "But I didn't really feel a connection with any of them. Not that I need that connection for a one-time hookup, but I won't go there with anyone who works with my brother."

"I get it." Fiona nodded her head in agreement. "For anything long term, you want that connection like our parents have, and the couples have in all the romance novels we read."

"Gross! Don't mention our parents and romance novels in the same sentence." Charlotte gagged at the thought of her parents doing anything like she read about in romance novels. Even though she knew they had to have an active sex life to have six children, she wanted none of those images in her head. "For long term, I'd need the connection. But I wouldn't mind the passion of a romance novel for a night or two, even without the connection."

"Okay, if you could have a hot hookup with a real-life version of a passionate book hero, who would it be?" Fiona made Charlotte think back to the most recent series of books she'd read after Kay recommended them.

If she was thinking long term, her homebody self wouldn't have even considered one of the men in Lexi Blake's *Masters and Mercenaries* series. But since it was a fantasy for only a night, Charlotte immediately imagined the tall, blond Viking of a man that was always in way more danger than she'd ever want in real life. Between being dominant in the bedroom, or anywhere else he had sex with his wife, and having a hidden gooey center that would do anything for his family and friends, Ian Taggart was Charlotte's idea of hot, without even considering how handsome he was described as looking in those books. She also liked his sarcastic side, though she wouldn't admit it to anyone but herself for fear her friends might let it slip to her siblings, who would then show their sarcastic tendencies even more often.

"Ian Taggart," Charlotte stated matter-of-factly.

"That is definitely not whom I expected you to pick," Fiona giggled.

"No? Whom would you have thought I'd pick?"

"Someone more studious, like that librarian in the Pippa Grant series we read last year," Fiona replied.

"Yeah, I could see that." Charlotte nodded as she thought back to how hot she got for the character when she read the book about him. Truth be told, even her one-night stands had always been the studious type, guys she could maintain control with, who weren't imposing or intimidating in any way. "And if we were talking about forever together, I'd probably agree. But since you said it was only for a hot hookup, I figured I could handle the excitement of Ian for a night. I mean, the opportunity to spend the night in a dungeon being dominated by a Nordic God, former spy, is too rare to pass up. So, if I ever met a real-life Ian, I wouldn't be able to say no."

"I guess I can see your point," Fiona admitted, giggling. "And your name is Charlotte, so Ian certainly fits with you."

"Yeah, but I'm no Russian assassin, so I wouldn't have to worry about either of us falling in love." Charlotte giggled at the thought of herself ever comparing to one of the strong women in Lexi Blake's books, much less the most alpha female character in the series. *Although if it's really as good as Ian gives it to Charlotte in those books, I'm pretty sure I could fall in extreme lust pretty darn quick. And maybe he could bring out my more adventurous side that's been dormant since I was a kid. Or at the very least, the sarcastic side I hide most of the time.*

They talked some more about the books they wanted to read next and had to order another round of drinks before turning on their stools and scoping out the place to play their usual game of people-watching and making up stories for the strangers around them. It was something they did to keep their creative juices flowing, since neither one of them actually took up writing like they'd previously talked about doing when they got tired of teaching.

"One o'clock, blue dress, and bad toupee." Char pointed out a couple across the bar to start their game. "Go."

"Midlife crisis, hired a hooker for the night." Fiona slapped a hand over her mouth after saying it. Fiona always did that when she felt she was being too harsh in her assessment.

"You are so, one-hundred percent, right on that one," Charlotte laughed, hoping to ease her friend's guilty conscience.

"Ten o'clock, red dress between the two suits. Go." Fiona pointed out the next group of people for Charlotte to figure out their story.

"In town on business, and the two bosses are planning to share their secretary for the night." Charlotte pictured the threesome from one of the Lexi Blake books they were discussing earlier. "Far right corner, black dress, sitting alone."

"Oh, she looks sad." Fiona's empathy was apparent in her expression and softened tone of voice. "I bet she's here for work and missing her family back in Tupelo."

"Tupelo?" Charlotte chuckled. "You could pick any city in the world for the narrative, and you pick Tupelo, Mississippi?"

"It was the only place that popped into my head." Fiona shrugged.

"And I don't think she looks sad." Charlotte tilted her head to examine the woman more closely. "Though I could understand being sad if she actually lived in Tupelo."

"Quit picking on me about Tupelo and give me a better narrative." Fiona chuckled lightly and shook her head.

"She's bored, stuck here for work when she'd rather be somewhere like New York or Los Angeles, where she'd be the life of the party."

"I can see that," a deep voice on Charlotte's right said, causing her to turn in his direction to see who had spoken. "She's definitely bored, not sad."

Holy shit! It's like I imagined a night with Ian Taggart, and he showed up in the flesh! Although I always pictured Ian Taggart in head-to-toe black, the navy-blue slacks and button-down this guy is wearing are close enough. His hair is a little darker blond than I imagined for Ian, too, but it's definitely a shade lighter than my light brown. And those baby blue eyes are panty-melting.

"And not from Tupelo." Charlotte smiled at the stranger. *Yeah, maybe I will get lucky tonight, after all. Or maybe this is the butterfly feeling my mom, Aunt Susan, and Memmaw all described upon meeting* **The One**.

"Definitely not from Tupelo," the guy chuckled and extended his hand to Charlotte. She placed her hand in his to shake. "Name's Ian. Mind if I join in your game?"

No fucking way! He had to have been sitting here a while, heard our earlier conversation, and is now feeding me a fake name, Charlotte thought, turning to look at Fiona at the mention of his name. She tried to ask Fiona with her eyes how long the man had been sitting on the stool beside her, but Fiona didn't seem to be getting the message, just laughing in response.

"You are definitely welcome to join the game." Fiona seemed to struggle to get her laughter under control. "In fact, I think I'm going to let you take my turn. I have an early morning tomorrow and think it's time for me to head up to my room."

"Fiona!" Charlotte growled her name with her hand still clutched in Ian's, wishing her friend would give her a clue as to whether or not he was lying after overhearing them, or if it was fate that put her and Ian together for the night.

Did Memmaw actually find my Mr. Right and send him to me tonight? Surely, Memmaw wouldn't give me the love-at-first-sight butterflies for someone who's lying about whom he is because of overhearing my hot hookup, book-boyfriend fantasies earlier. Right?

Are these the love-at-first-sight butterflies everyone warned me about? They have to be. Right? The flutters I'm feeling when I look at him are like nothing I've ever felt before, so I'm sure they are the butterflies that even Kay has mentioned feeling when she first met my brother.

Maybe? But only if his name is really Ian, and he's not feeding me a line after hearing our conversation earlier. I don't think even Memmaw would give me butterflies for a guy who is feeding me a line.

"Yeah, I'm not going to stick around and be a third wheel on your once-in-a-lifetime opportunity." Fiona downed the last of her drink and tossed some cash on the bar to cover her tab. "I'll call before I leave in the morning to see if you're up for going with me. Night."

"Sorry, I didn't mean to run your friend off," Ian apologized, bringing Charlotte's attention back to him. He looked down at their joined hands before finally releasing hers.

"It's fine." Charlotte waved in the direction Fiona just walked away. "I'll deal with her tomorrow."

"Do you need to go, so you can get up early tomorrow, too?" Ian looked at her like he really hoped she didn't, but he would let her go if she wanted to call it a night.

"I, uh," Charlotte stuttered out. Part of her wanted to head up to her room because she was planning to get up early the next day to go volunteer at the shelter with Fiona. But she was way too intrigued by Ian to walk away right then.

She was more attracted to him than she'd ever been attracted to any man before, and knew she would kick herself later if she didn't at least spend a little time getting to know him. Whether it was just for a one-night stand, or if they could be more, didn't matter at that point. She just couldn't walk away. "How long have you been sitting here?"

"Just a few minutes." Ian gave her a panty-melting smile. "Why?"

"Just wondering how much of our conversation you overheard." *Are you for real? Or are you using a fake name because of what I said earlier about not being able to say "no" to a guy named Ian?*

"Not long enough to catch your name." Ian was still smiling, and not giving her any clue as to whether or not he'd heard her earlier conversation with Fiona.

"Sorry, I'm Charlotte. Is your name really Ian?" She couldn't stop herself from asking, unable to decide if he was real or not. She might want to imagine her memmaw had sent her Mr. Right straight from Heaven, but she also knew to keep Memmaw's other lessons about being safe in all situations at the forefront of her mind.

"Yes, would you like to see my driver's license to prove it?" He smirked as he reached into his pocket and pulled out his wallet.

"If you wouldn't mind showing it to me." Charlotte returned his flirty grin. *Guess this will tell me if tonight is just a hot fantasy come to life or the real deal. Or maybe a bit of both?*

He flipped open his wallet and showed her a California driver's license with the name "Ian Campbell" on it. The picture was clearly him, so she had to believe it was just a twist of fate to bring them together that night.

Holy Shit! My family wasn't pulling my leg when they said love-at-first-sight hits hard and fast. Thank you, Memmaw, for sending Ian my way.

<div align="center">~~~</div>

Ian couldn't believe his luck at sitting down in the hotel bar next to the most beautiful woman in the room, only to hear her talk to her friend about her fantasy one-night stand with a book character who seemed to share a lot of Ian's own traits, as well as his name. While he wouldn't actually classify himself as a Nordic God, Ian had to admit his light hair and eyes, along with his six-foot-four height, seemed to indicate he'd descended from the same region of the world. *My grandparents claimed we were Scottish, so is that close enough to make me Nordic? And does being a former DEA agent classify me as a former spy? I mean, I did go undercover to catch a few criminals, but I've never spied on foreign governments.*

"Are you satisfied that I am whom I say I am, sweet Charlotte?" Ian closed his wallet and put it back in his pocket, grateful she seemed to be focused on looking at his face during the majority of their interaction, so she didn't notice how hard he'd been since sitting down beside her.

Since he lost his wife, Ian hadn't thought he could even find another woman attractive enough to arouse him. He had actually resigned himself to a life of celibacy, figuring taking care of his son and sister didn't leave him any free time for moving on romantically, anyway. But when he walked into the hotel bar and saw the profile of the gorgeous woman at the bar with her friend, his whole body had noticed her, and he'd quickly changed his mind about being celibate. At least for that night, since he still thought he had too much going on in his life to romance the beautiful Charlotte the way she deserved.

"Yeah, I guess I'll believe you're not lying to me for now." Charlotte gave him a tentative smile.

Ah, she thinks I'm lying because of not being sure if I overheard her earlier or not. That's okay, sweet Charlotte. I'm more than happy to fulfill your fantasies without you having to give me all the details about them. No point in spoiling the illusion of the night by telling you I heard you earlier and making you question my honesty again.

"I would never lie to you, sweet Charlotte." Ian brushed a lock of her caramel-brown hair out of her face, tucking it behind her ear. "I might not be able to tell you everything about my life, but I'll be completely honest about the things I am able to share with you."

Seeming to finally believe him, Charlotte changed the subject. "So, California, huh? What brings you so far from home?"

Ian was torn about what to tell her. On the one hand, he could be honest by saying he was there for the job interview he'd had that day. But if he did that, he risked her wanting to keep in touch after their night together, when she found out he'd be moving to the area in the next couple of weeks. On the other hand, he could also be honest by telling her he was there tracking Rojo for the DEA, which might help fulfill her fantasy of spending the night with Ian, the spy.

Fuck, she's hot, and it's been a long time since I've been this attracted to anyone. But as much as I could see myself pursuing more with her if we'd have met a few months ago in California, I can't risk her life by trying to start a relationship now that I'm back on Rojo's trail. This has to be a one-night thing for now. If we're meant to be more, then maybe fate will intervene, and I'll see her again after Rojo is behind bars, where he belongs.

"I'm on the trail of a cartel kingpin that was recently traced to this area." Ian took a sip of the scotch he'd been nursing all evening as he watched Charlotte's eyes widen. *Yep, definitely fulfilling her fantasy tonight.* "I've been with the DEA for the last decade, and trying to bring in the head of this cartel for most of that time."

"Wow!" Charlotte picked up her wine glass, but she didn't take a drink. It was almost like she just needed the prop to hold on to while she absorbed what he'd said. "How close do you think you are to finally catching him?"

"Very close." Ian shrugged, not wanting to appear too cocky, but also not wanting to sound like the failure he'd felt like for the last couple of years. "As of two weeks ago, all the other major players in the cartel were rounded up. So, while he's on the run, he doesn't have the support system to stay hidden much longer."

And hopefully, I can catch him before he rebuilds his organization.

Charlotte nodded in response before looking shyly down at the drink in her hand.

Not sure what had happened to the confident woman he'd sat down beside earlier that caused her to suddenly appear so coy, Ian decided not to let the silence linger between them. Letting her put up her defenses between them wouldn't allow either of them to live out their fantasies for the night. And Ian had been fantasizing about getting between her thighs since the first moment he saw her.

"So, you never answered my question earlier." Ian sat his drink down on the bar and extended his hand to lift her chin, gently forcing her to look into his eyes. He was so mesmerized by their hazel depths that he forgot to repeat it for her.

"What question?" Charlotte licked her lips and sat her drink down as well.

"Your friend said you have an early morning tomorrow. Do you need to call it a night and go up to your room soon?"

"Oh, um, Fiona has a lot more to do tomorrow than I do." Charlotte shook her head, her lips barely tipping up at the corners as she spoke. "She's starting a new job next month, so she's having to train her replacement at the shelter where we volunteer on the weekends because she won't be here regularly anymore. I'm just serving lunch, so I don't have to be there as early as she does."

Ian smiled at how thoughtful and compassionate Charlotte and her friend, Fiona, were for volunteering their time at a shelter.

"So, I don't have to go to sleep anytime soon," Charlotte continued when Ian didn't say anything more. "But I wouldn't mind going on up to my bed, if you're interested in joining me there."

There's the confident siren I saw in her earlier. Ian grinned as he pulled his wallet back out to pay for their drinks. "I would love to join you, sweet Charlotte."

After waving over the bartender to run his card for their tabs, Ian leaned in to whisper in Charlotte's ear. "But I have to warn you that if I go to your room, you won't be getting any sleep until I've had you on every flat surface in the room, and made you come so many times that you have to beg me to stop because you've given me all your pleasure."

"Hmmm," Charlotte made a whimpering noise deep in her throat that made Ian harden even further in his slacks.

Fuck, if we don't get upstairs and undressed soon, I'm going to have a permanent zipper impression on my dick.

Thankfully, the bartender was back with his card. Ian added a generous tip and scribbled his signature on one copy of the receipt, before shoving the second copy in his wallet with his card and slipping the whole works back into his pocket.

"Ready, Princess?" Ian extended his hand to Charlotte, unsure why he'd used the term of endearment he'd never thought to use with any other woman, including his late wife.

"Yes," Charlotte squeaked, placing her delicate hand in his much larger one.

She was obviously nervous, so Ian smiled to try to relax her as she slipped off the barstool. Once they were standing side by side, Ian realized just how petite she was. He guessed she would be almost a foot shorter than him if she wasn't in her low heels.

Though I guess most women are petite compared to Mari's five-foot-ten. Ian wanted to kick himself for comparing Charlotte to his late wife. But as he was about to have sex for the first time in years, he supposed it was only natural to think of the last woman he'd been with.

Don't go there, man, Ian mentally ordered himself. *Mari would understand that I have needs. She would want me to move on and fall in love again. Not that I'm going to fall in love with Charlotte when we can only have tonight together, but still, she'd understand.*

Shaking off the mental meltdown, Ian laced their fingers together and escorted Charlotte to the elevator. *I need to focus on the beautiful woman beside me,* he mentally berated himself, as he punched the button for the elevator before grinning at her once more. *Not my late wife.*

I guess she's really closer to average height since her heels bring her up to about the same height as Caitir, who complained about being too short to be a model until she hit five-foot-eight as a teenager. His smile widened at the memory of his sister from a decade ago.

"What's that look for?" Charlotte asked just as the elevator doors opened.

"Just looking forward to being alone with you, Princess." Ian didn't classify the statement as a lie, since it was one of the things he was thinking. He just didn't want to distract from their time together by mentioning his other thoughts as well, especially not as they were stepping onto the elevator to take them to her hotel room. "What floor?"

"Five." Charlotte smiled up at him as he pulled her to his side while he pushed the button for her floor. "Room five-oh-nine."

Ian didn't mention that his room was right across the hall, preferring to spend the night in hers, so he could leave her sleeping in her bed when he had to leave for his early morning appointment with the realtor in Heart's Destiny. Originally, he'd planned to fly back to California right after his interview. But things had gone so well in the interview that his new boss had offered him the job immediately. That meant he had to start making arrangements for the move, starting with securing a place for them to move to before he went back to California to start packing.

As soon as the doors to the elevator closed and they were alone in the car, Ian spun her against the wall. "I was beginning to think I'd have to wait until we got to the room to kiss you," he growled, before crushing her lips with his.

Charlotte wrapped her arms around his shoulders as she opened her mouth to him. Ian took advantage, claiming her with his tongue. He gripped the globes of her ass that were modestly encased in her navy pencil skirt, lifting her slightly, so he didn't have to bend as far to keep kissing her. Though, to be honest, he'd have probably bent further to dip her back as he kissed her if they weren't pressed up against the wall of the elevator.

Later, he mentally chastised himself as he pictured their second kiss once they were in her hotel room while still ravaging her with their first.

There was nothing shy about the way Charlotte kissed him back. The demure woman he'd briefly witnessed in the bar and on their walk to the elevator was replaced with a sex kitten he couldn't wait to tame.

Just as Ian was thinking about slipping his hands under her sexy as fuck pencil skirt to remove her panties before they exited the elevator, the door opened with a ding. *Fuck, too late now,* he thought as he released her from the kiss to usher her off the elevator.

He kept his hand on the small of her back as he escorted her down the hall to her room. Charlotte pulled the keycard out of her handbag and deftly unlocked the door.

As soon as they were inside the room, Ian kicked the door shut behind them, pulling Charlotte back into his arms as soon as she placed her purse and the keycard on the table just inside the door. With one arm around her waist and the other hand in her long caramel tresses, he dipped her back and kissed her hard, need for her shooting through him like he'd been struck by lightning.

Charlotte wrapped her arms around his neck, her fingers not finding much purchase in his short hair that he now kept military short, since he didn't have to keep it long to fit in undercover with the cartels anymore. She returned his kiss with fervor. Their tongues tangled in a duel for dominance. As much as he liked seeing the strong side of her take what she wanted, he was going to enjoy taming her even more. Teaching her how to be passionate while giving over control to him.

You're not the one in charge with me, Princess, Ian thought as he dropped his hand down from her waist to cup her ass. He wasn't into any of the hardcore kinks he'd seen in the cartel brothels while infiltrating their ranks, but he did need to be in control at all times during his sexual encounters. *And sweet Charlotte is about to learn that lesson the hard way. Good thing her fantasy included being sexually dominated.*

Ian squeezed her ass before lifting his hand and slapping it back down.

Charlotte's head jerked back from his as she squealed, "Ow! What was that for?"

"Just showing you who's in charge, Princess." Ian smiled down at her, knowing the light spank over her skirt didn't really hurt her. He couldn't quite read her expression as anything more than shock, but on the off chance she wasn't turned on by the swat, he knew he needed to give her an out before they went any further. "Unless you're not ready for me to take charge of your pleasure tonight. If that was too much and you'd rather I leave, then we can stop now."

"No," Charlotte quickly protested, tightening her hold on him, almost like she was afraid he'd really leave. "I, uh, I was just surprised by it. But it wasn't too much. I don't want you to stop. Or leave."

"Good, then you follow my commands and I'll give you the best night of your life." Charlotte's hazel eyes widened at Ian's bold statement. The amber flecks toward the center of her mostly green irises seemed to glow with excitement at the thought of following his commands. She nodded her agreement, but otherwise held still in his arms. "I need the words, Princess. Tell me if you agree to obey me tonight."

"Yes, Sir," Charlotte whispered softly.

"Good girl." Ian brushed his lips over her forehead before releasing her from his hold. He stepped over to the bed and took a seat on the end before motioning for her to follow him. "Strip for me."

Charlotte stepped out of her sexy as fuck navy stilettos as she closed the distance between them. She stopped a couple of feet in front of him, bringing her hands to the back of her skirt to unfasten it.

Since there was no music playing for her to dance to, Ian hadn't expected a sultry striptease, but Charlotte still titillated him by taking her time to slowly wiggle the skirt down over her hips.

Ian palmed his cock over his slacks when she finally dropped the skirt to the floor and revealed her white satin panties. *Fuck! She looks way too innocent for all the dirty things I want to do to her. Way too fucking innocent!*

She lifted the hem of her light blue blouse to pull it off over her head, revealing a matching white satin bra encasing the most perfect breasts he'd ever seen. She wasn't too big or too small.

Two perfect handfuls that I can't wait to get my mouth on, Ian noted as she reached behind her back to release the bra clasp. He was rapidly leaking precum into his boxer briefs from the sight of her tight, pink nipples when she dropped the bra to the floor.

"Fuck, you're gorgeous." Ian was barely keeping himself in check, struggling to stay seated while she shimmied out of her panties.

"And you're still wearing too many clothes," Charlotte playfully chided.

"Are you pushing for another spanking, Princess?" Ian raised an eyebrow at her.

"I'm not pushing for anything, Sir," Charlotte purred, giving him a slight smile. "But if you feel that's what I deserve, then I'll gladly lay over your lap for it."

Ian's dick twitched in his pants at the thought of her sinfully sexy body draped over his lap while he lightly spanked her before finger-fucking her. *No, I need to get my mouth on her first.*

"We'll have to save that for later to let you earn more than one swat." Ian returned her slight smile as he reached for her hands to pull her closer. Once she was standing between his splayed feet, Ian dipped his head to latch onto her right hard-candy peak.

Ian released her hands to cup her left breast with his right hand, while wrapping his left arm around her waist to pull her in even closer. Charlotte's hands went to the back of Ian's head as he suckled. He couldn't quite tell if she was trying to hold him in place or move him to the other breast to give it equal treatment.

"That's two," he barked as he popped his mouth off her turgid tip. "Clasp your hands together behind your back and let me play with my fuck toy."

"Ye, yes, Sir," Charlotte stuttered as she released her grip on his head and followed his command.

Ian could tell she was nervous, but from the smell of her arousal, she was also turned on by following his directives. Needing to know just how wet she was, Ian slid his left hand down, running a finger between her ass cheeks to lightly skim her puckered hole before moving between her thighs to find her soaked pussy.

"You like being my fuck toy, don't you, Princess?" Ian slipped his fingers through her folds, spreading her cream up to coat her clit.

Though Ian's words came out as a statement, Charlotte answered him with a breathy, "Yes, Sir," as if they were a question.

He rewarded her honest admission by closing his lips over her other nipple. He nipped the tip lightly with his teeth before soothing the sting with his tongue. Charlotte moaned in pleasure as her pussy gushed with more of her natural lubricant.

Ian continued to work her up to the edge by teasing her cunt with his fingers while alternating his oral onslaught between her tantalizing tatas.

"Oh, God, Ian," Charlotte cried out as her tight pussy clamped down on his fingers. Her whole body shuddered and spasmed as she climaxed.

Ian lifted his head from her glorious mounds to watch her face the first time he made her come. Luckily, he wasn't so mesmerized by the expression of ecstasy on her face to miss the moment she went boneless from the pleasure. He snaked his other arm around her just in time to hold her up when she collapsed against his chest.

He slipped his fingers from her channel as she came down from her high and spun her in his arms to cradle her on his lap. He sucked her sweet cream from his fingers while he held her as she recovered.

"Hmmm, delicious. But I bet your honey will taste even better straight from the source."

Charlotte lifted her head to look him in the eyes before giving him a wicked smile. "Don't I get to taste you next?"

Ian shook his head at the little minx. "That's four, Princess."

"Four?" Charlotte's voice raised an octave in her incredulity. "But we were just at two before, so shouldn't that be three?"

"Three was coming without asking for permission, Princess. I just didn't want to miss your O face by pointing it out then." Ian tapped the tip of her nose with his still slick finger before standing with her cradled in his arms to walk around to the side and lay her out on the bed. "And you're up to five for sassing me. Now spread your legs and let me eat my fill of my pretty little fuck toy."

"Yes, Sir." Charlotte stuck her bottom lip out in a pout as she spread her legs, but Ian could see the glint in her eye that told him how much she liked their game and wasn't really pouting.

Ian crawled on the bed, positioning himself between her thighs to get his first good look at her pink pussy. She had a neatly trimmed, thin strip of curls the same caramel-brown shade as the hair on her head.

As he ran his nose up the inside of her thigh, Ian picked up the faintest hint of blackberries and vanilla, along with something flowery he didn't recognize, mixed in with the musk of her arousal. He had a vague memory of similar smells on his grandparents' farm when he was a young child, but pushed it aside to focus on the beautiful woman with him at the moment.

When he reached the apex of her thighs, Ian swiped his tongue through her folds, lapping up his first true taste of Charlotte's tangy-sweet cream straight from her cunt. *Fucking amazing!*

Charlotte writhed as he devoured her. He alternated between licking her, sucking her clit, and fucking her with his tongue. Her breathing became ragged as he kept eating her pussy like a starving man and working her up to the edge once more. "Oh, yes, Ian!"

"Oh, no, Princess." Ian lifted his head, shaking it as a form of light reprimand. "You're not going to steal a second orgasm. You need to ask permission first."

"Please don't stop. Please, Ian, please may I come on your glorious tongue?"

Fuck! I love the way she begs. Ian didn't answer her as he lowered his head and pushed his tongue back into her creamy cunt.

Charlotte continued to beg, whimpering her pretty pleas as she ground her pussy on his face.

Ian licked his way from her slit to her clit, shoving two fingers inside her as he sucked her needy nub. When he felt her inner walls starting to flutter, he knew she wouldn't be able to hold her climax back much longer.

He lifted his mouth off of her just enough to be able to speak, ordering her to "Come now, Princess" at the same time he stroked over her G-spot. He latched onto her bundle of nerves once more, just as she squirted her release into his mouth. Ian drank down her tangy-sweet girl cum as wave after wave of ecstasy passed from her to him.

He couldn't fight his need to be inside her any longer. Glad he'd already removed his jacket and tie when he first got back to the hotel and left them in his room, he started stripping off his button-down as he pushed up from the bed while Charlotte laid there recovering. He toed off his loafers and socks as he pulled his shirt from his waistband and dropped it to the floor. Ian unfastened his belt and slacks, pushing them and his boxer briefs to the floor in one fell swoop.

Fuck! Condom!

Ian quickly retrieved his wallet and was glad to find he hadn't ever thought to remove the three he'd stashed there from the last time he planned a date night with Mari. Since they'd been there for over two years, he double-checked the expiration dates before suiting up, tossing the other two on the bedside table for easy access later.

Charlotte lifted her head just as he was rolling the latex down his length. Ian enjoyed watching her eyes go from heavy-lidded to practically bugging out at seeing him stroke his cock. He knew he was well endowed, but it had been a while since he'd felt that sense of pride at the way a woman responded to seeing his dick for the first time.

And she can't even see the dydoe piercings from that angle.

"See something you like, Princess?" Ian continued to stroke his cock as he stalked back onto the bed, positioning himself between Charlotte's spread thighs.

"I'm not sure that's gonna fit," Charlotte sputtered, licking her lips.

"Oh, it'll fit," Ian smirked. "Now reach up and grab the headboard. You'd better hold on tight for this first ride. It's going to be a hard one."

"Yes, Sir." Charlotte grinned as she followed his directions.

Ian lifted her legs to prop her ankles on his shoulders. Then he rubbed the head of his cock through the pool of moisture coating her lower lips, making sure she was ready for him before he slowly pushed inside her for the first time.

"Holy fuck! You're so tight." It took every ounce of willpower he had not to impale her on his cock, but he didn't want to hurt her, no matter how bad he felt he needed to be inside her right then. "How long has it been for you, Princess?"

"Too long," Charlotte moaned, shaking her head, obviously not comfortable talking about her previous experiences right then.

Yeah, I guess that is something to be avoided on a one-night stand. But, fuck, this feels like so much more than the one night I have to give her.

Ian pushed his feelings down, knowing he couldn't explore them with Charlotte. He needed to focus on memorizing every moment of his time with her to have the memories to carry him through the long, lonely nights ahead.

With their gazes locked on one another, he pushed into the tightest pussy he'd ever experienced until he was balls-deep. She fit him like a custom-made glove, and Ian was really wishing he never had to leave the depths of her body. Instead of pulling out to pound her as he'd originally planned, Ian swiveled his hips, rooting around deep inside her to find her hidden trigger point.

"Wha, what are you doing?" Charlotte stuttered, her eyes widening when his dydoe piercings stroked over her G-spot.

Ian had gotten the two parallel piercings on the dorsal ridge of his cock head, back when he first went undercover with the cartel, as a way to cover for why he couldn't fuck the women in the brothel during his initiation into the group. He still ended up having to lie about the healing time when he was undercover for more than Charlotte actual three-month healing time of the piercings. But once he was home, and his wife reaped the benefits of the piercings during sex, Ian was glad he'd gone to such extremes to preserve his fidelity.

"Rubbing my piercings on your G-spot, Princess," Ian smirked, rubbing his thumb over her clit to double the stimulation and get her back to the edge faster. "Gotta get you relaxed a little more before I fuck you the way I want."

"Piercings?" Charlotte's grin widened, curiosity lighting up the amber flecks in her hazel-green eyes. "I didn't see any piercings."

"Don't worry, sweet Charlotte, I'll let you get a close-up look at them when you suck my cock later," Ian growled, fighting to hold back his desire to rut into her like a wild animal until she started to come once more. "But first you need to come again, Princess. Now!"

He swiveled his hips again, while circling his thumb over her clit and reaching out to tweak her nipple with his other hand, to push her over the edge as soon as he possibly could.

"Oh, fuck, Ian!" Charlotte shouted as her next orgasm barreled through her.

"Fuck!" Ian joined her in shouting the expletive as her pussy squeezed him like a vise, surprising him at how much tighter she could grip him.

He had to wait for the contractions of her inner walls to pass before he could finally move. But once she relaxed and became pliant with satisfaction, he pulled halfway out before shoving all the way back in, finally starting to fuck her the way he craved. He pistoned in and out of her, not letting her fully recover from the climax before giving her yet another.

"That's it, take my cock. You like being fucked hard, don't you, Princess?" Ian had to bite his tongue to keep from telling her to come again, but he had to have a reason to increase the count of the swats to her ass that she was so obviously craving.

"Yes, Ian!" Charlotte's breathy way of crying out his name could have been in answer to his question, or it could just be the result of her next orgasm. Either way, Ian loved hearing his name on her lips as she shuddered and spasmed in yet another climax.

He moved his hands to grip her hips, anchoring her in place for him to ride her like a man possessed. Charlotte writhed and moaned beneath him, screaming his name every time she came, but she never let go of the headboard as he'd instructed.

Ian examined her closely, cataloging every freckle and feature of her perfect body beneath him while he fucked her, until the intensity of their connection became too much for him to focus on anything other than how fucking awesome it felt to be inside her tight, wet pussy. When she closed those mesmerizing green-gold eyes as she came for the seventh time that night, Ian completely let loose.

He pounded into her as they both fell over the edge to oblivion. He shoved inside her to the hilt, holding as deep as he could get while he exploded into the latex, filling the condom with more cum than it could hold.

"Fuck! Charlotte!" Ian clamped his hand around the base of his cock to seal the condom to his skin, trying to keep his cum contained until he could pull out of the tight clutch of her cunt.

He was seeing stars as he pulled out and collapsed on the bed beside her, the aftershocks of the intense orgasm still hitting him hard. They were both breathing hard and fast as they recovered from the best sex of his life.

"Wow," Charlotte breathed out the barely audible word.

"And we're just getting started, Princess." Ian grinned as he sat up, still holding on to the condom, trying to prevent any leakage. He slowly stood from the bed and made his way toward the ensuite bathroom. "Once we clean up in the shower, I have ten swats to give you before letting you examine my piercings with your tongue."

"Ten? I thought it was only five!" Charlotte glared at him as she sat up and watched him walk through the bathroom doorway.

Ian removed the condom and wiped up a little of the mess he'd made before poking his head back out of the bathroom door. "We were at five, but then you came at least another five times without permission. Now get your sexy ass in here for our shower before you earn more."

"Yes, Sir!" Charlotte gave him a jaunty salute before scrambling to the edge of the bed and running to join him.

Damn, I wish we could have more than just tonight. It would be so easy to fall for her mix of innocence and sex kitten.

But it wouldn't be fair to her to put her in danger while I'm on the hunt for Rojo. Not to mention the fact that I'm also juggling taking care of Brody and Caitir, so I don't really have the time to devote to a relationship the way she deserves.

Leah Mae Wright

I'll just have to make the most of the few hours we have together right now. And try not to long for her once I've put Rojo away and have no idea how to find her again.

Chapter Two

Charlotte awoke the next morning to a cold, empty bed, disappointed when she looked around and saw there were no signs of Ian in the room. She stretched out the soreness in her muscles as she thought back to the events of the night before.

After their first time together in the bed, Ian had moved their activities to the shower. Charlotte giggled at the memory of him dubiously arching an eyebrow at her when she insisted on him using her Falling In Love bodywash, instead of the soap provided by the hotel. But he had complied with her wishes, with his only comment about it being that he was confident enough in his manhood to wear her scent home.

"But only if you're the one rubbing it all over me, Princess."

Charlotte smiled as she remembered back to how she'd enjoyed running her hands over every part of his body, returning the torment of how he'd teased her mercilessly as he washed her body with only her bodywash between her skin and his bare hands. He was in excellent shape, with the chiseled, muscular body of an athlete. He had a few scars, but they didn't mar the perfection of his body, only enhanced it. Char's nipples hardened as she recalled how the light dusting of his chest hair felt rubbing against them before it was matted down with the water of their shower.

Charlotte hadn't ever showered with anyone before, but she had to admit it was a decadent experience with Ian Campbell. *Too bad he didn't stick around to shower with me again this morning.*

Leah Mae Wright

Once their shower was over, he'd dried her thoroughly before scooping her up into his arms and carrying her back to the bed for the sensual spanking she hadn't really thought she'd enjoy before he slapped her buttocks the first time. He'd started off exceptionally light with the swats, teasing her with his fingers running over her labia after each one to make sure she was aroused by the act before moving on to the next harder smack against her backside.

Char had been undeniably aroused, dripping wet before he even got to the fifth strike. She had wiggled and writhed on his lap. Not because it was painful, even though she did feel a little heat in her butt cheeks by the time he was done adding more swats to her tally from all her moving around. No, her squirming had all been from her vain attempt at applying pressure on her clit by rubbing against his muscular thigh.

Charlotte rolled to her side to rub her hand across her butt cheek, surprised she wasn't sore there from the spanking. But then again, he hadn't really slapped her bare ass very hard, even on the last of the twenty-five swats her final tally added up to with the ten she'd originally earned before their shower, five added in the shower for the way she teased him as she washed his body, and the final ten that had been added for wriggling around and trying to steal another orgasm. When she questioned him at the time about going soft on her, since none of the swats really hurt, he'd made it clear that the spanking was meant to be fun and arousing, not painful in any way.

"I want to get us both off, but I don't want to hurt you. I don't enjoy hurting anyone, but it's fun to play around with things like spanking when it's arousing for everyone involved. But only light spanking, not anything that would leave lasting marks. I might leave marks on your body from my mouth, but never from my hands, sweet Charlotte."

They had both left marks with their mouths as they'd explored each other orally after that. He might be more tan than she was naturally, but she'd still left little love bites on his neck and chest. *I should have tried to see if I could mark his glorious, pierced dick, too. But I was too distracted by the jewelry decorating the head to think about it at the time.*

She came back to the present from her mental musings when her phone rang. Groggily, she rolled her naked body to the other side of the bed, so she could reach her cell phone on the bedside table.

"Hello," she croaked into the phone when she swiped to answer Fiona's call.

"Morning, chica." Fiona sounded way too chipper for such an early call on a Saturday morning. "Just wanted to check if you're coming to the shelter with me this morning, or if you're staying in bed with Ian all day."

"I'm still planning to come volunteer with you this morning, but I need at least an hour to get ready first." Charlotte stood and walked to the restroom to begin her day.

"Oh, well, I'm already downstairs and heading out. I'm trying to get as much done there as I can, since I won't be able to volunteer regularly after this month, so I was planning to go in early. Meet me there when you get ready?"

"Will do," Char agreed before they disconnected.

After emptying her bladder, Charlotte stood in front of the mirror in the bathroom and took in the sight before her. She almost didn't recognize herself with her hair wild and her makeup gone. The marks Ian left on her neck and chest were evidence of the wanton woman she'd been the night before. She looked nothing like the polished, sophisticated school teacher she usually portrayed to the world.

I was certainly not my normal self last night, Char thought as she started her morning routine. *Ian made me feel like I was actually one of those strong, sexy women in my favorite romance novels with everything we did last night.*

I still can't believe we used all three condoms he had on him. He must have a magic cock to be able to recover so fast and come that many times in one night. Too bad his magic didn't last past dawn. I could probably be more adventurous in other aspects of my life if I could have him by my side for the rest of it.

Charlotte shook off her momentary wishful thinking to start her shower, knowing a fantasy man like Ian would never want to settle down for a quiet life on the ranch with her. *But damn, I wish we'd have at least exchanged numbers for the occasional booty call until I do find my Mr. Right.*

It didn't matter that she'd thought their instant connection the night before meant he was *The One*, just like all the stories of her ancestors she'd heard all her life. Charlotte knew it wouldn't work between them if he didn't feel that same instant connection. *And obviously, he didn't feel it, since he didn't bother to ask for my number or leave me his.*

A single tear slipped from her eye as she washed the smell of sex from her body. She wouldn't allow herself to think about the fact that she was also washing away all traces of Ian's masculine, woodsy musk from her skin as well.

It was just a one-off. I'm not going to cry over the fact that I can't keep him in my life. The marks on my body might not allow me to forget him for the next couple of weeks, but it's not like he marked my heart as his.

A few hours together isn't long enough to fall in love with him. I'll be fine without him. And who knows, maybe in a couple of months, I'll meet an even more perfect man for me.

Charlotte kept up her internal pep talk, lying to herself as much as she had to in order to make it through her day without crying. She robotically went through the motions of dressing, doing her hair and makeup, and checking out of the hotel to drive over to the shelter to meet Fiona.

As soon as she saw her, Fiona pulled Charlotte into an unexpected hug. "You're not glowing nearly as much as I expected this morning," she whispered so nobody else could hear. "Did Ian not live up to your dominant fantasies last night?"

"Oh, no, he definitely did," Charlotte whispered back, quickly returning Fiona's embrace while thinking back to all the decadent ways they'd made love the night before. *Had sex!* Charlotte mentally corrected. *One-night stands are not making love.* "Just a little bummed to not get another round this morning."

Though I don't suppose we really could have, since the condoms in my suitcase are standard-sized and not the Magnums he needs.

"Sorry, I shouldn't have called and interrupted you," Fiona apologized as they released each other from the hug.

"You didn't interrupt a thing." Charlotte shook her head to show her friend there was no need for an apology. "He had already left by the time you called."

"Oh, well, as much as I hate that you missed the morning with him, I'm glad you're here earlier than expected." Fiona turned to look around the room before turning back to Charlotte. "We have some new residents since the last time you were here, and I hope you can help me with one of them when I'm not able to be here in the new year."

"Yeah, sure." Charlotte didn't hesitate to volunteer, already planning to increase her hours at the shelter to make up for Fiona not being able to be there every Saturday once she started her new job.

"You see the man with his little boy over in the far right corner?" Charlotte looked where Fiona indicated and nodded her head in acknowledgment. "That's Roberto Reyes and his son, Antonio. They're working on getting their immigration paperwork in order after their village in Mexico was caught in the crossfire of a war between two rival cartels. Anyway, Antonio is almost five years old and hasn't had any kind of preschool to prepare him for starting kindergarten next year. I've spent a couple of hours with him the past two Saturdays to try and at least teach him colors, letters, and numbers. But he's so far behind in his speech development that it's going to take a lot more than just the couple of weeks I have left here to prepare him to start school in the fall."

Charlotte had taken a semester of speech therapy coursework in college before deciding on her career goal of being an English teacher, so she had a little bit of knowledge that might help the little boy. "I'm not a speech therapist, but I'll do what I can."

"Yeah, I know, but you know more about speech therapy than anyone else we have volunteering here. And I doubt Roberto will be able to afford a speech therapist until he gets his immigration paperwork straightened out to be able to get a job."

"Then take me over to meet him now, so I can schedule a time to work with Antonio every week." Charlotte motioned for Fiona to lead the way to the two newcomers to the shelter.

As they walked across the room, Charlotte put Ian Campbell and his perfect, pierced penis out of her head. *I just need to focus on the good I can do in the world for now. And pray that, maybe one day, I'll feel like I've met* **The One** *again.*

~~~

Saturday, December 29, 2018

Ian was irritated by being dragged to a late Christmas celebration by the proprietors of the boutique hotel where he and his family were staying until their things arrived, so they could move into the house in Heart's Destiny, Texas, he was renting from his new boss's husband. But Mandi Hunter had apparently told his sister, Caitir, that she could possibly find a job on the ranch that would allow her to bring Ian's son, Brody, with her since he was still too young to start school. So Caitir wanted to go, and Ian couldn't refuse his little sister's request.

While he had plenty of money saved to be able to provide for his sister, even with the pay cut he was taking to work at Heart's Destiny Middle School, he understood her desire to work outside their household. He just wished her desire to do so hadn't come back until after he had Rojo Rodriguez behind bars, where he couldn't hurt anyone in their family again.

Caitir had always been a strong, independent woman, until the day their family was ambushed by the Rodriguez Cartel. After healing from her injuries, Caitir hadn't been herself, preferring to stay at home with Brody instead of going back to work. After losing his wife, Ian needed his sister's help to take care of his son, so he hadn't thought twice about taking his sister up on her offer to be his live-in nanny.

Over the course of the last couple of years, however, Ian had started to realize that Caitir was using the job he gave her to cover for the fact that she was uncomfortable leaving the house without him accompanying her. Since she was suddenly wanting to work and interact with new people again, Ian realized she wasn't truly agoraphobic. She just hadn't wanted to leave their home in San Diego because she was afraid of another cartel attack. But now that they were in another state, and over a thousand miles away from San Diego, Caitir was no longer afraid.

Damn, maybe I should have told her the real reason for our move, Ian thought as he followed the Hunters to the ranch where they were having lunch and meeting a few of the locals. *But, shit, I can't have her scared to live here either.*
~~~

Resolved to keep his sister as in the dark as the rest of the people in town about why he was really there, Ian put on a fake smile to cover the way his head was on a swivel to look for Rojo. They turned off of Walker Road and onto Rogers Road before making the right into the driveway leading to a wrought-iron gate with a stylized B in the middle. Above the gate was a wooden sign that read, "Burleson Ranch."

Shit! I hope Jake is ready to pretend not to know me, Ian thought as he followed the Hunters through the gate and around to a large, white, plantation-style house, where they parked along with the rest of the guests coming from the bed and breakfast.

As he remembered back to his conversation with Jake the month before about being able to send his sister and son to the Burleson Ranch to keep them safe when he found Rojo, Ian relaxed a little about his fear for his sister while working outside his home. *Maybe if Caitir can get a job here, she'll be able to regain some of her independence without actually being at risk, with Rojo still on the loose in the area.*

"Maybe this wasn't such a good idea," Caitir mumbled as they got out of the rental car they'd gotten when they flew into San Antonio a couple of days before.

Ian would be glad when his Range Rover arrived, along with all the rest of their belongings that were being shipped to the rental house, so he wouldn't have to feel cramped in the sedan any longer.

"It'll be fine, Cait," Ian reassured his sister, using the abbreviated name she preferred since the shooting, as he lifted Brody from his car seat to carry him into the gathering. "If there isn't a job you're comfortable with here, then at least we'll have made some new friends by the end of the day."

"Maybe." Cait seemed to revert back to the reserved woman she'd been the last couple of years in San Diego, instead of the more confident woman she'd been before the attack and that he'd started to see coming back in the few short days they'd been in Texas.

Ian gave his sister a reassuring smile as they walked into the mansion-sized home behind the Hunters. As the Hunters started making introductions, Ian looked around at the crowd of people around them. He easily spotted Jake across the room, his Navy high-and-tight haircut standing out among the longer-haired individuals around him.

Maintaining his cover, Ian didn't acknowledge the only person he sort of knew in the group. He shook hands with Jon and Bob Burleson and nodded in agreement to find out from one of their wives where they should sit for the meal.

As he followed his sister, who was following Mandi Hunter, through the dining room toward the kitchen, where the matriarchs of the family were working to put the finishing touches on lunch, his eyes locked with a set of hazel orbs he thought he'd never see again.

Charlotte?

The sight of her momentarily took his breath away. He couldn't believe the woman he'd been dreaming about every night for the last two weeks was standing across the room from him. The instant he saw her eyes widen at recognizing him, Ian turned away to continue following his sister.

What the hell is Charlotte doing here? I mean, I figured out she was local to the San Antonio area based on what she said about volunteering at the shelter. But what are the odds she's actually from this small town? Or attending a Christmas party at the Burleson Ranch?

Oh, Fuck! What if she is a Burleson? Jake said he has two sisters and a couple of female cousins who live here on the ranch. I should have fucking asked for their names before I even came here for the interview.

Hell, I should have asked Charlotte's last name when I met her two weeks ago. But, no, I had to try to avoid the temptation of looking her up when I moved here by keeping things anonymous.

Fuck! What am I going to do to maintain my cover when I pretty much told her the real reason I'm moving here? There's no way she didn't recognize me just now. That was blatantly obvious by the way her eyes widened and her mouth opened in shock at seeing me here.

Maybe I can pretend I don't know her just like I am with Jake? I can't just pretend to not remember our night together. That'll just make me look like an asshole player, and might cause her to blow my cover by mentioning what I said that night in front of this crowd of people.

Fuck! I have to play it off as never having met her. And if she says anything about that night, I'll insist she must have had a one-night stand with my doppelganger. Surely, that will work. Right?

Ian was so far in his own head about seeing Charlotte again that he missed the introductions to the women in the kitchen and had no idea whom he was following back to the dining room.

He tapped his sister on the shoulder and asked, "Which Mrs. Burleson are we following?"

"Susan," Cait whispered in response. "Jon's wife."

~~~

Charlotte couldn't believe her eyes as she watched Ian Campbell walk through her parents' dining room following a woman and carrying a child. *Is that his wife? His son? I mean, the boy does have a darker complexion and darker brown hair than either Ian or the woman he's with, so maybe they're not blood related. But then again, they could have adopted him, so even if they share no blood, they're still obviously his family. No wonder he didn't bother exchanging numbers with me two weeks ago!*

Feeling like the room was spinning at the revelation that her one-night stand was a cheating bastard, Charlotte made her way over to the table to take a seat. If it wasn't for the fact that she was looking forward to watching her newly adopted nieces opening their Christmas presents after lunch, she would have snuck out of the house to head into San Antonio to spend more time working with Antonio Reyes than the couple of hours she'd already promised his father for that evening.

But since her family would never understand her sneaking away, instead of being there for the first time Anthony's family celebrated Christmas as Burlesons, Charlotte had to come up with a plan for how to deal with Ian if she had to talk to him in the middle of the party. *I'll just pretend I don't know him,* she thought as Amy Lawton took the seat across from her.

Surely, he won't acknowledge me with the little woman with him. So, we should be able to get through lunch and opening presents without exchanging more than general pleasantries.

And if I see him somewhere else, when nobody else is around, I'll call him out on being a low-life, cheating bastard.
~~~

"Hey, friend. How was the move?" Charlotte's cousin, Justin, took the seat beside Amy. Charlotte continued to listen to their conversation, trying to distract herself from her thoughts about Ian Campbell being in her childhood home.

"Tiring," Amy replied, smiling shyly at him. "Even with caravanning with Randi and James, and him having his brother and coworkers help us unload everything when we got here, I was so worn out I could have easily continued sleeping all weekend."

"You should have called me. I'd have come help, too."

"I know, but we already had more people than we really needed. It took James, Randi, and I all day Wednesday to load the U-Haul. But when the GWA crew unloaded it, they had everything out of the truck and stacked in the garage within thirty minutes. I felt useless to do more than direct traffic at that point." Amy shook her head and let out a self-deprecating chuckle. "Who knew driving for twelve hours straight could be so exhausting?"

"Ya'll didn't take turns driving?" Justin looked incredulously at Amy as he asked the question.

"No, it was just the three of us." Amy shook her head again. "And with moving both my car and Randi's, and also having the U-Haul truck, we each had to be behind the wheel of a vehicle."

Charlotte was about to ask Amy where she was staying since her move to town when her thoughts were derailed by her Aunt Susan walking up with Ian and his family in tow.

"Oh, let me introduce you." Aunt Susan directed Ian and his family to sit between Charlotte and her brother, Jake, who had left two empty seats between them when he sat down. "Family, this is Ian Campbell, his sister Cait, and his son, Brody. Beside you, Ian, is my niece, Charlotte, and across the table is my son, Justin. Beside Justin is Amy Lawton. She's starting work with Justin in the lab next week. On his other side is my other son, JJ. Then we have my nephew, Josh, and across the table from Josh, and seated next to Cait is Josh's twin brother, Jake."

His sister? Well, that's better than being married. But that's still his son, so where is the little boy's mother?

"Nice to meet you all." Ian looked around the group to acknowledge each of them as he took his seat with his son on his lap, his eyes lingering on Charlotte a little longer than she felt comfortable with considering the last time she'd seen him.

Amy leaned over and whispered something to Justin, but Charlotte couldn't hear their conversation. That was fine by her, since she was still trying to come to terms with all the strange emotions she was feeling while sitting next to Ian.

Still no ring and no wife in tow, so maybe our night together wasn't a mistake after all. Maybe my butterflies were real that night and he really is **The One**? *I mean, why else would I run into him again so soon? It has to be fate pushing us together.*

But he didn't look at me like he recognized me, so maybe he's not really interested in more with me.

How on earth am I supposed to tell if the feelings are real or not, when he doesn't seem to reciprocate them? Should I flirt a little and see how he responds?

No, I can't do that because then Mom and Aunt Susan will try to take credit for getting us together if it does work out. And we can't let them get their way with all their matchmaking.

So, I have to play it cool and act indifferent. If he's interested and actually worthy of my time, he'll pursue me. Lord knows, I don't want a man I have to chase down to catch.

Justin raised his voice, getting Charlotte's attention as he spoke to the newcomers. "What brings ya'll to Heart's Destiny?"

Charlotte watched from the corner of her eye as Cait looked up as if she was going to answer before looking back down at Brody, who was demanding his aunt's attention by crawling from Ian's lap to hers.

"I'll be starting a new job in town in a little over a week," Ian replied to Justin's inquiry.

No way! What are the odds of that?

"Oh, what do you do?" Amy asked enthusiastically.

"I'm a middle school English teacher," Ian replied curtly.

"Of course you are," Charlotte mumbled under her breath, shaking her head. *Just my luck! My hot one-night stand is Fiona's replacement. Work is going to be super awkward now, whether we end up getting together or not.*

"What about you, Cait?" Justin turned the questions to Ian's sister. "Are you just visiting your brother for the holidays? Or are you moving to town as well?"

"I'm, uh, moving here, too." Cait didn't lift her eyes from her nephew as she replied.

She seems too shy to be related to the man I met two weeks ago.

"Cait helps me out by taking care of Brody while I'm working." Ian reached over to pat his sister's shoulder.

Charlotte wondered why Cait seemed to need so much reassurance from her brother to even have a conversation with new people. Not that she would ever ask them to find out why.

"Looks like you've definitely got your hands full with that little cutie." Amy waved at Brody, who was shyly looking up at her from across the table. "How old are you, Brody?"

Brody held up four fingers before burying his face in his aunt's shoulder, but he never said a word.

Amy got that right. Ian's son is a cutie. Charlotte had to ignore her biological clock ticking in her ear, reminding her that she was just a little over a year away from thirty, with no prospect of motherhood on the horizon.

"Sorry, he's shy around new people." Ian tousled his son's hair as he smiled across the table at Amy. Charlotte felt a sudden jolt of jealousy when Ian smiled at the other woman, but she did her best to squelch it before anyone noticed. "He's four, but it'll be an hour or two before he'll tell you that himself."

"Oh, I understand that," Amy laughed, wiggling her fingers at Brody, who was twisting on his aunt's lap and peeking out shyly. "I was the same way when I was a kid."

"Susan said you're starting a new job next week," Ian stated, triggering another wave of jealousy in Charlotte with the look he gave Amy as he spoke. "What do you do?"

"I'm a chemical engineer." Amy's smile beamed at Ian before she turned to direct it to Justin. "When I was here last month for Anthony and Kay's wedding, Justin told me about all the R and D projects he has going on to try and make Burleson Incorporated into a more environmentally friendly company, and I couldn't turn down the opportunity to help make that happen."

Justin returned Amy's beaming smile before speaking. "Don't let Amy fool you. It took me a whole week after she schooled me on how I could do more than I already had planned in the lab before I convinced her to move here and implement her ideas to improve our projects."

The twinge of jealousy Charlotte had felt at seeing Ian and Amy smiling at one another dissipated once she realized Amy's focus was solely redirected to Justin.

"No, you were only vaguely hinting that I should come work at Burleson. Once there was an actual offer on the table, I accepted immediately."

Justin and Amy's playful banter and flirtatious looks were sickeningly sweet. While Charlotte was happy for her cousin to seem to find the woman for him, she couldn't handle being around another crazy-about-each-other couple while sitting next to Ian and not knowing where they stood. "Ya'll need to stop with the lovey-dovey eyes and fussing at each other like an old married couple. Or our mothers will let their matchmaking success go to their heads and keep trying to set the rest of us up."

"Oh, no, we're not," Amy sputtered, motioning between Justin and herself while looking across the table at Charlotte with wide eyes. "There's no lovey-dovey anything with us. We're just friends. And, um, coworkers starting next week. Or I guess, technically, Justin's my boss starting next week. So, we can't ever be anything more than friends."

"Is that why we were seated here instead of with the Hunters, who actually invited us to this dinner? So your mothers could play matchmaker?" Ian looked pointedly at Charlotte before turning to glare at Jake, who was seated beside his sister.

Don't glare at me! Charlotte mentally screamed. *If it was up to me, you wouldn't even be here, much less sitting beside me as one of my mom's matchmaking plots.*

"Technically, it was our aunt who seated you between my sister and I," Jake pointed out, smirking at Ian. Charlotte barely stifled a giggle at the way her brother was looking at Ian. "But, yeah, I'm sure Ma enlisted the help of her best friend, Mandi Hunter, and our Aunt Susan to try to pair us up."

"They've been doing it for years," JJ chuckled from his seat across from Cait. "They've just stepped it up a notch with any new people in town, since Anthony found his new bride outside of Heart's Destiny."

"Most of the time, we just laugh it off and appreciate making a new friend, like Justin and Amy." Josh motioned to them before pointing across the room at Bobby and Brooklyn, whom Charlotte was surprised to see wasn't wearing her colored contacts to hide her true identity. "But since Ma's matchmaking seems to have worked with Bobby and Brie, she and Aunt Susan are hoping that success snowballs into marrying us all off. But unless lightning strikes the instant you meet someone in our family, you don't have to worry about a trip down the aisle. It's either love at first sight or not at all for the Burlesons."

Charlotte pointedly looked down at the table, so she didn't give away how instantly she'd fallen for Ian just two short weeks before, to him or anyone else at the table.

"You all really believe in love at first sight?" Charlotte barely noticed in her peripheral vision that Ian looked at her brothers as he asked the question. But she felt his gaze when it landed on her, as if he had lasers in his eyes, trying to disintegrate her.

Charlotte just shrugged, not wanting to give Ian an honest answer to his question. *Yes, and I thought I felt it two weeks ago with you, Jackass!*

"I've never felt the tingles myself, but it's common knowledge that our family tends to know immediately when they've met their mate." Jake drew Ian's attention off of her with his statement.

I'll have to figure out how to thank him for that later. If I can without giving away why it matters so much to me to be able to thank him.

"For as long as there have been Burlesons on this land, they've fallen in love at first sight." JJ took over for Jake in explaining the history of how Heart's Destiny got its name. "Our third-great-grandfather, Jonah Burleson, saw Emma Rogers on the train out of San Antonio going to Laredo, declared her his heart's destiny, and followed her off the train to settle here. Twenty-some years later, when there were finally enough people here to form a town, he named the town Heart's Destiny to honor her and their love."

"Their son, Joshua, who I'm named after, fell in love with our second-great-grandma, Sarah, the first time he met her at a cattle auction in Dallas." Josh continued the family history lesson that Charlotte wished they would all drop while Ian was present.

"Joshua and Sarah's son, Robert, who our dad and brother are named after, met our great-grandma, Sylvia, while on a business trip to the east coast. He stayed a little longer than planned on that business trip and had her moved home and married to him within six months." Jake grinned before continuing. "I know he fell in love at first sight, but since it took him a little while to seal the deal, I have to wonder if she took a little convincing before she fell for him."

"Our Pappaw Jerry told us stories about how he had to keep making several trips to Oklahoma to court Memmaw Judy." JJ nodded his head at Jake. "While he knew the moment he met her, it took him almost a year before he won her heart."

"And of course, there's our parents." Josh motioned between himself and Jake.

"And our parents." JJ motioned between himself and Justin. "They all fell in love at first sight, too."

"Not to mention Anthony and now Bobby in this generation," Jake added.

"Gracious, did the Burlesons only have boys until the current generation?" Amy's eyes were wide at hearing all the love-at-first-sight stories in the family tree.

"No, there were a couple of girls before us," Charlotte replied, glad for Amy's change of subject. "Our great-grandpa, Robert, had a sister, Elizabeth, who died during a flu outbreak when she was fourteen. And Jonah and Emma had a daughter, Mary, whom my house was originally built for, but we don't have a clue what happened to her after she left the ranch to serve as a nurse during World War I."

"She went off to serve and never came back?" Cait gave Charlotte a similar wide-eyed look to the one Amy had just had on her face. "Do you think she died in the war?"

"No." Charlotte shook her head, surprised at Cait not seeming as shy as before when she asked the questions. "I found boxes of her stuff that were sent home at the end of the war, including a stack of love letters. I think she fell in love with someone she met while serving in France, and either stayed there to marry him or went back to his home after the war."

"So, ya'll could have some distant cousins out in the world and not even know it." Amy's face was practically glowing from the thought of their second-great-grandaunt possibly finding true love a hundred years ago, and producing a line of descendants that could still be alive and not know they're related to the Burlesons. *And she doesn't even know about the billion-dollar trust they're set to inherit if we can find her descendants.*

"Yeah, I think so." Charlotte nodded her head. "When Tia was staying with me a couple of weeks ago, she suggested we all do one of those online DNA tests to see if we can find our long-lost family. I've been thinking about it, but I don't want to be the only one doing it, ya know?"

"I'll do it with you, Char." Justin dipped his chin at Charlotte.

"Yeah?" Charlotte looked at Justin quizzically, unable to believe he would volunteer to submit his DNA for testing.

"Of course." Justin grinned at her before turning to look at their brothers. "We should all do it, don't you think?"

"Sure, why not?" JJ chuckled.

"Absolutely," Josh exclaimed before pointing to Jake. "Maybe it'll explain how we're twins, but nothing alike."

"We'll probably find out you were switched at birth," Jake joked with their brother. "What about ya'll? Any of you wanna spit in a tube with the rest of us to see if you can find any long-lost family?"

Cait looked over at Ian with an almost scared expression. Ian shook his head at his sister before looking back up at Jake and saying, "I know all I need to know about our family, but thanks anyway."

Hum, I wonder what that's about?

"What do you say, Amy?" Justin turned his attention to the woman beside him, who was looking back at him with an expression that appeared nervous, but her eyes were also lit with excitement. "If I order a bulk lot of DNA tests, will you take one with me?"

"I, uh, I don't know," Amy stuttered. "I mean it would be kind of cool to find out about my dad's side of the family that I don't know anything about, but it's kind of scary to think of what I might possibly find that I don't really want to see."

"Like what?" Justin looked at Amy with an expression of curiosity.

Charlotte looked at the African American woman across the table from her and felt a wave of empathy at the horrors Amy was probably imagining happened to her ancestors in their journey to freedom.

"I mean, those things don't just tell you who you're related to." Amy's expression turned extremely tentative. "They also give you a detailed racial breakdown. And while I know I'm mixed with both my dad and grandpa being white, I'm not sure I want to know if the mixing started back when one of my Black ancestors was raped as a slave. Things don't always go well for Black people on *Finding Your Roots*, ya know."

"Yeah, I've worried about what we'll find in our family history before Jonah and Emma started this branch of the family, too." Charlotte reached across the table and placed her hand on Amy's, hoping to comfort the woman, who might one day be her cousin-in-law, with her theory about Jonah Burleson's race based on the few pictures of him she'd seen over the years. "Since Jonah was born in eighteen-sixty, we could find that he was the product of one of those rapes and given the last name of the man who tortured his mother, which would taint the Burleson name as being on the wrong side of our American history. Or his parents could have been plantation owners, which would still put them on the wrong side, even if his father wasn't a rapist. But even as hard as all that will be to learn, I still want to know how much of Memmaw Judy's Native American ancestry flows through my blood, and if I have a Black fourth-great-grandma that I would be proud to claim in my family tree for the strength she showed to live through that horrible time in history and raise a man as good as our third-great-grandpa, Jonah. Not to mention all the possibilities on the Rogers' side of the family that we know nothing about."

Before anyone else could say anything more about the DNA tests, Charlotte's mom, Hazel, called everyone to line up to fix their plates.

"Okay, I'll think about it." Amy squeezed both Justin and Charlotte's hands before releasing them both and standing to join everyone else in filling their plates.

Luckily for her, when they came back to the table, Ian had taken her seat and put Brody in the chair he'd previously occupied. So, Charlotte moved down to Jake's other side to sit with her cousins, Jen and Julie, and the wrestlers from the GWA, who had decided to come to town for their holiday break. She successfully avoided any further interaction with Ian for the rest of the time she was at her parents' house, and didn't stay to help with the clean-up because of having committed to spending time with Antonio later in the afternoon.

Chapter Three

Saturday, January 5, 2019

As tired as Ian was after spending the last week moving his family into the four-bedroom, three-and-a-half bath, Victorian-style rental house where they were staying while living in Heart's Destiny, Texas, he was also just as eager to get out of the house and follow the first lead his former partner, Trent Jones, sent him to try to track down Roberto Rodriguez. Unfortunately, he hadn't thought about what he was going to have to tell his sister to keep her from wanting to come with him when he left the house to explore the area.

Fuck! I should have realized that her newfound feeling of freedom would make her want to go sightseeing today, too. But I can't let her and Brody come along this time.

While I doubt I'll find Rojo the first time I go out looking, I can't take the chance with their lives to have them with me when I'm going to check out the last place he was spotted.

Ian knew he was being broody over breakfast, but he didn't want to have the discussion he was about to have with Caitir while Brody was sitting there at the table with him. So, he held his tongue as his sister rambled on about the places she wanted to visit after talking to the Hunters at the bed and breakfast the previous week and chatting with his new boss, Lisa Walker, and her husband, Tully, when they came by to see how the move was going the evening before.

Once they were finished eating, he got Brody cleaned up and sat him down in front of the television with Saturday morning cartoons, hoping that would be enough of a distraction that he could have a conversation with his sister while they cleaned up the kitchen.

"So, um, Cait," Ian mumbled as he walked back into the kitchen, where she was already washing the breakfast dishes. "I, uh, haven't been completely honest with you about why we moved here so suddenly."

"What do you mean?" Cait looked warily at him, reverting back to the fearful young woman she'd been the past couple of years in San Diego.

"I didn't just want a change of scenery to help us all get over what happened…" Ian's voice trailed off when he was unable to specifically mention the day they were attacked by the Rodriguez Cartel.

Caitir gave him a side-eye, but she didn't say a word, making him feel like an ass for having to bring this up now. Ian stalled his explanation by taking over the task of loading the rinsed-off dishes into the dishwasher.

"I got a message from Jones back in November about someone who needs to be tracked down being in this area."

"So, we moved here for you to go back to work with him, tracking someone down?" Caitir's voice was little more than a whisper from her obvious trepidation at his revelation.

"Yes, and no." Ian couldn't look his sister in the eyes as he made his confession. "I'm not officially back on the DEA payroll. But I did volunteer to move here to keep an eye out for the one person who wasn't captured in the raid Jones ran here in November, since he doesn't have enough manpower to leave a full-time agent in the area."

"So, you're just watching for this person the same way you were watching for drug dealers in San Diego?" Caitir arched an eyebrow at him as she handed him the next plate she'd just scraped off and rinsed. "And reporting anything you see to local law enforcement?"

"Obviously, I'll be doing that if I see anything going on around the school." Ian nodded, then shook his head. "But I'm also following the leads the local police aren't equipped to handle in hunting down this fugitive."

"Okay, what is it about this fugitive you seem to be afraid to tell me?" Caitir shut off the water and turned to face him straight on, propping her hands on her hips to show her irritation at him for not fessing up sooner.

"It's Rojo," Ian admitted. "He's the only person in the cartel that wasn't captured back in November.

Caitir's face paled as realization dawned. "And you're going after him without backup?"

"No, I'm just doing surveillance. Following the leads Trent can't, checking out the places he's most likely to be hiding out, and reporting back to Trent when I think he should send in a team to capture him." He might have been forced to tell his sister who he was after, but Ian wasn't about to admit to her that he would be asking to be on the team to capture him when the time came.

"And what if he recognizes you? What if he tracks you back here from wherever you spot him?" Caitir started pacing the room, obviously worried about the whole situation.

"He's not going to recognize me." Ian reached out and pulled his sister into his arms as soon as she came close in her pacing. "I've cut my hair and let it go back to its natural color from the black I dyed it while undercover in the cartel. I've scrubbed Michael Campbell from existence, so even if he sees my name somewhere, he won't have a clue who Ian Campbell is, much less figure out I'm still alive and after him. As far as he knows, I died when Mari did, and the DEA covered it up, trying to maintain my cover with the cartel."

"But what if he sees me out in town and recognizes me from that day?" Caitir shuddered in his arms, sobbing into his shirt as she clung to him in fear.

"Oh, Cait, you don't have to worry. He wasn't there that day. He's a coward, who just sent his underlings to do his dirty work. And your name and picture were never released to the press, so he has no idea whom you are to still be looking for you." Ian rubbed a hand up and down his sister's back, trying to comfort her and feeling like an ass for causing her fear in the first place.

"Besides, you aren't going to be running around the slummy areas between here and San Antonio, where we think he's hiding, for him to be able to find you. You'll be safely going about your days at work on the Burleson Ranch, which I've been told is the Heart's Destiny version of the presidential bunker when it comes to keeping people safe."

"The Burlesons know you're here to find Rojo?" Caitir looked up at him with hope written all over her face.

"Jake does," Ian admitted, knowing he had to trust his sister with more information than anyone else around him to keep her and Brody safe. "I've worked with him before, a few years ago, before I left the DEA. He's the one who helped me get the job at the middle school and set up my cover with all the local authorities. His brother, Bobby, knows the DEA has someone in the area. But, since Jake didn't blow my cover by acknowledging he knows me or introducing me to him at the late Christmas thing we went to last week, I don't think Bobby knows it's me."

"Okay." Caitir took a deep breath and slowly blew it out, obviously gathering her courage before asking, "Since Jake doesn't stay on the ranch all the time, are you sure we'll be safe there when nobody else knows what's going on?"

"Yes." Ian nodded, grinning down at his little sister. "He's an overprotective brother, just like me. Only he's also a computer whiz with more hidden cameras around that ranch to watch over his family than I've put up here." Ian circled a hand in the air to indicate he was talking about the cameras he had hidden in and around the house they were staying in since the move. "Plus, he told me about how everyone there is prepared to watch for rustlers and armed to protect the women, children, and animals if needed. Remember, Sis, we're in BFE, Texas, where kids learn to shoot right after they learn to walk, and outsiders stick out like a sore thumb. Even if they don't know to watch for him, Rojo won't be able to step foot on the ranch. Hell, I'd be surprised if he could even come into this small town without everyone being alerted there's another newcomer in town, which would put him on the local authorities' radar."

"No, that would just lead to Hazel and Susan inviting him to dinner to try to fix him up with their daughters," Cait joked, chuckling.

"Probably," Ian laughed with his sister, though he found nothing funny about Charlotte possibly being fixed up with Roberto Rodriguez. "But then Bobby would catch him because I know he has his department watching for him to make a reappearance. Besides, Trent's intel seems to indicate he's hiding amongst the crowd in San Antonio, since it's easier to hide in plain sight in a bigger city."

"Okay." Caitir took another deep breath before plastering on a fake smile. "I'll trust that we're safe here in town and on the Burleson Ranch. But you'd better hurry up and call Trent and his team in, so they can capture him, and we can go sightseeing in San Antonio."

Leah Mae Wright

"Will do, Sis." Ian brushed his lips over the top of his sister's head, reassuring himself that she would be fine at home with Brody while he went to check out the first area of San Antonio that Trent and Jake suggested as a likely place for Rojo to hide.

He drove his Range Rover out to the small airport outside of town, where Jake had set him up with an unused hangar to use as a temporary tactical operations center, where he could hide his undercover vehicle, wardrobe, and weapons. After swapping his Range Rover and attire for something more likely to fit in as a local in the slums of San Antonio, Ian holstered his nine-millimeter Glock in his waistband under the back of his shirt. He didn't think he'd need the weapon on his first time out looking for Rojo, but he wasn't about to go unarmed either, just in case.

He pulled up the map on his phone, showing the areas of San Antonio with the highest crime rates. "Shit, this is going to take a while," he grumbled when he recognized the size of the city and how many square miles he would be searching, if he had to visit every neighborhood and not just the ones with high crime rates that Jake suggested. Finally, he double-checked the message from Trent about where he had intel that Rojo had been spotted, and wasn't surprised it was the neighborhood with the highest crime rate, which was also the closest high-crime area to Heart's Destiny.

Hopefully, I'll find him before I get too old to keep searching.

~~~

Monday, January 7, 2019

As she walked into her classroom at Heart's Destiny Middle School on Monday morning, Charlotte wasn't sure if she was looking forward to going back to work after the winter break or not. Usually, the spring semester was her favorite of the school year. With half the school year behind them, the students were well established in the routine of her classroom and tended to enjoy their more in-depth discussions of the novels she assigned them at this time of the year. But with her best friend, Fiona, no longer teaching in the room next door, and Ian
~~~

Campbell taking her place, Charlotte was afraid she'd be more distracted than her students, which could be disastrous.

No, I'm not going to let him derail my routine on his first day working here by worrying about having to interact with him. He's just like anyone else I have to work with daily. The fact that he's seen me naked doesn't matter.

Or that he gave me more orgasms in one night than every other guy who's screwed me in the last ten years combined. Even if we find a private moment to discuss our liaison a few weeks ago during our planning period or at lunch, it's not like we can have a repeat in the middle of the school day.

Considering the way he ignored me at Mom and Dad's last week, and hasn't reached out since, I doubt he wants a repeat, anyway. Or if he does, he expects me to pursue him. And that's definitely not going to happen.

After the lies he told me, and then ghosting me the next morning, he's going to have to do a lot of groveling before I give him a second chance.

Charlotte pushed her thoughts of Ian out of her head and started setting up the space for the school day. She was unpacking the first box of novels for her eighth-grade classes and placing one on each of the desks for her first class of students when Lisa Walker breezed into her room with Ian in tow.

"Before we go to your classroom next door, I want to introduce you to our other English teacher, Charlotte Burleson. If you have any questions or issues arise with where to find your supplies or whatever, Char is the person to ask."

At the sound of Lisa's voice, Charlotte's head popped up, just in time to see the shock on Ian's face at seeing her in the classroom next door to his. *Oh, well, this might not be so bad after all.*

Charlotte was grateful she'd studied a little acting with her sister, Becky, to be able to hide her glee at seeing how uncomfortable Ian was at realizing he'd be working with her. *Surprise, Ian, you didn't escape the talk we need to have by avoiding me since moving to town.*

"She and Fiona have been working together for the last few years, updating our syllabi, and getting the schedules worked out when we went down to only two teachers for three grades of students, while also coaching our softball team." Lisa continued singing her praises to Ian, not noticing the look of recognition that passed between them. "You'll want to coordinate with her during your planning period, so you stay on the same lessons with the seventh graders being split between the two of you in the afternoons."

Lisa paused to take a breath as Charlotte walked back to the front of the room, from where she'd just placed the last copy of **Lord of the Rings** in her hands on a desk for her first class of students.

"Char, this is Ian Campbell, our new sixth- and seventh-grade English teacher. Please help him out by going over everything with him to start the new semester off right. I have to get back to the office, so you'll need to start by showing him where to find the novels ya'll are starting the students on today." With that, Lisa rushed out of the room as quickly as she'd waltzed into it.

"Did she at least give you a key to the storage closet?" Charlotte didn't look at Ian, choosing to focus on going to her desk to grab her keys instead.

"Yes, and to my classroom, which I still haven't seen yet." Ian shifted the handle of his leather satchel from his right hand to his left before sticking his right hand in the pocket of his khaki pants. He then pulled his extra-large hand back out of the pocket and held it out toward her with a small keyring held between his thumb and forefinger to show her the two keys dangling from the keyring.

Oh, the glorious things those thick fingers can do...

Charlotte tried not to let her perusal of his body appear obvious as she walked toward the doorway where he was standing. But she couldn't help noticing how he seemed to have chosen his outfit to match her vision of the studious librarian she'd told Fiona back in December would be her choice of a book boyfriend for a long-term relationship. From the loafers on his feet and his khaki slacks, up to his slightly darker brown tweed jacket over a crisp, white button-down and necktie with a bookshelf design printed on it, he looked exactly like the image in her head of her ideal mate. Even the leather satchel he carried fit the image in her head from that night three-and-a-half weeks before.

"You were listening to our conversation that night," Char accused, waving her finger at him, as if his choice of clothing was her evidence.

"What night?" Ian tilted his head and looked at her like she was speaking a foreign language he didn't understand.

"The night we met in December when I didn't believe your name was really Ian. I have to admit it was fun to role-play a little, but you didn't have to lie to me about being a federal agent on a manhunt. You could have admitted to overhearing my conversation with Fiona about my favorite book heroes and let me know it was only role-playing for the night. Because now, seeing you dressed for the role of my long-term dream guy totally makes you seem like a creeper."

"I have no idea what you're talking about." Ian shook his head, acting like he didn't recognize her or remember their night together. "And since we only have fifteen minutes before the students arrive, I'd appreciate it if you'd show me where my classroom and supplies are, so I'm not late starting on my first day."

Irritated by his asshole attitude, Charlotte wanted to argue with him. But, unfortunately, he was right about the students arriving soon, and she didn't want to discuss their naked, naughty time in front of them. So she pushed past him and sauntered out of her classroom.

"That's your class." She pointed at the door beside hers as she passed it in the hall on the way to the storage closet for the books they assigned to their students each year. She used her key to unlock the door to the small storage room, glad for the automatic lights so she didn't have to stay close to the door, and Ian, to turn them on. "And this is the room where our supplies are stored."

She stepped into the small room, moving as far away from him and the door as possible, and pointed to the shelf with the boxes he needed first. "You'll need *Black Beauty* for your sixth-grade classes, so take all those boxes first. We have lunch and a planning period between grades, so we'll have time to come back for *Where the Red Fern Grows* for our seventh-grade classes this afternoon during our planning period. And we each get half of those."

"Are these our only choices for the books we're teaching?" Ian made a face as he stepped further into the room and looked at the shelves filled with boxes of books.

"For this year, yes. If you want something different for next year, I'll show you the form to fill out to requisition the books for next year during our planning period. You'll be able to pick what you want for the sixth-graders, but since we split the seventh-graders, we'll have to agree on the book choice for them next year." Charlotte turned and exited the storage room to walk back to her classroom, hoping he was smart enough not to argue with her about the books she liked to teach for the next school year. "Be sure and lock the room back up when you're done getting **Black Beauty**. And if you have any other questions, I'll answer them when we're not rushed to prepare for class during our planning period and lunch break."

She didn't give him a chance to say another word as she rushed back to her classroom. Even though she felt like a bitch for not staying to help him carry the boxes of books back to his classroom as she had with Fiona every year, she couldn't handle being in that small space with him for a moment longer.

She'd realized her mistake as soon as they'd stepped through the door to the storage room. With limited space, she felt crowded by him as soon as he'd followed her in there. His masculine, woodsy scent overwhelmed her, causing her to have flashbacks to their night together.

And I can't think about any of that at school!

His sexy smell seemed to follow her back to her classroom, making her panties wet against her will. She also felt like she might drool at the memory of how he'd tasted when he finally let her get her mouth on him. He was salty and all man, with just the slightest metallic twang when she ran her tongue over his piercings.

Lord, his pierced cock was a fabulous surprise!

Having never been with a man of his stature before, she'd thought she hit the jackpot when she saw his size. But when she felt the piercings rubbing her G-spot, even through the latex barrier between them, she felt like she'd died and gone to Heaven.

He didn't seem to take as much pleasure from her playing with the piercings with her tongue as she'd expected, but she sure had fun with them. Even the memory made her need to fan herself as she finished putting out the books for her first class of students. If she didn't figure out a way to push him out of her head, she was afraid her ever-observant eighth-graders would call her out on her crush before the end of her first class of the day.

And I've really got to get a handle on this attraction before lunch and our planning period, when I know I'll have to sit beside him to go over everything for our afternoon classes. With him actively trying to deny our hot hookup in December, I really can't let him know I'd like to have a repeat.

Though what is up with the way he went from acting the part of my ideal hot hookup in December to dressing like my long-term dream man today? Did he not know he was going to get the job that night, so he only offered me what he thought he could at the time? Did he realize we could be more now that he knows we're going to be working together, so he's trying to show me he can fit that role, too?

No, the look of shock when he walked into my classroom was too real for him to have planned to dress for me today. Though maybe, after seeing me again last week, he could've bought the jacket and tie to try on the role before he saw me again.

That would explain why he didn't acknowledge our first meeting. He was too shocked to see me before he was ready to make his move, so he went with denial to keep from having to explain himself.

Although, I suppose he could always dress like that and didn't do it for me in any way, shape, or form. He could be denying our night together because he thinks I'll be clingy, and he doesn't want anything more with me. But if that was the case, why was he sporting a hard-on the whole time we were near each other this morning?

All I know for sure is that if he wants another chance with me, he's going to have to work for it. And pretending he didn't lie to me that night isn't the way to do it.

~~~

Ian couldn't believe his luck at not only seeing Charlotte again, but also having to work closely with her in his new job. He felt like it was both a blessing and a curse. A blessing because he wouldn't have to search all of San Antonio and the surrounding area for her once he had Roberto Rodriguez locked up. And a curse because he couldn't act on his attraction to her again until after he had Rojo behind bars without risking her safety.

When he'd first walked into Charlotte's classroom that morning, Ian was glad his new boss was in front of him, so she didn't see his reaction to seeing Charlotte's caramel-brown hair and lithe body gliding through the rows of desks while placing a book on each one. His jaw had dropped in shock at the same time his dick stood at
~~~

attention from just the sight of her in navy-blue slacks, a light blue sweater, and another pair of blue fuck-me pumps.

Damn, if I didn't want to do exactly as those sexy shoes asked, and bend her over her desk to fuck her right then and there.

Luckily, he was able to school his features and hide his boner behind his briefcase before either of the women noticed. He had to look around her classroom instead of at Charlotte to get his dick to deflate while Lisa Walker was telling him about the woman of his dreams, but he only managed to get it down to a half-chub before she left for her office.

Of course, he went right back to rock hard as soon as he was alone with Charlotte, but she seemed too focused on putting him in his place to notice. Ian had to grin at how she'd called him a creeper for dressing the part of her long-term dream guy.

I know she said something about a librarian in a book being her type for a long-term relationship, but fuck, I didn't think my collection of ties covered in books would be such a turn on for her. Hopefully, she'll ditch the bulky sweaters as soon as the weather warms up a little, so I can see when her nipples pebble under her shirt while she's scanning my body the way she did this morning.

The way she called him out on lying about their first meeting showed the sexy spitfire he'd first met and wanted to tame. The Charlotte he'd missed when he saw her again with her family. He was glad to see the way that feisty side came out whenever they were alone, so he decided to push her buttons a little when they were sitting in the teacher's lounge for lunch and going over the lesson plans for the afternoon classes to keep bringing it out in her. Even though he wanted more with her, he couldn't do more than enjoy antagonizing her with Roberto Rodriguez still on the loose.

He didn't actually have a problem with the books she and his predecessor had already planned for him to teach or following the schedule they already had set up. He just liked to see her riled up, and messing with the seventh-grade syllabus and lesson plans was an easy, non-sexual way he could irk her. *And maybe seeing her flushed with anger will be enough to get me through all the nights I'm going to have to jerk off to thoughts of her, when I can't see her flushed from arousal.*

"What's wrong with ***Where the Red Fern Grows***?" Charlotte glared at him as she stabbed her salad with her fork rather aggressively.

"You mean besides the fact that it's older than our parents?" Ian fought to keep from smiling at Charlotte's irritated expression. "The plot is totally outdated. People don't go hunting anymore, so the kids can't relate to it. Instead of reading books about life a hundred years ago, I'd rather have them read something more recent that would inform them about the goings on in the rest of the world now. Like maybe ***I Am Malala***."

"No, while that's an excellent book for high schoolers to read, and maybe some of my older eighth graders, it's too much for the twelve, thirteen, and fourteen-year-olds in sixth and seventh grade." Charlotte vehemently shook her head.

Fuck, she's right! I can't teach sixth and seventh graders the same things I taught tenth graders back in San Diego. Guess I'll be getting online tonight and doing some research on age-appropriate books.

"Besides, people do still go hunting, especially people in rural Texas. So, not only can our kids relate to it here, but the age of the book means it's likely their parents have read it to be able to have discussions with their kids about what they're reading at night."

Damn, she's fucking hot when her eyes light up like that. Ian had to shift in his seat, trying to subtly adjust his erection without any of the other teachers who were milling about noticing. Though he enjoyed the way Charlotte's eyes widened when she noticed. *Fuck, it's going to be hard to keep from taking her behind the stacks in the library before catching Rojo.*

"Regardless, I'm stuck with it for now." Ian held up his hands in surrender to get her to quit ranting about all the reasons she'd chosen that book. "I'll put together a list of books I'd prefer to teach and see which ones I can get approved before next year. In the meantime, we're going to have to adjust the lesson plans by a couple of days."

"What do you mean we have to adjust the lesson plans by a couple of days?" If looks could kill, Ian knew he'd be six feet under from the look Charlotte gave him as she asked him to clarify his request.

"I mean, you need to come up with something else to do with your seventh-grade classes for today and tomorrow." Ian shrugged and hid his smile at fucking with her schedule at the last minute behind taking a bite of his sandwich. He slowly chewed as she fumed, shaking her head, and floundering for words. "I didn't even get through half my introductory stuff this morning, so my seventh graders are going to be a couple of days behind yours on the reading and a week behind yours on the spelling lists, since I'm going to have to skip them this week."

"You're skipping the spelling lists this week?" Charlotte's fair skin turned a pretty, peachy pink as she got worked up.

Damn, I wish she was blushing like that because she's aroused instead of angry. But, fuck, I'm still going to enjoy having the image of her right now in my spank bank for later when I'm jerking off in the shower.

"Why on earth would you skip the spelling lists? All you have to do with those on Mondays is pass them out."

"Yeah, well, nobody told me I had to go print them out. Or where to go to print them out since I don't have a printer in my classroom." Ian shrugged once more and took the time to take another bite of his lunch before continuing. "So, I don't have them to pass out. That actually helped me get off on the right foot with the sixth graders this morning, since they were thrilled to find out I'm not going to hit them with a spelling test on Friday. Oh, and the same goes for the vocabulary list, since I couldn't even find that folder of lists on my computer."

"It's the same list of words." Charlotte rolled her eyes at him. "How long have you been teaching?"

"Two years. Why do you ask?" Ian didn't elaborate on how he started as a substitute teacher starting in January of 2017, a month after his wife was killed, to get his foot in the door at the local high schools.

"How have you taught English for the last two years and didn't realize the spelling and vocabulary lists are the same words?"

"I taught high school English Literature," Ian smirked. "Spelling and vocabulary lists aren't included in the lesson plans for high school English Literature."

"But at Christmas, you specifically said you're a middle school English teacher. Did you lie to Lisa about your experience with teaching middle school to get this job?"

"No," Ian chuckled at her indignant expression. "She knows I've only taught at the high school level before today."

"Then why did you say you were a middle school teacher and not a high school teacher at Christmas?" Charlotte was back to stabbing her salad like a serial killer, and Ian had to wonder if she wished she was stabbing him with her fork instead.

"Because I'm not teaching high school here," Ian shrugged. "And while we're on the subject, why didn't you mention your job that day, when you found out we'd be working together? Seems to me that the polite thing to do would have been to mention we'd be working together when we first met." He wasn't sure how he managed to keep a straight face as he said those final two words, but he stoically tried to keep from showing any signs of remembering their actual first-time meeting two weeks before the time they were talking about right then.

"Oh, but I didn't know we'd be working together when we *first met*." Charlotte practically spat the words, putting special emphasis on the last two, which seemed to indicate she was referring to the hotel bar in mid-December and not their second encounter at the end of the month, as he had implied. "But since you didn't seem to be acknowledging the first time we met during our second meeting, I didn't think you'd be too happy with finding out we'd be working together, so I didn't say anything so as not to ruin Christmas."

Ian knew he was playing with fire, but he couldn't seem to help himself. "Is that another reference to some night we supposedly met before? I still have no idea what you're talking about."

"Like hell you don't," Charlotte mumbled under her breath as she packed away her lunch. "How about we discuss that back in the classroom while using our planning period to prepare for the afternoon classes?"

Without giving him a chance to argue, Charlotte got up and stomped out of the room. Ian quickly shoved the last of his sandwich in his mouth and cleaned up his space at the table before following her from the room.

He had no sooner stepped into her classroom and heard the door click closed behind him before she whirled around and wagged her finger in his direction. "You know damn well we met on December fourteenth and spent the night together in my hotel room," she whisper-shouted, her cheeks pink with anger. "So, quit acting like an ass who doesn't remember fucking me."

Leah Mae Wright

Damn, she's sexy as fuck when she's mad, Ian thought, grateful she was looking him in the eyes and didn't seem to notice his dick blatantly announcing that he remembered their night together all too well and was more than ready for a repeat. As much as he would love to fuck her again right then and there, Ian still wasn't willing to risk her life by getting involved with her before he caught Rojo. So, he had to keep being the ass she'd just called him for a while longer.

"While I'm flattered that you wish I was the guy you had a hot night with, it wasn't me." Ian held his hands up in surrender, feigning his innocence. "Maybe I have a doppelganger out there somewhere that enjoyed that night with you, but it couldn't have been me because I'm still grieving my late wife, Marisol, and haven't been with anyone else," *until I met you in December,* "since she passed away a little over two years ago. Hell, I haven't wanted to be with anyone else," *but you,* "since I first met Mari over six years ago."

Ian could kick his own ass for infusing his denial with that little bit of truth. He had fallen hard and fast for Mari and hadn't even looked at another woman until the night he met Charlotte, when he realized lightning could strike twice. At least, it felt like he'd been struck twice as he fell in love at first sight for the second time in his life. Not that he could admit that to Charlotte right then.

But oh, how I wanted to tell her last week when her family told me all those stories about how the Burlesons always fall in love at first sight.

He watched her as her expression changed right before his eyes, from anger to confusion, before finally settling on what he could only construe as sympathy for his loss.

Damn, we need to get off this subject fucking immediately. I can't handle her pity when I'm being an ass of epic proportions. And I definitely don't want to give her a chance to say something lame like "Sorry for your loss," when we both know we wouldn't have met if Mari hadn't died.

"Now, if you don't mind, I'd appreciate it if you'd show me where to print off the spelling and vocabulary lists for my classes, so I can at least keep up with that much of the seventh-grade lesson plans this afternoon."

I can always pass them out the same way I passed out the books this morning.

"Yes, I can do that." Charlotte locked her lunch bag in her desk before leading him down to a teacher's workroom. She pointed out the printer to send his stuff to before they went back to the storage room from that morning to get the books for their afternoon classes.

As they were carrying the first boxes back to their classrooms, he decided to throw her a bone on the schedule changes he'd demanded earlier, as well. "And don't worry about changing your lesson plans. I'll just assign the first day of reading as homework and use the time you have down for reading aloud in class for my introductory activities."

He left *"the same way I did with my sixth graders this morning"* off his statement to keep from giving away how he was already trying to stick to her schedule. He couldn't let down his one defense against trying for more with her just because he was feeling guilty for being an ass and lying to her.

"Thank you. I appreciate not having to change my schedule at the last minute." Charlotte gave him the slightest smile as she passed his classroom to carry her box of books into her own.

Ian went into his room and sat his things down before printing off the lists he needed for the afternoon and going back to get them and the rest of the books he needed. He let silence fill the space between him and Charlotte for the rest of the day, hoping she'd forgive him for his not-so-little lie once he caught Rojo and could finally tell her the whole truth.

And I'll just keep satisfying my need for her by jacking off to thoughts of her, the same way I have every night since I had to leave her in that hotel room.

Chapter Four

Saturday, January 12, 2019

Ian was anxious to check out the next lead he had on Rojo as he geared up at his temporary tactical operations center at the small airport between Heart's Destiny and San Antonio. After torturing himself all week by making up excuses to spend his lunch and planning period with Charlotte each day, when he couldn't touch her the way he wanted, he felt desperate to capture Roberto Rodriguez, so he could drop the indifferent act and actually start to pursue her.

"Fuck, I hope this lead is better than the one last week," he grumbled as he donned a San Antonio Stallions ballcap and climbed into his undercover truck.

Unfortunately, the previous week, he didn't see Rojo when he went to the neighborhood where he'd supposedly been spotted. Ian had scoped out the house Trent's informant told them was where he was staying, but only saw two women who appeared to be living there. So, he drove around the neighborhood to see if he saw anything suspicious, but without a resident to provide him cover for why he was there, he had to split pretty quickly to keep from standing out as an outsider as he drove around. He'd made a few more trips to the city in the last week to drive by there at different times, but there were still no signs of Rojo, or even the lower-tier dealer he was supposedly staying with at the house.

Jake had assured him that the older model pickup he was using as an undercover vehicle wouldn't stick out in the city, whether he was in the slums or in the parking garages near the more upscale clubs along the RiverWalk. But Ian was starting to wonder if it didn't stick out like a sore thumb, as he drove off the private airfield and saw the looks he was getting from the people in luxury cars headed onto the airport toward their private hangers.

"Yeah, I'm not sure this was the best place to store my shit. Even if nobody in the slums made me last week, these rich guys are liable to blow my cover if they get too curious about why I'm coming here to swap vehicles all the time."

Ian took evasive measures as he drove to the dive bar, where he was supposed to be meeting the informant, making sure nobody followed him from the airport to the meet. Once he got to the bar, he pulled out his phone and texted Jake.

> **Campbell: I think we need to move the TOC.**

> **Jake: Why?**

> **Campbell: Too much traffic.**

> **Jake: Damn. Okay, I'll see what I can set up from here.
> May have to loop in a brother to assist.**

With that taken care of for the time being, Ian pocketed his phone to go into the bar to meet Trent's informant. It felt a little weird to go into a bar in the middle of the day, when it wasn't actually open for business, but he supposed it made sense when the informant was the bar owner, who didn't want to spook his customers by obviously cooperating with the feds.

Ian wasn't completely comfortable with the cover story Trent had set up for him to use, if anyone questioned why he was talking to Levi Nash whenever they might have to meet up during this operation. It wasn't just that Trent had given the guy his real name and teaching job details, in case Levi needed to introduce Ian to anyone else, that bothered him. Trent had also filled Ian in on Levi's military record to use the old Army buddy story as a cover for how they knew each other. Ian realized he needed a cover story for how he met Levi, but he hated pretending to have been in the military when he hadn't ever served.

Ian had gone the police academy plus college route right out of high school, starting to work in law enforcement as soon as he had enough academy time under his belt to be able to work with the local police department, while still finishing his bachelor's degree in criminal justice. While it hadn't been his choice in life, he had a lot of respect for the men and women who went the military route and felt pretending to have served, even though it was done for the greater good, disrespected the service of the men and women actually in the military.

Ian pushed back his uneasy feeling and got out of the truck to go meet the informant. As he walked into Levi's Bar, Ian had to shake his head at the lack of creativity in naming the place. *Though, I guess there's not much point in creatively naming the place when it's as plain and nondescript as this building.*

He was surprised to see there were a few people milling about the room. There were two men behind the bar stocking the coolers with bottled beer, one of whom he recognized as Levi Nash from the photo Trent had sent him. There was also a woman running a vacuum cleaner around the booths on the opposite side of the room.

"Ian?" Levi feigned surprise at seeing Ian walk into his bar. "Damn, man, it's been a while. What the hell are you doin' in San Antonio?"

"Moved to the area for a new job, and couldn't resist looking up an old buddy." Ian went along with the act, extending a hand to Levi when he walked around the bar.

Levi took his hand, but instead of shaking it, he pulled Ian in for a one-armed bro-hug. "Damn, man, you haven't changed a bit since leaving the service."

Ian chuckled uncomfortably as he pulled back after returning the half-assed embrace and motioned toward the other man's beard. "Yeah, my hair is too light to pull off the mountain man look like you."

"Too bad for you, 'cause that baby face will never pull in the ladies like my beard," Levi laughed, running a hand over his straggly beard. Ian chuckled along, slightly shaking his head at how wrong the man was without saying a word to risk blowing his cover. "Let's go back to my office to catch up, so we don't have to keep shouting over the vacuum."

When Ian nodded his agreement, Levi led the way behind the bar and down a hallway to an office in the back. Once they were inside, with the door closed between them and Levi's employees, the two men sat down and got down to business.

"So, what's the latest info you have on Rojo?"

"Just that he's trying to reestablish his network in the area. Did anything pan out with the address I gave Jones last week?"

"No." Ian shook his head, not wanting to give the informant any details on the times he'd driven by that address to see if he could catch Roberto Rodriguez there.

"Damn, I was afraid they might have realized I overheard them talking about it, but I hoped I got the info to ya'll in time to catch him there. Sorry, I'll try to be a little stealthier next time the local dealer gets drunk and chatty."

"What can you tell me about the local dealer?" Ian was curious about how Rojo was supposedly linked to this dealer, who was too low on the hierarchy of the organization to have been captured in the raid in November.

"He's new to the area and goes by the name Big John, but I don't know his last name, or if John is his real name or not. Honestly, he looks more like a Juan than a John to me, but maybe he Americanized it." Levi went on to describe the Hispanic man in detail to try to help Ian recognize him, if he happened to see him while searching for Rojo.

Ian was glad for the wire he had in the lining of his ball cap, so he could play back this conversation later to keep from forgetting a single detail of Levi's description.

"From what I could tell, he wasn't getting very far in working his way up the ranks, until the bust in November that took out the top-tier guys. Then he just happened to be in the right place at the right time to get Rojo out and has been acting as his number two ever since."

"What was he saying about that address last week that made you think Rojo was staying there?" It didn't make sense to Ian that Big John would be openly discussing a hideout when he was so new to the inner circle.

"I didn't hear the whole conversation, just bits and pieces." Levi backtracked, holding up his hands and acting like he wasn't as positive Rojo had been staying there as he'd told Trent the previous week. "I caught the name Roberto, the address, and the mention of liking what they saw there, but I have no clue how they fit together, what they saw, or who saw it."

Fuck! If Rojo saw what I did at that house, he's not just trying to get his drug network back up and running. He's looking for women to traffic. That means we're going to have to bring in some other agencies to assist in shutting him down for good.

Ian made a mental note to pass the address on to Jake as soon as he left the bar to have him get all the info he could on the two women who lived there, so they could arrange to protect them better than Ian could on his own. He quickly finished up his conversation with Levi, making sure the other man knew to contact him first with any new info now that he was local.

When he left the bar, he called Jake as he drove over to another high-crime neighborhood to scope out the area.

"No, I don't have a new TOC set up yet," Jake popped off in lieu of a greeting when he answered the call.

"Damn, man, and here I thought you were a super-agent, capable of doing things we mere mortals would deem impossible in such a short amount of time," Ian quipped, knowing the mood of their conversation wouldn't be light for long.

"Well, I do have the location of where your TOC will be already, but I'm waiting on the other Wonder Twin to land in Texas before he can help you move everything, which will probably be about ten o'clock tonight."

"Seriously?" Ian was shocked to hear that Jake's twin, Josh, would be arriving that night to move the tactical operations center in the middle of the night. "I was joking about you having superpowers, but damn, man, now I'm a believer."

"Yeah, well, don't tell anyone about my secret lair and I won't use my superpowers against you," Jake chuckled. "And you need to be at the airport to get Josh at ten tonight and get him back to his plane before dawn, so nobody knows he was in town. His CO doesn't like it when I pull him from the team for outside ops, so we're doing this one covert."

"Couldn't you have just had your other brother, the police chief, help me out instead of sending Josh here from Virginia?" Ian was surprised Jake hadn't already looped Bobby Burleson in on his side gig to catch Rojo.

"Nope, big brother doesn't know about our secret lair, and I have no intention of sharing it with him until I know he's outgrown the asshole-who-picks-on-his-little-brothers stage of life. Hence the threat to use my superpowers against you if you tell him about it."

"Gotcha," Ian chuckled. "I won't say a word. But I do need you to use your cyber superpowers to help me out after my talk with Levi Nash just now."

"Oh, what did he say and how can I help?" Jake's tone turned serious, realizing the jovial part of their conversation was over.

Ian filled Jake in on his discussion with the informant, as well as his suspicions based on what was said. With just the address and the barest information about the two women Ian had seen at the house, Jake was able to identify them and loop in the FBI. He was apparently good friends with the agents who would reach out to the women and make sure precautions were taken to keep them safe.

Jake was also looking for more information on Big John. So, even though this endeavor in Ian's search for Rojo wasn't fruitful for the ultimate goal, there was a possibility the information could lead to more promising results in the next few weeks.

After they signed off and Ian unsuccessfully searched another neighborhood, he went home to spend the evening with his son. He needed the joy his little boy brought to his life to balance out the disappointment of not feeling like he was any closer to catching Rojo than he was back in San Diego.

And maybe a nap before I'm up all night moving weapons and tactical gear to Jake's secret lair.

<center>~~~</center>

Sunday, January 13, 2019

As distracted as Charlotte was after Ian's first week working at Heart's Destiny Middle School, she wasn't sure how she was going to get through the whole semester. After what he said about grieving for his late wife the first day, she'd been struck dumb with no idea how to respond to his declaration that seemed to hold a lot of truth behind his lie about not being with her in December. They'd avoided each other the rest of the day, but the more she thought about his words, the more they stuck in her craw. She was sympathetic to his loss at first, but

77

there was something about the way he worded his statement that felt off. She decided her unease was because he was lying to her once again.

At the very least, he was stretching the time frame of his grief to keep from admitting to our one-night stand in December. Though for the life of me, I can't figure out why.

If he's really still that torn up over her loss and feeling guilty for our night together, he should at least be able to man up and admit it. Pretending it never happened isn't going to absolve him of his guilt.

Honestly, though, I don't think he has anything to feel guilty about from that night. Well, other than the lies. But if she's passed away, he wasn't cheating, so he shouldn't feel guilty for being with me. And if he's going to feel guilty, shouldn't he feel guilty for the way he keeps lying to me?

Charlotte thought back to the rest of the week, especially to the way Ian insisted on spending their planning period each day discussing the things he wanted to change in the lesson plans for the rest of the semester and the books he wanted to request for the next year. He still had too many books on his list that were better suited for older students, but at least he'd started trying to make changes to the lesson plans a month or two out, instead of trying to spring them on her at the last minute the way he had on Monday. But she couldn't fathom why someone who felt guilty for being with her in December would be so pushy about spending every minute of their lunch and planning periods in her presence.

Unless I'm wrong and he doesn't really feel guilty. Charlotte groaned and dropped her head to her desk on top of the essays she was trying to grade. *Well, hell, maybe guilt isn't his problem.*

Guess it's a good thing I didn't tell my siblings about more than the school issues this morning at church. Bobby would have loved to gloat about how I've been handling Ian all wrong this week because of thinking he was feeling guilty for cheating on his dead wife, when that's clearly not the case.

But why else would he deny being with me in December while acting like we're besties every day at school? I know he feels the sexual chemistry between us. It's obvious in his pants every time our discussions go from friendly colleagues trying to compromise to mortal enemies in a heated debate.

Is he just turned on by the confrontation? Did he just not outgrow the little-boy-picking-on-his-crush-on-the-playground phase of life? If that's the case, how do I get him to grow up? Or move on to a woman who actually likes that kind of foreplay?

As soon as she thought of him moving on to someone else, Charlotte shut down all thoughts of Ian. She didn't want to deal with the jealousy she felt at the thought, especially on her birthday.

She redirected her mental energy, focusing instead on grading the essays about the activities of winter break that she'd had her students write until it was time to go to her parents' house for her birthday party.

Her only thought about Ian, while she celebrated turning twenty-nine, was relief that he hadn't come to the party. Instead of dwelling on her attraction to the lying ass, she focused on enjoying her time with her family and friends.

Luckily for Charlotte, nobody else brought up Ian Campbell as they enjoyed dinner and birthday cake. Oh, there were questions about how things were going at school now that the spring semester had started, but nobody specifically mentioned his name. So, Charlotte focused on talking about her classes and the novels she had her students reading, and blocked out thoughts of Ian as best she could.

Unfortunately, that was easier said than done, especially when she was opening presents, and her cousin Justin's thoughtful gift reminded her of the vehemence Ian had shown at Christmas about not wanting to do a DNA test with his sister to find out more about his family.

No, he doesn't get space in my head. I don't care what he knows or doesn't know about his family. It's none of my business. Even if whatever upset his sister about the thought of researching their family is also the cause of his lying nature, I'm not going to worry about it. Or him. He doesn't want to admit to being with me, fine. I'll just ignore him as best I can, and eventually, my vajayjay will get the message that we're moving on to other dicks. Dicks that aren't attached to walking assholes like Ian Campbell.

"Geez, Justin, how many DNA tests do you think Charlotte weeds?" Charlotte's cousin Jen shook her head at her brother as she peered into the box that had to hold at least three or four dozen DNA testing kits. "This looks like you ordered kits for one of those daytime talk shows to test every man in town to see who's the baby daddy."

Leah Mae Wright

"Oh my word!" Aunt Susan clucked at her daughter, smacking Jen's hand out of the box. "I hope none of you would ever need tests for that!"

"Don't worry, Aunt Susan," Charlotte laughed, glad her period had come like clockwork on Christmas Eve after her night with Ian. Though her biological clock was ticking pretty loudly, she still wanted to find her Mr. Right before she went to baby town. "That's not why Justin got so many of these tests for me. We were talking at Christmas about doing these tests to see if we can track down our second-great-grandaunt Mary's descendants. But since our DNA link to them will be small after so many generations, we need to all take the tests, so we can narrow down how we're related to our DNA matches on the site to be sure we have the right line of the family tree."

"And since it was easier to order in bulk than to go through and order individual tests for each of us, I figured I'd get enough for a few of our friends to do the tests, too." Justin grinned at his mom before turning to look at Charlotte. "But I put the family tree membership in your name, so your present is really more the hours and hours of fun you're gonna have figuring out our family tree from our DNA matches."

"The hours and hours of work figuring out our family tree, you mean?" Charlotte grinned as she pulled the first test kit out and tossed it at Justin.

"I'll help you with it, Aunt Char." Tia smiled at Charlotte as she offered her assistance.

"Me, too." Maria turned and stuck her tongue out at Justin.

"Thanks, girls!" Charlotte smiled at them as she grabbed two more test kits from the box and tossed them at her nieces. "You can start helping by spitting in a tube with me."

As the girls got excited and started opening their kits to read the directions, Charlotte started passing out the DNA tests to everyone else at her birthday party.

"I bet I can spit faster than all three of you and fill my tube up first," Anthony challenged his wife and daughters.

"Oh, no, we're gonna spit much faster than you," Maria argued, an ornery gleam in her eye.

"Wait, let Aunt Char pass out all the tests before we start, so we can all race to fill our test tubes." Tia directed her sister and dad.

"But we have to get a head start or Aunt Amy and Uncle Justin will beat us," Maria pouted.

"How am I going to beat you?" Justin looked confused as he questioned Maria.

"You might not, but I will," Amy interjected, quickly opening the box Charlotte had just handed her as she looked at Justin mischievously. "You spend too much time in your office to be as quick as I am working with test tubes of liquids."

Oh, those two are going to make great parents one day, whether they want to admit to liking each other now or not.

As Charlotte handed Bobby and Brooklyn their test kids, Bobby took both of them and set them aside to do the tests later. Charlotte nodded and gave him an understanding smile, knowing he was supporting Brooklyn by waiting until she was out from under the issues with her father in Georgia to do their tests, so his girlfriend could stay safely hidden until everything was all cleared up for her back home.

It was strange to see her older brother being the staid stoic one, when he was normally the jokester of the family, while her youngest brother was acting like a kid again with his new family, after years of being quiet and reserved. While she understood their behavior was being dictated by their circumstances, both now and in the past, she couldn't quite figure out what was going on with her nerdy cousin Justin responding to Amy's taunting and getting in on the childlike antics with Amy, Anthony, Kay, and the two children in their midst.

"So, what else do you think we'll find when we all do these tests?" Charlotte's mother, Hazel, asked as Char handed her a test.

"I think the racial breakdown information will be nice to know." Charlotte smiled at her mother. "Especially to see how much of Memmaw Judy's Native American blood we have, and to find out where your family came from, since we don't know much about the Clark line of our family tree."

"We'll probably see if those pictures of Jonah and Emma we found were just bad quality because of how old they are, or if he really was mixed race like we think," Charlotte's sister, Becky, added.

"My kids will also see a lot of Scottish, Irish, and English in their blood," Aunt Susan said with a faux British accent. "Since that's where I was always told my ancestors came from before crossing the pond."

"I imagine mine will see a lot of the same from my side of the family," Hazel added with a chuckle at her sister-in-law's antics before turning to look over at Anthony's family, who had all finished filling their test tubes with spit. "Kay, what do you think you'll see in your racial breakdown?"

"Being from Oklahoma, definitely some Native American, but other than that, I have no idea." Kay shrugged.

"You'll probably be a Heinz 57 mix, like my mom says we are." Amy grinned at Kay.

"What's a Heinz 57 mix?" Maria gave Amy a questioning look.

"Heinz 57 sauce is a steak sauce that my mom thought got its name from having fifty-seven ingredients, so she uses that reference for the mix of races in our blood from the time in history when our lighter-skinned African ancestors blended in with the Native Americans who walked the Trail of Tears to escape a life of slavery and intermarried with every other race of people who were adopted into the tribe for whatever reason," Amy explained. "It turns out she was wrong about the number of ingredients in the sauce, which actually got its name from a marketing slogan and the favorite numbers of the couple who started the company. But I hope when I do this test, it'll prove my mom's theory about our ancestors correct."

"It's a plausible theory." Tia nodded as she outlined the history of the Trail of Tears and the settling of Oklahoma, confirming Amy's belief in the various tribes assimilating people of all races into their families.

Yeah, I'm definitely going to take advantage of Tia's offer to help me with our family tree research. Her crazy-huge memory ability will come in handy when I'm trying to keep the different lines of the family tree straight, while sorting through our DNA matches.

After passing out DNA kits to everyone in attendance, Charlotte finally sat down and opened one to spit in the test tube to be able to send in her sample for testing. *And maybe focusing on finding our long-lost family will help me stop thinking about Ian all the time, so I can finally get over him and move on with finding my real Mr. Right.*

~~~

Saturday, January 19, 2019

Charlotte was surprised to see Fiona's name flashing across her phone screen as she was walking into the restroom at the bowling alley, while out with her friends and family after spending her midday at the shelter working with Antonio. But her friend calling was a welcome surprise, causing her to excitedly swipe to answer the call regardless of the fact that she was standing in a public restroom at the time. She just wouldn't actually go into a stall and use it until after their conversation. "Hey, world traveler! Finally have time between seeing the sights to actually talk?"

"Yeah, something like that." Charlotte could hear Fiona's smile in her tone of voice. "I'm actually taking time from my dinner break tonight to call you, since you're always busy in the middle of the day when I have time for sightseeing."

"What did you see today? And what's your favorite place you've visited so far?" Charlotte might not want to go visit any of the places Fiona was seeing in her new job, but she liked hearing the joy in her friend's voice as she talked about her travels.

"Today I saw the Gateway Arch in Saint Louis…" Fiona trailed off, obviously having to think about her favorite place she'd been in the last two-and-a-half weeks, since starting her new job traveling with the GWA.

"And?" Charlotte prompted when Fiona let the silence stretch too long. "Your favorite place so far?"

"I can't pick a favorite," Fiona sighed. "I've enjoyed everywhere I've gone so far. Though Tijuana might be the most memorable, since it was my first time out of the country."

"From what Kay said last week, I'd have thought Vegas would be your most memorable." Charlotte cringed at the memory of Kay telling her how bad her attempt at matchmaking had bombed.

"Yeah, it probably would have been if not for how the night ended."

Aw, shit. I didn't mean to bring her down. I may be bummed about how bad things are going between me and Ian, but I don't want my
~~~

friend to feel the same way about her chances with Rick. But I'll still be a good friend by listening to what she's really feeling and trying to be supportive, so maybe I can find a way to improve her mood before hanging up.

"So, did the drunken rambling kill the attraction, or are you still pining for your DILF boss?"

"I'm still attracted to him, but I wouldn't say I'm pining for him. I know it's a one-sided attraction, so I'm not going to let my feelings go any deeper than thinking he's hot."

"Sorry to hear that." Charlotte wasn't sure how best to help her friend feel better. "I was hoping you'd found *The One*."

"Speaking of *The One*, what's going on with you and Ian?"

Guess we'll go with commiseration, since Fiona's ready to change the subject. Char looked around the room, making sure there wasn't anyone else in one of the stalls before talking about her issues with Ian. She knew she could talk to Fiona about everything that had happened since meeting him, but she didn't want to share with her other friends or family members just yet.

"Don't even go there with suggesting he's *The One*," Charlotte groaned. "He's a total *PITA,* but definitely not *The One*. I've spent the last two weeks fighting with him daily about the seventh-grade syllabus. And he still won't admit it was him at the hotel last month. He claims he never met me before our late Christmas celebration and that I'm not his type, so he wouldn't have gone to my room that night, even if it was him."

At least, that was the latest iteration of Ian's excuses for why it wasn't him. Charlotte didn't think it was any more believable than his lie about still grieving his late wife.

"Darn, guess neither one of us has found *The One*," Fiona sighed. "So, what else is going on with you? Is Antonio becoming any more vocal since you've been working with him?"

Grateful her friend was changing the subject once more, Charlotte relaxed, blowing out a breath she hadn't realized she'd been holding. "Antonio is a little more vocal, but not as much as I'd like to see. Roberto has been really hands-on trying to help me with the sessions on Saturdays, but I think he's too busy with immigration paperwork and trying to find a job during the week to work with him as much as Antonio needs."

"I hate to hear that he's not progressing as quickly as we'd hoped. Maybe once Roberto finds a job, you can get Paige to work with Antonio while he's in the childcare center. I'd suggest having her work with him now, but Roberto only leaves him there sporadically, so she couldn't do anything consistently to be much help."

"Yeah, I've already talked to her about that." That was actually one of the first things she'd suggested, but Roberto didn't like letting his son out of his sight, so he rarely used the childcare at the shelter. Charlotte had tried to point out that it would be harder for him to get a job when he brought his son to interviews, but he waved off her concerns, saying he was still working on the immigration paperwork and not going on interviews yet, so it wasn't a big deal. She had to hope that when the time came for Roberto to start interviewing, he'd actually leave Antonio with Paige in the childcare center.

"So, anything else exciting going on back home?" Fiona sounded a little more upbeat, but Char couldn't tell if it was real or put on to cover how depressing their conversation had been so far.

"The only really exciting thing that happened this week was seeing Anthony and Kay's ultrasound pictures Monday night." Charlotte couldn't make out much in the grainy black-and-white images, but they were still exciting to see. She couldn't wait to meet her new niece or nephew in a few more months.

"Yeah, I got to see them yesterday when the girls insisted on showing their friends the pictures of their baby brother." Fiona paused to giggle for a second before continuing. "I still don't see how they can tell the baby is a boy from those pictures."

"Oh, that's not why they think they're having a boy," Charlotte explained, chuckling with her friend. "Anthony dreamed about his family for over a year before he met Kay, and in those dreams, they had two daughters and two sons. So, now they're convinced that the baby is a boy because his dreams were so accurate when he saw Kay and the girls before meeting them. Truth be told, I'm kinda hoping they have another girl, so the whole family will drop their belief in prophetic dreams."

"You don't believe in prophetic dreams?"

"No," Char replied adamantly, sick of hearing about how her family members only dreamed about good things that were supposedly going to happen in their lives. "If God really allowed us to see our future in our sleep at night, then we'd have some forewarning about the bad events in life as well as the good. How can I believe Anthony saw his future wife and children in his dreams, when he didn't get any warning before losing Nancy and AJ? If he'd have dreamt about losing them, maybe he could have done something to prevent it."

"So, you'd believe prophetic nightmares, but not good dreams?" Fiona sounded skeptical, but Charlotte couldn't tell if she was skeptical about prophetic dreams in general or just Charlotte's opinion of them. "I don't think I could sleep at night if I had nightmares that came true."

"No, I don't believe in either being signs of what's to come." Charlotte shook her head, even though her friend couldn't see her through the phone. "But if they were real, they wouldn't always be good dreams with positive outcomes. Life doesn't work that way. We have to take the good with the bad. Just like we all have bad days, we all have bad dreams. So, I don't think we can pick and choose which ones to believe will come true."

"But it would be really nice if we could pick the erotic ones to come true," Fiona sighed.

"If you'd have said that a month ago, I might have agreed with you," Charlotte chuckled. "But since all my erotic dreams lately have included a certain PITA English teacher, who lied to me about who he was before the best sex of my life, I really don't want them to play out in real life now."

Damn, I probably shouldn't lie to my best friend like that. But I hate admitting I want to jump Ian's bones again every time I see him, even to myself, so there's no way I can admit it to Fiona yet.

"Really? If it was the best of your life, I'd think you'd want to have a repeat." Again, Fiona sounded skeptical.

Yeah, you're right to be skeptical because I want a lot more than one repeat with his pierced peen.

"Well, he did have a glorious dick, so maybe. If I could gag him and put a bag over his head." Charlotte barked out a laugh to cover the lies passing her lips. "But only if there was no way for me to know it was him, since his asshole attitude has killed any attraction I had to him as a person."

Fiona laughed along, so Charlotte thought it best to leave that part of the conversation on a high note, changing the subject once more. "So, when is your first break to come home for a visit?"

"There's a pay-per-view in San Antonio the weekend before Valentine's Day, so I'll be in town then. But we don't have a holiday break until Memorial Day."

"Any chance you'll have some time off on that weekend? Maybe we can sneak in a girls' night?" Not that Charlotte thought she'd be able to find a one-nighter that soon when she was still caught up on Ian, but it would be nice to see her friend, regardless. "Or maybe a book club meeting while Kay and Randi are both in town, too?"

"I don't know. I'm not sure how my schedule will change with being in the same city for a few days, if it changes at all."

"Well, let me know if you find out before then, so we can try to plan something together."

"I will, and if nothing else, I'll be able to volunteer at the shelter when everyone else is going sightseeing in San Antonio, so we can catch up there."

"Oh, yeah, that'll be good. Everyone's been asking how you're doing every Saturday when I'm there." Fiona had only missed three Saturdays so far, but the staff and residents still asked about her every time Charlotte stepped through the doors.

"Then I'll definitely make time to volunteer that Saturday. And I'll let you know if I can plan anything else that weekend, but I've got to go grab dinner now before the kids come back for more classwork."

Once they said their goodbyes, Charlotte finished her business in the restroom before going back to join her friends at the bowling alley. They soon decided to head over to Tully's for the rest of the night, but Charlotte wasn't really feeling the party atmosphere, so she stayed just long enough to keep up appearances before heading home relatively early.

She changed into her PJ's and fixed herself a bite to eat. Then she went to spend the rest of her night reading in bed. She wasn't really tired enough to need to be in bed already, but after spending every night that week working on the family tree online, she needed a break from it for the night.

Besides, the book she was currently reading had some extra steamy scenes, so she preferred to read it in bed in case they aroused her enough to need a release. As she reclined against a stack of pillows pushed up against her headboard with her Kindle resting on the pillow-like tablet stand resting on her lap, Charlotte found herself slipping a hand under her pajama pants to rub over her clit while she read an exceptionally sexy scene.

With the hero of the book giving his woman multiple orgasms from behind, Charlotte pictured her night with Ian. Specifically, she remembered back to when he'd woken her after a brief nap to use that final condom.

"What are you doing?" Charlotte had sleepily asked the question as she shifted her hips for him to enter her from behind.

"Sporking you, sweet Charlotte," Ian had whispered in her ear before nibbling her neck as he filled her.

Charlotte had giggled at his silly term even as she enjoyed the way he combined spooning and forking to get her off three more times that night. Ian had wrapped his arms around her, so he could play with her breasts with one of his large hands while rubbing her clit with the forefinger of the other. He moved inside her with slow, gentle precision, all the while whispering dirty thoughts interspersed with romantic sentiments in her ear.

With her mental image of Ian fresh on her mind, Charlotte put her Kindle to sleep as soon as she finished that chapter, moving it and the pillow-like tablet stand to the floor beside her bed as she rolled to her side. She readjusted her pillows to give her the illusion of Ian being behind her once more and got her vibrator out of her nightstand.

She slipped off her pajama pants and panties before getting back into position to use her toy while imagining it was Ian again. While she hated that she'd only been able to get herself off while fantasizing about him since the night she met him back in December, she also wasn't going to deny herself the only form of sexual pleasure she had available to her at the moment by trying to block him from her mind.

It took her a lot longer to reach her first small release with her vibrator than it had taken Ian to make her come with their last round of sensual pleasure that night. *Probably because my vibrator isn't as big as Ian's almost-a-footlong cock,* she thought as she adjusted the setting and stroked her purple rabbit in and out of her pussy just enough for the rabbit ears to rub her clit the way she liked, which only allowed it to go in about four or five inches.

Or pierced. I wonder if they make vibrators or dildos with piercings like Ian's? Maybe as big as him, too? I'll have to do an Amazon search later.

As she settled into the rhythm of playing with her toy, trying to see if she could achieve multiples while thinking about Ian the same way he'd given them to her the one night they had together, Charlotte decided to do that search for a footlong pierced dildo the next morning. She had better things to do before falling asleep for the night.

Chapter Five

As the weeks wore on, Ian was getting more and more frustrated with almost every aspect of his life. The only bright part of his days was the time he spent with Brody before his son went to bed each night. Even his sister was driving him nuts by urging him to hurry and capture Rojo, so she could have more freedom to go out with the friends she was making on the Burleson Ranch.

Like I'm not doing everything in my power to find him! Ian grumbled in his head as he drove from the middle school over to the sports complex on the other side of the high school and across Brahman Blvd. from the subdivision where he was currently living. In addition to being irritated by not having any luck in finding Rojo, he was also irritated by having to spend some of the time in the afternoons and evenings, when he would normally be searching, to go coach a middle school baseball team.

Lisa Walker hadn't told him during his interviews that he would have to take over the coaching duties of his predecessor, or he might have looked for other options of schools looking for teachers, so he could keep his schedule open for the manhunt he moved to the area to do. He'd tried to use the excuse of not knowing anything about softball to get out of coaching. But Lisa had worked around that by moving one of the baseball coaches over to work with the softball team and assigning him to coach the baseball team. Since he'd played baseball in school, he couldn't use the excuse of not knowing the rules of the game to get out of it.

Not wanting to give up all of his prime manhunt time between the end of the school day and the time he had to pick up his sister and son at the ranch to coach baseball on Tuesdays and Thursdays, Ian decided to compromise by shortening the practice time to only an hour right after school and adding Monday, Wednesday, and Friday practices. He thought of it as the perfect solution, since the team would get an extra hour of his time each week and he still had a couple of hours each day to work on finding Rojo.

Unfortunately, when he put together his plan and told all his students to spread the word about tryouts starting a day early, he hadn't realized there were only two ball fields that had to be shared between the four baseball and softball teams at the middle school and high school. He also hadn't thought to even ask about the softball schedule, or who the softball coaches ended up being, just making sure his assistant baseball coach knew about the change a week in advance.

Needless to say, he was surprised when he parked in the lot at the corner of Brahman and Clydesdale to find both ball fields filling up with girls there to try out for the middle school and high school softball teams, along with the boys there to try out for his baseball team.

Fuck! Ian inwardly cursed himself for being so focused on his own needs that he didn't think about the other teams in the area to realize the schedule was set the way it was for a reason. He got out of his Range Rover and made his way over to the field, where the boys seemed to be congregating, to explain his screw-up and apologize to the parents for the confusion. Then he saw the woman coaching the middle school softball team and decided he'd rather rile her up by sticking to his five-days-a-week practice plan.

After arguing with him over his lesson plan changes and book suggestions for the first two weeks of school, Charlotte had started sneaking away from her classroom during their planning period and not eating lunch in the teachers' lounge to avoid him. While he knew he still couldn't act on their mutual attraction until after he caught Rojo to keep her safe, Ian still needed to see her daily, or as close to daily as he could get, so he couldn't pass up the opportunity to spend some time with her while he had it.

He knew he had it bad for her, when he missed their school day arguments so much that he sat his atheist ass on a church pew the day before, just so he could see her from across the room. Not that he would ever admit to anyone that seeing Charlotte was the only reason he'd given in, when his sister asked him to take her to church.

Ian slowly took her in, as he walked past the field full of high school girls to the chaos on the field designated for the middle school practices. She had changed out of the dress he'd barely caught a glimpse of as he passed her classroom that morning and into a burgundy tracksuit with a white "Cowpokes" logo on the back of the jacket and down the right leg of the pants.

Ian was glad he'd opted to wear a cup under the sweats he'd changed into, when she turned around and he saw that her jacket was open to reveal her cleavage in a matching burgundy v-neck t-shirt under it. He'd added it at the last minute, just in case any of the boys coming to try out for the team had aim as bad as Brody did when they played catch.

Theoretically, he knew these kids were three times his son's age and should have outgrown the uncanny ability that children seemed to have to hit him in the nuts when tossing a ball. But he'd opted to protect himself, just in case reality didn't live up to the theoretical. The fact that the cup kept him from broadcasting his reaction to seeing Charlotte to half the middle school students and their parents was just a bonus. Though as painful as it was to keep his erection contained, he wasn't sure it was much of a bonus.

"I should have known you're the one who caused this fiasco!" Charlotte shouted, stomping her foot like an indignant child as he approached her on the pitcher's mound.

"Sorry you didn't get the memo about the schedule change," *Princess*. Ian barely stopped himself from using the pet name he'd called her in his head since the first night he met her back in December as he smirked down at her. "But you and your girls can have the field at four when the first day of baseball tryouts is over."

"No, you and the boys can come back tomorrow for your baseball tryouts," Charlotte huffed, fisting her hands on her hips in frustration. "We have this field reserved for softball tryouts and practice from three to five on Mondays and Wednesdays all spring."

"No, the middle school has it reserved from three to five all week, but since I have other things to do and can't stay until five, the baseball team is practicing from three to four every weekday, and your softball team can have it from four to five. Now, please, have your girls wait in the stands while I get my boy's tryouts started." Ian didn't give her a chance to reply as he turned toward the crowd of kids milling about the dugouts to take charge of his first baseball tryout. "Boys, line up on the first base line with your paperwork in hand!"

Ian tried to contain his smile as Charlotte babbled behind him, trying to extend the argument. When the boys started lining up as he'd instructed, Ian took two steps toward home plate where the line started. He only got two steps before Charlotte darted around him and stopped him from going any further by slapping both of her hands on his chest.

The feel of her touching him again after six long weeks of longing for her momentarily fried Ian's brain. He couldn't focus on anything else but the exquisite feel of her palms on his pecs, not comprehending anything else about their surroundings as she ranted about his presence on the field.

"Look, I get that you're new around here and don't know how things work, but we have a schedule set that has been working wonderfully for years. And we're not going to change it just because you don't like it." Charlotte's cheeks were pink from anger and that tantalizing blush he loved seeing stretched down her neck to the valley between her glorious tits, drawing Ian's attention.

Fuck! She's hot when she's riled up. Ian struggled to fight his growing desire for Charlotte as she continued to rant and rave at him. He couldn't make sense of what she was saying, much less that they had an audience of students and parents watching their heated exchange. All he could see was the woman he wanted more than he'd ever wanted anyone or anything in his life.

Her hands on his pecs felt more like an intimate caress than the angry barrier to him starting baseball tryouts that she intended her actions to be. The feel of her hands on him through his thin t-shirt was his undoing. He couldn't fight his need for her a moment longer.

Ian stepped in, closing the distance between them as he cupped her cheeks with both hands and lowered his mouth to hers. Charlotte tried to push him away at first, but Ian slid one hand behind her head and wrapped his other arm around her low back to pull her body flush with his, not letting her escape the kiss they'd both been aching to repeat for the last six weeks.

It only took a moment for Charlotte to quit fighting it and open her mouth for him to deepen the kiss. Ian didn't waste a second, plundering her mouth with his tongue as soon as she gave him access.

Charlotte's hands slid up from Ian's pecs, over his shoulders, finally settling in the short hair on the back of his head as she wrapped her arms around his neck. Ian weaved his own fingers through her long walnut-colored tresses as he slipped his other hand down from the small of her back to squeeze her ass. They made out as if they were the same age as the teenagers around them, not caring that half their students and their students' parents were observing them.

Slowly, the catcalls of the boys there for baseball tryouts penetrated Ian's brain, causing him to have to fight not to groan as he lifted his head and released his hold on Charlotte. She stood there, still in a daze, as he got his bearings and took charge of the situation.

"Ladies, Ms. Burleson will meet you on the bleachers to start going over your paperwork!" Ian physically turned Charlotte toward the bleachers and slapped her ass to get her moving before making his way to the line of boys waiting to show him their skills for a chance to play on the baseball team.

Ian pointed down the line as he started collecting the permission slips. "Don't even think of making rude comments, unless you want to automatically be cut from the team!"

"Wow!" Tori Collins, his assistant coach and one of the history teachers at the middle school, looked shocked when the boys straightened up in line and stopped talking. "With you coaching, we might get these boys to focus well enough to win a game or two this season."

Ian just smiled as he started handing the permission slips to Tori to match up with the evaluation forms she held. He took enough time to look at each one to see the student's name and preferred position, so he could match them up with the faces before him. But he was glad to let his assistant coach handle the paperwork portion of the tryouts.

~~~

Charlotte was fuming by the time she finally left the ball field. She'd been so flummoxed by Ian's kiss in the middle of the field that she'd walked in a daze to the bleachers. When she came back to the present, she found herself sucked into the crowd of girls and parents, who
~~~

overwhelmed her with permission slips and pointed questions about her relationship with Ian Campbell.

Stupid man and his talented tongue! Not to mention those damn gray sweatpants, showing off his biteable ass and the outline of his extra-large cup covering his pierced dick.

It took the entire hour Ian was on the field with the boys trying out for the baseball team for her to shut down all the questions and get the permission slips matched up with the evaluation forms she had on her clipboard to, finally, start running the girls through a warm-up before evaluating their performance during batting and throwing drills.

It wouldn't have taken her nearly as long if Fiona had still been her co-coach. Instead, Carrie Adkisson, one of the middle school math teachers, had been reassigned from being the co-baseball coach to Charlotte's assistant softball coach. And someone had actually informed her of Ian's asinine schedule change, so Carrie didn't arrive at the fields until four o'clock, thinking that was when the softball tryouts would start.

Though she supposed having to handle everything by herself for the first hour, at least, kept her busy enough to not spend the whole time being jealous of how Tori Collins, the other co-baseball coach and one of the history teachers at the middle school, kept fawning over Ian. Oh, Charlotte had caught more than one glimpse of how Tori had flirted with him by putting a hand on his forearm or pointing out something on the forms while holding them directly in front of her cleavage. But she didn't have a chance to react when she was dealing with the rowdy group around her at the time.

Thankfully, the parents mostly quit coming to practice once tryouts are over, so the chaos will be manageable next week when it's just the players I have to supervise. The damn, gossipy women in this town are going to make this week miserable, though. Unless, maybe, I can get Lisa to override Ian's schedule change, so I only have to deal with them again on Wednesday and not every day the way he wants our practices to go.

"Call Lisa," Charlotte instructed the hands-free feature of her phone via the Bluetooth connection with her car.

"Hey, Char," Lisa chipperly greeted her as she answered the call. "How'd the first day of softball tryouts go?"

"They went to hell in a handbasket thanks to the pain in the ass you hired to replace Fiona," Charlotte griped, not caring that she was cussing at her boss.

"Whoa!" Lisa sounded shocked at Char's harsh words. "It's not like you to use language like that. What happened to upset you that bad?"

"I've been trying to work with Ian. Really, I have. But our religious differences are preventing me from being able to work with him any longer."

"Religious differences?" Lisa sounded confused at Charlotte's reference.

"Yeah, he thinks he's God, and I disagree!" Charlotte chuckled at her own joke, feeling like she either needed to find a reason to laugh or she was going to start screaming and crying. When Lisa chuckled along, Charlotte continued, finally starting to explain the issues she was having with Ian. "I understand he's used to working with an older age group and needs help adapting to the additional tasks of teaching younger kids. But apparently, he can't handle following the plans we had in place before he came to work here, or my explanations of why we can't change things to add in his ideas. So, to get back at me for not agreeing to change our lesson plans and reading lists to things that aren't appropriate for the age group we're teaching, he decided to change the baseball and softball practice schedules without informing me in advance."

"Wait, he didn't tell you about the schedule changes?" Lisa huffed, sounding as irritated as Charlotte. "I thought it was a mutual decision. At least, it seemed like a mutual decision when I talked to Tori and Carrie about it last week."

"Oh, it might have been mutual between Ian, Tori, and Carrie, but none of them bothered to ask me. Or to inform the girls coming to try out for softball today. So, when I got to the ball field today, it was overrun with students and parents expecting tryouts for both teams at three. He wouldn't listen to me when I tried to explain our schedule. Then he had the audacity to kiss me to shut me up before he and Tori took over my field to do baseball tryouts." Charlotte inwardly cringed at her admission, wishing she'd skipped over telling her boss about the kiss.

She quickly shook it off and continued explaining her complaints to her boss. "And Carrie wasn't there at three, so I was stuck trying to calm down the mob of irate parents and girls, who were relegated to the bleachers for the first hour of our normal time slot for tryouts, by myself. I ended up having to keep them an extra hour on the field to get through the first round of evals, so now we're all late going home. Don't be surprised if your day starts tomorrow with an office full of upset parents, whose schedules were screwed up tonight, or teacher complaints all day from the girls not having time to complete their homework tonight."

"Shit," Lisa cursed under her breath, but Charlotte still heard it clearly through her car stereo.

My thoughts exactly!

"Yeah. I'm not the only person whose schedule was screwed up by his little stunt. So, you need to make sure he goes back to our regular practice schedule by tomorrow, and get the word out to everyone affected, or you'll be fielding complaints all week. Starting with having to be the one on the field tomorrow afternoon to make sure nobody shows up for softball practice without a coach. I already have plans to go to a birthday party tomorrow, and can't change them to conform to the almighty Ian's wishes."

Charlotte barely stopped herself from mentioning it was Brooklyn's birthday party, not wanting to get into the issues with the press release that went out that morning about Brie actually being Brooklyn with her boss, when she was already inundating her with issues from Ian screwing with the schedule.

"I understand," Lisa sighed. "And I'll take care of it. The practice schedule will go back to normal tomorrow."

"Thank you."

They said their "good evenings" just as Charlotte had to weave around a large news truck on the side of Rogers Road, approaching the gate to the Burleson Ranch.

Thank goodness, the reporters didn't know I'd be at the ball field today to add to the mess there.

She stopped to make sure the gate closed behind her without the reporters trying to get the scoop on Brooklyn's story sneaking onto the ranch. Once the gate was closed, she took the gravel road to her house, passing Ian, who was leaving after picking up his sister and son, as she drove by her parents' house to pull into her driveway. Charlotte resisted the urge to flip him off, but only because Cait and Brody were in the SUV with him.

That didn't stop her from mumbling the word "asshole" under her breath, though. After the stunt he pulled on the field, Charlotte was determined to get over her attraction to him, effective immediately.

And that starts with not masturbating to thoughts of him anymore. I can't get over him if I'm constantly imagining it's him touching me or fucking me when I use my toys.

I'll just focus on my family tree research and take a break from reading the erotic romance novels that always lead me to touch myself before bed. Surely, it won't take that long to get him out of my head.

~~~

Tuesday, January 29, 2019

Ian felt like an ass all day, after being reprimanded by Lisa Walker for changing the baseball and softball practice schedules without consulting Charlotte as soon as he got to school on Tuesday. He'd apologized profusely and volunteered to spend his lunch and planning period time personally calling to apologize to the parents who had been put out the day before.

On his way to the Burleson Ranch to pick up his sister and son after his longer baseball tryout time on the ball field that afternoon, he tried to come up with a plan for how to apologize to Charlotte. He didn't think the generic apology he'd given the parents he had to call earlier in the day would suffice for her, especially after that hot-as-hell kiss they'd shared on the field the day before.

Unfortunately, he didn't come up with any decent ideas in the short drive to Bob and Hazel Burleson's home. Only more questions when he saw yet another news van driving by as he turned off of Rogers Road to go up to the gate, where he had to enter a code to enter the property.

His questions started to answer themselves once he parked and approached the door he'd been instructed to enter without knocking from the first day he came to pick up his sister from work. There were
~~~

a lot of voices coming from the home, way more than just the family that he often ran into while picking up Caitir and Brody.

As soon as he entered the home, he noticed the balloons and streamers hanging all around the dining room to the right of the foyer. In addition to the Burlesons who were in town, the place was filled with several other extended relatives and friends of the family, most of whom Ian had only met in passing in the month he'd lived in Heart's Destiny. Though, as he looked around, he wondered if he'd even met some of them at all.

In addition to the three tables that were set up the same way Ian remembered from the late Christmas celebration he'd attended at the Burlesons' home, there was a fourth table set up against one wall, holding a birthday cake and presents. Right beside the largest sheet cake Ian had ever seen was a vase of red roses, presumably for the person whose birth they were celebrating.

Ian found his sister among the crowd, hoping they'd be able to sneak out before the party officially started. Unfortunately for him, Hazel spotted him before he could escape.

"You absolutely must stay for Brooklyn's birthday party," Hazel insisted.

Before Ian could explain that he didn't even know who Brooklyn was, Hazel started dragging him along with everyone else going to shout "Happy Birthday" as the woman he thought was named Brie entered the house with Bobby Burleson.

As they sat down to a meal of barbequed brisket, baked beans, potato salad, coleslaw, corn on the cob, a leafy green salad, a couple of different varieties of pasta salads, and fresh rolls, Ian whispered to his sister to find out what was going on with the different names. Unfortunately, Caitir just shrugged, so Ian had to try to piece things together from the other conversations going on around them.

As the plates were cleared from their dinner, Ian maneuvered his way around the room to stand off to the side and listen in on what was being said by Bobby Burleson, since he had come into the party with the birthday girl, who Ian thought was Bobby's girlfriend.

"Ya'll doin' okay?" Ian didn't recognize the older man who approached Bobby and started the conversation.

"Doin' great, Uncle Doug." Bobby reached out to shake the older man's hand with his right arm while keeping his left around Brooklyn's shoulders.

"Figured with as much work as you gave me today that you'd be worn out from dealing with twice as many reporters as you've arrested and sent to my courtroom." The man Bobby referred to as Uncle Doug smiled at the police chief.

"Naw," Bobby chuckled. "I only personally arrested the first one. I've put Dusty in charge of scheduling the other officers to patrol out here and making sure their paperwork is in order when an arrest has to be made. Don't want to risk my last name being on the paperwork to affect the outcome in the courts, or look like anything improper is happening if the reports end up on the news."

"Smart thinking," Doug nodded, his smile starting to spread across his face. "Come to think of it, maybe it's a good thing I've had to remand them to Medina County, since we don't have a big enough jail here in town. Maybe I should transfer all their cases to the county-level judge, too, seeing as how being related to the Burlesons could be considered a conflict of interest for me, as well."

"Wait," Brooklyn interjected, appearing as confused as Ian felt. "Just how many reporters have tried to get on the ranch?"

"Only the one actually made it on the grounds." Bobby squeezed his hand on Brooklyn's shoulder to comfort her.

"The other six I saw today were charged with harassment and obstructing a roadway." Doug reached out to pat Brooklyn's hand to reassure her as well. "Did you tell your guys to add the obstruction charge because of the larger fine than harassment or trespassing?"

"Nope," Bobby grinned. "I didn't even mention how the roads around town are too narrow to accommodate large news vans parking on the shoulders. But I'd be willing to bet that charge was recommended to the other guys by Dusty. He's always threatening to arrest his cousin for it, when they pull the fire truck out to clean the bay and block off half of Thoroughbred. So, I'm sure he can see the problem with news trucks parked alongside Rogers, Walker, and Burleson when they can't get past our gates."

"Any chance the reporters will back off after being arrested?" Brooklyn looked worried, making Ian wonder if the two news trucks he'd seen in the last two days were nothing compared to how many had been swarming the ranch for whatever reason.

Shit! I should probably go check my TOC to make sure it hasn't been compromised by whatever news story seems to have broken about the Burlesons while I was dealing with baseball tryouts. While Ian was slightly worried about his temporary tactical operations center, he hoped the dirt road on the south side of the ranch that led to it looked enough like the overgrown hunting trail Josh had described it as the night they moved the TOC that the reporters wouldn't attempt to take their large news vehicles over the rough terrain.

"Well, the ones who are sitting in county lockup won't be back." Doug smiled. "But I can't imagine they'll all stop poking around until everything is settled."

"And they'll probably be even worse when you go back to Georgia," said the older woman, who walked up and looped her arm through Doug's, her expression wary.

"That's why I have security lined up for us when we're there." Bobby smiled reassuringly. He opened his mouth as if he was going to say something else, but he was interrupted by Hazel announcing it was time for cake and presents.

They all gathered around as Bobby and Brooklyn stepped over to the table with the cake that read, "Happy Birthday, Brooklyn/Brie."

"I guess everyone in town knows who I am now, huh?" Brooklyn pointed at the cake.

"Well, I'd ordered it with just Brie." Hazel smiled at Brooklyn. "But when the story broke yesterday, I called Kara and told her to change the name since I figured everyone knew. I guess I confused her, so she put both names."

"Guess it's a good thing I've gotten used to answering to either," Brooklyn replied, still chuckling lightly.

Ian pulled out his phone and slipped off to search for whatever story had broken about Brooklyn or Brie in the last couple of days, while everyone else started singing an off-key version of *Happy Birthday*. He read through the articles about the heiress, Brooklyn Brielle Barns, releasing a statement about escaping from her father's estate in Georgia to prevent being forced to marry one of her father's associates, while the woman in the articles opened her birthday presents in the next room.

So the Burlesons have been hiding Brooklyn here on the ranch under the assumed name of Brie. Guess my pursuit of Rojo isn't the only case Jake's been working on outside his jurisdiction in Naval Intelligence for the last couple of months.

Fuck! No wonder he hasn't wanted to loop Bobby in on the Rojo hunt, when he's already dealing with the emotional side of everything going on with his girlfriend. Now I feel like even more of an ass for giving Charlotte a hard time recently, when she has to be worried about the news vans stalking her family and concerned about her brother and his girlfriend.

Too bad I still can't tell her why I'm being an ass and really ask for her forgiveness. But I've got to keep pushing her away to keep her safe from Rojo.

When Ian stepped back into the room, he noticed Brooklyn tearing up and wondered what he'd missed.

"What's wrong, Brie-Baby?" Bobby reached out to brush his thumb under Brooklyn's eye to prevent any of the tears from falling.

"Nothing's wrong," Brooklyn cried. "It's just, so much. You guys didn't have to buy me all these presents. Just having you all here to tell me happy birthday was more than I ever imagined. Especially when I'm causing so many problems with reporters and..." Her voice trailed off when she couldn't stop sobbing to finish her sentence.

"Oh, Brie-Baby." Bobby pulled her into his arms and kissed the top of her head. "You aren't causing any problems. And none of this is because we have to. It's because we want to. I love you, Brie-Baby."

"We all love you," one of the women Ian didn't recognize said. "But we can't all show you how much we love you with hugs and kisses like Bobby does."

A chuckle went around the room as Brooklyn pulled out of Bobby's embrace and wiped her eyes. "I love you all too." Brooklyn leaned into Bobby. "Thank you for all of this. I can't express just how much it all means to me."

"You still have one more present to open." Bobby handed her a rectangular gift box with "Brie-Baby" written on it. Ian assumed it was from him, since he was the only one who called her that. Everyone else had been calling her Brooklyn or Brook all evening.

Brooklyn opened the present to reveal a beautiful silver necklace with a heart-shaped lock and key dangling from it. "Oh, Bobby, it's beautiful," Brooklyn barely breathed out the words. She wrapped her arms around his neck and pulled him down to give him a peck of a kiss. "Thank you. Will you help me put it on?"

"Of course." Bobby smiled at Brooklyn, lifting the delicate chain out of the box, and using the attached key to unlock the heart-shaped lock that was essentially acting as the clasp at the ends of the chain.

Brooklyn lifted her hair for Bobby to put the chain around her neck and smiled up at him as he locked the heart in place at the base of her throat.

Ian felt like a voyeur for watching such an intimate moment between the couple, but he couldn't turn his eyes away. He longed to have a similar moment with Charlotte, but feared he'd never get to have a relationship with her the way her brother had with Brooklyn.

"I didn't realize we were going to a collaring ceremony tonight," JJ Burleson chuckled.

Ian stifled a grin at the implication, but he was unable to resist looking for Charlotte to see her reaction. Their eyes locked on one another for a brief moment, and Ian thought he saw the same longing in her eyes that he felt deep in his chest.

He was so focused on Charlotte, Ian almost forgot anyone else was in the room. Until a shrill ringing broke the spell between them.

"Chief Burleson," Bobby greeted his caller when he answered his phone. His eyes narrowed and his mouth turned down in a grimace as his tone of voice garnered everyone's attention. "Yes. We're in the middle of a family gathering at the moment."

Bobby paused to listen to whoever was calling him, while the rest of the room quieted and focused on watching his angry expression turn to one of resignation. "No, I'm not going to open the gate to allow you to interrupt her birthday party, when you're outside your jurisdiction."

Bobby closed his eyes and ran a hand through his hair in frustration as the other person spoke. "I can have her there tomorrow afternoon," he barked into the phone, his voice sounding dark and menacing. "But she will remain in my custody at all times. No, I haven't arrested her. She hasn't committed a crime."

Bobby blew out an obviously aggravated breath before raising his voice as he continued his conversation with whoever had called him. "You can consider her in protective custody with the Heart's Destiny Police Department. And I will maintain jurisdiction, even when we leave the city of Heart's Destiny, because my department is the only one involved that she feels she can trust. And quite frankly, with demands like you're trying to make right now, I agree with her assessment of not being able to trust the Macon Police, GBI, or FBI at this time."

Brooklyn reached out and clasped Bobby's free hand in hers, obviously trying to calm him down some with the comforting gesture. He squeezed her hand as he looked down at her and gave her a small smile.

"Actually, I am the police chief here," Bobby smirked. "So, as the highest-ranking police official in the department protecting Ms. Barns, I am officially denying your request to remand her to your custody for extradition to Georgia. As I said earlier, I'll gladly accompany her to a meeting with your department tomorrow. But after the gross ignorance of the law you've shown tonight, Detective Johnson, I will be speaking with your chief tomorrow morning to make sure they are not only present for any interviews Ms. Barns gives to your department, but also aware of my suspicions regarding you and the false charges you're trying to bring against her."

False charges? Damn, this case sounds about as fucked up as mine.

Bobby lifted their joined hands to his mouth and kissed the back of Brooklyn's while listening to whatever was being said on the other side of the phone conversation.

"That sounds like the first good decision you've made all evening." Bobby smiled and winked at Brooklyn. "I'll set an appointment time with your chief tomorrow, and let them decide if you need to be present for the meeting." With that, Bobby hung up his phone without even saying goodbye to the caller.

"Everything okay, Son?" Bob Burleson asked as soon as Bobby pocketed his phone.

"Yeah, Pop, everything's fine," Bobby answered his father, not taking his eyes off Brooklyn. "But I have to make a few phone calls and charter a plane for tomorrow."

"Do we need to come with?" Julie Burleson looked between Bobby and Brooklyn. "In case we need to present our backup plan to the Ashbury board?"

"Not yet," Bobby sighed. "Tomorrow we have to talk to the Macon PD to clear up the mess Detective Johnson has apparently made there. It'll be at least a day or two before we'll be able to set up a meeting with the Ashbury board, and probably not until next week, after we've met with the attorney about requesting a new trustee for Brie's inheritance."

"Wha-what were you saying about false charges against me?" Brooklyn slightly stuttered her words, probably afraid of what she might be facing the next day.

"Nothing to worry about, Brie-Baby." Bobby hugged her to him and kissed the top of her head. "You can't be charged with kidnapping yourself, no matter how that idiot tried to spin it just now."

Damn, that's a charge I never thought I'd hear brought. Ian chuckled, along with several other people in the room. There were a few people questioning how the man had made it to the rank of detective with that lack of common sense, when Ian made their excuses to Hazel and pulled his sister and son from the room.

"What's the rush to leave?" Caitir grumbled her question as he loaded Brody into his car seat in the back of the Range Rover.

"I feel bad enough for letting idle curiosity keep me there all evening." Ian shook his head as he shut the back door and got in the driver's seat. "The Burlesons don't need an audience while discussing their strategy for clearing up Brooklyn's situation."

"But as a fellow law enforcement officer, couldn't you have helped them strategize?" Caitir gave him a curious look.

"Since nobody in that house knows I'm former law enforcement," *except Charlotte who probably thinks I was lying about my DEA experience when we met last month after I've denied even meeting her for the last few weeks,* "no." Ian was glad his sister finally dropped the subject as he drove them home for the night.

But now that I know everything else she and her family are going through, I need to quit antagonizing Charlotte so much. Maybe I can just avoid her completely by focusing on work and hunting down Rojo.

Chapter Six

Charlotte was enjoying the reprieve she'd had from Ian the past couple of days. Or at least that's what she was telling herself, in the hopes that she'd eventually believe it.

Since the fiasco on the field at softball tryouts on Monday, she'd only seen him in passing at school and had successfully stayed on the opposite side of the room when he was at her parents' house for Brooklyn's birthday party on Tuesday evening. There had been a moment when their eyes had locked on one another as Brooklyn was finishing opening presents that still haunted her two days later. But the longing look he gave her, as if he wanted to be with her the way Bobby was with Brooklyn, was fleeting, so she'd convinced herself it was only in her imagination.

She still couldn't bring herself to risk reading a romance novel, knowing it would lead her to a setback in her attempt at recovering from his rejection by tempting her to masturbate to thoughts of their night together. So, she was keeping herself busy each evening by working on her family tree, until she was tired enough to fall straight to sleep as soon as her head hit her pillow.

Since she was back to her normal softball practice schedule of only Monday and Wednesday practices, she was glad to go back to her normal life. Starting with spending her free afternoons the rest of the week with the only male she needed in her life who wasn't a blood relative. Her horse, Westley. If the physical activity of horseback riding didn't keep her from thinking about Ian, then she, at least, knew she could count on Westley to keep her secrets as she confided in him how brokenhearted she felt over Ian not being her Mr. Right.

As she was carrying her saddle from the tack room to Westley's stall, Charlotte was surprised to see Brody chasing one of the barn cats down the aisle in the center of the stable.

"Whoa, little man," Charlotte whisper-shouted, hoping to slow him down, so neither of them spooked the horses, her by being too loud, or him by running past their stalls. "What are you doing out here?"

"Memmaw said I could play with the kitties." Brody turned to look at her when the cat disappeared into one of the horse stalls. "But Speckles took off and won't stay in the yard, so I'm trying to catch him to bring him back."

Charlotte stifled a laugh at the determination on Brody's face as he turned in circles to look around the stable, trying to figure out where the kitten went.

"Speckles, huh?" Charlotte knew Brody had been calling her mom "Memmaw" since meeting her at their late Christmas celebration and had rapidly come out of his shell with everyone on the ranch in the month he'd been coming to work with Cait. But she didn't realize he'd joined her nieces in naming the feral cats that kept the rodents at bay in the various outbuildings around the ranch.

"Yeah, I wanted to name him Spot because he's white with black spots," Brody explained. "But Maria said that's a dog's name, so she picked Speckles instead of Spot for his name."

"Makes sense," Charlotte nodded as she stepped into Westley's stall with the saddle that was getting too heavy for her to keep holding while talking to Brody.

"Your horse looks like the horse on the book Daddy's reading for school." As she saddled her horse, Charlotte had to fight not to giggle at Brody's revelation that Ian had to read *Black Beauty* to be able to teach his sixth-grade classes. "What's its name?"

"Westley," Charlotte replied, explaining how she came up with his name as she adjusted the girth to secure the saddle. "I named him after a character in the movie *The Princess Bride*, who wears all black clothes throughout most of the movie."

Technically, Westley wasn't a black horse. He was a dark bay American Quarter Horse, but the brown part of his coat was so dark that it appeared black in any light lower than the brightest sunlight. But when the other foal born that year was a white female American Quarter Horse, it seemed fitting to Charlotte to name them after

Princess Buttercup and Westley. Her suggestion had led to an argument between all her siblings and cousins when the boys suggested naming him Dread Pirate Roberts, but thankfully, her mother had stepped in to settle their dispute in the girls' favor.

"Are you gonna ride Westley?" Brody shifted on his feet, fidgeting in the doorway to the stall like he wanted to come closer to the horse, but he wasn't sure he could. "Can you teach me how to ride horses, so I can ride with you?"

"Yes, I'm getting ready to ride him." Charlotte smiled down at the curious little boy. "But we should probably ask your Aunt Cait if it's okay before I take you horseback riding."

As much as she would miss her solitude on a trail ride by taking Brody along, Char was almost as excited as Brody at the prospect of teaching him about the horses and how to ride. She finished tacking up Westley before walking Brody and her horse over to her house on the other side of the smallest of the paddocks that surrounded the stable.

She secured Westley to the fence as Brody ran ahead into the house, hollering, "Aunt Cait!"

Charlotte walked into the house to find Cait looking flustered as Brody begged to go horseback riding.

"I don't know." Cait shook her head at her nephew as she pulled her cell phone from the back pocket of her jeans. "I'll have to call your dad and ask him if it's okay."

"I'll be supervising him." Charlotte hoped her confidence and reassuring smile would alleviate any trepidation Cait had about allowing Brody to ride with her. "Actually, I'll be holding on to him, having him ride on my horse with me. So, there's no chance he'll get hurt on the trail."

"Yeah, I still have to call Ian." Cait looked anxious as she dialed her brother's number. She put the phone on speaker just as it started to ring.

"Hey, Cait, everything okay?" Ian sounded as anxious as Cait when he answered the call.

What's up with all the nervous energy between them? Charlotte wondered, remembering back to how Ian had seemed to need to soothe Cait's anxiety at Christmas.

"Everything's fine," Cait answered her brother. "I just wanted to check if it's okay for Brody to go on a horseback ride with Charlotte."

"Are you going with him?"

"No, I'm still working." Cait shifted nervously from foot to foot.

"You know I don't want him out of your sight, Cait," Ian groaned through the phone.

"And you know I can't keep him cooped up in whatever house I'm cleaning all the time," Cait argued with her brother. "He has way too much energy to sit still all day, no matter how many coloring and activity books you send with him every day. So, I have to let him go outside and play like the other kids on the ranch, even on the days the other kids aren't here."

"Yeah, but he's still supposed to stay in the yard where you can look out the window to keep an eye on him," Ian grumbled.

"I'll be watching him," Charlotte interrupted, hoping to keep them from arguing anymore by reassuring Ian that his son would be properly supervised. "I'll have more than an eye on him when I'm literally holding him in the saddle to ride my horse with me."

"I don't know," Ian groaned again. "He's never been around horses before, so I think he needs Cait or me there to supervise him."

"Are you kidding me?" Charlotte couldn't believe Ian thought he or Cait could do a better job supervising a child around horses than she could. "Have either one of you been around horses before?"

Ian was silent on the other end of the phone, but Cait answered Charlotte's question with a very definitive shake of her head in the negative.

"I've been riding horses since I was younger than Brody. In addition to teaching at the middle school, I volunteer at the youth center in town, teaching kids how to ride and take care of their horses. Not to mention all the trophies and ribbons I won barrel racing in the rodeo as a teenager. So, Brody will be safest riding with me, whether ya'll are there or not." Charlotte couldn't believe the audacity Ian was showing by insisting he or Cait had to supervise Brody around the horses they knew nothing about.

"While I'm sure you're much more qualified to teach him to ride than Cait or I, I still want him to stay in the corral where Cait can see him through the window," Ian insisted. "And he has to wear a helmet anytime he goes near the horses."

Leah Mae Wright

While Charlotte could understand Ian's desire for his son to wear a helmet while learning to ride, especially since he didn't know how gentle her horses were, she still thought he was being unreasonable for not allowing her to take him on a trail ride. When she tried to explain how the trail ride was actually safer than teaching him how to ride in the paddock, since she'd be on the same horse with Brody the whole time, Ian interrupted her, speaking over her to demand she only worked with Brody in the corral where Cait could see them, or Brody could stay inside with Cait and not get to go near the horses at all.

"Fine!" Char shouted, fuming at his piss-poor way of mansplaining his incorrect opinion on what was the safest way to learn to ride. *Arrogant fucking asshole!* "Come on, Brody, let's go find you a helmet that fits."

It took every ounce of self-control Charlotte possessed to calmly walk out of her house with Brody, instead of yelling at Ian and hanging up on the prick the way she really wanted to at that moment. But somehow she managed to calm down by the time they got to the barn where they stored their four-wheelers and all the old protective gear she and her siblings and cousins wore when they were kids just learning how to drive them.

Brody had her laughing as he tried on every single helmet in the barn before deciding which one he liked best. She didn't know whom it had originally belonged to, but she was glad he'd found one small enough to fit him, so Ian couldn't complain if he saw his son wearing it when he came to pick him up that evening.

Though I'm sure he'll find something to complain about if we're still in the paddock when he arrives tonight.

Charlotte shook off the negative thoughts about Ian, focusing instead on having fun with Brody as she started teaching him the basics of good horsemanship.

~~~
~~~

Ian wasn't sure how he got roped into going to the Burleson Ranch on a Sunday afternoon, when he really should be spending his time more wisely working on finding Rojo.

I probably shouldn't have given in when Cait said she wanted to go to church again. But no, I had to think with the wrong head and go just so I could see Charlotte. Since she's done an even better job of avoiding me after our phone argument on Thursday, hearing my son sing her praises every night after she started teaching him to ride horses just made my need to see her worse.

As his son practically bounced out of his car seat from the excitement of getting to go for a "real ride," instead of staying in the paddock like he had to do on Thursday and Friday, Ian realized his sister and the Burleson matchmaking matriarch had gotten their way by bribing the part of his heart that lived outside his body.

If Hazel had invited them while they were mingling between church services, when Brody was off in the four-year-old classroom with the other kids, Ian could have declined. But she was too conniving for that, so she waited until Brody was sitting right beside him during the potluck lunch after church to ask them to come horseback riding.

With the way Caitir was talking up all the Burleson women and wanting to go riding with them, Ian was beginning to think Hazel had recruited her to try to fix him up. Although, Hazel did mention her son, nephews, and granddaughters would also be going on the trail ride, so maybe she was trying to fix Caitir up, too, under the guise of their families all going.

Ian wasn't sure what he thought about the matchmaking that seemed to be happening everywhere in town since they'd moved there. On the one hand, it was rather annoying to be manipulated into these situations all the time. But on the other hand, he thought it was a good thing. Not only because Caitir seemed to start opening up again and was behaving more like her former self due to her friendships with the Burleson women, and maybe a little at thinking about being fixed up with the Burleson men, but also because of how the matriarchs of the family seemed to be pushing him and Charlotte together.

At least I know I can trust the Burleson men with my sister, since they all seem to be cut from the same cloth as Jake. If only Hazel could hold off on some of her matchmaking until after I find Rojo and get him locked up, so it would be safe for me to go along with her plans for me and Charlotte.

"Park at Charlotte's house," Caitir instructed as he drove into the cluster of houses she cleaned as her job with the Burleson family. She pointed to a small brick house on the opposite side of the gravel drive from the large, white, plantation-style home where he normally parked when he came to the ranch to pick her up from work. "It's a shorter walk to and from the stables, and I have a feeling we might need that after horseback riding."

Ian wasn't sure his sister knew what she was talking about, but he pulled into the driveway she indicated. *Seriously, how hard can it be to ride a horse? I doubt we'll be as sore as she thinks. And certainly not so sore that we'll have a hard time walking afterward. It's the horses that will be tired, not those of us sitting the whole time.*

As soon as he got out of the Range Rover and saw Charlotte walking across the yard in a pair of skintight blue jeans with her cowgirl boots hugging her calves over the jeans, Ian worried his need for a shorter walk had more to do with the fact that he'd have a hard time walking to the stable with his hard-on pressing against his zipper than any discomfort he might have after riding the horses. *How the fuck am I supposed to get on a horse with her ass on display like that?*

Her appearance kept him so distracted that he completely missed what his son was saying as they walked to the stables no more than twenty paces behind Charlotte. Once they got inside, she turned around and started talking to Brody and Cait, but Ian had no clue what was said. He was too centered in on the way her turquoise blue western shirt was open just enough at the top to reveal the valley between the tops of her breasts.

He didn't even notice anyone else was in the stables until she turned to walk over to a room on the left side of the stable to grab a helmet that she handed to Brody. As Brody put on the helmet, Charlotte walked back to the room on the side of the stable and loaded up with all kinds of other equipment that she carried to the stalls, where the horses were waiting.

Ian turned to see that several of the Burlesons were already gathering their supplies the same way Charlotte was and was happy to see Justin and JJ among them, since he'd spent more time talking to them at Christmas than the other Burlesons there for the ride. "What do we need to do first?"

"Grab a brush and follow me," Justin answered with a smile as he carried a couple of strappy things that kind of reminded Ian of the harnesses he'd seen police dogs wearing in the past.

Ian moved to the room where the equipment seemed to be stored and picked up a couple of the brushes on the shelf just inside the door. He handed one to Caitir and one to Brody before grabbing a third for himself and following Justin.

"We have to groom the horses before we put the saddles on, so we make sure there's nothing in their hair that might cause saddle sores while we're riding," Justin explained, showing them how to brush the brown and white horse he'd just put one of the harnesses on and attached to a strap on the wall of the stall.

"Miss Char already taught me how to do this with Westley." Brody surprised Ian with how outspoken he was with the Burlesons, since he normally acted super shy for the first couple of hours around anyone but him and Caitir. He hadn't said much in the few times Ian had been on the ranch for events or when he picked Brody and Caitir up after work each day, which was Ian's only experience with seeing his son with the Burlesons in the last few weeks. "What's this horse's name?"

"This is Michelangelo." Justin smiled down at Brody as he continued to brush the horse. "He's a little younger than Westley and the horse I rode the most growing up."

"Nice to meet you, Michelangelo." Brody presented his hand to the horse for it to smell him before he started brushing his hand over the side of the horse's neck. He turned to look up at Justin. "Which horse do I need to start tacking up to ride?"

"We can get you set up to ride Michelangelo if you want," Justin stated, grinning down at Brody. "Or we can see which of the other horses are available to let you pick your favorite."

"We're tacking up Pocahontas for Cait." Jen poked her head into the stall and motioned for Caitir to follow her.

Ian watched his sister follow Justin's sister out of the stall and over to another stall across the aisleway in the center of the stable.

"Which horses are still available for Brody and Ian to pick from?" Justin asked as he followed the girls out of the stall.

"Tornado and Raphael," Charlotte answered from a stall farther down on the opposite side of the stable.

Justin motioned to the next stall down from the one they'd been standing in with Michelangelo and introduced them to Raphael, another brown and white horse that looked similar to Michelangelo, who had his head sticking out over the top of the half-door.

"Michelangelo and Raphael?" Ian chuckled and quirked a brow at Justin as Brody started petting Raphael. "You guys named your horses after the *Teenage Mutant Ninja Turtles*? Where are Leonardo and Donatello?"

"I'm riding Leonardo." The oldest of the Burleson granddaughters stuck her head out of a stall two spaces down and waved at them. "And Daddy is riding Donatello." She motioned to the stall in between Leonardo and Raphael, where the man he recognized as Anthony Burleson was saddling his horse.

"Well, then we have to ride Raphael, so all four of the *Turtles* can stick together," Ian chuckled.

Justin opened the stall door for them to step in. He then put a harness on Raphael and instructed them to start brushing him while he finished tacking up Michelangelo. Ian followed his son's lead to become acquainted with the horse before the father and son worked together to brush him.

He felt a little stupid when his four-year-old son had to instruct him not to walk behind the horse to get to the other side to be able to finish brushing him.

Fuck, I hope he didn't say that loud enough for Charlotte to hear how inept I am around horses.

A few minutes later, Charlotte and JJ joined them in the stall to help them finish getting the horse ready to ride. Ian was once again struck deaf by her appearance in front of him.

He saw her lips moving and knew he should be focusing on what she was instructing him to do to saddle the horse. But all he could think about was how perfect her pink lips looked around his cock back in December. His cock quickly did an impression of a steel spike in his pants as he remembered back to their one night together.

"Now be a good girl and get on your knees to thank me properly for your spanking, Princess." Ian struggled to maintain a

straight face as he helped Charlotte stand from where she'd been draped over his lap while he spanked her, though it was hard with her smiling wickedly at him as she dropped to her knees between his feet on the side of the bed.

"Yes, Sir," Charlotte purred, reaching for his erection with both hands.

"Uh-uh, just your mouth, sweet Charlotte. You're going to need your hands to play with your pussy and tits while you suck me off."

Charlotte obeyed him beautifully, her right hand diving to her pussy while she pinched her nipple with her left hand. She stuck her tongue out and licked him from the root to the head, as if she was sampling her favorite flavor of ice cream piled high on a cone.

She spent a little time running the tip of her tongue over and around his piercings before sucking the curved barbells and his coronal ridge between her lips. With her leaning to one side to reach his piercings without blocking his view of what she was doing, he'd had to lean the other way to see her fingers rubbing her clit at the same time he watched her titillating him with her tongue.

The mischievous way she started the blow job while playing with her pussy was incredible, but not nearly as amazing as the feel of her lips when she finally closed them over the whole head of his cock and started moving down his shaft with strong suction.

Ian could practically feel her lips around his cock again as he relived the first moment she had him in her mouth.

Fuck, she was amazing with the way she alternated between deep-throating me and teasing me with her tongue playing with my piercings.

Ian knew it was completely inappropriate to be popping a boner while the woman of his dreams was talking to his son on the other side of the horse between them, so he closed his eyes for a moment and hoped the horse smell would wipe away his erotic thoughts for him to be able to come back to the moment.

He inhaled deeply and still caught a whiff of her blackberry, jasmine, and vanilla scent mixed in with the hay and horse that should have overpowered every other scent in the stall.

Leah Mae Wright

Fucking Falling In Love bodywash.

After their sensual shower together, Ian had been so infatuated with her scent that he had to look up the products she used to find out what flowers he couldn't identify before he even left the hotel to go house hunting the next day. He may have also ordered a bottle of it to have in his shower to jerk off with when he got home, too, but he wasn't about to admit it to anyone.

They certainly got the name right on that product.

He probably took longer than he should to recenter himself before opening his eyes, but it was all he could think of to do to be able to get through the rest of the day, even if it didn't actually work to get Charlotte off his mind.

When he opened his eyes, Ian was surprised to see that Charlotte and Brody had left the stall, leaving him alone with JJ and the horse, whom JJ was saddling. *Shit! Now's not the time to think with the wrong head. I need to forget Charlotte's here and focus on keeping Brody safe around all these animals that are at least ten times his size.*

"Where's Brody?" Ian heard the panic in his voice, but there was no way he could stop it.

"Char took him to meet the other horses while we finish tacking up Raphael." JJ gave him a concerned look over the back of the horse. "You seemed to need a minute to mentally prepare for riding, and we figured you wouldn't want Brody to see how nervous you are about it."

"Thanks." Ian wasn't sure if JJ's assumption that he was nervous about riding the horse portrayed him in a better light than if he'd realized the real reason Ian had taken a moment to close his eyes and take a few deep breaths, but he was pretty sure it wasn't worse, so he played along. "This is my first time around horses, so it's more the not knowing what to do to keep Brody safe while we're riding than a fear of the horses or riding. That and being overwhelmed with all the steps to prepare for the ride before even learning how to get on the horse to ride."

"Yeah, we don't expect you to do any of this," JJ chuckled as he cinched the straps of the saddle tighter around the horse before moving to trade out the harness that Justin had put on Raphael for a different one with straps of leather that he draped back over the horse's neck to the saddle. "But when we have so many people going riding, it takes a

116

while to get all the horses tacked up, so we usually let newbies bond with their horse for the day by brushing them while we get all the others ready."

"Oh, good, that makes me feel better about not remembering any instructions you guys have given me other than the way Justin showed us to brush the horses."

"Yeah, I'm not surprised with the way your eyes kinda glazed over when Charlotte started reviewing the stuff she taught Brody earlier this week." JJ grinned as he finished tightening the straps on the equipment he'd put on the horse. "But from what she said about his equestrian skill level already, all you'll have to do on this ride is sit in the saddle behind him while he holds the reins."

Ian wasn't so sure about that, but he followed JJ's directions as they exited the stall and walked the horse over to line up with the others. Brody ran up, took his hand, and practically dragged Ian to the front of the line of horses to introduce him to each and every one.

JJ was leading the trail ride on his horse, Hurricane. Jen was right behind him on her horse, Belle, followed immediately by her twin, Julie, on her horse, Jasmine. Caitir was next in line on Pocahontas, followed by Becky on Ariel.

Ian started to recognize a pattern of Disney princess names for the female horses ridden by the Burleson women. Well, except for Charlotte, who was next up in line on Westley, the horse Brody hadn't stopped talking about since Charlotte first started teaching him to ride on Thursday.

Ian recognized Raphael in line behind Charlotte's horse and hoped JJ was right about him not needing to do anything but sit in the saddle while Brody directed the horse on what to do on the ride. *Maybe I should have worn a cup for this like I do at baseball practice? It wouldn't make the ride any more comfortable, but at least my erection from watching Charlotte's ass the whole time would be contained and not obvious with my son in the saddle with me.*

Before they were instructed how to saddle up, Brody had to introduce Ian to the rest of the horses, as well as the two little girls he'd been playing with whenever they were in town while he was on the ranch with Caitir. Tia was riding Leonardo directly in line behind Ian and Brody, followed by her sister, Maria, on Princess Buttercup.

Ah, now Westley makes sense. They're named after the characters in **The Princess Bride**. *Fitting since Charlotte's horse is almost solid black while Maria's is bridal white.*

Anthony was in line right behind his daughters, or at least his horse, Donatello, was in line. Anthony was actually standing beside the split-rail fence while his daughters climbed it to mount their horses.

Finally, bringing up the rear was Justin on Michelangelo. Ian was about to ask for his assistance in figuring out how to get both himself and Brody on Raphael, but he didn't get the chance to say a word to the first person who'd helped him that afternoon as Brody quickly changed directions to head back to their horse.

Ian vaguely registered Charlotte turning around on her horse and saying something to Brody as they passed by Anthony and his daughters to get back to the horse they were about to ride, but he focused in on the other parent among them to ask for help, knowing he'd be too distracted by looking at Charlotte to hear her instructions.

"Hey, Anthony, can you help me out with instructions for how you taught your girls to get on the horses using the fence?"

"Yeah, sure, it's easy." Anthony waited until his girls were both on their horses before he walked up to where Ian was holding Brody back from climbing the fence to get on the horse before he was properly supervised. Anthony squatted down from his full height, at least a couple of inches taller than Ian's own six-foot-four, to be closer to eye level with Brody's three-foot-four. "Have you done this before, little man?"

Yeah, much better to get the help of a fellow dad.

"Miss Char's been teaching me this week," Brody nodded.

"Well, then let's let you teach your dad," Anthony smiled at Brody, giving him a fist bump before standing back up. "And I'll spot you both, so neither of you fall off the fence."

"Thanks," Ian chuckled at Anthony's mirth-filled statement.

"It's easy, Dad." Brody grinned up at him before pulling away to start climbing the fence and demonstrating each step as he told his father what to do. "You climb up to sit on the top of the fence first. Then hold on to the saddle horn while you put your foot in the stirrup. Oh, Mr. Anthony, can you shorten the stirrup for me?"

Ian chuckled at seeing his son standing on one foot in the stirrup and his chest barely coming up to the top of the saddle, making it impossible for him to put his other leg over the horse.

"Oh, yeah, I guess those are a little long for you," Anthony drawled. "But since it's not a tandem saddle, we should probably leave them long enough for your dad to use."

"Miss Char just shortened it enough for me to get on the horse the other day and then moved it back to where she needed it to get on behind me."

"Yeah, well, Char's small enough to squeeze between the horse and the fence to make that adjustment, and I'm not." Anthony made a face at Brody as he tickled his waist while moving him back to sit on the top of the fence. "So, I'll just have to let you step on my hand instead of the stirrup, so it can stay at the length your dad needs."

"Cool," Brody grinned at Anthony before turning his head toward Ian. "Dad, you'll use the stirrup like I'm using Mr. Anthony's hand."

Anthony held his left hand out close to the front of the saddle while keeping his right hand on Brody's back. Brody continued to tell Ian what to do to get on the horse as he stepped up with his left foot on Anthony's hand, held onto the saddle horn with both hands, and threw his right leg over the saddle to settle into a seated position on the horse. Ian hoped he could get on the horse as gracefully as his son, but was afraid he'd been shown up by a four-year-old when he heard giggles coming from the ladies, both in front of and behind him.

Once Ian was successful with mounting the horse, Anthony made sure Brody had the reins and knew what to do with them before instructing Ian to "just keep holding on to the saddle horn" and walking away to mount his own horse. While Ian was grateful all the Burlesons were building up Brody's self-esteem by showing confidence in his riding ability, he felt like an idiot for having no riding ability of his own.

Thank fuck, Charlotte is in front of us, Ian thought several times on their ride around the ranch. *At least she's not seeing my incompetence the whole time we're out here.*

Brody babbled on and on about everything he'd learned about the horses and named each piece of equipment on the horse, while the others carried on conversations all around them. Ian tried to pay attention to the things his son was saying, but he found it hard to keep his eyes off Charlotte's ass bouncing in the saddle right in front of him.

The sight of her in the saddle would have kept him hard the whole time, with thoughts of her riding him instead of the horse. That is, if it wasn't for the bouncing of his balls against his own saddle being so painful, especially combined with Brody bouncing so precariously close in front of him.

Yep, definitely should have worn a cup. And some compression shorts to keep my dick and balls tighter against my body than these boxer briefs are at the moment.

When the torturous ride was finally over, Ian was especially grateful his sister had suggested parking close. He wasn't sure how he made it through taking care of the horse before rushing home to ice his groin at the end of the day. *Yeah, I'll stick to riding Charlotte, or Charlotte riding me from now on, and leave the horseback riding to Brody and the Burlesons.*

Chapter Seven

Ian's second week as the middle school baseball coach was going a lot better than his first. He'd like to say it was because going back to the original schedule for practice times kept his mind off of Charlotte, so he could focus on the kids since she wasn't on the field at the same time as him. But since he couldn't look at the spot on the field where he'd kissed her without getting hard at the memory, he knew that was a lie.

As much as he might have to lie to her about only kissing her to shut her up that day, he couldn't lie to himself. He'd kissed her that day because he couldn't go a moment longer without her in his arms.

He'd thought giving himself just a little taste of her would help him stave off the hunger for her that he constantly felt. But a week and a half later, he was beginning to wonder if his strategy had backfired. Since it seemed his craving for her had only intensified, Ian feared that small sip from her lips was more like an alcoholic thinking it was okay to take a little nip and ending up falling completely off the wagon.

He'd never thought he had an addictive personality before he met Charlotte. He certainly didn't when it came to alcohol or drugs. He drank socially, but he never felt like he had to have a drink. He could take it or leave it, and neither option really mattered to him. And he'd never even been tempted to try narcotics in any way. Thanks to his mother's drug-addiction issues, he'd seen the devastation they could cause in a family, which was why he'd chosen to work with the DEA.

But unlike alcohol or drugs, Ian was beginning to think he could easily become addicted to Charlotte. After their one night together almost two months before, he'd ached for her in ways he'd never felt previously, not even with his late wife. He'd jerked off to the memories of her less than an hour after leaving her bed and every day since, sometimes multiple times a day.

He thought he could quell his desire for her by satisfying himself to thoughts of her after he walked away from her to keep her safe from Roberto Rodriguez. But he was so drawn to her that he couldn't stay away once he ran into her again. He tried to be satisfied with feeding his need for her with snark and banter until he caught Rojo and was finally free to safely be with her in all the ways he really wanted. But it just wasn't enough. Not to mention how bad he felt about being an ass to her when he learned about the other issues stressing her out.

After that kiss had reawakened the beast inside him that wanted to come out and claim her, Ian was trying to convince himself that he only wanted her so badly because he couldn't have her. *Surely, once I find Rodriguez and don't have that barrier between us, this fiery desire for her will burn out. So, it's probably best for both of us if I just douse it now.*

With his resolve to put her out of his mind artificially shored up, for the time being, Ian called his team back to the field after their final water break of the day. He focused on taking them through some base running drills for the last fifteen minutes of practice. As he was acting as a first base coach to get the players used to reading his signals to know what they were supposed to do in different situations on the field, Ian felt eyes on him. And not the hazel eyes of the woman he secretly wished was stalking him.

He looked around surreptitiously, hoping the eerie feeling was from the parents arriving a few minutes early to pick up their kids. Unfortunately, none of the parents that were already there appeared to be looking in his direction.

Ian kept his head on a swivel for the rest of the practice, trying to spot anyone suspicious without alerting them or any of his students that he was aware of being watched. There were a couple of cars parked in the lot in front of the vacant building on the other side of Clydesdale Street that were too far away for him to determine if they were occupied or not, but other than that he saw nothing out of the ordinary.

Fuck! I'm probably just being paranoid, Ian hoped as he finished up practice and walked with his team as they carried the team equipment to the field house. They put everything away before he started releasing the kids to their parents. Once the kids were all off with their families, Ian waved goodbye to his assistant coach and carried his gear bag to his Range Rover.

Normally, he would have gone straight to the Burleson Ranch to pick up his sister and Brody, but Ian needed to have a private chat with Jake before being surrounded by either of their families. Besides, if he was being observed by Rojo or one of his minions, he didn't want to lead them to the ranch any more than he wanted to lead them to his home or the out-of-the-way cabin that was his temporary tactical operations center. So, Ian drove around town as he activated the hands-free option on his secure phone to call Jake, watching for a tail the whole time.

"Damn, Campbell, I talk to you more than I do my own brothers," Jake grumbled instead of a traditional greeting. "I'm beginning to feel like you might have a crush on me or something."

"Or something," Ian chuckled, wondering if he should admit to having more than a crush on Jake's sister. *Fuck! Since Jake is more like a friend than just a colleague on this operation, is that breaking Bro Code?* "More like I'm crushing on your cyber skills than on you, though. And I'm hoping you can use them to hack into any cameras around town to see if I've been made, or am just being paranoid that someone's surveilling me while I'm supposed to be surveilling them."

"Fuck! Where were you when you felt eyes on you?" Jake's voice turned serious as Ian heard his fingers clacking on his keyboard in the background.

"On the baseball field in Heart's Destiny, just a few minutes ago." Ian hoped telling Jake when he felt that eerie feeling would also be helpful. "I saw a dark blue sedan and a black SUV in the parking lot of the vacant building on the other side of Clydesdale at the time, but I couldn't tell if they were occupied or not from that distance. While neither of them tailed me when I left there, I can't be sure if they were watching me or not."

"Did anyone else tail you when you left?"

"No, and I followed procedure to evade a tail to make sure I lost them on the off chance I just didn't see them."

They were silent for a few minutes, other than the sound of Jake's fingers flying over his keyboard.

"Damn, Bro, I think the evasive procedure training is different in the DEA than in the Navy," Jake laughed. "I don't see anyone tailing you, but since you also lost me, I can't be certain of that. Where the hell did you go?"

"If you're looking for me now, you're not going to find me in Heart's Destiny," Ian chuckled. "I'm damn near in Lytle now."

"Damn, you're good at this game. Last I saw you on camera was by City Hall, headed south. Where'd you go after that to end up ten miles north?"

"I'm not about to tell you all my secrets," Ian quipped. "But I'm guessing there aren't as many cameras in the subdivisions around town as there are on the main roads and in the business districts."

"You'd be surprised, but I don't have time to hack all the doorbell cameras in town to figure out your route. As for the two vehicles you questioned, the SUV was occupied. But it pulled out when you walked to the field house, so I can't say if they were watching you or not. And the cameras on Clydesdale that I was able to follow them on until they got on I-35 don't give me a clear enough image of the driver for facial recognition."

"What do you think the chances are that it was Rojo or one of his halcones?" Ian didn't think he'd done anything to be recognized in the time he'd been in Texas hunting for Roberto Rodriguez, but he supposed anything was possible. "Or that my cover's been blown?"

"Since the lot they were in is only a couple of blocks from the building that was raided back in November, I'd give it higher odds of being someone in the cartel, who wasn't there during the raid, scoping the area for loose ends more than anything else. And after seeing you at Christmas, I think they'd have to get a lot closer than that to recognize you without the long black hair and beard you had when you were undercover."

Ian sighed with relief as he exited the highway to turn around and drive back to Heart's Destiny. They talked for a few more minutes about the case, Ian's next steps, and the cyber-sleuthing Jake had done to identify Rojo's most recent associates in San Antonio.

Once Ian had a plan for the weekend surveillance he would do in the area that Jake had narrowed him down to in San Antonio, they said their "goodnights" and Ian headed to the Burleson Ranch to pick up his sister and son. Somehow managing to not think about Charlotte again until he turned onto her family land.

Fuck! Just seeing her house and knowing she spends part of her time in there naked shouldn't be enough to make my cock hard.

~~~

Saturday, February 9, 2019

Charlotte was struggling with controlling her sexy thoughts and dreams about Ian, even though they'd settled into a pattern of avoiding each other at school since he'd infuriated her the previous weekend on the ranch. She wished she could avoid him as easily over the weekend, but after her mother's comments at their family breakfast, she had a feeling that wasn't going to be as easy as she'd hoped.

I hope Mom's wrong about him volunteering to chaperone the middle school dance tonight, Charlotte grumbled in her head as she walked into the shelter to work with Antonio Reyes. She normally would have gone in a little later to help with lunch and then work with the little boy who'd just turned five years old two weeks ago. But since she had to chaperone the Valentine's dance at the middle school that evening, she had to leave the shelter early that day. Thankfully, Antonio's father, Roberto, was happy to reschedule their speech session to a mid-morning time for her when she'd explained why she couldn't stay later the way she usually could.

After spending every Saturday for almost two months working with Antonio, she was thrilled with the progress he was making in his speech development and learning the things he would need to know to be able to start kindergarten in the fall. Thinking of the little boy she was about to spend a couple of hours with, like she did every Saturday, helped to cheer her up.

If I had to develop an uncontrollable attraction to a single father in the last two months, why did it have to be Ian? Roberto is a really nice man. He's handsome and actually trusts me with his son. So, why didn't my libido stand up and take notice of him, instead of irritating Ian?
~~~

Charlotte shook off the frustrating thoughts as the man she wished she could be attracted to greeted her.

"Good morning, Charlotte." Roberto smiled at her as he waved her over to the table where Antonio was already seated and waiting to start their lessons. He stood and pulled out a chair for her beside his son as she approached the table.

"Good morning, Roberto." Charlotte smiled at Roberto before turning to grin at Antonio as she took the seat. "Good morning, Antonio."

"Good ma, morning, Char." Antonio's words were stilted, but he managed to get them all out, even if he still only called her by the abbreviated nickname she'd first taught him, instead of trying to say her full name unprompted.

Charlotte was okay with that, though. She was just happy Antonio said anything unprompted, since he had basically quit talking after the trauma of losing his mother. It had been a struggle to get any kind of vocalization out of the boy when she first started working with him. So, having him speak to her at all without anyone instructing him what to say was a major step for him.

After working with him for a while now, she knew he needed more help with coming out of his shell than he needed the word games they played each week to get him to talk. But since that was well beyond her scope of education, she did what she could with him each week, knowing she'd recommend a child psychologist as soon as Roberto was able to get Antonio in to see one.

She'd actually already made that recommendation, but Roberto refused to talk about it until after he got their immigration issues settled and found a job to be able to pay for the medical professional his son needed. Charlotte had even tried offering to pay for it herself, but Roberto was too prideful to accept her monetary assistance. So, Charlotte just had to be grateful that he at least accepted the help she could provide through spending time working with Antonio every Saturday.

They started off their session by playing a matching game with a set of cards with basic reading words and pictures that Charlotte had picked up. They covered the table with the picture cards lying face down and the word cards lying face up. As they flipped over each picture, Antonio had to say the word identifying the object on the card, and then look through the word cards to match the sounds of the word with the letters on the card. The activity was actually a little advanced for his age group, but she'd figured out quickly that Antonio was more advanced than his lack of motivation to speak portrayed.

"Good morning!" Fiona surprised Charlotte as she walked up to the table where she was helping Antonio sound out any words he struggled to get out.

"Good morning." Roberto stood as Fiona approached.

"Oh, don't get up for me." Fiona waved off his attempt to pull out a chair for her. "I'm headed to the kitchen. I just wanted to say hi and see how things are going for ya'll before I make it in there."

"Everything is going well. Thanks to everything you helped set up when we first got here." Roberto's smile widened as he sat back down next to his son.

"Antonio, can you say hi to Fiona?" Charlotte prompted, knowing her friend would be surprised to hear how much Antonio had started to talk in the six weeks she'd been away with her new job.

"Hi," Antonio said shyly. "Fi. Fi." Antonio turned to look at Charlotte for assistance in pronouncing her name, since it wasn't a word they'd worked on previously.

Fiona smiled widely as she heard him speak clearly for the first time.

"Fi-oh-na." Charlotte broke down her friend's name into three distinct syllables and over-exaggerated the movement of her mouth as she spoke them to Antonio.

"Fi-oh-na," Antonio repeated, watching Charlotte to make sure he had it right before smiling brightly at Fiona and waving. "Hi, Fi-oh-na."

"Hi, Antonio." Fiona returned his huge grin and little wave. She then motioned to the cards spread out on the table. "What kind of game are you playing?"

"It's a matching game," Charlotte explained. "Antonio, why don't you show Fiona how it works?"

Antonio nodded and turned over the next card, which had a picture of a cat on it. "Cat," Antonio said easily before looking at the word cards to find the match. He picked them both up off the table and held them up for Fiona to see as he said "Cat" again.

He went on to demonstrate with the cards for "Ball" and "Lamp," earning lots of praise from all three of the adults around him before Fiona excused herself to go into the kitchen to start the meal prep.

Charlotte helped Antonio finish the matching game before moving on to the animal flashcards she used to get Antonio to say some bigger words he couldn't quite read yet. After going through those, she moved on to the sight word cards that didn't have pictures, before finally having him read her a Dr. Seuss book.

Once they were done with everything she had for Antonio that day, Charlotte joined Fiona in the kitchen to see if there was anything left for her to do to help with the meal prep. As they worked on putting everything together to go in the oven or simmer on the stove, Charlotte asked her friend about the cities she'd visited since they last talked.

Fiona regaled her and the other two volunteers with stories about the various museums, historical sites, and attractions she'd seen so far. When everything was in the final stages of the cooking process, the other two volunteers left the room to go set up the dining room for feeding all the residents of the shelter, leaving Charlotte and Fiona to pull the food when it was done and clean up what they could of the prep bowls, cutlery, and cutting boards they'd used in preparing the food.

As soon as they were alone, Charlotte was ready to find out what was really going on between Fiona and Rick. Fiona hemmed and hawed for a moment before finally filling Charlotte in on the nights she shared a bungalow with Rick and his daughter Britney while in the Caribbean.

"Wait, so you actually shared a bungalow with him for two nights and *nothing* happened between you?" Charlotte raised an eyebrow at Fiona, unable to continue drying the dishes as she stared at her friend in shock at the revelation. "I don't buy it. You've got that guilty look you get whenever your mom asks about what book you're reading and it's smutty."

"Well, nothing *really* happened." Fiona kept her eyes averted, not looking at Charlotte as she continued. "We sat up watching a movie after his daughter went to bed the first night. And after I told him about Jax being gay, he got really quiet. Like all conversation stopped, so I tried to focus on the movie. But the next thing I know, I'm waking up from a dream about him while laying on top of him on the couch. And while I might have O'ed in my sleep, he didn't even kiss me."

Charlotte just stared at her friend, confused by how "nothing really happened" turned into "I might have O'ed in my sleep" in the span of five sentences.

"I'm not sure if him squeezing my bottom was real or part of the dream," Fiona continued, still not looking at Charlotte. "But we both admitted to rubbing against each other the next morning, thinking we were dreaming. He called me Fifi again, but I'm not sure if it was real or part of the dream. And after the embarrassment of his apology, while trying to get away from me as fast as possible when his alarm went off and woke us up, I wasn't about to ask him to find out. Then we went for a run and decided to forget about it and pretend it never happened. Instead, we talked more about Jax, and his crush on Cage, and went back to our normal friendly interaction."

Charlotte opened her mouth, thinking she was about to respond, but couldn't come up with the words. Not that she really got the chance to speak as Fiona continued rambling.

"And then Britney embarrassed him by talking about tampons in the middle of Customs to set it up where she and I could talk alone, so she could ask me about helping find her dad a wife and her a mom. So, the second night after she went to bed, I had to tell him about that. I had to rush off to the bunk beds in Britney's room as soon as I could, so I didn't volunteer to be the one to marry him and adopt her."

"And since then, we've only been sort of alone together in the car with Britney and Cage from San Antonio to Heart's Destiny yesterday, which isn't really alone. It was more like our outing in Tijuana that kinda felt like a date and kinda felt like family time. But all our outings since have been with other families going sightseeing, so we haven't really had the opportunity to talk, much less kiss or do any of the things I dream about doing with him alone every night."

"Not that I'm sure he'd want to do any of that with me, no matter what Jax and your matchmaking sister-in-law say about him being interested in me. Although, for the last week and a half, he has been innocently touching me as we're walking through various places and our conversations have turned a little more personal, even with everyone else around. Britney says that's his way of flirting, so I tried returning it to gauge his interest in me. But he didn't step it up even then, so I asked him over for dinner at my place tonight. I originally thought it would be a nice first date, but I'm not sure it'll really be a date, since Britney is coming, too."

Fiona sucked in a deep breath after not pausing to breathe as she rambled. Charlotte opened and closed her mouth several times like a fish out of water, still trying to wrap her head around everything Fiona had revealed to come up with the right words to respond.

"So, what else is new with you? Anything interesting with Ian? Have you got the results of your DNA tests back yet?" Fiona quickly tried to change the subject.

Oh, no, we're not changing the subject just yet!

"No, not yet." Charlotte shook her head as she answered the DNA question before going back to everything else Fiona had just hit her with. "But we'll come back to what I've found on the family tree after we break down everything you just spit out at me."

"Can we not and say we did?" Fiona gave Charlotte a pleading look as she rinsed off the cutting board that she'd been scrubbing the whole time she was rambling.

"No." Charlotte reached over, took the cutting board from Fiona's hand, and started drying it, so her friend could focus on clarifying what she'd said. "I'm not going to make you tell me about every sightseeing trip or which ones felt like dates, but you are absolutely going to explain sleeping on top of him and how you ended up asking him on a date that might or might not be a date tonight."

"I thought I explained both of those things pretty well already," Fiona giggled as she washed the next bowl. "But I guess I can try again."

Charlotte grinned at her friend as Fiona explained once more how she fell asleep on January twenty-eighth in Nassau and woke up early the next morning in the middle of a dream about being intimate with Rick.

"So, you were really dry-humping him when ya'll were dreaming about having sex with each other? And you cried out his name when you came, and he called you Fifi when he came?"

"Yes, we were both rubbing each other while having dreams about S-E-X, but I don't know for sure that he was dreaming about me," Fiona admitted. "The only times he's called me Fifi were when he was asleep then and when he was drunk in Vegas. So, I don't know if he was referring to me, or if I just reminded him of someone in his past named Fifi when he was in an altered state of mind."

"What are the chances he'd know both a Fiona and a Fifi in his lifetime?" Charlotte shook her head as she reached for the bowl Fiona just rinsed off, knowing the chances of Rick being with two women with similar names were extremely slim. "No, Fifi is definitely the pet name he calls you in his head. He's just not ready to use it all the time yet."

"You think?" Fiona gave Charlotte a skeptical look.

"I don't think, I know." Charlotte nodded to emphasize her point. "So, did he O too? Or was that part of your dream?"

"I think he did." Fiona half-shrugged one shoulder, like she wasn't totally sure one way or the other. "He had a wet spot on his pajama pants when he stood up, but he didn't really shrink much when he was still laying there under me afterwards. So, I can't say for sure that he did, since the wet spot could have been from me."

"Maybe he's a shower and not a grower?" Fiona barked out a laugh at Charlotte's crass question. Char laughed along with her before changing the subject. "So now that we know he's into you and probably O'ed from dry-humping while dreaming about you, tell me about asking him on a date for tonight and how it ended up not necessarily being a date."

"As everyone was getting off the plane yesterday, I went and sat down in the seat facing him and asked him two questions," Fiona explained as they finished up the dishes. "First, about taking Britney shopping without him or Cage tagging along. Then if he'd like to come to my place for dinner."

"And Britney wasn't sitting right beside him to think you were including her in the invitation?" Charlotte asked for clarification.

"No, she was back with the other kids." Fiona waved her hand behind her as if she was indicating where Britney was on the plane at the time of the initial invitation. "But while he was thinking over his answers, Britney walked up and started trying to talk him into saying yes to me taking her shopping, since that was the only thing she knew I was asking him. Once he agreed to our shopping trip, he insisted on driving us to my place, so he'd know where I live. When I said it was the house by the church, he asked if dinner would be with my parents. I then explained it would just be *us* in my apartment over the garage."

"And you specifically used the word *us*?" Fiona nodded to answer Charlotte's question. "I wonder if he realized you just meant the two of you when you said *us*?"

"I don't know," Fiona shrugged. "But Britney jumped on the opportunity to spend time in the kitchen with me once dinner at my place was mentioned in her presence, and I couldn't tell her that I was inviting him on an adults-only date."

"Ah! I get it now." Charlotte bobbed her head. "And while I agree that ya'll need some one-on-one time, maybe it's better that your first few dates include his daughter."

Fiona tilted her head as she thought over what Charlotte said before finally speaking. "I feel selfish for wanting him all to myself during his very limited free time, when he would normally be with his daughter."

"That's not selfish," Charlotte disagreed, not wanting to delve into the fact that she'd wondered if part of the reason Ian refused to admit to their attraction and time together in December was because of feeling guilty for not devoting all his free time to his son. She also wondered if part of the reason he didn't want to let her take Brody on a trail ride was because he didn't like the idea of her bonding with his son. "You absolutely need to have one-on-one time with each of them to develop the individual relationships and not just the overall family dynamic you feel like you're falling into when ya'll do things together. But with ya'll's crazy schedule, your one-on-one time is probably going to be limited to late at night after his daughter goes to bed. So, you might as well enjoy the family bonding time while you can and work up slowly to the overnight dates."

Their conversation was interrupted by the timer going off to alert them that the food was ready to come out of the oven. They didn't bother trying to talk while they moved the various dishes to the buffet table in the dining room and served lunch alongside the other volunteers.

After all the residents ate, Charlotte and Fiona tackled the dishes once more. Since it was just the two of them in the kitchen yet again, Charlotte finally opened up about the last month with Ian. She rehashed the changes he wanted to make to the seventh-grade lesson plans and reading list before getting into the details of their more recent interactions.

"Oh, and get this!" Charlotte exclaimed, her anger over the incident on the first day of softball tryouts reignited. "He insisted on coaching baseball instead of softball, which was fine by me, so I don't have to coach with him. But instead of taking the normally scheduled days of Tuesday and Thursday field time for the baseball tryouts and practice days, he wants to use the field five days a week. It's frustrating enough trying to juggle our game schedules with the high school teams to make sure we don't double-book the fields on Saturdays during the season. But we've had our practice schedules coordinated for years, so there's no point in making our schedules more frustrating by changing up what already works."

"And what did he do on the first day of tryouts to try and stop me from arguing with him about it not being his day on the field? He kissed me! Right there in the middle of the field in front of all the kids coming to try out and their parents. Now everyone in school is talking about us being a couple." The rumors around the school were almost as annoying as her mother's matchmaking antics.

"And Mom's matchmaking is getting even more out of hand. Since Ian's sister started working on the ranch and brings his son with her every day, Mom has been sending him to the barn every time I go out there. It's not that I don't enjoy spending time with Brody and teaching him about the horses. The kid is adorable and much more fun to be around than his father. But I can't go on a long ride to clear my head and destress because Ian insisted he can only ride with me in the corral where Cait can see him from whichever house she's working in at the time. Like I'm not good enough on a horse to supervise his son on a trail ride."

Charlotte had thought that might change after the trail ride Ian had gone on, but alas, it had not. So, now she was stuck in the small corral and paddock spaces between the stable and the houses on the north side of the ranch every afternoon that she wasn't at softball practice, teaching Brody all about the horses. She really didn't mind spending the time with Brody, and knew she could go on her longer, more relaxing trail rides on the weekends when he wasn't on the ranch. But the kid was a natural on a horse and she could tell he would soon get bored with the limited space in the paddock, where the horses couldn't run at top speed.

God forbid, Ian ease up his restrictions, so I can at least take him to the arena-sized area we have set up on the other side of the barn to teach him about barrel racing.

"And Mom, bless her heart, thought she could fix the issue last weekend by inviting Ian to go on a trail ride with me, so he could see how safe Brody would be with me. That ended up being a nightmare because Ian, the idiot, would only listen to Anthony, JJ, and Justin the whole time we were out on the trail. He has absolutely no respect for women."

"And the guys let him get away with that?" Fiona looked shocked at hearing how her brother and cousins let Ian disrespect her the previous weekend.

"Oh, no," Char fumed, shaking her head, convinced her youngest brother and cousins only let him get away with it because they didn't hear her already telling him what to do before he asked them. "He was so subtle with his selective hearing that I don't think they even noticed he was ignoring my directions just to get one of their attention later to ask how to do what I just told him."

"I'm sorry, Char. I wish I knew how to help you deal with him." Fiona gave her a sympathetic look.

Not wanting her friend to pity her, Charlotte decided to change the subject. "Just listening to me rant about him is the most helpful thing you, or anyone else, can do for me at this point. But once I convince my vajayjay that there are other dicks in the sea, we'll have to schedule another girls' night out on one of your holiday breaks from traveling the world."

"Deal," Fiona agreed, laughing once more.

They finished cleaning up the kitchen at the shelter just in time for Fiona to leave to get ready for her dinner with the Robertsons and Charlotte to put on a dress to go chaperone the Valentine's dance at the middle school.

Lord, please help me get through this unscathed tonight, Charlotte prayed as she drove to the middle school. *Maybe set it up where we can chaperone from opposite sides of the gym, so we're not tempted to argue half the night. And, please Lord, keep me from being tempted to climb him like a tree and kiss the living daylights out of him the instant I see him in a suit.*

~~~

Ian regretted his decision to chaperone the middle school Valentine's dance as soon as he walked into the gym. Back in San Diego, he'd caught wind of quite a few drug deals going down when he chaperoned the school dances, so he thought he might have similar luck in learning about the lower-level dealers who might be getting their stock from the Rodriguez Cartel by doing the same in Heart's Destiny. Unfortunately, he didn't take into consideration the differences in demographics between an inner-city high school and the small-town middle school where he now worked when he made that decision.

With the girls huddled together on one side of the gym and the boys congregating on the other, he could see that it wasn't very likely that he'd find any leads there. From what he could tell, the kids were having the same conversations he overheard in school each day. The boys were talking about the latest video games and the local sports teams, while the girls were discussing hair and makeup trends and the latest celebrity gossip.

If it wasn't for the fact that the music blaring through the speakers was the same current pop hits he heard at the high school dances he chaperoned in San Diego, Ian would think he'd gone through some kind of time warp when he crossed into the city limits of Heart's Destiny, Texas. The whole town reminded him of the idealized television version of life in the 1950s that he remembered seeing as a child when he watched reruns of classic television shows with his grandparents.

Damn, I should have stayed at Levi's Bar tonight to see if Big John ever showed back up. Maybe I could have at least identified some of the other dealers in the area there.

Ian shook off any thoughts of following leads on Rodriguez that night and made his way around the room, trying to at least do a decent job supervising the activities of the students. A couple of his baseball players stopped him to ask his opinion on the local minor league ball team's players, who might move up to the majors when spring training started in a couple of weeks. Luckily for him, he actually knew a little about the San Antonio minor league team, since it was affiliated with
~~~

his favorite major league team in San Diego. So, he was able to have a decent conversation with the kids before moving on to see what was going on in the rest of the gym.

As he got close to the refreshment table, he saw Charlotte for the first time that night. Dressed in a red, knee-length cocktail dress and matching fuck-me pumps that made her legs look a mile long, with her hair up in a fancy updo that he desperately wanted to tangle his fingers in and mess up, she was a Valentine's vision.

He had to quash his instant jealousy at seeing her talking to Ryder Deere, the middle school physical education teacher that Ian had thought he might become friends with before seeing him flirting with Charlotte beside the refreshment table. Although, the good thing about the jealousy he was feeling was that it killed the boner he'd popped the instant he saw Charlotte.

"You'd better not be spiking the punch, Coach," Ian joked as he walked around the table to stand on the opposite side of Charlotte from Ryder.

"Like I'd try it with Char here to narc on me to her brother or my cousin at the police department," Ryder chuckled, extending his hand to Ian to shake. Ian squeezed the other man's hand with a little more force than necessary as they shook. "But hit me up later when the other chaperones aren't around, and I'll share my flask with you to help us get through the night without our ears bleeding too bad from all the teeny-bopper music we're gonna be tortured with tonight."

"Yeah, I doubt we'll hear any Queens of the Stone Age played tonight," Ian chuckled, not wanting to touch the flask comment with a ten-foot pole. He focused on the music reference, assuming Ryder had similar taste in music to his own.

"No, probably not, but if that's the music you're into, you're welcome to DJ next time I have a party," Ryder grinned at Ian before turning to look at Charlotte. "But ya gotta promise not to let Char near the stereo, so we don't end up listening to the sappy country she always plays on the jukebox at Tully's."

"Whatever, Ryder," Charlotte scoffed. "We all know you only complain about country music because you're too uncoordinated to dance to it."

"Oh, no, that's not the problem, Char. Well, not the whole problem anyway," Tori laughed from the other side of the table. "Ryder complains about country because the buckle bunnies turn him down after seeing his lack of rhythm, knowing it means he can't give them a good ride on or off the dance floor."

"Har, har," Ryder sneered at Tori as the ladies laughed. "I'll be glad to prove you wrong on that, Tori. Anytime you're ready to go for a ride."

"No, thanks," Tori rolled her eyes at Ryder before turning her gaze to Ian. "I was actually coming to see if you might wanna help me get these kids to start dancing, Ian."

Ian was a little uncomfortable as he realized his assistant baseball coach was asking him to dance. He'd thought her behavior during practice was a little overly flirtatious, but he'd just brushed it off as part of her personality, thinking Tori was that way with everyone. But seeing the way she looked at him right then, and in light of the way she'd just dissed Ryder, Ian was beginning to wonder if the history teacher was actually hitting on him.

Fuck! How do I turn her down without making things awkward at practice for the rest of the season?

When Ian realized how Charlotte stiffened beside him, he turned to look at her and saw the jealous glare she was shooting at Tori. While he was glad to know he hadn't totally killed his chances with Charlotte by being an asshole since reconnecting with her, he didn't want to give her any more reasons to shut him down when he was finally able to pursue her after capturing Roberto Rodriguez. So, Ian quickly came up with a plan to take advantage of the rumors that had started to spread around the school since their kiss on the ball field.

"Actually, I was just about to ask Charlotte to dance," Ian smirked as he slid his arm around Charlotte's waist. "Since we're taking advantage of chaperoning the dance together for our date, I've already promised her all my dancing time tonight."

"Ah, so that's why ya'll are dressed to match tonight," Ryder chimed in, pointing at Ian's red tie that was the exact same shade as Charlotte's dress. Ian had decided to add a touch of Valentine's flair by wearing the tie with his black suit and dress shirt, not realizing it would help sell his lie by making them look as if they'd matched their clothing, as if they were teenagers going to prom together.

Before Charlotte could protest, and out him as a blatant liar to their colleagues, Ian pulled her around the table and onto the dance floor.

She opened and closed her mouth several times, like a fish out of water, but she didn't fight him when he pulled her into his arms and started dancing to the bubble-gum pop song currently playing. She actually clasped his hand when he gripped hers to get into the proper position for one of the ballroom-style dances his wife had taught him years ago. She placed her other hand on his shoulder when he put his hand on the small of her back and followed him beautifully as they whirled around the dance floor.

Ian enjoyed having Charlotte in his arms again, even though there was more space between their bodies than he liked due to their surroundings. They made it around the floor a couple of times before Charlotte finally spoke.

"Why did you tell them we're on a date?" She looked so cute as she stared up at him with a confused expression.

"It was the first thing I could think of to get out of having to dance with Tori," Ian admitted truthfully, leaving out how getting to dance with Charlotte was a bonus he couldn't indulge normally for fear of putting her at risk if they were seen by Rojo or one of his underlings.

"But I thought I wasn't your type, so why is it okay to dance with me but not Tori?" Charlotte arched an eyebrow as she kept dancing in sync with him.

"Because you already know why I don't date," Ian lied, again. "So you know this doesn't mean anything, where Tori would think it meant I was reciprocating her advances. Besides, the school is already overrun with rumors about us, so I figured I'd take advantage of those rumors, and maybe add to them a little bit, to keep the rest of the thirsty women of Heart's Destiny from hitting on me."

"Uh-huh, sure," Charlotte scoffed, rolling her eyes. Ian would have taken offense, but her lips turned up in the slightest smile, proving she didn't believe what she was about to say. "I think you might be feeding your own ego by imagining all these thirsty women that are supposedly hitting on you. Trust me, Campbell, you're not that great a catch. In fact, if you'd actually asked me on a date, I'd have said no."

"I'm not that great a catch?" Ian dropped his jaw in mock outrage, enjoying Charlotte's feisty side making an appearance.

"Nope, you're not," Charlotte smirked. "But go ahead and keep thinking I'm helping you out by being your beard tonight, when I'm really just helping the other women in town keep from wasting their bait on a fish they'd throw back for being too small."

Ian barked out a laugh at how Charlotte had perfectly timed her statement to end it by patting his chest and walking away just as the song ended.

Oh, Princess, we both know I'm anything but small, Ian thought as he watched her weave between the kids that had joined them on the dance floor. *But I'll be glad to show you again just how perfectly my big cock fills you up, just as soon as I can make it safe for us to be together.*

And in the meantime, I'm going to enjoy getting to spend the evening acting as your date when I know there's nobody in the Rodriguez Cartel around to identify you as mine to make you a target.

Chapter Eight

Charlotte was looking forward to a night with her sister, cousins, and single girlfriends for a Galentine's celebration, instead of going to the Sweetheart's Ball her matchmaking mother was trying to rope them all into attending. Since the house her sister and cousins shared was larger than Charlotte's, they were all meeting there for wine, pizza, and commiseration over their singledom.

Since none of her childhood friends had come back to Heart's Destiny after college to be included in the various get-togethers, Charlotte had felt a little like an outsider in the group when she'd first started hanging out with her siblings and cousins and their friends after college. But after getting to know Fiona through teaching together, she'd gradually gotten closer to the group of women a year younger than her that had stayed in town. She just had to block out the memories of the ladies she now considered friends dating her brothers and cousins in high school.

It hadn't taken long to start inviting the Fab Five from the Heart's Destiny High School graduating class of 2010 to every event and group get-together the Burleson women had, especially when they helped balance out the estrogen-to-testosterone ratio of all her brothers and male cousins inviting so many male friends along. The Fab Five consisted of Fiona Harrison, Kara Thompson, Cassidy Reilly, Kayla Scott, and Lexi Wilder.

While Charlotte counted them all as friends now, she hadn't felt comfortable confiding in Kara, Cassidy, Kayla, or Lexi the way she did with Fiona. She had thought about talking to them about everything going on with Ian when they went bowling the month before. But with the guys all being there, she hadn't had a chance to have any real girl-talk time, even with Cassidy and Kayla bowling in her lane. They also had her cousins, Julie and JJ, in their lane, along with Dalton Walker, so they had no privacy whatsoever.

Maybe I can actually open up to the girls tonight since Galentine's is a guy-free night.

It wasn't that she couldn't confide in her sister or female cousins that was holding her back from wanting to tell all that night. It was that she knew they had invited some of their other friends that she wasn't as close to, including Becky's best friend, Sierra Sadler, Amy Lawton, who had moved to town after coming to Anthony and Kay's wedding, accepting a job with Burleson Incorporated, and becoming besties with Charlotte's cousins, the three younger women her future sister-in-law, Brooklyn, had become fast friends with since moving to town, who had also come bowling the previous month, and Ian's sister, Cait, who had apparently started hanging out more with Becky, Jen, and Julie since starting work on the ranch.

Since Brooklyn wasn't going to be at their Galentine's get-together because of going to dinner with Bobby after getting engaged that morning, Charlotte wasn't sure if any of her friends would come by or not. Charlotte would probably be okay talking about her feelings for Ian with Sierra, whom she'd known through her sister for years, and Amy, who was probably going to eventually be her cousin-in-law, there. But there was no way she'd be able to confide in anyone with Ian's sister there, so she resigned herself to limiting her discussion of him to her irritation that she'd already shared publicly with her sister and cousins, when Cait might feel uncomfortable with being part of the discussion.

Regardless of who was coming over that night, Charlotte knew it was a night for dressing comfortably, washing off her makeup, and going with her hair in a messy bun. After changing into yoga pants, with a tank top under a college hoodie, and slipping on a pair of Birkenstocks, Charlotte grabbed three bottles of wine from the built-in wine cooler in her kitchen. She picked a chianti, a rosé, and a chardonnay to make sure she had the right pairing regardless of what toppings they ended up ordering on their pizzas.

Then she made the short walk next door to the house that had been her grandparents for many years before her sister and cousins moved into it after their grandparents passed. As always, she had a momentary pang of loss when she walked into the house to see the mix of several generations of furnishings, instead of Memmaw and Pappaw's house as it had been when she was a child.

Miss you Memmaw and Pappaw, she silently spoke to their spirits as she made her way to the family room where she already heard voices.

"Yes! More wine!" Lexi shouted when she saw the three bottles Charlotte was carrying. "I was worried we wouldn't have enough when Jen and Julie said they didn't have time to stop for any on their way home from work."

Charlotte added her three bottles to the six already on the side table her sister was setting up as a bar for the night, bringing the count up to a bottle each for all nine of the women who were already there. "One of these days, they'll get a wine cooler and keep it stocked like I do," Charlotte teased her cousins. "And if we need more when the other ladies get here, we can just run next door to raid my wine cooler."

"Yeah, I don't think anyone else is coming." Becky shook her head as she uncorked the first bottle and started filling glasses.

"Really?" Charlotte was surprised that Amy, Cait, Ashley, Heather, and Kenzie weren't there. Even though she hadn't expected the three younger women to come since Brooklyn wasn't attending, she thought for sure Amy and Cait would attend.

"Yeah, Ashley had to oversee the food at the Sweetheart's Ball," Sierra explained.

"And Heather and Kenzie came in for me to do their hair for the ball today," Kayla continued Sierra's explanation.

"And we didn't even get the chance to ask Amy because she left work early for some reason," Jen shrugged.

"Justin left early, too." Julie wagged her eyebrows suggestively as she picked up one of the glasses of wine Becky had poured. "So, maybe they're going out tonight."

"Or maybe they both got roped into going to the Sweetheart's Ball by your matchmaking mommas," Kara giggled, waving her wine glass in the direction of the Burleson women.

"I'm surprised none of ya'll caved to the pressure to go to the ball tonight," Cassidy chuckled with Kara. "I barely escaped being roped into going, and I only see the matchmaking mommas on Sundays at church, and maybe once a month in the store."

"I guess Cait took one for the team, since they probably badgered her about it every day since it was announced." Thinking about Cait being talked into going to the ball made Charlotte wonder if Ian was also there that night.

"Oh, no, Cait couldn't go to the ball for the same reason she couldn't come to our Galentine's party." Becky shook her head as she explained. "She had to go home to watch Brody because Ian apparently already had plans to go out tonight."

"Seriously?" Charlotte fumed, hating that she was both pissed and jealous at hearing he was going out for Valentine's Day with someone else after the way he'd been flirty with her at the dance they'd chaperoned over the weekend. "That bastard!"

"Whoa! Sis, why are you so mad about Ian having plans tonight?" Becky looked shocked by Charlotte's outburst.

"Because he's a lying bastard, who keeps sending mixed signals about what he wants!" Charlotte yelled while fighting not to cry.

"I didn't think you were into him." Jen shook her head before taking a sip of her wine.

"Yeah, it seemed like you've been trying to avoid him as much as possible," Julie added.

"I thought you were irritated by Mom and Aunt Susan pushing the two of you together because of all the issues you've had with trying to work with him." Becky topped off Charlotte's glass that she'd just drained trying to calm her nerves. "But that reaction seems to indicate you're more interested in him than you've let on."

"I was," Charlotte admitted with a huff before downing her second glass of wine. "When I met him on December fourteenth."

"December fourteenth?" Becky's eyes widened in surprise. "You met him two weeks before he showed up at Christmas and didn't tell anyone?"

"Technically, Fiona knows about it," Char admitted sheepishly, afraid she might blush as she told her friends about the night she first met Ian. "But only because she was there when I met him."

"Wait, you met him on one of the girls' nights she roped you into doing at a hotel in San Antonio?" Lexi fanned herself. "Now I understand why having them at Tully's isn't good enough. Ya'll aren't having girl talk. You're picking up hotties without the scrutiny of the gossip grapevine here in town."

"Oh, we are so going to San Antonio next time we get together for girls' night!" Kayla nodded before high-fiving with Lexi.

"So, did you hook up with him that night?" Cassidy leaned in, obviously curious about the details of that night.

"Is that why you're pissed at him? Because ya'll hooked up but then he acted like he didn't know you at Christmas?" Jen leaned forward, her face lighting with interest as she questioned Char.

"And now he's going out with someone else for Valentine's Day instead of you?" Julie continued the line of questioning started by her twin.

"Whoa, guys, give her a chance to tell us the whole story before you overwhelm her with questions," Kara interjected, reaching over to rub Charlotte's back to ground her enough for her to be able to tell them about her relationship with Ian.

"Wait," Becky interrupted, holding up a hand to Charlotte to stop her from speaking. "Let's get our pizza ordered and on the way, while Charlotte has another glass of wine, so she can tell us the whole story without being interrupted by our growling stomachs."

"Smart thinking." Sierra pointed at Becky and grinned, before making her request for pizza toppings.

Once they'd all decided on a variety of pizzas and Becky placed the order on her phone, they turned the floor back over to Charlotte to relay her tale of O's and woes with Ian over the last two months.

"So, you know I was at the hotel bar with Fiona," she started, settling into a comfortable position on the sofa with her wine glass in hand. "We ordered food and drinks and started talking about her new job and all the hot wrestlers she's now traveling with daily. After talking about her prospects for meeting Mr. Right in the GWA, she asked me to pick a fantasy book boyfriend for a hot hookup."

"Oh, what a fun fantasy to think about." Jen fanned herself, obviously having someone in mind for herself. "Who did you pick?"

"Ian Taggart." Charlotte wasn't sure how she maintained a straight face as she said the name, knowing none of her friends or family would expect her answer.

"Oh my God! They have the same first name and the hottie teacher kinda looks like the description of Ian Taggart in Lexi Blake's books!" Sierra squealed, bouncing in her seat with excitement.

"Yeah, and when Fiona questioned why I picked him, instead of the librarian from that Pippa Grant series we read a while back, I may have described a few of the attributes I find most attractive about Ian in the books." Charlotte shook her head, even more convinced that Ian had heard her talking about the book-character fantasy before introducing himself to her later that night than she was before. "And said that if I ever met a real-life Ian, I wouldn't be able to say *no* to him."

A couple of her friends gasped and covered their mouths with their hands as she went on to explain how they'd continued talking and eating before turning around to play the people-watching game when Ian interrupted them to introduce himself. As well as how Fiona had left almost immediately to keep from being in the way of Charlotte's once-in-a-lifetime opportunity.

"So, do you think he heard you and decided to take his shot before you picked another guy in the bar for the night?" Becky barely got the words out just as the doorbell rang signaling their pizza had arrived. "Hold that thought!"

Becky held up a hand to stop Charlotte from answering her question before running out of the room to collect the pizzas. Everyone sat silently as Julie refilled all their wine glasses while they waited for Becky to get back with the pizza. Once they all had a slice or two on a plate and had retaken their seats, Becky motioned for Charlotte to finally answer her question.

"At the time, I wasn't sure because I didn't realize when he came in and took the empty seat at the bar beside me, since I was turned facing Fiona most of the night. But I did ask for his identification to confirm his name was Ian, thinking he might have lied to me after overhearing our earlier conversation." Charlotte shook her head at how she'd been fooled into thinking they were fated to be together that night.

"Since his driver's license listed his name as Ian, I chalked it up to a twist of fate," she shrugged between bites of pizza.

The other women stared at her, silently eating, and waiting for her to continue the story.

After washing down her first slice of pizza with a big gulp of chianti, Charlotte continued the story. "But once we ran into each other again at Christmas, and I realized his reason for being in town that night was all a lie, I knew he had to have overheard me and made it up to fulfill the fantasy of book Ian."

"What did he say was his reason for being in town?" Cassidy arched an eyebrow before taking another drink.

"That he worked for the DEA and was there hunting down a cartel kingpin that got away during a bust a couple of weeks before." Charlotte rolled her eyes at how obvious his lie was, berating herself for being so gullible and falling for the man who pretended to be the epitome of her fantasy. "I still can't believe I was so caught up in the fantasy that I fell for such a line."

"Don't feel bad about that, Char." Becky reached over and patted her sister's hand reassuringly. "With that military-style short hair and fit physique, I could totally see casting him in the role of a DEA agent. So, I probably would have been fooled by that lie, too, especially if reality lived up to the fantasy when ya'll got to the good stuff in the room."

A few of the other women agreed, nodding along as they continued eating.

"So, what did he say when you called him out on his lies?" Kara asked, being the sensible one among them to know Charlotte didn't want to give them details about what happened once they were in her room for the night.

"Oh, he denies it was him," Charlotte huffed before continuing on to tell them all the different stories he'd given her about why it couldn't have been him. "But he can't make up his mind if it couldn't have been him because he's still grieving his late wife and hasn't wanted to be with anyone else since the day he met her, or because I'm not his type, or because he doesn't have time to date with all his other commitments to his family and the school, or because he doesn't want to date to keep from confusing his son with a string of women who could never replace his wife."

"Wow, that's a lot of excuses," Lexi giggled. "Sounds like someone's protesting too much."

"Oh, yeah," Charlotte agreed, nodding her head at her friend. "And that's been obvious multiple times in the six weeks since he moved here. But just as soon as he seems to be finally acting on the mutual attraction, he turns around and acts like an asshole. His hot-and-cold act is enough to give me whiplash."

Charlotte went on to tell them about noticing his erection when he first saw her on the first day back to school, and then how he'd complained about the books that had been scheduled for them to teach months ago and wanted to make changes to the lesson plans at the last minute. She told them about the first day of softball tryouts and how he'd messed up everyone's schedules without properly discussing it, or notifying her, and then kissing her in the middle of the field to coax her into going along with his schedule. She explained how they'd seemed to come to a truce at school after Lisa stepped in, but then he'd been an ass again when she wanted to take Brody for a trail ride.

"Didn't ya'll settle that when he came on a trail ride with us a couple of weeks ago?" Jen looked confused as she asked the question.

"Oh, no." Charlotte shook her head. "He basically ignored everything I said that day, and only followed instructions when one of the guys gave them to him. And we're still stuck in the paddocks between the stable and the houses whenever I get to work with Brody, so Cait can watch him through the window."

"I did notice how he didn't listen to you that day," Becky confirmed, rolling her eyes. "I just thought it was because he was nervous about the horses and didn't hear you."

"Oh, he might not have heard me," Charlotte chuckled. "But based on the way he was filling out his jeans every time I caught him looking in my direction, I think it was because he was listening with the wrong head anytime I spoke."

The ladies all giggled and made rude comments about needing to check him out the next time he was in a pair of jeans. Of course, that conversation quickly devolved into a few more questions about what he was packing, since Charlotte had gotten a better look at his dick in December.

"I'm not describing his dick for ya'll," Charlotte protested, laughing with her friends to cover her blush while thinking about his piercings. "But I will say it's the best I've ever seen, and now I'm in the market for a bigger B-O-B, 'cause mine's too small after being with Ian."

"Ah, now I get why you're pissed that he's all hot and cold with you. He's got that magic peen that ruins a woman for all others," Cassidy sighed.

Charlotte was silent as the ladies around her discussed Cassidy's magic peen theory, including their own experiences with Charlotte's brothers and trying to decide who else in town was rumored to be blessed with a magic wand in his pants. She wished she could disagree with her friend's assessment of her ruined status, but unfortunately, her body seemed primed to only want Ian.

"So, who do you think he's out ruining tonight?" Sierra carelessly asked.

"I don't know." Charlotte shook her head, not wanting to think about all the women she'd seen taking notice of Ian at school and during that first day of baseball and softball tryouts. "After the way he feigned being on a date with me Saturday, when we were chaperoning the middle school dance to get out of dancing with Tori Collins, I don't think it's her. But since she's his assistant baseball coach, she's certainly had the opportunity to wear him down since then."

They went on to discuss a few of the other women around town whose heads Ian had turned during his time in the area before the subject finally changed to the other ladies' dating disasters. While Charlotte liked knowing she wasn't alone in finding the duds of dating, she hated hearing that her friends and family were faring no better than she was in finding Mr. Right.

Thank goodness, at least, none of them are having these issues with my brothers or cousins. I don't need to hear any more about their supposed magic peens.

~~~

Saturday, February 16, 2019

Ian hoped the conversations he'd overheard the last two nights at Levi's Bar would finally lead him to the right part of San Antonio, where Roberto Rodriguez was staying. He had been skeptical when he'd gotten word from Levi Nash that Big John was back at the bar after disappearing for a few weeks. But he'd dropped everything to go see the guy for himself, including his favorite nighttime ritual of reading to Brody before tucking him into bed.

Luckily, losing time with his son didn't seem to be for naught, when Ian was able to get a picture of Big John on his cell phone that was clear enough for Jake to run it through facial recognition. After
~~~

hearing him Thursday night when he was discussing a meeting with his supplier on Saturday at a warehouse just a few blocks over from his house, Ian needed to find out Big John's real identity to have any hope of locating his residence.

Ian had immediately sent the photo to both Jake and Trent, hoping at least one of their departments would have him in their database to be able to identify him if the other didn't. He hadn't been able to get close enough to hear any more of their conversations that night, so he'd gone back to the bar on Friday night to see what else he could find out.

After hearing about the meeting on Saturday once again when he was listening to Big John talking with his buddies on Friday night, Ian was even more convinced his supplier was Roberto Rodriguez. So, he'd been thrilled when he got the call on Saturday morning that Jake had identified Big John as Juan Gomez, and had an address for his last known residence.

Ian knew they didn't have time to assemble a team to back him up to possibly capture Rojo at the meet, so when he conferenced Trent into the call with Jake, he wasn't surprised that he was ordered to surveil from afar just to confirm Rojo's identity. But as he turned off the dirt road that bordered the southernmost portion of the Burleson Ranch after gearing up at his temporary TOC, he kind of wished he was picking up Jake or one of his brothers as backup.

Unfortunately, the only one of the Burlesons there who was qualified to back Ian up was Bobby. But after Jake filled him in on Bobby's recent engagement and impending fatherhood, Ian didn't feel right asking him to accompany him on what could be a dangerous surveillance situation. Yeah, he knew Bobby's job as the police chief could be dangerous, but it was rare that officers in small towns like Heart's Destiny faced off against criminals as bloodthirsty as Roberto Rodriguez.

Ian wasn't comfortable being the one to burst Bobby's happy, domestic bubble, when he hadn't even had a week to enjoy being an engaged father-to-be. So, he was headed into San Antonio alone and would let Jake decide when they needed to bring his brother into the investigation.

After his hour-long drive into the city, Ian drove by the neighborhood where Big John supposedly lived. He didn't go into the neighborhood to verify Juan Gomez still lived at the address Jake had given him because he didn't want to be recognized and jeopardize his ability to find Rojo. Instead, he tried to figure out which warehouse nearby they might be meeting at by watching his odometer to drive a mile away from each exit from the neighborhood as if he had made a left turn from each of them, since those were the basic directions Big John had given his associate the night before.

Unfortunately, that led him to four different warehouse districts in the city. *Guess I'm driving around between all four to see if I recognize Big John's car near one of them.*

He kept his sunglasses on and his ball cap pulled low to help conceal his identity as he made the rounds driving around trying to figure out where the meet was happening, grateful that the excessive city traffic didn't seem to slow on the weekend to help him blend in even more.

Though he was constantly on alert for any signs of Roberto or Big John, Ian couldn't keep his mind from wandering to thoughts of Charlotte. He kept thinking back to dancing with her on Saturday night and wishing he could have a real date with her, instead of just pretending to date her while safely behind the closed doors of the school to get the other teachers to back off on their advances.

Ian told Charlotte the ruse was to keep Tori from hitting on him, but in reality, it was to get Ryder to stop trying to put the moves on Charlotte. Unlike Tori, who seemed to realize he was already spoken for and quit flirting after the first time Ian danced with Charlotte, Ryder had continued to hang around as if biding his time to get Charlotte alone.

After their first dance, Ian and Charlotte had made the rounds to check on the kids before congregating with the other teachers once again. Or at least that's how he'd tried to play it off to Charlotte. In actuality, he'd planned to give her some space for the rest of the dance, until he saw Ryder following her around like a love-struck puppy. After that, he stuck to Charlotte's side like he was glued there to keep the other man from moving in on his woman.

Ian had kept a hand on her every chance he got, whether it was resting on her back or taking her hand while they sat to talk with their colleagues, just to make sure Ryder got the message that Charlotte was his. They had also danced a couple more times before the parents started collecting their kids at the end of the night.

He wasn't sure how effective all his posturing was, though, because he didn't get to end the night with a kiss when he walked Charlotte to her car the way he really wanted. Oh, he'd leaned in for it, aching to taste her once more, but Charlotte had quickly shut him down.

Ian couldn't stop his smile as he remembered how she'd pushed him back with both hands on his chest.

"Sorry, I don't kiss on the first date."

He'd wanted so badly to call her out on doing a whole lot more than kissing on the night they met, barely biting back the words since they were outside with an audience that didn't need to know about their sexual escapades. While he wouldn't mind cluing Ryder in as a means of getting him to back off of Charlotte, he knew she would be mortified if word of their first night together was made public in the gossipy small town.

Besides that, he hadn't been able to shake the feeling of being watched whenever he was outside, since that day on the ball field a little over a week before. While he hadn't seen anyone not affiliated with the middle school there for the dance, he couldn't be sure one of Rojo's subordinates wasn't hiding in the dark wooded area on the other side of Rogers Road from the middle school parking lot that night. So, he'd backed off and smiled, stepping into the role of a friendly colleague, who had just escorted one of the ladies to her car to make sure she was safe, just like any gentleman would do, even if he didn't actually know the woman in question.

Hopefully, I'll spot Rojo soon, so I don't have to keep playing that disinterested role much longer.

As he pulled up to a stoplight, Ian looked across the intersection to see a black Suburban pulling out of the warehouse on the other side. When the driver turned in his direction to make sure it was clear to pull out onto the road, Ian was almost positive it was Rojo.

Ask and ye shall receive, Ian mentally quoted the preacher from the sermon he gave the week before. *Maybe I should pay more attention to Pastor Harrison, instead of ogling Charlotte in church. If I'd have known spotting Roberto would be as easy as asking for it, I'd have done it a month ago.*

Ian had to wait for the light to change before he could follow, but that was probably good to keep Rodriguez from being suspicious of being tailed. He talked through the route he was taking to follow Rojo turn by turn, just loud enough to be picked up by the recording device in his ball cap, so he could retrace his steps accurately in the report he knew he'd have to turn in to Trent later. He tried to cover his note-taking by acting like he was singing along with the radio, in case any of the cars between him and Roberto were affiliated with the cartel.

They weaved through an industrial part of town for several miles before moving toward another residential area. Unfortunately, Roberto didn't turn into the neighborhood, sticking to the main thoroughfare that ran past it, which was heavy with traffic.

As they got closer to downtown, Ian noticed a building that looked like an old mission that was now acting as a homeless shelter. *I wonder if that's the one where Charlotte volunteers?*

He didn't see her bright blue Equinox nearby, but by the time the building registered as a shelter in his mind, he'd already passed the public parking lot, two plots down from the old mission. Not that he could have seen her vehicle if she was parked in the parking garage half a block down, either. When he turned his attention back to the vehicles in front of him, he could no longer see the black Suburban he'd been tailing.

"Fuck!" Ian slammed his hand on his steering wheel as he cursed his momentary distraction from his task, due to thinking more about Charlotte than the vicious criminal he was supposed to be surveilling. "Lost visual at Travis and Navarro."

He continued driving around the area for the next several hours, but he didn't see the Suburban again. Finally, writing the day off as a semi-fruitless effort, Ian drove back to Heart's Destiny to report in to Trent with the DEA and update Jake on where he might be able to pick up Rojo's trail on traffic cameras.

Once he'd changed back into his more typical attire and swapped the pickup for his Range Rover, Ian went home to spend some quality time with his family. He needed the mental reset of time with his son to be able to get through the stress of getting so close to Roberto Rodriguez, only to lose him again.

Chapter Nine

Charlotte was excited to enlist her family's help in reviewing their DNA matches, now that most of them had their results back on the website. She was still waiting on her brothers, Jake and Josh, to come back into town to give them their kits to send off their samples. And Bobby had just sent his sample off with Brooklyn's, now that they were home from dealing with her daddy drama in Georgia. But with seven of the ten members of the Burleson family in their generation and all of their parents having their results, she was sure they could at least come up with a few shared matches that were potentially the descendants of their second-great-grandaunt, Mary Burleson, who had left the ranch to go serve as a nurse during the first world war.

As soon as they got back to the ranch after church, everyone changed into their more comfortable clothes before meeting in the dining room of her childhood home with their laptops. Well, all of the Burlesons who were in town at the time, anyway. Obviously, Jake and Josh weren't there because of being off with their jobs in the Navy. Anthony and his family weren't there either, since they were currently off with the GWA.

Charlotte was surprised to see that of all the people who didn't share her last name that she'd given one of the kits on her birthday, only Brooklyn and Amy came by to compare notes about their results. She'd known Brooklyn would be there because she went practically everywhere with Bobby. And she'd known Amy was coming over after talking to her at Bobby's birthday party on Friday night and discussing the issues she was having with setting up her family tree. But she was surprised none of the Walkers or the girls she'd seen at their Galentine's party on Valentine's Day opted to join them.

"Before we get started going over the DNA matches, I wanted to ask you about the ethnicity results." Charlotte's sister, Becky, pointed to her computer screen, where she had the page brought up that showed her ethnicity breakdown from the website. "I don't see any of Memmaw's Native American, but I do see some African. Do you think her ancestors were adopted into the tribe and not really native?"

"No," Charlotte shook her head and hid her disappointment at what she'd learned about her Memmaw's ancestors while looking through the paper trail on the family tree section of the website. "I'll have to show you all the records that show her ancestors weren't native later, but I have them all saved to the family tree. I also have the records that seem to prove our African DNA comes from Jonah's mom."

Becky's eyes bugged out, just as Bobby called out to remind her to give him editing privileges on the family tree, so he could work on adding Brooklyn's family branches to the tree, since he didn't have any DNA matches to compare yet.

Charlotte logged into the site, added Bobby's email address to the tree as an editor, and stood to direct everyone else in the steps to authorize her to look at their DNA results to link them to the Burleson family tree.

"You too, Amy." Charlotte pointed at Amy's computer when she took her seat and noticed her friend wasn't following the directions.

"Me too, what?" Amy looked confused as she turned to look at Charlotte.

"Go in and authorize me to link your DNA to the family tree." Charlotte pointed at Amy's computer once more.

"But I'm not on your family tree," Amy protested.

"Maybe not yet, but you will be." Charlotte shrugged and smiled, knowing that if Justin had his way, Amy would soon be added the same way Anthony had added Kay and Bobby was adding Brooklyn. "So, we may as well go ahead and add you from the start, since your DNA test is already linked to my account, with Justin putting them all on my account when he bought them. And it'll save us from having to try and figure out how to merge our family trees later when ya'll get married."

"Ma-married?" Amy stuttered, looking around nervously. "We, we're jus-just friends."

"Char, don't push," Justin ordered from beside Amy as he reached over and squeezed her hand reassuringly. "Amy already has her family tree started. She just wanted our help in learning how to link her DNA test to her tree, and figuring out how to trace back through the branches to find ancestors she doesn't know about, not for you to join in with the Matchmaking Mommas before your time."

"Oh, no, don't even lump me in with our mothers!" Charlotte exclaimed, lifting her palms up in surrender. *Just because I can see you want to marry her, doesn't mean I'm going to actively try to help you win her over by acting like my mother!*

Several people around the table laughed at Charlotte's abject horror at being compared to the Matchmaking Mommas before Char finally gave in and laughed along with them.

When their laughter died down, Charlotte walked Amy through the steps of linking her DNA test with her profile on the family tree she'd started.

"Okay, now that we got that fixed, what are you having trouble with on your family tree?" Charlotte might not have a ton of experience with the site just yet, but hoped the month she'd been working on her own tree would be helpful to give Amy some pointers to help her fix whatever issues she was having.

"I'm not getting any hints to be able to trace back." Amy showed Charlotte her screen displaying a six-person tree with no leaves. "I think it's because I don't have enough information on my dad and grandparents. So, maybe once my mom gets here next week to give me full names with proper spelling, and birth and death dates, and locations, it'll improve, but I'd kind of like to figure out how I'm related to some of my DNA matches before then."

"Oh, well, the best way to do that is to look at your matches and check out their family trees if they're public." Charlotte walked everyone through the steps of how to do that, since that was the main reason the Burlesons were meeting.

Once everyone had their DNA match lists up and could start looking at their matches' trees, Charlotte, Becky, and each of their cousins picked a match they all had in common to start scouring the other trees on the site. They were finally looking for their second-great-grandaunt's descendants, with the hope of being able to pass on the trust fund that their third-great-grandfather had left them.

As Charlotte was searching through the first of several family trees they planned to review that day, and the rest of her family was quietly working on reviewing similar trees, Amy started giggling beside her.

"What's so funny?" Justin asked from Amy's other side.

"Just a silly thought about my grandchildren inventing time travel and coming back in time to put their DNA on this site for me to see them as a match long before they're born." Amy pointed to her screen and Justin chuckled with her.

"Wow, that's a close match." Justin pointed to Amy's screen. "That's like twice as much as I share with my cousins and slightly more than I share with Uncle Bob."

"Really?" Amy leaned over to look at Justin's screen.

Oh, but they're just friends. Charlotte stifled her giggle at how cozy they were acting for friends.

"Yeah, see." Justin turned his computer, angling his screen toward Amy.

Curious, Charlotte looked back at her match list to see that she shared thirteen percent of her DNA with Justin before looking at Amy's screen over her shoulder to see that Amy was on a page showing her match shared twenty-eight percent of her DNA.

"Okay, so Donna is definitely closer than a cousin." Amy's voice rose, giving Char the impression that she sounded excited about finding a close relative.

"Hey, you okay?" Justin reached over to rub his hand up and down on her back.

That's definitely more of a boyfriend gesture than a just-friends gesture.

"Yeah," Amy sighed. "Just overwhelmed by the possibilities. With so many private people listed on her tree, and no personal information on her profile other than her name, I'm not sure how to figure out how we're related."

"You can send her a message through the site to ask about her parents and siblings to see if any names are familiar." Charlotte pointed out the message button on the page showing their shared DNA details.

"Yeah, maybe later." Amy gave Charlotte a little smile. "Maybe Mom will recognize her name and be able to tell me how we're related. I know there was some animosity between my mom and my father's family, so I'd rather wait to see if any of my matches are people who still have hard feelings for Mom before messaging them."

"Yeah, okay, that's understandable." Justin smiled reassuringly before removing his hand from her back and pointing to her computer. "Let's move on to the next match, then. Maybe the next one will have a tree with more people you can look at to see if you recognize any names."

Charlotte turned back to her computer, spending the next hour or so comparing her DNA matches with her sister and cousins as they went through family trees for their shared matches, who were listed as distant cousins.

When she pulled up the Avington family tree, she noticed several shared DNA matches were linked to the tree.

"Is anyone looking at the tree for the username B.J. Av.?" Charlotte's cousin, Julie, looked around at her siblings and cousins.

"Yes, I am," Charlotte answered. "I'm guessing the Av. is short for Avington, since that's the family name on the tree. And there are four other matches linked to their tree, but their usernames are all initials that don't make sense to me."

"Yeah, I saw those strange initials lower down in the list," Justin said, scrolling on his screen, presumably to look at the main list with all his DNA matches to find the initials. "You're talking about B.B.A., B.A.A., B.J.A., and M.A.A.B.A., right?"

"Yeah, those are the ones showing up on the Avington family tree, along with B.J. Av., whom we seem to have twice as much DNA in common with than the other initials that I'm assuming are his children."

"How do you know B.J. Av. is a he?" Justin looked at Charlotte like he was confused.

"I don't know for sure, but I'm assuming based on the fact that the icon for that username is blue." Charlotte pointed to the icons used in place of photos for some of the people on the various trees. She wasn't sure if they hadn't uploaded pictures of themselves, or if the site only showed the pictures to authorized users when the person in question was still alive.

"Wait, did you just say you're looking at the Avington family tree?" Bobby jumped up out of his chair and shouted his question over to Charlotte.

"Yes," Charlotte replied, wondering what was up with the strange expression on Bobby's face. "Why?"

"You think it's the same Avingtons?" Brooklyn tugged on Bobby's shirt sleeve.

"Who are the Avingtons?" Jen asked from the other side of Justin.

"Avington, that's the name of the security firm you hired in Georgia, right?" Julie nodded excitedly at Bobby from her seat across the table from her twin.

"Yes." Bobby returned Julie's nod before turning to look down at Brooklyn beside him. "I don't know if it's the same family, Brie-Baby, but it's certainly possible. Back when we were in training together, one of the things we learned about was how common certain last names were for trying to track people down. Being curious when neither of our last names was on the list of common last names we reviewed, we looked them up. Burleson is like the two-thousand-seven-hundred-something most common last name in the US, and the twenty-nine-thousand-eight-hundred-something most common in the world. Blake couldn't find a listing for how common the last name Avington was in the US, but it was over a million down the list for the world. With it being that rare of a last name, I have to wonder if Blake or his brothers are the common matches everyone is finding."

"Blake's that boy you brought home for supper a few times when you were training in San Antonio, right?" Hazel, their mother, questioned from her spot on the other side of the room beside their father.

"Yes," Bobby agreed, nodding his head at their mother.

"Guess it's a good thing we didn't try to match him up with one of our daughters back then, if he's the one all the kids are matching up with then," Aunt Susan chuckled at Hazel's mortified face.

"Goodness, I didn't even think about needing to check these DNA lists to make sure we're not trying to match our kids up with their distant cousins." Hazel covered her mouth with her hand.

"Yes, Mom, please make sure you get Ancestry usernames for anyone you want to push us toward dating." *Maybe the fact that Ian won't do one of these tests will keep her from continuing her matchmaking with the two of us.* "So I can make sure they're on my DNA match list."

Amy giggled beside her, obviously remembering the same thing she did about Ian not wanting to do the tests back in December. "Why don't you call your friend and ask him if he's on the site?"

"Yeah, Bobby, call Blake and see if he or his brothers have done their DNA and are using these usernames." Justin reinforced Amy's suggestion, pointing to his screen where his match list was still on his screen.

Bobby walked around the table to look at Justin's screen as he pulled out his phone and dialed a number. He put the phone up to his ear as the call went through.

"Hey, Blake," Bobby greeted his friend through the phone. "Not much, just hanging out with the family and trying to trace our ancestry." Bobby paused, apparently so Blake could speak. "Yeah, have you or your brothers done one of those online DNA tests?" Another pause, combined with a chuckle. "Yeah, maybe. Most of the family did it last month, but Brie and I just sent ours in this last week, so we don't have our match lists yet. But there are several people linked to an Avington family tree that are showing up as matches to those of us who've gotten their results."

"Looks like the closest match is B.J. Av. But there's also a B.B.A., a B.A.A., a B.J.A., and an M.A.A.B.A. that are all on the same family tree and matching with my sisters and cousins." Bobby paused for only a brief second before exclaiming, "Holy shit! Seriously? Yeah, let me put you on speaker, so you can talk to all your newfound cousins."

Bobby pulled the phone away from his ear and tapped the screen to switch it to speaker mode, holding it out between Amy and Justin and slightly above their heads.

"So, I guess it's a good thing I never broke Bro Code and asked one of your sisters to go out with me?" A deep chuckle rumbled out of the phone, following Blake's question.

"I take it one of these usernames is yours." Charlotte leaned into Amy, so her voice could be heard through Bobby's phone.

"Yeah, I'm M.A.A.B.A.," Blake chuckled again. "And which of my new cousins am I speaking with?"

"I'm Bobby's sister, Charlotte. And according to what I'm looking at on here, you and I share fifty-four centimorgans on two segments of our DNA."

"Shit! Seriously? Let me pull my list up. I thought Bobby was joking around that we were matching up with ya'll."

"Dude, why would I joke around about being related to your ugly mug?" Bobby deadpanned.

"Holy! Wow! You got a lot of Burlesons on this site," Blake exclaimed. "Bob, Jon, Anthony, JJ, Charlotte, Becky, Justin, Jen, and Julie are all showing in my match list. And we thought we were nuts when all six of us took the tests. How many of ya'll took it?"

"Yeah, well, our moms, Anthony's wife, and daughters, Brie, and our friend, Amy, also took the test, but none of them should show up as a match with you," Bobby chuckled into his phone. "And you'll probably see me show up on your list in a few weeks, and then Jake and Josh whenever they come home on leave and take the test, too."

"Damn, I can't wait to tell Dad to look at his results again." Blake sounded excited at the prospect of finding the kinship between their families, not even realizing just how big a deal it could be if they were related through the right line of the family. "He's gonna flip to find out we're related. Now we just have to figure out how."

"That's what we're wondering about most." Justin seemed just as excited as Blake, and his excitement was contagious around the room. "Since you're not showing as related to us through our mothers, it has to be through the Burlesons somewhere further back."

Everyone started pushing in to see Charlotte's computer screen, where she was looking at the Avingtons' family tree. Bobby laid his phone down on the table beside Charlotte's computer as he knelt down beside her to look closer at the screen. "Do you have any Burlesons on your family tree?"

"Not that I know of," Blake replied. "But if B.J. Av. is a closer match than me or my brothers, then it's gotta be from Dad's side of the family here, too."

Charlotte clicked back to the page that showed her match with B.J. Av. to see the list of shared surnames on their family trees. Once she saw they had the surname Davis in common, she clicked back to the Avington's tree to look for that surname, assuming it would make it easier to find the link to their family there, since Davis was her great-grandmother's maiden name. Unfortunately, as she looked over the branches on the Avington tree, she didn't see anyone with the last name Davis listed.

"I don't understand why this says we both have Davis as a shared surname in our family trees, but I can't see it in the people I can see on your tree." Charlotte leaned toward the phone as she spoke to make sure Blake could hear her over the whispers of her family all around her.

"That's because Davis is my aunt's husband's last name," Blake sighed. "So, he's on the tree, but we don't share any DNA with him. Once I get Dad to give you administrator rights on our tree, you'll be able to see him along with the rest of our living relatives."

"Yeah, that will come in handy to get to know who all we're related to," Becky chimed in from her seat that she'd scooted in close to Charlotte's side. "But with as little DNA as we share with each other, our common ancestors are more likely to be a few generations back and long dead."

"Yeah, well, it's obviously not on mom's side of the family, so we have fewer branches to look at since we've hit a few dead ends on the Avington side. You haven't been able to find any names you recognize on the Langston or Miller branches of the tree?"

"No, but I've just been searching the last names of our grandmothers, since you don't have a Burleson on your tree." Charlotte clicked her mouse to expand the Langston branch of the Avington tree out a few more generations. "I need to pull together a list of all the surnames on the Teague, Davis, and King branches of our tree to search them in your tree."

"This is going to take forever," Jen grumbled, shaking her head as Justin squeezed in closer beside his sister to see the Avington's tree over Charlotte's head.

Bobby walked back over to his computer and started calling out names for Charlotte to look for, where he was in the Burleson tree since he and Brooklyn had been working on adding her branches to it. Charlotte jotted them down on a notepad beside her as she scanned the Avingtons' tree for them. When she couldn't find any of the names Bobby gave her on the Langston branch of the Avington's tree, she collapsed it back to Blake's grandmother, Carolyn Langston, who was married to his grandfather, Aaron Avington, and expanded the Miller branch that started with Blake's great-grandmother, Shirley Miller, who was married to his great-grandfather, Jack Avington.

"Wait," Justin shouted, pushing forward to point at the end of the Avington line of their tree, Benjamin Avington, who was listed as Jack's father, and was Blake's second-great-grandfather. "You don't have a second-great-grandmother listed on your tree. Do you know who was married to Benjamin Avington?"

"Dude, I only know my first-great-grandmother's name because Dad found it when he was putting together the family tree." Blake chuckled before continuing. "I'll have to ask Dad if he didn't find anything on the second-great-grandma, or if he just didn't get it added before his subscription expired. Maybe he knows who she was."

"Oh, wow!" Charlotte exclaimed, turning to look at Justin after she noted the dates on Benjamin and Jack Avington's leaves on the Avington family tree. *Those letters I found addressed to Mary were just signed with a B... Could they be from Benjamin Avington?* "Are you thinking what I'm thinking?"

"Yeah." Justin nodded at her, smiling with what appeared to be hope shining in his eyes. "From looking at the birth years that are showing on this screen for Benjamin and Jack, and with us all sharing about the right amount of DNA to be fourth cousins, I think it's possible that Benjamin Avington married our second-great-grandaunt, Mary Burleson."

"Holy shit!" Uncle Jon shouted, jumping up from his seat on the other side of the room and running around the table to see Charlotte's computer screen. Charlotte was as surprised to see her uncle move so fast as she was to hear the expletive come from his mouth. "Bob, get over here. You've got to see this. If our kids are right…"

It was an emotional moment when Charlotte watched her uncle tear up to the point he couldn't complete his sentence. Her Uncle Jon wasn't the only one in the room with tears in their eyes. Everyone who had gone back to their seats after initially crowding Charlotte while she looked at the Avington's tree made their way back into a huddle, hugging and crying at the possibility that they'd just solved a hundred-year-old family mystery.

Blake was quiet on the other end of the phone line until Charlotte and a few of the other girls in the family broke into sobs as the happy tears flowed. "Hey, now, being related to me isn't so bad that ya'll need to start crying about it." He obviously didn't realize that the

Burlesons were all overwhelmed with joy at possibly finding the daughter that Jonah Burleson went to his grave missing.

"It's all happy tears, Cuz." Bobby picked up his phone from the table beside Charlotte. "But you might want to tell your dad to renew his subscription to verify how we're related. If it's really through our great aunt Mary, then life as you know it is about to change."

"Oh, man, sorry, I didn't realize this was such a big deal for ya'll." Blake sounded remorseful for his joking comment.

"Yeah, our family has been trying to find out what happened to Mary for the last hundred years." Bobby hugged Brooklyn to his side as he spoke to his friend. "And if our hunch is right, your dad might just be able to finally solve the mystery of where she went after World War I, when she didn't come home to the ranch."

"Wow, yeah, okay. How about I head over to Dad's now and see if I can get the whole family there for a Skype session to meet everyone?"

"Sounds good," Bobby replied, looking around the room to see the rest of the family nodding in agreement.

"How long do you think it will take you to get everyone together?" Hazel pushed in closer to Bobby to direct the question at Blake.

"I can be at Mom and Dad's in about fifteen minutes," Blake replied. "But it might take an hour or two to get all my brothers there."

"Then let's plan the Skype for two hours from now, so I have time to get everyone through the kitchen and fed first."

Only Mom would think about food at a time like this!

"That works for me. Maybe I can get a home cooked meal from Mom before we solve our DNA mystery, too."

They said their goodbyes and put away most of their computers before heading to the kitchen to fix plates.

"Hey, where did Amy go?" Charlotte asked Justin as they sat back down at the dining room table to eat. She didn't remember seeing Amy during the conversation with Blake, except at the very beginning, and wondered why she would have left in the middle of the phone call.

"She had some things she had to get done at home." Justin shrugged.

"You don't think us connecting with some of our matches bothered her, do you?" Jen inquired from his other side.

Oh, I didn't think about how uncomfortable it might be for her to witness us connecting with family, when she's struggling with getting hints on her tree. I'll have to make time this week to go by her house and see if I can help her with researching her DNA matches.

"I don't know," Justin finally said, shaking his head. "She just said she had some things to do at home and she'd see me tomorrow at work."

"Oh Justin," Jen sighed, reaching over to pat his hand. "If you ever want to be more than friends with her, you're going to have to learn how to listen to more than just her words."

Justin ducked his head sheepishly, and Charlotte cringed at her cousin's obvious discomfort about discussing his feelings for Amy with the rest of the family.

When Justin didn't respond, Jen dropped the subject. The conversation around the table turned to how to figure out if Mary Burleson married Benjamin Avington, either during or immediately after World War I.

"I think I'm going to start by looking at Benjamin's profile on the Avington family tree." Charlotte pointed to her computer that she'd just moved into the chair beside her where Amy was previously sitting.

"I already texted Blake to give him Mary's full name, birth date, and what we know about her time as a nurse in the war." Bobby gestured with his fork between bites. "I figured if he's already at his parents' house, they might be able to look at the hints on Benjamin and see if her info lines up with his."

"Now that I have an idea of where she might have gone after the war, I can do a search for her in records from Georgia, too," Charlotte added. "Maybe I can find a marriage license or something to link them together."

"Did you not have any hints on her from the site already?" Becky asked between bites.

"Yeah, but they were all from before the war," Charlotte replied. "Without knowing where she went after the war, I couldn't narrow down the search to a specific state, so all I could say for sure was that she didn't come back to Texas. Or if she did, she didn't leave any records for me to find when I searched. And I searched Texas' marriage records, birth records, census records, and even death records and couldn't find her."

"Have you had a chance to go over all the hints for Memmaw Judy's family branch on our tree?" Justin changed the subject as they all continued to eat their dinner.

"Not all of them, but I've gone a few generations back there," Charlotte replied, hating that she was about to disappoint her family when she revealed all about their not-so-native ancestors.

"Did you find anything in the paper trail about the Native American ancestry she told us stories about?"

"Oh, yeah," Charlotte laughed to cover her disappointment. "Apparently, there were some not-so-scrupulous members of the Teague family back in the day. I found some Teagues on the Dawes Rolls, but they weren't in Memmaw's direct lineage. Memmaw's third or fourth-great-grandpa apparently tried to claim he was Cherokee on his mother's side of the family but was found to be lying about it, thinking they'd get free land in Oklahoma."

"Seriously?" Charlotte nodded in affirmation at Justin's question. "So, why did Memmaw think she was part Cherokee, if they were proven wrong so many generations back?"

"I guess he was bitter about not being able to claim the free land and continued to claim his supposed heritage, and later generations didn't realize it was all lies." Charlotte shrugged, unable to come up with any other plausible excuse for their ancestors who'd tried to cheat the system so long ago. "And her second-great-grandfather has a criminal record in Arkansas, but he wasn't all bad since he fought for the Union in the Civil War."

"You've found records for our ancestors going back to the Civil War?" Charlotte's dad, Bob, looked at her with surprise, like he wasn't sure how far back the records went online.

"Oh, yeah, and way farther back than that," Charlotte answered her dad. "I haven't followed all the hints to verify everything, but the potential parent hints took me all the way back to England in the fifteen-hundreds on the Teague line and several of the lines that married Teagues to lead down to us. I think I went back as far as our fifteenth great-grandparents on a few of them. And only back to the late sixteen-hundreds on the Burleson line."

"So you found Jonah's parents?" Uncle Jon arched an eyebrow, obviously curious about what she'd found.

"Yes," Charlotte confirmed once she swallowed the bite of food she'd just taken. She turned to her computer and clicked a few times, bringing up the specifics about their Burleson ancestors. "Jonah's mother's name was also Mary, and the census records I found for her listed her as mulatto. I couldn't find anything about her parents, but it appears she was born to a slave mother and later sold with her mother to a John Burleson, who owned a farm in Alabama. I can't find anything for certain about his father, but knowing the atrocities of American history, I'm assuming Jonah's father was that John Burleson. It's his lineage that I traced back to an Aaron Burleson born in sixteen-ninety-five in Wales."

"So the first Mary Burleson is where we got our Southern Bantu Peoples listed in our ethnicity?" JJ asked the question from his seat across the room.

"I'm assuming since she's the only person I've found in our tree that wasn't listed as white on the census records," Charlotte answered, then grinned. "Well, and Jonah. He was listed as mulatto on the eighteen-seventy census records with his mom, but when he left Alabama and moved here, he started claiming white. I guess he was light enough to claim he was just tan from working outside all the time to be able to get away with the change in an area where nobody knew his mom."

"So, Memmaw's ancestors weren't the only ones who lied to the government about their race," Julie giggled.

"Yeah, but at least Jonah was doing it to avoid persecution and not for material gain," Jen giggled along with her twin. "I'm actually kinda proud of him for getting away with it."

Several heads nodded in agreement around the table, including Charlotte's. They finished their meal with Charlotte going through the family tree to tell them a little about the various ancestors she'd found fascinating in her first month of research. Once the table was cleared and the dishes were done, the laptops made a reappearance. Though it seemed to Charlotte that everyone was crowding around hers once more, since she was actively looking for hints about the second Mary Burleson, Jonah's daughter, to see if they were right in their hunch about her marrying Benjamin Avington at the end of World War I.

First, she went to Mary Burleson's profile on the Burleson family tree to search for hints about her life. Once she put in the state of

Georgia as Mary's possible state of residence after the war, the hints started showing up.

"Oh, yes, yes, yes!" Charlotte shouted, throwing her arms up in a V with each "yes" she screamed, like back in her high school cheerleading days. "Marriage records, birth records, they're all popping up now!"

"Don't keep us in suspense." Her mom, Hazel, motioned for Charlotte to continue telling the family what she found. "Tell us who she married."

"Give me a minute to look, Mom." Charlotte smiled and rolled her eyes at her mother before clicking the first record. Unfortunately, her smile was wiped away when she saw it wasn't the right Mary Burleson in the record. "Okay, well, that's disappointing."

"What's disappointing?" Becky leaned in to look over Charlotte's shoulder at the record on her screen.

"The first marriage record is for a Mary Fulton who married a John Burleson in the eighteen-hundreds. I guess I should have narrowed down the years I was searching for before hitting the search button." Charlotte went back and made the change before checking a few more records that came up in the new search, only to click the "ignore" button and move on to the next one.

They were all on pins and needles, watching her go through the records when Bobby's computer chimed with a Skype notification.

"Hey Blake." Bobby accepted the video conference on his computer. "Or I guess I should say, hello to all of the Avingtons. We're not all going to be able to get close enough together to fit us all on the screen at once like that, so how about I walk around and introduce everyone before we start trying to figure out how we're related."

"Sounds good," someone chuckled from Bobby's computer.

It took a few minutes for Bobby to walk around and make introductions multiple times before he finally settled in the seat between Justin and Charlotte. Bobby set his laptop on the table angled toward Charlotte, so she could review the records on her computer with Blake's father, Byron Avington.

"When Blake first got here, he insisted on renewing my subscription, so I could look at the hints I hadn't followed yet." Byron poked the son seated next to him, whom Charlotte had recognized before the introductions as Blake from when Bobby had brought him home on leave when he was in the Navy.

"And were you able to find out whom Benjamin was married to?" Charlotte hoped it was easier for him to find a marriage record than her search for Mary's had been.

"Well, yes, and no," Byron replied. "I found his marriage certificate, but it's in French. Though the names are handwritten in English, whoever filled out the paperwork had horrible handwriting, so I can't make out the name for certain."

"Why would the marriage certificate be in French?" Becky furrowed her brow in confusion.

Charlotte would have rolled her eyes at her sister, but she was too focused on going back to the search parameters and putting in France as a location for Mary to see if she could find the same record.

"If they got married while they were both in France during the war," Justin answered, saving Charlotte from having to explain to her younger sister.

"Oh, yeah, didn't think about that," Becky replied, shaking her head at herself for not seeing the obvious reason for a French marriage certificate. "Can you tell when they got married? Maybe that will help us find it, too. If Benjamin married our Aunt Mary, then we should come up with the same certificate when we search for her records in France in the same year."

Charlotte had already assumed it was sometime either during the war or just after, so she'd narrowed the dates down to encompass the time they knew Mary was in France from the postmarks on the letters she'd found in her attic and a couple of years after the war ended.

"Nineteen-nineteen," Byron replied.

As soon as the parameters were changed and Charlotte clicked to run the search again, the marriage record showed up first in the search. "This is it!" Charlotte exclaimed, excited when she realized what she was seeing on her screen. "Bride, Mary Burleson, groom, Benjamin Avington, married November seventh, nineteen-nineteen."

"You can actually read that?" Byron gave her a shocked look through the computer screen.

"Well, no, I can't read it on the actual document, but the citation for the document gives me the details in English." Charlotte couldn't stop the tears from flowing as she realized what she was looking at on the screen.

This is the proof we need to show the Avingtons are Mary Burleson's descendants to be able to release the trust Jonah left for them.

"I must have missed that screen." Byron turned to fiddle with the laptop on the table beside him.

"This is it, Daddy," Charlotte blubbered as she turned to look at her father. "The first piece of proof you need to release the trust."

"Wow, you did it," Bob said softly, his words conveying his sense of awe at the revelation. She saw a single tear slip down her normally stoic father's cheek as he smiled at her. "Thank you, Char."

There was a lot of crying and more hugging and even a few squeals of delight at finally solving the mystery of where Mary Burleson went after the war before Jon and Bob Burleson took over the conversation with Byron Avington. Not wanting to make the Avingtons uncomfortable by seeming to listen in on the conversation about the trust and their interest in Burleson Incorporated, Charlotte stayed in her seat when her father and uncle walked away with Bobby's computer. She followed the new hints that popped up on Mary Burleson's profile that helped her start adding the Avingtons to the Burleson family tree.

Once she added Benjamin and Mary's son, Jack Avington, she followed his hints to add his wife, Shirley Miller, and their son Aaron Avington. Continuing to follow the hints led to adding Aaron's wife, Carolyn Langston. She managed to add their son, Byron, but couldn't find much about him on the site since it blocked a lot of the records for living people.

I bet that's why Amy's having such a hard time finding any hints on her family tree. Maybe I should wait until after her mom comes to visit to try to help her again, so we have more information to go by and I can actually help instead of just frustrating her more.

Instead of worrying about her friend right then, Charlotte focused on what she needed to do to add on to the newest branch of her family tree. Since her father and uncle absconded with Bobby's computer, where they were talking to Byron about the trust in another room, Charlotte asked Bobby to call Blake, so she could get all their new cousins' pertinent information to manually add them to the family tree, the same way she'd added all her other living relatives that she knew about.

It ended up being a late night of celebration and exchanging information with her new cousins, which Charlotte was grateful for in more ways than one. Not only had she played a major role in solving a hundred-year-old family mystery, but she'd also found another way to distract herself from thinking about Ian Campbell.

Chapter Ten

After talking to Jake a few times in the last week to find out what he was able to see on the San Antonio traffic cameras from the previous week, Ian went back to the same area to retrace his steps. He specifically wanted to check out the parking garage connected to a luxury hotel, where Jake saw the black Suburban Ian was tailing turn in while Ian was momentarily distracted by the shelter. Or rather, he was distracted by wondering if Charlotte was volunteering at that shelter.

When he pulled into the parking garage, he searched through the rows of vehicles on each floor to see if he spotted the Suburban that Jake hadn't seen leave the structure the previous weekend. Since he knew Jake wasn't able to watch the traffic camera covering the only entrance and exit from the parking garage twenty-four-seven, Ian assumed he'd just missed the vehicle leaving sometime later in the week. So, he was pleasantly surprised when he spotted the large SUV parked in the middle of the garage.

He's got to be staying in the hotel, or sneaking through the hotel to go out a back exit that's not covered by the traffic cameras to walk to wherever he's staying nearby. There are plenty of places he could stay in this general vicinity, including a couple of other hotels within walking distance, as well as the shelter a couple of blocks back.

Fuck! Surely, he wouldn't hide out in a homeless shelter when he's driving a brand-new, sixty-thousand-dollar vehicle. Would he?

No. It's more likely that he's hiding in the hotel, thinking nobody would be looking for him here. But, fuck, I'm not willing to bet Charlotte's life on that theory. I need to make sure she's not volunteering at the shelter closest to here, just in case.

Ian exited the parking garage after double-checking it for Charlotte's Equinox. He drove around the blocks surrounding the parking garage to make note of any other hotels where Roberto Rodriguez might be hiding out. Since he wasn't technically back on the DEA's payroll, he didn't have a badge to be able to show the hotel managers to make inquiries about their guests' identities, so he had to turn that task over to Trent and his team.

Or maybe Jake knows someone with the San Antonio PD, who can make those inquiries?

As he finished making his list of hotels to check out, he decided to loop back around to check out the parking lot nearest the shelter for Charlotte's vehicle. Ian also made a mental note to give her brother, Jake, the same list of hotels he was giving Trent, so Jake could check into the guest records. It wasn't that he didn't trust Trent and his team to do a thorough search. He just knew the DEA's resources were stretched too thin to be able to send an agent to the area in a timely manner.

He also knew that Jake Burleson had more contacts in the local law enforcement agencies that he could call on to do the leg work if his brother was still otherwise occupied. *Or he might just hack into the hotels' computers if he can't get someone to physically search them in a timely manner. Or, hell, just so he can narrow down the search area for whomever he gets to check them out in person, so he doesn't waste too much of another department's time.*

Once he had all the hotels in the area noted, Ian doubled back to look for Charlotte's SUV in the parking lot closest to the shelter. He knew there was more than one shelter in a city the size of San Antonio, so Charlotte might not be volunteering at the one closest to where Ian had tracked Rojo. But he couldn't shake the feeling that she was nearby the whole time he was driving around the area, so he had to check it out to make sure she wasn't there.

Since the lot was rather small, it didn't take him long to discern she wasn't parked there. *But it's also a full lot, so she could be parked in the parking garage across the street.*

Ian pulled out of the lot and circled the block to be able to pull into the parking garage on the other side of the road from the lot he'd just left, and the mission that was now being used as a shelter. It didn't take him long to find her bright blue Equinox on the third floor of the parking structure.

Fuck! Not only is she here, but she's also parked in the darkest corner of the place, where she'd be an easy target for Rojo or one of his halcones to grab without witnesses.

Ian parked his undercover truck a row over from where Charlotte was parked, hoping she wouldn't notice he wasn't in the Range Rover she would recognize as his vehicle. He took off the ballcap he always wore while searching the city for Roberto Rodriguez and finger-combed his hair to hide any signs of having worn it all afternoon.

Ian also took off the garish short-sleeved button-down he was wearing over a plain white t-shirt, knowing Charlotte would question why he was wearing something so diametrically opposed to his normal classic style. She might also question the t-shirt, jeans, and sneakers, since she'd only seen him in similar garb the day he went horseback riding with her family. But since he didn't have time to drive all the way back to Heart's Destiny to change into his standard attire of slacks, a button-down, and loafers, he planned to play it off as clothing he could work in while volunteering alongside her.

He removed his nine-millimeter Glock from the back of his waistband, knowing the white t-shirt wouldn't conceal it well enough for him to be able to carry it into the mission. He locked it in the center console, grateful that Jake had thought to upgrade to a locking unit in the older model Chevy.

He got out of the truck and straightened his clothes, double-checking in the side mirror that he looked as close to his normal self as possible. Then he locked up the truck and walked to the exit from the garage. He had to walk down a block and wait for a traffic signal to be able to cross the street to get to the old mission with the small sign identifying it as the Community Mission Shelter.

Just as he approached the short set of stairs leading to the door where he planned to go in and ask for information about volunteering to cover for looking for Charlotte, the woman in question came out the door. She was a vision in a pink floral print dress with short sleeves, a modest, scoop neckline, and a hemline that came down almost to her ankles. It was flowy and sexy, even though it was conservative, as it swirled around the straps of her sandals that crisscrossed up her lower legs.

Ian was momentarily struck dumb, both from the surprise at seeing her walking down the stairs toward him and from the instant wave of lust that hit him at the sight of her.

"What are you doing here?" Charlotte's accusatory tone of voice brought him out of his stupor.

"Checking into volunteer opportunities." Ian wasn't sure how he managed to remember his cover story as Charlotte stomped up to where he'd stopped dead in his tracks at first seeing her, but he thought it had to have something to do with his years of undercover experience. "What are you doing here?"

"This is the shelter I volunteer at every Saturday." Charlotte motioned over her shoulder with her thumb to indicate the shelter behind her. "And since I told you about it in mid-December, I have to wonder if your showing up here is another ploy for you to stalk me."

"You didn't tell *me* anything about this place in mid-December," Ian lied, holding up both hands to feign his innocence. "I thought we already agreed your mysterious lover was my doppelganger."

"Whatever!" Charlotte pushed her way past Ian and headed straight for the crosswalk he'd just used a minute or two before.

He quickly turned and followed her, needing to make sure she got safely back to her vehicle, even if that was all he could have go his way that day. When he caught up with her, he resisted the urge to take her hand or wrap his arm around her to escort her back to the parking garage, not wanting to take a chance that Roberto Rodriguez was watching through a hotel window to see them acting like more than acquaintances. "Where are you headed now?"

"Home, not that it's any of your business," Charlotte huffed, refusing to look over at him. "I'm done for the day here, so you're welcome to go volunteer for the evening. But please skip Saturday afternoons for any volunteer hours you spend here in the future."

Ah, so she wants to avoid spending any time with me here, too, huh? Too bad that's not going to work out for her with Rojo on the loose in this area.

"Yeah, I thought picking someplace in San Antonio to volunteer would insure I wouldn't run into you, too," he lied again. "This isn't exactly a safe neighborhood for a woman to be walking around alone. Since, apparently, there aren't any gentlemen around here to walk a lady to her car to keep her safe, maybe you should stick to volunteering at the youth center in Heart's Destiny, so you don't put yourself at risk, and we can continue avoiding each other."

Though he hated how they'd settled into a routine of mostly avoiding one another since the dance, Ian knew it was the safest thing for her until he finally put Roberto Rodriguez behind bars, where he belonged.

"Oh, I volunteer at the youth center in Heart's Destiny, too." Charlotte waved a hand dismissively at him as they walked into the parking garage. "But because of softball season, I just don't have a set schedule there in the spring, the way I have my Saturday afternoons here since December. Once the season's over, I'll be back over there after school all week."

As they took the stairs up to the floor where they were both parked, Ian made a mental note to know where to find Charlotte in the future, hoping to volunteer with her once Rojo was no longer a threat.

"Well, why don't you spend your Saturdays there now, instead of coming all the way into San Antonio to volunteer here?" Ian knew he sounded like an ass for suggesting she quit volunteering at the shelter to free it up for him to take her place, but he couldn't think of another excuse to give her to not be there without telling her the real reason he didn't want her near the shelter at the moment.

"Since you know I won't be there, why don't you go volunteer at the youth center on Saturdays?" Charlotte insolently spat the question at him as she pulled her keys from a hidden pocket in her skirt.

"Because I'm a man and capable of handling a dangerous situation, should one arise in this dark as fuck parking garage, better than you can," Ian growled, waving an arm around to get her to see how unsafe the area around her Equinox could be for her if she was there alone. "There are too many places for a predator to hide and sneak up on an unsuspecting woman in here, so you should stick to safer places to volunteer."

"Seriously?" Charlotte stopped as they rounded the back of her vehicle to turn in his direction and slap both hands on his chest. "The only predator I see here is you. So, if you'd just go away, I'd be perfectly safe."

"You think I'm a predator?" Ian stepped closer to her, causing her to back up into the darker space between her driver's door and the concrete wall of the building.

Oh, Princess, you have no idea how right you are in that assessment. Only I don't think you'd really protest if I feasted on you right here and now.

The fire he saw in Charlotte's eyes told him all he needed to know about what she wanted to happen between them. The desire, the passion, and the need he saw in her green and gold depths were his undoing. He lost all consciousness of their surroundings. The world was swept away as his own lust for her took over the moment.

Without giving her a chance to respond to his question, Ian reached out and pulled Charlotte into his arms, covering her mouth with his and taking what he'd craved for the last two months.

~~~

Charlotte couldn't believe Ian was actually there at the Community Mission Shelter, when she was leaving after working with Antonio, much less that he was kissing her like he was claiming her. She'd thought she was well on her way to getting over him after they'd steered clear of each other since the middle school Valentine's dance. Yeah, she'd still seen him at school daily and dreamed about him nightly. But they'd barely spoken, and he hadn't pulled any more stunts to aggravate her, so she thought they were both moving on.

With the asshole attitude he'd given her when they ran into each other on the steps of the shelter, Charlotte assumed he wanted to keep avoiding one another. The rejection hurt, but it also fueled her ability to walk away from him, while giving him back some of that asshole attitude.

But apparently, fighting with her was a turn-on for him, since he was once again kissing her with more passion than she'd ever experienced from another man. And, of course, her traitorous body responded to his, with more ardor than he deserved.

Charlotte tried to fight the urge to return his kiss, but with the way her body felt on fire from his touch, she couldn't stop herself from plunging her tongue into his mouth to explore every crevice, the same way he was exploring hers. Her nipples felt as hard as diamonds in her bra, and she felt the instant need to change her soaking-wet panties.
~~~

She vaguely registered the sound of her keys hitting the concrete as she dropped them from her hand, when she wrapped her arms around Ian's neck and weaved her fingers through his short, sandy blond hair. The world around them seemed to disappear, as all Charlotte could focus on was her connection to Ian.

They continued devouring one another's mouths, as Ian gripped her hips and lifted her off the ground. Charlotte wrapped her legs around his waist, relishing the hard ridge of his erection pressing into her core. Ian pressed her back against the driver's door of her car, using it to help hold her up as his hands roamed her body.

Needing to feel as much of Ian as possible, Charlotte released his hair to rub her hands over his shoulders, back, and chest. The soft cotton of his t-shirt wasn't enough. She needed to feel his skin to know they were really together in this incredible moment between them. She untucked the t-shirt from his jeans and slid her hands under it to feel him. She skimmed her hands over his washboard abs, up across his chest, then down and around the muscular planes of his back.

They didn't say a word as they ground their bodies against one another, breathing through their noses because they couldn't stop kissing to even come up for air. Ian palmed her breast with one hand while the other pushed the front hem of her dress up to her navel, exposing her pink satin bikini panties to the rough denim of his jeans where he was humping her through their clothes.

In the back of her mind, she briefly registered it wasn't the proper time or place for what they were doing, especially with the animosity and his lies between them. But the wanton woman inside her, who'd been awakened back in December on her one night with Ian, didn't care about any of that. Char needed to feel the passion that only Ian had ever been able to bring out in her.

As Ian found her clit through her panties, Charlotte fumbled with the buttons on his jeans. He stroked her to the point of madness as she freed his magic, pierced peen from the confines of his pants. Ian was already leaking precum, which Charlotte gladly spread down the length of his shaft.

She broke the kiss long enough to demand what she needed. "Inside me, now!"

"Fuck," Ian groaned, ripping away her panties to rid them of the last barrier between them.

Charlotte wasn't sure where he put the scrap of satin as he covered her mouth with his once more, plunging his tongue in her mouth at the same time he plunged his cock into her pussy. She thought she screamed at the sudden invasion, but any sounds she was able to make were swallowed down by Ian, as he took her against her vehicle with wild abandon.

Charlotte tried to rock her hips in time with his powerful thrusts, but all she could do was hold on for the wildest ride of her life. She had to tear her mouth away from his to suck in air as he pounded into her like a man possessed. Ian paid attention to her cues, kissing and sucking down her neck while she panted for breath, never ceasing in their primal mating. He fondled her breasts as he shifted his hips to make sure his pubic bone stimulated her clit with every stroke of his piercings against her G-spot.

Their coupling was more intense than it had been two months before, but it was exactly what Charlotte needed at that moment. Ian growled, what Charlotte presumed was dirty talk since his voice was so low she couldn't hear his exact words, against her skin, sending her over the edge for the first time that day.

As her body convulsed in climax, Charlotte dug her nails into Ian's back, vaguely aware she was leaving marks with her hands under his shirt. She cried out his name as he commanded her to "keep coming on my cock" and "tell me you're mine, Princess," making her smile with the same pet name he'd called her back in December.

After this, he can't deny that it was him anymore. Not that Charlotte was going to mention that and ruin the moment.

Following his directives prolonged her orgasm to the point that Charlotte thought it might have counted as two or three O's instead of just one. "I'm yours, Ian!"

"Fuck, yeah, you're mine," Ian rumbled as he continued to fuck her into the side of her SUV. Charlotte was pretty sure they were leaving body-sized dents in her door with every thrust, but she couldn't care less about her Equinox, as Ian claimed her with both his body and his words.

"All. Fucking. Mine." Ian punctuated each word with a forceful stroke inside her before shoving as deep as he could go to release his load straight into her womb. "Fuck! Charlotte!"

The feel of his orgasm was so awe-inspiring, it caused Charlotte to go off once more. She shuddered in his arms as wave after wave of ecstasy washed over her. Ian collapsed against her, resting his forehead on her shoulder as their bodies twitched with aftershocks from the earthquaking orgasms they'd just shared.

Charlotte clung to Ian like a monkey in a tree, afraid the only reason she hadn't hit the ground was because of his weight holding her against her car, since her whole body felt limp with satiation. She wanted to bask in the afterglow as they caught their breath, but reality crashed in around them, crushing her dreamlike moment.

"Fuck," Ian groaned as he stepped back and lowered her feet to the floor. He didn't even bother to make sure she was steady on her feet before releasing her and letting her dress fall down to cover her. "What the fuck was I thinking?"

Ian tucked his spent dick back into his boxer briefs before pulling up his jeans that had slipped down to his thighs while they were fucking. "I'm fucking smarter than this. I don't make mistakes like this."

"Mistakes?" Charlotte screeched, angry at his quick rejection so soon after their semi-public copulation. "Are you seriously calling what just happened a mistake? Like you just tripped, and your dick accidentally ended up inside me because I'm not your type? Or am I just not good enough for the almighty Ian Campbell?"

"Fuck, Charlotte, that's not what I meant," Ian grumbled, running a hand through his hair in frustration as he paced back and forth around the back of her vehicle. "I can't... Fuck!"

"You know what, never mind!" Charlotte threw up her hand in the universal sign to stop with a little frustration of her own as she felt his cum dripping down her thigh. She looked down and scanned the ground to find her keys, grateful her phone seemed to still be in the pocket of her dress.

She was glad she'd had the foresight to lock her bag in her vehicle before helping with lunch after working with Antonio earlier in the morning. Otherwise, she'd have probably had a mess to clean up from the contents spilling out when she dropped it before she could leave.

She pulled her phone from her pocket and used the flashlight app until she spotted her keys. She bent down and picked them up before turning to face her car door as she clicked the unlock button on her key fob.

"Just stay the hell away from me, so neither one of us has to worry about making that *mistake* again." Charlotte got in her car and buckled her seatbelt before pushing the button to start the engine.

She glanced in her rearview mirror to make sure she wouldn't hit Ian as she backed out of the space. But she was proud to say her eyes didn't linger on his dejected form, leaning against the wall to watch her drive away.

"I can't believe that bastard had the audacity to fuck me without a condom, and then call it a mistake," Charlotte fumed the whole way home to the family ranch in Heart's Destiny. "That's not a mistake. It's a fucking catastrophe! The arrogant asshole didn't even bother to ask if I'm on birth control or reassure me that he's clean."

The fact that she also hadn't thought about the need for a condom wasn't lost on her. She was mentally kicking herself just as much as she was berating Ian, if not more.

"Ugh! Why haven't I ever gotten over the ick factor of talking about sex with the doctor who's treated me since I was a child? If I had, I could have at least had the reassurance of being on birth control before losing my head and forgetting the need for a condom."

Charlotte blinked away the tears that threatened to blur her vision as she continued her self-deprecating rant. "Thankfully, my period just ended yesterday, so I'm probably not close enough to ovulating to get pregnant this time. But now I'm going to have to try to keep from cringing when I book an appointment to ask Doc Hayes to do an STI panel. I just know he's going to ask why I need another test so soon when that was all just covered at my yearly physical last month."

"Why didn't I pay more attention last week when Kay and Brooklyn were talking about picking an OB-GYN? Oh, because I knew I wasn't pregnant, so I didn't think I really needed one. Stupid, stupid, stupid! If I could find a female OB-GYN, I could ask her all the embarrassing questions about extra STI panels and getting on birth control. But if I ask either one of them whom they're seeing now, they'll think I'm knocked up, too."

Charlotte groaned when she realized she might have to confess her sins with Ian to one of her sisters-in-law if she went to ask them for a recommendation for a female doctor. "Female doctor," she giggled, opting to laugh at the situation she found herself in instead of crying. "Yes, that's the correct term in more ways than one. I need a doctor of the female gender to treat my female issues that were caused by my female parts taking over control of my brain whenever Ian's around."

"Too bad I'll probably die of mortification from talking about this with Kay or Brooklyn before I'd even be able to make an appointment," Charlotte sighed, resigning herself to setting an appointment with Doc Hayes to limit her embarrassment to behind his closed office door. "Maybe Summer or Jeri will be at Bobby and Brooklyn's wedding shower tomorrow? If so, I'll try pulling one of them aside to ask about when I should set an appointment. I know they won't have the schedule with them, but maybe they can tell me how long I should wait after unprotected sex to schedule the STI tests. Or give me a referral to an OB-GYN?"

With a plan in place for dealing with those issues, Charlotte's mind wandered back to her Ian issues for the rest of her drive home. She really wished she could somehow wipe him from her memory, so his rejection would quit hurting her so much.

"I was doing so well the past couple of weeks with us avoiding one another. Yeah, it was hard dreaming about him every night and not being able to act on our attraction to each other, but I wasn't miserable without him in my life. At least, I didn't feel like my heart was being ripped from my chest, like I do now."

Charlotte brushed away the tear that escaped the confines of her watery eyes. "If he hates the thought of being with me so bad, why did he act like he wanted me as much as I wanted him today? For that matter, why did he hunt me down in San Antonio in the first place? And what was up with all that *'you're mine'* bullshit he was spewing in the throes of passion? I swear, it's like he has some kind of mental disorder that manifests as multiple personalities. And I'm definitely not qualified to help him integrate them, like on that soap opera Memmaw used to watch."

Charlotte cried even more at the thought of Ian actually having a mental issue that caused him to run hot and cold with her all the time. Even if she wasn't qualified to help him with whatever was going on in his head, she felt such a strong connection to him that she wanted to be able to help him.

"Memmaw, why'd you have to send me a crazy man to fall in love with? Couldn't you find a nice, normal, mentally stable man for me?" Charlotte knew if anyone heard her talking to her dead grandmother, they'd think she was the mental patient, but she didn't care. Her talks with Memmaw helped her feel better, even if they weren't real.

Though when the song on the radio changed to Lady Antebellum's *Crazy Love*, Charlotte had to wonder if Memmaw was communicating with her from beyond the grave. Charlotte burst out laughing at the irony as she wiped her tears away.

"Fine, I'll keep trusting you to know what you're doing up there in Heaven. But you might want to have a shrink or two help Ian out with his bipolar personalities before we both end up in the looney bin. And while I'm waiting on him to quit acting crazy, I'll keep doing research on your unscrupulous ancestors."

Chapter Eleven

Saturday, March 2, 2019

Over the course of the last week, Ian practically drove himself insane, trying to figure out how to make things right with Charlotte. He felt like an utter and total ass for the way he let his lizard brain take over his body the previous Saturday. There was no excuse for the way he behaved, or the risk he took by letting his lust for Charlotte take precedence over keeping her safe while he completed his mission to locate Roberto Rodriguez.

Of course, his feelings of guilt after the crazy, intense fuck in the parking garage didn't stop him from using what was left of her torn, pink panties to jerk off with that night. He'd been too grateful to find them in his pocket when he got undressed for bed to worry about whether or not he should be ashamed of keeping them like a trophy.

Once the fog of lust had lifted in the parking garage, Ian had felt that eerie feeling of being watched again. That feeling caused him to freak out at the thought of Rojo spotting him on the street with Charlotte, and possibly following them into the parking garage to see some of their intimate time together.

He had looked around the best he could to see if they'd been observed, but he hadn't been joking about there being too many dark hiding places between cars in that particular garage when he mentioned it to Charlotte. So, he couldn't be certain that nobody else was on that floor of the parking garage, while they were otherwise occupied and wouldn't notice a voyeur. Or Ian's worst nightmare, a criminal like Roberto Rodriguez, or one of his associates, who might want to do them harm.

Because he was a paranoid bastard, Ian had waited for Charlotte to turn toward the ramp down to the next lower level before running over a row, jumping in his truck, and following her at a discreet distance to make sure nobody else followed her home. Considering how pissed she was when she left, he was glad he was in his undercover truck, so he didn't think she'd recognized it was him, even if she figured out she was being tailed.

Ian hadn't noticed anyone else shadowing them, especially not the black Suburban he'd seen Rodriguez in the week before. So, once he knew she was safely back on the ranch, Ian went to his temporary tactical operations center and made a few phone calls to get both Trent and Jake working on narrowing down where Roberto was staying in San Antonio. He also checked in with Levi Nash to see if his presence was necessary at the bar that night before reading over the updated files Jake had sent him on Big John and the guys he'd been meeting with the past couple of weeks at Levi's Bar.

Most of that time was routine and helped him get his mind off of his colossal fuck up with Charlotte. But Ian was sweating bullets while talking with Jake, uncomfortable with having to ask him to check into the shelter clients and volunteers. And especially with having to mention seeing Charlotte there. Needless to say, Ian was rather tense going into the conversation with his friend.

Ian had to finally come clean to Jake about the first time he met Charlotte and why he was trying to keep his distance from her to keep her safe. He glossed over their insane sexual chemistry and only admitted to kissing her in the parking garage. But he needed the opinion of someone who knew Charlotte better than he did to try to figure out how to apologize to her and keep from completely blowing his chances at ever having a relationship with her after Rojo was no longer an issue.

Jake had been surprised by the revelation and had seemed to enjoy giving Ian the requisite brother-speech about not hurting his sister. But once those uncomfortable few minutes were over, he'd quickly jumped over to the supportive friend role and wished Ian lots of luck at making things work with Charlotte.

Unfortunately, Jake hadn't had any better ideas for how he could apologize than Ian had in the last week. In fact, he'd agreed with Ian that the only way Charlotte would forgive him for the hot-and-cold routine would be if he told her everything about what was going on with both his feelings for her and the case he couldn't walk away from until it was over. He also agreed that telling her before Rojo was behind bars put her at greater risk of being targeted by the cartel because of being seen with him.

So, now, a week later, Ian was standing on the ball field for the first games of the season, watching the woman he wanted to be with on the other field while unable to even talk to her. He was trying to leave her in peace as she'd asked, while also watching to make sure nobody had seen them together to target her. But he was dying to be able to apologize and tell her everything.

While he knew he still couldn't tell her about the case, or even his history with Mari because of how the Rojo case had been the cause of her death, he knew he needed to figure out how to apologize for his asinine behavior soon, so they could at least talk about the possible consequences of his lust-fueled lapse of thought about protection.

Ian still couldn't believe he'd forgotten to put on a condom. He was normally diligent about using them, having previously only skipped them when Mari was pregnant with Brody.

Hell, I even wore one when we conceived Brody, only stopping using them after Mari told me they weren't necessary because she was already pregnant. Once he was born, the love gloves went right back on. So how did I forget it last week with Charlotte?

Fuck, maybe I was subconsciously trying to tie her to me, so she can't pick another guy before I'm free of this Rojo mess to be with her without risking her life.

Ian pulled off his ballcap and ran his hand through his hair in frustration at being such a dick, as he called a time-out to pull his first-string pitcher. They were ahead by three in the seventh inning, so he swapped out to let his second-string pitcher get some game time, too.

Once the switch was made and the game resumed with Ian back at his position just outside the first base line to call the plays, his mind wandered back to Charlotte. Specifically, he started thinking about the possibilities he could see for a future with her.

The possibility that she could be pregnant sent his mind reeling with images of them all together as a family. He imagined having a little girl with her, one who looked as much like Charlotte as Brody looked like Mari.

He also wondered if Charlotte would want to adopt Brody if he could convince her to marry him someday. She obviously adored

Brody and Brody loved her. At least, Brody acted like he loved her when he talked non-stop every night over dinner about what she had taught him with the horses.

Apparently, the Burlesons had recently purchased a couple of new horses that they trained to become working horses for the ranch hands that worked with the cattle every day. Once they were ready to work, they pulled two of the previous working horses out of the stable used by the ranch hands working with the cattle and brought them over to the family stable. They were retraining them for trail rides and giving each of the kids in the youngest generation of Burlesons a horse of their own. And since Charlotte was helping her father teach the horses what to do in their new role on the ranch, as well as Brody how to ride and care for the horses, she was doing double duty by teaching Brody while working with Lightning and Thunder.

Ian hadn't been sure he was comfortable with his four-year-old son learning to ride a horse that had been named Lightning because of its speed. But then Cait had reassured him that he was perfectly safe with the way Charlotte was teaching them to work together.

Would Charlotte consider me allowing Brody to go on trail rides with her without Cait or me going along as an olive branch? Should I make that a part of my apology for the way I've been a jackass to her? I really should show her I trust her with my kid, now that there's a possibility she's carrying my baby.

Though I should also probably start doing things to show her I want to take care of her and the baby, too. I could pick up an extra coffee on my way to school for her without drawing too much attention from anyone outside the building.

Shit, no, not unless I go with decaf until I know if she's pregnant or not. I know, a treat from the bakery in the middle of town instead.

Hell, maybe I'll just do both. I'll have to ask Jake if he knows her favorites, so I don't pick something she doesn't like and just piss her off even more.

As the baseball game ended with the Cowpokes beating the Sandcrabs, seven to three, Ian decided to sit in his Range Rover and call Jake while he was waiting for the softball game to finish. Once Charlotte was finished coaching, Ian planned to follow her to the shelter to make sure she was safe, whether she wanted him there during her volunteer time or not.

And just to be sure neither Roberto Rodriguez nor one of his associates recognized his undercover truck from the previous two weekends, Ian was taking his Range Rover. Since he knew he wouldn't have time to go to his TOC to grab his weapons after the game and before Charlotte left the sports complex, Ian had already moved a couple into the lockbox in the back of his Range Rover, so he was prepared to keep her safe.

If she lets me keep her safe. As pissed as she was last weekend, I'm not sure she'll forgive me enough to let me hang around and volunteer with her. But all I can do is apologize with as much sincerity as I feel. And hopefully, I won't stick my foot in my mouth again when I try to apologize to her for last week.

"Hey man, what's up?" Ian couldn't get over how laid back Jake always sounded on the phone, no matter what he was dealing with for both work and his family.

"Not much, just finishing up at the baseball field and waiting for Charlotte's team to finish up, so I can follow her to the shelter."

"Ah, a day at the ball field brings back some good childhood memories." Ian could hear the smile in Jake's voice, even over the phone. "You got the family with you to help soften Char up about letting you volunteer with her?"

"No," Ian sighed, hating that he couldn't let Brody come watch the team he coached while Roberto Rodriguez was still a free man. "I'm not taking any chances with their safety by going on public family outings with Rojo still on the loose. But hopefully, you'll figure out where he's staying soon, so they can quit hiding at my house or on your family ranch all the time."

"Damn, yeah, I guess you wouldn't want to take any chances on a repeat of the last time you were at a park with your family." Jake's tone turned serious as he mentioned the day of the ambush.

Ian absentmindedly brushed his hand over the scar on his shoulder from the bullet he took that day while shielding his son. "No, I definitely don't want a repeat of that day, which is why I wish I could convince Charlotte to stop volunteering at the shelter for a little while."

"Yeah, me too," Jake sighed. "But short of telling her all about Rojo, there's no way either one of us can convince her to stop. I even thought about calling her and telling her that I've gotten word about a fugitive hiding out near the shelter."

"Yeah? You think she'd listen to you?" Ian hoped a call from her brother would save them from having to worry about Charlotte crossing paths with Roberto Rodriguez.

"Maybe if I'd have said something before she saw you at the shelter," Jake huffed. "But now she'd figure out that you're in on the case if I mentioned it. And with her not knowing the whole story, she'd be just as likely to blow your cover as she would to stay away from there until we catch this bastard."

"Damn, you're probably right about that." Ian shook his head. "As pissed as she is at me right now, she'd likely blow my cover on purpose, thinking it would make me move back to California."

"You're probably risking that now by shadowing her at the shelter today."

"You think?" *Damn, I didn't think about the attention she could draw by getting pissed at me for being there.*

"Maybe," Jake drawled like he wasn't sure if it was a risk for Ian to go to the shelter or not. "It might be safer for both of you if you just follow her to make sure she gets there safely. Then check out a couple of other leads I have for you in town while she's doing her thing inside. And then trail her home without actually getting close enough for her to hit Rojo's radar, if she isn't already on it after last weekend."

"Fuck," Ian cursed under his breath at the realization that Jake was right. *Maybe I'm too emotionally involved in this case to be discreet enough to keep us both safe.* "You're right. What have you got for me to check out?"

"You know I haven't found any record of Rojo at the hotels you sent me, under his real name or his known aliases," Jake repeated his update from earlier in the week. "But I did get a couple of contact names from my buddy in the S.A.P.D. of people who weren't sure if they recognized Roberto or not. I thought you might want to set up some meetings with them to show them some different pictures than the one he took to the hotels to see if you can get a positive I.D."

"Yeah, if you think they'll talk to me since I don't have a badge to flash to compel them to talk to me."

"They'll talk to you," Jake chuckled. "Rico asked if they'd be willing to meet with the undercover agent working the case when he talked to them, making sure they knew it wouldn't be possible for you to carry a badge in case you're searched while you're under. And they both agreed to let him pass on their contact info."

"Cool, text me the info and I'll make contact as soon as Charlotte is safely inside the shelter." Ian started his Range Rover as soon as he saw Charlotte getting into her car.

They said their goodbyes, so Ian could focus on following Charlotte without being spotted. As they made the hour-long drive into San Antonio, Ian wondered if maybe his history with the Rodriguez Cartel and his feelings for Charlotte were making this case too risky for him to continue working on, even with him trying to avoid actual contact with Roberto.

Maybe I should back away from the Rojo case altogether? Thinking about Charlotte is keeping me from focusing a hundred percent on the op, and the op is keeping me from being able to see where things could go with Charlotte. So, maybe I should let Trent and Jake and their teams focus on getting justice for Mari, while I move on with my life with Charlotte.

~ ~ ~

Monday, March 4, 2019

Charlotte was flummoxed by yet another shift in the dynamic between her and Ian. She thought they'd settled back into the routine of avoiding one another after their angry fuck in the parking garage a little over a week ago. It wasn't ideal and didn't seem to be helping her get over him, but at least she wasn't getting worked up by him daily the previous week.

Actually, she'd had a lot of other things going on in her life that kept her from thinking about him as much. On Sunday, the day after their angry fuck, she had Bobby and Brooklyn's wedding shower to keep her too busy to think about Ian most of the day.

Well, other than when she'd talked to Jeri about getting an appointment at the Heart's Destiny Clinic. She'd found out that they were bringing in an OB-GYN on the first of April. And since her research had basically shown she needed to wait until she missed her period, which was due on March eighteenth, to get a pregnancy test, and that it could take up to three months for some sexually transmitted diseases to show on tests, she figured she'd be fine waiting until after the new doctor started at the clinic, so she could feel more comfortable speaking with a woman about all her concerns.

She was able to put all of that out of her mind again on Monday the twenty-fifth, when she had to get a substitute to cover her classes, so she could spend the morning at the Burleson Incorporated corporate office in San Antonio signing paperwork to transfer part of her share of the company to the new cousins they'd found. Having her share of the company go down from five percent to three-point-five-seven percent wasn't much of a difference to her, but that transfer of a portion of the family business and the trust fund Jonah Burleson had originally set up a hundred years ago for his daughter's descendants would change the Avingtons' lives dramatically.

Not that the Avingtons were doing all that bad with their security company before finding out they were Burleson heirs, but now their combined net worth was in the billions to match their Texan cousins. Charlotte had to wonder if her new cousins would step back from the riskier aspects of their business, now that they were more financially stable. Or if they'd be like her brothers, who continued working in high-risk vocations while letting their share of the Burleson billions keep earning them more money than their grandchildren could spend.

If she really thought about it, Charlotte could understand part of why her brothers continued to work in their dangerous jobs, even though their positions on the board of directors and dividends from their shares in the company paid enough they didn't have to work. They'd all been raised to want to give back to their community and take care of others. She was doing the same thing by working as a teacher, but her job wasn't nearly as dangerous as her brothers' jobs.

Well, I guess Anthony's job isn't that dangerous anymore. Flying the corporate jet for the GWA is way safer than when he was flying fighter jets in the Navy.

Thinking about her brothers and how they'd all spent time in dangerous positions in the Navy made Charlotte wonder if Ian had ever served in the military. *That would certainly explain the military short haircut and the scars he didn't want to talk about back in December.*

Remembering him naked brought her back to thinking about the more recent time they'd been together, even though neither of them actually got naked the previous Saturday in the parking garage. She still hadn't figured out how to deal with his Dr. Jekyll and Mr. Hyde personality shifts, which seemed to kick in again two days earlier when she caught Ian staring at her from across the fields when both the baseball team and softball team had their first games of the season.

After that, she noticed him following her to San Antonio when she went to volunteer with lunch and work with Antonio at the shelter. Since he didn't actually come inside or attempt to volunteer alongside her, she assumed he was just making sure she was safe going into what he considered a dangerous area of the city, but he was actually going to respect her boundaries by not actually interacting with her.

He'd apparently spent the whole afternoon in the parking garage, waiting to follow her home, but he didn't say a word to her. She was okay with that. In fact, having him follow her to and from the shelter actually made her feel a little safer, knowing he was watching out for anyone who might cause her harm as she went about her day. And not having to speak to him meant she wasn't likely to climb him like a tree and ask for a repeat of the parking garage pounding, which she still got wet thinking about nine days later.

She'd thought they'd finally settled into a decent compromise that would work best for both of them. Not speaking to one another meant she could keep her heart safe from him and could maybe keep her vagina from leading her into trouble with him. It would also keep him from acting on their chemistry, just to lash out later when he got angry about feeling that attraction with her, since he clearly didn't want to feel it.

She didn't know why he'd followed her, but she thought it might have something to do with the safety issues he'd brought up the first time he found her at the shelter. She hadn't ever thought she was unsafe there before he pointed it out. But now that she had those images in her head, she was almost comforted by him following her, so she knew she wasn't alone there, just in case he was right about the risks.

That was the ideal way for us to deal with each other. Knowing he was there to be a safety net for me without having to talk to him to deal with his hot-and-cold attitude toward me.

But then he flipped the script on her again this morning by showing up in her classroom bearing gifts. She wasn't sure how he'd figured out how she took her coffee or that chocolate long johns were her favorite donut from Kara's Kakes. But somehow, he'd showed up with a perfectly prepared cup of joe from the Caffeinated Cowpoke and two long johns in a bag from Kara's. He'd given her a panty-melting smile as he placed them on her desk, saying, *"Just a couple of sweet treats for my sweetie,"* before heading right back out of her classroom.

She'd been too dumbfounded by his odd behavior to say a word in response before he was out the door. But as she'd enjoyed her coffee and donuts while preparing for her day to begin, Charlotte's mind filled with questions she had for him and things she wished she'd said.

His sweetie, my ass! I should have shown him just how Not Sweet I can be!

Though she knew she probably wouldn't say any of the mean things she'd come up with earlier, Char decided to take advantage of some private time during their planning period to ask the questions she had for Ian. Once she finished eating the salad she brought for lunch at her desk, she put her things away and walked next door to his classroom.

He was apparently just coming back from the teacher's lounge, where he'd been eating lunch, and hadn't even sat down before she started in with her interrogation. She had to start questioning him as soon as she saw him in yet another literary tie with his gray button-down and slacks, or else she just might give in to her vajayjay's desire to jump his boner.

Damn, those things shouldn't be that sexy on him.

"Why did you bring me coffee and donuts this morning?" Charlotte stomped right up to his desk as he took his seat behind it.

"I thought you'd like them," Ian shrugged.

"Did my mother tell you my favorite donuts and how I take my coffee?" Charlotte placed both palms on his desk and leaned over it, trying to be intimidating.

"No," Ian chuckled, his lips turning up in that way too-cute half-smile, half-smirk that made Charlotte's panties wet. "But I'll have to remember to ask her for suggestions of other things you might like in the future."

Not feeling like she was really getting anywhere with that line of questioning, Charlotte changed tactics. "Are you finally ready to admit it was you at the hotel in December?"

"I am not at liberty to confirm or deny that just yet, Princess." Ian, the asshole, had the audacity to wink at her.

Ugh! What a jackass answer!

"Are you ever going to stop lying to me? Or are you just going to keep going back and forth between the Ian I want to like and get to know, and Ian the lying asshole?" Charlotte stomped her foot like an insolent child and instantly felt ridiculous for being suckered back into his games by her favorite chocolate coffee and donuts.

"I'm not intentionally lying to hurt you, Charlotte." Ian reached forward and lifted her hands from his desk to hold them in his. "I have…stuff going on in my life that I can't tell you about right now. I'm truly sorry if my way of dealing with that stuff has seemed like I'm lying to you. I thought trying to distance myself from you was the best course of action to be able to get through this mess as quickly and painlessly as possible for both of us. But I can't keep fighting this…whatever it is between us any longer. Especially if we made a baby last weekend."

Charlotte jerked her hands out of his, taking a step back at the realization that he knew a baby between them was a possibility. *Shit! I didn't expect him to bring that up!*

Her surprise at his unexpected turn to the conversation kept her from responding to his bold statement, much less comprehending everything he'd just said. It also gave him an opening to continue speaking.

"I want to apologize for losing control last week. I'm normally very diligent about using condoms. The only time I haven't worn one was when Mari was pregnant with Brody. We were both tested for everything then and were both clean. As were all my tests since losing her. And I haven't been with anyone else since I first met her, until you. So, you don't have to worry about any other consequences other than pregnancy."

Charlotte took a deep breath as his words sank into her brain. *He's clean, so I don't have to worry so much about the STI testing.* While that revelation was a relief to her, Charlotte still felt a little twinge of jealousy that the other woman had been the first he'd gone condomless with, and she didn't want to admit that she wished he'd saved that first-time honor for her.

"I'm clean, too, as of my annual physical in January." Charlotte didn't think it was necessary for them to get into their sexual histories while at school, where anyone could walk in on their conversation, so she didn't bother to tell him it had been close to a year since her last sexual partner before she met him in December.

She took another deep breath and made sure the door was securely closed behind her before addressing the baby possibility. "As for pregnancy, I don't think there's much of a risk. According to the ovulation calendars I've looked at, I wasn't at the right point in my cycle on the twenty-third to conceive, so I expect to have my period as normal this month. But I'll let you know if there's any indication that those calendars and calculators are incorrect, and it doesn't come as expected."

Charlotte couldn't be sure, but she thought she saw a look of disappointment cross Ian's face just before he nodded and said, "Thank you. Even if I can't ever get you to forgive me enough to give me a chance to be the man in your life, I'll want to be a part of our child's life should he or she come along in nine months."

After seeing him with Brody a few times in the last couple of months, Charlotte already knew he was a good father. She'd assumed he'd be the same with their child, if they'd conceived. But as images of him holding their infant flashed through her mind, she couldn't bring herself to say anything to him about how she'd want him to be a part of her child's life should they have conceived a baby in their reckless romp a little over a week before. So, she just nodded once and turned on her heel to leave the room.

As Charlotte went back to her classroom to finish out her day teaching, she vowed to herself that she wouldn't let her libido override her brain again when it came to Ian Campbell. Or her biological clock.

No matter how much my vagina wants his pierced peen or my eggs clamor to become his babies, I'm not giving him a chance with me, until he comes clean about our night in December and whatever is keeping him from being honest about it now. Even if I have to badger him about our first night together every time he tries to talk to me to get him to finally tell me the truth.

Chapter Twelve

Ian was feeling pretty proud of himself for how well his plan to get back in Charlotte's good graces was working. Oh, she'd badgered him with questions he couldn't answer the first day he brought her coffee and donuts and seemed more irritated than appreciative at first. But over the course of the week, she'd quit asking him the same questions over and over that he kept telling her he couldn't answer yet. She'd even started saying "thank you" when he dropped off his morning deliveries and smiled back at him when she saw him in the halls of the school, instead of scowling the way she had before he started plying her with sweets.

Since they were on friendlier terms, Ian decided to try once again to talk her into skipping her weekly trip to San Antonio to keep her out of the area where he suspected Roberto Rodriguez was hiding out. While he wasn't completely convinced that going on a lunch date with him was any less risky for her than going to volunteer at the shelter, he had to trust that Jake was right in saying they'd be safe to be out in public together as long as they stayed in Heart's Destiny.

In the last couple of weeks, Jake had taken to trying to convince Ian that he was being paranoid when he thought he was being watched while at baseball practice. He chalked it up to PTSD from the ambush in the park when Mari was killed and both Ian and his sister had taken bullets.

Ian already knew he suffered from PTSD, so he didn't feel like he really needed Jake playing armchair psychologist to tell him that, especially since he'd seen an actual psychologist right after the surprise attack by the Rodriguez Cartel. Actually, he and Cait had both seen a therapist for the first year after the incident to deal with their flashbacks and nightmares. But he thought they'd mostly moved past the worst of those issues when the frequency of the flashbacks and nightmares decreased to only rare occurrences.

Now, after seeing how Cait only felt comfortable enough to relax in certain environments, and with him starting to feel that eerie feeling at the ball field, which was the closest thing to a park that Ian had been at since his son's second birthday on December 3, 2016, he was starting to wonder if they'd both quit therapy prematurely. *Could that feeling of being watched really just be paranoia, or a weird almost flashback?*

When Ian walked into Charlotte's classroom to see her bent over her desk reaching for something, he hoped he was just in need of more therapy and not actually being followed, so he really could relax a little and go out with her somewhere public without putting her at risk. The sight of her heart-shaped ass encased in a skirt the same bright blue color as her car made his mouth water more than the smells in the bakery he'd been visiting every morning before school.

Damn, if only I could take a bite out of her right now.

"What color is your skirt?" Ian couldn't stop himself from inquiring, needing to know the specific name of the shade of blue as much as he needed to know everything else about her. He assumed it was her favorite color, based on how often he saw her wearing an article of clothing that shade and the fact that she'd had her Equinox painted in the custom color that wasn't standard from the factory.

"Azure blue," Charlotte replied, straightening from her bent position, and turning back to look at him as she clutched a book to her chest. "Why?"

"Just wanted to know the specific shade of blue that seems to be your favorite color." Ian smiled as he held out his morning offering to her.

"How'd you know it's my favorite color?" Charlotte arched an eyebrow as she placed the book on her desk to reach for the coffee and donuts.

"The same way I've learned most of the things I know about you, Princess," Ian grinned. "Through my excellent observation skills." *And asking your brother and friends.*

"Uh-huh, sure." Charlotte rolled her eyes at him as she lifted the decaf coffee to her lips and took a sip.

Ian wasn't sure how she could choke down the sweet concoction that included more sugar, cocoa powder, and caramel-flavored creamer than coffee, but the smile it put on her face when she took the first taste made Ian glad he'd gotten it for her.

"But if you'd rather we spend some time talking about all our favorite things, instead of me just guessing from watching you all the time, maybe we can go to lunch tomorrow after our ball games are over," Ian suggested, trying to be smooth as he segued into the discussion of her Saturday afternoon plans.

"I might be persuaded to sit and talk to you at lunch in the teacher's lounge this afternoon, but I already have plans for tomorrow after the game." Charlotte tilted her head as she studied his reaction to her rejection. "But you already know I have plans to volunteer at the shelter tomorrow afternoon, so I have to wonder why you're inviting me to lunch when you know I'm not available to go. Is this just another game to make it seem like you like me, when you really want nothing to do with me? A way to seem like you're into me by asking me out, but then not actually having to go through with a date you don't want to go on with me?"

"No, no games, sweet Charlotte." Ian held his hands up in surrender. "I just want to spend as much time with you as possible, so we can both get to know one another better. And I'll gladly do that wherever and whenever you want. Today in the teacher's lounge sounds like a good start. And maybe if all goes well, I'll be able to convince you to let me go with you to volunteer at the shelter tomorrow, too."

It's not as good as convincing you to stay away from there for a while, but at least I'll feel better if I'm there to protect you.

"We'll see," Charlotte smiled as she placed her coffee and donuts on her desk and picked up the book she was reaching for when Ian walked in earlier. "Depends on how much you're willing to share at lunch today."

"I'll share as much as I possibly can, Princess." Ian stepped closer to Charlotte and used one finger to tilt her chin up. He dipped his head and lightly brushed his lips over hers. "I'm through fighting whatever this crazy thing is between us, whether I'm free to share everything with you yet or not."

He lightly pecked her lips once more before turning and exiting the room. He needed a few minutes alone in his classroom to get his cock under control again before his first class arrived for the day.

A few hours later, after getting through all his sixth-grade classes for the day, Ian practically strutted into the teacher's lounge, where he was meeting Charlotte for lunch. He knew she'd only agreed to a conversation in a room full of their colleagues, but Ian was confident this mini-date was just the first step toward the real dates that he hoped would eventually lead to a lifetime together.

Fuck! I'm so ready for our life together to get started. Hopefully, this case won't keep that from happening for too much longer. And if I can lay a little groundwork with getting to know her better while we're finishing it up, then maybe it won't derail Charlotte and me any more than it already has.

He hadn't ended up deciding to walk away from the Rojo case just yet. As much as he wanted to be able to turn it over to Trent and Jake and their teams, he had to stay on board as long as Charlotte was insisting on volunteering at the shelter in the same area of San Antonio, where he'd confirmed Roberto Rodriguez had been spotted. Besides wanting to keep Charlotte safe, Ian felt he owed it to his family to bring Rodriguez in to pay for his crimes against them. Bringing the man responsible for Mari's death to justice would be his final way of saying goodbye to his first love.

I'm sure Charlotte will understand my need for closure after the way we lost Mari before I'm able to fully move on with giving her my heart.

When he saw Charlotte already sitting at a table off away from the other teachers, he flashed her a smile before striding over to join her. "Are we hiding in the corner for privacy, Princess?" Ian wagged his eyebrows suggestively at her as he took the seat beside her.

"What? No," Charlotte sputtered, her eyes widening in surprise at his innuendo as she waved her arm toward the rest of the room. "This was just the only empty table when I got in here and it's not exactly private."

"Maybe not private enough for what we did a couple of weeks ago in a parking garage," Ian whispered as he leaned in close to keep their fellow teachers from eavesdropping. "But it's private enough for a quiet conversation to not be overheard."

"Well, since you won't answer the questions I really want answers to when we're alone, I figured we'd stick to innocuous topics in a room full of our gossipy colleagues." Charlotte grinned after not keeping her voice down at all.

Ian stifled a chuckle at how she'd basically called out the school busybodies, who were clearly leaning in trying to hear them. "Good point."

They unpacked their lunches and got set up to eat while giving the gossips in the room no fodder for their entertainment. Once the rest of the tables in the room started to go back to their normal level of conversation, Ian finally turned to look at Charlotte. "So, what innocuous questions do you have for me?"

"I figured we'd start with the basics," Charlotte shrugged between bites of her steak salad. "Like how old you are, where you're originally from, and any of your favorite things you can think of off the top of your head."

"I'm thirty-three," Ian replied with a smile. "Well, for a few more months, anyway. I'll be thirty-four on July twenty-ninth. I'm originally from California. I was born in a small town a couple of hours east of San Diego and spent the first few years of my life on my grandparents' farm there. But we moved to San Diego when they passed away." Ian didn't mention that losing his grandparents wasn't the whole reason for the move.

Ian also didn't mention how the scent of her bodywash reminded him of the farm he hadn't seen in over twenty years, knowing if he did then she'd realize he remembered her bodywash from their night together at the hotel the night he came for his interview.

"As for my favorite things…" Ian trailed off, thinking about which favorites he could tell her that weren't related to her or sex with her to keep the conversation friendly and safe for their current environment. "I've never really thought about a favorite color or anything like that. I like rock music, but I don't have a favorite song or band. My favorite food is pizza. What else should I have a favorite of that I can't come up with off the top of my head right now?"

"Oh, I don't know. How about a favorite book? Or a favorite author? You know, since literature is such a big part of our jobs."

Charlotte's flirty smile told him she was teasing him for not thinking about books.

"Oh, man, I can't narrow it down to one favorite book." Ian shook his head as the titles of his favorite crime thrillers swam in his head. "But I'd say Lee Child is my favorite author. Anything in his *Jack Reacher* series would be on the list of my favorites for personal reading. I'm more into the current crime thrillers than I am the classics we have to teach for our classes."

While Ian was happy to share these little details about himself, he wanted to know the same things about Charlotte. So, while she was chewing her food, he took the chance to turn the subject back on her. "What about you? Care to share the basics I don't already know?"

Charlotte quickly finished chewing and swallowed her bite while Ian took a bite of his sandwich to give her the opening to speak. "Well, you already know I was born and raised on the ranch and that my favorite color is azure blue. My favorite food is barbequed brisket. I prefer country music, but there are too many good songs to pick a favorite."

Yeah, I figured you liked country music more after watching you at the Valentine's dance last month.

"My favorite genre for personal reading is romance," Charlotte continued, telling him something he'd already assumed.

Of course, she prefers romance novels. Don't most women?

"And while *Pride and Prejudice* will always have a special place in my heart as the first romance novel I ever read, I'd have to say I prefer more contemporary romance now. I'd have to pick Lexi Blake as my current favorite author, with pretty much all of the books in her *Masters and Mercenaries* series on my list of favorite books. Although, I'm also enjoying several of her other series set in the same literary universe. What else? Oh, I just turned twenty-nine in January."

Twenty-nine. Four-and-a-half years younger than me. That's not too big of an age difference, is it? Nope. Seems just right to me.

"Wait, how'd I miss your birthday party?" Ian couldn't believe he'd missed Charlotte's birthday when he'd been pulled into several of the parties for her other family members on the ranch in the last couple of months while picking Cait up from work.

"I got lucky that it was on a weekend when Cait wasn't working, so you didn't get coerced into attending by my mother." Charlotte gave him a mischievous grin.

"It wouldn't have taken much coercion." Ian grinned back. "I only stayed at the other birthday parties to get to watch you from across the room."

"Stalker," Charlotte teased, her grin widening.

"I'll have to plead the fifth on that charge," Ian quipped back, raising his hands in surrender as he smiled back at her. "But don't be surprised if I bring you a belated birthday present tomorrow, since I missed the most important birthday party of the year."

"You don't have to do that," Charlotte protested, shaking her head at him.

"I know I don't have to. I want to." Ian smiled at her, hoping he looked sincere enough to cover for the fact that he already had plans to find a piece of jewelry he could put a tracker in to give her the next day.

He already had a few of the little microchip trackers that looked like charms embossed with the letter C for a bracelet or necklace at home in case Brody somehow lost or damaged the ones Ian had hidden in his shoes. Ian still wasn't sure how his four-year-old managed to damage them so easily when his sister hadn't needed a replacement of hers in the two years she'd been wearing one on her anklet. But now that he was thinking about what he could put one on for Charlotte, Ian was glad he'd stocked up to be prepared for Brody to keep busting them as he played. While the initial C had been chosen for their last name of Campbell, it would work for Charlotte as well.

While he knew Jake thought Charlotte was perfectly capable of protecting herself well enough that he didn't think she needed to be observed twenty-four-seven, Ian couldn't shake the nagging fear that she could be taken for trafficking by Rojo or one of his men, even if she wasn't a target because of the budding relationship between her and Ian. So, just like he was making every effort to keep her safe when she went into San Antonio, he would take the opportunity to put a tracker on her to keep her safe when he couldn't be with her. Or at least to be able to find her if she ever went missing.

"What are you going to do? Embarrass me in front of all the kids and parents again by giving me a present in the middle of our ball games in the morning?" Charlotte glared at him as she finished her lunch.

"No, I was actually thinking of giving it to you on the drive to San Antonio before we spend the afternoon volunteering at the shelter together." Ian popped the last bite of his second sandwich in his mouth before giving her a closed-mouth grin.

"Do you think you've actually shared enough during lunch to earn the right to volunteer with me?" Charlotte arched an eyebrow inquisitively at him.

"I've answered every question you've asked with a hundred percent honesty and transparency, so yeah, I do," Ian smirked at her.

"True, but we haven't exactly been able to go very deep with the questions while having an audience, so I'm not sure it's enough."

"Then think of the drive between here and San Antonio tomorrow as the perfect time to ask the deeper questions when we don't have an audience." Ian just hoped she'd stick to questions about his childhood or college years to keep from having to evade topics that were too close to the Rojo case for him to be able to discuss them openly.

"Okay, I guess I can give you a one-time chance to volunteer with me, but if you're not open and honest enough with me on the drive over there tomorrow, you won't get a second chance."

"You drive a hard bargain, Princess, but I'll take it." *And hopefully, I'll convince you to let me hang around the shelter with you more than just tomorrow.*

<div align="center">~~~</div>

Saturday, March 9, 2019

Charlotte wasn't sure what she was thinking when she agreed to let Ian drive her to San Antonio and volunteer with her at the shelter. It certainly wasn't sticking to her plan to not give him a chance to get close to her again until he told her all his secrets and admitted to being the man she was with at the hotel on the RiverWalk back in December. But as she was in the locker room of the fieldhouse changing out of her burgundy and white tracksuit that she wore for softball and into yet another maxi dress, this one her favorite color of blue, for her afternoon with Ian, Charlotte was having a hard time remembering why she should be sticking to the plan instead of letting Ian accompany her to the shelter.

Oh, yeah, it might have something to do with the way he fills out his baseball pants, causing me to think with my vagina. Stupid magic, pierced peen!

She still hadn't mentioned anything to her friends about his piercings, even though she had put in a request for a pierced dildo on Amy's sister, Ashlyn's website, after meeting her at Bobby and Brooklyn's wedding shower. She also hadn't admitted to her friends about how she often referred to Ian's equipment in her head with her modified version of Cassidy's term for a really good dick. Nor had she confessed to hooking up with him again a couple of weeks ago.

She probably would have told Fiona all of those things by now, if she'd still been living in town. But with Fiona's schedule taking her to Europe just a few days after their most recent hookup, Charlotte hadn't had the opportunity to talk to her since she realized she needed to talk to someone to help her with her confusion about everything with Ian. *Maybe I can schedule another girls' night in the next couple of weeks?*

But I doubt they'd want to plan something so close to Brooklyn's bachelorette party next weekend. Since I won't be able to control who might overhear us talking at Tully's next Saturday, maybe I can get Becky to come over for some sisterly bonding to talk to her this week?

She may be a little more adventurous than I am, but she knows me well enough to offer advice about how to navigate my feelings for him and keep my heart safe from shattering without trying to push me outside my comfort zone.

And hopefully, I can keep myself from hooking up with Ian again between now and when I'm able to talk to her about developing a more solid plan for how to deal with everything between us.

Charlotte looked in the mirror to double-check that she looked casual and confident enough for her volunteer time at the shelter and not done up as if she were going on a real date with Ian. Once she was satisfied that she looked like her normal, relaxed, weekend self, and not date-night Charlotte, she exited the locker room to find Ian waiting for her just outside the fieldhouse.

He had also changed into a pair of jeans and a blue Henley, which she assumed he'd picked out to wear because it was her favorite color of blue. *Ugh! Not only do we match each other, but his shirt also makes his blue eyes appear more azure to match both of us. Why do his eyes have to be my exact favorite shade of blue?*

She ignored his comments about them obviously being a couple since their outfits matched, trying to shake the image of coupledom with Ian from her mind. She walked right past him to her Equinox, so she could swap out her softball gear bag for her bag of word games to play with Antonio when she got to the shelter. She made sure her wallet, phone, and keys were transferred into the correct bag before locking up her vehicle and turning to look for Ian.

She was tempted to insist on driving, but she knew Alpha Ian wouldn't submit to riding shotgun across the parking lot, much less all the way to San Antonio. So, once she verified one more time that she had everything she needed for the afternoon, she dutifully walked over to Ian's car without saying a word, almost feeling like she were walking toward a torture chamber instead of going on an almost date.

"Relax, sweet Charlotte," Ian cooed at her as he opened the passenger door of his silver Range Rover for her to get in. "I promise, we're going to have a fun afternoon together."

"Yeah? Are we stopping to get Brody to bring the fun?" Charlotte meant the question to playfully insinuate that Ian's son was more fun to be around than he was when she first put it out there. But as she thought about the possibility of bringing the little boy along while getting into Ian's vehicle, she wondered if it wouldn't be a good idea to help her get Antonio to open up a little more.

Brody was a little younger than Antonio and tended to be shy when he first met someone, but he was very outgoing, inquisitive, and well-spoken once he got to know the people around him. He also got along great with Charlotte's nieces, who were two and three times his age, so Char believed he might be a big help in getting Antonio to engage more with his peers.

"Not this time. I want to spend a little time there first to make sure I'm comfortable before bringing Brody along." Ian smiled as he reached across her to buckle her seatbelt before stepping back and closing the door.

What was that about? Charlotte wondered as Ian walked around the vehicle and got in on the driver's side.

She wasn't sure how to take the whole buckling-her-in thing. She was used to the men in her family opening and closing doors for her, as that was what they'd all been taught was the gentlemanly thing to do for any lady in their presence. But she hadn't been buckled in by anyone since she was a small child, and as the second oldest of six kids that hadn't lasted long, when her parents were preoccupied with buckling in the four youngest before double-checking that she and Bobby had already buckled themselves in when they were only four or five years old.

She didn't get the chance to question Ian about the seatbelt issue because he sidetracked her by handing her a small box wrapped in silver paper with a blue bow on it. "Happy belated birthday, Charlotte."

"You really didn't have to get me anything for my birthday, Ian. It's not like we're a couple or anything, and we definitely weren't when it was actually my birthday two months ago." Charlotte shook her head, trying to refuse the gift.

"I know I haven't earned that status yet," Ian smirked, pushing the box into her hands. "But hopefully, this will help me move a step closer to earning it. Now quit being rude and show me the southern grace I'm sure your mother taught you by opening and accepting the gift."

"What do you know about southern grace?" Charlotte quipped as she untied the bow to begin unwrapping the present.

"Only what I've learned since moving here," Ian chuckled as he started the vehicle and pulled out of the parking lot at the ball fields. "Which means I've learned that it's rude to reject a gift or say no when invited to eat."

"So, just the things my mom has used against you so far," Char chuckled as she finished opening the gift. Inside she found a silver necklace with four charms dangling from the links at the very front, a book, a garnet with the word January under it to indicate it was her birthstone, a disc with the letter C engraved in it, presumably for her first name, and a softball nestled in a glove.

It was more her style when she was in high school than now, but Charlotte couldn't contain her smile as she pulled the necklace from the box and put it on. *I'm just wearing it now to be polite. Not because I want to wear it all the time for the constant reminder of who gave it to me.* Charlotte mentally lied to herself as she turned to look at Ian and smiled. "Thank you. I love it." Somehow, she stopped herself from admitting aloud that she had no intention of ever taking it off.

She tucked the box, wrapping paper, and bow in her bag and almost missed seeing the sincere smile Ian gave her upon seeing her wearing the necklace. She wouldn't admit it to anyone else, but she secretly loved the way her heart seemed to do a flip in her chest at seeing the emotion in his eyes as they had a poignant moment.

Too bad that look of love probably won't last long. I could really appreciate seeing that all the time from him. But I know he's going to be denying our attraction and pushing me away anytime now, since that behavior from him is about a week overdue.

Charlotte shook off the negative thoughts and smiled at Ian. Ready to see how much he was actually willing to share with her about himself and his life prior to meeting her, Char decided to fill the hour-long ride into San Antonio with more questions. "So, now that we don't have an audience, I think it's time to delve deeper into getting to know one another."

"I did tell you to consider this drive as interrogation time, didn't I?" Ian's chuckle came out sounding like it was more of a moan than laughter, causing Charlotte to cackle with glee.

"Yes, you did. So, let's get into the good stuff." Charlotte wiggled her eyebrows at him suggestively as she grinned. "When and why did you get your dick pierced?"

"Four years ago," Ian groaned, shaking his head. "Right after Brody was born. A couple of my buddies had piercings and a lot of stories about how their ladies loved the feel during sex, so I figured it'd be a nice treat for Mari after childbirth. And the timing was perfect since we both needed the healing time at the same time."

"Oh, yeah, I guess that would be convenient timing," Charlotte cringed at the thought of healing time, both from the piercings and childbirth. Not that she really thought she'd need the healing time in nine months or anything, but she still didn't want to hear about Ian's former wife's healing time after having Brody.

While she was curious about the other woman, she was afraid Ian would withdraw from their easy conversation and getting to know one another if he thought too much about her. Seeing him already getting quiet instead of asking her a reciprocal question, she tried to think of a different topic that would steer their discussion away from his married life.

Nothing about the last six years, since that's how long he indicated he knew his wife. Or I guess the two years since she passed away are okay to ask about. Maybe something about his time teaching?

No, because he's only been teaching for two years, too, which means he probably started teaching right around the time she died. Could that be why he became a teacher? Damn, I can't ask that either.

Okay, back to before he met her. His childhood. That's got to be a safe topic to ask about, right?

"So, what was it like growing up in California?"

"I imagine my early years weren't much different than yours being raised here. I remember playing on the farm with my grandparents. My grandma had a hard time keeping me out of the chicken coop when I was little." Ian's smile was blindingly wide as he told her tales of getting in trouble for chasing the chickens and wanting to play ball with the eggs. He talked in detail about the produce stand where the bus dropped him off after school and eating his weight in blackberries as an after-school snack while doing his homework while his mother and grandmother sold the fruits of their family's labor on the farm.

He had a lot of stories about living with his mom, Lorna, and his grandparents, Keith and Carol Campbell, but he never mentioned his dad. Charlotte assumed there was a story there as to why he had his maternal grandparents' last name and didn't mention anything about his father, but she sat back and let him tell his story at his own pace.

He went on to tell her about being seven years old when his sister was born, and hating having to be quiet all the time, so the baby could sleep during the day, especially when she cried and woke him up in the middle of the night. Then he turned the questioning back on her without telling her about moving to San Diego.

"With so many siblings, I imagine you had more than a few sleepless nights with babies crying growing up, right?"

"Not really," Charlotte disagreed, shaking her head. "We were all born pretty close together, so I was too young to remember when any of my siblings were born. My earliest memory of them was when my youngest brother, Anthony, was learning to walk, so he was past the middle of the night feedings at that point."

"Yeah, you all do seem to be pretty close in age," Ian nodded. "Where do you fall in the birth order?"

"Number two. Bobby's the oldest and eleven months older than me. Then the twins, Josh and Jake, were born fourteen months after me. Becky was next, eighteen months later, when I was three months shy of turning three. And Anthony was last, ten months after Becky, when I was about three-and-a-half." Charlotte shrugged, mentally blaming hitting her head on that fallen tree branch when she was thirteen for her lack of memories as a toddler. Not that she would tell Ian about that accident and give him another reason to keep her from taking Brody on trail rides. "But I don't have any strong memories until I was at least four years old, so they were all past the middle of the night feedings by then. Which is probably good, so I don't worry too much about the lack of sleep when I eventually have kids of my own."

"Possibly," Ian chuckled. "Though it's not nearly as annoying when it's your own kid. At least then you can do something to take care of what the baby needs and cuddle them back to sleep, which is pretty sweet."

"Yeah, that does sound sweet," Charlotte sighed, imagining Ian cuddling their baby one day.

No! I can't think about what a great Dad he is to Brody and would be to our children. Time to change the subject before I succumb to the urge to jump his bones and try again to make a baby with him.

"So, how old were you when you moved to San Diego? And what was different about living in the city?"

"I was ten when we moved to San Diego," Ian choked out, his tone of voice turning more somber than the light-hearted tone he had while discussing his earlier childhood. "Caitir was three. That's why she doesn't have any memories of the farm or our grandparents."

Oh, yeah. He said he moved to San Diego when his grandparents died. Shit! Time to change to another new subject, so I quit bringing him down with my questions.

"Caitir? I thought Cait's unusual spelling was short for Caitlyn, but I think I like the exotic sound of Caitir better." Charlotte was always fascinated by unusual names, wishing she had an interesting name instead of plain old Charlotte Anne.

"It's Scottish," Ian explained, his smile coming back slightly. "I remember my grandparents talking about their roots in Scotland, and how they helped our mom pick the names Ian and Caitir to show their heritage. So, when Brody was born, I honored their tradition by naming him after a Scottish castle."

Seeing the opportunity to figure out why Ian had been against the DNA tests at Christmas, Charlotte leaped on the subject of family heritage. And hoped she wasn't stepping on another landmine in Ian's history. "Our DNA tests came back showing we have some Scottish ancestors, too."

"You ended up doing the DNA tests that were mentioned at Christmas?" Ian looked surprised as he asked the question, though she couldn't figure out why he would be surprised after hearing how adamant they were about doing them at Christmas.

"Yeah, Justin gave me like four dozen of the test kits and a membership to an ancestry site online for my birthday. I still have a few extras if you change your mind about wanting to do one." Charlotte stifled a giggle at the look Ian gave her at the mention of him taking a DNA test. "Since we both have Scottish ancestors that we know about, you probably should take one to make sure we aren't related. I mean, we found out Bobby's best friend from the Navy is actually related to us, which mortified my mother when she realized she almost tried to fix me up with him when Bobby brought him home on leave back then. So, it's possible we could be related and should avoid dating."

"Seriously?" Ian looked alarmed as he arched an eyebrow at Charlotte before taking the exit ramp from the highway into San Antonio. "Like how closely related are you?"

"Fourth cousins," Charlotte grinned at Ian's wide-eyed look. "Our second-great-grandaunt is their second-great-grandmother. Finding the Avingtons is actually a pretty big deal for the Burlesons because we've been holding their share of Burleson Incorporated in trust for them since the family lost contact with Mary at the end of World War I. That was why I had to have a sub a couple of weeks ago. To go sign all the paperwork releasing their trust and adding them to the board of directors."

"I've heard mentions of Burleson Incorporated a few times around your family, but I have no idea what the company does."

Charlotte spent the rest of the time they were driving on the city streets of San Antonio to get to the shelter giving Ian a little bit of a Burleson family history lesson combined with a rundown of the family company and all its subdivisions. By the time she was done, he looked shell-shocked at hearing all about the vastness of the company, presumably because he was figuring out just how wealthy the Burlesons were, even though none of them showed off that wealth.

"I guess it's a lot more than just the ranch, refinery, and gas stations I've seen around town then." Ian pulled into the parking garage where they'd had their rendezvous two weeks before. "How'd you get out of having to work in the family business?"

"I'm on the board of directors, as all my kids will be one day." Charlotte got a little melancholy thinking of the losses her family would have to suffer before her kids would inherit those board seats as Ian parked. "But that's the only way we're required to work with the company. We were also encouraged to pursue our own dreams and find jobs we find fulfilling, whether they're with the family business or not. And while the family was able to start the entertainment division of the company, so Becky has an outlet for her passion for performing, I preferred just teaching at a school I went to as a kid, instead of letting them start a school. I knew I'd end up having to run the whole thing if my family had anything to do with setting up a place for me to teach, and I prefer being in the classroom with the kids."

"Yeah, your love of working with kids is obvious." Ian smiled as he parked the Range Rover.

"Speaking of working with kids, I should probably tell you about the little boy I work with here on Saturdays before we go in. Antonio had some trauma in his life before he came here about three months ago, so he stopped talking for a while. I've been working with him to get him talking more and prepare him for kindergarten this coming fall. So, after we serve lunch, I'll leave you and the other volunteers with the clean-up, so I can spend a couple of hours working with Antonio."

"No problem." Ian smiled at her as he turned off the vehicle and they unbuckled their seatbelts. "I look forward to meeting him."

Charlotte thought about how Antonio tended to shy away from the male volunteers as she and Ian walked from the parking garage to the shelter. She started to warn Ian not to expect too much interaction with Antonio when he tried to introduce himself. But then she thought about how Ian was with Brody, and wondered if being a father to a little boy not much younger than Antonio would give him a little insight into how to deal with Antonio, without inciting the reticence in the child that the other male volunteers seemed to bring out.

Since she didn't see Antonio or his father when they first walked in, she didn't get a chance to find out as they started their volunteer time. Charlotte introduced Ian to Faith, Paige, Kendall, and Nate, the other volunteers there for the day. Faith, being the manager of all the programs at the shelter, directed Charlotte to have him fill out the volunteer information form they kept on file in the office and enter his information into the computer.

Once he was officially in their system as a volunteer, Charlotte showed him to the kitchen and put him to work chopping vegetables for a salad while she started putting together a casserole. They made small talk as they put together lunch for the shelter residents and the other area homeless, who often stopped in for a meal, even if they preferred not to sleep inside the shelter.

As they were finishing up the prep work and started setting up the serving line, Faith pulled Charlotte aside and whispered, "Is this the Ian you were talking to Fiona about last month?"

Charlotte tried to cover her shock at realizing the other woman had overheard her conversation with Fiona when she thought they were alone in the kitchen, but she wasn't sure she was completely successful. She looked around to make sure neither Ian nor anyone else was near enough to hear her soft-spoken reply. "Um, what do you know about that?"

"Just enough to know you were irritated with him last month, though you seem to be on friendly terms with him now." Faith grinned and implored Charlotte with her eyes to tell her how friendly those terms were now.

"Yes, I was talking about him. No, I don't want him to know I've talked about him to anyone. And that irritation level varies on a daily basis, depending on whether or not he's being a PITA. So, now can we drop this subject to keep my irritation level on low for the rest of the day?" Charlotte could hear the annoyance in her own voice and wasn't sure if it was directed at Faith for asking about her and Ian, or at herself for not feeling comfortable talking about personal matters to a woman she'd grown friendly with since spending the past few months working with her every week.

"Consider it dropped." Faith pretended to lock her lips. "But just know that I'm here for you if you need to talk, since Fiona's off with all those wrestling hotties."

"Thanks," Charlotte said sincerely, leaning in to give her relatively new friend a one-armed side hug, so she could whisper in her ear. "I may take you up on that later, but only when the PITA in question isn't around to, possibly, overhear us."

They finished stocking the serving line and Charlotte enjoyed watching Ian interacting with the residents as they served lunch side by side. He was a naturally charming guy, who elicited smiles from every person he met, young or old, male or female. Though Charlotte did notice the women seemed to smile bigger than the men while chatting with Ian.

She was surprised that she didn't see Antonio or Roberto come through the line. As the lunch service was winding down, she looked around the dining hall to see if she saw them sitting in the usual spot where she met them to work with Antonio. When she didn't see them there, she started to wonder if something had happened that prevented them from coming to their usual meeting time.

Knowing Ian wouldn't know what they looked like to be able to help her find them, Charlotte turned to Nate, the volunteer on her other side, to ask, "Have you seen Antonio and Roberto today?"

"Yeah, they were here earlier," Nate replied as he looked around. "But I don't think they've gotten a plate yet."

"Who are you looking for?" Ian leaned toward her section of the serving table.

"Antonio, the little boy I work with every Saturday," Charlotte replied, looking around to scan the whole dining hall for the father and son duo. "And his father, Roberto. Nate said they were here earlier, but I haven't seen them since we got here."

"Roberto?"

Charlotte wasn't sure why Ian said the name like a question, but she didn't have it in her to discuss what she presumed were his jealous feelings toward the other man while she was concerned about why Antonio wasn't there for their normal time working on his speech. So, she ignored Ian to step away from her station at the serving table to ask the other volunteers if they'd seen the Reyes family.

Neither Kendall nor Faith had seen them in the last couple of hours. Paige had stepped away from the table, so Charlotte went back to her station and finished serving the last of the people in line before starting to return the leftovers to the kitchen to be packed up for the residents to snack on later.

When she walked into the kitchen and found Paige already starting to transfer the leftover food into Tupperware to go in the refrigerator, Char finally got the chance to ask her, "Have you seen Antonio and Roberto today?"

"Yes, they were here this morning, but they left not long after you got here." Paige never looked up from her task as she explained what had happened. "I thought Roberto waited just long enough to tell you they couldn't stay."

"No, I haven't talked to him today." Charlotte shook her head before setting down the tray of mixed vegetables she was carrying and moving over to grab a couple of plastic bowls and their lids to put them in while she continued talking to Paige. "I didn't even see them."

"Oh, huh. That's strange. I wonder why he'd leave and take Antonio before your session without saying a word to anyone?"

"No clue," Charlotte replied as she scooped the leftover mixed vegetables into the container in front of her. "Did he mention having a job interview or anything? Though he usually leaves Antonio with me for our sessions when he has interviews or other job leads to check out on Saturdays, so I don't know why he wouldn't do that this week, too, if that's where he went."

"No, he didn't say anything to me about where they were going." Paige shook her head as she looked up after putting the lid on a container of pears.

Ian came in carrying the last of the chicken and broccoli casserole, with Kendall, Nate, and Faith right behind him carrying dishes. "You still talking about Antonio and Roberto?" Kendall asked as he sat down the stack of empty serving trays he was carrying.

"Yeah, trying to figure out why they would leave without telling me they couldn't stay for my session with Antonio," Char confirmed as she continued putting away the leftovers the others were carrying into the kitchen. "I thought Roberto might have been checking about a job, but he normally leaves Antonio with me for our session when he has an interview on a Saturday."

"I don't think he had anything scheduled this weekend." Faith shook her head. "He seemed to be waiting to hear back about that farm job he was talking about last week that included lodging and meals in the benefits."

They spent the rest of the time cleaning up after the meal speculating as to what happened with Roberto and Antonio. While nobody seemed to have any solid ideas for the unusual vanishing act, Char felt like Ian was especially tight-lipped on the subject. He was there helping with whatever tasks he was asked to perform, but he didn't participate in the conversation as long as Roberto and Antonio's strange disappearance was the main topic.

He also seemed to be in quite a hurry to get back to Heart's Destiny and drop her off at her car as soon as the cleanup was completed. They didn't even talk much on the drive back as Ian brooded beside her.

Yep, it's time for asshole Ian to make a reappearance. Hopefully, he doesn't stick around for a whole week before the charming, likable Ian takes back control of his body.

Chapter Thirteen

Ian realized he'd screwed up by freaking out the previous Saturday and trying to cover his anxiety by quietly thinking through the possibility that the man Charlotte referred to as Roberto Reyes was actually Roberto Rodriguez. He'd spent all week trying to make it up to Charlotte by continuing to bring her breakfast treats every morning, along with a few more charms to go on the necklace he'd gotten her.

The sterling silver knife-and-fork charm to commemorate their first time volunteering to feed the homeless together didn't go over as well as he'd hoped. Apparently, it just reminded her of how he'd been a brooding asshole on the way home. He'd apologized and came up with an excuse of getting a text from Caitir about a stomach bug that had him worried, but he wasn't sure she believed him.

She probably didn't since I was lying through my teeth and didn't think to text Caitir to back me up with the lie before Charlotte got home and talked to her Monday before I got there to pick Caitir and Brody up for the day. But I couldn't exactly tell her the truth about what I was worried about that had me freaking out last Saturday.

The number-one-teacher-apple charm had at least brought a small smile to her face. As had the coffee mug charm. But it took the last two days of the week, when he brought her a saddle charm, and finally, a horse charm, to convince her to forgive him and let him have another chance at volunteering with her.

Although, it may have been the fact that those charms came with permission to take Brody on trail rides alone that actually won her over. But thank fuck, she's willing to let me go with her again now that I know Rojo has been hiding out at the shelter, so I can keep her safe while she's there.

The other positive thing that had come out of the past week was Jake confirming Ian's suspicion about Roberto Rodriguez using the alias of Roberto Reyes. Though Ian wasn't sure he wanted to know how Jake got his hands on the Immigration and Naturalization Service's file on Roberto Reyes to see that the picture they'd taken of him in December was actually Rojo.

As soon as he had confirmation from Jake that his hunch was correct, Ian had gotten in contact with Trent to let him know the new information on the last time Roberto had been spotted. But unfortunately, Trent couldn't get authorization to send in a team to capture Rojo, until he had confirmation from Ian that Rodriguez had returned to the shelter after disappearing the first time Ian had been there to volunteer.

Fuck! I hope my being there wasn't the reason he disappeared last weekend.

He knew shaving his beard, cutting his hair, and letting it all go back to his natural light brown, almost a dark blond, color had changed his look dramatically. But no matter how much he tried telling Jake and Trent that he didn't look like the same person Roberto had known, he wasn't completely convinced it was enough of a change to truly conceal his identity from the cartel ringleader that he'd been trying to get close to with his former undercover persona.

Knowing he couldn't change his size, shape, body type, or voice, Ian worried that he'd been made when he walked into the shelter the previous weekend. Unfortunately, he knew if that was the case, he'd also made Charlotte into a target for the Rodriguez Cartel just by being seen with her there.

Fuck! If only I'd had the foresight to check out the shelter residents when she wasn't there, I could have captured him by now. Hell, if I'd have followed my first instinct and checked for him at the shelter the day I first ran into Charlotte coming out, I might have still been made, but I wouldn't have put her at risk at the same time.

But no, I had to think with my dick that day and followed her instead of going inside, first to the parking garage to fuck her, and then home to make sure she got there safely.

When he had that realization, Ian wanted to tell Charlotte everything immediately, thinking it would be the only way to get Charlotte to step back from volunteering at the shelter to keep her safe.

But after talking to Jake, he'd decided to listen to her brother's opinion on how Charlotte would take the news.

According to Jake, Charlotte was less likely to have a dramatic reaction than their other sister or female cousins, but it was still a real possibility. Remembering back to the way she seemed more reserved around her family when they first met, and how he'd been bringing out her feisty side whenever they were alone, Ian realized that the chemistry between them would make her reaction to anything he told her more volatile than she would have if she was told the same things by a family member like Jake. And volatile, dramatic reactions, like pushing him away when he was the only person in town who knew she needed protection from Rojo, could end up getting them both killed.

Not that sticking to her like glue was a guarantee that he'd be able to keep her safe, but it was the only option that felt right to Ian. Jake had briefly suggested that Ian might just be imagining he'd been made as a symptom of his PTSD from the attack on his family. But when they discussed whether Charlotte would be safer with him by her side or backing away, even Jake had to admit he wasn't willing to risk Charlotte's life by not trusting Ian's gut that he'd been recognized. And if he'd been identified by Roberto, then Charlotte would be a target, whether Ian was with her again at the shelter or not.

So, they'd decided it was best for Ian to accompany Charlotte to the shelter to keep her safe without alerting her to what was going on just yet. They also planned to finally let her in on the whole situation when Jake and Josh came to town in a couple of weeks, so maybe they could control her reaction to the news.

Apparently, that family meeting wouldn't just include Charlotte and her twin younger brothers meeting with Ian, either. After talking with Jake, Ian had learned that the cousins they'd recently connected with were in the private security business. And they were all going to be in town for a quarterly board meeting at the end of the month. They were all staying a couple of weeks for Bobby's wedding and a few family birthdays, so Jake wanted to bring them in on the investigation, since Trent couldn't get approval for a team yet. He would also be including Bobby in the discussions of how to handle Rojo, since he was the local police chief.

Ian knew they needed at least one law enforcement agency involved when they captured Roberto Rodriguez, but he hoped he'd be able to get the confirmation that he was back at the shelter, so he could have Trent's team come in, instead of possibly messing up Bobby's wedding and honeymoon.

Ian hadn't spent as much time getting to know Charlotte's older brother as he had her younger brothers, but he still didn't think the expectant father needed to add this risky op to his already full plate. So, he was going to do everything he could to keep Charlotte safe, while finding out if anyone at the shelter had heard from Roberto in the last week.

For now, that meant Ian was once again changing his clothes after the baseball game and waiting on Charlotte's softball team to finish up, so he could drive them both over to San Antonio for the afternoon and another day of volunteering. He had already gone into the fieldhouse to change his clothes, but he was waiting until Charlotte was in there and the parking lot had cleared out of families there for the games to get his weapons out of the lockbox in the back of his Range Rover for the afternoon.

The previous week, he'd left his Glock in the lockbox and only carried his Colt thirty-eight special in his ankle holster under his jeans, not thinking his thin shirt was enough to conceal the weapon in his waistband. But now that he knew a vicious criminal had been hiding out inside, Ian needed to know he was fully armed to protect Charlotte, and the other innocent people in the shelter, if Roberto tried to pull his own weapon.

Carrying both his Glock nine millimeter in the small of his back, under both a gray t-shirt and a navy-blue button-down to conceal it, and his Colt thirty-eight special in the ankle holster under his jeans was probably more firepower than he needed at the shelter. But after not having either to be able to return fire and protect his family when his wife was killed, Ian needed the mental reassurance he felt from feeling their weight against his body to feel like he was more prepared this time.

As soon as he was ready to go, he walked back over to the fieldhouse to meet Charlotte. A few minutes later, she came out wearing yet another classy, yet casual, dress. This one was a sunny yellow that wrapped around her body to create a vee neckline and asymmetrical hem.

As gorgeous as Charlotte looked in the dress, Ian wished he was seeing it on his bedroom floor, instead of on her. He had a brief vision of unwrapping her in his bedroom to find her wet and ready for him, but he had to shake it off to focus on their plans for the rest of the day.

"Wow, you look amazing." Ian wasn't surprised to see her lightly blush at his compliment. "Too bad we're needed at the shelter and can't just go somewhere for some time alone this afternoon."

"Knock it off, Casanova." Charlotte rolled her eyes at him. "Just because I'm willing to spend more time getting to know you and letting you volunteer with me at the shelter, doesn't mean I'm open for anything more with you."

"Understood." Ian held his hands up in surrender as he smiled sincerely at her. "I'm more than willing to put in the work to earn another chance with you, sweet Charlotte."

Ian then reached out and took her softball gear bag from her shoulder. He looped the strap over his own shoulder before placing his opposite hand on the small of Charlotte's back to escort her to her vehicle, assuming she needed to swap bags again this week, like she had the previous week.

"I'm also capable of carrying my own things," Charlotte protested, trying to reach around him for her gear bag.

"More than," Ian agreed, but he didn't allow her to take her bag back. "But I heard Texas girls prefer men to be gentlemen, so I'm trying to step up for you in that way, too."

Charlotte rolled her eyes once more, but she quit fighting him for her bag as they walked over to her Equinox. Once she swapped her softball gear for a large purse that she refused to let him carry for her, they went over to his Range Rover.

Ian opened the door for her, helped her in, and made sure she was buckled in before walking around to the driver's side and getting in. He wasn't sure where the urge to buckle her in like a child came from, but he couldn't stop himself this week any more than he could the previous week.

They were quiet as they started the drive to San Antonio. But once they were on the highway, Ian decided to break the silence. "So, last week while we were driving, I told you all about my grandparents. Why don't you tell me about yours this week?"

"I suppose turnabout is fair play." Charlotte smiled at him as she turned in her seat to look at him as she spoke. "I was a lot closer to Memmaw Judy and Pappaw Jerry than I am to my mom's parents. Grandma and Grandpa Clark moved to Corpus Christie when I was fifteen, so we only see them a couple of times a year."

Charlotte went on to fill the entire drive with a Burleson family history lesson, including what seemed like a retelling of several stories she'd heard from her Memmaw Judy when they snuck off for alone-time with the horses when Charlotte was a child. She also regaled him with tales of what she'd found on her family tree since starting the research in January and how finding them had made her question her memmaw's beliefs. Ian tried to be reassuring that the beliefs were valid while understanding how disconcerting finding out they weren't actually Native American was for Charlotte.

The more she talked about the things she found through the ancestry site, the more Ian wondered if he should do one of the DNA tests. The only family history he knew was from what his grandparents had taught him, and that only covered his mother's side of the family. He didn't know anything about his father other than that he'd been his mother's high school sweetheart and left their small hometown right after graduation, never to be seen again.

Having never actually met his father, Ian knew more about Caitir's father than his own. He had been one of the men hired to help their grandfather on the farm, though he left shortly after Lorna informed him she was pregnant.

Ian's mother had gone through a string of short-term boyfriends for as long as he could remember. One of which she followed to San Diego before they broke up a few months later. After that, the quality of the men his mother dated went even more downhill. To the point that Ian insisted on sharing a room with his little sister to make sure none of them tried to touch her in the middle of the night while high as a kite.

It was because of knowing the low caliber of men their mother dated that both he and Caitir were leery of doing the DNA testing to find out about their biological fathers. He fully expected to find out that the two men responsible for impregnating Lorna Campbell were also junkies that he'd want to protect his sister and son from ever knowing. Just like he'd been taking care of Caitir since their move to San Diego as children.

When he graduated high school, Ian chose a college close to home, so he didn't have to live in a dorm to stay and be Caitir's protector. Luckily, he had a wonderful guidance counselor, who helped him get grants and scholarships to pay for school. Ian had put any extra money from those scholarships and grants in his dining account and took Caitir to the campus dining hall on the regular to keep her from having to be around their mom and her boyfriends.

Then, when Ian was about halfway through college and able to start working as a police cadet while going through the academy, he could finally afford to move out of the crappy apartment where his mother lived. He'd barely saved up the deposits for a place of his own, just in time to take custody of his sister, when their mom and her man of the month were arrested on drug charges.

Basically, becoming a father to a thirteen-year-old when he was only twenty himself, Ian had to grow up fast. But he was grateful that neither his, nor Caitir's birth certificates had a father listed, so he didn't have to fight anyone for custody of his sister.

They had pretty much decided they didn't want to know anything about their sperm donors, since neither one of them were man enough to step up and be a dad. But hearing about the stuff Charlotte was learning about her family history made Ian wonder about what he could learn about his Campbell ancestors that even his grandparents hadn't known, especially when Charlotte told him about the records from around the world she'd been able to find for her family going back hundreds of years.

Just because my biological father's information would possibly show up, doesn't mean I'd have to research that branch of the family tree. And if nothing else, doing the test will keep Charlotte from using the excuse of us possibly being related to fight our sexual chemistry.

"Alright, you've convinced me of the merits of a DNA test," Ian announced as he turned into the parking garage at the shelter.

Charlotte raised an eyebrow in surprise at his sudden change of heart when it came to DNA testing.

"I'd love to be able to double-check the stories my grandparents told me when I was a kid." Ian grinned as he pulled into the first parking space he saw open. "And I do believe you said something about proving we're not related before agreeing to really date me. So, if taking one of those tests is what I have to do to improve my chances with you, then I'm more than willing to take a test."

"Yeah, I might have to watch you spit in the tube to make sure you don't cheat to prove we aren't related," Charlotte chuckled as she unbuckled her seatbelt and grinned at him mischievously.

"I'd much rather swallow your sweet cream, Princess." Ian gave Charlotte a suggestive smile as they got out of the vehicle. He rushed around to the passenger side to catch up with Charlotte before she got too far away from him on the walk between the parking garage and the shelter. He reached out and grabbed her hand, pulling her in close, so he could whisper into her ear, "But, sure, if you're into watching me spit, I'll do it for you."

"Really? I thought I was supposed to be the one to swallow," Charlotte retorted, causing them both to chuckle as they walked the short distance to the shelter, hand in hand.

Ian tried to hide his cautious and alert state as he observed the residents of the facility throughout the afternoon under more flirty banter with Charlotte. Because there were kids around, they tabled the more raunchy innuendo. But he was happy to watch his woman hold her own in their witty repartee all afternoon.

He was disappointed when the other volunteers confirmed what he feared had happened the previous weekend — that Roberto had left the shelter with all his things and hadn't been seen since. Ian didn't know how Roberto ended up with Antonio in his custody to be able to use him as cover to land a spot in the shelter in the first place, but he worried that the boy's life was now in danger, since Roberto would probably think he was no longer useful to help him hide from the authorities.

Not that he would share that possibility with Charlotte or any of the other volunteers, who were all speculating on where Roberto and Antonio went a week before. Their guesses ranged from Roberto having taken a job on a farm that included room and board to possible immigration issues that caused them to be deported.

Ian knew the immigration problem wasn't a factor, since Jake had looked at the file to see that the supposed father and son were given asylum status to be able to stay in the country. He also highly doubted that Roberto Rodriguez had taken a job as a farm laborer, even though it would be an excellent way to stay under the radar of the authorities. But he'd pass that theory on to Jake to see if he had any way of checking the local farms and ranches for recent hires.

Though he was frustrated that he couldn't confirm Roberto was back in residence to be able to bring Trent's team in to capture him, Ian was able to relax a little, knowing Rojo wasn't there to be a threat to Charlotte. Therefore, he was able to have a pretty good time getting to know the other men who volunteered there regularly and a few of the resident families, as he helped keep the kids entertained after being kicked out of the kitchen for being useless at any kind of food prep other than chopping vegetables.

Ian was glad that Charlotte was able to see a little of his goofy side when those same kids came through the line while they were serving lunch. Those interactions led to more flirty banter and lighthearted teasing that seemed to indicate she was coming closer to agreeing to give him a chance at being her man. So, Ian decided to ask her on a real date while on the drive back to Heart's Destiny, when their time at the shelter was done.

Hoping to ease into the conversation about dating, and maybe get a few date ideas that Charlotte would like, Ian asked her what hobbies she had besides softball, horseback riding, and reading, once they were ensconced in his Range Rover and back on the road.

"With working and volunteering both at the shelter and the youth center, I don't really have time for other hobbies," Charlotte shrugged. "Even my usual leisure reading time has been replaced with ancestry research for the last couple of months."

"Yeah, I can see that," Ian nodded in agreement while he tried to think of how else to lead into asking Charlotte to go out with him. "What about when you go out with your girlfriends or on dates? Where do you like to go and what do you like to do?"

"Well, the last time I had a real girls' night out was mid-December," Charlotte smirked. "But even though you still won't admit to meeting me that night, I'm sure you know enough about where I go and what I've done on a night out in San Antonio. Since Fiona was the only one of my friends who pushed me to drive into the city for girls' night, I've stuck to things around town since then. Bowling at Lover's Lanes and dancing at Tully's Roadhouse are about the only things to do when going out in Heart's Destiny. Well, unless there's something the town is putting on for holidays, like the Fourth of July picnic and fireworks. Or whenever my mom convinces Mandi Hunter to host something like the Sweetheart's Ball or New Year's Eve in the B and B ballroom."

"Is that what you did for Valentine's Day?" Ian regretted going to Levi's Bar looking for Rojo, if he missed the opportunity to dance with Charlotte at the Sweetheart's Ball.

"No, we had a Galentine's party with all our single girlfriends on the ranch to keep Mom from playing matchmaker that night," Charlotte giggled.

Thank fuck!

Satisfied that he at least had a couple of ideas for activities for them to do later in the evening, Ian finally got up the courage to ask Charlotte to go out with him that night. "So, uh, it's been a little while since those snacks on the ball field. What do you say to going with me for an early dinner before bowling tonight?"

"Sorry, no can do." Charlotte shook her head and gave him a look that told him his lackluster invite held no appeal to her. "I already have plans tonight at Tully's."

What the fuck? She already has a date tonight?

Ian opened his mouth to ask about another day for them to go out, but he promptly shut it to keep from interrogating her about whom she was going out with that night. He knew showing his jealousy and possessive feelings for her would only give her another reason to reject him.

"But keep working on proving you're worthy of my time. And if I'm still single after tonight, I might go out with you when my schedule clears up." Charlotte gave him an apologetic half-smile, as if her rejection of him was no big deal.

If she's still single after tonight? Does that mean there's a possibility her date tonight could become her boyfriend? Or that she's expecting a proposal?

Fuck! She'd better not get engaged tonight!

Ian spent the rest of the drive back to Heart's Destiny quietly brooding as he tried to figure out whom Charlotte was going on a date with that night. He knew it could be anyone from Ryder Deere to one of the Walkers.

Frustrated with his lack of progress with both Charlotte and the case, Ian dropped her off before heading over to his temporary tactical operations center to swap out vehicles and head back to San Antonio for another night at Levi's Bar.

Too bad I have to be alert while I'm there and can't drink away my feelings for Charlotte.

~~~

Monday, March 18, 2019

Charlotte was miserable dealing with cramps while on the field coaching softball practice. Her period had shown up like clockwork that morning, and it was making her feel wretched. Unfortunately for her psyche, it wasn't just the cramps, bloating, and bleeding that were upsetting her. She was also feeling dejected with the comprehension of the fact that her condomless copulation with Ian the previous month hadn't resulted in a baby.

Not that she was really ready to have a baby with the way her relationship with Ian was going. But after seeing the second ultrasound for Anthony and Kay's baby the previous week, Charlotte was definitely having a case of baby fever.

Getting confirmation with that second ultrasound that her brother's dreams were coming true in the form of a little boy being born in a few months had also discombobulated her a bit. She thought for sure that the way her family was raving about Anthony's dreams foretelling the birth of his and Kay's son was what instigated her most recent dreams.

Well, at least the ones with Memmaw coming to talk to me about my future, anyway. I'm still blaming Ian's magic, pierced peen for the sex dreams he keeps starring in regularly.

Charlotte wasn't sure how to take the dream conversations she was having with Memmaw Judy the past few nights. Mostly because they didn't always make sense. One minute they'd be sitting on her bed where her grandmother woke her up to talk, and the next minute they'd be on the backs of a couple of horses on one of the trails around the ranch. The topics of the conversations jumped around, too.
~~~

They talked about a little of everything, from the stories Charlotte was finding about their ancestors online to the current couplings on the ranch. Then they'd jump to a story Charlotte remembered Memmaw telling her when she was a child, and right back to how many Burleson babies were going to be born in the next couple of years, and more adoptions than the two that had recently happened with Anthony and Kay's girls.

Charlotte felt like she was going crazy trying to decipher the convoluted messages, but she thought she vaguely remembered something from her recent dreams about Memmaw being excited for a baker's dozen of great-grandchildren in the next couple of years, and over three dozen when all the current generation of Burlesons finished building their families.

Considering the only kids she knew about that her memmaw would call her great-grandchildren were Anthony & Kay's two girls and their little boy on the way, and Bobby & Brooklyn's baby on the way, Charlotte didn't believe there would be thirteen by the time Christmas 2020 rolled around. Her skepticism wasn't just based on the fact that she didn't believe in dreams predicting the future. She also didn't think it was numerically possible to get from four great-grandchildren to thirteen in twenty-one months.

Although, one of her future nephews being named Antonio in her dreams seemed like proof enough that her worry about the sudden disappearance of the little boy she'd been working with for the past couple of months had seeped into her subconscious to taint the predictions her memmaw was telling her in the dreams.

But thirteen would require all ten of us to have a baby or adopt or both. And with at least a couple more multiples, whether they're twins or adopted like Anthony's girls. But there's no way Jake and Josh are ready to give up their Navy careers to fall in love and have kids yet. So, the rest of us would almost all have to have multiples, which isn't likely to happen.

While Charlotte didn't agree with her brothers' risky career choices, she knew them well enough to know that they'd give up their risky careers for true love and to build a family. So, while she thought it was possible everyone in her generation could fall in love and have kids, she didn't think the timeline was feasible because her brothers still needed to grow up a little more to get all their adrenaline-junkie jobs out of their systems first.

But maybe not, since Bobby isn't giving up his dangerous job for Brooklyn and their baby. But then again, his job isn't as risky as Jake's or Josh's, since we don't have much real crime here in Heart's Destiny. He also hasn't seen the first ultrasound of his baby yet. So, he might still change his mind about how risky his job is when he first sees a picture of their baby.

Thinking about her brothers and their risky jobs made Charlotte wonder if Ian started teaching to be home for his son after losing his wife because his former career was dangerous. He still hadn't told her what he did before he became a teacher, and that made her wonder if the DEA line he gave her in December was partially true, just of his former life before his son was left with only one parent.

That would explain why it seemed so believable. And with what I've seen of him as a father, I can definitely see him giving up a career he loved to be home for his son.

Thoughts of Ian made her feel a little guilty for not being completely honest with him about her plans for Saturday night. Char still wasn't sure what had come over her to make her push his buttons by not admitting she was going to Bobby and Brooklyn's bachelor and bachelorette party. But as much as she'd enjoyed seeing him getting jealous at the thought of her dating someone else, she also hated the distance she'd inadvertently put between them with her little stunt.

I probably should have invited him to come along, so we could have danced again. But, no, I had to try to give him a taste of his own medicine with the hot-and-cold act.

Clearly, since he's back to being standoffish so far this week, he didn't learn the lesson I was trying to teach him. And now I have no idea how to apologize to get us back to the fun we were having together before he asked me to dinner on Saturday.

Charlotte had to push thoughts of Ian out of her mind to focus on the next drill she was running her girls through on the softball field. But no matter how hard she tried to block him from her thoughts, he kept creeping back in.

By the time they were about two-thirds of the way through with practice, Charlotte was beginning to wonder if Ian kept crossing her mind because he was watching her on the field. When the strange feeling of being watched crawled along her spine, she started to look around to see if she could spot him. But she didn't see him or his Range Rover anywhere near the sports complex.

She tried to shake off the eerie feeling as she went through the motions of conducting softball practice, hoping her assistant coach didn't notice anything was wrong with her. Carrie Adkisson was nice enough to be friendly on the field, but Charlotte didn't consider her as more than an acquaintance. So, she really didn't want to have to explain her issues with Ian, or why she was scanning the area looking for him.

Carrie was a couple of years older than Char and was way too interested in the gossip around town for Charlotte to feel comfortable sharing anything personal with her. Carrie was also one of the single women at school who were clearly interested in dating Ian, so Charlotte thought it best to avoid any mention of him or the things she'd done with him in Carrie's presence.

As she walked across the field to get the girls to line up for their end-of-practice stretching routine, Charlotte finally noticed a black SUV parked across Clydesdale with someone in the driver's seat she thought she recognized.

Why would Roberto be in Heart's Destiny? And in what looks like a brand-new vehicle? Geez, was it him I felt watching me this whole time?

She went through the whole stretching routine with the girls, trying to figure out the potential answers to her mental questions. None of her possible options for explanations made sense, though. So, as soon as she finished with practice, she started to walk over to the parking lot where he was still sitting. But before she even made it to the street she'd have to cross to go talk to him, he started the SUV and drove away.

That's really freaking weird, Charlotte thought as she stopped in her tracks with a hand on her hip. *Why would he sit there watching me all that time, just to leave without talking to me?*

He wouldn't. I mean, I don't know him that well, but surely, he'd have given me the chance to check on Antonio if he'd realized who I was, right? Right. So, it must not have been him.

Great! Now I'm not just having dreams about Memmaw mentioning Antonio. I'm actually imagining seeing Roberto because of being so worried about what happened to cause the two of them to leave the shelter so abruptly.

Maybe I should look into seeing a shrink instead of an OB-GYN? Maybe they could give me some ideas of how to fix things with Ian after they tell me how to stop having hallucinations.

Chapter Fourteen

Ian was having the week from hell. After only a couple of days of not eating lunch with Charlotte, the other teachers had pounced on his obviously single status. Well, the single female teachers anyway.

Ian didn't understand why they'd backed off on the flirting after he danced with Charlotte at the school Valentine's dance, even though he and Charlotte were only cordial to one another in passing at school for the rest of the month of February. But then, after seeing him spending a couple of weeks bringing her coffee and breakfast every morning, they thought they had to be all coquettish again practically the instant he stopped doting on Charlotte.

Tori, Carrie, and a couple of the others, whose names he couldn't even remember, had each taken the opportunity to invite themselves to sit way too close to him in the teacher's lounge at lunchtime for the last four days. And, of course, they leaned over to touch him right when Charlotte walked into the room, making it impossible for him to get the chance to talk to her all week. So, since he couldn't talk to Charlotte yet again, Ian extracted himself from the blonde, whose name escaped him at the moment, and made his way back to his classroom as soon as he'd finished eating, claiming he needed to get a head start on his planning period to grade the spelling tests he'd just given that morning.

He'd tried to talk to Charlotte a couple of times when he picked up Caitir and Brody at the ranch. But on Tuesday and Thursday, she took off on her horse as soon as Brody was finished with his riding lessons for the day, so Ian didn't even get the chance to see her.

And on Wednesday evening, he'd only briefly seen her vehicle when she got home from softball practice and changed clothes before leaving again. Since he'd noticed only the older Burlesons were still home, he'd asked Hazel where everyone was off to for the evening. Only to be disappointed to hear they were all going to a birthday party for one of the Walkers.

He'd been even more disheartened that night when he got his family home and heard that Caitir had also been invited to the party, but she had declined the invitation. She gave an excuse of not knowing the Walkers well enough to feel comfortable going to a party for one of them, but Ian didn't believe that was the real reason. He knew it was because he was no closer to finding Roberto Rodriguez, and his sister didn't feel safe going anywhere but their home, the Burleson Ranch, the local church, and the bed and breakfast. And she only felt safe going to church and the B and B when he went with her.

In addition to his issues with needing to talk to Charlotte and not knowing how to help his sister feel safe, other than by capturing Rojo, he was also struggling with feeling like a failure for not having found the man yet. All his leads on Rojo had seemed to dry up. Even Big John had seemed to disappear, not showing up at Levi's Bar or his last known address since Roberto had skipped out of the shelter. But that left Ian feeling like he was back to square one in the investigation, no closer to finding the man who ordered the hit on his family than he had been on his first day in town.

From what Jake had told him about the FBI's investigation into the warehouse where Ian had spotted Rojo in February, they weren't faring much better at shutting down his operation. Apparently, the warehouse was vacant, and the meeting Ian had heard about was Rodriguez meeting with a realtor about buying the warehouse. With the feds sniffing around as soon as Ian had passed on the lead, he'd backed out of the deal and even the realtor hadn't heard from him since.

As much as Ian wished that meant Rojo had left the area and was no longer a threat to Charlotte or his family, he knew in his gut that wasn't the case. Roberto Rodriguez was still out there, somewhere nearby, plotting his next move. And probably planning to target Ian or someone he cared about after recognizing him almost two weeks ago.

Ian was at the point he was ready to tell Jake to take over the investigation, or give it to someone who wasn't as emotionally involved as Ian felt he was. But he had to wait until the next week when he could talk to Jake face-to-face. He just couldn't handle spending another afternoon out looking for Roberto in San Antonio when he wanted to be in Heart's Destiny, watching over Charlotte and trying to earn her affection.

Thank fuck, our games tomorrow are away games, so I won't have to worry about her going to the shelter alone after. I might not be able to ride on the same bus as her, since the teams have separate buses, but at least I can keep an eye on her at the games and know she's safe on the other bus on the drive to and from Luckenbach.

Ian was just sitting at his desk, still looking at the first of the spelling tests he needed to grade, when his alarm went off on his phone inside his briefcase. He pulled it out to silence the blaring noise, instantly on alert from the notification that something was happening at his house. He pulled up the camera view to see that someone dressed in all black and wearing a ski mask had kicked in his back door and was ransacking his home office.

"Thank fuck, Caitir and Brody aren't home," Ian growled as he stood and gathered his things. *And that I don't have anything related to the investigation at the house for them to verify my identity.*

He walked quickly to the principal's office. He didn't give Lisa Walker the chance to even say a word before he started explaining. "I've got an emergency at home and need to leave. Like now. Do you have someone who can cover my afternoon classes? Charlotte knows the lesson plan and can help them with what they need to do for the spelling test and writing assignment."

"Go, I've got you covered." Lisa waved him away, so Ian didn't stick around long enough to hear if she said anything else.

He rushed to his Range Rover, stopping just long enough to get his weapon from the lockbox in the rear cargo compartment before hopping in the driver's seat and heading home. He called nine-one-one on the way home, knowing he needed to alert the authorities that he was coming in armed. Since they were probably already on their way to his house with the alarm signaling the police department of the break-in at the same time it alerted Ian, he was unsure if they would answer the non-emergency line with such a small staff to handle everything else during the alarm call.

"Heart's Destiny Police Department. This is Paisley." Ian was surprised by the unusually calm greeting when calling an emergency services line.

"Yes, my name is Ian Campbell. You've probably already dispatched officers to my house because of being alerted by my alarm of a break-in."

"Oh, yes!" Paisley squealed enthusiastically. "That was so exciting. It's the first time we've had that kind of alert here, so half the department is on the way to your house. Well, the half that's working this shift, anyway. Do I need to call in the other three to assist Bobby and the two officers already there?"

"No, I only saw one perp on my camera feed, so three should be plenty if they get there before he leaves." Ian shook his head, wondering why he was having to decide how many officers the dispatcher sent to his home. "I just wanted to let you know to notify your officers that I'm almost there, and I'm coming armed to assist them if needed. I have my concealed carry permit, but I don't want them to mistake me for the intruder if they see my weapon in hand when I get there."

"Oh, yeah, okay. I'll radio Bobby now."

Ian didn't even have the chance to say "thanks" before Paisley disconnected the call. "Wow! Small towns really are different."

Ian pocketed his phone just as he pulled up to see two patrol cars with their lights flashing and sirens blaring in his driveway. He was surprised they were unattended as he parked on the street in front of his house and approached his front door with his Glock in his hand.

Just as he stepped up onto his porch to enter his home, Bobby Burleson strode out the front door with his radio in hand. "House is clear," he said into the radio before nodding at Ian's weapon. "Hey, Ian. Didn't know you had a concealed carry."

"I have a feeling there's a lot I need to fill you in on about me." Ian lowered his Glock, but he wasn't putting it away until he knew the whole area was clear and not just his house.

Before he could elaborate, another officer came running around his house. "I lost him when he got in a black SUV on Roper," the officer shouted as he got to the bottom of the steps up to the porch. "But I pointed Jagger in the direction he headed."

Before Bobby could introduce the officer or radio Jagger to get an update on the search for the perpetrator, the radio roared to life with someone, presumably Jagger, calling out the last known sighting of the suspect in a black Suburban and giving a tag number Ian recognized from seeing Rojo driving that Suburban in San Antonio.

When he realized Jagger had lost the vehicle, Bobby keyed his radio to instruct him to head back to the office to run the tag.

"Don't bother tracing the tag," Ian sighed, shaking his head. "It's a stolen tag that doesn't match the vehicle. But the driver is most likely Roberto Rodriguez, or someone he sent to see what I have on him."

"Fuck!" Bobby cursed, looking to the sky for a moment while keying his radio to change his instructions for Jagger to go back on patrol. Finally, he turned to look back at Ian. "Are you DEA or Homeland?"

"Neither, at least officially." Ian grinned at Bobby's perplexed look. "I'm former DEA, with a vested interest in this case. But we should probably go somewhere private to discuss all the details of whom I am and why I'm here."

"Yeah, we should probably get your back door secured first and dust for fingerprints to prove it was someone from the Rodriguez Cartel." Bobby motioned to the front door for the men to walk inside. He introduced the officer who'd run back to the house after chasing the suspect on foot as his cousin, Dougie Whitman, whom Ian remembered seeing at a couple of Burleson birthday parties over the last few months, but hadn't formally met yet.

"There won't be fingerprints." Ian secured his weapon in his waistband before opening the front door and walking inside. He pulled out his phone and pulled up the video feed before handing it over to Bobby. "As you can see from the video, he was wearing gloves."

"If there's not going to be any fingerprints, what do you want me to do, Chief?" Dougie followed the other men inside.

"Just go back on patrol, Dougie," Bobby instructed. "And keep an eye out for that Suburban."

Dougie nodded and left as Ian inspected the damage to his back door.

"Where are your monitors to get copies of all footage from the different cameras you have covering the house?" Bobby clicked around on Ian's phone to see a couple of the camera views as they walked toward the back door.

"I have a temporary TOC set up with all that, but I'm not sure Jake wants me to show you where that's at." Ian almost chuckled at the incredulous look Bobby gave him. "But he can probably get you the feeds from the cloud. Or get you the original feeds when he gets here next week."

"My fucking brother," Bobby grumbled under his breath as he handed Ian's phone back to him. "Of course, I should have known he was in on this as soon as you said Rodriguez's name. I can't believe I didn't figure out ya'll knew each other at Christmas."

Ian cringed, wondering if he should fill Bobby in on who else he knew before being introduced to the Burleson family at Christmas. *Fuck, yeah, I should probably fill him in on everything, so he knows to help me keep Charlotte safe, too.*

"I, um, also kind of met Charlotte a couple of weeks before I met everyone else at Christmas, too."

Bobby just arched an eyebrow at Ian, not commenting on the coincidence.

"She was out for girls' night at the same hotel bar where I was staying while here for my interview at the school," Ian shrugged.

"Stop!" Bobby held up a hand in the universal symbol for stopping. "I don't need any details about what's goin' on between you and my sister. Fill me in on the case and why you're here when you aren't with the DEA anymore."

"I was first brought onto the task force working the Rodriguez Cartel case at the San Diego field office about eight years ago. It took a while to make any progress on their drug operation, but then just when we thought we were starting to get a handle on it, we found out they were also into trafficking women and guns. We put together a task force with several agencies, and I got tapped to go undercover in the organization about four years ago."

Ian went on to explain how he changed his appearance to fit in with the local dealers and worked his way up to guarding the brothels as he was trying to get closer to the cartel leaders. He also told Bobby about the brief visits he had with his family in the two years he was undercover before finally detailing the ambush on Brody's second birthday.

Leah Mae Wright

"Wait, so the DEA made it look like you died along with your wife that day?"

"Yeah, it was clear my cover was blown, so we changed my identity and put out the word that Mari and I both died to keep the cartel from coming to look for me and finding Brody and Cait. Anyway, after that, I moved to the opposite side of the city, cut my hair, and went back to my normal look. As soon as my injuries were healed, I started working as a substitute teacher to feed the agency any info I could find on the lower-level dealers in the area. I knew I had to be home for my son and take care of my sister after her injuries, but I still wanted to help fight the problem if I could." Ian shrugged.

"So, how did you end up here?" Bobby gave him a questioning look.

"My former partner messaged me at the end of November and told me about a bust here that got most of the cartel rounded up. And when he said there weren't enough resources available to leave someone from the team here to look for Rojo, I volunteered. He hooked me up with Jake, whom I know from another joint task force right before I went under with the cartel. And I've been coordinating with Jake for everything I've done to look for Roberto since moving here, especially after I found out Charlotte has been in contact with Roberto every weekend at the shelter where she volunteers."

"Fuck! Tell me you're joking about Char being caught up in this mess," Bobby demanded.

"Wish I could." Ian shook his head. Ian went on to explain to Bobby about the kid Roberto had with him at the shelter, and how Charlotte had been tasked with working with him on his speech. Finally, he reviewed the surveillance that led him to finding Charlotte at the shelter, and how Roberto and the child both disappeared the day Ian stepped foot in the shelter to volunteer for the first time.

"Alright, as much as I hate to have to ask this, I need to know what's going on with you and Char. I thought you were avoiding Ma's matchmaking by annoying her as much as possible whenever ya'll are in the same place. But obviously, that's not the case if she's letting you go with her to the shelter to protect her."

"She doesn't exactly know I'm there to protect her." Ian inwardly cringed once again, as Bobby gave him a scathing look that obviously said, *You'd better not be playing games with my sister.*

Ian held his hands up in surrender. "I'm not messing with her, I promise. I felt something for Charlotte the first night we met, but didn't think it could go anywhere at the time because of my commitment to catching Rojo. Then when I saw her again two weeks later, I tried to fight it to keep from putting her at risk. But our connection is too strong for me to keep fighting it, so now I'm taking advantage of it to stick close to her, when she insists on going to the shelter where Roberto has been hiding out, trying to keep her as safe as I can without scaring the shit out of her by telling her everything that's going on with the case."

"Oh, fuck, man, you gotta tell her everything if you wanna chance at a relationship with her." Bobby didn't actually roll his eyes, but the way he shook his head, and his tone of voice, clearly implied an eye roll of epic proportions.

"I know," Ian agreed. "But Jake seemed to think she'd take it better coming from a family member than from me, so I was planning to tell her when he gets into town next week. We figured that would keep her from getting so pissed at me that she'd head to the shelter alone and be at risk of Rojo or one of his guys grabbing her after seeing her with me."

"Damn," Bobby cursed and looked up at the ceiling. "Yeah, he's probably right about that. Char's a lot more cautious than the rest of us, but if she gets pissed, she's definitely likely to act without thinking."

He huffed out a breath before continuing. "Alright, let's get things taken care of here. Then you need to pack bags for you and your family to come stay on the ranch until we catch this bastard, since he obviously knows where you live now. And I'll figure out how to help you break the news to Char, either over dinner tonight or breakfast in the morning."

Ian opened his mouth to protest staying on the ranch, but he promptly closed it again when he thought of what could happen if Rojo or his cartel members came back when Caitir and Brody were home. He nodded in agreement before pulling up the number to call Tully Walker about what needed to be done to get the door fixed since he was renting the house from him.

While Ian was on the phone with Tully, Bobby took photos and started his paperwork for the police report of the break-in at Ian's house. They called Jake and filled him in on what had happened while waiting on one of Tully's sons to come fix the door. Then Bobby went back to the police station to finish up his paperwork and get all the video feeds from Jake electronically.

Aiden Walker reintroduced himself to Ian and mentioned missing Cait at his birthday party before getting started on replacing the back door. Though Aiden seemed like a decent guy, Ian gave him the typical big brother spiel about not hitting on his sister.

It wasn't that Ian particularly cared whom his sister chose to date that caused him to tell Aiden to back off. He just thought that after everything Caitir had been through, she needed someone who could make her feel safe and be a steady presence in her life. And Aiden struck him as more of a laid-back, party guy than Caitir needed in her life.

Once Aiden was finished, Ian packed a week's worth of clothing and all the toiletries he thought his family would need to stay away from the house. He could always come back to get something if Caitir or Brody complained that he'd missed important items, but he didn't want either of them to leave the safety of the ranch until Roberto Rodriguez was locked up where he belonged.

Then he met Bobby at the police station to figure out the plan for where exactly they'd stay on the ranch, and how to inform the Burlesons of what was going on without causing a panic among the family members that didn't need to know all the details. They ended up calling and talking to both Bob and Hazel Burleson to set up their accommodations and loop them in without Brody being able to overhear the conversation. They raised the point about not worrying anyone else in the family by giving them more details than they needed about what had happened that day. Ian agreed, knowing he didn't want to discuss any of it in earshot of his son. So, they ended up concocting a story about a burst water pipe flooding their house as a cover for why the Campbells were staying with the Burlesons for a little while.

Ian also called and talked to Caitir on the phone to let her know as well, filling her in on the real story, as well as what would be used as their cover story. After all those calls, they ended up having to make a couple more calls to keep Trent and Jake looped in on the latest updates of the case, and didn't get back to the ranch until almost seven that night.

Ian was disappointed to find out that Charlotte wasn't at dinner at her parents' house because of having a book club meeting that night. But as Ian sat down to eat with his sister and son, along with Bob, Hazel, Bobby, and Brooklyn, he welcomed the opportunity to get to know more of her family, without her there causing him to be distracted by thinking of all the dirty things he wanted to do with her. He learned a little more about the Burlesons, feeling more like part of the family than the unwelcomed outsider he thought he'd be after they heard the whole saga that brought the Campbells to Heart's Destiny.

After Ian took Brody upstairs to put him down for bed in the room that joined the one he'd be staying in with a Jack-and-Jill bathroom, and Caitir decided to go soak in a bath in her room across the hall, Ian went back downstairs to continue the conversation with the Burlesons about which of their family members still needed to be informed of what all was actually going on and which of their family members would get the burst water pipe story.

He informed the family about Jake and Josh already knowing what was going on, how they'd helped him set up his temporary tactical operations center, and how Jake had been providing his cyber services all along. He also mentioned Jake's suggestion of bringing in the Avingtons when they got to town the next week.

He knew Charlotte would still need to know what was going on because of her involvement with Ian, and her volunteer time at the shelter, putting her at risk. But Ian figured he was going to have to find a way to pull her aside the next morning at breakfast to speak privately, so her parents wouldn't worry about her safety. Well, until Bobby informed his parents that Charlotte would need to know everything.

"I told Ian I'd help him tell Char what's going on, so she doesn't break up with him over this and rush off to the shelter where Rojo or his goons might target her. But since they have to leave so early in the morning for the away games they're coaching, he's probably gonna need one of ya'll to help him break the news to her before they leave."

"You're dating Char?" Of course, Hazel quit listening to Bobby's explanation as soon as she heard the words about breaking up and leapt to the conclusion that they must be officially dating.

"Not really," Ian grumbled, shaking his head.

"Then what's *really* goin' on between you and my daughter?" Bob Burleson was still a rather imposing man for someone who had to be close to sixty years old, if not a little older. His glower at Ian made it apparent that their age differences wouldn't mean as much as their similar sizes, if Bob decided Ian had wronged his daughter and needed to be dealt with physically.

Ian buckled under the older man's scrutiny so fast that nobody in the room would ever guess he'd undergone training to endure torture before working undercover. "I fell for Charlotte the night I met her, two weeks before I met all of you at your Christmas party. Unfortunately, I couldn't pursue anything with her because of this case, and trying to fight our connection by pretending it wasn't me she met that first night has pissed her off to the point that she can barely tolerate me most of the time. Now that misstep with her is coming back to bite me in the ass because Roberto Rodriguez has seen us together. So, my timeline for coming clean with her and making things right between us has sped up dramatically, so I can keep her safe. Because even if she can't forgive me for being stupid in my first attempt to protect her from the risks of this case, and I've lost my chance with her, I can't let Rojo and his gang harm another woman I love."

Ian snapped his mouth shut, realizing he's screwed up once again by admitting his feelings to her family before he told Charlotte. Bob only nodded in response to Ian's rambling declaration.

"I knew you two were perfect for each other." Hazel clapped excitedly as she smiled at Ian. "Though if I'd have realized you were gonna fight all my matchmaking attempts, I'd have pulled you aside at Christmas to warn you not to make such a boneheaded move with my Char. But don't worry, we can still fix this."

Ian wasn't sure what he'd gotten himself into by informing Charlotte's parents of his feelings for her, but as he looked across the room at the smirk on Bobby's face, he feared it might be as dangerous as going up against Rojo unarmed.

Yeah, maybe I should sneak over to Charlotte's house in the middle of the night to talk to her before her mother can interfere.

~~~

Saturday, March 23, 2019

Charlotte wasn't quite sure what was going on when she woke up around three in the morning to find someone sitting on the side of her bed. At first, she thought it was just another dream about Memmaw Judy coming to talk to her, like so many others she'd had recently. But then she recognized Ian's deep, baritone voice and felt comforted by his large hand softly brushing her hair away from her face.

"Relax, Princess, it's just me. I know it's way too early to wake up, but we really need to talk before breakfast with your parents."

Breakfast with my parents? What's going on? This isn't how my sex dreams normally start out.

"No, I imagine not," Ian chuckled, shaking the bed. "And I can assure you that if I was here for sex, I wouldn't mention your parents."

"Shit, did I say that out loud?" Charlotte rolled over and turned on the bedside lamp before sitting up to look at Ian. She couldn't quite comprehend that she wasn't dreaming him up.

Why on earth would he sneak onto the ranch and into my bedroom in the middle of the night?

"Yes," Ian replied, smiling at her. He was already dressed for the ball games they had in Luckenbach that morning, and the sight of him in his coaching clothes confused her even more.

"We don't have to leave until seven," Charlotte pointed out as she waved her hand in his direction to indicate his baseball attire. "Why are you waking me up four hours before we have to meet the buses?"

She wasn't sure if she wanted him to say he was there for sex with her or not. She was a little upset with him after the way he'd seemed to take her implied date the previous weekend as a sign that he should move on to date half the single teachers at the middle school.

"Because I have a lot of stuff to tell you and know you're going to need a little time to process it all before six, when we have to be over at breakfast with our families." Ian trailed his hand down her bare arm where she was wearing a silk nightgown with spaghetti straps.
~~~

Leah Mae Wright

Why did he have to show up on the morning after I've slept in something slinky to feel sexy, instead of my PJ pants and a t-shirt like I normally wear?

Charlotte shivered from the goosebumps his light caress produced. Ian took her hand in his as he sat there staring at her, as if he forgot what he was about to tell her.

"Okay, I'm awake. Start talking, so maybe I can get a couple more hours of sleep when you're done. And start with why our families are having breakfast together at six."

"Sorry," Ian smiled. "Our house was broken into yesterday, so we're staying with your parents until the perp is caught. I wanted to tell you what was going on last night, but you weren't home. Anyway, after explaining everything to your parents and Bobby, we decided to tell most of the family that we're only here because of a water pipe bursting and flooding our house, so they don't worry. But you need to know the truth because you're in danger otherwise."

"I wondered why you left school early yesterday." Charlotte was confused about why she'd be in danger because Ian's house was broken into, when she'd never even been to his home. "Okay, start over from the beginning, because that doesn't make sense."

"Okay, the beginning was about eight years ago, a couple years after I first started working with the DEA. What I told you the night we met was all true, with the exception of the fact that I actually left my job with the DEA a little over two years ago."

Charlotte nodded, realizing she'd been right in guessing that earlier in the week. "So, you're finally ready to admit to hooking up with me at the hotel in San Antonio in the middle of December?"

"Yes, and I regret not being completely open and honest with you when we met again at Christmas. But I had what I thought were good reasons at the time for keeping my distance from you."

"Yeah, we'll come back to that later." Charlotte waved her free hand at him to get him back on the original subject of the conversation they were having at three in the freaking morning. "Finish explaining the whole danger-and-breakfast-with-my-parents thing first."

"One of the major cases I worked on in my time with the DEA was the Rodriguez Cartel. It was a huge operation with branches throughout Mexico and in several states here in the US. Not just with drugs, but trafficking women and guns as well. The head of the cartel is Roberto Rodriguez, who earned the codename Rojo for how many people he's either killed or ordered to be killed. Each time we'd send agents in and get part of the operation shut down, he'd slip away and move to another location in his vast organization."

"Okay, so what's all that have to do with what's going on now?" Charlotte didn't understand why Ian thought she needed a DEA history lesson before getting to the point.

"I'm getting there, Princess. Just be patient and listen." Ian smiled as he rubbed his thumb over her hand, sending more goosebumps through her body. "A little over four years ago, I was the agent sent in to infiltrate the cartel. I grew my hair out, grew a beard, dyed it all black, and spent way too many hours in a tanning bed to change my appearance to blend in with the cartel dealers. It was gut-wrenching work, but I was able to move pretty high up in the organization over the next eighteen months. Then my progress stalled out. I couldn't quite make it up from brothel security to protecting the major players in the cartel."

Ian huffed out a sigh and looked down at their joined hands for a moment before continuing. "I thought it was just standard procedure. That I'd be stuck there for a year or more before they trusted me to move up. So, I went about business as usual with only short visits with my family, when I thought nobody would realize I'd gone back to San Diego for a day or two. But apparently, seeing my wife and kid for a few stolen moments in a park was noticeable, or ended up on the cartel's radar when Mari posted a picture of the three of us on social media."

Ian closed his eyes and took a few deep breaths. "I don't know if they figured out that Mike Smith was an alias, or if they actually figured out my real name was Michael Campbell from Mari being online as Mari Campbell."

"Well, duh, Mike Smith is way too white-boy of a name to pass as a member of a Mexican cartel. Wait, so Ian isn't really your name?" Charlotte shook her head, trying to figure out how he'd picked that name and produced identification the night they met with it listed.

"Yeah, well, no matter how much I tan, I can't change my race, so a generic, white-boy name seemed appropriate," Ian chuckled. "And Ian was my middle name. Now, I don't have a middle name and neither does Brody because I wiped all traces of Michael from our lives after I realized my cover was blown."

Charlotte just stared at him in surprise as he continued explaining.

"I was born Michael Ian Campbell and named my son Brody Michael Campbell. On Brody's second birthday, I met my family in the park for his birthday party and realized my cover was blown when the Rodriguez Cartel ambushed us with a spray of gunfire in a drive-by. Mari was killed. Caitir and I both took bullets in the arm and shoulder. She also suffered a concussion from hitting her head, diving for cover. And I almost smothered my son from trying to cover his body with mine."

"Oh, Ian," Charlotte gasped in shock at the revelation. She quickly composed herself and lifted her free hand to wipe away the tear that escaped from Ian's watery eyes. *That's what the scar on his shoulder is from?*

"When all was said and done that day, there were two casualties and thirteen wounded, most of them innocent bystanders, who were just unlucky enough to be at the wrong place at the wrong time, when the cartel tried to take me out. And the worst part is that I was there unarmed, so I couldn't even stop the shooters to prevent any of it."

"Of course you were unarmed. Nobody would ever think it was appropriate to carry a weapon to a toddler's birthday party. You can't beat yourself up over that." Charlotte tried to soothe him, scooting closer to wrap her arms around him.

"But I knew the danger of the assignment I was on at the time, so I should have thought to carry at least one weapon that day to protect my family." Ian wrapped his arms around her and held on tight as emotion overwhelmed him.

Charlotte tried to comfort him as best she could, though she knew her softly spoken words, about how even if he'd had a gun that day, he wouldn't have been able to do much against multiple gunmen, weren't much reassurance.

"Sorry," Ian mumbled as he released his hold on her and pulled back to wipe his eyes.

"Don't be. I completely understand needing a shoulder to lean on sometimes." Charlotte gave him a circumspect smile, unsure if he was really ready to go on with his explanation of why he was at her house in the wee hours of the morning or not.

"Anyway, back to the point," Ian stated, standing to pace around her bedroom. The room she usually thought of as spacious seemed much smaller with him stalking around. "The agency reported it as three dead and released a statement that Michael and Marisol Campbell both died that day. They helped me with everything that needed to be done to backstop our modified identities and moved us to a suburb north of the city. I changed jobs, starting as a substitute teacher before getting a permanent position in the school where I was working before moving here. And while I was teaching, I took every opportunity I could to feed information to my former partner about any lower-level dealers I heard about at school."

"So, while you weren't actually employed by the DEA anymore, you still felt like you were doing something to help fight the cartel." Charlotte nodded as she spoke, understanding dawning that Ian needed to leave the agency to take care of what was left of his family, but he also needed to have a hand in bringing down the cartel that had killed his wife.

"Yeah," Ian agreed, nodding along with her. "It wasn't much in the grand scheme of things, but it wasn't as dangerous as continuing to be an agent, so I could be home for Brody and Cait."

Ian walked back over and sat down on the edge of her queen-sized bed. He took her hand once more and looked into her eyes as he continued his tale. "The week after Thanksgiving, I got a message from my former partner about a bust here in Texas. They captured most of the higher-level members of the cartel, but Roberto Rodriguez got away. Since the local PD doesn't have the manpower to keep hunting for him, and both the DEA and Homeland Security have too much red tape and rules to follow before being able to send in a team to keep searching, I volunteered to move here and scope out the area to see if I could find the cartel head before he could regroup and get away."

"So, the story you told me the night we met about hunting a fugitive was all true?" Charlotte hated that her statement came out sounding like a question, but she also kind of needed him to reiterate that point to let it fully sink into her brain.

"Yes," Ian said simply, nodding. "I told you I wouldn't lie to you, but I also couldn't tell you everything. That's because I knew what I was about to embark on was too dangerous for us to have more than that night. I wanted more, even then, but I couldn't take the chance on getting involved with you, when I knew I could be putting you at risk of being gunned down like Mari was just for being seen with me. That's why I didn't ask your last name or for your phone number. I knew I'd be too tempted to see you again once I moved here."

"And surprise, you saw me again two weeks later," Charlotte chuckled at the irony.

"Yeah, and had no idea how to deal with my conflicting feelings," Ian groaned, shaking his head. "So, of course, I pushed you away thinking I was protecting you, when I really wanted to hold you close and enjoy every moment I could spend with you."

"And confused the hell out of me with the hot-and-cold, Jekyll-and-Hyde act. You know it's infuriating to be attracted to someone who makes you want to slap them just as often as you want to kiss them, right?"

"No, I didn't know that," Ian chuckled. "But I do now, so maybe I can quit making you want to slap me all the time."

"Yeah, I'll believe it when I see it," Charlotte laughed with him. "Anyway, back to what all this has to do with why you're here now and having breakfast with my parents."

Ian took a deep breath and blew it out before continuing his account of the events leading up to that morning. "So, in the midst of trying to keep my distance from you to keep you safe, I've also been searching for Rojo in the areas where either my former partner, Trent, or your brother, Jake, have reports of him being spotted."

"Wait, you know Jake? And he's been in on this with you?"

"Yeah, we met a few years ago on another joint task force. So, when Trent said the bust happened in Jake's hometown, he gave Jake my number to help me find a job here and to provide some cyber backup when I'm following the various leads we've had on Roberto's whereabouts." Ian held up a hand to stop her from asking the questions that were on the tip of her tongue.

The bust happened in Jake's hometown? Does he mean here in Heart's Destiny? When? How did I not hear about it? Is it just Jake that's been working with him? Has Bobby been in on it the whole time, too? Or anyone else in my family?

"Anyway, one of the informants I've met with owns a bar in San Antonio where some of Rojo's associates have been spotted. And where I've had to spend way too much time the last few months, trying to get an idea of where to look for Rodriguez. I got lucky on Valentine's Day to overhear some info about a meeting a couple of days later. I scoped out the warehouses most likely to be the site of the meeting, and managed to spot Roberto as he was leaving. I trailed him to the area around the shelter before I lost him. Then the next weekend, when I retraced my steps to see if I could spot his vehicle and figure out where he might be staying, I ran into you coming out of the shelter."

"Holy shit!" Charlotte gasped before covering her mouth as realization dawned that not only had Ian been working on this case, instead of dating someone on Valentine's Day, but also that the following weekend, when they hooked up in the parking garage, their sexual encounter was partially driven by his fear for her being in the same area as the man he was hunting down for the DEA. "That's why everything got so crazy the first time you came to check out the shelter."

"Yeah, I was freaking out about you being in the same area as Rojo, and completely lost control of my need to be with you." Ian ran a hand through his hair nervously. "We still need to discuss the possible ramifications of that afternoon, too."

"No need." Charlotte waved away his worry about a baby in the middle of this mess, hoping he didn't recognize her disappointment about them not creating a life that day in February. "My period was normal as usual this month, so unless you were lying about being clean, there won't be any ramifications."

"Oh, um, okay." Ian nodded before going back to tell her about the investigation. "So, anyway, over the next couple of weeks, I continued searching the area and figured out that Roberto was hiding out in the shelter."

"That's why you followed me there, and then insisted on volunteering with me…" Charlotte's words trailed off as she wondered if the coffee, donuts, and flirtation were more about getting into the shelter for the case than him actually being into her.

"Yeah, I couldn't stand the thought of you being anywhere he might see you and decide to grab you, either to traffic you like he has other women, or because he saw us together and recognized me."

"You sure it wasn't just to use me as a way into the shelter to get closer to catching him?" Charlotte closed her eyes, hating that her insecurity was showing so plainly as she asked the question.

"Absolutely not," Ian growled vehemently. "I honestly thought he was holed up in one of the hotels nearby until the first day I volunteered with you, and you mentioned someone named Roberto suddenly leaving the shelter around the same time we walked in together. Then I gave Jake the name you mentioned and figured out it's an alias being used by Roberto Rodriguez."

Ian pulled his phone out of his pocket and pulled up a picture. "Open your eyes, Princess. Look at his mugshot and tell me if I'm right or not."

Charlotte automatically followed his command and was surprised to see a picture on Ian's phone that was very clearly a younger version of the man she knew as Roberto Reyes. She reached out and took his phone to get a better look before nodding. "Yes, you're right. This is definitely the man we were talking about leaving with his son that day."

"From what we can tell, the boy isn't actually his son." Ian shook his head in disgust. "We're not sure of the particulars of how he managed to come to have custody of a child while on the run, but unless he was born in one of the cartel brothels, Jake should be able to find his birth certificate, eventually."

"Roberto had Antonio's birth certificate," Charlotte shouted, realizing that he had to show it to the INS agents working on their asylum status. "I never actually saw it myself, but Faith might have a copy from helping Roberto get all the paperwork together for INS."

"You've been working with Antonio for a while. Did he ever mention anything about his mom, or where he lived before coming here?"

"No, not really." Charlotte really wished she'd tried to get him to talk more about his life before the shelter, now that she knew he wasn't actually Roberto's son. "But we were told he saw his mother die in the crossfire of a cartel war in their village in Mexico, and that was why he quit talking, so I didn't want to retraumatize him by asking about any of that."

She went on to tell Ian everything she remembered about her time working with Antonio, both when Roberto was present for the sessions and the times over the last few weekends when she worked with him that Roberto left the boy with her to go on job interviews. Or at least what he told her were job interviews. After hearing about Roberto meeting with his cartel cronies on one of the Saturdays when he'd left Antonio with her for his speech session, she had to wonder if the man had ever gone on a job interview the whole time he was staying at the shelter.

After talking for quite a while about the search for Roberto Rodriguez, including calling Jake for Char to fill him in on the whole backstory the shelter volunteers and employees had been given, she somehow managed to get out of breakfast with her parents because she had to use that time to shower and get ready for her day. She had already let Faith know she wouldn't be at the shelter in time to help with lunch that day because of the road trip to Luckenbach with her softball team, so she hadn't argued with either Ian or Jake when they tried to convince her to stop volunteering there until after Roberto Rodriguez was arrested.

As much as she hated feeling like she'd be letting the other residents and volunteers at the shelter down by not volunteering for a while, she had no desire to be anywhere near the scene when that arrest went down. So, she acquiesced to Ian's domineering demand rather quickly. She only wished they'd have had time for him to show her some of that dominance in sexier ways in her bedroom before they had to rush across town to catch the buses that would take them to their games.

But maybe, now that he's finally told me the truth about everything, we'll be able to figure out our romantic relationship soon. And hopefully, I won't have to wait too long to get another taste of his magic, pierced peen.

Chapter Fifteen

Sunday, March 24, 2019

Charlotte only got a one-day reprieve from dealing with her family and the fall-out of Ian, Cait, and Brody staying with her parents for the foreseeable future. For the most part, her family all bought the busted water pipe story and mostly talked about how long it had taken to get the south bunkhouse repaired after the same thing happened there back in November. But unfortunately, her mother was privy to the whole story and was clearly using it to further her matchmaking agenda.

While she didn't mind being seated next to Ian at every meal and activity all that much, and actually hoped they'd end up together when all was said and done, she didn't want her mother taking the credit for getting them together, which put her in the uncomfortable position of not knowing how to respond to his flirty behavior for the majority of the day. As much as she wanted to flirt back and start working toward a meaningful relationship with him, she just couldn't make herself follow that instinct with half her family watching their every move.

To make matters worse, everyone was getting excited about the upcoming quarterly board meeting, family birthdays, and the wedding that her brothers and newfound cousins were coming to the ranch for beginning in just a couple of days. Not that she wasn't excited about having them all there and enjoying the family celebrations, but she knew she'd have even more eyes on her and Ian at each and every one of those get-togethers.

Just the thought of everyone watching as they worked through their relationship issues made her feel like they were a life-sized science experiment, with their every move being examined under a microscope. It felt like a lot of pressure to put on a new relationship, especially one with so many early missteps already.

Yeah, she understood why Ian hadn't wanted to pursue more with her while he was dealing with everything else he had going on when they first met. She also understood how emotional the case was for him after hearing how the cartel had killed his wife. But since he wasn't able to be honest with her about everything from the very beginning, she still struggled with wondering if their connection was strong enough to form a lasting relationship. Or if it was just lust that would soon fade.

She was seriously afraid that it was just sexual chemistry, heightened by the dangerous situation surrounding them because of Ian's former job with the DEA, and that they didn't have enough in common to build a life together after the threat of the cartel was dealt with by Ian, her brothers, and the other authorities on the case. The more time she spent seeing him interacting with her family, the more she saw their differences as possible hindrances to them lasting as a couple long term.

From the talks they'd had, both at school and while driving to and from the shelter, Charlotte knew they didn't have a single favorite thing in common. The one thing they did have in common was a love of reading. But even though they both enjoyed reading before going to bed at night, they had vastly different tastes in books.

While that wouldn't be a problem for most people, Charlotte wanted a man who was at least willing to read her favorite romance novels to get some ideas for them to play out in the bedroom. She also wanted a man who was passionate about his own reading choices and would sit down with her and have meaningful discussions about the books he found most enthralling. But her conversations about books with Ian barely glossed over their favorite authors and book series, and were mostly about the books he wanted to teach that she still believed were too advanced for their middle school classes.

Even as they sat at dinner that night with her family and the conversation around the table turned to the books Kay and Brooklyn were working on, both individually and the series they wanted to do together, Ian had clammed up as soon as the genres were mentioned. It was like he realized he had no interest in romance or children's books, so he had nothing to add to the conversation. Charlotte thought he should really pay attention to the discussion about Brooklyn's children's books because they could be appropriate to add to the reading lists for his sixth-grade classes.

Guess it's a good thing I've already added her last one to the seventh-grade reading list, so this year's sixth-graders won't miss it entirely. And I can do the same with her latest release if I need to, so his students don't miss out.

"So, have you figured out what pen name you're going to use when you're writing the adult novels with Kay?"

Charlotte was cataloging the next Brie Brooks book she needed to read before adding it to her class reading lists and missed who asked Brooklyn about her pen name. But she quickly tuned back into the conversation around her.

"Yes, I'm going with Brie Roberts," Brooklyn stated between bites. "That way I'll be listed as Roberts, Brie whenever my books are catalogued by the author's last name, so I can appease Bobby's need for me to broadcast to the world that I'm all his."

Is he going to make her spell it with the apostrophe to denote his possessiveness of her? If so, it's going to look wrong on the book cover listed as Brie Robert's.

"Are you spelling it with or without the apostrophe?" Ian inquired, causing Charlotte to choke on the bite of steak she'd just taken. Ian reached over and patted her back to help her dislodge the food.

"What apostrophe?" Bobby looked at Ian with confusion at the same time Brooklyn answered Ian's question, "Without."

Charlotte took a drink of her tea to finish washing it down as everyone's attention turned to her and the "you alright, Char?" comments commenced around the table. She nodded that she was fine as she finished swallowing everything completely before answering verbally. "Yes, I'm fine. Just surprised to hear Ian ask the same thing I was wondering. Though I guess I shouldn't be since we're both English teachers."

Huh? Something we actually have in common? I wonder if the incorrect apostrophe on the book cover would be an annoying pet peeve for him, too?

"Now ya'll really need to explain the apostrophe thing." Bobby waved a finger between Charlotte and Ian.

Charlotte looked at Ian, who looked back with a half-shrug and seemed to be deferring to her to explain.

"If it's meant to show possession, it should be spelled Robert-apostrophe-S to show that Brie belongs to Robert. But the surname Roberts doesn't have an apostrophe and would look incorrect if one was used anywhere the author's name was listed first name first," Charlotte clarified.

"Exactly," Brooklyn agreed, nodding her head at Charlotte. "So, instead of turning off readers with an incorrect apostrophe on my book covers, I figured the surname originated to mean the family of Robert, so it still got the same message across without the apostrophe."

"Actually, the surname Roberts originally meant son of Robert," Tia corrected. "But considering that's the same way the surname Robertson originated, I can see why that would be confusing."

After a brief discussion about the blatant sexism in the origins and propagation of surnames, it was decided that the Burlesons would consider Roberts as meaning "family of Robert" to stop the celebration of sons over daughters that was so prevalent throughout history and support Brooklyn in her choice of a pen name. Luckily, in all her ancestry research, Charlotte had found that their last name was originally derived from the village of Burleston in Dorset, England, and didn't mean "son of" anyone, even though the name ended with the syllable   -son. So, they were able to change the subject to more of her research finds for the rest of the meal.

After dinner, Ian pulled her aside, so they could talk privately. "Hey, um, can you give me the information on where to get one of those DNA test kits to be able to trace my Campbell ancestors and find out where our last name originated?"

"I can do better than that," Charlotte snickered, surprised that he really was following through with wanting to do a test. "I can go grab one from my house, so you can do the test tonight if you want. And the website information is in the kit, so you can trace your family tree while you're waiting on the results."

"I can just order one," Ian objected, shaking his head. "I don't want to leave you running short when I know you're holding onto the last of them for your brothers."

"Don't worry about it," Charlotte waved off his objection. "I have like ten left, not counting the ones I have set aside for Jake and Josh. And yeah, I'll probably talk Fiona or the Hunters into doing them when they come home for their next holiday break, but I still have plenty for you, Cait, and Brody, if you want them."

"No, uh, just for me is fine. The one test is enough to trace the Campbell lineage, which is all we're interested in looking into." Ian looked across the room at his sister and son, setting up to play a game with Charlotte's nieces before turning his gaze back on Char.

"Yeah, I'll go get it now." Charlotte smiled at him reassuringly. *And hopefully, one of these days, you'll trust me enough to tell me why ya'll don't want to know anything about your father's family.*

"Thanks, but, um, don't hand it to me in front of Cait." Ian's eyes darted back over to his sister once again before he looked back at Charlotte. "Can you, maybe, put it under my pillow, so she doesn't see it?"

"Sure," Charlotte agreed, not wanting to make Cait uncomfortable just to satisfy her curiosity about their family. "Which room are you staying in?"

"The first one on the left on the second floor." Ian inclined his head toward the foyer, so she assumed he meant the first room on the left from the front staircase.

Of course, Mom put him in my old bedroom. Charlotte almost rolled her eyes at the irony, but she didn't want to explain the action to Ian with her family just a few feet away.

Char excused herself as Ian walked over to participate in the game the rest of their family members were setting up to play. She ducked into the restroom as cover for where she was going, but just stayed in there long enough to keep anyone from noticing when she escaped to head out the front door.

After she grabbed one of the DNA tests from her house, she decided to sneak back in the back door and go up the back stairs, thinking the rest of her family would all be in the family room and might see her go through the foyer. Unfortunately, she was wrong about the kitchen being empty when she returned to her childhood home.

"Char? What were you doing outside?" Her mother raised an eyebrow at her as she was putting cookies on a plate at the island in the kitchen.

Of course, the nosiest person in my family would be the one to catch me sneaking this test to Ian. But Mom's also really good at keeping secrets, so maybe I can tell her what I'm really doing without her making a big deal about it.

Whom am I kidding? She's going to make anything I do for Ian into a big deal, but at least I know she won't tell Cait about it.

"All our family heritage talk finally convinced Ian to take a DNA test to trace his Campbell ancestors." Charlotte held up the test kit to show her mother. "But for some reason, he doesn't want Cait to know, so I'm sneaking this up to leave it in his room."

"Oh, I wonder why that is?" Charlotte shrugged in response, but she didn't have a clue how to answer her mother's question. "Well, whatever his reasoning, it's wonderful to see you helping him out while keeping his secrets. Just make sure he fully confides in you about all of them before you break out the book to start implementing your wedding plans."

Charlotte's jaw dropped at her mother's declaration. She wasn't sure if it was from realizing her mother knew she still had her wedding plans book from high school, or from her mother's unexpected advice about knowing everything about Ian before jumping into marriage.

With as eager as Hazel Burleson was to marry off all her children, nieces, nephews, and friends' adult children, Charlotte expected her mother to push for a quick wedding without taking the time to really get to know one another. Sort of like the way Hazel had pushed for Charlotte's brothers to quickly plan their weddings to Kay and Brooklyn.

"Oh, don't look so shocked, Char," her mother chided with a grin. "A mother knows these things, especially about her daughter. While I knew Ian would be perfect for you as soon as Lisa told me she'd hired him, and wasn't surprised at all to see your wedding book out the first time I took Cait over to your house a week after seeing you and Ian together at Christmas, I know you well enough to know that you need to know absolutely everything about him before you'll be ready to walk down the aisle."

Charlotte was speechless as her mother continued to tell her what else she knew about her and Ian. Apparently, Ian had really spilled his guts to her parents the night his house was broken into, and he already had them convinced that he'd fallen in love with her at first sight the night they met in the hotel bar.

"He stopped short when he realized he'd told us he loves you before actually tellin' you, but I fully expect him to ask for our blessing to marry you as soon as this whole cartel mess is cleared up. So, don't let him use that excuse for stayin' away from you any longer. Use this time to get to know everything you need to know to be able to say *yes* when he proposes."

Hazel paused in her monologue to put the plate of cookies on a tray with a stack of plastic cups and a pitcher of sweet tea, obviously planning to carry them into the family room for everyone to snack on while having a family game night. "Now hurry up and sneak that up to your old bedroom before anyone else notices you're not in the family room with the rest of us."

"Yes, ma'am." Char snapped out of her daze to finish her errand before joining in the family fun.

If he's already trying to convince Mom and Dad that we're in love and going to get married, then I'd better show him what life on the ranch is really like, so we both know if he's really the right man for me. Hopefully, he'll share more about his past while proving he can be happy in my normally boring routine of life.

And what better time to show him all about life on the ranch than our spring break? Hope he's prepared for a couple of days of sitting in a saddle this week.

~~~

Thursday, March 28, 2019

Ian was glad to finally get a meeting with the Burlesons and Avingtons to brainstorm some fresh ideas for how to find Roberto Rodriguez, but he was surprised that they'd decided to have this meeting at the Heart's Destiny Police Department.

Damn, I guess Jake and Josh really don't want their brother to know about their hidden TOC on the ranch, since they didn't think this meeting would be more productive if we held it there where all our intel is stored.

As soon as he walked in the door, Ian recognized Mabel, the receptionist at the HDPD, from meeting her the previous week when
~~~

he'd been in the office after the break-in at his house. He thought it was adorable how the grandmotherly woman insisted on wearing a uniform to make sure the townspeople gave her the respect of an officer whenever they came into the building.

"Good morning. Nice to see you again, Mabel." Ian smiled at the matronly woman as he approached her desk.

"Good morning to you, too, Ian." Mabel smiled back before her expression turned concerned. "Please tell me you're here for a friendly visit and not because your house has been broken into again."

"No, not another break-in," Ian reassured her with a small shake of his head before winking at her. "But I am here for a meeting with Bobby, so I probably won't be able to get away with sitting out here flirting with the beautiful women of the HDPD today."

"Hey, are you flirting with my girlfriend?" Jake walked up and threw his arm around Mabel's shoulders. "You'd better knock that off, or I'm gonna tell my sister on you."

Ian lifted his hand to his chin, miming thinking about whether that was a good idea or not. "Hum, maybe making Charlotte jealous will bring out her feisty side. This could be a good plan."

"Sorry to burst your bubble, man, but Char doesn't have a feisty side." Josh slapped a hand on Ian's back as he walked up. "You picked the wrong sister for that."

"Oh, you boys, quit picking on Ian," Mabel interjected. "He's a good man and perfect to bring Char's feistiness back out."

"Oh, I think he already has," Bobby chuckled as he walked up from his office in the back of the building. He nodded at Ian as he stopped beside Mabel's desk. "Or at least her sadistic side. You still walkin' bowlegged after she made you spend the first two days of spring break on the back of a horse?"

Ian groaned at the memory of how he'd had to ice his groin after Charlotte's attempt at getting him caught up with Brody in his horse riding lessons on Monday and Tuesday. While he'd enjoyed spending the time with Charlotte and Brody together, he'd been glad to hear she had to spend the day at the Burleson Incorporated board meeting on Wednesday, so he had a day away from the horses. He clearly needed to find a better way to protect his balls while on the back of a horse before he let Charlotte and Brody talk him into another extended day of riding lessons. "Seriously, guys, you've got to tell me the secret to lessening the impact on the boys while riding."

"There is no secret," Jake shrugged. "Ya just gotta toughen up."

"And this is why we're not going to be spending our time here on the back of a horse," Barrett Avington laughed as he and his brothers joined them.

"Oh, boy, Paisley is gonna be so disappointed that she's working the night shift this week and missed out on all the handsome men ya'll brought with you for this meeting." Mabel fanned herself before extending her hand in Byron Avington's direction. "Hi there, handsome. I'm Mabel. Welcome to Heart's Destiny."

"Byron Avington. Nice to meet you, Mabel." Byron lightly shook her hand, but the oldest of the Avingtons looked slightly uncomfortable.

"Back off, Mabel. He's married," Bobby warned.

"So's your daddy, but I can still enjoy the view whenever he comes around without poachin'." Mabel waggled her eyebrows at Bobby. "Now, ya'll head on up to the briefing room before you get me in trouble. Dusty's already taken the donuts up there and corralled Dougie and Jagger before they left for patrol."

Ian was surprised to hear the other officers of the HDPD would be sitting in on their meeting. He thought this was just an informal meeting to get some different perspectives on how to generate new leads on Rojo's whereabouts, not a formal meeting to coordinate the efforts of the various departments that could possibly be involved in capturing him.

As they took the stairs up to the second floor of the building where the briefing room was located, Ian sent a message off to Trent to see if he was available to Skype into the meeting. He just hoped the fact that it was two hours earlier in San Diego would work in his favor. It might be best if they caught Trent before he started his day, but didn't upset him by waking up his friend, who was more of a night owl, too early.

"You know I already have him scheduled to Skype in, right?" Jake nodded his head at Ian's phone in his hand.

Ian arched an eyebrow in surprise at Jake as they took seats around the conference table.

"Dude, you've either been out of the game too long, or my sister really has you distracted," Jake laughed as he hit a few keys on the computer in front of him and Trent and his team appeared on a large screen at the front of the room.

"Maybe a little of both," Ian sighed, wondering if he should just step back and let the rest of the guys take over the operation.

"Don't worry man, we've got ya covered," Jake whispered to Ian as he slapped a hand on his shoulder. Then he turned to the rest of the room and took over, starting the meeting by introducing everyone in the room.

Ian finally had faces to put with the names Dusty Deere and Jagger Youngblood on the Heart's Destiny police force, nodding at each of the two men he hadn't been formally introduced to before then when their names were mentioned. Trent then took the time to introduce everyone on his team in San Diego, most of whom Ian already knew from his time with the DEA.

Ian was surprised when Byron Avington then took over the meeting. Again, thinking the Burlesons just brought their cousins in because of their security company and to get some different perspectives on ideas for finding Rojo, Ian had expected to have to debrief everyone on what he'd been doing for the past three months, not hear that Byron had already read over all the files.

As the oldest of the group of men and women gathered to work on the case, and the owner of Avington Security, Ian knew Byron would have years more experience than anyone else on the various teams of people working on the case. But he thought it would be experience in protecting clients that would help them keep Charlotte safe. He had no idea that Byron and Avington Security had so much experience working investigations with the FBI and ATF in Atlanta, along with several local and state police forces and the various branches of the military.

Damn, so much for thinking all they did were little bodyguard jobs like they did for Bobby when he and Brooklyn went to Georgia.

"Yeah, I should probably get the director in here to negotiate a contract with you before we actually start coming up with a plan for our next steps in tracking Rojo," Trent confessed, shaking his head. "But since Jake said he was bringing in his cousins to brainstorm, not hiring an investigative team, I didn't think to ask Director Jameson to come in early today."

"Can you authorize us to go in without your director signing off beforehand?" Byron asked Trent.

"Yeah, but I can't authorize an expenditure over five-thousand dollars, which an investigation of this magnitude would obviously be." Trent shook his head as he explained the need for a contract through the director of the DEA for outside investigators due to budgetary reasons.

"If your only concern is the money, then you don't have to worry about a contract. I just need to know my men won't be treated as vigilantes or charged for whatever happens when we go in and capture this guy. If you can give us the authorization to work on behalf of the DEA to bring in your fugitive, then we're good."

"Yeah, I can authorize that," Trent nodded.

"And even if he couldn't, I could just swear all ya'll in as officers before we get started," Bobby quipped, causing a few chuckles around the room.

Byron smiled before looking around the room at his sons, then the Burlesons, before turning back to look at the screen at the front of the room to see Trent's reaction to his next statement. "Since my family likes to keep financial matters private, I'm sure you haven't heard all the specifics of how we recently found out my great-grandmother was the long-lost Burleson heiress. But because of finding that out about six weeks ago, there's been quite a few changes to our family business. One of which is that we're now able to take on cases with law enforcement agencies on a pro bono basis."

Holy shit! Ian thought at the same time several people in San Diego seemed to say the same thing.

"That's not even the best change in the company," Blaine Avington chuckled.

"No? What's the best change in the company?" Josh arched an eyebrow at his cousin.

"Turning all the accounting, human resources, and other paperwork we hate doing over to the pretty ladies at the Burleson headquarters," Blaine smirked.

Barrett reached over and smacked his brother in the back of the head. "I thought when you turned thirty, you'd mature enough to quit being a sexual harassment lawsuit in the making."

Byron gave his sons a look that made them all straighten in their seats, even the ones not horsing around, before bringing the meeting back on topic. "Well, now that we know there's no need for a contract, let me tell you my plan for finding Roberto Rodriguez and bringing him in."

Byron explained how he planned to send a couple of his employees from Georgia undercover in San Antonio to see just how much of the operation Rojo had recovered since the bust in November. Since Ian had obviously been recognized at the Community Mission Shelter and had possibly put Charlotte on Rojo's radar, Byron wanted him to stay in Heart's Destiny, working as close cover for Charlotte while his team took over the search for Rodriguez in the San Antonio area.

Yeah, I'm going to enjoy covering her very closely.

Ian agreed wholeheartedly, glad he didn't have to be the one to make the call on when it was time for him to back off on the case. Though he still felt a little like he was letting Mari down by not being the one to avenge her by capturing Rojo, he knew it was time to move on with his life with Charlotte and let this team of vastly more qualified individuals deal with dispensing justice.

Chapter Sixteen

Friday, April 5, 2019

Charlotte felt exceptionally emotional as she walked into the rehearsal dinner for Bobby and Brooklyn's wedding at the Hunters' Bed and Breakfast. She knew the most likely cause was probably where she was in her monthly cycle. But since she had ten more days until her period was due to start, she really wished she could figure out how to decrease some of her PMS symptoms, or at least their duration. She wished she could shrink the time down to just a couple of days, or maybe a week before her period, like her sister and cousins, instead of the almost two weeks of moodiness she seemed to suffer from lately. *Hopefully, this new doctor can give me some ideas for how to do that when I go for my OB-GYN appointment on Monday.*

Apparently, Dr. Magnum was the doctor that both Kay and Brooklyn were seeing for their pregnancies, so Charlotte had already heard them both sing her praises. Bobby and Brooklyn had also gone that morning to have their first ultrasound in the newest part of the Heart's Destiny Clinic and were raving about the experience as they were getting ready for the rehearsal.

Charlotte figured some of her overly emotional feelings this evening were from seeing the pictures that were being passed around at the church during the rehearsal. Even though the grainy, black-and-white image was hard to make out as a baby, the picture of her future niece or nephew was more than enough to trigger another round of baby fever in Charlotte.

Which is absolutely crazy, since I don't even know what's going on between Ian and me right now.

She had thought having him living on the ranch would give them numerous opportunities for some alone time to work on their relationship. Or to at least act on their mutual attraction with a quickie or two. But even with both of them being off work for spring break the previous week, they'd only managed to have some one-on-one time that first Saturday when Ian snuck into her house to tell her all the details about what was going on with the DEA case that brought him to Texas. And there wasn't time for more than talking that morning, no matter how much they both might have wanted more.

They'd had away games both Saturdays, so they'd been surrounded by two teams of young teenagers and their parents, who came along on the bus rides to help supervise the rowdy bunch. Then their Sundays had been overrun with relatives and fellow church-goers that prevented them from having any meaningful conversations, even though they were seated side by side most of those days.

Char had thought she'd get some alone time with Ian by inviting him to spend the first two days of spring break learning proper horsemanship. The plan was to take Ian on a trail ride while Brody was down for his nap, but apparently, not all four-year-olds take daily naps. And Brody was among the forty percent who no longer napped regularly, especially on days when he was too excited about riding horses to settle down to sleep.

Then on Wednesday, Charlotte spent the whole day at the Burleson Incorporated office in San Antonio for the quarterly board meeting and to tour the facility with the family members who hadn't ever been there before. It had been a while since Charlotte had ventured out of the conference room where the board meetings were held, so she enjoyed seeing the changes since the last time she'd toured the facility. The Avingtons didn't seem as enthusiastic about seeing everything there as Brooklyn, Kay, Tia, and Maria were, but then again, Charlotte knew that not many people showed excitement as avidly as her sisters-in-law and nieces.

When Charlotte thought she could spend some time with Ian on Thursday and Friday while they were off for spring break, he disappeared with her brothers and cousins. Well, most of her brothers and cousins. Anthony and his family flew off to work with the GWA, and her Burleson cousins continued to work at the corporate offices as usual. Since her sister still went to work at the Destiny Playhouse as per her usual schedule, Charlotte found herself hanging out with Brody and the horses for the rest of her spring break.

Then, of course, they were back at school this week with softball and baseball practice keeping them occupied on alternate afternoons, and they only saw each other for meals, when they were once again surrounded by people. Even at school, she'd had to share their lunch table with the other teachers, making it impossible to talk about the possibility of them starting to date officially, or see what else might develop between them.

She had at least given up on her attempt to stop herself from masturbating to thoughts of Ian every night. Once she got the email from Ashlyn that It's My Pleasure had taken her suggestion to stock a pierced dildo, she pretty much had to order it and try it out. While the rubber cock had a different type of piercing than Ian, it was closer to his size than her rabbit vibrator, so it worked for her. At least, it did a decent enough job with the addition of a clitoral stimulator and lots of dirty thoughts about Ian while she was trying to figure out how to get her hands on the real thing again.

As Ian finally finished mingling with her Avington cousins and took his seat beside her for the meal, Charlotte wondered if there was a possibility of them sneaking away for a quick tryst once the meal and speeches were over and the dancing commenced. She wasn't sure that would be very likely with Cait and Brody also at their table, but she was hopeful.

As the rest of their closest family and friends arrived, Charlotte was glad when her girlfriends filled the other four seats at their table. Cassidy, Kayla, Lexi, and Kara apparently weren't kidding about wanting to check out Ian after their Galentine's party, and finally saw the opportunity since there weren't place cards to designate where anyone should sit at the rehearsal dinner.

Ian looked slightly uncomfortable as the only man at the table, which Charlotte found exceptionally amusing. Especially since Ian didn't get much help balancing the estrogen-to-testosterone ratio from Brody, who was too shy to speak to the ladies as dinner was served.

"I still can't believe this place was here for over a hundred years and we didn't even know about it until they started the renovations back in the fall," Kayla spoke in awe as she looked around the ballroom.

"I remember hearing about it as a teenager when the twins came over to play with Anthony and talked about the haunted mansion hidden in the woods," Char admitted with a slight lift of one shoulder. "But I never would have imagined the dilapidated ruins they described could be restored into such a beautiful location for weddings and events like this."

"Yeah, if I had known, I'd have been bugging Mandi to fix it up sooner," Kara revealed, with a mischievous gleam in her eye. "Since she's started promoting the use of the ballroom for weddings and other events, my monthly cake orders have doubled."

"Wow, and only two of those have been Burleson wedding cakes," Lexi exclaimed with a giggle. "Well, so far. I'm sure that number will be increasing with the Matchmaking Mommas on the loose."

There was a chorus of words of agreement around the table as her girlfriends all looked at Charlotte and Ian a little too closely for her comfort at the moment. *Back off, girls. We're nowhere near ready for wedding cake yet. If ever.*

"I imagine quite a few of us in town have revised our wedding dreams since the ballroom became available for use," Cassidy sighed wistfully. "After Anthony and Kay's wedding, I actually swapped a picture of this ballroom for the one I had of Garden Ridge on my wedding vision board."

Hearing Cassidy talk about a wedding vision board made Charlotte feel a little better about still having her wedding book from her freshman year of high school.

"Yeah, I put one of their wedding pictures in my wedding book, too," Kayla admitted, nodding along.

"Is that why you had your wedding book out the first time your mom showed me around your house?" Cait looked over at Charlotte with an inquisitive expression.

"Nah-no," Charlotte stuttered, not wanting to admit having gotten it out to look through after meeting Ian because of wanting to see if she could picture him in the groom role in her mind. "I was going through some boxes from the attic, looking for some old family letters with Tia, and ran across that silly book from when I was in high school. I looked through it to reminisce, but I didn't change anything in it."

But only because I didn't have any hard copies of Anthony and Kay's wedding pictures to add the ballroom to my reception section.

Her wedding plan book didn't actually have any pictures of a reception venue, just the cakes, flowers, and other decorations she'd chosen as a teenager. She'd actually thought her reception would be held in the fellowship hall at the church, like the other weddings she'd seen in Heart's Destiny as a kid.

"Oh? Nothing in your wedding book that you want to change now that your tastes have matured since high school?" Cassidy arched a brow at Char. "That's why I switched mine to a corkboard, so I can swap things around on it whenever I see something I like better than what I had up there. Since what I picked as a teenager in home economics no longer reflects my sense of style, it's a lot easier to swap pictures if they aren't glued into a book."

Charlotte tilted her head as she thought about the things in her wedding book. She pictured the strapless gown with an almost bustier style bodice. The pearl buttons up the back made it seem classier than the corset it was styled after, even with the lace overlay on just the bodice of the gown to show off the corselette style.

No, I absolutely still want to wear that dress on my wedding day.

She thought of the navy-blue tuxedos she had picked out and cringed slightly at the realization that they were similar to the ones her brothers had picked up earlier that week for Bobby and Brooklyn's wedding. *But I did have a different style of shirt and tie picked out for the guys than what Bobby and Brooklyn picked, so maybe nobody would notice that we have practically identical tastes in tuxedos. And if nothing else, at least they are a classic style that shows we have decent fashion sense.*

Besides that, the navy-blue was the only option to have the tuxedos semi-match the bridesmaids' dresses she picked out. Unless she wanted her groom and his groomsmen to wear the brighter, royal blue tuxes like Anthony and Kay had the Hunters wear in their wedding.

No, definitely the navy-blue. I can't see serious Ian wearing a royal blue tux to get married. Especially since the navy-blue suit he's wearing tonight is extremely similar to the tux I'd want him in for our wedding. Shocked at how easily she'd slipped into casting Ian as her groom in her fictional future wedding, Charlotte quickly went back to thinking about the other things she'd picked out as a teenager.

The dresses she'd picked for her bridesmaids were navy-blue from the sleeveless shoulders down across the v-neckline and through the waist, then the asymmetrical skirts had an ombre effect that lightened to as close to her favorite shade of azure blue at the hem as she could find in a bridesmaid's dress.

I suppose I could check to see if the dress designers have updated their color choices in the last fourteen years to pick different dresses for my bridesmaids. But having so many shades of blue in the dresses opened up so many more options for flowers in the bouquets and reception centerpieces.

"No, I think the selections I made as a teenager are pretty classic," Charlotte finally answered her friend with a small side-to-side movement of her head. "Or at least, they are still in style. Not that I'll need to see if they're still available anytime soon."

"Oh, yeah, they're definitely still in style," Cait giggled. "At least the clothing options Hazel took pictures of with her phone are still available through the dress shop, where she texted the pictures, anyway."

"Char, you might want to check with Louella to make sure your mom hasn't already ordered your wedding attire," Lexi chuckled.

"No, I'm sure she hasn't ordered anything yet," Kara commented with a slight grin. "She was just checking with everyone to see if your first choices were still available. Or in my case with the cake, if I could do the delicate design work you have picked out."

"Geez, how many pictures did she take of the things in that book from freshman home economics?" Charlotte rolled her eyes as she thought of her mother already planning her wedding.

"Oh, she took pictures of every page," Cait proclaimed, causing a round of laughter around the table.

"Look on the bright side, Princess," Ian taunted with a chuckle. "When it comes time for your wedding, you won't have to do anything but pick a date and go be fitted for the dress. Your mom will take care of everything else, so you don't have to worry about a thing not being perfect."

"Keep laughing," Charlotte glowered at Ian. "If she has her way, while I'm having the dress fitted, you'll be next door being measured for the tux."

She wasn't quite sure how to interpret the expression on Ian's face. *Is that trepidation? Maybe a little wariness? But there's something else there in his eyes, too. Is that wistfulness? No, more like hope.*

Fuck! We'd better change the subject before I end up engaged without seeing the love I need to see in his eyes first.

~~~

Ian spent most of the evening enjoying listening in on the conversation around the table between Charlotte, Cait, Kara, and their three friends. He recognized Kara from his trips to the bakery, but he hadn't met Cassidy, Lexi, or Kayla before that night, which was rather remarkable in a town the size of Heart's Destiny.

But then again, the only times he really socialized since he moved to town were at the Burleson Ranch or the middle school. Since the ladies in question were single, didn't work at the school, and had no children to drop off or pick up at the middle school, he had no reason to have met them there. Since they were friends with the Burlesons, they could have been at one of the birthday parties on the ranch. But the Burleson birthday parties were so crammed with people that he couldn't be sure if they'd attended or not, especially the one the previous Sunday for Jake and Josh.

As Ian looked across the room at the two Burleson men that he felt like he'd become the closest friends with over the last few months, who were being pulled onto the dance floor by the bridesmaids they were escorting down the aisle the next day, Ian wondered whom Charlotte would pair up with them as bridesmaids in the wedding he pictured when the ladies were discussing their wedding planning books earlier. He had to smile as he remembered how quickly Charlotte had changed the subject to whether or not there were any hidden passages in the restored B and B building her youngest brother had claimed was haunted when they were kids.

Even as the conversation turned to wanting to explore the building and whether or not the Walkers would know if there were any secret rooms or passages, since they'd done the restoration, Ian had continued to imagine marrying Charlotte. He wondered what all she'd picked out as a teenaged girl and how likely Hazel Burleson would be to share the pictures she'd taken of Charlotte's wedding planning book with him if he asked her about them.
~~~

Ian hadn't ever thought much about wedding planning or having an elaborate celebration the way the Burlesons seemed to plan weddings and other events. With his family being down to just him and Caitir, and Mari not having any close family in the area, his first wedding had been a simple courthouse ceremony with a cake from the grocery store at their apartment when they got home.

With it being summer in San Diego, he hadn't even worn a suitcoat, much less a tux. He'd worn black slacks, a white button-down, and a yellow tie to match Mari's yellow sundress to make it seem like they'd at least dressed up for their wedding. But they'd picked clothes from their closet instead of going shopping for wedding attire.

Caitir and Trent had attended as their witnesses, but they didn't really act as either a maid of honor or best man. After the ceremony, they'd only stayed at Ian and Mari's apartment long enough to eat a piece of cake and say "congratulations" before leaving the newlyweds to honeymoon at home.

Ian couldn't fathom having a similar wedding with Charlotte. No, he pictured the tuxedos, formal dresses, and lots of flowers for the day he married Charlotte. He pictured Charlotte in a long, princess-style, white dress with her hair pulled up in one of those fancy styles women did for weddings in movies.

He envisioned both the church for the ceremony, and the ballroom of the bed and breakfast for the reception, decorated in her favorite shade of azure blue and bridal white. He didn't know what kind of flowers they'd have to match that color scheme, but he imagined them on every table.

After Kara mentioned delicate design work on the picture of Charlotte's dream wedding cake earlier, he'd envisaged a multi-tier cake with a blue base frosting color with thin lines of white frosting making up Charlotte's chosen pattern over the top of it. He imagined it would take at least seven layers of cake to feed everyone in Heart's Destiny who would want to attend the Burleson-Campbell wedding.

Thinking of their wedding in those terms, Ian had started to speculate whether or not Charlotte would want to hyphenate her name. As much as he would want her to take his last name, he could see why she would want to retain the Burleson name. Between the family legacy they had in town and the vast holdings of Burleson

Incorporated, he knew she'd want to maintain that link between her and the rest of her family.

Hell, she'll probably want me to change my name to Burleson, Ian inwardly chortled. *But maybe I can talk her into both of us, and our kids, hyphenating as the Burleson-Campbell family.*

"What's so funny?" Charlotte leaned in close to whisper the question, bringing Ian back to the moment.

Ian looked around to realize they were the last two at the table with everyone else, including Caitir and Brody, out on the dance floor. *Damn, I can't believe I was so into daydreaming about marrying Charlotte that I haven't even asked her to dance yet.*

Although, maybe I should take advantage of the fact that Caitir and Brody are occupied at the moment to get her alone for some private dancing, where I can touch her a little more than I can on the dance floor in front of her whole family.

"I was just thinking that maybe we should go looking for those secret passages while everyone else is dancing," Ian smirked and extended his hand to Charlotte in invitation as he stood from his seat. "What do you say, Princess? Want to find someplace we can *dance* with maybe a little less clothing?"

Charlotte's emerald and gold eyes went wide at his innuendo. "I don't know where we can find a place private enough to lose any clothing," she purred, taking his hand to allow him to pull her up from her seat and out of the ballroom. "But maybe we can find someplace private enough we can at least move it out of the way to *dance*. But we probably can't stay gone longer than a song or two before people start to notice."

"Well, considering you've made me wait for six weeks, I'm sure I can make it a quickie," he teased as they made their way down a deserted hallway in the opposite direction of the kitchen and dining room, which he remembered from his stay at the B and B at the end of December.

"Who said I've made you wait? Maybe you should have made a move to realize I was waiting on you," Charlotte bantered back flirtily.

It wasn't that Ian hadn't wanted to make a move on Charlotte in the last six weeks. It was more that he'd felt like he had to atone for his lapse of good judgment in February before he could earn another chance to be with her. But he wasn't about to argue the point when he was about to finally be with her again.

"My bad," Ian grinned, holding his free hand up in surrender as they ducked out of the hallway into an empty parlor on the opposite end of the building from the ballroom. "Let me rectify that right now."

Ian quickly shut the door before spinning Charlotte back against it and dipping his head to cover her lips with his. As always, their kiss swiftly turned passionate, both of them exploring the other's mouths with their tongues, as if they'd forgotten the familiar terrain after so much time apart.

Ian couldn't keep his hands off Charlotte, gripping her ass to lift her up. She wrapped her arms around his shoulders and her legs around his waist as he ground his rock-hard cock against her pussy. Neither of them cared about how they were wrinkling their professional attire as they clawed at the garments to get as close as possible to one another.

Ian took advantage of the door behind her, assisting him in holding Charlotte up, to move his hands from her ass to push the navy-blue pencil skirt she was wearing up even further than it had already ridden up for her to get her legs around him. As he was trying to get to her pussy, she was unbuttoning his blazer and pushing it out of the way, so she could unfasten his pants.

"No time for foreplay," she growled when he teased her clit through her silky, light blue panties. "Inside me. Now!"

"Yes, ma'am," Ian acquiesced, ripping her panties out of his way at the same time she freed his cock from the confines of his slacks and boxer briefs. "But first, condom."

He shifted his hold on her to cradle her now bare ass in one hand and shoved her torn panties in his jacket pocket with the other. He then pulled his wallet out of his pants pocket to get out the condoms he'd bought and stashed there after his faux pas of forgetting one in February.

Charlotte took the gold-foil wrapper out of his wallet and opened it while Ian put his wallet back in his pocket. She deftly opened the package and rolled the condom down his length, as Ian slipped his fingers through her dripping wet folds to make sure she was ready to take him.

"God, you're soaked, Charlotte," Ian groaned as he slid two fingers inside her to open her up for his dick. "Is it this position you like? Or the semi-public location where we could get caught?"

"Both," Charlotte breathed out the word as she lined his cock up with her slit. "Now move your fingers and fuck me already."

"Bossy," Ian bantered as he removed his fingers from her tight cunt and took hold of his dick to tease her with the head. "I'm torn between obeying because I like it when you're bossy once in a while, or swatting your ass for telling me what to do when we both know you prefer me being in charge when we fuck."

"Why choose when you can do both?" Charlotte leaned in and nipped his bottom lip as she tried to wiggle down on his cock.

"Excellent point," Ian agreed, their lips brushing over one another as he gradually pushed forward into her and moved his hand out from between them to lightly swat her hip.

Charlotte moaned as her arms wrapped around his shoulders once again. Ian swallowed her sounds, kissing her ardently as he made love to her against the door. He wanted to go hard and fast, but was afraid the banging against the door would alert someone of their indiscretion.

Besides, he wanted to savor the feeling of being inside her again, and going slowly made him feel like he was showing her how he felt about her, even though they hadn't had a chance to talk about their feelings yet. He wanted to be all in with her. Hell, he felt like he was already all in with her. But he knew she needed time to come to terms with the danger he'd inadvertently put her in by falling for her so fast and to figure out what she felt for him before she'd be ready to discuss their future. So, he wanted to show her his love in every way he could possibly show it, and would wait for her to be ready to hear those three little words.

"More, Ian. Harder," Charlotte moaned, pulling her lips from his to trail them down his neck. "You've got to make this a quickie. Remember?"

"Don't want to make too much noise and get caught," Ian murmured against her throat, continuing to stroke in and out of her leisurely, as his hands roamed her body from her ass to her tits. He teased her nipples through her blouse and bra, wishing they could be skin to skin, so he could suckle her breasts to take her over the edge.

"But if you take too much time, we're going to get caught anyway," Charlotte breathed out as she delicately nipped his earlobe. "And we absolutely can't get caught."

"Fine, you want it hard and fast, then that's what I'll give you," Ian growled as he gripped her hips and lifted her off his dick. As soon as he pulled out, he put her down on her feet and spun her around as he took a step back. "Bend over. And hold that door closed without letting it bang in the frame while I bang you from behind."

Charlotte did as Ian instructed, obeying him beautifully. He pushed her skirt the rest of the way up to her waist, so he could see her gorgeous ass and watch as he fucked her tight, wet pussy.

"Oh, Ian," Charlotte cried out softly, as Ian gripped her hips and went balls-deep in one powerful thrust.

"Fuck, Charlotte," Ian grunted as he pulled halfway out before plunging back in. He increased his rhythm as his lizard brain took over control of his bodily movements, causing him to rut into her harder and faster with each stroke. His only thought as he continued to pound his cock into her pussy was the word he didn't even realize he was chanting aloud. "Mine! Mine! Mine!"

"All yours, Ian," Charlotte confirmed as her inner walls clamped down on his dick when she came. "And you're all mine!"

"Fuck, yes, Charlotte!" Ian shoved in as deep as he could go and let her orgasm milk his from him. Not that he could pull out or fight the climax when her cunt clutched him like a vise with each wave of her release.

He felt slightly lightheaded as the aftershocks incessantly washed over him for several long minutes. Recognizing he wasn't alone in that feeling, he finally pulled out, wrapped an arm around Charlotte's midsection, and drew her over to a sofa for them both to collapse on it.

They sat there catching their breath for a few moments before Charlotte stood and adjusted her skirt back into place. Ian removed the condom, tied it off, and straightened his own clothing as Charlotte looked around the room.

"Looking for these?" Ian pulled her ripped panties from his coat pocket.

"Yes, though I guess I can't really put those back on." Charlotte shook her head. "You really need to stop ruining my panties."

"Maybe you just need to quit wearing panties, so I have easier access," Ian taunted playfully.

Charlotte rolled her eyes at him. "Please dispose of them when you dispose of the condom, so there's no evidence of what we've been doing in here." She flounced toward the door, trying to leave without him.

"Hey, where are you going?" Ian rushed to catch up, hiding the evidence of their quick copulation in his coat pocket until he could get to a men's room to toss the condom. "Wait on me, Princess."

"No," Charlotte hissed, giving him a wide-eyed look of mortification. "If we walk back in there together, then everyone will know what we've been doing. It's bad enough I have to try not to let on that I'm no longer wearing my panties. I'm not going to make things worse by giving my mom a reason to gloat about her matchmaking schemes working."

She turned on her heel and stomped out of the room. Ian held back, giving her the space she wanted to make their separate entrances back into the party.

"She should probably not stomp in there all pissy either," he chuckled. "But damn, she's sexy as fuck when her attitude shows like that."

~~~

Saturday, April 6, 2019

Ian was surprised at how much fun he was having at Bobby and Brooklyn's wedding reception. After getting distracted at the rehearsal dinner and not participating much in the conversations going on at their table, he was afraid the actual wedding day would be an extended repeat of his fantasies about marrying Charlotte. While he had pictured his and Charlotte's wedding during the actual ceremony, having a couple more guys at the table during the reception seemed to help him stay in the moment throughout the reception.

Though I'm not really sure what Hazel was thinking in seating the two youngest of the Walkers between Cait, Kara, and Summer, who are all obviously more mature than Hayden or Hudson. They don't
~~~

seem to have any common interests to make them compatible, much less good candidates for her matchmaking.

Ian had recognized Summer Deere when she sat down at the table because of meeting her when he'd taken Brody into the clinic in town, where she worked as a nurse, for his vaccinations right after they moved to town. He had also briefly met Hayden and Hudson Walker at one of the Burleson birthday parties he'd attended. They were all nice and friendly, just like everyone else he'd met in Heart's Destiny. But Hazel was nowhere near hitting her mark if seating them together was part of her matchmaking plans.

As the Walkers talked about a car show that was coming to town the following weekend and a rodeo the weekend after that, Ian could see the eyes of the women at the table glassing over. He had to wonder if that was part of the reason they were seated at the same table with him and Charlotte. To make him seem more appealing to Charlotte since he was more mature, worked in the same field, and had more chemistry with her than the two younger men.

When Summer mentioned hearing about Ian from her brother, Ryder, the middle school physical education teacher, and started low-key flirting with Ian, he noticed a brief flare of jealousy in Charlotte's eyes. *Huh? Maybe they aren't here to be matched with each other. Maybe Hazel knows what she's doing to get Charlotte to quit trying to hide our relationship after all.*

Ian had to admit, even if it was only to himself, that he was more than a little irritated by Charlotte refusing to even talk to him about their relationship. Yeah, he understood that they couldn't have a deep discussion about their future together when they were constantly surrounded by other people, most of whom she was related to in one way or another. But her constant denial of them being anything more than friends and work colleagues was really starting to wear on him.

We were way more than that when I was balls-deep inside her yesterday, he mentally grumbled while only half listening to the speeches going on after dinner. *Hell, if Bobby and Brooklyn had taken much longer to show up for the reception, we'd have been heading for a repeat performance in that parlor, just so I could prove her introduction of me wrong earlier.*

And the next time I fuck her, I need to explain what I mean when I'm calling her "mine," so she gets that it's more than as friends.

Thinking about fucking Charlotte again distracted Ian enough that he missed the announcement that caused all the ladies at the table to stand and walk over to the dance floor. Though the sway of Charlotte's hips as she walked away from the table quickly drew his attention back to the moment. Yeah, he might not want her to ever leave his side, but he sure enjoyed watching her perfect ass in her form-fitting azure blue sheath dress as she walked away.

"What are they doin', Dad?" Brody moved over into the seat Charlotte had vacated and tugged on Ian's sleeve.

"The bride is about to toss her bouquet," Ian explained, picking his son up and holding him on his arm, so the little boy could see over the other wedding guests. "And the single women are all trying to catch it."

"Why is Brook throwing her flowers? And why do the other ladies want to catch them? Shouldn't they get a ball to play catch?"

"It's a wedding tradition," Ian chuckled at his son's confusion. "Whoever catches the bouquet is supposed to be the next woman to get married."

"Who is she gonna marry?"

"Whoever catches the garter, I suppose."

"What's a garter?"

Damn, how do I explain garters to my four-year-old?

"It's something brides wear during the wedding," Ian finally replied as he watched the bouquet sail straight into Charlotte's arms. "And the groom tosses it after the bride tosses the bouquet for the men to try to catch it."

"Can I catch the garter? You know I'm a good catcher and I want to marry Char when I grow up, so I need to catch the garter since she caught the flowers."

"I think you might be a bit too young to start planning your wedding," Ian chuckled. "But you can help me catch it if you want."

"Then you get to marry Char?" Brody looked at Ian thoughtfully as Ian joined the rest of the men walking onto the dance floor with his son still seated on the crook of his arm.

"I sure hope so," Ian said wistfully.

"Okay, since I'm not old enough to marry her yet, I'll help you be the one to marry her now. And I'll wait to catch the garter when Maria catches the flowers, so she can't tell me I'm too young to marry her anymore."

"Dude, don't let Anthony hear you say you want to marry Maria," Josh chuckled as the single groomsmen joined the rest of the men on the dance floor.

"Naw, it'll be funny watching him figure out how to keep Brody and Maria from being kissin' cousins," Jake snorted.

"What are cousins?" Ian was glad his son was distracted by asking about cousins while Bobby practically crawled under the skirt of Brooklyn's full wedding gown and a few of the men on the other side of the dance floor made lewd comments.

"Cousins are your parent's brother's or sister's kids. So, when your Aunt Cait has kids, they'll be your cousins," Jake explained before Ian could. "And when your dad marries Char and she becomes your mom, then all our kids will be your cousins, including Tia and Maria."

"Oh, okay." Brody apparently didn't grasp the possibility of becoming legally related to Maria and unable to marry her. But Ian wasn't about to enlighten his son at that moment.

Bobby finally crawled out from under Brooklyn's wedding dress, whispered something to his new bride that made her blush, and gave her a peck of a kiss before standing up and turning toward the men on the dance floor. He surveyed the scene before looking at Ian and nodding.

Ian wasn't sure if Bobby was aiming for him or Brody, but the navy-blue garter shot straight at them, making it an easy catch for Ian when Brody fumbled it.

"I wonder what Ma had to do to convince Bobby to rig that," Josh quipped as the other men walked away for Ian and Charlotte to pose for pictures with the garter and bouquet.

Ian sat Brody down beside him, so he could follow the photographer's instructions.

"Oh, no, Daddy!" The photographer, who introduced himself as Philippe, wagged his finger at Ian. "You bring that boy with you. Half the people in here got baby fever from seeing him assist you in catching the garter, so we have to include him in the pictures."

Brody wrinkled his nose and furrowed his brow, obviously confused by Philippe's statement, but not wanting to ask about it since he'd just met Philippe. Finally, he tugged on Ian's jacket sleeve to get him to squat down to his level before whispering to his dad, "How'd they get a fever from me dropping the garter in your hand? Fevers are bad, and I don't want to keep doing something to make people sick."

"No, it's not that kind of fever," Ian chuckled. "He just means that seeing you being your adorable self makes some people want to have kids like you. He just called it baby fever because they want to have babies who grow up to be like you."

"So, they're not sick with a fever?" Brody still looked confused.

"No, they aren't sick. They just want cute kids of their own." Ian stood when his son finally seemed satisfied with his answer.

Philippe had Charlotte sit down in the chair Brooklyn had been seated in for Bobby to remove the garter. Then he directed Ian and Brody to each go down on one knee in front of her to present the garter to her together.

"Oh, I hope that new baby doctor is prepared for all the immaculate conceptions that just took place from seeing this," someone in the audience shouted. Ian thought it sounded like one of the Walkers, but he couldn't be sure with such a big crowd.

"Dude, the girls might have all just ovulated, but I don't think they can actually get pregnant without…" another man argued before he was cut off by a feminine shout of "enough!" and a roar of laughter from the rest of the crowd.

Ian had to stifle a chuckle of his own as he watched Charlotte roll her eyes at the commotion.

"Oh, come on, Char," Philippe scolded impishly. "Don't ruin my shot by rolling your eyes at that, when we both know you were among the ovulators."

"Philippe!" Charlotte screeched in shock.

"What?" Philippe shrugged. "You know Nico and I would have both joined you if we had that equipment. As it is, I'm going to have to hope showing our surrogate these pictures will speed up our baby-making process."

"What are they talkin' about, Dad?"

"Something you don't need to know about until you're older," Ian chortled as Philippe instructed them all to smile once more.

"We should have just left Ian out of these pictures," Charlotte grumbled as Philippe directed them to change poses to make it look like she was trying to decide between Ian and Brody. "Since Brody's the one who actually caught the garter to be my future groom."

"But Dad said I'm not old enough to marry you yet, so he's gonna marry you first, so you can get married next."

"Actually, Kay's sister, Randi, is going to be the next woman I know to get married," Charlotte disagreed, shaking her head. "So, I guess I'll get a do-over on finding my future groom at her wedding."

"You don't need a do-over," Ian growled without thinking.

"You're right, I don't," Charlotte smirked as she pulled her hand from Ian's. "I'll just wait for Brody to grow up and marry me."

Philippe continued to snap picture after picture, as Charlotte turned her back on Ian and leaned down to kiss Brody on the cheek, making it look like she'd chosen his son over him.

Cute, Princess. Real cute. Ian played up the jilted lover role for the camera and hoped his real feelings of rejection weren't obvious to anyone else. *You can keep running and wanting to hide what's happening between us for now. But I'm not giving up on winning you over. It may take longer than I want it to, but you will be my wife, eventually.*

Chapter Seventeen

Monday, April 8, 2019

Charlotte had to turn the last hour of softball practice over to her assistant coach, so she could drive over to the Heart's Destiny Clinic in the middle of town for her first appointment with the new OB-GYN. She felt a little bad about leaving Carrie with all the clean-up tasks at the end of practice. But with what seemed like every woman in town clamoring to get an appointment with the new doctor, Charlotte hadn't been able to pick the time and day for hers.

So, regardless of whether Carrie wanted to take over or not, Charlotte had to leave at four o'clock. *If she complains about it to Lisa to try to get our assignments changed, I'll just remind everyone of the hour I had to handle alone on the first day of tryouts and how much easier it is to deal with an hour of practice with just our team than it was to deal with that mob scene.*

She made the announcement to the team and waved goodbye to Carrie from across the field, not giving her another chance to bitch about it right then. Char didn't bother going to the fieldhouse to change, knowing she only had fifteen minutes to make it to her appointment. With it only being a couple of miles between the parking lot at the sports complex on Brahman, over to the clinic at the corner of Mustang and Angus, she knew it would take her about the same amount of time to walk to her car in the parking lot as it would take her to drive to the clinic. And she fully expected to be at the clinic with at least five minutes to spare before her appointment.

As she walked to her car, she devised the questions she wanted to ask her new doctor. While she and Ian hadn't had much alone time to discuss their relationship over the weekend, she did think it would probably be in their best interest for her to look into her birth control options. Even if Ian was ready for them to become an exclusive couple, she wanted to wait until after getting married to have babies.

She may have had a serious case of baby fever, but she didn't really want to make the decision to have a child unilaterally. She wanted to talk to her spouse and plan out the timing of their children. That meant she needed to know what birth control options were effective, yet easily reversible, just in case their relationship moved at Heart's Destiny speed, and they got to the talking-about-marriage-and-babies stage sooner than she expected.

She was so distracted thinking about the questions she needed to ask Dr. Magnum that she didn't realize someone was coming up behind her as she put her gear bag in the back of her Equinox. She had just dropped the bag and didn't even have the chance to shut the hatch before she was grabbed from behind.

Charlotte tried to fight off her attacker, but he was both bigger and stronger than she was, so it was a mostly futile effort. With only one big, tan arm banded around her, she thought she might have a chance to get away by elbowing him and running. But as soon as he used his other hand to put a bag over her head, he had both arms around her and lifted her clean off the ground.

She screamed for help at the top of her lungs, hoping the dark, canvas hood didn't muffle the sound too much to be heard. She continued to kick, flail, and scream, hoping someone would see what was going on and call for help.

Dear Lord, please don't let any of my softball girls try to come rescue me themselves! Surely, they're smart enough to know to call nine-one-one and not intervene to put themselves in danger, too.

"Knock it off, bitch," her attacker growled in her ear as he walked away from her vehicle.

That's good. Maybe someone will notice the back hatch open and call it in, even if they didn't see him grab me.

She didn't recognize his voice, but she hadn't ever heard Roberto lower his voice to a menacing growl to know for sure it wasn't him. But even if it wasn't Roberto himself, she knew her kidnapper was somehow associated with Roberto Rodriguez.

Less than a minute later, she was tossed unceremoniously into the back of a vehicle. She barely got her hands out in front of her to keep from face-planting on the carpet that was either in the back of an SUV or a car trunk. Her assailant quickly grabbed her and flipped her onto her back, so he could slap a pair of handcuffs on her wrists before slamming the trunk closed.

Idiot! He must not be an experienced kidnapper, or else he'd know better than to leave my hands in front where I can still feel around my surroundings. And hopefully, get my phone out of my pocket and this hood off my head, so I can see to call for help myself.

She scarcely lifted her hands to feel the trunk lid less than a foot above her. She felt more than heard one of the car doors slam before the engine revved and she slid across the carpet with the movement of the vehicle peeling out.

Think Char! At least, now I know where I am in the trunk. With the way he took off, I have to be right at the back to be able to find the emergency latch and possibly make a scene, even if it's not safe to jump out of the trunk of a moving vehicle to make an escape. She felt around the space, at least what she could reach between her waist and the few inches above her head to the sidewall, but couldn't find anything that could be the emergency trunk release all cars are supposed to be equipped with. *Shouldn't there be a trunk release here somewhere? I mean, even if they cut it out trying to disable it, I should feel the wire to try to pull it. Right?*

When her efforts to find the emergency trunk release proved to be futile, she started to try to maneuver her hands into her pocket to pull out her phone when she remembered it was in the pocket of her warm-up jacket. The warm-up jacket that was laying over the top of her gear bag in the back of her vehicle back at the ball field.

Shit! Now what do I do? She took a couple of deep breaths. *Stay calm. First and foremost, freaking out won't do me any good right now.*

She lifted her joined hands up to her face, trying to figure out what was going on with the cloth bag and whether or not she could remove it.

Although, maybe I shouldn't take it off. As of right now, I haven't seen his face to be able to identify him. But if I remove this hood, I'll see him as soon as he opens the trunk again. While it would be good to be able to identify him in a lineup, being able to identify him will give him even more reason to not let me live to tell anyone who he is and what he's done.

She lowered her hands away from the cloth covering her face, settling them to rest over the charms on her necklace. It was probably silly, but she needed to feel the charms, to feel her connection to Ian, as she thought about the best way to get out of this predicament.

No, I need to be smart about this. Stay calm. Don't remove the bag, keeping me blinded. And once we get to wherever he's taking me, I have to continue being calm, so I don't give him any other reason to kill me.

She absentmindedly ran her fingers over the individual charms, self-soothing by remembering when he gave her each and every one of them. She started with tracing the letter C embossed on the disc that hung in the center of the other eight charms and laid just below the top of her sternum before moving over to feel the open book beside it. But it was the feel of the horse charm on the other side of the book charm that triggered her brain to come up with an idea for how to ensure her safety in this precarious situation.

Hell, I'm a Burleson! I need to point that out and use it to my advantage. Even if Roberto is behind this, I'm sure he'd rather have the money my family would pay in ransom for me than just taunting Ian by hurting me.

Charlotte lost track of time as she laid in the trunk of the strange car, plotting how to behave when they made it to their destination in order to get the best possible outcome at the end of the day. She tried to focus only on what she needed to do to make things go her way, blocking out the horrible possibilities that could happen if she was kidnapped to be trafficked instead of for ransom.

She knew it was naïve to think those things couldn't happen to her, but acknowledging the possibilities was all she was capable of without freaking out right then. And she knew freaking out about the possibility of being raped and beaten would only increase her chances of screwing things up and not getting out of this horrendous mess alive.

Getting home to Ian and my family is all that matters. We can deal with whatever I have to endure during this ordeal later, once I'm safely in Ian's arms again. She continued rubbing her fingers over the charms Ian had given her, praying he could somehow feel their connection to be able to find her. And knowing he'd come to her rescue if there was any way he possibly could.

Leah Mae Wright

Maybe I should have thought to ask Ian to come to the doctor with me, so he could have kept this from happening. Not that we're really at the point in our relationship to go to doctor's appointments together, but at least I wouldn't have missed this one if Ian had been with me.

<p style="text-align:center">~~~</p>

Ian took the long way home after staying late at school to chaperone a study group, when two of his sixth-grade students flagged him down as he was passing the ball fields on Rogers Road. Considering the ball fields were in the opposite direction from the middle school as the Burleson Ranch, where he and his family were currently staying, he figured it was pretty obvious that he was looking for Charlotte as he drove by to check on her since she wouldn't let him shadow her at practice in his role as her bodyguard. So, he wasn't surprised when the girls on her softball team flagged him down, probably to tell him where to find their coach.

Ian pulled over to the side of the road just before he got to Clydesdale and shifted his Range Rover into park. He subconsciously remembered to turn it off and grab his keys before getting out to see what Sage and Bristol were so excited about. "Hey, girls, what's up?"

"Mr. Campbell!" Both girls screamed in unison as they ran up to him.

"You have to help Ms. Burleson!" Bristol shouted.

"What happened to Ms. Burleson?" Ian looked around to see if he could spot Charlotte to figure out why she needed help.

"That creepy guy grabbed her!" Sage screeched.

"Fuck!" Ian cursed without thinking, pulling out his phone to pull up a picture of Roberto Rodriguez to verify his worst fear. "Is this the creepy guy?"

"Yes," Sage nodded at the same time Bristol pointed at Roberto's photo on Ian's phone and shouted, "that's him!"

Fuck! Fuck! Fuck! Ian barely stopped himself from cursing aloud again, looking around for the girls' parents as he swiped away the photo, pulled up Bobby Burleson's contact info, and hoped the police chief was back in town from his short honeymoon. "Where are your parents?" Ian asked the girls as he punched the call button and lifted the phone to his ear.

"My mom's in the car over there waiting for us." Bristol pointed in the direction of the parking lot off of Brahman on the other side of the fields.

"What's up, Campbell?" Bobby asked over the phone as Ian directed the girls to walk with him toward the softball field, where the rest of their teammates were still congregated, and the parking lot on the other side of the field where Bristol's mom waited in her car.

"Rojo kidnapped Charlotte. I don't have details yet, but I have a positive I.D. from two witnesses." The girls jogged along beside Ian as he walked briskly across the ball field in the direction of the parking lot.

"Fuck!" Bobby cursed. "Where are you? Where was she taken from?"

"The ball fields. I have to make sure the softball players are secure before I can follow, but you might want to get here and bring backup." Ian didn't wait for Bobby to confirm he was on his way before he disconnected the call and pocketed his phone.

As they got halfway across the field, Ian realized the rest of the team was still there for practice, so he whistled to get their attention, along with that of their assistant coach, Carrie Adkisson, who was trying futilely to get the rowdy bunch under control. "Huddle up, girls!"

"Oh, Ian, thank goodness you're here," Carrie blurted as she ran up to where the softball team had started to surround him. "Char had to go to the doctor, and I've had a terrible time keeping the team on task..."

She didn't get a chance to finish whatever she was about to say as the girls all started shouting over her.

"He put a bag over her head..."

"He carried her off..."

"...put her in the trunk..."

Ian couldn't catch everything that was being shouted as the whole team started trying to recount the events they'd just witnessed. He held up a hand in the universal sign for stop, so he could get them to speak one at a time to be able to understand what was going on. "One at a time, please. Carrie, why don't you start telling me what happened?"

"I didn't see what happened because I was watching the girls practice," Carrie snapped, shaking her head. "Char had just left for her doctor's appointment when the girls started acting out and trying to run off the field. I've been trying to get them to calm down and continue practicing while one person tells me what happened, so I can call someone to help Char if she needs it."

"She needs it," Ian growled, irritated by Carrie's incompetence. "And I've already called Chief Burleson to get the police out here."

He turned his attention back to the team of girls around him. "Raise your hand if you actually saw what happened to Ms. Burleson."

Only half of the girls raised their hands. "Okay, those of you who didn't see anything, go with Ms. Adkisson to meet your parents. Practice is over for today."

He gave Carrie a pointed look as he instructed her. "While you're at the fieldhouse to release the girls to their parents, have any parents, whose children are still here to give a statement about what happened, meet us here on the field."

"Yeah, I can do that." Carrie nodded as she led the girls, who hadn't seen what happened, over to the fieldhouse.

He was just about to start asking questions to see if any of the girls could identify the vehicle Charlotte had apparently been carried off to when he saw the flashing lights of the police cruisers showing up on site. He waved Bobby over from the parking lot on Brahman as soon as he saw him get out of his official vehicle.

Bobby pointed the other two officers, who had pulled in right behind him, in the direction of Charlotte's Equinox, which Ian now realized was parked in the lot with the back hatch still open, before jogging over to the field where Ian was standing with the girls who'd witnessed the abduction. "Catch me up, Campbell!"

"These are the girls who witnessed what happened." Ian motioned to the remaining team members, who were nervously fidgeting around him. "I was just about to start asking about what they saw and which direction the vehicle went when I saw you. Figured I should probably wait for you and maybe their parents, who are now on their way over here, before getting too far with that. Are your brothers and cousins on the way?"

"Yeah, they should be here any minute," Bobby affirmed with a nod.

"Then I'm going to let you take over getting witness statements," Ian indicated to the girls around them. "And I'm going to go grab my laptop to pull up the tracker I hope Charlotte is still wearing."

Bobby started to nod in agreement before his expression turned to one of shock as he shouted, "Wait! You have a tracker on my sister?"

"Yeah," Ian called back as he jogged back over to his Range Rover.

He couldn't hear what Bobby said in response to finding out Ian was tracking Charlotte, but he didn't really care at that moment. He was too focused on pulling up his laptop and connecting to his vehicle's Wi-Fi hotspot to pick up the tracker's signal to worry about what Charlotte's brother thought of him tracking her whereabouts.

Just as he brought the program up to see the three dots on the map where Charlotte, Brody, and Caitir were at that moment, Jake, Josh, and their Avington cousins pulled up behind him, hopped out of their vehicles, and surrounded his driver's door.

"What are you doing on the computer when my sister was just kidnapped?" Josh growled the question angrily.

"Pulling up her location from the tracker in her necklace," Ian admitted, unable to pull his eyes from the green dot on the screen that was moving away from Heart's Destiny on the map.

"Damn, and ya'll called me a cyber stalker for accessing the traffic cams on the way over here," Jake quipped as he leaned in to look at Ian's screen. "I'm guessing, since the pink dot and blue dot are both on the ranch, Char's the green dot moving away from town on one-thirty-two."

"Yeah," was all Ian could say in response as the dot indicating Charlotte's location turned off the two-lane state highway into an area not marked as a road on the map used by the program. *Green to match the majority of the color of her eyes, since I couldn't select a green and gold dot.*

The Avingtons were talking about gearing up and making a plan to free Charlotte from her captors, while Ian and the Burlesons watched the tracker's movement slow down on the screen.

"That's all farmland out that way, isn't it?" Josh pointed to the area on the screen where Charlotte and her abductor appeared to be stopping.

"Yeah, let me grab my laptop and see if I can find the land records to get an idea of what we're going into out there." Jake turned and walked back to the truck he had pulled up in, just as Bobby walked up.

"I've got Dougie and Chase taking statements and processing Char's car, and Dusty, Jagger, and Gabe are on their way here to assist in going to rescue Char, if you have a location pinpointed." Bobby nodded toward Ian's computer.

"I've got an idea of a location." Ian handed his computer over to Bobby, thinking the top cop in town would know the area better than anyone else to know who might own the property in question, and have the best idea of how many entry points they would have available to do the rescue.

"Fuck! I should have thought to check there back in November," Bobby snapped before explaining. "That's the old Gruber farm. Mac Gruber died a few years back, and the place has been abandoned ever since. His kids moved out of state like twenty years ago and haven't ever come back to deal with selling the place."

"Any idea how many structures are on the premises that we'll have to search to find Char?" Josh asked his brother.

"Only two that I can find in the land records," Jake answered as he walked back over with his laptop in hand. "The house and a barn. But who knows what might have been added without a building permit?"

"Too bad we can't get permission to fly a drone over the place." Josh looked at Jake with what could only be described as a mischievous expression on his face.

"Bro, you know the drones I have on the ranch don't have near the capabilities of the ones I use for recon when sending in a SEAL team." Jake shook his head at his twin.

"They have cameras," Josh shrugged. "All we need is a visual of the structures we need to breach to make a plan."

"Don't we need a warrant to fly a drone over a private residence?" Ian wasn't sure about the FAA rules for using drones in police surveillance, but he was pretty sure a warrant would be required. Just like he knew Bobby would have to get a warrant for them to raid the farm and arrest the kidnapper.

"I'll add that to the request I'm taking to the judge while everyone else is gearing up," Bobby stated matter-of-factly before pointing at

Jake. "And I'm assuming that your license for flying Navy drones is valid in Texas."

"Of course," Jake smiled. "Hell, that FAA license is probably a lot more valid here than it is in the Middle East."

"Then let's all head over to the PD to finish up the paperwork and gear up while Jake goes back to the ranch to get his drones," Bobby directed.

They finalized the plan for raiding the farm and rescuing Charlotte while donning their Kevlar and weapons at the Heart's Destiny Police Department. Ian was astonished at how promptly Byron Avington had been able to get his company equipment moved from Georgia to Texas after hearing about the case. But while preparing to go on a raid they hadn't expected to have to complete, Ian was damn glad to have Avington Security on his side.

~~~

Char was doing the only yoga breathing exercise she could think of to slow her heart rate and keep herself calm, when the car she was riding in came to a stop and the engine turned off. Not that the slow, deep breathing did much when the trunk opened, and she was callously hoisted over the shoulder of her kidnapper.

She would have offered to walk wherever he wanted her to go, but the impact of his shoulder against her diaphragm knocked the wind out of her. So, she let her body go limp, trying to silently impart that she wasn't going to fight him again.

She listened intently, hoping to hear some kind of recognizable sound to get an idea of where he might have taken her. Unfortunately, there were no sounds of city traffic or other indicators that they were anywhere near civilization. She only heard nature sounds, like birds chirping and wind rustling nearby trees. Sounds she might hear on the ranch, minus the occasional horse neighing or barn cat meowing.

She heard the boards creak at the same time it felt like he was walking up a couple of steps. Then the screech of old hinges on a screen door opening. She recognized the hum of a fan as he moved through what she assumed was a farmhouse.
~~~

Leah Mae Wright

Great! Even if I could get my hands on a phone at some point to call for help, all I could say for sure is that I'm in a rural area. In Texas. Which would only narrow the search area down to about eighty percent of the land in the state.

She registered muffled voices, both male and female, as her captor carried her through what felt like a maze of hallways and staircases from her upside-down and blindfolded vantage point. When her kidnapper stopped walking, she heard the distinct sound of him unlocking a door before he took another dozen or so steps and callously dumped her off his shoulder. She wasn't sure what she landed on. It wasn't quite soft enough for a bed, but it wasn't as hard as a table either.

"Get her ready to see the boss later," her abductor ordered before stomping away and slamming the door.

Or was that someone else? His voice sounded a little different at the sports complex. Maybe the guy to get me out of the trunk wasn't the same one who actually grabbed me?

Char wasn't sure to whom he'd given the order, but since she heard the lock engage when the man left the room, she realized whoever it was that was supposed to "get her ready" was obviously locked in as well. She didn't have to wait long before the hood was removed, and she found herself in a room with four other women and a couple of children. One of which she recognized instantly.

"Antonio," Charlotte gasped, unable to hide her shock at seeing him, even though she'd already suspected Roberto was behind her kidnapping.

"Cha, Char," Antonio stuttered her name as he ran over to the ancient Army-green cot she was sprawled across and threw his arms around her.

She couldn't really hug him back with the handcuffs still on her wrists, but she pushed him back just enough to lift her arms out from between them and looped her arms over his head to return his hug the best she could. Charlotte twisted to sit up on the cot and adjusted Antonio to sit on her lap as he cried into her shoulder.

"He knows you," the woman who had removed the hood from Charlotte's head pointed out, waving her hand with the black canvas still clutched in it at the two of them embracing awkwardly and sobbing.

"Yes." Charlotte didn't elaborate further, focusing instead on trying to comfort Antonio as best she could while taking in her surroundings. The room was fairly large for an older farmhouse, with enough space for ten of the cots to fit without being too cramped together. The wallpaper was peeling and looked like it hadn't been replaced since the 1980s. And there appeared to be a doorway into a bathroom on the other side of the room.

I guess they converted the master bedroom into their dungeon for the women and children they abduct?

"He hasn't said a word in the month or so he's been here. We were getting worried that he wouldn't acclimate to earn any privileges like the rest of us."

"Privileges?" Charlotte looked over the only woman in the room who had spoken to her since her arrival, noting how she looked cleaner and more put together than the other three women who were watching her warily.

"Yes, better clothes, more food. Things like that have to be earned around here. And the boy can't earn them when he can't talk or do the chores he's assigned."

"He's five," Char barked indignantly. "The only chore he should be assigned is to pick up his toys when he's done playing with them."

"Quiet down or you're gonna make things worse for all of us," the woman hissed, holding up her hands in a placating gesture. "Look, I agree with you. The kids should be able to go outside and play and not have real chores. But I learned early on that all fighting with these guys will do is earn me a beating. So, now I do as I'm told and keep my mouth shut. And I suggest you do the same. It'll be safer for both you and the kid. Now, you need to go to the bathroom and wash your face and hands. The boss will be sending someone to get you for orientation soon."

Charlotte wasn't sure what orientation entailed, but she was more concerned with taking care of Antonio than preparing for it. She held him and comforted him as best she could until his sobbing subsided. Once he was calmed down, she somehow managed to maneuver him onto her hip, so she could stand from the cot and carry him with her into the bathroom.

Since she didn't need to do anything more than wash her hands and face, she decided it was best to keep the little boy close for his peace of mind, if nothing else. She also wanted to wash him up to keep the evidence of his crying jag from being a reason for their captors to punish him further. So, she sat him on the bathroom counter to set about the task of cleaning them both up.

Charlotte didn't want to frighten Antonio any further, so she talked him through everything she was doing as she washed both their faces and hands. She tried asking him questions about what had happened in the month since she'd seen him last. But all she gathered from his broken account of what had happened was that he'd seen her enter the shelter with "a big, scary man" before Roberto insisted they leave.

"Ian's big, but he's not scary." Charlotte disagreed with Antonio's description of Ian, assuming it had come from Roberto, and not Antonio actually being afraid of Ian because of his size. "He was there to help that day. And I'm sure he's doing everything he can to help us get out of here now."

"Not mean like Sir?" Antonio's brow furrowed as he contemplated the differences between Ian and Roberto.

Charlotte had always thought it was strange that Antonio called Roberto Sir, instead of Dad or Padre, like the other kids in the shelter had called their fathers. But as she was realizing that Ian's assumption that Roberto wasn't Antonio's father was probably true, the Sir moniker made more sense.

"No, he's not mean. He's a big teddy bear, who likes to play games and have tickle fights with his little boy." Since she hadn't actually witnessed any negative behavior between Roberto and Antonio, Charlotte wanted to ask when Roberto had been mean to him. But she also didn't want to trigger him into another crying spell, when she could be pulled away from him at any moment. So, she focused on telling Antonio about Brody and how she hoped they'd get to meet and be friends, once they were all allowed to go home.

"I don't have a home," Antonio pouted, his eyes welling up with tears once more.

"Not yet, but you will." Charlotte could kick herself for upsetting him with her wording. She looped her arms over his head once more to hug him close. "Once Ian and my brothers come and get us from here, I'm going to see if you can come home with me. It might take me some time to get through all the paperwork, so it might not happen immediately. But I'd love to have you live on the ranch with me."

Antonio hugged her tighter as he started asking her questions about her brothers, the ranch, and the horses she'd told him about in their sessions together at the shelter. She picked him up and carried him back out to sit on the cot, describing each of her brothers and the horses, and getting him to repeat each of their names to keep his mind off of the horrendous situation they were currently in at the moment.

Unfortunately, she didn't have long to sit and talk before a man she didn't recognize entered the room and demanded she come with him. Antonio didn't want to let her go, crying to come with her when the man grabbed her arm.

"It's okay, Antonio," Charlotte placated him with a wary smile. "I need you to stay here and be my big, brave boy while I go talk to Sir about when we can go home to the ranch."

She knew it wasn't likely that what she said to Antonio would actually be what transpired in this meeting, but thankfully, neither the goon who came to get her nor any of the other captives contradicted her, so Antonio let her go without further complaint.

Charlotte walked along willingly, grateful this guy seemed less inclined to get rough with her than whoever had actually grabbed her at the ball field. He kept a firm hold on her upper arm, but he didn't grip her too tightly or drag her along when her strides were smaller than his.

She tried to make note of her surroundings as they walked through the hallways and stairwells, while also keeping her head down to make it appear that her gaze was focused solely on the floor. Since the hood had been removed, she knew the men moving about the place would consider her a threat if she looked them in the eyes and made it obvious she was noting features to be able to identify them in a lineup later. So, she hoped the submissive posture would make them think she was less of a threat to their continued freedom and keep them from wanting to kill her before she could escape.

She followed along quietly as the man escorted her to what appeared to be a home office. The ornate desk in the middle of the room seemed to clash with the rest of the farmhouse style of the rest of the furnishings she saw as she was ushered through the house, but she assumed it was something these men brought with them and not original to the old home.

Leah Mae Wright

The henchman stopped about three feet in front of the desk, halting her forward movement before releasing his grip on her arm. "Anything else, Boss?"

"No, that will be all. Thank you." Roberto dismissed the guard, who promptly turned and left the room.

Charlotte immediately recognized Roberto's voice this time, even without looking up to make eye contact with the man seated at the desk. She stood there, nervously fighting the temptation to look up into the eyes of the cartel kingpin she now knew was a cold-hearted killer.

Thank God, I wasn't attracted to him like I wished I could be a couple of months ago. Ian's hot-and-cold act might have had me all mixed up, but at least I didn't make the mistake of trying to get over him with a criminal like Roberto.

"You surprise me with your compliance. I expected you to put up more of a fight."

Since he didn't ask a question, Charlotte wasn't sure how to respond to Roberto. Therefore, she kept her mouth shut, waiting for him to ask her a direct question before replying. *No point in pissing him off by talking back, when I know he doesn't care how I feel about this whole mess.*

"Have you chosen to adopt Antonio's strategy of remaining mute to deal with the tragedy of your life not going your way any longer?"

"No," Charlotte answered succinctly, not wanting to piss him off further by explaining her logic. She continued to keep her eyes focused on his feet, which barely showed under the edge of the desk from where she was standing. *Damn, I should have taken my hair out of the French braid I put it in for softball practice, so I could look around a little more without it being obvious.*

"Such a pity. I was looking forward to breaking your spirit myself before sending you to the brothel to earn your keep. But I prefer a woman who fights me when I fuck her, not a cold fish who would just lay there."

A cold chill went up Charlotte's spine at his words. *Oh, I'll definitely fight you if you try to fuck me! And I'll remember the dirty tricks my brothers taught me to get away, too. Especially the various methods to rip your balls off!*

Even as her mind whirled with ideas for how to hurt him in a fight, Charlotte stood there stoically, expressionless, maintaining her cool, calm demeanor to lull him into a false sense of being in control. She might have enjoyed giving control over to Ian the night they met, and pretty much every other time he touched her, but he was the only man she would ever trust with control over her, sexual or otherwise.

"Maybe I'll have to use Antonio to bring out the fight in you. I don't normally go for the kids like some of my associates, but I bet his tight little ass will feel just as good on my cock as a virgin pussy…"

Roberto's words trailed off as the lights flickered off, plunging the windowless room into total darkness. Charlotte was glad he didn't have the chance to finish his monstrous thought, but she didn't waste time thinking about it before turning to flee through the door that she remembered being just a few feet behind her. She didn't want to run full speed, knowing she'd just run smack into the door before getting it open. But she swiftly walked back the way she'd entered with her hands extended out in front of her to feel for the doorknob.

Damn, I wish I could have seen more of the room to be able to find a weapon before the lights went out.

Just as she found the wall and started feeling for the door, she heard gunfire from somewhere nearby. She also heard Roberto cursing from behind her as he stumbled around, obviously trying to find her in the dark.

Shit! Now what do I do? Ian will be devastated if I walk into the middle of a gunfight and end up with the same fate as Mari. But I can't stay in this room where Roberto is looking for me, either.

Her hand bumped into a table up against the wall, giving her an idea. She felt around and realized it was open at the bottom. So, she crouched down and curled into a ball underneath it, scooting as close to the wall as she could while making herself as small a target as possible.

Hopefully, Roberto won't realize I'm not still standing to look under here. Dear Lord, she silently prayed. *Please keep Ian and my family, whom I'm sure he brought with him to rescue me, safe from harm as they fight their way in here. And please don't let any of those bullets come through this wall to make their rescue effort fruitless.*

~~~

Ian couldn't believe how fast an impromptu raid by a small-town police department could come together with the backing of Avington Security. It seemed like they were running at lightspeed compared to the hurry-up-and-wait situations he'd had to deal with in putting together a bust with the DEA.

I'm sure the fact that the only judge in town is the uncle of the police chief makes getting warrants much easier to be able to rush into an emergency situation like this, too.

They had everything together so fast that the Avington team in San Antonio didn't have time to get to Heart's Destiny to go with them, leaving them with only twelve men going in to rescue Charlotte. The four Avington brothers and their father, three of Charlotte's brothers, three additional HDPD officers besides Bobby, and Ian. He hoped they wouldn't find themselves outmanned when they got there, but there was no time to waste waiting on the other Avington Security guys or calling in Trent and his team with the DEA.

But I guess it's easier to work with military precision when most of the team going in are former or current SEALs or other naval operators. Maybe with their military expertise, it won't matter how many guys Rodriguez has guarding the place.

Ian shook off his thoughts as he followed the caravan of police vehicles and pulled off the road into an overgrown field a half-mile away from the entrance to the old Gruber farm. Jake immediately launched his drone, barely waiting for Ian to get the Range Rover in park before sending it out the window.

Ian stayed seated, looking over at Jake's computer screen where the drone footage was displayed, as everyone else gathered around the passenger side of the vehicle to get updated on the intel from the drone before dividing up into groups to simultaneously hit the various buildings on the farm.

As the drone made the first pass over the farm, they made note of three structures on the premises. The farmhouse that Bobby identified as Mac Gruber's former residence, the barn that Jake had already told them should be there, and a newer metal building set off by itself that
~~~

reminded Ian of the brothels he'd seen while undercover with the cartel.

"Fuck," Ian cursed under his breath, garnering the attention of all the men trying to figure out which building was most likely where Charlotte was being held.

"What pissed you off about that third building?" Byron Avington asked from the back seat of the Range Rover.

"That's most likely where they've set up a brothel," Ian explained, pointing to the screen where Jake had the drone focusing on the metal building. "Or where they're trying to set up a brothel if it's new since the raid in November."

"So that's where they've got Char?" Josh raised an eyebrow in question.

"Not likely." Ian shook his head. "Not this soon after kidnapping her. Even if they were hosting a party tonight, they'd only bring the women they already have trained to the brothel. If I had to guess, she's being held in the farmhouse and they're using the barn to hide their vehicles."

Jake maneuvered the drone to get a closer look at the area surrounding the buildings to see if they could figure out how many people were milling around on guard duty. They only found one person walking around outside the brothel. Ian told them that was standard procedure for when the girls were there, but the johns hadn't arrived for the night yet.

"Barrett, you take the brothel with one of Bobby's officers," Byron instructed, pointing to his oldest son.

"Gabe, you go with Barrett," Bobby directed Gabe Garcia, the officer Ian had just met that day. "Arrest the guard if you can, but your most important job is to communicate with any women who've been trafficked from Mexico that don't understand English, so we can help them get home safely."

As they were giving out those instructions, Jake flew the drone around the barn to see that it appeared unguarded, which Ian found strange since it also appeared that they had a generator running power from beside the barn to all three of the buildings.

"I'll head over to the barn to disable the generator," Byron announced. "Cutting their power will cause just enough confusion to put them at a disadvantage when ya'll go into the house. But I'd like an officer with me, just in case there's a guard in the barn."

"Jagger, you go with Byron." Bobby pointed to Jagger Youngblood. "Secure the barn before he goes to cut the power at the generator."

"You got it, Chief," Jagger saluted Bobby.

"There's at least two guards walking around outside the house," Jake alerted them. "I don't want to take the drone down low enough to see on the porch in case they figure out we're coming from seeing it. And the visuals aren't close enough for me to determine if the two I saw on the last pass are the same two I saw on the first pass."

"What can you tell us about their typical numbers from when you were undercover?" Byron looked at Ian as he asked the question.

"If that's a training house for the brothel, then there can be up to a dozen guys there to guard it and keep it running. The master bedroom would be used to house the women, with the secondary bedrooms set up for the guards to train them before they go to the brothel. If there's an office in the house, they'll set it up for whoever's in charge of the local operation. And if there's not an office in the house, they'll set one up in the dining room or another room in the common area of the house. But I'm not sure how that might change if Rojo is using the house as his headquarters." Ian ran a hand through his hair in irritation at not having the intel on the setup of Roberto's typical residence, since he hadn't made it that far up in the organization when he was working undercover.

"Okay, we'll treat it as a training house and deal with whatever adjustments we have to make on the fly," Byron stated, patting a hand on Ian's shoulder. "The rest of you divide up, half going in the front and half going in the back. I'm guessing the bedrooms are upstairs, so Ian should focus on heading there to look for Charlotte. Bobby, you and Dusty need to look for the office. That way, you can arrest Roberto."

"We're with Ian to look for Charlotte," Jake insisted, waving a finger between himself and Josh.

"Perfect. That leaves Blaine, Blake, and Brady to cover you if there are more guards inside than what we've seen out on the grounds."

They made sure they all had everything they needed, from handcuffs and zip ties, in case they had to secure more than a dozen prisoners, to their protective gear and weapons with plenty of ammo. Josh even put a pair of night-vision goggles around his neck in case the lights going out in the house made seeing who was in a room difficult. They left their vehicles in the field, hiking through the overgrown fields to their target buildings with weapons drawn.

They coordinated their movements via earbud two-way radios, so they all knew when Jagger secured the barn. He had one guard in cuffs and reported the barn clear, allowing Byron to cut the power and give the rest of them an upper hand as they made entry into the other two buildings. Ian followed Bobby, Jake, and Josh Burleson to the back of the house while Dusty Deere, Blaine, Blake, and Brady Avington prepared to make entry from the front.

Ian was impressed with the way Josh snuck up on the guard patrolling the back and knocked him out without making a sound. He cuffed him and added a gag, just in case the man woke up before Byron and Jagger made it over to finish securing him with the other prisoner.

Dusty and Bobby took turns on the coms, alerting the others that the guards patrolling outside in front and back of the farmhouse were secured and ready to be taken to transport back to the jail.

Bobby led the way through the back door as soon as the power was cut, announcing "HDPD, we're here with a warrant" at the same time Dusty made the same announcement as their half of the team made entry from the front. Ian recognized Barrett Avington on the coms next, reporting that the guard at the brothel was in custody, just as he walked through the back door into a kitchen, but he couldn't focus on the other communication in his ear as the gunfire started.

He fought the flashbacks to that day in the park as he returned fire. He wasn't sure which of the four of them actually took out the guard who'd opened fire, but he had a feeling that the autopsy would show at least four bullet wounds from four different guns.

"One down, kitchen clear," Bobby barked, his voice echoing through Ian's earpiece since he was only a few feet away.

One of the Avingtons reported in that two more guards were eliminated in the living room, just as they exited the kitchen into a dining room where they took out another guard, who thought he could lie in wait for them. Ian didn't think the man had even gotten off a shot, having barely raised his gun when Josh put a bullet between his eyes.

As they continued moving through the farmhouse, the eight men inside continued to communicate with the rest of the team as they cleared a room. They split up even further to search the other floors once the main floor was completely cleared. On the second floor, Bobby called for Josh and his night vision goggles when he found the room he thought was the office, since it was centrally located and wouldn't have any light coming in with no windows to the outside.

Since the bedrooms on the second floor seemed to be set up as barracks for the guards, the Avingtons started clearing them while Ian and Jake continued up to the third floor, hoping to find the bedroom where Charlotte was being held. After going through a few more bedrooms that were obviously used for training the trafficked women and making sure they were all clear of the men in the cartel, they finally came to a locked door.

Ian knew that had to be where Charlotte and anyone else the cartel had kidnapped for trafficking were being held. He didn't waste a second thinking about how to make entry. He swiftly lifted his foot, kicking the door down, glad he'd changed into steel-toed, combat boots when he swapped his typical business-casual clothing for tactical gear.

He scanned the room, noticing four women and two children, but Charlotte wasn't among them. "Fuck!" he cursed, not realizing his outburst would scare the hostages they were there to rescue. "Where's Charlotte?"

Jake reported in that they'd found some of the cartel's hostages, but not Charlotte, while Ian checked the ensuite bathroom in case she was hiding there.

"Ian, calm down man," Jake tried to cool Ian's frustration, holstering his weapon. "We'll find her."

"You're here for the new girl?" With just a little bit of light coming in through a window on the opposite side of the room, Ian couldn't tell which of the women huddled in the darkest corner had spoken, but he nodded to answer her question. "They took her down to meet with the boss just before the lights went out. Before that, she was telling the boy that you were coming to get her."

"E-on?" Ian barely heard the little boy phonetically saying his name as the woman's words sank in.

She knew I'd come find her.

"Charlotte is probably in the office with Rojo," Ian practically shouted into his com to alert her brothers, who were making entry to the office at that moment. He wanted to run back down the stairs to find her, but he couldn't move when a little boy not much older than his son stepped up to him.

"E-on? Char okay?" The look on the little boy's face brought Ian to his knees, both to appreciate the child's concern and to be closer to his level while they talked, so he didn't scare the child any more than he already had by making entry to the room. It was clear the little boy was afraid, but he was also more worried about Charlotte than his own safety at the moment.

"Yes, I'm Ian. Char is going to be fine," Ian reassured the little boy using the nickname her family called her, so the little boy wouldn't be confused by his usage of her full name. He then holstered his weapon, not wanting to frighten the little boy any more than he already appeared to be. "Two of her brothers are downstairs looking for her now. Jake here is also her brother and the two of us are here to help you and your friends get out of here, so you can go home."

"Jake?" The little boy's face lit up as he turned to look at Jake. "You ride Raphael."

"Yeah, I do," Jake chuckled. "When I'm home on the ranch, anyway. What's your name?"

"Antonio. Is Anthony here? We have close names."

Antonio. Fuck, this is the little boy that was with Roberto at the shelter that Charlotte was working with on his speech development.

"No, Anthony isn't here. He had to go out of town for work yesterday. But if you know about me and Anthony, then you probably know about Josh and Bobby."

"Bobby is police," Antonio nodded. "Josh rides Leo, Leo."

"Leonardo," Jake finished the horse's name when Antonio seemed to falter in remembering the whole thing.

"Leo-nar-do," Antonio carefully enunciated each syllable.

"Yeah, Josh rides Leonardo. Josh and Bobby are both downstairs helping Char."

At Jake's statement, Antonio bolted toward the door. Ian barely reached out and grabbed him around the waist to keep him from heading down to the middle of the mess he could hear unfolding on the coms. "Sorry, little man, you've got to stay up here until the rest of the bad guys are taken care of, and it's safe for us to take you down to Char."

"I gotta help Char. Sir no kill her like Mommy." Antonio fought to get out of Ian's arms.

Fuck! Fuck! Fuck!

Realizing the little boy had probably witnessed his mother's death at the hands of Roberto Rodriguez triggered more of Ian's flashbacks to the death of his wife under the orders of the same man. As he listened to Bobby in his ear, trying to negotiate with Rodriguez to lower his weapon and come into custody with no more bloodshed, Ian fought to keep his shit together and not succumb to an extremely ill-timed panic attack.

"I know, Antonio," Ian consoled the boy, and possibly himself even more than Antonio. "I want to be the one to go rescue her, too. But her brothers are already helping her, and if we were to run in there now, it would just put more lives at risk. So, we need to trust that her brothers will keep her safe while they arrest Roberto."

Ian tried to look to Jake for reassurance that he was doing the right thing by staying put to protect the hostages, if any of the other cartel henchmen came back to the scene. But with Jake on the other side of the room trying to gain the other victims' trust, so he could check them for injuries and figure out how to help them get home at the end of this ordeal, he didn't notice Ian's uncertainty.

That uncertainty was momentarily amplified when Ian heard another gunshot ring out from the floor below them, followed by the bloodcurdling scream of a woman. Without even thinking, Ian ordered Antonio to go to Jake, releasing the boy, so he could run from the room.

Hang on, Princess! I'm coming.

~~~
~~~

Charlotte wasn't sure how long she stayed huddled under the table praying before the gunfire stopped, but it was long enough for Roberto to quit cursing as he stumbled around, trying to find her. Even though she couldn't see him in the dark room, she still had an idea of where he was from hearing him bumping into the furniture.

She considered herself lucky that the sounds were coming from the other side of the room. Since she hadn't really gotten a good look around before the lights went out to be able to guess what he was running into, she wasn't sure if their being on opposite sides of the room was because his sense of direction was as discombobulated in the dark as hers, or if he was actually closer to the door than she was because she'd been too turned around to find it on her initial attempt to flee the room.

As she heard muffled, masculine voices behind her and slightly to the left, she decided that she hadn't been that far off in her estimation of where the door was after all. A few moments later, she was glad she hadn't actually found the door when it came crashing down just a few feet to her left.

"Eleven o'clock," announced a voice that sounded a lot like her brother, Josh.

Not even a second later, a light shined from the doorway, illuminating Roberto across the room. "Roberto Rodriguez, you're under arrest. Lower your weapon," Bobby's voice boomed.

Holy shit! How the hell did he find a gun in the dark?

Charlotte stayed huddled under the table, knowing the flashlight didn't throw off enough light for anyone to see her, as three large figures entered the room. Even with the little bit of light coming into the room from the doorway behind them, it was still too dark in there to verify their identities. Since she recognized both Josh's and Bobby's voices, she assumed the third person was Jake, since he was an inch shorter than Josh and two inches shorter than Bobby.

Why isn't Ian with them? She knew that the third person couldn't be Ian because he was the same height as Josh and the third person who entered the room was clearly a little shorter than the other two. Not that she would ever refer to any of the over six-foot-tall men she knew as short in any other way than compared to even taller men, especially not to their faces.

As she tried to figure out where Ian was and why he wasn't there to rescue her with her brothers, Charlotte missed what was said between Bobby and Roberto. She also didn't notice how the other two men moved slowly through the shadowed sides of the room, trying to get closer to Roberto as Bobby continued to try to negotiate Rojo's surrender.

She would have alerted her brothers to her presence, but she didn't want to give away her position to Roberto, as long as he was still holding that gun. So, she continued to sit there, silently praying that Ian hadn't been injured in the gunfight she heard earlier.

Oh, dear God, please, please, please don't let him have been killed trying to rescue me. We're just starting to work things out to finally be together. I can't lose him now.

Not to mention how devastated Brody would be to lose both of his parents because of this bastard Roberto.

As all her memories of her time with Ian flashed before her eyes like a movie, Charlotte continued to pray for his safety, along with that of her brothers, not even realizing what was going on around her while her tears soundlessly flowed down her cheeks.

It wasn't until Bobby shut off the flashlight that she realized one of the men had moved close enough to tussle with Roberto for his gun. In the darkened room, she couldn't tell who was across the room fighting for all their lives when the sound of a gun discharging echoed through the room.

Charlotte involuntarily screamed at the same time she jumped in fright, bumping her head on the table she was hiding under.

Chaos reigned as Bobby turned his flashlight back on while barking at someone to "get the lights back on now!" Three more men stormed in with flashlights, scanning the room as Bobby crouched to check on Charlotte. "Have you been hit?"

"Nah-no," Charlotte stuttered, unsure if she was shaking her head or just shaking from fear. "Just scared."

"Stay there," Bobby ordered just as Josh announced, "Target eliminated."

"Or don't, since it's safe to come out now." Bobby extended his hand to Charlotte to help her out of her hiding place.

"The rest of the room is clear, Chief," Dusty Deere reported as Charlotte took her brother's hand to let him help her stand up out from under the table.

Bobby pulled a key from his pocket and removed the handcuffs from her wrists as soon as he saw them.

Oh, I guess that wasn't Jake. Wait, where's Jake? Charlotte rubbed her sore wrists as soon as they were free of the shackles.

She looked around to see if Jake or Ian were part of the second group that barged in, recognizing three of her Avington cousins holding flashlights as they searched the room. "Where are Ian and Jake?"

"I'm here, Princess," Ian announced, running into the room, and scooping her up into his arms. "And Jake's upstairs with Antonio."

He didn't take the time to explain any further before kissing the daylights out of her. Charlotte was so relieved to see that he was alive and well that she returned his kiss with equal fervor, not caring that they were being observed by two of her brothers, three of her cousins, and one of her childhood classmates, who now worked with her brother at the police department.

As the rest of the world faded away, Char wrapped her arms around Ian's neck, wishing he'd have picked her up straight on instead of bridal style, so she could wrap her legs around his waist, too. She never wanted to leave the safety of Ian's arms, needing the reassurance that he was really there kissing her and hadn't been injured in the rescue after all.

Regardless of her desire to take things slow as they worked out the particulars of their relationship, or whether they actually tried for a serious long-term relationship or not, Charlotte needed him to be the one to comfort her as they dealt with the aftermath of the ordeal she'd suffered through over the past few hours. Her family would be there for her. She knew that for a fact, as was evidenced by her brothers and cousins being there to rescue her. But her love for her family was different than what she felt for Ian.

Though she hadn't ever personally felt it before meeting Ian, she knew they had the soul-deep connection of true love because she'd seen the same looks they shared when looking at one another on the faces of her parents all of her life. Knowing what those looks meant was why she'd been so devastated by Ian's rejection of their connection, when he was trying to fight his feelings in a misguided attempt to keep her out of the cartel crosshairs.

Even though she knew he still wasn't sure of more than their sexual chemistry, she had to have him by her side the rest of the night. She knew they both had a lot to deal with emotionally after the evening's events, things they probably needed to discuss with a therapist before they could truly come together as a couple, who were capable of lasting the test of time. But as her brother, Bobby, interrupted their lip lock to start the process of taking statements and seeing to the medical care of Charlotte and the other hostages, Charlotte didn't feel strong enough to go through everything again without Ian by her side.

I just hope that by needing him to be my rock to lean on tonight, I'm not pushing for too much, too fast from him. I know we need to take things slow to build our relationship. And I'm willing to go back to that. Tomorrow, after I have a night of reassurance that he can be there for me without me being an albatross around his neck.

Dear Lord, please don't let the taste of excitement he got tonight remind him of what he's missing from his old life as a DEA agent. I don't want to hold him back, but I can't live with this much danger in my life all the time.

Though if he wants to wear this all black tactical gear for a little role-play once in a while as my super-spy Ian, I'd certainly be on board.

Chapter Eighteen

Ian dragged himself into school the next morning after being up all night dealing with everything that had to be taken care of after Charlotte was rescued, including reporting to the DEA that Roberto Rodriguez had been killed in the raid to rescue her. He would have normally called in and asked for a substitute teacher after such an ordeal, but since Charlotte insisted on going to work, as usual, he had to follow her lead. Luckily, since her car was still in the impound lot until they found the time to go pick it up, the fact that she needed him to drive her to work that morning worked nicely with his need to stay by her side constantly. Even knowing that Rodriguez was dead didn't lessen his fear that something might happen to her if he let her out of his sight.

The night before, when he'd finally gotten Charlotte in his arms, he hadn't been able to let her go. He knew it went against regulations, but he insisted on staying by her side the whole time she was giving her statement to each of the local law enforcement agencies that had been called in, as well as when she was taken to the hospital with the other hostages to be checked over by medical professionals.

Since the former Gruber farm wasn't technically in the Heart's Destiny city limits, the Medina County Sheriff's Department had been called in to take over the containment of the scene and the investigation into how long the brothel had been in operation. With confirmation from one of the cartel underlings that had been arrested outside the farmhouse that Roberto had personally kidnapped Charlotte from the ball fields in Heart's Destiny before having one of his lieutenants take her to the room where she was held with the other hostages, the kidnapping case opened by the Heart's Destiny Police

Department was officially closed. So, the other issues they'd uncovered on the farm had to be turned over to the departments with jurisdiction.

Ian had been slightly surprised when the Texas Rangers were called in before the DEA and Homeland Security, but he went along with the way things worked a little differently in Texas, as long as they let him stay by Charlotte's side. He was sure that courtesy was only given to him in light of his status as a former DEA agent and at the request of the Burlesons, who had extensive contacts in the local and state agencies.

He knew when Trent got into town to start questioning everyone involved in a couple of hours, he could also talk his former partner into letting him sit in on the meeting with Charlotte as well. The Homeland Security agents were the only ones he was worried about trying to block him from being by her side when she was questioned later. Ian wasn't sure any of his friends or her family had enough clout with Homeland Security to get the rules bent just a little.

Although he also hadn't been sure any of them had the authority to insist he stay with Charlotte at the hospital the night before either, he hadn't been forced to sit in the waiting room with Charlotte's brothers and cousins the way he expected. He was pretty sure that had more to do with the way Charlotte was clinging to him all night than anything else, though.

It had been difficult for him to sit by and watch as every bump and bruise on her body was documented. He wanted to go back and kill Rojo again, slowly and painfully, when he saw the handprint-shaped bruises on her arms and the abrasions from the handcuffs he'd put on too tight.

Though the rest of her bruises were from bumping around in the trunk of the vehicle Roberto had transported her in, and the worst of her injuries was the bump on her head from hitting it on the table she was hiding under when the gun went off in the scuffle between Roberto and Josh, Ian was still fuming with anger for each and every mark left on her. Since he didn't have an outlet for that anger with Roberto dead, Ian was struggling with how to contain it.

Charlotte not needing to see another act of aggression after the ordeal she'd been through was the only reason he hadn't lost his temper the night before. But as they walked hand in hand to her classroom together, Ian could feel it bubbling back to the surface at the thought of letting her out of his sight to go next door to teach his classes.

"Are you sure we can't combine all our classes today?" Ian set his coffee down on her desk at the same time Charlotte did the same with hers, so he could pull her into his arms and just hold her for a moment.

"No, my eighth graders and your sixth graders don't have the same lessons planned for the day, so it would just be chaos," Charlotte objected even as she looped her arms around his waist and rested her head on his chest, right over his heart.

"But I know I'm going to have several students throughout the day who will want to come over to your classroom and check on you after seeing what happened at the ball field yesterday." Ian knew it was a weak excuse, but he couldn't think of any other reason why they might need to combine their classes other than his paranoia, which he really didn't want to burden Charlotte with after everything else.

"And I'll gladly let you send them over during the first five minutes of each class to reassure them that I'm fine," Charlotte acquiesced. "But I'm not a counselor, so if they need more than physically seeing that I'm okay and back in one piece, then I'm not the person to help them. That's why I had Bobby notify Lisa of what happened, so she can have counselors available all day, if any of the kids need to talk about what they witnessed."

"Yeah, I know," Ian conceded with a sigh as he rested his chin on the top of her head. "And I plan on utilizing those counseling services for any of the kids even minimally affected by what happened yesterday."

Hell, I wonder if the school counselors are equipped to handle the therapy I need after yesterday? If not, maybe one of them can refer me to a therapist in the area who can help me deal with this intense need to keep Charlotte glued to my side, so I don't suffocate her.

She might have submissive tendencies in the bedroom, but I'm sure she doesn't want me to be clingy and controlling twenty-four-seven.

Charlotte hadn't said a word about the tracker in her necklace the night before, when he mentioned it was how he'd found her to the various law enforcement agencies they had to give statements to after the ordeal was over. But he knew it was just because she was so overwhelmed by everything that she'd been through. He knew once everything really started to sink in, she'd balk at the thought of him keeping track of her whereabouts with the tracker.

So, I have to get this shit under control before she kicks me to the curb to find someone more supportive of her independent tendencies.

They spoke for a few more minutes about their plans for lunch, and Trent coming by to take their statements during their planning period, before Ian finally gave her a quick kiss and reluctantly walked next door to get his teaching day started. As he went about his day, he started realizing just how much he needed to slow things down in his relationship with Charlotte to keep from suffocating her with his need to keep her close, so he felt like she was safe.

Fuck! I don't want to slow things down. But I know she's going to need a little time and space to deal with the trauma she endured yesterday before she'll be ready for everything I want to happen for our future together.

Hell, I probably need just as much time to wrap my head around everything, too. I certainly can't be the man she needs me to be when I'm a basket case, worrying about her and having flashbacks of losing Mari that morph into Charlotte in her place.

Damn it! As much as I hate it, we need to take our time and build a strong foundation of friendship for our relationship to be able to stand the test of time.

Since Charlotte had already wanted to keep their mutual attraction to themselves to keep her mother from taking credit for getting them together with one of her matchmaking schemes, Ian was sure she'd agree that it was best for them to slow things down for a little while. He didn't care one way or the other if Hazel claimed credit for their relationship, but he needed to take some time to manage his PTSD before he could be the man Charlotte needed him to be.

Fuck! I can't be a good boyfriend, much less her husband, when I can't spend the night with her because I'm worried I'll accidentally hurt her in the throes of a nightmare. So, it's time to find a good therapist here before I push for more than quickies when we can sneak away while we're hanging out, with everyone around us thinking we're just friends.

~~~
~~~

Charlotte hadn't realized just how rough the day would be when she insisted on going to work as usual that morning. She had vastly underestimated the number of students who would want to check up on her throughout the day. And with Ian's former partner at the DEA coming to the school to interview her during her planning period, she also hadn't allotted enough time in her day to speak to the counselor at the school about her state of mind after the events of the previous afternoon and evening.

Maybe Ian had the right idea when he suggested combining our classes today. At least if we'd done that, we could have taken turns napping while the other one taught, so we could both catch up on some of the sleep we missed while at the hospital all night.

It had been a while since Charlotte had pulled an all-nighter while studying for finals in college, but she certainly didn't remember the lack of sleep kicking her butt quite this bad back then. She found herself fighting a yawn throughout the whole time she sat with Ian and his former partner in the DEA, Trent Jones, recounting the events of the previous day for what felt like the billionth time since she was rescued.

Between the constant fight to stay awake and her mind wandering to thoughts about Antonio, when she'd get a chance to call and check on him, what she'd need to do to be able to foster him to get him out of the Children's Protective Services' group home he was taken to after the hospital, as well as all the other things she needed to do, like picking up her car from where Bobby had it towed and rescheduling her OB-GYN appointment that she missed, Charlotte wasn't sure her statement to Agent Jones was very coherent. But thankfully, her part of the interview seemed to be over, so she just had to sit there patiently while Ian gave his statement.

With everything else weighing on her, she really wished she'd called for a substitute teacher and taken the day off to rest before trying to play catch-up with her life.

I probably shouldn't try to call the social worker from CPS while I'm this tired, so maybe it's a good thing this meeting with Trent is eating up all my free time to make the call today. But I hate that I'm not going to get to see Antonio today to check up on him.

Leah Mae Wright

The night before, Charlotte only saw Antonio briefly before they had to be separated to go be examined at the hospital in Hondo, along with all of the other women and children that had been held by the Rodriguez Cartel. When she was finally released to go home at four in the morning, she wasn't allowed to take Antonio with her. She was given a card for Children's Protective Services and told to check with them later in the day to determine if it was possible for her to visit with him at the group home he was taken to the night before. The number on the card would also be her point of contact for going through the steps to become a foster parent, if they couldn't find Antonio's birth family.

She hated that she hadn't had a chance to tell Antonio what she was planning to do to see him again in the craziness of everything else going on with the various law enforcement and other agencies that were called in to handle the situation. But at least they got to see each other for a few minutes to have the reassurance that they'd both made it out relatively unscathed.

But that precious five-year-old boy shouldn't have to go into the system and deal with this all alone.

She was brought out of her mental musings as Trent shut his laptop when he was finished making notes on Ian's debrief.

"So, now that Rojo is no longer a threat and the rest of the Rodriguez Cartel is either behind bars or dead, are we going to restore your identity?" Trent arched an inquisitive eyebrow at Ian. "I, for one, would like to quit tripping over my tongue when I forget I can't call you Mike anymore."

"I hadn't really thought about it," Ian chuckled. "But even if the powers that be don't want to go through the trouble of restoring everything they wiped out two years ago, I won't mind if you go back to calling me Mike. Hell, Cait still calls me Mikey on occasion, especially when she's really tired and not thinking about it."

Char also hadn't thought about the possibility that Ian would go back to using his full, original name once the cartel was no longer a threat to him or his family. But as she sat there with *Mike, Michael,* and *Mikey* cycling through her brain, she couldn't decide if she'd be able to switch to calling him anything but Ian after knowing him as such for the last four months.

Besides the hard-to-change-now factor, she liked the way his use of the name Ian had led to their meet-cute story. Granted, most of her family didn't know they had a meet-cute story, but still, it made the name somewhat special to her.

Aw, hell, if he decides to go back to Michael, or some variation thereof, and doesn't like that I still call him Ian, then he can spank me for it.

Charlotte couldn't contain her grin at that thought as she shook hands with Trent, who was leaving the school to head over to the police department to meet Bobby to finish up his part of the paperwork.

"What's that grin for, Princess?" Ian arched an eyebrow at her as he turned to face her, once Trent had left them alone for the last few minutes of their planning period.

Charlotte debated whether or not to be completely honest with him for a moment before deciding that she had to be totally transparent with him if she wanted him to be as utterly open with her. "First I was trying out the different variations of your real name in my head to see which one I might be able to call you. But then, when none of those felt right, I wondered if continuing to call you Ian would earn me a spanking."

"No," Ian chuckled, pulling her out of her chair and into his arms. "I've gone by Ian long enough now that I'm cool with using either name. So, it's fine if you want to keep calling me Ian, even if the DEA restores my full name legally. Of course, I'd also be okay with you only calling me Ian when we're fulfilling some of your fantasies about sex with a spy."

"You did overhear our conversation that night," Charlotte scoffed, slapping both hands against his chest. "All this time, you've let me believe you didn't hear us and take advantage of using the same name as my fantasy book character hookup to get in my panties. So much for fate bringing us together."

"I think fate still brought us together," Ian disagreed, squeezing her close enough to feel his erection pressing into her belly. "I mean, I probably wouldn't have gotten brave enough to introduce myself to you that night if I hadn't heard you talk about wanting a hot night with a guy, who not only had the same name I've been using, but also sounded a lot like me physically."

"You wouldn't have made a move?" Charlotte's eyebrows furrowed, showing her skepticism of Ian's belief that he wouldn't have made a move without hearing her conversation with Fiona earlier in the night.

"No, I wouldn't have." Ian shook his head, his lips turning down as he released Charlotte to run a hand through his hair. "I wasn't in a good place that night. I was barely a week and a half out from the second anniversary of losing Mari, and had gone to the bar to wallow in my memories as much as the scotch. On top of that, I was trying to mentally prepare for getting close to the cartel again. So, even though I was instantly attracted to you, I wouldn't have been able to even convince myself to talk to you, if not for seeing how I could fulfill your fantasy while giving myself a night off from reality as well."

"A night off from reality?" Charlotte fumed, his opinion of their first night together feeling like a dagger to her heart. "That's all that night was for you?"

"That's what I had to tell myself at the time," Ian backtracked at seeing her angry reaction to his hurtful words. "But we both know it means a lot more than that to both of us now. I just couldn't let myself hope for more at the time because that would mean I needed to walk away from the hunt for Rojo to keep you safe. But now that Rodriguez and the cartel are no longer a threat, we can actually pursue what I really wanted with you that night."

"Oh, and what's that?" Charlotte slammed a hand on her hip as she glared at Ian. Charlotte wasn't sure why she was suddenly so mad at him, but the way he was talking to her, going back and forth between seeming to want something with her and seeming to negate their instant connection in December was making her head spin.

"Dating," Ian replied earnestly. "Seeing how far we can go as a couple. Slowing things down to really get to know one another, so we can see if we're more than just hot, sexual chemistry."

Slowing things down? Geez, if we go any slower, we'll be going backwards.

Charlotte opened her mouth to reply, but promptly closed it when the bell rang to signal it was time for classes to change.

"Fuck," Ian cursed, looking up at the ceiling as he huffed out a frustrated breath from their conversation being interrupted. "Let's talk about it some more after school to figure out where we go from here."

"Can't." Charlotte shook her head. "I have to go meet with the Homeland Security agents, and you have baseball practice."

"Then we'll sneak off by ourselves to talk after dinner," Ian suggested.

"I figured you'd be too busy with your own meeting with Homeland Security, and then moving your family back home to stay for dinner on the ranch." Charlotte shrugged as the first students in her next class entered the room.

"Then I'll text you this evening and what we don't work out tonight, we'll talk about tomorrow over lunch," Ian declared as he turned to leave her classroom.

And I'll make sure I'm home alone for that text conversation, so my mom doesn't get her hopes up for there being more between us than a few hot hookups. It's bad enough I'm starting to hear wedding bells when Ian wants to slow things down. I don't need to hear more of her delight at how wonderfully things are going in our relationship, when it's obviously not going as wonderfully as she thinks.

~~~

Friday, April 12, 2019

Ian wasn't sure if he'd played things right with Charlotte since her kidnapping or not. But after talking to the counselor at school, and then the therapist the counselor referred him to for his PTSD, he was as convinced as he could be that he needed to slow things down with her to give him time to get his head on straight before pushing for more in their relationship. Unfortunately, her lack of enthusiasm for the date he'd planned for them on Friday afternoon seemed to indicate that she wasn't fully on board with the go-slow plan.

Ian assumed it was because of their lack of time to really converse since Tuesday that prevented them from being on the same page. He'd wanted to talk to her right after school that day, either while he was taking her to the police station or home. But then Bobby brought her Equinox to her during their last class on Tuesday, so he hadn't even had the chance to see her after school, much less chat with her.
~~~

Since he barely had time to talk to the school counselor to get the therapist referral before baseball practice, Ian assumed he'd see her at dinner and would get to talk to her that evening. But Charlotte had been right about his evening being filled with other obligations. Not only had he spent more time than he wanted with the Homeland Security agents, but he'd also had to have a long talk with Caitir about the events of the previous day, and reassure her that Rojo was dead before she was willing to move back to their rental house. Ian had tried texting Charlotte when he finally got settled back at his home for the night, but she hadn't replied.

On Wednesday at school, she'd given him an excuse about her phone having died from not being charged since Sunday night, which made sense with it being in her vehicle when she was kidnapped on Monday. Then, when their lunch and planning period rolled around, she spent the whole time on the phone trying to find out about Antonio and didn't have time to talk. After school on Wednesday, Charlotte was back to her normal schedule with softball practice, so Ian took the opportunity to meet with the therapist he'd been referred to in San Antonio.

That first session was intense, with him having to rehash his entire life story. Ian went all the way back to his childhood, explaining how he grew up wanting a relationship like his grandparents had, his mother's drug and boyfriend issues, raising his little sister when their mother finally went to jail, why he chose to go to work with the DEA, his whole history with the cartel, his marriage to Mari, losing her, recapping what he'd worked with the therapist in San Diego on after the shooting there, explaining how he ended up in Texas to track down the man responsible for his wife's death, telling him about meeting Charlotte, his instant feelings for her, how she'd been kidnapped by the same man responsible for his first wife's death, and finally how he was having flashbacks and nightmares again. Ian had gotten lucky in being Dr. Ryan Edwards' last patient of the day, so it wasn't as big a deal when the session went way past the normal hour-long appointment time. But it did make for a later-than-normal evening for Ian by the time he drove back to Heart's Destiny from the psychologist's office in San Antonio.

It was actually a suggestion of Dr. Edwards that led to the plans Ian had for his date with Charlotte that he finally got her to agree to on

Thursday at lunch. She had been trying to rush him out of her classroom, so she could meet with her own therapist on a telehealth appointment from her desk, when he pushed for her to agree to the date.

He hated feeling like he had to force her hand, but the way she was avoiding him wasn't going to lead to the outcome he wanted for their relationship. He knew he needed some time to deal with his PTSD first, but he wanted to be all in with Charlotte for the long term. He wanted marriage, her adopting Brody, and more babies with her, but he was willing to wait and put in the work to make that perfect life happen.

Ian also knew she needed the therapy time to deal with the trauma she endured on Monday before she'd be ready for everything he wanted with her, too. He hoped her therapist had helped her start to reach that realization, as well. But if not, he planned to explain in more detail why he needed to slow things down as they walked through the Japanese Tea Garden, which Dr. Edwards had recommended as a good place to spend some time talking with her in a tranquil, neutral setting.

"So, now that you've got me on this date, where are we going?" Charlotte still didn't look like she really wanted to go anywhere with Ian as she glared at him from the passenger seat of his Range Rover while he drove along the interstate into San Antonio.

"Our first stop is the Japanese Tea Garden." Ian's lips turned up in the slightest smile as he continued to keep his eyes on the road while explaining. "The therapist I started seeing this week recommended it as a good place to go for a walking meditation, or to have an uninterrupted conversation. He seemed to think it would be a good place for you and me to talk about our feelings without risking being overheard. But it's also not private enough to keep our communication from being derailed by acting on our sexual chemistry."

"Oh, um, okay." Charlotte seemed lost in thought for a moment as she pondered his words. "I suppose we do need to talk some before we have sex again. I'm assuming our second stop is somewhere we can be alone to explore that more, though. Right?"

"No." Ian shook his head. "Our second stop is wherever you want to eat an early dinner before we go back to Heart's Destiny, so I can pick up Cait and Brody from the ranch by seven."

"Wait, so we basically only have four hours for this *date*? And we're *not* having sex?" Charlotte's eyes were wide with shock at the realization.

"Exactly," Ian affirmed, nodding his head. "But hopefully, now that the cartel is no longer an issue, I'll be able to convince Cait to pick out a car and start driving herself to and from work in the next couple of weeks. Then we won't be limited to Friday afternoon dates."

He didn't mention that the time limit on their dates would be the only thing to change when he no longer had to be back in town early enough to pick up his sister. He didn't think Charlotte was ready to hear his plan to hold off on sex until he got his nightmares under control, so he could feel safe in falling asleep with her after they made love. But he figured he could wait until later in their date to explain all that, after their talk about everything that had been stirred up in his psyche by recent events.

Charlotte grumbled something about short, afternoon dates being a waste of time, but with her turned away from him to look out the side window of the vehicle, she obviously didn't intend that statement for his ears. So, Ian ignored it, changing the subject to the acceleration tests they'd had to send several students to take in the last week. They ended up talking about innocuous subjects, mostly related to their jobs, for the rest of the drive.

Once they arrived at the garden and were out walking around with plenty of space between them and their fellow park patrons, Charlotte wasted no time in changing the subject back to the reason for their date. "So, why did your therapist suggest we come here to talk?"

"Because I spent three hours in his office Wednesday evening telling him all the ways I'm fucked up in the head," Ian replied with a self-deprecating chuckle as they strolled by exotic plants he didn't even notice. "After hearing my whole life story, including how everything that's happened since meeting you has brought back some issues I had after Mari died, he thinks I need to spend some time telling you everything I told him before we decide to be more than friends."

"Oh." Charlotte's pretty, pink lips formed a perfect O, as she laced her fingers together behind her back, as if she needed something to hold onto to ground herself for what all he had to say. "Since we're here to talk, I guess you agree with him."

"Yes and no," Ian floundered with how to explain his feelings to her. "Intellectually, I understand the need for complete transparency in a relationship. I should be able to tell you everything about me, especially since I want to know everything about you. But emotionally, that's a scary proposition for someone with as much baggage as I carry around from my past."

Charlotte looked at him inquisitively, but she didn't say a word, waiting for him to elaborate.

"Like I told Dr. Edwards on Wednesday, I'm afraid if I unload everything on you all at once, the way I unloaded it all on him, then you'll run as far and as fast away from me as you possibly can." Ian nervously ran a hand through his hair. "And even though I feel guilty as fuck for being the reason Rodriguez targeted you, I'm also a selfish bastard, who doesn't want to lose you when you realize I'm not worthy of a woman as wonderful as you."

"Oh, Ian," Charlotte sighed, shaking her head. "That's not true at all. You're an honorable man, who lost your wife and still wanted to do more than your fair share of the work to bring down the cartel."

"No, I'm a vengeful asshole," Ian bellowed, unable to see himself through Charlotte's rose-colored glasses. "A pissed-off prick who wanted revenge on Rojo so bad that I didn't even stop hunting for him when I realized I was putting you, Cait, and Brody at risk by doing so."

"No, I don't believe that," Charlotte argued, stopping their walk by stepping in front of Ian and resting her palms against his chest. "Did you want justice for Mari? Yeah, probably. But you didn't want revenge. If that's what you wanted, you'd have been the first one through the door to that office, where ya'll expected him to be hiding, guns blazing. But that's not what you did. Instead, you went looking for me and let the two highest-ranking police officers on the scene go after Roberto to arrest him."

Ian tried to look at the situation from her perspective, unsure how much of his anger after the fact was tainting his memory of the events to make him think he went on the raid with the intention of killing

Roberto Rodriguez. "If I wasn't more focused on revenge than justice, why do I keep having dreams of bringing him back to life, just so I can have the honor of being the one to kill him?"

"Alright," Charlotte conceded, raising her hands from his chest in surrender. "There might be a little bit of a need for revenge in there, but it wasn't your primary motivation for anything you've done in trying to bring him to justice. And if wanting a little bit of revenge makes you unworthy of anything, then I'm just as unworthy, and so are Bobby, Jake, and a few of my cousins. 'Cause I can guarantee you that we've all had a dream or two this week about being the one to pull that trigger."

Ian let out a breath he hadn't realized he'd been holding, relieved to hear her defend him instead of wanting to walk away from him. He thought for sure his need for revenge for Marisol's death taking precedence over Charlotte's safety would be the reason he'd lose any chance he ever had at a future with Charlotte.

"Okay," Ian capitulated, reaching out to take Charlotte's hand, as they started walking around the lily pond once more. "I'll try to accept that you're right about this, but I still need to slow things down with us. I want you to know exactly what you're getting yourself into before we commit to more than friendly outings together. So, we need to take the next few weeks, while we're both still in therapy to deal with the mental aspects of what happened earlier this week, to just get to know each other better."

"Yeah, I can do that," Charlotte agreed. "Let's start with you telling me more about your childhood, and why you and Cait don't want to know about your father's side of your family tree."

"Damn, going right for the hard stuff, huh, Princess?" Ian chuckled wryly, deciding that letting her in on the worst parts of his childhood was as good a place to start getting to know one another as any. "First of all, we don't have the same father. Mine was my mom's high school boyfriend, who left town right after they graduated, and she told him she was pregnant with me. Cait's was one of my mom's many boyfriends over the years. And we don't want to know about them because they were both, most likely, as strung out on drugs as our mother. After working so hard to get away from that scene, to the point of dedicating a decade of my life to bringing down as many of the dealers and cartel leaders as possible, neither one of us wants to invite that element back into our lives by finding our sperm donors."

Ian went on to tell her the horror story of his and Caitir's childhood, with their mom dragging them to San Diego to live with one druggie after another, losing their grandparents shortly after they moved off the farm, how their mom spent the proceeds from selling the farm on drugs, and her eventual arrest that led to him raising Caitir through her teenage years.

He then went on to explain how he'd minored in English Literature in college, thinking that after he retired from a career in law enforcement, he'd spend his time writing crime novels. But then, after losing his wife and needing to find a safer career to be around to raise his son, he used the knowledge gained from his minor in college to pass the tests necessary to earn his English education certification.

Charlotte told him about her own journey through multiple changes of major in college before finally deciding to become an English teacher. She, too, had a goal of becoming an author after retirement, though her genre of choice was romance.

She went on to tell him more about both of her sisters-in-law's books, as well as how her sister had plans to turn their books into movies. She mentioned how she was second-guessing her plans to write romance, since that genre was already covered in her family. Not wanting to see her discouraged or give up on a dream, Ian suggested they collaborate and write romantic suspense novels, so they would fall into a different sub-genre from her sisters-in-law.

That led to Charlotte telling him that the book character she mentioned the night they met was from a book series she classified as romantic suspense, and that he needed to read it before she would agree to collaborate with him on any future writing projects. By the time they finished walking through the Japanese Tea Garden, she had him convinced that he needed to read the book series that brought them together based on her description of the books as much as to get her to collaborate with him in the future.

Charlotte picked a casual restaurant on the RiverWalk for their early dinner, where they talked more about their therapy sessions to learn that they were both referred to the same psychology practice by the school counselor. They were seeing two different doctors, however. A husband and wife team that started their own practice after meeting and getting married while in their doctoral program together.

They also discussed more aspects of their lives, specifically their childhoods. He wasn't surprised to hear that she'd been more adventurous as a child. Though hearing that Hazel had been the one to primarily rein in Charlotte's adventurous urges after an accident on the back of a horse was quite shocking.

Not that Hazel wanting her child to be safe while out riding was all that surprising. But that safety became such an issue that Charlotte had spent the last half of her life almost fearful of stepping outside her comfort zone because of the way Hazel had freaked out about her daughter not doing anything she deemed too dangerous. Considering how impetuous Hazel could be while matching her kids up with perfect strangers, it seemed out of character for her to stifle those same impulsive tendencies in her daughter.

Ian had several ideas for ways he could bring out that feisty, adventurous side that Charlotte had buried in her teens, even if it was only with him. Not that he could tell her about them at the moment, when he was trying to back away from their sexual connection to build a foundation of friendship to be the base of their relationship in the future.

They ended up having a great time, even though their only physical interactions were holding hands throughout the date and chaste kisses when he dropped her off at her car in the middle school parking lot at the end of their afternoon together.

It's just the first of many days together for the rest of our lives. We have plenty of time for more intimate moments together once we've both healed emotionally, and are fully prepared for marriage and babies and all that life together entails.

And in the meantime, I'll just keep jerking off twice a day in the shower.

Chapter Nineteen

As Charlotte took two over-the-counter pain relievers to deal with her menstrual cramps that came along with her period starting that morning, she remembered she still needed to call and reschedule her appointment with the new gynecologist in town. Unfortunately, she didn't have time at the moment because she had to login to her telehealth therapy appointment during her lunch and planning period at school.

I should probably write myself a note to remind me to do that tomorrow, she thought as she finished the sign-in procedure on her laptop.

Before she could grab her pad of sticky notes to put a reminder beside her computer on her desk, her psychologist, Dr. Ariel Edwards, appeared on her screen to start their session. They went through the standard greetings and check-in questions before getting into the more pertinent discussion about how Charlotte was dealing with the stress of being kidnapped the week before.

"Honestly, the worst of it is worrying about Antonio," Char admitted. "I mean, I wasn't really there long enough to suffer through the atrocities the other women were subjected to at the hands of the cartel. But there's no telling what all that little boy went through in the time he was there."

"In our sessions last week, you mentioned your abductor threatening to sexually abuse the little boy to get a reaction from you," Ariel reiterated their previous conversations from the notes she'd taken in their first couple of sessions. "Have you changed your mind about the sexual abuse of Antonio just being a threat?"

"I don't know," Charlotte sighed. "From the way Roberto worded it, I don't think he personally sexually abused Antonio. But with the way he mentioned his associates' proclivities, I can't say for sure that they didn't. I'm pretty sure that's why I can't see the faces of the men in my nightmares."

"The ones where you're forced to watch?"

"Yeah," Charlotte nodded. "And not being able to see Antonio, or even get an update on him, has me so worried about him that I'm having those nightmares more often than the ones about actually being kidnapped."

They talked for a few minutes about why CPS wouldn't let her see Antonio, with Ariel trying to help her understand that the social workers were doing what they thought was best to take care of Antonio. While Charlotte appreciated they had Antonio's best interest at heart, she didn't agree with their belief that keeping her away from him was actually in his best interest.

"Have you had any dreams or flashbacks about the rescue?"

Charlotte took a deep breath while thinking about her answer. "Yes, and no."

Ariel tilted her head inquisitively, but she didn't say a word to interrupt Charlotte's train of thought.

"No, I haven't had any flashbacks or dreams that are accurate to what happened during the rescue," Charlotte told her honestly. "But I have had nightmares about the rescue going awry."

"Tell me about them."

"It's all pretty accurate up to the point that the lights go out and I hide under the table," Charlotte admitted with a sigh. She reached for a tissue from the box on her desk and dabbed it on the inside corners of her eyes, hoping to stop her tears from actually streaming down her face as she finished her overview of the recurring nightmare. "But then it's Ian coming through the door, without my brothers or cousins or police backup. And the scuffle for the gun ends with Roberto shooting Ian."

"And what do you do when you wake up from those nightmares?"

"Freak out," Charlotte scoffed, feeling like an idiot for letting her nightmares get to her. "Cry into my pillow, wishing Ian was there, so I'd know he was alive and well and perfectly safe."

"Have you talked to him about these nightmares?" Charlotte shook her head in response to Ariel's question. "Why not?"

"Because I'm trying to forget them," Charlotte shrugged. "And with him wanting to slow things down between us right now, I don't want to come off as a clingy psycho by calling and waking him up in the middle of the night, when my nightmares make me worry that something's happened to him."

"Why do you think something has happened to him when you have this nightmare?"

Charlotte just looked at her psychologist on her computer screen with a blank stare, trying to figure out how to explain her family's belief in prophetic dreams and how the nightmares, along with her other dreams have made her start to question whether or not they're right. "There have been multiple incidences in my family where my mother and brother claim their dreams have been fairly accurate in predicting future events in their lives."

"But you know Roberto is dead and can't come back as a zombie to kill Ian, so why do you believe this nightmare is going to come true?"

"I don't believe it's going to come true exactly as I see it in my nightmare," Charlotte swore defensively. "But I'm afraid that now that this cartel is no longer after him, Ian's going to want to go back to being a DEA agent, and some other criminal could kill him. Or if my family is right about dreams foretelling the future, then maybe I'm dreaming about his death because he's going to die soon by some other means, and I'm just picturing it in my nightmares in the only way I've actually seen someone die."

Ariel nodded, jotting down some more notes before asking her next question. "What other dreams or nightmares do you have that you fear might come true?"

"I'm only truly afraid of the nightmares coming true," Charlotte admitted. "It'll just be humiliating to have to admit to my family that they were right about dreams being able to foretell our futures, if my good dreams start happening in real life."

"I take it you've had discussions with your family in the past where you've disagreed with their belief in their dreams coming true?"

"Oh, yeah," Charlotte chuckled. She went on to explain the conversations that had transpired at several family dinners since Anthony announced he'd been dreaming about his future family before he met Kay, and their mother corroborated his belief that he was dreaming about his actual family by mentioning the dreams she had before having her six children.

"So, let me make sure I understand this correctly. Your argument is that the good dreams can't come true without the nightmares also coming true?"

"Yes, exactly," Charlotte nodded, feeling vindicated by her therapist understanding her point of view when her family didn't seem to get it. "So, if my sex dreams about Ian start coming true, or if my life starts to follow the path my dead grandmother told me it will follow in my dream last night, then I have to worry about my nightmares happening in real life, too."

"And have any of your good dreams actually happened in real life?"

"Well, no, not yet," Charlotte admitted sheepishly.

"Then I don't think you have any reason to worry about your nightmares coming true."

"But given our history," Charlotte pointed out. "I fully expect the sex dreams with Ian to eventually happen. Well, whenever he gets over this *going-slow thing* he's got going on since the kidnapping, which I hope will be sooner rather than later."

Ariel quizzically arched an eyebrow. "Tell me more about your history with Ian, and this *going-slow thing*."

"I already told you that we met back in December when he came to town to start setting up his job and that he moved here to track down the guy who kidnapped me, but what I didn't mention is that we actually had a one-night stand the night he was here for his interview at the middle school." Charlotte paused to decide just how graphic she wanted to be with her therapist.

"We had an instant connection, and the sexual chemistry between us is off the charts. But he didn't think we could have more than one night because of the danger the cartel would pose to anyone he got involved with, so he ghosted in the middle of the night."

Charlotte went on to explain how they'd run into each other two weeks later, and then started working together a little over a week after that. She talked about how Ian had denied being her hot, hotel hookup in December while also looking at her with obvious interest. She glossed over the fact that she knew he was interested in her because it was impossible to completely camouflage an erection that size, even in loose trousers. But she did mention how his hot-and-cold act made her feel conflicted about their relationship.

She mentioned how neither one of them could fight their attraction for long, leading to their second hot hookup in February. Then went into detail about how his calling it a mistake had hurt her. She also mentioned how she'd forgiven him for his boneheaded way of trying to protect her, once he came clean about everything going on with the cartel and how he'd lost his wife.

"While he was staying on the ranch after his house was broken into by Roberto or one of his men, we were chaperoned practically twenty-four-seven by our families, so there wasn't much opportunity for dates or hooking up again. We hadn't committed as a couple or anything, but it was obvious that was the direction we were headed. And we did manage to sneak off for a quickie the Friday evening before I was kidnapped, so it seemed like we were both on board for a sexual relationship."

Charlotte paused to take a deep breath and blow it out before getting into the most recent turn of events in her relationship with Ian. "But for the last week, he's decided we need to slow down and not do anything sexual while we're both in therapy to deal with what happened last Monday."

"And you don't agree that slowing down is a good idea?"

Charlotte didn't know how to answer, so she just shook her head.

"You don't think it might be better if you're both at least partially healed from this trauma before you embark on a new relationship?"

"If I hadn't met Ian before the kidnapping, I'd say yes. Now isn't the time to meet someone new and jump into a sexual relationship with them from day one. But we started our relationship four months ago and went through this trauma together. Him wanting to slow things down now feels like he's deserting me when I still need him to lean on, as I'm dealing with the emotional fallout." Charlotte grabbed another tissue and dabbed at her eyes once again, fighting to keep the tears from falling.

"When you say you 'need him to lean on,' do you mean by having sex with him?"

"It's not the only way I want to lean on him," Charlotte defended, suddenly feeling uncomfortable about discussing her sex life in her therapy session. "But when we have sex is when I feel the most connected to him, and I need that connection. It helps build a foundation of trust that we can build on with the long talks and friendly outings we're also doing together. I mean, it's easier to strip yourself emotionally bare to someone, when you're also physically getting naked with them."

"Okay, yeah, I see your point," Ariel chuckled. "I just wanted to make sure you weren't trying to use sex as a way to forget what happened, instead of talking it out and dealing with the feelings."

"I doubt I'll ever forget everything that happened last Monday, or stop worrying about Antonio and what happened to him during the time he was in that madman's clutches. But if it's done right, I don't think a break from having all that stress at the forefront of my mind is a bad thing. And the health benefits of releasing endorphins are pretty impressive."

"Agreed." Ariel smiled as she shifted her eyes to look at something else in the room with her other than her computer. "I just wanted to make sure you weren't self-medicating with sex, to the exclusion of building a healthy relationship with Ian in other ways before I agreed with you. Unfortunately, our time is up for today, so we don't have time to discuss this further. I already have you down for an in person appointment on Friday, so we'll pick this conversation back up then."

"Sounds good." Charlotte smiled at her psychologist, feeling a little lighter after talking through a few things, even though Ariel hadn't given her any new suggestions for how to stop the nightmares or deal with what they might mean. "See you Friday."

~~~

Friday, April 19, 2019

Since they were out of school for Good Friday, Charlotte decided to go to San Antonio to spend a few minutes at the shelter before her therapy appointment. She needed to face her fear of flashbacks to her interactions with Roberto before she'd be able to volunteer at her normal time slot with the lunch prep. While she was there, she hoped to get more information about Antonio from Faith, so she timed her
~~~

visit to the mid-morning, when Faith was less likely to be busy with juggling meal prep and her other duties.

Surely, CPS has been more forthcoming with her than they have with me. At least Charlotte assumed that the program manager of the shelter where Antonio had lived would be included in the short list of people CPS deemed worthy of getting updates on his case status.

She was really frustrated with the runaround she'd gotten from the social workers for the last ten days. Apparently, having also been held by the Rodriguez Cartel for a few hours disqualified her from being able to even get any information about Antonio. Never mind that she was the only other hostage that the little boy would speak to, or that they never would have found him if she hadn't been kidnapped. The CPS social workers believed that seeing anyone who had also been a hostage would be traumatizing for him, so Charlotte was out of luck when it came to finding out how he was doing.

The crushing part of the authorities' refusal to tell her anything was that it meant she had no chance of being allowed to become his foster mom. Regardless of whether or not she ever moved forward as more than friends with Ian, she knew she had plenty of room in her heart for adopting a couple of kids in addition to any she might eventually give birth to, and she knew in her heart of hearts that she wanted to include Antonio in her family, no matter how the rest of it came together.

That sweet little boy had stolen a piece of her heart the first time he attempted to say her name, and it was slowly killing her to not know how he was dealing with everything that had happened to him. So, she hoped Faith would be able to reassure her that he was being well cared for in the CPS group home.

As she drove through the parking garage, she couldn't stop herself from parking in the same place she'd parked almost two months before. *Too bad Ian's not here to have a redo of how that encounter ended. Though I'm sure Ariel would say I was self-medicating with sex, if I had that kind of endorphin release before going into the shelter today. Yeah, I probably won't confess to wanting it right now, when I meet with her in an hour.*

Knowing her time to talk to Faith was limited, she quickly parked her Equinox and made her way down the stairs and across the street to walk the half a block to the shelter. She felt herself shaking as she walked up the stairs to the front door, feeling nervous about being back there for the first time since she was kidnapped. She found herself watching over her shoulder, as if she expected Roberto to jump out at her any second.

Get a grip, Charlotte! She mentally scolded herself, taking a deep breath and steeling her resolve to get through this first visit back. *He's not here. None of his cartel cronies are here. I'm just going to go talk to Faith. I don't have to be afraid to walk inside.*

She took one more cleansing breath before blowing it out and opening the door. Once inside, she waved at Paige in the childcare center before making her way to Faith's office. She knocked on the doorframe as she poked her head in the open door to see if Faith was free to chat.

"Hey, stranger!" Faith exclaimed, waving her into the office. "Long time no see. How are you doing after…you know?"

Charlotte wasn't sure how much Faith knew about what happened, but she knew she'd been informed about the kidnapping when Ian mentioned talking to her during their various debriefs with law enforcement that night. "I'm doing okay. More worried about how Antonio is doing than anything that happened with me."

"You and me, both," Faith frowned.

"Please tell me that CPS has, at least, been more open with you about how he's doing than they have with me," Char implored, though based on Faith's expression, she thought her hope might be futile.

"Sorry, wish I could." Faith shook her head from side to side. "But when they found out that I'd helped Roberto with his INS paperwork without verifying the authenticity of the Mexican birth certificates he showed me, they cut me out completely." She paused, then huffed, "Like I have the resources or contacts to verify the authenticity of documents issued by a foreign country."

"You're not in trouble for that, are you?" Charlotte hadn't even thought about the legal issues Faith could be facing if Homeland Security or Immigration thought she was aiding and abetting a human trafficker.

"No," Faith sighed. "Well, not anymore. It was touch and go there for a while, but then a certain, former DEA agent stepped in on my behalf and convinced them I was acting as a good Samaritan. They ended up confiscating my files on Roberto and Antonio and made sure

I know to refer anyone needing help with INS paperwork to an immigration attorney in the future, but I'm not in any legal trouble."

Charlotte could only smile at hearing how Ian had intervened on Faith's behalf, not even the slightest bit surprised that he'd gotten to know Faith well enough in the brief time he'd volunteered at the shelter to vouch for her character. She'd known from the first moment she met him that there was an innate goodness about him. And even when he was acting hot and cold about his attraction to her, he was always kind and thoughtful.

She talked to Faith for a little while longer, with Charlotte explaining that she needed a little more time in therapy to get her flashbacks and nightmares under control before she'd be ready to volunteer regularly again. Faith understood and told Charlotte to take all the time she needed to take care of herself first. She also offered to be there to talk to Char whenever she needed, whether she came back as a volunteer or not.

She managed to leave the building without having a flashback, as she'd feared. But she also didn't go into the areas of the shelter where she'd had the majority of her interactions with Roberto and Antonio, which was what she assumed would be the trigger to those flashbacks. With as high as her anxiety was just walking into the building, she considered the small step she'd just taken by going into the building to talk to Faith as a win, even if it wasn't a very big one.

Charlotte made it over to the building that housed her psychologist's office with ten minutes to spare before her appointment. She used that time to check in with the office manager and pay her co-pay, not even having to sit down in the waiting room before she was called back to meet with Ariel in her office.

As they'd done with each of the telehealth appointments they'd had, they went through the standard greetings and basic mental health questions before getting into the nitty-gritty of the therapy session. Char knew it was time to talk about the messy relationship stuff when Ariel's first question was, "How do you feel about the talks you've had with Ian and your family this week?"

Charlotte pondered the question for a moment, realizing that her psychologist was asking about more than just the conversation they'd had to cut short on Monday. Since they had ended the second session the previous week by talking about how her family was smothering her after the kidnapping, she decided to address that topic first. "Thankfully, they've all backed off on the hovering this week. My mom still checks on me more often than normal each day, but it's mostly via text while I'm at work and more casually brought up in conversation when she pulls me aside on the ranch. Apparently, your advice to set some boundaries with her was spot on. She hasn't made a big deal in front of the family, or shown up out of the blue since I followed it."

"And the rest of your family?"

"Are pretty much back to normal," Char affirmed.

"And what about the *going-slow thing* with Ian?"

"It's going so slow that I'm worried we're going in reverse," Charlotte sighed. "I mean, I'm enjoying the time we spend together every morning before school having coffee and donuts, and the one afternoon date we went on so far to the Japanese Tea Garden last week. I feel like we've really started getting to know one another on a deeper level since we're spending all that time talking about our lives. But since we aren't doing anything together that we couldn't do with my parents watching, it's starting to feel like we're stuck in the friend zone."

"Have you discussed the abduction or the nightmares you've started having since then with him?"

"Only superficially," Char admitted. "We've acknowledged that we're both in therapy to deal with the trauma, but we haven't discussed the details of our sessions. The only other thing that's been mentioned in our conversations pertaining to that day is my lack of progress in finding out about Antonio from CPS."

"So, you haven't told him about the nightmares?"

"No." Charlotte shook her head. "I'm sure he's having plenty of nightmares of his own. I don't want to burden him with piling mine on top of them."

"You don't think it might help both of you to talk about your nightmares with each other?"

Char sat quietly for a moment, pondering the question. On the one hand, she knew that talking about her nightmares with Ariel had helped her decrease their frequency, which would be an outcome she'd want for Ian if he was suffering from the same issue at night. But on the other hand, she already knew Ian was talking about his issues with his therapist and she didn't believe rehashing the worst of what had happened to them, or what they dreaded might happen to them, repeatedly with different people would help either one of them heal from the trauma any faster than they were by just talking to their individual therapists.

But when she really thought about it, she wasn't confident in her reasoning that repeatedly talking about something traumatic would make the trauma more pervasive in someone's mind, which was why she wanted to avoid retelling her nightmares. She wasn't an expert in the field of psychology by any means, so she decided to ask Ariel's opinion.

"I guess, I assumed that repeatedly talking about what happened and the nightmares that I've had since would give those horrible events more space in my head. And I'd rather try to get those images out of my head and not by passing them on to someone else to have to deal with in their head. But you're the expert, who probably hears about a lot of horrific nightmares daily, so if I'm wrong in that assumption, you'd be the one to tell me the benefits of talking about our nightmares with more than just our therapists."

"I can definitely understand your trepidation. But I'm not suggesting you go into detail, reliving the traumatic events or describing the nightmares. I'm talking about building a support system. Only instead of going to a support group for trauma survivors, you and Ian could be a support group of two. Having gone through this event together, you don't have to know the details of his nightmares to know he's having them."

Charlotte nodded along, as Dr. Edwards explained how beneficial it is to an individual's well-being just to know they aren't the only one suffering from whatever they are dealing with, even when the other people going through the same thing can't offer any suggestions for how to ease the burden.

"In our previous session, you said something about how slowing things down in your relationship with Ian felt like he was abandoning you when you needed him to lean on after all this."

"Yes," Char sheepishly agreed, recalling the conversation about their sex life vividly.

"What if that's his way of trying to be there for you emotionally, or to lean on you a little while dealing with his own issues from all this, without the physical aspect of your relationship getting in the way?"

Charlotte tilted her head as she stared across the desk at her therapist. She hadn't thought of those possibilities as motivating factors for why Ian was friend-zoning her. She'd thought his whole spiel about being unworthy of her because he'd wanted revenge on the man responsible for his wife's death was a cop-out, when he didn't want to reveal that he felt guilty for being with Charlotte while still feeling married to Mari. But she hadn't thought he might have any other reasons for backing away from their sexual attraction.

When Char mentioned all that to Ariel, the psychologist shrugged. "You could be right, and I could be completely off base. I don't know Ian. I haven't met him, spoken to him, or even reviewed his file to know what he's talked about in his sessions. I just tried to imagine how I'd feel if I were in his shoes. And if I'd just rescued someone I'd recently started a sexual relationship with from human traffickers, who are known for sexually abusing their victims, I wouldn't want to push to continue the sexual side of the relationship until I knew it wouldn't be a trigger for them."

"Wow, that makes a lot of sense." Charlotte leaned back in her chair, trying to comprehend everything from Ian's perspective.

He's definitely the type of man who wouldn't want to pressure me if he thought it could trigger a bad reaction after being held by the cartel. But he knows I wasn't sexually assaulted by them after sitting in on all the statements I had to give to the various law enforcement agencies on the scene that night. So, there has to be another reason why he's holding back sexually.

Is he having flashbacks to the rescue, the same way I am? Only having a much worse outcome in his nightmares than actually happened, the same way I am?

Or is he feeling guilty that he was able to bring in my brothers and cousins to save me, when he couldn't save his wife? Shit! I bet that's it! He doesn't want to be with me now because he's wishing he'd have been able to save her.

I really need to talk to him to find out what he's thinking and feeling. If he's still missing her so much that he feels guilty for moving on with me, then we're not meant to be together. At least, not right now, anyway.

But until I talk to him about his nightmares, I won't know if slowing things down between us is his way of breaking things off with me, or just him giving me space to heal, so we can build a strong foundation for our future relationship.

"So, my point in all that is to help you realize that you can't assume what his thought process consists of, or how any of the events ya'll have been through are affecting him without talking to him. And to help you be a little more patient and understanding, so you don't pressure him into more than he's ready for in your relationship at the moment. I want you to be able to take this *slow-down thing* as the gift it can be for both of you. And while ya'll are talking about everything else in your lives, add in some conversations about how you're each dealing with the nightmares."

They went on to discuss some coping strategies that Charlotte could try in the middle of the night when she awoke in a panic, as well as more visualization exercises she could do when she had to fight the flashbacks she had at the ball fields when she was coaching her softball team and to prepare for volunteering at the shelter again.

Once again, she felt lighter at the end of the session and actually looked forward to talking to Ian about the coping strategies she'd just learned while on their afternoon date. She even smiled the whole way over to the RiverWalk, where they were meeting to explore the area while they talked.

~~~

Ian spent his morning off playing catch in the park with Brody before dropping his son off with his sister to go to his therapy session. He was still on edge while at the park with his son, worried about flashbacks as much as another ambush. Thankfully, Brody didn't seem to notice that his father spent as much time watching their surroundings as he did watching his son catch the ball.

Theoretically, he knew the Rodriguez Cartel was no longer an issue with their members being dead or in jail. But after almost two-and-a-half years of avoiding parks with his son to keep him safe, Ian knew
~~~

he'd need more than a couple of weeks to get used to not having to watch for another drive-by shooter situation. Thankfully, that's what therapy was for — to help reduce his anxiety and get him back to a more normal life.

After therapy, he had another afternoon date with Charlotte scheduled. During their early dinner at one of the restaurants on the RiverWalk the previous week, they'd decided that it would be another great option for where they could walk and talk without interruption on an afternoon, when most people would still be at work. So, that's what they had planned for their afternoon.

But before Ian could meet Charlotte at the parking garage they'd designated the previous week as where they'd start their date before picking a restaurant for lunch on the RiverWalk, he had to get through his therapy session with Dr. Ryan Edwards. When he signed in for the appointment, he saw Charlotte's name on the line above his on the sign-in sheet. He looked around for her, but assumed she'd already been called back to speak with her therapist, when he didn't see her in the waiting room.

Guess we both planned to use our day off for a therapy session before our date. Thinking of Charlotte going through the same steps he was to move past the ordeal with the cartel relaxed him a little. It was good to know they were both on the same journey to healing before progressing in their relationship. *Hopefully, she's not struggling with nightmares and flashbacks as bad as mine.*

As soon as he finished the check-in procedures, he was called back to Ryan's office for his session. Once they were seated across the desk from one another and the cordial greetings were dispensed with, Ryan got straight to the point. "Have the nightmares eased up any this week?"

"No," Ian huffed, frustrated with his lack of progress. "If anything, they're getting worse."

"Why do you say that?" Dr. Edwards made a note on the tablet in front of him.

"Because I'm barely getting to sleep before I'm waking up from the first one of the night. Then I struggle to go back to sleep. And if I somehow manage to get back to sleep, I'll have another nightmare. And it doesn't seem to matter how many times I wake up in the middle of the night. If I go to sleep at all, even for a short nap, I have a nightmare. Some nights, I have four or five." Ian shook his head, wishing he could shake the memories of the horrific visions that haunted him from his mind. "And the flashbacks during the day are just as bad. If I hear a car backfiring, or a kid drops a book in class, I'm right back in that park in my head. Only Mari isn't the only one dying. I'm seeing Brody, Caitir, and Charlotte dying, too."

"And what do you do to try to get back to sleep?"

"I go peek in on Brody to make sure he's still in his bed, sound asleep," Ian admitted. "Then I'll go downstairs to the home gym to lift weights, trying to wear myself out, so I can sleep. If that doesn't work, then I'll try lying in bed reading. And as a last resort, I'll have a stiff drink."

"Let's look at those things one at a time," Dr. Ryan Edwards suggested. "When you go check on Brody, do you also check on Caitir? Or think about calling to check on Charlotte?"

"I learned the first time around not to check on Caitir," Ian chuckled. "She's a light sleeper, so I can't even open her bedroom door without waking her. And I know if she realizes I'm having nightmares again, then she'll start having nightmares again, too. I wouldn't wish these on my worst enemy, much less my sister, so I can't even talk to her about them."

"And what about calling to talk to Charlotte?"

"I don't want to wake her up either." Ian shook his head.

"What about texting her?" Ryan gave Ian a moment to think about the suggestion before adding, "that way you might not wake her up. But if she's up from her own nightmares, then she might need someone to talk to about them at the same time you do. Maybe it could strengthen your bond by leaning on each other."

Ian contemplated the suggestion, not sure he really wanted to risk scaring Charlotte with the nightmares he was having since she was abducted. "I don't want to scare her," Ian voiced his objection. "Besides, it would be pretty awkward to talk about my dreams about Mari with Charlotte."

He didn't mention how uncomfortable he'd been whenever he'd occasionally mentioned Mari to Charlotte over the past few months. But his biggest issue with talking to Charlotte about Mari was that he was afraid it would make Charlotte feel like he was comparing the two of them. And since he had compared them some when he first met Charlotte, he couldn't outright deny doing it to spare her feelings.

He'd also quickly realized they were drastically different women and his feelings for each of them weren't comparable. While he would always have a special place in his heart for Mari because of their time together and the fact that she gave birth to his first child, meeting Charlotte showed him that his love for Mari was based on thinking it was time to settle down more than anything else.

His feelings for Charlotte were drastically different. Yes, he wanted the whole package with her. Marriage, family, and happily ever after. But he also needed to be with her in a way he'd never felt before. He felt an all-consuming, almost overwhelming, emotional, soul-deep connection with Charlotte. It was like she was his missing piece. And he wanted to give her inner peace, not traumatize her further by sharing his nightmares with her.

"Before we go back to the other things you've tried to help you sleep, tell me what you're thinking right now."

"Ugh," Ian groaned, not wanting to divulge his feelings for Charlotte to his psychologist before he actually told her how he felt about her. But he knew therapy wouldn't work, unless he was completely open and honest with his therapist. "I was thinking about how my feelings for Charlotte are different than what I felt with Mari."

"How so?"

"They're deeper. More intense," Ian confessed. "Which is strange considering we're just getting to know one another, while I had several years with Mari."

"Do you think those differences are affecting your nightmares?" Dr. Edwards made a few more notes on his tablet.

Ian wondered if the psychologist was just making notes of what Ian said, or if he was also logging his opinions on how everything linked together to be a root cause of Ian's nightmares.

"Maybe," Ian supposed, trying to figure out how his feelings for both Mari and Charlotte could be impacting the content of his flashbacks, both when he was awake and when he was asleep. "You think it could be that I'm feeling guilty for replacing Mari in my life with Charlotte, so that's why I'm also swapping them in my nightmares?"

"Possibly," Ryan nodded. "With losing Mari so tragically, it's feasible you haven't completely healed from the loss yet to be ready to move on with Charlotte."

Ian thought back to his previous therapy sessions, when he'd talked to his therapist in San Diego about not feeling like he had closure, since they hadn't had a public funeral for Mari when she passed. With Michael Campbell needing to stay hidden to appear to have died at the same time, a funeral for Marisol Campbell wasn't an option because the cartel would have easily found him.

Ian had followed his therapist's advice on the one-year anniversary of Mari's passing and had a private ceremony with just him, Brody, Caitir, and Trent, scattering her ashes at the beach where he'd first met her. Trent had insisted on having a couple of agents shadowing them, just in case the cartel caught wind of being duped by his unreal demise. But when the day went by without incident, Ian thought he had closure, both in letting Mari go and in worrying about the cartel finding and harming his remaining family.

Did coming here to try to finish shutting down the cartel reopen the wounds? Is that why I had to give myself a pep talk the night I met Charlotte to convince myself that Mari would be okay with me moving on with my life?

Ian knew he couldn't answer those questions himself, so he explained to his therapist how he thought he'd had closure before voicing those questions out loud. When Dr. Edwards agreed with his assessment, they spent the rest of their time talking about how Ian might be able to finally get closure on his time with Mari.

At the very end of their session, they finally went back to the discussion about the things Ian had tried to go back to sleep, with the psychologist suggesting he drop the activities that could be waking him up more, instead of relaxing him to be able to sleep. Ryan offered a few suggestions for promoting peaceful sleep that Ian could try that wouldn't require a referral to a psychiatrist for medicinal intervention.

By the time he made it to the RiverWalk to meet Charlotte, Ian felt much better about his potential to eradicate his nightmares in the near future. Unfortunately, that feeling didn't last long. As soon as they started walking along the RiverWalk, Charlotte's choice of opening topic put him right back on edge.

"In my session this morning, my therapist suggested you and I form our own support group to have someone other than our therapists to talk to when we have nightmares or flashbacks or whatever," she casually mentioned, as if she hadn't just dropped a bomb on him.

Fuck! Fuck! Fuck! How do I tell her I don't want to talk to her about my nightmares without hurting her feelings?

"Um, okay," Ian sputtered. "What, um, what does starting a support group entail?"

Hopefully, she's thinking about finding a location and setting up meetings with other people who suffer from nightmares after traumatic events, so I can put off actually having to talk about them while we search for a venue.

"She wasn't talking about a typical support group like they host in their offices for people with depression or anxiety or whatever," Charlotte explained as they continued walking. "But just the two of us being able to lean on one another to have someone to call in the middle of the night, or whenever we have a flashback and need to hear the calming voice of someone else who understands what we're going through."

"Oh, um, okay." Ian nodded, even though he hated the idea of appearing weak to Charlotte by needing to call her in the middle of the night after a nightmare. *But this isn't just about me and my nightmares. This is about Charlotte and her nightmares, too. And I want to be there for her to help her heal after the trauma she suffered, so I need to quit worrying about my own shit, and man up to be there for her the way she deserves.* "You know you're more than welcome to call me anytime you need that, right? We don't have to make it a support group. That's just being a good friend."

"But we haven't really talked about the kidnapping, or how it's affected us," Charlotte sighed, her shoulders slumping as if she felt defeated. "So, I didn't know if you even realized I'm having nightmares about it, too."

"I'm sorry, Princess." Ian reached over and took her hand in his, hating that he'd been so oblivious that he didn't realize she needed him to talk to the past couple of weeks. "I haven't wanted to make things worse by bringing up the subject. I figured you were dealing with everything in therapy, the same way I am, so we could keep our conversations more friendly and fun. And maybe we could both forget about the cartel and their actions for a little while when we're together. But I'm here for you whenever you're ready to talk about all of it."

"I don't think I need to talk about all of it, so much as I need to know I'm not the only one having nightmares about how that rescue could have gone wrong," Charlotte admitted, squeezing his hand as she leaned her head on his shoulder.

Fuck! Ian involuntarily groaned, unable to bite it back with the curse in his head as he realized he couldn't honestly be that person for Charlotte. Charlotte stiffened beside him before slowly lifting her head and turning to look at him. Ian closed his eyes as they stopped walking, knowing she'd be able to read the truth in his eyes, even though he wanted to lie to make her feel better.

"You don't have nightmares about how the rescue could have gone wrong." Charlotte's words were an obvious declaration. She knew without question that they weren't dealing with the same issues since her abduction to be able to lean on one another.

"No," Ian admitted, wishing he didn't have to tell her the details of his nightmares. "The gunfire that night actually triggered a return of my flashbacks to the shooting in San Diego before we even had the first floor cleared to start searching for you and Roberto upstairs. And my nightmares since have all been back in that park without a weapon or backup. Only Mari isn't the only person I love who dies in my dreams."

Ian was too choked up to continue, unable to tell her that he watched her, his sister, and his son die four or five times a night.

"Oh, Ian," Charlotte consoled him, reaching up to wipe away the tears he hadn't even realized had started falling. "I'm so sorry. I shouldn't have brought it all up now."

"No, I'm glad you did." Ian sucked in a deep breath and forced his watery eyes to dry up, uncomfortable showing so much emotion in a public place. "And I meant what I said earlier. I want to be here for you to talk to whenever you need to, even if it's when you wake up from a nightmare in the middle of the night. While our nightmares aren't the same, I still understand what you're going through with having them."

"Okay," Charlotte tentatively agreed. "And you can call me when you have nightmares, too. But maybe we can talk about something else to get our minds off the bad dreams and help us go back to sleep afterward."

"Deal," Ian agreed wholeheartedly, deciding to change the subject of their current conversation, too. "Now, where are we eating lunch?"

"I was thinking with your love of rock music, you might enjoy the Hard Rock Café," Charlotte suggested with a grin.

"Ah, finally!" Ian cheered in an overdramatic fashion to lighten the mood. "Someplace that won't be playing country music!"

Chapter Twenty

After the past few weeks, Charlotte was glad to get back to a more normal family activity of helping her brother and his family move on the bye week she had off from softball games. While her regular therapy appointments and talks with Ian had helped her get over the majority of the trauma of the day she was kidnapped, she was rapidly growing frustrated with only going on platonic, Friday afternoon dates with Ian for the last three weeks. But no matter how hard she tried to follow Ariel's advice to be patient and understanding of Ian's need to slow things down, she still struggled with fighting her attraction to him.

If a man can think with the head of his dick, can a woman think with her vagina? If so, then I think my vajayjay is trying to override my brain and sending me all these signals to forget this friend-zone shit he's insisting on by mounting up and riding him.

She was beginning to wonder if he needed a reminder of their sexual chemistry, since he kept everything so platonic between them lately. Even the sweet little things he did, like bringing her coffee and donuts at school every morning, were starting to feel like friendly gestures, instead of romantic ones like they'd felt at first. When she barely got a peck of a kiss out of him, and sometimes just a hug, not even a peck, at the end of their time together, she was really starting to feel romantically rebuffed.

So, making plans with her family instead of him on the day they both had off from ball games seemed like her best course of action to keep from having to fight her libido to avoid another rejection from him. Thankfully, Anthony's new house being completed gave her the perfect excuse to not spend any time with Ian on their otherwise free Saturday.

Anthony and Kay had come home earlier in the week on leave from the GWA and wouldn't be leaving town again until after having their baby boy. And Char was looking forward to spending more time with her baby brother, sister-in-law, and nieces as they prepared for baby boy Burleson's arrival, even though she was still a little discombobulated by Anthony's dreams about his family seeming to be coming true.

Her own recent dreams about Memmaw Judy coming to visit her in the middle of the night were weighing heavy on her mind, as she helped pack up the dishes and other kitchen items for them to be moved first thing by the women of the family while the guys were upstairs preparing the bedroom furniture for the move, so they could sleep in their new house for the first time that night. While she was grateful that the strange dreams about Memmaw had replaced the majority of the nightmares she'd been having since the kidnapping, she still struggled with anxiety about the meaning of the nightmares and her fear that they might play out in real life.

Since she couldn't shake the weird vibe she had about Dream Memmaw's predictions for her life coming true, she still worried about the nightmares coming true, too. Charlotte tried to put her brief relapse of concern about the nightmares out of her mind by focusing instead on the other recurring dreams she'd been having. Not wanting to blush and give away her thoughts to her family by thinking about the sex dreams with Ian, she revisited the dream she'd had the night before with Memmaw Judy telling her about her future instead.

If everything Memmaw said in my dreams about me getting pregnant before marrying Ian comes true, then I'm naming that little girl Judy after her. Charlotte giggled at the thought of taking revenge on her Memmaw posthumously for proving her wrong about prophetic dreams by giving her daughter the name her grandmother disliked.

"What's so funny?" Kay inquired when she heard Charlotte's giggles.

"Just thinking about a dream I had last night." Charlotte waved a hand in front of her face to stop the uncharacteristic giggles.

"Oh, this must have been a good dream. Now you've gotta share it, Sis." Becky leaned across the island between her and Char, resting her chin on her hand as she implored her sister to dish the deets.

"It wasn't really the dream that was funny," Charlotte admitted, shaking her head at her sister. She didn't want to divulge she was the slightest bit hopeful Dream Memmaw's prophecy would come true after the way she'd argued with her family about dreams coming true in the past.

"Then what was funny?" Brooklyn joined them in taking a break from packing.

"You know how I don't believe our dreams can tell our futures," Charlotte sighed, surprised she was about to confess such a thing to her sister and sisters-in-law. Although she was relieved that they'd all stopped asking her how she was doing after the kidnapping, she wasn't completely convinced that talking about her dreams and the possibility of them coming true was a better option. *I just won't think about the nightmares. And I definitely won't mention them.*

"Yeah," they all nodded in unison.

"Well, last night I had a dream that Memmaw Judy came to visit. She woke me up to sit on the side of my bed and tell me all about the birth of my first child." Charlotte cringed at the looks of surprise and delight on the faces around her. "And I was just thinking that if what she told me actually comes true, I'd get back at her for proving me wrong about prophetic dreams by naming my daughter Judy because I know she disliked her name."

"Geez, Char, if you do that, you know Memmaw will haunt you forever in your dreams," Becky teased, laughing as if she thought being haunted would be a fitting punishment for Charlotte.

"Boy, you Burlesons really don't like being wrong, do you?" Kay chuckled. "Trying to get revenge on your memmaw's spirit sounds even crazier than Anthony insisting we have to wait until we hear about an orphan named Antonio before we look into adoption for our fourth child, just so he knows we'll end up with the little boy he dreamed about."

Charlotte's jaw dropped at Kay's revelation that they were actively expecting to adopt an orphaned little boy named Antonio. She stumbled back and flopped into a kitchen chair that she was grateful hadn't already been moved when some of her memmaw's words from a previous dream ran through her head.

"Protect Antonio. He's gonna be your nephew one day."

"Holy shit!" Charlotte wasn't sure if she said the words aloud or only in her head as she stared at her sister-in-law in shock.

"Are you okay?"

"Geez, Char, you're white as a ghost."

Her sister, sisters-in-law, and cousins all gathered around her, trying to make sure she wasn't going to pass out or something. But Charlotte couldn't make out who was saying what, or even half the words being spoken all around her, as she tried to wrap her mind around the possibility of her dreams overlapping with Anthony's and actually becoming reality.

When Kay pulled another chair in front of Charlotte and took the seat to start wiping her face with a cool washcloth, Char finally started coming around to all the activity around her. She looked deep into her sister-in-law's bright blue eyes as she reached up and took both of Kay's hands in hers.

"I know who your Antonio is," Charlotte whispered reverently. "I worked with him at the shelter, and Memmaw told me to protect him in a dream because he was going to be my nephew. I'd forgotten about the dream in all the chaos when I was kidnapped and found out Antonio was also being held at the same place. But you saying his name just now made me remember."

"Holy shit is right!" Tears sprang to her eyes as Kay squeezed Charlotte's hands three quick times. "I knew you'd worked with a little boy at the shelter, and he was with you when you were rescued, but I didn't ever hear his name. Do you know where he is now?"

"No," Charlotte sobbed, shaking her head. "He was turned over to CPS while they try to figure out his citizenship situation, and I haven't been able to get any other information about him."

Char had been getting the run-around for the last three weeks whenever she tried to call CPS to ask about Antonio. The social worker who came to the hospital the night of the kidnapping had seemed like it would be no big deal for Charlotte to get set up as a foster parent to take care of him. But then the other people in the CPS office had shut that idea down, citing her single status as not favorable for fostering, along with saying it might be traumatic for him to see her after being held in captivity by the cartel together.

Faith had at least been able to confirm that the Mexican birth certificate that Roberto had presented to the shelter and INS was fake, after talking to the Homeland Security agents she'd turned her files over to during their investigation of her involvement with Roberto's criminal activity. But even she'd been shut down from getting any information about Antonio's situation in the system, when the CPS officials found out she'd helped Roberto with the paperwork for his and Antonio's political asylum status with the Immigration and Naturalization Service.

"Maybe I can help with that," Brooklyn interjected, kneeling down between Charlotte and Kay, and covering their joined hands with hers. "Surely, all that paperwork I've been doing with the state to get the Madeline Ashbury House approved as a group home gives me enough of an in with CPS to find my nephew, right?"

"I'm sure it does." Kay nodded at Brooklyn before squealing at the top of her lungs, "Anthony!"

The ladies heard a crash of some kind before the stampede of heavy footfalls that signaled Anthony and the rest of the Burleson men rushing to the kitchen from where they were upstairs taking apart the beds.

"I should have probably grabbed my phone and texted him, huh?" Kay giggled as she turned to see her husband stumble into the room.

Charlotte had to laugh at seeing both her youngest and oldest brother rushing in, followed by her father, uncle, and a couple of cousins.

"Baby, what's wrong?" Anthony fell to his knees beside Kay before reaching over to wipe the tears off his wife's face.

Char had a momentary jolt of jealousy at seeing the love between her brother and sister-in-law. She wanted that soul-deep connection with Ian, but she wasn't sure when they'd heal enough to be more than friends. Since he confided in her that he couldn't be more with anyone until he stopped having nightmares about losing his wife, she didn't think it would be anytime soon.

Her heart had plummeted when he first made that revelation the previous week, thinking they'd be stuck in the friend zone forever. But in their middle-of-the-night talks since then, he'd clarified that the worst part of the nightmares was that he also lost Brody, Caitir, and Charlotte in that ambush. Realizing she was included in the list of people he loved and lost in his nightmares gave Charlotte hope that they could eventually move past the trauma to openly love one another.

"Nothing's wrong." Kay shook her head as she pulled her hands from Charlotte and Brooklyn's to reach for Anthony. "But we need to go ahead and get started furnishing Antonio's room, so it's ready for whatever site visits CPS has to do before we can adopt him."

"What?" Anthony looked shell-shocked as he squeezed Kay's hands, the same way Kay had squeezed Charlotte's a few minutes before.

I'll have to remember to ask them the meaning of that three-squeeze thing they do so often later.

"I've already met your son," Charlotte blubbered, tearing up once again. She was overwhelmed with emotion at the thought of the little boy she already loved joining her family.

In trying to comfort Antonio during the time they were being held captive, she'd told him that he'd have a home soon. Little did she know at the time that she was talking about her brother's home. Or that he'd not only have a home, but also a whole, loving family that could give him all the love and support he needed to heal after the ordeal he'd suffered through for months.

I can't wait to be his favorite aunt and hear all the stories Antonio is going to share with me after Anthony and Kay adopt him. He's going to love all the adventures he'll be able to go on as a part of their family.

As much as she'd thought she wanted to foster and adopt him herself, Charlotte realized Anthony and Kay could provide things for him that she couldn't. If any of their dreams had to come true, then Anthony and Kay adopting Antonio was definitely the one that she would choose to make into reality.

"And I'm going to help you find him in the system, so you can start the adoption," Brooklyn added, bringing Char out of her mental musings.

"You are, huh?" Bobby questioned his new wife as he pulled her up from the floor.

"Fine, *we* are." Brooklyn rolled her eyes at Bobby as she wrapped her arms around him. "With the help of the whole Madeline Ashbury Foundation."

"Seriously?" Anthony's gaze roamed first to Charlotte, then up to Bobby and Brooklyn, before settling on Kay once more. "For real?"

"Yeah, for real." Kay nodded, grinning at Anthony.

Charlotte started filling them in on the details she knew about Antonio Reyes, so they could all get on the same page regarding what needed to be done to find him in the system and start the adoption process. She barely finished telling her brother about his potential new son when her mother burst in through the back door.

"What's this I'm hearing about getting another grandson via text?" Hazel Burleson shouted, slamming her hands on her hips with her phone still held in one.

Charlotte could only laugh at her mother's indignant excitement. She quickly relayed the whole sordid tale, glad to finally find the silver lining to the kidnapping, so she could move on with her life. And so could the rest of her family, including a special little boy who might soon be her favorite nephew.

But first, we actually have to get started moving his future family into their new home.

~~~

Sunday, April 28, 2019

After three weeks of sessions with Dr. Ryan Edwards, where he'd started discussing more than just his PTSD issues, Ian had finally taken the total-honesty-in-relationships message to heart, and came clean to his sister about submitting his DNA for testing to learn about their Campbell ancestors. Caitir still didn't want to take the chance that one of the druggie losers their mother had slept with might seek them out if she submitted her sample to a public site the way Ian had, but she supported him in learning more about their maternal grandparents' family histories. Since Cait wasn't interested in helping him with the research, though, Ian decided to use it as an excuse to
~~~

spend some time with Charlotte, without her family getting suspicious of them being more than friends.

So, while Cait and Brody went to see Anthony, Kay, and their daughters' new home on the Burleson Ranch after church on Sunday afternoon, Ian took advantage of the time his family wanted to hang out with friends to spend some time alone with Charlotte at her house on the ranch to review his DNA info on the family tree site. With everyone in her family knowing how she'd helped several of her other friends with deciphering their results, it made sense that she would help Ian, even though they were "just friends," at least according to what she was telling everyone, anyway.

And since we didn't have any ball games yesterday, I'll take any excuse I can to spend time with her today to make up for not getting to see her at all, when I normally would have, at least, been able to watch her from across the fields then.

"So, now that I've got my results, what do I need to do first to trace my Campbell ancestors?" Though Ian could easily figure out the site on his own, he liked the idea of having Charlotte lean in close to him to show him what to do on his laptop.

Fuck! I must be a masochist to torture myself by having her so close and not being able to touch her the way I desperately want to be touching her.

"Before we do that, we need to check your DNA match list to make sure we're not related." Charlotte pointed to a link on the screen to look at the list of his DNA matches on the site.

Ian clicked on the link and found an exceptionally long list of people who shared parts of his DNA on the site. "This is going to take a while to look through for your name," he pointed out.

"Not nearly as long as you think," Charlotte corrected, pointing to another link to look at the matches by location. Once the flattened-out world map came up, he saw markers for a lot of his biological relatives in Texas. "Now zoom in on the Heart's Destiny area to see if any of us show up."

He was relieved to see that the closest markers he saw to Heart's Destiny were twelve distant relatives in San Antonio, with none of the Burlesons or anyone else in Heart's Destiny coming up as having even one centimorgan of DNA in common with Ian. When he zoomed back out on the map to see around the globe, he realized the majority of his matches were in the United States and Canada, with a few showing up in places as far away as Australia and New Zealand.

He was surprised to find that there were only nine matches showing up in Europe, eight of which were in England and one in Germany. These numbers were even more astounding when Charlotte had him click over to his ethnicity breakdown to see that his DNA came up as forty-two percent from Scotland, thirty-eight percent from England & Northwestern Europe, seven percent from Ireland, four percent from the Jewish peoples of Europe, three percent from Wales, two percent from Sweden & Denmark, two percent from France, one percent from Finland, and one percent from Germanic Europe. With all of his DNA originating in Europe, he would have thought more than nine of his DNA matches who'd taken the test would still live there.

When he mentioned that to Charlotte, she explained that the map only listed the DNA matches who put their location on their profiles on the site. She also verified that Heart's Destiny, Texas, was listed on her profile. So, when she didn't show up on his map, she knew they weren't related.

"Now you need to start building your family tree to follow the paper trail of your grandparents' ancestors," Charlotte instructed, pointing to the correct section of the website to start a family tree. "The more information you can put in about them, the more hints you'll get to be able to trace their lives back to previous generations."

Ian followed her directions, feigning his need for her to show him the specific steps to add each person to his tree and link his DNA to him on the tree to keep her close. He basked in her blackberry, jasmine, and vanilla scent, wishing he was close enough to pick up a hint of her innate musk of arousal to go along with the smell he knew was from her bodywash and lotion.

Fuck! I've got to quit torturing myself with thoughts about fucking her, when I can't be with her yet.

Ian was struggling with following his therapist's advice to keep things platonic between them, until he felt like he was over the majority of his nightmares and had a handle on the rest of his PTSD issues. He'd followed Dr. Edwards' advice to write a letter telling Mari goodbye to help him feel the sense of closure he needed on their relationship. While he didn't believe the hokey part of the process that burning the letter after writing out all his feelings would send the message to her in Heaven through the smoke, he did feel the sense of closure that had been missing since his move to Texas after following the advice.

However, he still had to figure out how to deal with the night terrors that hadn't completely stopped. Changing his nighttime routine to promote better sleep seemed to be helping some, with the frequency of his nightmares dropping to only one a night. But he was afraid that melatonin, a white noise machine, and lavender essential oil in a diffuser in his bedroom wouldn't be able to rid him of them completely.

He was also still battling with his compulsion to always have an arsenal of weapons on him in case of another ambush, when he needed to be able to defend the people he loved. While his psychologist had managed to get him down to only carrying two concealed handguns and leaving his pocket knife at home, Ian feared it was only because he knew the pocket knife would be useless in a gunfight that he agreed to quit carrying it.

He wasn't sure what it would actually take to get him to feel at ease enough to quit carrying his thirty-eight special in his ankle holster and his Glock at the small of his back. *Though I suppose being able to get naked with Charlotte is the best reward Dr. Edwards could think of to convince me to leave my weapons in my gun case. I guess that's why he pushed so hard for me to keep us in the friend zone for now. So he can help me decide when I've hit the right milestones to be rewarded with making love to her again.*

Charlotte brought him out of his thoughts by pointing to the next thing he should click to see if there were any hints about his grandparents that he could follow to find their parents in the records on the site. When he clicked where she instructed, it brought up his family tree with him at the home position. Looking at it from this view, it looked a little lopsided since he'd just put in the information for his mother and grandparents, without listing his biological father, even though he knew the man's name.

He started to ask Charlotte if she thought he needed to add his sperm donor's information to the tree to be able to see if any of his DNA matches were related on that side of the tree, but didn't get the chance when she pointed out the potential parent tabs that were showing for his grandparents.

He started clicking on them to add them to the tree instead. *I'll just look at the DNA matches that show up on these branches of the tree. And hopefully, I won't have anyone from my sperm donor's family contact me on here to find out how we're related.*

They had worked their way back through a few generations of his Campbell ancestors that they added to his family tree when Charlotte's phone rang. She pulled back from her seat close to him at her dining room table to answer it.

"Hey, Josh," she greeted her caller, whom Ian assumed was her brother, as she leaned back in her chair. "What's up?"

Ian continued to evaluate the potential ancestor tabs that popped up on his tree while listening to Charlotte's side of the conversation. Though he didn't have a clue what the conversation was about, he enjoyed the melodic tone of her voice as she kept agreeing with whatever Josh was saying.

"Seriously?" Charlotte screeched, drawing his attention away from the profile of his possible fifth-great-grandmother that he was reviewing before adding her to his family tree. "Yeah, give me a minute to get my computer, and I'll look at it on my account."

"Here, use mine." Ian didn't know why she needed her computer, but his was right there and already running, so he turned it in her direction and pointed at the keyboard.

"Thanks," Charlotte smiled at him as she pulled her phone from her ear, switched it to speaker mode, and laid it on the table beside the computer. She then logged out of his account on the family tree site and quickly logged in on her account. "You have to authorize me to look at your DNA matches, so I can see the one you're talking about."

"How do I do that?" Josh sounded distraught through the phone, making Ian wonder what he'd found on his match list that upset him.

Charlotte walked her brother through the steps to give her authorization to look at his DNA test results, and within moments, she was looking at his match list. Ian looked over her shoulder to see that Josh had three people listed in the Parent-Child category that shared fifty percent of his DNA. Two of them listed their first and last names and matched up with his parents, Bob and Hazel Burleson. The third was listed as "Triple J" with no family tree linked to the match. All his siblings were listed in the Immediate Family category just below those three with shared DNA between forty-seven and forty-nine percent.

"Um, Josh, this looks like you have a kid out there you don't know about," Charlotte sputtered, her face the picture of shock.

"You sure it isn't another brother? Like maybe Jake and I aren't twins, but triplets with one of us being stolen at birth? I thought maybe that could be the case since we were born in the hospital in San Antonio, and Jake comes the closest to fifty percent of his DNA matching mine." Josh sounded frantic as he laid out his theory.

"I mean, I suppose that could be possible," Charlotte hesitantly agreed. "Let me look for this Triple J on my match list, and see how much DNA I share with him to see if we have enough shared DNA to be siblings."

She clicked over to her DNA match list and scrolled down to find the profile in question in the Close Family category with twenty-eight percent of the same DNA as Charlotte. When she clicked on the profile name and then the amount of their shared DNA, a second window popped up listing the possibilities for how she could be related to the person.

"I only share twenty-eight percent of my DNA with Triple J," Charlotte told Josh. "And this says there's a hundred percent chance that he is either my grandparent, grandchild, half-sibling, aunt or uncle, or niece or nephew. So, it looks to me like someone has put her child's DNA up on here and you're coming up as the baby's daddy."

"Fuck," Josh groaned through the phone. "How am I supposed to find the kid to step up, when all she's listed on his profile is a username, which doesn't identify either of them in any way, and that they joined the site and last signed in on it last month?"

"I guess you have to hope you have enough information on your profile that she can identify you and reach out," Charlotte shrugged. "Maybe send them a message on the site to let them know you want to step up and give them your phone number to contact you, so they know how whenever they sign in on the site again."

"Yeah, okay, I can do that," Josh sighed, sounding a little less flustered by the revelation.

They talked for a few more minutes about what all Josh should write in his message, and agreed not to mention anything to the rest of the family until Josh figured out the identity of his unknown DNA match, before disconnecting the call. Charlotte then signed back out of her account on Ian's computer and turned it back over to him.

"So, I guess you have another nephew out there somewhere." Ian dipped his chin in the direction of Charlotte's phone still laying on the table. "That's got to be a shock. How do you think your family is going to take the news?"

"Yeah, it's definitely a shock," Charlotte chuckled. "But another Burleson baby is definitely going to be considered a blessing to my family. My mom's going to be thrilled. Though, Dad's probably going to read Josh the riot act for not knowing about his child to step up sooner. And if nothing else, it'll be interesting to see how the biggest player in my family handles having to grow up to be a dad."

As they went back to working on his family tree, Ian thought back to the conversations he'd had with his sister, which seemed to indicate to him that she had a little crush on Josh. He thought he'd seen sparks between Caitir and Josh all the way back on the first day they met at the Burlesons' late Christmas celebration at the end of December. Those sparks had seemed to amplify when they were all staying on the ranch after the break-in a little over a month before. But she definitely seemed to swoon over the guy when she found out he was the one to take down Roberto Rodriguez when they went to rescue Charlotte after she was kidnapped.

Ian wondered how Josh's newfound parenthood would affect Caitir's feelings for him. *Damn it! She's just starting to act like the outgoing young woman she was before the shooting. She doesn't need to have her heart broken now to send her back into the hermit stage she's been in the last couple of years.*

Chapter Twenty-One

Friday, May 3, 2019

Charlotte couldn't believe how quickly things came together for
Anthony and Kay to get custody of Antonio, once Brooklyn sicked the
Madeline Ashbury Foundation on the CPS officials in charge of his
care. They had not only informed them of where he was being housed,
but had also set up times for Anthony and Kay to meet him, and
rushed the paperwork to set them up as his foster parents, while they
were tracking down his birth certificate to enable them to adopt him.

Since the little boy had refused to speak to anyone the entire time
he was in the care of CPS, they quickly saw the light when Anthony
introduced himself to Antonio, and the boy spoke for the first time in
the three weeks he'd been in their charge. All Anthony had to do was
tell Antonio who he was, and the child had opened up to him
immediately.

Charlotte liked to think it was because of the bond she'd built with
Antonio while working with him at the shelter, and the fact that she'd
told Antonio enough about her family that he knew he was safe with
Anthony. But she wasn't sure enough of that being how the CPS
officials would see it to risk her brother and sister-in-law's ability to
adopt him by not disclosing their familial relationship to the court
beforehand.

She didn't want the people who could still stop the adoption at any
point to think she was trying to skirt the system to see Antonio. So,
she'd taken the afternoon off from work to go to court with Anthony
and Kay to let the judge decide when, or if, she'd be allowed to
interact with her soon-to-be nephew.

She wasn't sure how they'd deal with family get-togethers if the
judge agreed with the CPS officials, who thought being around her

would be detrimental to Antonio's mental well-being. But she was willing to keep her distance from the boy if it meant he'd get the family and proper care he deserved.

She straightened her navy-blue skirt and brushed a piece of lint off the matching blazer she wore as she got out of her vehicle at the Medina County Courthouse in Hondo. She was nervous as she made her way into the courthouse, where she was meeting her brother and his family before speaking with the judge in his chambers.

Apparently, this was an unusual situation that didn't fall under the normal parameters of the courtroom procedures for a petition for adoption, so the judge wanted to meet with all parties involved in his chambers before the hearing in the courtroom. Charlotte wasn't sure how it would all work, specifically if they would all go into the judge's chambers at once, or one at a time to speak privately with the judge, so that was the first thing she asked her brother, once they finished greeting one another in the hallway of the courthouse.

"I'm not sure," Anthony shrugged. "When I adopted the girls, we all went into the judge's chambers together as a family to sign the final paperwork. But Kay's ex had already signed away his parental rights in their custody hearing the day before, so we didn't have to do a hearing for the adoption, like we're having to do now with Antonio being a ward of the state."

"Okay, so I guess we're just supposed to sit here and wait until they call us back to know if we go back one at a time or not," Charlotte sighed, taking a seat on the uncomfortable bench beside her nieces.

She didn't have time to engage the girls in conversation before the door opened beside them and a professionally dressed woman, who appeared to be in her forties, stepped out. She looked in the opposite direction down the hall first before turning to look at the group that included not only Anthony, Kay, their daughters, and Charlotte, but also Bob, Hazel, Bobby, and Brooklyn. "Are you the Burlesons?"

"Yes," the nine of them answered in unison.

"Wow, okay," the flustered woman sputtered as a wide smile spread across her face. "While I'll probably be calling you all back eventually, I think I only need Anthony and Kay right now to convince Antonio to talk to the judge. The social worker said he actually talks to you when you come to visit him, so hopefully, having you in the room will help him relax enough to answer the judge's questions."

"Of course," Anthony agreed before helping his very pregnant wife stand up from the bench, so the two of them could follow the woman to the judge's chambers.

While neither her brother nor sister-in-law directed their daughters to stay with any of the other family members in attendance, it was understood by all of the Burlesons that whoever wasn't called into the judge's chambers was tasked with watching the girls while they all waited together. The way everyone in the family watched over one another and their children was one of the many things Charlotte loved about her family. She was looking forward to the day when she'd entrust her own children to her brothers, sisters, and cousins in a similar manner, with them all raising their families on the ranch.

I really hope Ian ends up being the man I end up marrying and having those babies with, eventually.

She started to drift off to memories of the last week, with Ian continuing to keep their interactions friendly and their few kisses chaste. But she didn't get far into her thoughts before her family pulled her into a discussion about the next two weddings that would be happening in Heart's Destiny. They speculated about the differences in the guest lists between Randi and James's wedding and Fiona and Rick's wedding with them all working with the GWA, as opposed to Bobby and Brooklyn's recent wedding, which had been composed of primarily family and friends from in town.

I still can't believe Fiona actually warned me not to reference our conversation about Rick being a DILF in the wedding toast I'll have to give as her maid of honor. Obviously, her man of honor is the one of us who needs to be warned about stuff like that.

Then again, who'd have thought the preacher's daughter, who can't even say DILF without blushing, would have such an unconventional bridal party? Maybe she's thinking I'll do something out of character that day, too?

The only thing I might do out of character for me is bring a plus one, so Mom can't pull any matchmaking stunts on me. Like I'd ever bring anyone to a wedding who wasn't already invited. Although, since I'll be walking back up the aisle with Rick's daughter, I should probably have a plus one at their wedding, so I have someone to sit with when they have their families at the main table.

Charlotte contemplated inviting Ian to be her plus one for the weddings if he wasn't already invited, thinking that might keep her mother from trying to match her up with another of the wrestlers, the way she had at Anthony and Kay's wedding. *But with her not being directly involved with the planning the way she was with Bobby and Anthony's weddings, then maybe she won't have a say in the seating charts at the various events to push her matchmaking agenda.*

Oh, who am I kidding? I'm sure she's already recruited both Mandi Hunter and Kathy Harrison to her Matchmaking Mommas Club, so I'm sure they'll all be in on planning the seating charts to fit their agenda.

And while I'm sure Mom will cackle with glee at me inviting Ian to be my plus one, at least, it'll keep her from trying to match me up with anyone else.

Charlotte had to drop her distracting thoughts when the same woman as before stuck her head out the door and called her name. "That's me," she said as she stood.

"The judge wants to see you next." The woman led her through an outer office to another door.

Charlotte followed the woman into the judge's chambers, which just looked like another office and not nearly as ornate as she expected his chambers to be. Before she could be directed where to sit, Antonio jumped up off of Anthony's lap, squealed "Char," and ran over to hug her, pressing his face into her stomach.

Char couldn't stop her grin as she ran a hand over his back to return the embrace.

"As you can see, that relationship is the exact opposite of detrimental," Anthony chuckled as Kay grinned and pointed to the chair beside her for Charlotte to take a seat.

"Hey Antonio, let's go sit down, so I can talk to the judge. Okay?" Charlotte coaxed Antonio to release her legs, so she could take the seat and not delay the proceedings any longer.

When she finally got settled with Antonio on her lap, she looked up to see a smile on the judge's face to match the ones on the faces of her brother, sister-in-law, and their attorney, Tyler Reilly, her friend Cassidy's father. She relaxed a little then, knowing the scowls on the faces of the CPS social workers and attorneys to her right didn't matter.

Leah Mae Wright

"Ms. Burleson, please state your full name for the record and then tell me about your relationship with Antonio Reyes," the judge directed after informing her that while this was an informal meeting, she was to give her statements as if she'd been officially sworn in during a court proceeding.

"Charlotte Anne Burleson," Char stated while looking at the placard on his desk that read, "Judge Adam Collins" and wondering if he was any relation to Tori Collins, the middle school history teacher, who was Ian's assistant baseball coach. *If so, I hope he doesn't know about her crush on Ian, or recognize my name from conversations with her.* "I actually met Antonio in December at the Community Mission Shelter in San Antonio, where I was tasked with helping him with what we initially thought was a developmental speech delay. As I worked with him for a couple of hours every Saturday, I discovered it wasn't a developmental delay, but rather his reaction to a traumatic event that caused him to regress."

"Are you a speech therapist?" Judge Collins arched an eyebrow as he looked down at the paperwork in front of him.

"No, sir, I'm an English teacher." Charlotte smiled at the judge.

"As we stated earlier, Ms. Burleson isn't qualified to diagnose Antonio's speech issues, which is why we feel he needs to stay in our custody to be treated by our speech therapists," one of the CPS officials interjected.

Seriously, I thought Anthony and Kay fostering him was a done deal, and this was just to decide if I'd be able to see him while he's in their custody and they're going through the adoption process.

"And as I stated earlier," Kay shouted at the CPS social worker, sounding sterner than Charlotte had ever heard her sister-in-law. "If Antonio needs a speech therapist, then we're more than capable of providing him with the best speech therapist in the world. But after talking to Charlotte about everything Antonio has been through, we believe a child psychologist would be more beneficial. That's why we've already researched the local options and have one picked out, who is just waiting on the court to award us custody of Antonio to schedule his first appointment."

Wow! She's a rather formidable Momma Bear, even though she's short enough to still be allowed on the kiddie rides at amusement parks. Char stifled her chuckle.

360

"You'll have to excuse my wife, your honor." Anthony reached over and took Kay's hand, squeezing it in their secret code that Charlotte had recently learned was their silent way of saying "I love you" to one another. "The pregnancy hormones have increased her aggression when defending our children to the point that she doesn't always realize she's not using her inside voice or following the rules of courtroom decorum to wait her turn to speak."

Charlotte had to fight to keep her expression blank when she really wanted to giggle at the backhanded way her brother had pointed out the rudeness of the social worker's interruption of Charlotte's discussion with the judge.

Realizing she hadn't finished her statement earlier, Char decided it was probably best if she continued explaining how she started working with Antonio before the shouting match escalated. "As I was saying, I'm an English teacher as well as a regular volunteer at the shelter. Since the shelter doesn't have the resources to pay a speech therapist, and I took a semester of speech therapy in college before deciding on my English major, I was asked to help until the man we believed at the time was Antonio's father could afford to get him in with a speech therapist. In working with Antonio, I found that it was more a matter of making him feel comfortable with someone to get him to talk to them. I made the recommendation to get him in with a child psychologist less than a month after I started working with him. But since we didn't know we were being lied to about his parentage and family circumstances, none of us at the shelter realized there were other reasons why he wasn't getting the services he needed. So, I continued to work with him every Saturday on language games and reading, which are very clearly inside my scope of practice as a teacher. During that time, I came to care for Antonio the same way I care for the middle school students I teach during the week."

Charlotte hoped her expression read as sincere and didn't give away the fact that she'd grown to love the little boy on her lap as if he were her own. She didn't want to do or say anything in these proceedings to jeopardize Antonio's adoption by Anthony and Kay.

"It's because I care about Antonio that I followed the directives of the CPS social workers to not visit him since the night we were freed from the cartel compound where we were held last month," Charlotte added. "But as I'm one of the only people he feels safe enough with to talk to, I disagree with their opinions that being around me now could bring back the trauma of being held there. The hour or so that we spent together after I was abducted was, most likely, the least traumatic time he spent there. Especially since it was because I spent that time telling him about my family that made him feel comfortable enough to talk to my brothers that night, as well as to start speaking again after meeting Anthony, Kay, and their girls this week. So, I hope you will see that it's actually in Antonio's best interest to be adopted by Anthony and Kay, without restricting which of our family members are allowed to be around him. We have a big family and a whole lot of love to share and help him heal."

"Thank you, Ms. Burleson." The judge nodded at her, signaling that he didn't need to hear anything more from her. "I think I've seen all I need to see in chambers. I will allow the hearing for the petition for the adoption of Antonio Reyes by Anthony and Kay Burleson to proceed. We shall reconvene in the courtroom in fifteen minutes."

Antonio was instructed to go with the social workers until it was time for him to testify in the hearing, as the rest of them were directed where to go for the courtroom portion of the proceedings. He wasn't happy about not being able to stay with Anthony, Kay, and Char, but he perked up when he was told the girls and their grandparents were in the hallway where he'd be waiting.

Charlotte expected the social worker to balk at letting the kids play quietly together outside the courtroom, but was happy to see the judge shut down any objections they might have by asking Antonio to bring the girls in with him when it came time for him to testify. Obviously, he knew the importance of sibling bonding in blended families and was encouraging it with Antonio, Tia, and Maria in preparation for if the adoption was granted.

When they walked back out of the office area, Bobby and Brooklyn joined Charlotte, Anthony, and Kay in going into the courtroom, while Bob and Hazel stayed with the kids in the hallway. It didn't take long for them to all be seated and then be called to rise for the judge to enter the courtroom.

The process wasn't really as formal as the courtroom scenes Charlotte had seen on television, but she assumed that was because it wasn't a criminal court. Instead of swearing in witnesses as people were called to the stand, the judge did a sort of mass swearing in of everyone in the room and informed them that the attorney's would do most of the talking for their clients, but if anyone was asked a question, they should answer from their seats as if they were sworn in on the witness stand.

Anthony and Kay's attorney presented the petition for adoption and made a brief statement about the Burleson family being ideal candidates to adopt. The CPS attorney then gave opening remarks stating that they needed more time to evaluate Antonio's parentage, immigration status, and medical needs before they could authorize an adoption. He also commented on the Burlesons trying to use their money and social status to circumvent the system, and the social worker's belief that being adopted into Charlotte's family could be detrimental to Antonio's mental well-being after they were held captive together.

Charlotte could tell by the clenched fists and jaws around her that she wasn't the only person on her side of the aisle that disagreed with everything coming out of the man's mouth. But the way the Burlesons were raised clearly showed in the self-control they displayed in not calling him out on the blatant inaccuracies in his statements. And both Anthony and Bobby were keeping their wives in check by holding their hands and whispering calming words in Kay and Brooklyn's ears.

It was strange watching the way the proceedings differed from what Charlotte had seen in criminal cases on television, but she could see how much time it saved by having the judge ask questions of the lawyers, who then answered for their clients without having to call individual witnesses. Judge Collins began by asking the CPS attorney about what they'd found out so far in their investigation into Antonio's biological parents and citizenship status.

"At this time, your honor, CPS has been unable to determine who Antonio's biological parents are or where he was born. They've been in contact with INS officials, who have tried to track them down through the birth certificate Roberto Rodriguez presented to them, but the INS agents have determined that it was a forgery. They have also been in contact with the Mexican government to locate a legitimate birth record. But without knowing where in Mexico he was born, that effort has yet to turn up any results."

"If I may, your honor," Mr. Reilly interjected. "After talking to Antonio on Tuesday, my clients informed me that he had given them his biological parents' names, as well as the city where they lived before the cartel tore their family apart last year. After finding out that they hadn't been living in Mexico as we'd previously believed, we've verified that Antonio was born in El Paso, and is in fact a US citizen. I've been in contact with the El Paso County Clerk's office and have copies of the digital records of Antonio's birth and his biological father's death. The certified copies are also on their way to my office, but as they were just mailed yesterday, I don't expect them until Monday."

"I'll accept the copies of the digital files for now." The judge motioned for the bailiff to take the papers Tyler pulled from his briefcase. "Did your clients also notify CPS of this information?"

"Yes, your honor."

The CPS attorney spoke quietly with the CPS director sitting beside him, who was flipping through a file of papers on the desk in front of her, before he turned to the judge and shook his head. "Ms. Anderson was not given this information, your honor. Nor is there a record of this information in the CPS file on Antonio."

Anthony raised his hand as if he was a child in school, indicating he wished to speak.

"Yes, Mr. Burleson?" Judge Collins nodded at Anthony.

"Your honor, I relayed the conversation I had with Antonio word for word to Ms. Hildebrand, the social worker present when we first met him, right after she informed us our time with him was up. She seemed shocked that he'd spoken with me since he hadn't spoken to anyone else while in CPS custody, but she assured me that she would pass the information on to her supervisor." Anthony lifted one shoulder in a half-shrug. "I'm not sure whom she spoke to, or why the information wasn't put in his file, but CPS was informed within minutes of Antonio telling me that he lived in El Paso with his mom, Maria, and his dad, Jorge, before the *bad men* came and killed his dad and took him and his mom."

"Did he also tell you what happened to his mother?" Judge Collins inquired of Anthony as he made notes, presumably of the names Anthony mentioned.

"Just that she didn't return to their room one night after being taken to work. But my brother," Anthony pointed to Bobby, "can tell you more about what happened to her according to the cartel members he helped apprehend last month."

Ah, so that's why Bobby's in his police uniform, Charlotte realized as the judge turned his attention to Bobby and reiterated the information at the beginning of the proceedings about forgoing a typical swearing-in for testimony and need to move to the witness stand, emphasizing that Bobby should understand he's under oath since he was obviously in law enforcement and knew the penalties for perjury.

"Yes, your honor, and they're a slap on the wrist compared to how our parents would punish us for lyin'," Bobby quipped, drawing a smile from the judge. "And since they're out in the hall with the kids, I can guarantee every Burleson you talk to today will tell you the whole truth and nothing but, even if you'd kept this whole thing informal and hadn't sworn in any of us."

"Very well," Judge Collins chuckled. "Then I'll trust you to tell me the things I need to know about the cartel involvement in this case that aren't listed in the police reports I've seen so far. And don't forget to state your full name and official title for the record."

"Yes, sir, I'm Heart's Destiny Police Chief Robert Adam Burleson, Jr. I actually go by Bobby Burleson, so that is how you'll see my signature on the reports you've most likely seen."

The judge nodded, acknowledging having seen his signature on the reports he'd already read over.

"Back in October of last year, I noticed some unusual activity at a bodega that opened in Heart's Destiny and reached out to my brother, Jake, who works in Naval Intelligence, to get him to put me in contact with the people he works with regularly in the DEA and Homeland Security to investigate."

Bobby went on to detail the raid in November that brought down the majority of the lieutenants in the cartel, as well as how Ian came to town to search for Roberto Rodriguez. He basically gave an overview of the last seven months of work by multiple law enforcement agencies and civilian contractors, like Ian, which Charlotte had no idea he was privy to before he laid it all out for the judge.

After telling the court about Charlotte's kidnapping and the rescue that freed not only her and Antonio, but also a dozen other women and children that were being held by the cartel to work in their brothel,

Bobby finally mentioned the cartel members who were arrested that night. "When they were interrogated, they passed along information about past crimes and identified key players still at large. That information included the details of the abductions of several women and children, along with multiple murders that coincided with those abductions. The Reyes family was mentioned, both when Maria and Antonio were abducted and Jorge was killed, as well as an approximate date and location of the death of Maria Reyes, and the name of the man responsible for her death at one of the cartel's brothels. The FBI sent agents and a forensics team to the area and located what they believe to be Maria's remains. They are currently working to positively identify her, so a death certificate can be issued."

Huh? I wonder if they're going to want Antonio's DNA to compare it? Charlotte made a mental note to let Bobby know she still had a couple of DNA kits at her house if the judge granted custody of Antonio to Anthony and Kay, so they could use one if it would help speed up the process.

"We were not informed of any of this either," the CPS attorney huffed.

"I'm sure the FBI is waiting to confirm the deaths of Mr. and Mrs. Reyes before they contact you." Bobby nodded to the table where the CPS attorney and director were seated. "I'm sure you understand how large, bureaucratic organizations take their time in making sure they have all the information before releasing it to other agencies."

My brothers are on a roll today with the subtle digs at CPS. Charlotte barely bit back a giggle at the irritated look on the face of the CPS director.

"Thank you, Chief Burleson." Judge Collins redirected the proceedings before any more words could be exchanged between Bobby and the CPS table. "At this time, I think I've had all my questions answered to my satisfaction. Now we just need to bring the children in and get Antonio's statement on record, so I can issue my ruling."

The bailiff stepped out of the courtroom to bring Antonio and the CPS social worker in, along with Tia, Maria, Bob, and Hazel.

Antonio was directed to stand up to talk to the judge, and reminded that he was to tell the truth the same way he'd been instructed in the judge's office. Charlotte thought he was meant to stand at his seat, but

Antonio apparently had other ideas. He turned and looked at Tia and Maria, who nodded to reassure him of their presence. He smiled back at them before running up to the witness stand and climbing into the chair.

"You don't have to sit up here to testify if you'd be more comfortable standing by your seat," Judge Collins pointed out.

"But Tia said I have to sit on the witness stand to testify." Antonio looked at the judge before turning his head to look back at Tia, his expression making it clear that he was confused.

"And who is Tia?" Judge Collins gently questioned Antonio.

"Tia's my oldest sister." Antonio pointed at Tia, who raised her hand and waved at the judge.

"Your sister?" Judge Collins' eyebrows raised in surprise at Antonio's insistent tone.

"Yeah, and that's my other sister, Maria, and Memmaw and Pappaw." Antonio pointed to Maria, then Hazel and Bob Burleson as he introduced them to the judge. "They've already 'dopted me in their hearts, so they're my family, even if you don't let Mom and Dad 'dopt me today."

"A-dopted," Tia softly corrected, causing Char to smile at how her niece couldn't hold back the assistance that Charlotte almost let slip from her own lips.

"A-dopted," Antonio corrected on the stand, surprising Charlotte that he'd caught the correction with how softly Tia had spoken.

He obviously still needed a little extra practice when learning new multi-syllable words, but Charlotte was proud of how easily Antonio was communicating with the judge. He was a very bright little boy, who showed amazing resilience after the events of the last year or so of his life.

"And is that what you want?" Judge Adam Collins asked Antonio.

Antonio looked at him with confusion, like he didn't understand the question. Then he turned his head to look at Tia. "Tia, you ask him, 'cause I don't know all the words yet."

"Oh, Tia," Kay gasped, holding a hand up to her face as she flushed from embarrassment at whatever Tia had done. "What did you do?"

"I just started trying to teach him what Grandpa Lee taught me to say to my teachers when their directions didn't make sense," Tia shrugged. "I was younger than Antonio when I learned it, so I thought it might help him know what to say when people confuse him or scare him into wanting to stop talking again."

"Oh, dear," Hazel giggled. "I thought all that was just a vocal exercise to help him speak clearly to the judge. I didn't realize all that gibberish actually meant something."

"We'll stop by Doc Hayes' office on the way home to have your ears checked, Baby," Bob chuckled, teasing his wife. "Because while they were speaking softly, they were loud enough that you should have been able to understand every word."

"Tia, would you please enlighten me as to what Antonio wants to ask me?" The judge redirected the conversation with an arched eyebrow at Tia.

"Would you kindly condescend to elucidate on the terms of that phraseology? Or do you fear to deviate from the true course of rectitude? I, too, would hesitate to articulate, but mind you, only for fear of pre-verification." Tia smiled brightly at the judge. "It just means, 'Would you please explain what you just said? Or are you afraid you can't say it correctly with words that make more sense? And that I would also be afraid of showing incompetence by speaking clearly about something I don't actually know about.' Antonio didn't understand your question about what he wants because you used the generic term *'that,'* instead of specifically asking if he wants to be adopted into our family or not. He's extremely intelligent for his age, but he's still a little kid who needs more explanation to comprehend things when he's feeling overwhelmed or nervous about a situation."

Charlotte wasn't alone in her slight giggle at how her niece had just schooled the judge, as even the judge seemed to be fighting a smile. He quickly lost the fight when Antonio piped up, "Would you kindly, uh, do what Tia said?"

"Yes, I will definitely do what Tia said," Judge Adam Collins laughed, along with half the people present in the courtroom. "Antonio, would you like Anthony and Kay Burleson to adopt you?"

"Yes, and Tia, and Maria, and Char, and Memmaw, and Pappaw…" Antonio trailed off, looking from the judge to the Burlesons in the courtroom. "And all my new family."

"Yes, the whole Burleson family," the judge agreed with a smile at Antonio. "But I only need Anthony and Kay to sign the paperwork."

"Okay," Antonio shrugged, showing he didn't care who signed the paperwork as long as he got his whole new family. "Can I go sit with my family now?"

"Yes, you may." The judge waited for Antonio to get down out of the chair and run over to Anthony and Kay at the table with their attorney before continuing. "A lot of variables factor into my decision-making process when it comes to cases such as this, and normally I would take my time to weigh all the facts and wait for more than copies of digital records before deciding to allow an adoption to proceed to the next step. However, after what I've seen today, I think waiting to place Antonio Reyes in the Burleson home would actually do more harm than good. While Children's Protective Services does an admirable job of ensuring the well-being of the children in their care, the two versions of Antonio that we've seen today have made it evident that their group home is not the environment that Antonio needs to be in at this time. Just having the Burlesons present today had a dramatic effect on him, and I believe that placing him in their home as a part of their family will help him not only heal from the traumatic events of his past, but will also help him thrive as he grows up. Therefore, I'm granting temporary custody of Antonio Reyes to Anthony and Kay Burleson, with all the rights that custody entails."

Temporary custody? What the hell?

Charlotte wasn't the only one who grumbled incoherently at the decision.

"I know you're all confused by the word *temporary* in my ruling." The judge held up a hand to stop the grumbling. "But as much as I would love to issue a final ruling in this adoption case, I still have to follow the laws of the state of Texas. And according to the law, we still have to wait for verification that no biological family members are available to come forward and care for Antonio. There are also five post-placement home visits that need to take place before I can issue that final adoption ruling. I'm ordering those to be scheduled once a month, so the reports can all be filed with me in six months, when I'm scheduling the final hearing in this case. Chief Burleson, I'm trusting that you will make sure the other law enforcement agencies you've been working with on this case will send me official copies of the paperwork I need on Antonio's biological family before then as well."

"Yes, your honor." Bobby nodded.

Leah Mae Wright

After the judge adjourned the proceedings, the Burlesons gathered in the hallway to discuss how they would celebrate the newest addition to the family.

"We have to have a welcome to the family party for Antonio," Hazel insisted.

"But we have Jen and Julie's birthday party tonight." Kay shook her head. "I don't want to take away from their day by stealing their spotlight to add Antonio's adoption celebration to their party."

"Nonsense," Charlotte reassured her sister-in-law. Knowing her cousins well, she knew they'd be upset that anyone would think they didn't want to share their special day with the newest addition to the family. "Jen and Julie will be honored to share their birthday with Antonio's Gotcha Day."

"Oh, absolutely," Hazel agreed with her daughter. "I'll call Susan on the way home to make sure they're in on the planning for combining the parties."

With that settled, they all headed to their cars. Anthony and Kay had to take Antonio back to the group home one last time to get his things before coming back to the ranch, so Charlotte had just enough time to meet Ian for a quickie date before the party.

If only it was for an actual quickie!

~ ~ ~

Ian was glad to hear from Charlotte that their regularly scheduled date didn't have to be completely canceled due to her appearance in court. Though he was concerned that she sounded on edge after the hearing, he hoped seeing him for even a shortened date would settle her mind about whatever was bothering her.

After she'd informed him of the hearing for her brother and sister-in-law to be allowed to foster and adopt Antonio, and her need to be there to testify earlier in the week, he'd rescheduled his normal midday telehealth appointment with his therapist for an in-person appointment at their typical date time after school. He wanted to be able to look Dr. Ryan Edwards in the eye when he informed him that he'd only had one nightmare in the last week and none in the last five nights.

The psychologist had been surprised at how much the nightmares had tapered off in such a short amount of time. But when Ian had explained how he'd been looking at making love with Charlotte again as his reward when they were under control, Ryan had laughed and told him, "Of course, the love of a good woman is the best kind of motivation to get a man's mind in line for healing."

So, now that he had his psychologist's approval, Ian sat in the little coffee shop in Lytle, Texas, trying to figure out when he'd be able to finally make love to Charlotte again. As much as he wished it could be on their date that evening, he knew they'd barely have time to finish their coffee with having to rush back to Heart's Destiny to Jen and Julie's birthday party.

He was glad he'd had a heads-up on their party, instead of being caught off guard by it the way he had for several of the Burleson birthdays at the beginning of the year. With Caitir becoming closer to the twins and their cousin Becky than the other Burlesons, she'd insisted he take her shopping for their presents the previous Saturday, when he had the week off from baseball games.

Truth be told, he was probably happier about seeing his sister finding her footing in a friend-group than he was about being informed of the party in advance. She was really starting to act more like her old, pre-shooting self, and he hoped that meant her mental wounds were finally healing.

He realized then that his relationship with Charlotte was helping him heal his own mental wounds. *Fuck, I hope I'm as good for her mental well-being as she's been for mine. I want to be the man to make her feel whole, the way she's been that woman for me.*

He didn't have time to ponder how he might go about making sure he was fulfilling all her needs, as Charlotte walked into the coffee shop. Ian held up the coffee he'd already ordered for her to show her that she didn't need to wait in line before joining him at the table in the back corner of the room.

"Thanks, I needed this." Charlotte sighed as she took the first sip of her coffee while taking her seat.

"No problem," Ian chuckled at the expression of relief that crossed her face as she sat her cup down. "How'd it go in court?"

"Good," Charlotte bobbed her head. "Nerve-wracking, but good. Anthony and Kay were awarded temporary custody of Antonio. Now they just have to do the home visits the state requires before the judge can finalize the adoption in six months."

"And how are you doing with your brother being the one to adopt him and not you?" Ian knew she had planned to foster and adopt Antonio herself the night they were rescued from the cartel, but she hadn't talked to him about her feelings since the plans changed.

"I'm good." Charlotte's eyes clouded up briefly, but she shook the momentary sadness away. "I admit, I kind of wish I was what he needed, but that's just because I'm fighting the baby fever that's spreading through my family like wildfire. After seeing Antonio with Tia and Maria today, I know he needs siblings and more than one parent, which I can't give him right now. So, he's definitely being adopted into the part of my family that's best for him. And I get to be his favorite aunt, so it's a win for all of us."

Ian was impressed with Charlotte's acceptance of the situation. Instead of letting it get her down that she couldn't adopt Antonio, or being resentful of her brother and sister-in-law for being able to step in and gain custody of the boy so easily, when she'd been hitting her head against a brick wall just trying to find out how he was doing in the CPS group home, she seemed genuinely happy that everything was working out the way it was.

"And just so you know, Jen and Julie's birthday party tonight is expanding to celebrate Antonio's Gotcha Day," Charlotte informed him.

"Gotcha Day?" Ian was confused by the strange term.

"Yeah, it's something I was reading about online," Charlotte explained. "Where adopted kids and their parents celebrate the day they *got* their adopted family member. They treat it almost like a second birthday and celebrate it every year."

"Aww," Ian understood the need for such a day to show adopted kids how much they're loved and wanted by their new families. "So, do we need to go shopping for presents for Antonio before we go to the party tonight?"

"Oh, geez, I didn't even think about that!" Charlotte reached down and dug through her bag to grab her phone. She sent a series of rapid-fire texts before looking back at him with a smile. "Okay, I've got everyone working on the presents now. My family seems to have clothing covered, but since Brody is only a little younger than Antonio, I offered to pick your brain for toy ideas."

"Oh, yeah, I can definitely help you out there," Ian chuckled, thinking of all the toys Brody had asked for at Christmas.

They did a quick internet search for places to shop in Lytle, since they'd met there with him coming from San Antonio and her coming from Hondo. With Lytle being a bigger city than Heart's Destiny, there were more shops, and even a mall that their small town lacked. Once they had a plan, they took off to raid the mall.

As they walked from store to store, picking out the coolest toys and books for the preschool and kindergarten age group, they talked about how hanging out with Brody could be good for Antonio. Ian agreed, thinking it would be just as good for Brody to make a new friend closer to his own age. Charlotte confided in him that she'd mentioned Ian having a son when she talked to Antonio in that room where they were being held by the cartel, and Ian realized that it was her having talked about him and his son that set Antonio at ease with him enough to talk to him during the rescue.

Once they were finished shopping and were loaded down with bags of gifts on their way out of the mall to their separate vehicles, Charlotte asked how his therapy session had gone, and why he'd opted to do an in-person session instead of telehealth.

"I wanted Ryan to be able to see how much better I'm sleeping with the drop in nightmares this week," Ian grinned, unsure if he should share the details of his session when they didn't have time to give him the reward he'd promised himself with his progress. "Since the bags under my eyes haven't completely gone away yet, and always seem exaggerated on my computer when I look at myself during the video sessions, I figured he needed to see me in person for that."

"Based on that grin, I'm guessing the session went well," Charlotte smiled at him.

"Oh, yeah," Ian agreed, his grin widening as he decided to share his reward system concept with Charlotte. "I shared my idea for rewarding myself for certain milestones with my progress. And he agreed that I've progressed enough to earn the reward I've chosen."

"Oh, that's a great idea," Charlotte beamed. "And what reward have you earned with your progress?"

"Moving us back out of the friend zone." Ian wagged his eyebrows suggestively, so Charlotte would know he meant bringing sex back into their relationship. "I wanted to get your input on just how far you'll let me go for every night I don't have a nightmare."

"You mean like a kiss for every night you don't have a nightmare?" Charlotte arched her eyebrow while grinning at him mischievously.

"I was hoping for more than a kiss," Ian admitted honestly. "But if that's all you're ready for, then I'll take it. But they'd better be good kisses, with tongue, not the chaste kisses we've shared for the last few weeks."

"Oh, they'll be good kisses." Charlotte's grin widened as she looked around the mall they were walking through, as if she was looking for someplace private to give him the first of those kisses right then.

"Since I haven't had a nightmare the last five nights, I think you owe me five kisses," Ian pointed out as Charlotte grabbed his hand and started dragging him toward the sign for the bathrooms.

"And what if I want more than kisses as my reward for not having nightmares?" Charlotte questioned in a teasing tone as they left the main walkway through the mall and entered a deserted hallway that led to the restrooms.

"Whatever you want, Princess," Ian adamantly agreed. "I'll give you whatever reward you want."

"Then I'll take my reward in orgasms, preferably on your cock," Charlotte announced in a breathy tone that turned Ian's half-chub from being in the same room as her into a hard-as-steel erection in an instant. "And you also owe me five."

Thank fuck! Ian mentally moaned as he followed Charlotte into what appeared to be a seating area outside the ladies' room. "That can definitely be arranged."

"Wait here," she commanded as she released his hand, dropped the bags she was carrying on the little loveseat in the room, and walked through another door without acknowledging his statement. Ian placed the bags he was carrying beside the ones she'd just dropped and stood there waiting for her to reappear with further instructions. When she returned, she walked to the door they'd entered and locked it. "Just had to check and make sure nobody was in the stalls to walk in on us first."

Yes! Ian's cock cheered as Charlotte started stripping. He quickly started removing his own clothing, starting with his shirt, and deciding that he definitely needed to quit carrying both guns on him when he realized he couldn't do more than lowering the front of his pants enough to get his cock out without removing his concealed carry holsters. He donned a condom as Charlotte bent over to place her clothing on one of the chairs in the little room.

"Stay bent over, just like that, Princess," Ian commanded, moving up behind her to rub his fingers through her folds. "Fuck, you're already dripping wet for me."

"Yes, Ian," Charlotte moaned as he stroked her sensitive flesh. "And we don't have time for foreplay, so fuck me already."

"As you wish, Princess." Ian gripped her hips with both hands, lined his cock up with her slit, and slid home in one firm thrust.

Being inside her again after almost a month felt exquisite, even though they were still separated by the thin barrier of the condom. They both moaned in pleasure as Ian pistoned in and out of Charlotte's slick pussy.

It didn't take long for the pressure to build inside him, bringing him to the edge of orgasm faster than he'd even gotten there as a teenager. Not wanting to go off before Charlotte, Ian reached around to rub her clit with one hand while tweaking her nipple with the other.

"Oh, fuck, yes, Ian," Charlotte panted as she rocked her body to push back in time with his strokes into her creamy cunt.

Her inner walls started to flutter as her first climax built. Needing to make her come more than once before finally going over the edge himself, Ian ordered her to, "come now, Charlotte," before biting his lip to keep from coming with her.

"Oh, yes, Ian," Charlotte chanted his name as she followed his directive, coming hard on his cock. He held still in her vise-like grip as she convulsed in pleasure, barely holding back his own release with her tight pussy trying to milk him dry.

As she shuddered and swayed, gripping the back of the chair she was bent over, Ian slid his hands away from her tits and pussy to grip her hips once more, planning to hold her up should her legs give out beneath her. Once Charlotte's first orgasm passed, and he knew she was steady on her feet, Ian reversed his path with his hands, tweaking her other nipple this time while rubbing her clit with the opposite hand as before.

"Oh, too much, too soon." Charlotte squirmed as if she couldn't decide if she wanted to move away from his tormenting hands or press harder into them.

"No, not too much, sweet Charlotte," Ian disagreed, not letting her get away from his titillating attention to her body. "Can't be too soon when we have to hurry to get in all five of your rewards."

"Not enough time for all five," Charlotte panted out breathlessly. "You'll have to give me some of them tomorrow."

"Deal," Ian chuckled, surprised to find himself laughing while in the middle of fucking his woman. "But you're going to get at least one more now, so I can get one of mine."

"Yes, Ian, yes!" Charlotte cried out repeatedly as he sped up his movements and increased the pressure on her sensitive spots to take her over the edge once more.

"Fuck, yes, Charlotte!" This time when Charlotte's cunt clamped down in climax, Ian joined her in reaching his release. He filled the condom with multiple jets of cum, and prayed they didn't both collapse from the intensity of their simultaneous orgasm.

Once he felt like they'd both recovered enough that he didn't have to hold her up, Ian stepped back, reluctantly pulling his still semi-hard cock from her body. He stepped through the door to the restroom stalls to dispose of the condom. He grabbed a couple of paper towels from the dispenser, wetting one before going back to the other room to clean her girl-cum from between Charlotte's legs. He dried her with the dry paper towel before going back into the other room to dispose of the used towels and repeat the process on his cock. He quickly pulled his pants back into position and zipped up, hoping she wouldn't notice the handgun still located at the small of his back.

When he got back into the outer room the second time, Charlotte had stood from her bent over position and started getting dressed. As Ian joined her in redressing by putting his shirt back on, they made plans to meet at the fieldhouse an hour before their games were set to commence the next morning to see if they could find a private enough place to dole out the rest of their rewards before anyone else arrived at the ball fields.

Once they were both decent enough to leave the ladies' room, Ian pulled Charlotte into his arms and kissed her. While they didn't have time for their tongues to tangle very long, Ian needed the taste of her on his lips to be able to get through the rest of the night surrounded by her family.

"Oh, yeah, you did say you wanted kisses as your rewards," Charlotte cooed teasingly as they picked up their packages to leave for the party. "Guess I still owe you four tomorrow morning."

"I suppose I could take mine as a combo," Ian quipped as they strolled back through the mall in the direction of the exit. He leaned toward her to whisper, so nobody else could overhear what he was about to say. "Since I can't come quite as often as you, I'll take half of my rewards as kisses and the other half as orgasms."

"Deal," Charlotte giggled. "But I want all of my rewards as O's."

"Of course," Ian agreed, opening the door for her to step out of the mall. "And I plan to give you more of them than you can handle, Princess."

Chapter Twenty-Two

Monday, May 13, 2019

Ever since the evening they rekindled the sexual side of their relationship with a semi-public quickie before going to Jen and Julie's birthday and Antonio's Gotcha Day party, Charlotte and Ian had been sneaking in daily quickies anytime they thought they could get away with it. From the supply closet at school, before anyone else arrived for the day, to the fieldhouse locker rooms, before and after practice and games when nobody else was around, they'd been desecrating public spaces to enjoy the element of risk at the possibility of being caught in a compromising position.

The only places they saw each other regularly that they hadn't even copped a feel were when they were at church or on the Burleson Ranch. Even with Ian coming to ride the horses with her and Brody and to work on his family tree with her assistance in confirming he was trusting the right documents to provide his link to his Campbell ancestors, they hadn't taken that chance on the ranch yet. There were just too many people around for Charlotte to feel like getting caught was a slim chance.

Between their families and the ranch hands, there was always someone else in the stables or on their trail rides. Solitary riding time was especially a thing of the past, since Brody and Antonio became fast friends and Anthony started spending every afternoon teaching all three of his kids more about taking care of the horses while home on paternity leave. Even when she was in her house alone with Ian working on family trees together, they knew there was a chance of someone walking in without bothering to knock.

For the first time in her life, Charlotte was starting to wonder if she might want to live somewhere other than on the family ranch. She'd always thought she'd spend her whole life living on that land, but the lack of privacy she was noticing since being with Ian was starting to become a definite drawback to continuing to live in such close proximity to the rest of her family.

Like, seriously, how did Mom and Dad manage to find time alone to have six kids? Charlotte mused as she walked into her classroom at the middle school to get an early start on her day. *I know Memmaw and Pappaw popped in on them unannounced all the time. Same with Uncle Jon and Aunt Susan. Hell, the lack of privacy was probably why Pappaw was an only child. And I'm sure Memmaw and Pappaw only had two kids because they were twins.*

I know Anthony and Kay sneak in alone time when they're on tour with the GWA and the kids have sleepovers with their friends. But maybe I can ask Brooklyn how she and Bobby keep from worrying about Mom walking in on them.

Not that I need to know this week, since Ian and I have to stop our quickies until after my period. But it would be nice to have some ideas for next week.

They had given up trying to keep a count of how many orgasms they were owed for nights without nightmares, deciding that being together daily was the real reward. Since Charlotte knew the way Ian kept giving her multiples meant she'd surpassed the number of orgasms she'd earned by being nightmare free, she decided she was more than okay with changing the reward system.

And I can still give him his rewards in the form of blow jobs this week. She giggled at the thought just as Ian walked into her classroom, carrying their morning coffee and donuts.

"What's got you so giddy this morning, Princess?" Ian arched an eyebrow as he placed their breakfast treats on her desk.

"Just thinking about how I can still reward you this week, when certain orifices are closed for business due to the red tide," Charlotte teased as she took her coffee from the drink holder and took a sip.

"Ah," Ian acknowledged her subtle reference to her period using the term for a harmful algae bloom in the ocean that closes beaches, which she'd learned about from him while discussing his surfing hobby on one of their friend dates. "You do know I don't mind swimming in *your red tide*, right? It's just the red tide that closes the beach that I don't want to surf in."

"Well, unless it happens in a shower, so we can clean up immediately, you can consider my beach closed," Charlotte quipped.

"The whole beach or just the cove?" Ian arched an eyebrow. "I mean, there's a certain spot on the beach I could focus on without getting in the red tide."

"The thought of doing anything I can't clean up from immediately grosses me out," Charlotte confessed, setting her coffee back down and stepping in closer to Ian. "But if you think you can push the right buttons without encountering the red tide, I'm willing to let you try."

"Don't worry, sweet Charlotte," Ian crooned in her ear as he pulled her into his arms. "I can play with your clit and suck on your tits to get you off without making a mess. The real question is whether or not you're willing to swallow to keep from making a mess when you give me my rewards."

"Oh, yes, Ian," Charlotte purred as she pressed her body against his, needing to feel his hardness against her. "But you know we can't do that here."

"No, but I think we might need to go inventory the storeroom to know what books we have available to teach next year," Ian pretended to suggest, kissing the top of her head before releasing her from his embrace.

"Yes, we should definitely get right on that," Charlotte agreed, practically floating in anticipation as they left her classroom to go to the storage closet for more privacy.

Ian quickly unlocked the door, ushering her inside before closing and relocking it to give them more of a semblance of privacy. If someone with a key came by, they could still get in the door. But at least the sound of a key in the lock would give them the chance to disengage and straighten their clothing before they got caught.

Charlotte reached for Ian's belt buckle, deftly unfastening it, and moving on to the button of his khakis.

"Oh, no, Princess," Ian growled, covering her hands with his to stop her from giving him his reward first. "You know the rules. It's always ladies first. Now open your blouse while I move your skirt out of my way."

Ian started to push her skirt up to her waist as Charlotte protested by stilling his hands. "Look, Ian, I appreciate that you always want to take care of me first, but it's not going to work this time. If this isn't as clean as you seem to think it will be, then I'm going to need to run straight to the bathroom to clean up after. And I don't want to take a chance on running out of time to take care of you."

"You know I don't care if I have to wait until later," Ian argued, still trying to push up her skirt.

"Yes, I know," Charlotte admitted, pushing up on her toes to give him a peck of a kiss. "But I already feel guilty enough for coming three times as often as you. Please let me assuage some of that by taking care of you first this time."

"Fine," Ian conceded, shaking his head, and smiling at her. "But I want it on record that I'm only agreeing to this because I can't say no to you, Princess. Your pleasure is way more important than mine, so this will not become our new order of things."

Charlotte disagreed with one of them being more important than the other, but she didn't argue the point, knowing they didn't have time for that discussion right then. *We'll just have to talk about it again later. Whenever we can find more than a few minutes alone to talk.*

With both his baseball and her softball season ending at the end of the week with a final tournament on both Friday afternoon and Saturday morning, they weren't going to be able to go on a Friday afternoon date this week. Since they had opted for a quickie after school, instead of a full afternoon together to go on a family horseback ride the previous week, Charlotte was beginning to wonder if their friend dates were a thing of the past now that they were having sex again.

She couldn't think about that at the moment though, as she was too busy focusing on getting Ian's pants and boxer briefs down around his thighs and her hands and mouth on his magic, pierced peen.

"Fuck, Charlotte, at least open your blouse, so I can see your tits," Ian commanded as she dropped to her knees and grabbed his dick with both hands. "And keep your eyes on mine. I want to see how much you enjoy sucking me off."

Char smiled as she released his shaft to do as he directed, extending her tongue to lick him from root to tip at the same time.

Ian moaned in pleasure, his baby blues sparkling with excitement, as she teased the tip of her tongue over his most sensitive spot, just below the head of his cock. He reached down and freed her breasts from her bra, pushing the cups down as soon as she had her blouse opened enough.

As Ian played with her breasts with his large hands, Charlotte brought her hands back up, circling his base with one while cupping his balls with the other. She wrapped her lips over the head and slowly sucked him into her mouth.

With his size, the tip of his cock hit the back of her throat before she had half of him in her mouth, but she used her hand to stroke the part of his shaft that wouldn't fit in her mouth. She knew he was watching her eyes to know when he pushed in as far as she could handle, but she loved seeing the desire in his eyes the whole time she pleasured him.

Charlotte focused on swirling her tongue around his piercings as she pulled back before quickly bobbing her head back down and sucking him as far back as she could take him. She repeated this sequence, getting into a rhythm that she knew would take him over the edge quickly. Ian started thrusting his hips in time with her bobbing head, fucking her mouth the way she wished he could fuck her pussy right then.

Ian moaned in pleasure as he whispered words of praise for her efforts. With him trying to keep quiet so they didn't get caught, Charlotte couldn't clearly hear what he said. But the way his dick twitched in pleasure whenever she hit his sensitive spots with her tongue made it obvious he was enjoying her oral ministrations.

She was enjoying the way he was fondling her breasts just as much, feeling each tweak of her nipples as if he was doing the same to her clit. She was so worked up from what they were doing that she was already on the edge of orgasm, and he hadn't touched more than her breasts.

Char felt Ian's balls tighten in her hand as his soft words of praise turned more guttural. "Fuck, Charlotte. Feels so good."

Knowing he was about to come ramped up Char's arousal. She sped up her rhythm briefly before sucking him as far back in her throat as she could, not wanting to risk a drop of his cum escaping through her lips.

"Fuck, yes," Ian groaned as the first jet of his cum hit the back of her throat. "Coming. Swallow. Every. Drop. Princess." Each word from his lips was punctuated with another spurt of his semen down her throat and a tweak of one of her nipples.

The whole scene was so surreal that Charlotte couldn't hold back her own orgasm as it careened through her. Her whole body spasmed, causing her to squeeze his cock and balls a little harder than she intended.

"Fuck," Ian growled, releasing her left breast to pull her hand from his balls. "Such a dirty girl. Coming from sucking my cock."

Charlotte hummed her agreement around his shaft, the vibrations in her throat eliciting a wave of aftershocks from his dick. When they finally started to subside, she pulled back, making sure to lick him completely clean before tucking him back into his boxer briefs.

Once his pants were back in place, Ian assisted Charlotte in standing once again. He dipped his head to suckle her breasts as he pushed her skirt up out of the way of his wandering hands.

"As much as I loved watching you come already, I need you to do it again," Ian whispered into the valley between her breasts as he quickly found her clit with his expert fingers.

He circled the nub over the silk of her panties while trailing feather-soft kisses over her breasts. Charlotte ran her fingers through Ian's soft, short hair, wishing it was long enough for her to grip to guide him to her nipples.

Not that he needed much direction, since Ian seemed to know her body as well as she did. Maybe even better.

Ian moved to suck one nipple while using the hand not fondling her clit to massage the other breast. Charlotte fought to keep her eyes open and focused on his as she succumbed to the pleasure he was giving her.

Ian alternated his attention between her breasts as he slipped his fingers beneath the thin piece of material covering her mound.

Thank God I use tampons and not a pad, so he doesn't have to touch it. Charlotte cringed at the thought, but as he swirled the liquid pool of her arousal around her clit, Charlotte second-guessed her thinking about pads. *Although, if he makes me squirt like he has before, maybe a pad would be better for containing the mess.*

She didn't ponder those thoughts for long as Ian lightly bit her nipple. His little nibble sparked a resurgence of the intense sensations he was stoking in her clit, bringing her back to the edge of orgasm within milliseconds. Char couldn't hold back her moan of pleasure when he soothed the sting of his bite by laving his tongue over her taut tip.

Reading her body like an open book, Ian repeated the titillating torture on her other breast. Combined with a light pinch of her clit, the exquisite sensations sent her careening into the abyss of orgasmic bliss.

"Oh, Ian," Charlotte cried out, not even thinking about needing to keep quiet to prevent being caught as the waves of euphoria washed over her.

Ian popped up from his bent-over position, covering her mouth with his and swallowing her climactic sounds. Char returned his lascivious kiss with all the love she felt for him but wasn't able to express with words just yet.

I need him to say those three little words first, so I don't ruin what we have going on by trying to move too fast.

They broke the kiss to breathe as she floated down from her orgasmic high. Ian pulled his hand from inside her panties, lifting his fingers to his lips to suck her cream from the tips.

"See, sweet Charlotte," Ian grinned and wagged his eyebrows as he turned his hand for her to look at his fingers. "No mess at all."

"Yeah, I still need to change my damp panties," Charlotte disagreed with a giggle, glad she actually carried extra in her bag in case of tampon mishaps the week of her period.

"Why? I'm just going to make them wet again at lunchtime," Ian quipped as they worked together to right her clothing, so they could leave the storage room.

Charlotte shrugged, unable to disagree with his very valid prediction, as Ian unlocked the door. They made it back to her classroom with nobody noticing that they'd spent so much time alone in the storage room doing things they probably shouldn't at school.

Charlotte grabbed her bag, preparing to run to the bathroom before the students started arriving, while Ian picked up his, now cold, coffee. He grimaced as he took a sip.

"We should probably switch to iced coffee," Charlotte joked as she gave him a peck on the cheek before turning to make her way to the restroom to change her panties.

"Naw, it'd just be watered down after we leave it sitting every morning," Ian grumbled as she walked away, leaving him standing in her classroom.

~~~

Saturday, May 25, 2019

Ian wasn't sure what was going on with Charlotte asking him to meet her at Tully's Roadhouse for a date night in town. Even though their relationship was progressing nicely, with both of them seeming to have banished their nightmares completely since they'd started having sex again, he thought she still wanted to keep their couple status a secret from her family for a little while longer. And he couldn't figure out how she intended them to have a date in the local bar without word getting back to her family, specifically her matchmaking mother.

But since he had no problem with openly admitting to dating her, he dutifully followed her instructions to meet her at the bar. When he got there and saw several rental cars in the parking lot, he wondered if there was a rodeo in town.

Maybe she thinks the bar will be so full of out-of-town guests that are only here for the rodeo this weekend that nobody will notice us? Or maybe with so many cowboys and buckle bunnies in attendance, it's not likely that anyone we know will be here?

His theory was dashed when he walked in and saw the banner congratulating James and Randi on their upcoming wedding. Remembering the couple, whom he met at the B and B when he first arrived in town, Ian realized he'd just walked into what looked to be their joint bachelor and bachelorette party.

He saw Charlotte sitting with her female relatives, along with the bride-to-be, a few women Ian only recognized in passing, and more than a few he didn't recognize at all. As the ladies all downed a round of shots, Ian walked up to the bar and ordered a beer from Leo Walker.

"The guys are all in the back." Leo nodded his head toward the doorway between the two areas of the bar. "If this one is anything like the other parties they've done like this, it'll only be about thirty
~~~

minutes before the ladies are through with their bachelorette games to free up the front room for dancing."

"Thanks for the heads up." Ian acknowledged the bartender's hint that he should go to the back room for the time being with a chin lift as he paid for his drink.

He arched an eyebrow at Charlotte, who only acknowledged his presence with a smile. Realizing she was sticking to their friends-only cover, he decided to join the group of guys scattered around the pool tables in the other room.

Feeling self-conscious about inadvertently crashing the man's bachelor party, Ian walked up to James Hunter and congratulated him on his impending nuptials.

"Thanks, man," James grinned as the two men bumped knuckles. "You'll be at the wedding next Saturday, right? We didn't really send out invitations. Just figured everyone in town would know they're welcome to come. But with you being new to town, I want to make sure you know you're welcome to join in the festivities, along with the rest of your family."

"Oh, yeah, thanks," Ian sputtered, shocked to be invited to a virtual stranger's wedding so casually.

James introduced Ian to a few of his fellow wrestlers, whom Ian instantly recognized from seeing them on television. They all seemed to welcome him with open arms. It was strange to feel like he was automatically being accepted into the inner circle of the only celebrities he'd ever met. But with the Hunters being born and raised in Heart's Destiny, he wasn't completely surprised by their friendliness. Or that of their coworkers.

Soon, though, he found himself wandering over to where Bobby and Anthony Burleson were playing a game of pool, feeling more comfortable hanging out with Charlotte's brothers than anyone else in the room.

"Hey, Ian," Bobby greeted him, shaking his hand while Anthony took his shot. "I didn't know you knew James and Randi."

"I don't really," Ian admitted with a shrug. "I met them at the B and B when I first moved to town, and saw them at your family Christmas party. But I had no idea when I decided to stop in here for a beer tonight that I'd be crashing their party."

"Aw, you're not really crashing the party," Anthony drawled. "They've pretty much invited the whole town to celebrate with them this week. You'll have to stay after church tomorrow for the wedding shower to get the whole list of events surrounding the holiday and leading up to the wedding next weekend, too."

"Wow, you all cram all the events leading up to a wedding into a week here?" Ian was surprised to hear how they were planning all of the traditional wedding events in such a short timeframe.

"Only when half the GWA has to be at every event," Bobby chuckled. "Brie and I had our wedding shower in February, our bachelor and bachelorette party in March, and then the rehearsal, rehearsal dinner, and wedding in April, since Anthony's schedule with the GWA is more flexible than the wrestlers' schedule."

"But since half our wedding party could only get time off from traveling for the week around Thanksgiving, Kay and I started this week-long wedding-fest schedule for the GWA couples. It'll be the same way when Rick and Fiona get married the weekend after Independence Day."

"I just met Rick a few minutes ago." Ian turned to look around the room to spot the man he thought Anthony was referring to, just as he wondered if the Fiona in that couple was the same Fiona he'd briefly met the night he met Charlotte. "And Fiona is Charlotte's best friend, the teacher who had my job at the middle school before me, right?"

"Yep," Bobby confirmed with a nod. "She's also Pastor Harrison's daughter, so we're all kinda in awe of Rick for gettin' his blessing to marry her."

The guys filled him in on how Pastor Harrison was known for warning all the guys away from his daughter from the pulpit on Sunday mornings when they were all in high school. They also told him about how their cousin Justin had only been able to date Fiona in high school because they hid their dates in group outings with friends and were almost always chaperoned.

Ian kind of felt like he and Charlotte were in a similar situation anytime they were in the same space in Heart's Destiny. Especially when he and his family were invited to the various events and activities on the ranch, or where her whole family was in attendance, such as the party that night.

But maybe we can sneak away for some alone time at the various wedding events this week, if they're not on the Burleson Ranch, like we did at Bobby and Brooklyn's rehearsal dinner.

As he talked to Anthony about scheduling some time for their boys to get together over the summer when school was out and Brody no longer had to go to work on the ranch with Caitir every day, Ian decided to see if there was some place in the bar where he and Charlotte could sneak off for a quickie. *She's too classy to fuck in a bar bathroom, but maybe they have a storeroom we could use?*

He got his answer a little while later when the ladies started mingling with the guys and he convinced Charlotte to dance with him. Once they were on the dance floor where he could whisper in her ear without anyone else hearing, he broached the subject. "Any chance we can sneak off to a storeroom in back, so I can kiss you the way I've been dying to all evening?"

"Don't tease me, Mr. Campbell," Charlotte whispered back, teasing him with a little extra brush of her hips against his erection. "If I sneak off into the storeroom with you, then I'm going to want to do more than kiss."

"Fuck," Ian groaned as he moved his hips to rub his dick against her belly. "Lead the way to the storeroom, Princess."

"We can't go at the same time, or my family will get suspicious." Charlotte shook her head, pulling back slightly from his close embrace. "But the storeroom is just down the hall beside the bar. The last door at the end, past the bathrooms. Once this song's over, we'll go mingle some more and then each excuse ourselves to meet there in, say, ten minutes?"

"Make it five minutes," Ian commanded, emphasizing his point by grinding his hard-on into her midsection once more. He wasn't sure how he was going to hide his obvious arousal while mingling as she suggested, so he planned to head for that storeroom long before her ten-minute plan.

"Deal," Charlotte agreed just as the slow song changed to something more upbeat.

They separated with Charlotte walking over to talk to friends as Ian decided to hide his erection against the bar while ordering a bottle of water. He made small talk with Leo and a couple of his cousins before asking where the men's room was located as cover for why he was walking away and excusing himself.

Just as he was about to open the door to the storeroom, he heard the distinct clicking of heels on the hardwood floor behind him. When he turned and realized it was Charlotte, he quickly opened the door and slipped inside. The door didn't even have a chance to get halfway closed before she joined him. Luckily, the light was already on in the room, so they didn't have to fumble to find it or worry about the light showing under the door to alert anyone of their whereabouts.

Unlike the storeroom at school, this one didn't have a lock on the door, so Ian pressed Charlotte against it to keep it closed as he claimed her mouth with a passionate kiss. Grateful she'd had the foresight to wear one of her flowy dresses, Ian lifted the skirt to her waist before gripping her bare ass to pick her up.

Holy Fuck! No panties? This woman is going to be the death of me. No matter how many times I fuck her against this door, I'm still going to be as hard as a rock when we go back to the party from knowing she's bare beneath her skirt.

Charlotte wrapped her legs around his waist and her arms around his shoulders, clinging to him as their tongues tangled. With the way she tended to mount him for standing sex in this same manner all the time, Ian was glad he'd worked through his issues enough in therapy to be able to leave his Glock in the lockbox since they'd added these illicit rendezvous back into their relationship.

With her hanging onto him, he was able to reach around her legs to unfasten his jeans, barely remembering to grab his wallet from the back pocket to get out a condom before pushing them down his thighs along with his boxers.

They continued to make out like horny teenagers as he rolled the latex down his length. Without being able to see what he was doing, he didn't realize he hadn't left enough of a reservoir at the tip to contain his cum. Not that he really cared about the condom right then with his overwhelming need for Charlotte driving him to plunge his cock into her pussy as soon as fucking possible.

He only took a moment to run a finger through her folds to make sure she was wet and ready for him before impaling her on his stiff rod. As she cried out into his mouth at the invasion, Ian slipped the digit wet with her arousal between her ass cheeks to tease her tightest hole.

He barely slid his fingertip past the strong ring of muscle, not even going in as far as his first knuckle. But the shocking stimulation was enough to make Charlotte's pussy gush, easing his movements inside her with the additional lubrication.

He used his other hand on her ass to bounce her up and down his length in perfect time with his powerful thrusts up into her scorching, hot sheath. Knowing he needed to keep their cries of pleasure quiet to prevent them from being caught in the act, Ian continued to kiss her, fighting his own instinctual drive for dirty talk.

Charlotte dug her nails into his shoulders through his Polo when the inner walls of her pussy started to flutter as her first climax approached. *Fuck, I hope she leaves marks,* Ian thought as he continued to pound into her while still teasing her asshole with the tip of his finger.

He lost his train of thought when her pussy clamped down on his cock as the waves of her orgasm peaked. Their moans of pleasure mingled as one while he continued pumping his hips to fuck her through the release.

Charlotte momentarily went limp in his arms as she floated away in ecstasy. Ian plunged his tongue into her mouth, mimicking the way he was fucking her pussy with his cock. His pillaging invasion of her mouth seemed to revive her as Charlotte matched him in the impassioned kiss and started to buck her hips in time with his thrusts once more.

Their mating was primal and intense, much like Ian's feelings for Charlotte. Ian was almost grateful they had to keep things quiet, so he didn't succumb to the overwhelming urge he had to confess his love to Charlotte right then. As much as he wanted to tell her how he felt about her, he knew the storeroom of the local bar while balls-deep inside her wasn't the time or place to make that declaration.

But maybe I can convince her to go on an overnight date with me in the next couple of weeks, so we can recreate a little of the night we met to make it more romantic when I tell her I love her for the first time.

In the meantime, Ian settled for telling her with his body what he couldn't yet say in words. As *"I love you, Charlotte!"* ran on a loop through his head, Ian conveyed the message to Charlotte with a four-count rhythm, expressing each word with a powerful stroke of his cock into her creamy cunt.

It didn't take long for her to reach her second crescendo. Her release was so intense, Ian couldn't hold back his own, shoving as deep inside her as he could get when the orgasm exploded through his body. The tight clutch of her pussy milked the cum from his cock as they simultaneously climaxed.

Their movements stilled as the waves of euphoria passed, leaving them clinging to one another while they reveled in the aftershocks. They took their time recovering, lightly trailing kisses down the other's neck as they caught their breath. Eventually, Ian softened enough to slip from her body, realizing that something was wrong the instant the air hit the tip of his dick.

He looked down as he placed Charlotte on her feet. "Fuck," he cursed at seeing the head of his cock poking through the end of the broken condom. He instantly dropped to his knees, lifting the hem of Charlotte's dress back up where it had fallen from her waist.

"What are you doing?" Charlotte seemed confused by why he was examining her pussy.

"The condom broke," Ian explained as he inserted a finger to feel around inside her. "I have to make sure there aren't any pieces still inside you."

"Oh," was her only reply as she took over holding her dress up, so he could use both hands to hold her lower lips open while feeling around for any stray latex in her vagina.

When he couldn't find any pieces of the condom in her pussy, Ian pulled his fingers out and reached over to a shelf that held extra bathroom supplies to grab some paper towels. He cleaned her up as best he could in the storeroom before standing and grabbing another paper towel to do the same with himself. When he pulled the condom off, he pushed the end back together to see if there were any pieces missing.

"It looks like a clean break, so I don't think there's anything left inside that could cause a problem," Ian informed Charlotte as he pulled his boxers and jeans back into place. He wrapped the messy bundle of the broken condom and used paper towels in a few more paper towels to be able to wad it all up and trash it in the men's room. "But you might want to use a douche when you get home, just to be sure."

"Yeah, I'll have to go to the store tomorrow for that," Charlotte admitted with a blush as she lowered the hem of her dress. "And I've been meaning to reschedule my OB-GYN appointment that I missed last month, so maybe I'll just have her double-check, too."

They didn't mention the likelihood of a pregnancy from their little mishap as they snuck out of the storage closet to their respective restrooms to clean up a little better than Ian could clean them up in the storeroom. As he was washing his hands after tossing the evidence of their rendezvous in the garbage can, Ian tried to remember what little he knew about women's cycles to determine the odds of conception from his incompetent condom usage.

With it not even being two weeks since she started her period, he didn't think it was likely that they'd just made a baby. *It's two weeks after her period ends that she ovulates, right? If I'm remembering correctly, then we've got almost a week before we can make a baby.*

Ian looked at his reflection in the mirror as he realized he was ready to plan a family with Charlotte. *Fuck! I really need to plan that romantic, overnight date to tell her I love her before I bring up having babies.*

Since I know it'll probably take a little while after that to convince her to let her family know we're dating, I'm sure she won't be ready to talk about marriage and babies before she ovulates at the end of the week. I guess I'll just have to be more vigilant with the condoms next weekend.

~~~

Sunday, May 26, 2019

Since she'd had to tell Ian to come to the bachelor and bachelorette party the night before so they could see each other, Charlotte was surprised to see him and his family staying after church for James and Randi's wedding shower. Once the Campbells were all seated at the same table as Charlotte, however, Cait quickly cleared up Char's confusion, when she mentioned how nice it was of the couple they'd briefly met at Christmas to invite them after running into Ian the night before.
~~~

It didn't take long for Charlotte's Aunt Susan to fill the other four seats at their table with Jen, Julie, and two of the GWA wrestlers in town for the wedding festivities. Jen and Julie didn't seem to mind being paired up with Liam and Dion yet again. But Charlotte couldn't get a read on whether or not Liam and Dion were actually interested in her cousins, or if they were just playing along with the repeated matchmaking attempts to be polite.

As she looked around the table, she noticed that the seating arrangement seemed off. Ian sat next to Charlotte with Brody seated between Ian and Cait, the same way they tended to always sit when they were seated together at these round tables for potlucks and other events. But on the other side of the table, Julie sat beside Cait, with Dion on her other side. Liam sat next to Dion, with Jen filling the last seat between Liam and Charlotte.

I wonder why Aunt Susan didn't change the seating arrangement to the standard boy-girl, boy-girl pattern she and Mom seem to always use? I would have thought they'd at least want one of the wrestlers seated between Cait and one of my cousins, even if they're dead set on pairing me with Ian.

Are they also dead set on pairing Julie with Dion and Jen with Liam? Or are they planning something else with Cait? Maybe pairing her with Jake? Or Josh? Are they not pairing her with anyone today, since the twins aren't here?

Charlotte tried to think back to when her brothers were last in town and Ian's family was staying on the ranch to recall any potential sparks between Cait and either Josh or Jake. But from what she'd remembered, Cait had been shy around both of them. She also hadn't caught either of her brothers looking longingly at Cait, so she didn't think either of those pairings would work out, no matter how hard the Matchmaking Mommas tried to push them.

Since she hoped to eventually be openly coupled up with Ian, Charlotte decided to try to spend more time with Cait to get to know her better. It not only made sense to build a closer friendship with her potential future sister-in-law, but it also might give her insight into whom Cait might be interested in dating.

I doubt it's one of my brothers, though. Not that Charlotte had any interest in following in her mother's footsteps to play matchmaker, but it would be nice to see Ian's sister connecting with someone other than her brother and nephew at the various events around town.

With that in mind, Char intentionally tried to pull Cait into the conversation going on around the table. Jen and Julie seemed to pick up on what Charlotte was doing, also intentionally including Cait in the ongoing discussion about the potentially embarrassing questions to be asked during the Newlywed Game later in the wedding shower.

Charlotte confessed how mortified she was to learn things about her parents during the wedding showers for both of her brothers. Her comment elicited groans of agreement from her cousins, who'd also learned more than they wanted about their parents, when Susan and Jon were recruited to be the fourth couple participating at Bobby and Brooklyn's wedding shower.

"When was Bobby and Brooklyn's wedding shower?" Cait looked around the table at the three Burleson women seated there. "And how did I miss it if it was held after church like this one, with the whole town invited?"

"It was the last weekend of February," Julie informed her.

The day after Ian and I banged in the parking garage, when he skipped church to avoid me.

"I, um, had some things to check out in San Antonio that day and that's why we missed it," Ian filled in, shifting uncomfortably in his seat at the reference to the situation they were in three months before with the cartel.

"Thank goodness, neither of our parents are participating today," Jen laughed, changing the subject back to the game they'd be watching as soon as everyone was through with lunch. "Although, I doubt the questions today will be as risqué as the questions Nana Marie asked at Bobby and Brooklyn's wedding shower."

"No, I think Pastor Harrison banned Nana Marie from participating after she asked about the first time the couples *made whoopie* for the bonus question," Julie chuckled, shaking her head. "Between that and Amy's sister promoting her website, I'm surprised that wedding shower wasn't the last one he agreed to have in the fellowship hall."

"What's whoopie?" Brody looked at his father as he innocently asked the question.

"Um," Ian floundered.

Julie quickly rattled off an apology. "Oops, sorry! I forgot about little ears."

"Whoopie pies are like giant Oreos, but with softer, more cake-like cookies on either side of the cream filling," Charlotte explained, grateful Julie had used Nana Marie's terminology for sex, so she could come up with an age-appropriate answer for Brody. Knowing from her time teaching him equestrian skills that Brody would follow up with another question, Charlotte came up with another false answer before he could pose the question. His first follow-up question would most likely be why asking about whoopie pies would get Nana Marie banned from participating in the game again, so that's the question she answered. "And since Nana Marie just said whoopie instead of whoopie pie, she confused everyone."

"Oh," Brody nodded, acting like he understood, even though Charlotte knew the real context of the conversation was way over his head. "He should get you or Dad to ask the questions. You're both good at explaining things since you're both teachers."

"I agree with Brody." Jen grinned at the little boy. "When it comes time for any of us to participate in the game, or our parents, I definitely think one of ya'll should ask the questions, so we know they won't be embarrassing. And I'll volunteer to ask the questions when it's your turn to participate."

Just as she had imagined her dream wedding at both of her brother's recent weddings, and specifically marrying Ian at Bobby and Brooklyn's wedding, Charlotte's mind quickly created a mental movie of her own wedding shower and who might participate in the Newlywed Game if she was to get her happily ever after with Ian. Now that she knew his family background, she knew she couldn't subject him to any of the games and events that would normally include his parents or other family members.

Geez, the only people he's close enough to even include in the bridal party are his son, his sister, and his former partner in the DEA. Guess we'll have a small bridal party, if we ever progress to walking down the aisle together.

"Yeah, I'm not having the Newlywed Game at my wedding shower." Charlotte shook her head. Her declaration was as much about avoiding embarrassment as it was anything else, but she hoped it would alleviate any of Ian's concerns about not having more of his family in his life to participate in wedding shower games as well. Not that he was showing any signs of thinking that far ahead for them.

"You really think your mom will let you get out of it?" Julie arched an eyebrow in Charlotte's direction. "I mean, even if we find grooms who don't have any family to participate, I think our mothers have already proven they'll just recruit more of our family and friends to play along."

"Yeah, like how James and Randi got roped into playing at Anthony and Kay's wedding shower," Jen agreed with her twin. "They had barely started dating then, so you know your mom will pull in your married brothers and sisters-in-law to fill any vacant seats in the game."

"Maybe it won't be so bad if you insist it's only younger couples and not your parents playing with you," Cait suggested.

"Maybe," Charlotte reluctantly agreed, still unable to read Ian's thoughts on the subject.

"Regardless of who ends up playing, it sounds like a good time to take the kids to another room to play some games they'll find more fun," Ian interjected, obviously ready to put the topic to rest.

"Actually, Mom has already planned to take the kids back to their Sunday school classrooms right after lunch," Charlotte informed him. She didn't mention that her mother had recruited the children's Sunday school teachers to stay with the kids because of Antonio's anxiety being amped up after meeting so many new people the day before, when all of the out-of-town guests had arrived for all the wedding festivities.

"Is Memmaw gonna stay with us like she has since Antonio moved here?" Brody looked at Charlotte with excitement written all over his little face.

"Of course," Charlotte returned his beaming smile. "And I'll walk up there with you when it's time, just to make sure they have enough teachers staying for all the classrooms."

They continued making small talk as they ate. It was an enjoyable afternoon, with all of them laughing as the whole table collaborated to write out their lines on the love story being passed around the room. Once it was time, Charlotte and Ian both walked Brody up to the four-and-five-year-old's classroom where her mother had all the kids in attendance set up with activities for the remainder of the afternoon.

Since it was mostly children from out of town, both from the GWA and the Lee family, her mother had more than enough help from the Sunday school teachers who had stayed for the afternoon. Realizing they weren't needed for the kids or the wedding shower at the moment, and that the adult Sunday school wing was unoccupied, Charlotte decided to take advantage of some time alone with Ian, when nobody would notice they were missing.

She took Ian's hand and stopped him from following the other parents back downstairs to the party. Once they were far enough ahead to not see where she and Ian were going, she redirected him away from the stairs leading to the fellowship hall. They circled around to the other side of the church, where they had their choice of adult Sunday school classrooms open.

"Where are we going? Shouldn't we get back downstairs to watch the Newlywed Game?"

"I really don't want to take a chance on hearing about when James's Meemaw and PopPop first made whoopie," Charlotte teased, shaking her head. "Especially when we have a half hour we can be alone without anyone missing us."

"Whoa! What happened to the woman who said we couldn't sneak off for a quickie in church?" Ian grinned as he quickened their pace into one of the secluded rooms.

"It wasn't that I didn't want to," Charlotte playfully protested, stepping into his arms as soon as the door closed behind them. They didn't bother turning on the lights, since the light from the windows on the other side of the room provided plenty of illumination for them to see what they were doing. "I just didn't see how we could escape our families until the special circumstances of today made it possible."

"Thank fuck, you figured it out today," Ian groaned just before he claimed her mouth in a scorching kiss.

As always happened when she was in an intimate moment with Ian, the rest of the world disappeared, leaving her feeling like they were the only two people on the planet. Char threw herself headlong into the flaming passion between them, returning his tantalizing licks as their hands explored one another's bodies.

Ian pulled up her dress and kneaded her backside like he was making bread. He slipped his hands under her panties, pushing them down out of his way, so he could slip a finger through her slippery folds and up between her cheeks.

"Such a dirty man," she teased as she moved to trail kisses over his clean-shaven jaw and down his neck. "Isn't it a little inappropriate to play back there in church?"

"Oh, Princess," Ian chuckled against her neck as he licked and nipped the column of her throat. "Nothing I'm planning to do to you in the next few minutes is appropriate to do in church. But we're both still going to enjoy every second of it."

"Oh, and just what do you plan to do to me?" Charlotte cooed seductively as she started to unfasten Ian's belt.

"First, I'm going to get on my knees and eat your pussy until you're begging for my cock." Ian kissed his way down her body as he pulled his pants from her grasp to drop to his knees. He pushed her panties to her ankles as he went before lifting the front of her dress to expose her for his mouth to explore. "Then, once you're begging me to fuck you, to make you come, I'm going to give you what you want. You're going to come in my mouth, then on my cock, letting the angel you portray to the world turn into my naughty girl. Now, spread your legs, Princess. Let me have a taste of your sweet pussy."

"Yes, please." Charlotte wasn't sure if she said the words aloud, or just thought them, as she followed his instructions without even a momentary second-thought. She was too lost in the glorious feel of Ian's tongue sweeping between her lower lips and lapping up her cream before he suckled her clit to care about anything but their pleasure at the moment, not even noticing that she stepped out of her panties.

Char ran her fingers through the short strands of his dark blond hair, needing to hold on to some part of him as he worshiped her with his mouth. With the way he expertly devoured her, it didn't take long for him to get her worked up and ready to explode. Just as she felt like she was about to go over from his very thorough tongue-fucking, Ian backed off, lightly licking her labia, and pulling her back from the precipice.

Realizing he'd backed her away from her orgasm because she hadn't started begging for it yet, Char capitulated. Her pride wasn't going to keep her from the heights of ecstasy she knew Ian could deliver. "Please, Ian, I need to come. Please, make me come. Oh, please, Ian."

Her panting words turned into a whimper as he inserted a finger and started teasing her G-spot while sucking on her clit. "Oh, please, Ian. Please make me come, so I can have your big cock. Please, please, please."

Ian added another finger, both of them stroking over her G-spot in time with his mouth sucking on her clit. She felt his other hand as he swiped one of the digits through her juices before moving to her back entrance. He barely had to touch her puckered hole before she felt the first waves of her orgasm rolling over her.

He continued to pump his fingers in and out of her in unison, finger-fucking both her pussy and ass in synchronicity with his suckling on her clit. As the intensity of her climax crested, Charlotte clamped her mouth shut, wishing she had something to bite down on to prevent the scream of pleasure that wanted to escape.

She felt like she was floating outside her body, her spirit having been knocked out of her physical being from the sheer force of the orgasm Ian had given her by stimulating her clitoris, G-spot, and anus at the same time.

"Wow," Char breathed out the words she didn't realize she was speaking aloud. "I thought the triple orgasms I've read about in romance novels were a myth."

"I take it we just proved the books correct?" Ian chuckled, gently pulling his fingers from her body as she came down from her euphoric high.

"Most definitely," she agreed as he stood and started to unfasten his pants.

"Fuck," Ian swore, stopping before he finished unzipping.

"What?" Charlotte looked around, twisting her head to listen from both directions of the hallway outside the room, trying to hear if someone was coming and about to catch them in the act.

"I used my last condom last night," Ian groaned, bowing his head. "I didn't want to stop for more this morning with Brody and Cait in the car, and didn't think it would matter since we wouldn't need one at church."

"Oh." Charlotte's heart sank, knowing she hadn't thought to bring a condom to church either, even though she had bought some of the correct size since she and Ian had started having sex regularly.

She thought for a minute about the last time they'd had unprotected sex and decided that with it just being a couple of days off from the same time of the month as back in February, they probably weren't likely to get pregnant, since they hadn't then. "Um, I'm still clean and haven't been with anyone but you in over a year."

"Same here." Ian looked up, their eyes locking on one another. "And we're probably not at any more of a risk going without today than we are from the condom breaking last night. If my calculations are correct, then you're not due to ovulate until the end of the week."

Charlotte was too aroused to think at the moment to do the calculations herself, so she trusted Ian's were correct. "So, you want to risk it without a condom?"

"Only if you're willing to risk it, Princess." Ian's hands didn't move from where he'd stopped unzipping his pants as he waited for her positive confirmation.

"Please, Ian, I need you too bad to wait for another time and place when we have a condom available." Char hoped she wasn't blushing too much from her whispered confession.

"Thank fuck," Ian groaned, quickly shoving his zipper and then his pants and boxers down. The silver jewelry in Ian's piercings glistened in the sunlight coming through the window, already coated in his precum. "There was no way I could make it through the rest of the afternoon without having you."

Ian pushed her dress back up, gripping her hips as soon as the hem was high enough and lifting her up to meet his cock. With one powerful thrust, he joined their bodies at the same time his mouth crashed down on hers.

Charlotte wrapped her arms around his shoulders and her legs around his waist, clinging to him as they kissed and bucked in a primal mating neither of them could control. She rocked her hips in time with his as their tongues tangled. She tasted herself on his lips and reveled in the dirty desires the mix of their tastes amped up in both of them.

Char sucked his tongue as if it was his cock while Ian pressed her back against the door and swiveled his hips to skim his piercings over her G-spot. *Greatest piercing ever! And even better without a condom between us!*

She dug her nails into his back as Ian masterfully played her body like an instrument only he could draw music from, working her up to the brink of another climax within moments.

He pulled back from their lip lock to grin at her and waggle his eyebrows suggestively while adjusting his grip on her hips to move his hand back to her ass. "Let's see if we can hit another triple."

"If you're going to attempt that again," Charlotte teased, wiggling her ass against his hand as he pushed against her puckered back entrance with the same finger he'd used there earlier. "I need something to bite down on to keep from screaming and broadcasting to everyone in the building where we are and what we're doing."

"Then unbutton my shirt and move it out of the way, so you can bite down on my shoulder, sweet Charlotte," Ian commanded, his voice deepening with arousal. "Because I'm absolutely going to make you want to scream."

"Yes, Sir." Charlotte skipped the playful salute she wanted to give him, needing both hands to loosen his tie and work the first few buttons at his collar free. Once the fabric was moved out of the way, she kissed her way down his neck before licking across his collarbone to find the meatiest part of his muscular trapezius to bite down on when he finally pushed her over the edge.

Ian synced up his movements, timing the way he was finger-fucking her ass with the powerful strokes of his cock into her pussy, so he could tap his pelvic bone against her clit with each plunge of his dick into her core. The added stimulation of her anus with his finger and her G-spot with his piercings was overwhelmingly exquisite.

"Fuck, I love fucking you, Charlotte," Ian groaned, his speed increasing as he, too, approached the verge of his orgasm.

I love you, too. Charlotte barely held herself back from speaking the words, realizing at the last second that he'd added an extra word that changed the meaning of the three she originally heard.

She couldn't dwell on the thoughts of love, or even comprehend the other dirty things Ian was saying, with the exception of the guttural, "Mine," he always included in his dirty talk repertoire, as her body started to convulse in the ultimate pleasure he was giving her.

Ian was a moment late in ordering her to, "Come, now, Princess." Charlotte was already starting to float away to nirvana when her inner walls started to spasm and squeeze his cock. She barely remembered to bite down on his shoulder, moaning her release against his skin as her body imploded.

Ian shoved in deep one last time, his whole body stiffening as he spilled his seed directly into her womb. "Oh, fuck, Charlotte," he whisper-shouted, burying his face in her hair as he came.

He pulled his finger from her ass, so he could wrap her in his arms to cuddle her close as they each recovered. His big body shuddered with each aftershock that hit him, causing another spurt of his cum to splash inside her.

Charlotte loved the way sex felt with Ian when there were no barriers between them, imagining his cum dripping into her panties for the rest of the day as his way of marking his claim on her. *I have definitely got to reschedule that doctor's appointment to get on birth control, so we can do this without condoms all the time.*

Once they caught their breath, they disentangled their bodies. As they adjusted their clothing back into place, they found Charlotte's panties on the floor next to Ian's tie. She'd been so caught up in the moment, she hadn't even realized she'd completely removed it from his neck.

"Damn, I'm never going to be able to get this knotted the same way it was before without a mirror," Ian chuckled as he looped it under his shirt collar. "Think I can get away with going back to the party without it?"

"No," Charlotte giggled, straightening her dress after putting her panties back on. "Brody will alert everyone when he comes back downstairs and notices you've taken it off. But we can stop at the restroom for you to tie it on the way back down."

She would take the extra time to wipe up the first round of Ian's escaped swimmers in the ladies' room while he dealt with his tie in the men's room. *And hopefully, nobody will notice when we sneak back into the party.*

Chapter Twenty-Three

After sneaking off at the other wedding events earlier in the week to covertly spend time with Charlotte, Ian's wallet was restocked with condoms, and he was ready for another repeat performance as he walked into James and Randi's wedding reception in the ballroom of the B and B. He wasn't sure it was going to happen though, not with all the speculation about what was going on between him and Charlotte that was spreading around the room.

Apparently, their more recent disappearing acts had been noticed by a couple of Charlotte's family members. *Yeah, sneaking off to have sex at church last Sunday probably wasn't our best idea. But, damn, it sure felt like it at the time.* Ian grinned at his memories of being inside Charlotte with no barrier between them, as he took his seat at the table beside her for the reception, glad for the long tablecloth to cover his instant erection from thinking about the glorious feeling of fucking Charlotte.

With Brody and then Cait on his other side, he wasn't surprised when the other half of the table filled up with Charlotte's cousins, Jen and Julie, and the two wrestlers that had been seated with them at the wedding shower the previous week. Ian found he liked Dion and Liam, as they weren't nearly as rowdy as some of the other men he'd met, both with the GWA and from Heart's Destiny, since he'd been in town.

While Ian would always prefer hanging out with Charlotte's brothers after they'd bonded while taking down the cartel, he understood that wasn't always possible at events such as this. Especially when the two Ian felt closest with, Jake and Josh, weren't even in town to attend the wedding reception.

Leah Mae Wright

Since Anthony and Kay were in the wedding party, they were seated at the head table with the bride and groom and the rest of the bridal party. Ian would have volunteered to sit with their kids, so Brody would have his friends to help occupy him. But Antonio, Maria, and Tia were all seated with their grandparents, Bob and Hazel, along with Bobby and Brooklyn.

Looking across the room and seeing how wary Antonio looked about everything going on around him, made Ian wonder if they might need to take the kids to a separate area of the building, the way they had at the wedding shower to ease the little boy's anxiety. Knowing how close she felt to Antonio, Ian turned to Charlotte to make the suggestion.

"How's Antonio doing with meeting so many new people this week? Is he more comfortable than he was on Sunday? Or do we need to find a room to take the kids to give him a break from the crowd?"

Charlotte's brow furrowed as she looked over at Antonio. "He's still pretty overwhelmed," she admitted with a sigh. "I wish he could have met Kay's side of the family and the GWA crew at separate times, so he could have eased into getting to know all of them. But Tia and Maria are both really good at trying to make sure he's comfortable with everyone around him. If it gets to be too much, he knows to let one of us know. And if he doesn't, I'm sure Tia or Maria will. Mom already has a plan for taking the kids into the library if necessary tonight, but we should probably let her know if you're willing to take Brody in there, too."

"Of course," Ian nodded. "I'm willing to take a turn in there watching the kids too, so she doesn't have to miss out on any of the festivities."

"I'll let her know." Charlotte smiled at him briefly before standing to walk over to the table where her parents were seated to whisper a few words in her mother's ear.

Hazel turned and looked straight at Ian, giving him a small smile and nod of acknowledgment for his offer. Ian lifted his chin as he smiled back.

When Charlotte returned to their table, she informed him that they planned to keep the kids in the ballroom through the meal that was currently being served, and then move to the library after the cake was cut. "I think wanting a piece of cake is the only thing keeping Antonio from wanting to run to the library right now."

"Well, of course," Ian agreed with a grin. "Cake is the most important part of all this to a little boy. Right, Brody?"

"Yes!" Brody excitedly agreed. "When do we get to eat cake?"

"After you eat your dinner," Ian chuckled just as a waiter placed a plate of roast beef, potatoes, and baby carrots in front of Brody.

Brody's eyes bugged out at the adult-sized servings, so Ian quickly reassured him that he only had to eat half of the food on his plate.

"We'll help you out, little man," Liam told Brody as he pointed back and forth between himself and Dion. "Pass your plate over here, and we'll take half off, so you can see it's not too much you have to eat before getting cake."

"Don't trust him." Dion shook his head at Brody while pointing his thumb at Liam. "If you pass him your plate now, he'll eat it all before you even get a bite. Eat as much as you want first, and then we'll clean your plate for you once you're full."

"I don't trust either of you." Brody wrapped his arms around his plate, pulling it as close to him as he could without it falling off the table into his lap. "I've seen the way you cheat when you wrestle."

"Smart boy!" Julie reached around behind Caitir to give Brody a high-five, as the rest of the table laughed at the two big, imposing wrestlers being called out as cheaters by Ian's four-year-old son.

"I only cheat when I'm playing a bad guy on TV," Dion protested, pretending to pout, which was hilarious coming from the imposing African American wrestler. "I'm really not a bad guy, I promise."

"Feck!" Liam slugged Dion in the shoulder, his voice taking on a distinct Irish accent, instead of his previous New Yorker inflection. "You better change dat I to we. I can't be partners wit a clown who throws me oehnder de boehs while defendin' 'imself."

Brody's brow furrowed as he looked at Liam. "Daddy, why's he talking funny?"

Ian had no idea how to answer his son. Thankfully, Dion was able to translate for his tag-team partner, which was surprising considering Dion's New Orleans accent. Or as he would put it — his N'awlins accent.

"Red's Irish tends to come out at odd times," Dion quipped, garnering chuckles from the ladies at the table. "Especially when he's upset, and right now he's upset that you think he's a bad guy. But we're only pretending to be bad guys when we're wrestling."

"I don't know." Jen shook her head as she waved her fork at Liam and Dion. "Bugging Brody and not letting him eat his dinner, so he can have cake later, seems like bad guy behavior to me."

"I agree with Jen." Charlotte reached across Ian to pat Brody's arm, which was still protectively wrapped around his plate. "Don't listen to Red Velvet," she instructed him, referring to the wrestlers by their tag-team name. "They're just trying to trick you into not eating your dinner, so they can have your cake later."

"Yeah, they're such big fans of cake that they use a type of cake as their tag-team name," Julie added with a giggle.

As Brody finally started eating his dinner, while giving Dion and Liam wary glances, the rest of the table had a lively discussion about the various names used by professional wrestlers. While Ian didn't think a tag-team named after a cake sounded as intimidating as the two wrestlers across the table from him looked, he had to agree with the reasoning that the ridiculous name gave the fans and their opponents on the shows plenty of fodder for taunting them without being vulgar in front of young fans.

That was something Ian could appreciate from the GWA. They tried to keep their shows family-friendly, so parents could watch with their children and enjoy the athleticism of the wrestling without worrying about the excessive violence and over-sexualism of other organizations.

Even the one sexual gimmick they had for the tag team known as Protection Detail was tastefully done. Parents with young kids, like Ian, could easily explain their name by telling their children that the wrestlers were protecting their manager, Chastity. While parents with older children, who might get the innuendo, could use it as an icebreaker to discuss safe sex with their preteens and teenagers.

The conversation around the table quieted down while everyone ate, and the various speeches were given. When they went through the special dances for the bride and groom, their parents, and the wedding party, Ian assumed they'd be opening the dance floor to the rest of the reception for a little while before cutting the cake and tossing the bouquet and garter.

Hopefully, they don't delay too long for Antonio to be able to deal with his anxiety around strangers.

He was surprised when they progressed straight to the bouquet toss instead of opening up the dance floor, but hoped that was intentional on Randi's part to help out her new nephew. Of course, he had to tease Charlotte just a little when the emcee asked all the single ladies to congregate on the dance floor.

"You caught the last one, Princess." He grabbed her hand, stopping her from walking away from the table as she stood with the other ladies. "So, you can sit this one out."

"Oh, no, I definitely need a do-over," she retorted, giving him a cheeky grin, and pulling her hand from his to join the other ladies in lining up for the bouquet toss.

Ian let out a sigh of relief when Randi took aim as if she was pitching a baseball and threw the bouquet straight at her best friend, Amy. Amy threw her hands up to protect her face, catching the bouquet in an act of pure self-defense.

"Jeez, Randi," Kay shouted while laughing. "I wasn't nearly that blatant when I threw my bouquet to you. Or as deadly with the toss."

"Sorry, Ames, didn't mean to almost poke your eye out with the roses," Randi yelled across the room, laughing with her sister.

"I'm just glad you had the foresight to have the thorns removed," Amy hollered back, laughing along with the rest of the people in the room.

"She throws like you taught me," Brody pointed out, causing Ian to chuckle even more.

"Yeah, she does," Ian agreed with his son.

"And now it's time for the single gentlemen to line up for the garter toss," the emcee announced.

Ian stood to go stand with the other guys, carrying Brody with him the same way he had at the last wedding they'd attended, though he had no intention of trying to catch the garter at this wedding. "We're not trying to catch it this time," Ian whispered to Brody, explaining why he was standing back away from the main crowd of guys. "Amy's boyfriend, Justin, needs to catch it."

Brody nodded his agreement before turning his head to watch what was happening.

Randi took a seat in the center of the dance floor as James got down on his knees at her feet. When he lifted the hem of her dress and bent further down as if he was going to dip his head under her wedding gown, Anthony called out, "Remember, there are children present!"

"Guess that means I have to use my hands and not my teeth to remove the garter," James joked, wagging his eyebrows up at his bride.

"Please don't slobber on it before you toss it at us, Bro," James's twin brother Dean yelled, inciting a round of laughter throughout the room.

"For real," the wrestler Ian only knew by his ring name of Crockett shouted. "Randi's the only one who wants your bodily fluids flying at her."

"Dude, I don't want him to spit on me either!" Randi squealed over the roar of laughter.

"I don't think that's what he meant, Angel." James chuckled as he slid his hands up under Randi's dress. "But I promise I won't be sharing any bodily fluids, even the ones I know you do want shooting at you, while we're here in front of an audience."

Randi's face turned beet red when she finally realized what the guys were referring to. "Oh" was all she said before covering her face with her hands and folding down to touch her forehead to the top of James's head.

When his son gave him a questioning look, obviously confused by the things being said, Ian just shook his head at Brody. "I don't get it either," he lied to his son, not wanting to use the same speech about Brody being too young to understand that he'd used at the last wedding.

James pulled his hands out from under Randi's dress, holding the garter in one and reaching up to move her hands away from her face with the other. He whispered something unintelligible before pressing his lips to hers briefly.

"Now, let's get this show on the road!" James stood up and looked around the room. "I'm ready to get started on our honeymoon!"

Without any warning, James wrapped the garter around his fingers as if they were a slingshot, aimed directly at Justin, and let it fly. It was an easy one-handed catch for Justin, with nobody else even attempting to catch it. With as inseparable as Justin and Amy had been since admitting to dating back at Justin's birthday party, Ian wasn't the only one who respected Justin's claim on his woman by stepping back.

"Fabulous! Time for the bouquet and garter photo!" Philippe, the photographer, clapped his hands to get their attention before pointing at Justin and Amy to direct them to the center of the dance floor, where the chair was now sitting empty. "Miss Amy, if you would please have a seat."

With most everyone going back to their seats, Ian could easily see what was going on as he carried Brody back to their table.

"Oh, I thought Justin was supposed to sit first with me on his lap, like at Kay and Anthony's wedding." Amy looked confused by the directions that were apparently different at the other recent wedding than they'd been when Ian, Charlotte, and Brody had posed for this same style of picture at Bobby and Brooklyn's wedding.

"Oh, but that pose is so last year." Philippe waved his hand around dismissively. "The trend now is for him to make it look like he's going to put the garter on you, as if you're getting ready for your own wedding."

"Oh, okay." Amy still looked slightly confused as she sat down in the chair for Philippe to arrange the bouquet in her lap the way he wanted it for the pictures.

When he stepped back, Justin dropped down on one knee in front of her. Instead of presenting her with the garter and pretending to put it on her the way Ian assumed he would pose, Justin put the garter in his pocket and pulled out what looked like a ring box from what Ian could see from his seat back at the table.

Justin took Amy's left hand in his, opening the box with his right hand before presenting it to her.

"That's not a garter!" Amy pointed out the obvious before Justin could even utter a word of what Ian assumed was going to be his proposal.

"No, it's not," Justin chuckled. "But I still hope you'll let me put it on you tonight."

Amy opened her mouth as if to speak, but quickly closed it and nodded at Justin to continue.

"Amy Edwina Lawton, I fell head over heels in love with you the first moment I saw you back in November. Getting to know you as a friend and coworker just made me fall deeper and deeper in love with you. Dating you these past few months has only shown me that I was right to give you my heart from day one. I know this is sooner than you expected and I'm willing to wait through a long engagement if that's what you need. But I can't wait a moment longer to call you my fiancée. Please, Sweetheart, will you marry me?"

"Yes!" Amy shouted, dropping the bouquet on the floor as she threw her arms around Justin's neck and fell to her knees on the floor beside him.

Their lips met in a kiss that quickly became too passionate for their audience. Ian redirected Brody's attention as Justin picked Amy up, stood with her in his arms, and spun her around.

Ian and Charlotte both joined in on the shouts of "congratulations" that spread around the room, along with the others at their table.

Justin placed Amy back down on her feet and withdrew the ring from the box.

"How did you get it to fit?" Amy's eyes widened as Justin slid the ring onto her finger.

"That was actually the work of your dad and Ashlyn," Justin confessed.

"Yeah, Dad called me and asked our ring size since you wouldn't tell Justin." Amy's twin pushed between Justin and Amy to hug her sister.

"It's not that I wouldn't tell him," Amy protested, even as she hugged Ashlyn. "I just don't know it and haven't had the chance to visit a jewelry store to have my finger sized."

As more people crowded around the newly engaged couple to offer their congratulations, Ian turned his attention back to the people at his table. "Guess I messed up by not popping the question when we caught the bouquet and garter at the last wedding," he teased Charlotte, wagging his eyebrows suggestively.

"Yep!" Charlotte popped the P at the end of her declaration. "And now you're going to have to wait until the next wedding to see if you can get the chance for a do-over to get it right."

Not if I can come up with a better idea for how to propose before then. Ian's mind flashed with ideas of how he could propose as Randi and James moved over to the cake table to cut their wedding cake. *I'll get right on planning that as soon as I get Charlotte to agree to our overnight date, so I can tell her I love her. And I'm sure, once Charlotte agrees to let her family know we're dating, Hazel will be more than glad to share her pictures from Charlotte's wedding book, so I can give my princess the wedding of her dreams.*

~ ~ ~

Monday, June 3, 2019

Charlotte was finally getting in for the appointment she'd rescheduled with the OB-GYN after she missed it back in April. While things were going great between her and Ian, they hadn't really made any solid plans for their future together, so she wanted to talk to her new doctor about getting on birth control until they both decided they were ready to build a family together.

While she was more than ready to become a mom, and Ian had seemed to be prepared to step up and be a dad if they'd have conceived back in February, Charlotte wanted to have a plan in place before they brought another child into their lives. And with the way they both got carried away and forgot condoms a couple of times, that meant she needed to pick another form of protection until they could come up with that plan as a couple.

She wasn't waiting long when a door opened on the opposite side of the receptionist's desk from the one she always went through to see Doc Hayes. A new nurse that Charlotte didn't recognize stepped into the waiting room and called her name. Charlotte stood from her seat and walked over to follow the nurse back to the exam room.

When she stepped through the door, she saw her cousin, Justin, and his fiancée, Amy, standing at the counter just inside the door that she assumed was where patients checked out after their appointments. Charlotte's eyes widened as they met Justin's, and Justin smiled at her as she walked past them, but they didn't otherwise acknowledge each other.

Why are they here together? I know he went with her to see Doc Hayes and a cardiologist back in March, but she got a clean bill of health. So, why is he at the doctor's office with her now? It's not like he still has to be with her constantly, in case she faints again. Or even has to go to every follow-up with her from back then.

But why else would he be with her here, if not because of that? Unless…oh, shit! This is the OB-GYN side of the clinic.

They're not here to follow up on her fainting spell in March. They're either here because they're pregnant, or they're here to go over their family planning options.

Since Arden Snyder introduced herself as Dr. Magnum's nurse as she escorted Charlotte into an exam room, she didn't dwell on her cousin and his fiancée or their possible reason for being at the doctor's office for long. The nurse went over all the basic new patient questions and had just finished recording Char's vital signs, when Dr. Magnum knocked once before entering the room.

"Good afternoon, I'm Dr. Devon Magnum," the doctor, who looked to be close to Charlotte's age, introduced herself.

"Charlotte Burleson," Char replied as the doctor took a seat at the computer to read over the information Arden had entered in her chart.

If the doctor recognized her last name from her other patients, she didn't give any indication of it. That put Charlotte a little more at ease, knowing that she could talk to Dr. Magnum without worrying about doctor-patient confidentiality being breached, no matter which of her family members might visit the same office.

"So, you're here to discuss your birth control options?" Dr. Magnum questioned when she was finished reading over the information in Charlotte's chart.

"Yes. I, um, recently started seeing someone and want to know our options besides condoms," Charlotte confided. "We had one break a little over a week ago, so I figured it's time to pick a better option."

"That's definitely a good reason to pick a different form of birth control." Dr. Magnum nodded in agreement, smiling at Charlotte. "And there are several alternatives to choose from, with a whole list of factors to consider for each of them before making the decision. But before we get into that, let's discuss the issue you had with the condom breaking."

The doctor turned to look at the computer, scrolling through Charlotte's chart before continuing. "Do you remember the exact date the condom broke?" Charlotte nodded, but didn't get a chance to state the date as Dr. Magnum asked another question. "When it broke, did you account for all the pieces of the condom?"

"My, um, partner felt to make sure there weren't any pieces left inside," Charlotte admitted, blushing at telling the doctor how Ian fingered her afterward. "And when he took it off, I looked and saw that he'd pushed through the end of it, so it fit back together like there weren't any pieces missing. But just to make sure we didn't miss a sliver, I bought a douche the next morning and used it to rinse everything out."

"We'll still do a pelvic exam today, just to be on the safe side, but it doesn't sound like you have to worry about any infection from a lost piece of latex." Dr. Magnum smiled once more. "Now, you said it was a little over a week ago. Do you remember the exact date?"

"Yes, it was Saturday, May twenty-fifth," Char informed her.

"And May thirteenth was when your last period started?" Dr. Magnum referred to the date in Charlotte's chart on her computer.

"Yes," Char confirmed the information she'd given Arden just a few minutes before was correct.

"That puts your fertile window between the twenty-third and twenty-eighth, with your most likely ovulation date of the twenty-seventh." Dr. Magnum announced the dates surrounding the weekend she was with Ian twice without any barriers between them, as if she wasn't dropping a bomb in Charlotte's brain. "Since I'm assuming your partner ejaculated on the twenty-fifth when the condom broke, we'll want to wait until your next period starts to confirm you're not pregnant before we start you on birth control."

I knew I should have looked that up before agreeing we were probably safe to skip the condom on Sunday, when neither one of us thought to bring one to the wedding shower. But no, I let my vajayjay override my brain, and agreed with Ian's assumption that we were probably safe for another week, just so I didn't have to wait a day to ride his magic pierced peen!

She was so busy beating herself up internally for having a second unplanned pregnancy scare in less than four months' time that she missed what the doctor said before she stood to leave the room. Luckily, she recognized the paper sheet that Dr. Magnum had pulled out of a cabinet and laid on the exam table, and realized she was supposed to undress from the waist down for the pelvic exam.

Charlotte went through the process like a robot on auto-pilot, wondering if this was the first step to the predictions she dreamed her memmaw told her about for her future coming true.

Oh, yeah, if I'm pregnant, then this baby is definitely going to be named Judy! And if it's a boy, I'll go with Jude, regardless of what the rest of my family thinks about there being too many J names in the family already.

Charlotte started to come out of her daze as the doctor finished with the pelvic exam, confirming that everything looked fine inside, with no signs of infection from stray latex. "You can't tell from this exam if I'm pregnant or not, though, right?"

"Sorry, no." Dr. Magnum shook her head while giving Charlotte a wry smile. "You have to wait until you're a day late on your period before we can even be sure with a pregnancy test. And we wouldn't even be able to see an embryo on ultrasound for several weeks after that."

"Okay," Charlotte sighed, sitting back up on the exam table.

"Don't worry," Dr. Magnum instructed. "You won't have to wait that much longer. Since you're due to start your period next Monday, let's schedule you an appointment for the middle of next week. I'm going to give you several brochures on the various forms of contraception to read over. If you've started your period, then we'll discuss them and pick the option that works best for you. If not, we'll do a pregnancy test and go over your other options."

Charlotte agreed, though she knew if she was pregnant, she wouldn't need to discuss her other options with the doctor. If she and Ian made a baby, then she only had one option she'd want to go with — having and keeping her baby.

Once she'd redressed, Dr. Magnum came back into the room with the brochures she mentioned on the various pills, shots, and other methods of birth control. She did a quick overview of each of the categories before instructing Charlotte to read over the pros and cons of each to see what would fit best in her life.

Charlotte was then released to go to the check-out desk, where she made an appointment for the following Thursday. She originally wanted the appointment on Tuesday, thinking the first day after her period was due would be best for taking a pregnancy test. But when there weren't any appointments available that day, she decided maybe it was better to give herself a couple of extra days. *Just in case the stress of all this causes me to be a couple of days late this month.*

Chapter Twenty-Four

Ian had finally come up with a plan for how to tell Charlotte he loved her. After almost slipping and saying those three little words several times over the past couple of weeks, and literally having to insert the word "fucking" between the words to keep from confessing his feelings in the middle of a quickie, Ian had decided to take her on the date he wished they'd had the night they met, only meeting a little earlier in the evening, so they'd have time for everything he wanted them to do.

He'd booked a suite at the same hotel, planning to end up back there for the night. But first, he wanted them to recreate meeting in the hotel bar, go on a carriage ride through the city at sunset, and have dinner in the revolving restaurant atop the Tower of the Americas, where he planned to tell her he loved her for the first time over a decadent dessert.

When he first told Charlotte about his plan to take her on the date he wished they could have had in December, she was skeptical of their ability to sneak away from Heart's Destiny for a night without anyone noticing. But when she started talking about the progress she'd made in therapy and feeling ready to go back to volunteer at the shelter, he convinced her that she could use the excuse of spending the night in a hotel in San Antonio the night before to recreate the times she'd volunteered with Fiona, if anyone in her family questioned where she was for the night.

While making her volunteer time seem more like the occasions she'd volunteered before Roberto came to the shelter was a good excuse to give her family, it wasn't truly what she would be doing, since Ian would be accompanying her the next day. Though when she argued about not being able to lie to her family, he pointed out that she was going to be volunteering with the other middle school English teacher, just as she had before, so it wasn't really a lie.

Once Ian had convinced Charlotte to meet him at the hotel bar where they'd first met for an early drink before their overnight date, he'd talked to his sister to let her know why he'd be out all night. He wasn't sure how Caitir would feel about him dating Charlotte, but when she found out they'd been secretly dating for months, Caitir responded with elation.

Ian had then made sure his sister knew she was sworn to secrecy about his and Charlotte's relationship. He didn't want her to say a word about them to Hazel and cause Charlotte to call things off with him. It had taken a promise of him not interfering when Caitir started dating again to get her confirmation that she wouldn't say a word to anyone. But Ian was happy to offer it, knowing the only man she seemed interested in at the moment had too many other things on his plate to date her anytime soon.

And if Josh ever figures out his kid situation to make a move on Caitir, then I trust she'll be safe with him. It'll only be if she decides to date someone other than one of the Burlesons or Avingtons that I might need to go back on that promise not to interfere.

He didn't have long to ponder the possibility of what he might do if Caitir decided to date one of the Walkers, the way he'd feared a few months back, as Charlotte sashayed into the room. She had apparently taken his silly plan to recreate their first meeting to heart, wearing the exact same navy-blue pencil skirt and white blouse that she'd been wearing that night. Ian had worn the same suit he'd worn for his interview that day, but he kept the jacket and tie on when he went to the bar this time.

"Hi, I'm Ian," Ian stood and introduced himself, feeling a little silly now that he was actively engaged in the role-play.

"Nice to meet you, Ian." Charlotte took his outstretched hand, which he then used to pull her hand up to his lips for a chivalrously light brush, instead of a handshake. "I'm Charlotte."

"May I buy you a drink?" Ian pulled out the barstool for her, still holding her hand as he assisted her to take her seat beside him.

"I'd say something about it being too early for a drink, but as nervous as I am about tomorrow morning, I need one too bad to complain about the time," Charlotte scoffed with a wry smile, bringing them out of the role-play of just meeting.

He didn't want to draw attention to her nerves about the two of them going back to volunteer at the shelter the next day, so he decided to skip replying to that portion of her comment. He just hoped his teasing innuendo would take her mind off of her fear of bringing back the flashbacks as well.

"Aw, it's close enough to five o'clock," Ian quipped back at her, waving at the clock above the bar before wagging his eyebrows at her suggestively. "But I'm sure we can come up with something else to do to pass the time, if you really want to wait the thirty minutes until happy hour."

"I'm not sure your suggestions would be appropriate to do with someone I've just met," Charlotte playfully scolded him.

"Yeah, I can't maintain that role-play," Ian chuckled, shaking his head. "I'll have to stick to writing, since I obviously suck as an actor."

"Good," Charlotte agreed, giggling. "I don't think I could maintain it either. Although it was an interesting trope in a book I read a few weeks ago."

"Oh? Tell me about the book." Ian had enjoyed the book series she'd referenced the night they met more than he expected, so he wondered if the book she was talking about now would be as entertaining.

"It was different than what I normally prefer to read. More of a novella than a full novel and by an author I hadn't heard of before. Through the whole thing, it seemed like these two characters met for the first time and were having a one-night stand. Then in the final chapter, they wake up the next morning and go pick up their kids from the babysitter, where they'd stayed the night while the parents had a date night. Come to find out, the characters were married for over a decade and using fake names for role-play to spice things up."

"Yeah, that's definitely different than the books you've recommended before." And didn't sound like something Ian would enjoy nearly as much as the spy games in the romantic suspense series in which he was eagerly awaiting the next book release.

"Oh, yeah, way different," Charlotte agreed, nodding her head. "And not something I think you'd enjoy, even though the sex scenes were hot."

"Yeah? As hot as you're going to make the sex scenes when we collaborate on a book?" Ian arched an eyebrow, daring her to answer as the bartender walked up to them to take their order.

Charlotte blushed in response, so he gave her an out, momentarily dropping the subject to let her choose from the wine menu. He wasn't exactly a wine connoisseur, typically choosing a beer or scotch on the rare occasion when he actually imbibed. Therefore, he followed Charlotte's lead when she chose a prosecco for their before dinner drink.

Once the bartender had served their drinks and walked away to tend to other customers, Ian brought the conversation back around to their future book writing plans. "The more I think about reading the scenes you'll be writing in our books, the more I think we should get started collaborating this summer, instead of waiting for retirement."

He really liked the idea of reading some of her sexual fantasies in what she wrote and already had plans to start making them come true. *If for no other reason than our need to research the feasibility of the positions she comes up with for our book characters.*

"I don't think the world is ready for the hotness level of the scenes we'd write just yet," Charlotte disagreed, smiling over the rim of her glass before taking a sip.

"We might not make any bestseller's lists, but I'm sure there are a few people who can not only handle the hotness level, but are actively looking for something hotter than what's currently popular. Though I can't say for sure, since I'm not really up on what's popular in the romance genre."

"Right now, it seems like there are two major themes that are the most popular," Charlotte informed him. "Sweet Christmas romance, like you'd see in a Hallmark movie, and at the opposite end of the spectrum, BDSM."

"So, if we write a Christmas themed, BDSM romance, will we hit the bestseller's list in both categories?" Ian quipped, thinking the brainstorming for story ideas would be funny, even if it never led to a book.

"Maybe," Charlotte giggled. "But we'd have to license the movie rights to a porn studio, instead of Hallmark. Or maybe the production company my sister is working on for Burleson Incorporated, if she's willing to make such steamy movies."

"I'm sure it can be tastefully done for theatrical release by your family business," Ian jokingly argued, waiting for Charlotte to set her glass down before finishing his thought. "Or maybe we could sell the rights to Skinemax."

The way she snorted at his bastardization of Cinemax made it evident it was a good thing he waited until after she'd swallowed her sip of wine to say it.

"Okay, say I'm on board with this idea," Charlotte teased, her voice light with a hint of laughter. "Plot it out for me, so I can get an idea of the scenes I'd have to write."

"Alright," Ian nodded, metaphorically putting on his thinking cap and coming up with an idea on the fly. "Since we're planning to write romantic suspense for me to be able to tap into my law enforcement background, we'll start by having our DEA agents unwind on weekends in the local BDSM club."

"Be careful," Charlotte warned, making an unnaturally stern face. "You can't steal ideas from other authors, so you'll have to come up with a creative name for the club."

"Easy," Ian boasted, grinning. "The Playground."

"The Playground?" Charlotte skeptically arched an eyebrow.

"Yeah, they call indulging in kink playing, so they'd naturally need to go to The Playground," Ian explained his reasoning.

"No, that sounds too much like someplace I'd take my nieces and nephew, or you'd take Brody," Charlotte objected, scrunching her nose. "You have to come up with something else."

Ian amended his BDSM club name idea in his head before elaborating to Charlotte. "How about The Pleasure Playground? That way, it's obvious it's a place for adults and not kids."

"Okay, I'll allow that change for now." Charlotte finally accepted his club name. "But if we ever write this book for real, we might have to amend it again." Ian nodded his agreement before Charlotte prompted him to, "go on with the plot of the book."

Ian took a sip of the surprisingly refreshing drink she'd ordered for them while he brainstormed some more, setting his glass back down before giving her an overview of the ideas that popped into his head. "To keep from seeming anything like a Hallmark movie, we'll have the club throwing a Christmas in July event. Maybe have some specialty floggers made up from tinsel and use ribbon instead of rope in the bondage area. Oh, and instead of having an *Elf on a Shelf*, they'll have a *Sub in a Tub* set up in the water play area."

"You are a twisted man, Ian Campbell," Charlotte snorted, roaring with laughter at his goofy ideas. "But I have to admit, I'd enjoy reading a book with your ideas in it. Though maybe you should plan to write comedy instead of suspense."

"I'd rather just add a few comedic moments to keep the rest of the book from turning too dark," Ian admitted. His biggest fear about writing a novel was that he'd write out too many of the harsher things he'd seen in his career, and the whole book would be a downer for anyone who read it.

Charlotte seemed to think for a moment before agreeing with him. They talked out a few more plot ideas, specifically the types of cases the characters would work for the suspenseful portions of the book they might one day write, as they finished their drinks.

Charlotte seemed surprised when Ian ushered her out of the bar and hotel to the area where they were meeting the horse-drawn carriage for their sunset ride. "Oh, Ian," she gushed, momentarily covering her mouth with her hand as they approached the carriage he'd reserved. "I've always wanted to do one of these rides."

"Really? I wasn't sure if you'd like it or not, since your horses aren't pulling it," he confessed, her reaction making him glad he'd seen them and gotten the idea.

"I love it," she beamed as the driver assisted them up into the carriage. "I've thought about taking one of these rides every time I've come downtown, but it's not exactly something I wanted to do alone."

"Well, I will gladly accompany you anytime you want to take a carriage ride, Princess." Ian wrapped his arm around Charlotte's shoulders as they settled in for the ride around town.

While the ride wasn't as romantic as Ian expected, due to the driver offering a running commentary about the history of the sights they were seeing, it was enjoyable to just sit and listen with Charlotte cuddled in close to his side. He liked the fact that he felt comfortable with her, no matter what they were doing. Whether they talked about the harder things in life, or kept their conversation light about topics that others might consider silly or irrelevant, they meshed in a way he'd never experienced with anyone else. That was just as true for the two of them when they were quiet together, saying nothing at all as they delighted in the other's presence.

As much as Ian was relishing the evening so far, he couldn't wait to get to dinner, so he could finally share his feelings with the woman he loved. *I just hope it's not too soon for her to feel a little of the same love I feel.*

~ ~ ~

Charlotte couldn't believe all the romantic gestures Ian kept surprising her with on their date. The little things he always did, like opening doors and pulling out chairs for her, didn't seem like such a big deal since he performed the gentlemanly behaviors all the time. As did most of the men she knew because of growing up in her old-fashioned hometown. But setting up the carriage rides to and from the restaurant, spontaneously buying her flowers from a street vendor as they walked between the carriage and the Tower of the Americas, and indulging her chocolate addiction by preordering the Hot Chocolate Lava Cake for dessert were most definitely romantic gestures that no other man had ever done for her before.

As was always the case when she was with Ian, their conversation flowed easily, and his undivided attention made her feel like the Princess he called her. It was such a fairytale date that she was starting to wonder what was going on that caused him to plan it.

June seventh isn't a special date, is it? I mean, I know it's not the anniversary of the date we met, since that was December fourteenth.

I know it's not his birthday because that's not until the end of next month. And it's not Cait or Brody's birthday, because they'd be with us for their celebrations.

But I can't think of anything significant about the seventh of any month that only he and I would celebrate. Unless he wants to celebrate the five-month anniversary of his first day teaching at the middle school?

No, that would be something we'd only celebrate during the school year. But what else would cause him to plan such an elaborate evening for us?

Unless he wants to talk about our future as a couple? This seems like something a guy would set up for a special night or maybe a proposal. But we haven't even officially labeled ourselves as a couple, so surely, he's not ready to propose tonight.

Of course not. If that were the case, then we'd have talked about more meaningful topics than silly book ideas and fun outings we can do with Brody this summer.

Finally giving up on her speculation, Char broached the subject with Ian just as the servers were finishing the presentation of their dessert. "So, what's the special occasion we're celebrating with all this tonight?"

"No special occasion." Ian slightly shook his head as he smiled at her. "Just my way of trying to show you how I feel about you, sweet Charlotte."

"How, how you fa, feel? A, about me?" Charlotte stuttered out the words nervously, wondering if he might share the same love for her that she'd been feeling for him.

"Yes, you know those emotions that develop when two people start dating." Ian reached across the table and took her hand in his, lightly rubbing his thumb over the back of her hand in a soothing circle. "I've been fighting not to shout it every time I see you, but I wanted to make it a memorable night with just the two of us the first time I tell you."

Ian ran his free hand through his hair, like he was nervous about his next words. "Hell, I had a whole speech planned and now that it's finally time, I can't think of a word of it."

"Don't worry about the speech," Charlotte reassured him, squeezing his hand in hers. "Just tell me what you feel."

"I love you, Charlotte. I think I fell in love with you the night we met. That's why I wanted to recreate it a little tonight." Ian gave her a tentative smile, tightening his hold on her hand. "I know it's fast, and I don't expect you to say it back just because I said it. I just didn't want to screw up and accidentally say it for the first time in the middle of a quickie."

"Well, then I'd better come clean and say it now, too," Charlotte teased, grinning at him. "Since there have been several instances when I've had to bite my tongue in the middle of a quickie to keep from screaming my feelings. I love you, too, Ian. And I'm pretty sure I fell for you the night we met, too."

"Oh, thank fuck!" Ian stood from his seat and rounded the table, pulling Charlotte up from her seat to seal their declarations of love with a passionate kiss.

Their tongues tangled, meeting in their joined mouths for a primal dance Char had only ever shared with Ian. The world around them disappeared as Charlotte wrapped her arms around Ian and gave herself over to his claiming kiss.

"Would you like your dessert boxed up to go?" The server's question brought Charlotte out of her Ian-induced fog, causing her to blush when she realized they were causing a spectacle in the restaurant.

"Yes, please," Ian responded to the server as he released Charlotte. He pulled out his wallet as they retook their seats, handing his credit card over to the server to handle their bill at the same time he boxed up their Hot Chocolate Lava Cake.

Charlotte was grateful there weren't any faces she recognized in the restaurant as they waited for the server to return so they could leave. She wasn't embarrassed about being there with Ian, but that their PDA came so close to getting out of hand in such an openly public place.

We definitely need to be more vigilant about finding secluded semi-public areas before doing more than holding hands in the future. I'd never live it down if we got arrested for public indecency and had to call one of my family members to bail us out.

Ian laughed when she said as much aloud. "Yeah, I'll be more careful and stick to chaste kisses in public from now on, so we never risk having to make that call."

They didn't have to wait very long before the server was back with their to-go box, Ian's credit card, and the slip for him to sign for their bill. Soon, they were back down from the top of the tower and on their way back to the hotel in the horse-drawn carriage.

The ride back was much shorter than the sunset tour around the city that they'd taken to the restaurant, getting them back to the hotel in record time. Ian surprised her once again when they got to the hotel, escorting her up to the fifth floor to the same room she'd been in the night they met.

"How did you get the same room?" Charlotte looked around the room they'd first used almost six months before, noticing the only difference in the room was that Ian's suitcase was in there instead of hers.

"I got lucky with a reservation agent who thought it was romantic that I wanted to recreate our first night together," Ian shrugged as he sat their dessert box on the table and picked up the ice bucket.

"Hopefully, not too lucky," Char quipped as he carried the ice bucket into the bathroom.

"Don't worry, Princess," Ian grinned, carrying the ice bucket full of water back out to the table and taking the flowers from her hand to put them in it. "I only get lucky the way you're thinking with you. Besides, I could tell from his deep voice over the phone that he wasn't my type."

Charlotte chuckled at the silly face Ian made as she sat her purse down on the table beside the flowers and their dessert. "I should probably go down and get my suitcase out of my car," she suggested, realizing she didn't have anything in the room for the next morning.

"I'll go get it for you in a little bit. Now, where were we before the waiter interrupted us at the restaurant?" Ian pulled her into his arms and covered her mouth with his, kissing her passionately once more.

Charlotte couldn't fight the pull to give in, letting Ian set the pace of their night. She loved the way he took control of their intimate moments, but treated her like an equal in most of the other aspects of their lives.

While he was definitely sexually dominating, he also made her feel like he was worshiping her body with the way he made love to her. He might be the one administering the sexy spankings, but he never treated her like she was subservient to him. Their light form of kink meshed their preferences perfectly, building a bond of trust between them that she hoped would never break.

Charlotte relaxed into the arms of her lover as Ian continued exploring the depths of her mouth while slowly starting to undress her. When she started to move to return the favor, he nipped her lip and grabbed her hands, holding them together at the small of her back.

"Hold still, Princess," Ian commanded, releasing her hands, and trusting that she'd keep them in place behind her back. "Let me unwrap you like the precious gift you are to me. I'll let you have a turn eating dessert after I've eaten my fill of your sweet pussy."

"Yes, Sir," Char responded breathlessly as her arousal increased with the anticipation of what he was going to do to her.

It was hard to maintain her position as Ian took his time touching and kissing every part of her he exposed as he removed her clothes. He alternated the way he tormented her with both pleasure and pain, mixing soft caresses with a hard pinch of her most sensitive areas, and soothed the sharper bites he took with a gentle laving of his tongue.

He didn't limit his erotic torture to the standard erogenous zones of her body, showing her that even her elbows and the backs of her knees could be sexually stimulated to make her pussy gush with her cream. The overwhelming sensations built her up to the precipice without so much as his finger stroking through her folds.

"Oh, Ian, please," Charlotte begged, needing him to quit teasing her and finally start to fuck her.

"Please, what, Princess?" Ian crooned as he trailed his tongue up the back of her thigh, lightly nipping her left butt cheek when he reached the top of her leg. "You have to tell me exactly what you need, so I can give it to you."

"I need you to fuck me, please," she pleaded, so aroused her juices were dripping down her inner thighs.

"Ah, but I haven't eaten your pussy yet, sweet Charlotte," Ian tisked, gripping her hips to turn her toward the table. "Bend over the table, spread your legs, and let me eat my dessert first."

"Yes, Sir Ian," Charlotte complied, pressing her bare breasts into the cool marble of the tabletop as she shifted her stance wide enough for him to fit his head between her thighs.

"Oh, I like that," Ian lightly chuckled, finally running his fingers over her pussy. "Sir Ian sounds so regal. You can keep calling me that anytime we're playing, Princess."

"Yes, Sir Ian," Char agreed, liking the sound of Sir Ian and his Princess for potential book characters as well as their pet names for one another.

She didn't get but a second to think about the book possibilities, however, when Ian bent to replace his fingers with his tongue, licking through her slit to lap up her cream. Once again, he alternated between gentle and rough, devouring her with his mouth and taking her to the brink in mere moments.

"Come, Princess," Ian ordered, his hot breath fluttering over her femininity just before he sucked her clit between his lips.

"Yes, Sir Ian!" Charlotte's orgasm exploded through her, the anticipation of all his teasing building it up to epic proportions with no internal stimulation. She continued repeatedly panting out the new honorific as wave after wave of bliss washed over her, carrying her away to a higher plane of existence.

She barely registered that he stopped sucking her clit as she floated peacefully while recovering, not understanding what she was hearing when he unzipped his pants to undress and ripped the foil packet containing the condom he used to sheath his cock. She crashed back into reality when he rubbed the tip of his dick through her folds to line up with her slit before impaling her on his stiff rod.

Now that his mouth was no longer otherwise occupied, Ian let loose with a litany of dirty talk. He started off with a few sweet utterings of "I love you" paired with gentle strokes to open her up to take his massive member. But as the fucking became more primal, so did his grunted out words claiming her as his.

While Charlotte still wasn't sure what exactly he meant when he growled out, "Mine!" as he unleashed his inner beast, she loved the feelings it always evoked in her. That one, simple word made her believe she was connected to Ian even more than their declarations of love. Like nothing could ever tear them apart because they were truly joined as one being.

"And you're mine, Sir Ian!" Charlotte shouted as her next climax snuck up and struck her.

"Yes. Fuck, yes! Come, sweet Charlotte," Ian commanded as her inner walls clamped down on his cock, slowing the pace of his persistent pounding. "Fuck, I love the way you milk my cock when you come."

As soon as the hardest waves of her release passed, Ian increased his speed once more, plunging into her relentlessly while gripping her hips to hold her in place. Charlotte was glad he'd instructed her to bend over the table, needing it to hold her up as her body seemed to liquify from the sheer magnitude of the pleasure he was wringing out of her with every deep thrust.

Just when she thought she couldn't take anymore, exhausted from the never-ending waves of orgasmic aftershocks, Ian slipped one hand down to stroke a finger over her clit. He bent over her back, gripping her hair with his other hand to move it out of the way so he could kiss her nape.

"Come one more time for me, Princess," he commanded, growling the words into her ear before nipping his way back down her neck.

"Yes. Sir. Ian." Charlotte panted breathlessly between each word, trying to suck in enough air to prevent her from passing out as Ian shoved as deep inside her as he could get for their simultaneous release.

"Charlotte!" Ian roared her name as he filled the condom at the same time she flew off to nirvana.

She wasn't sure if the other realm she floated in was what some romance novels described as subspace or not. But if it was possible to get there through their light style of dominance and submission, then she believed it to be her version of the phenomenon. Regardless of what it was called, she loved the sensation of extreme relaxation that she'd only ever experienced with Ian.

She floated in the heavenly clouds, only vaguely aware of Ian moving around the room to clean her up and settle her in the bed. She pointed to her purse when he asked for her keys, or at least she thought she did. She was too confused by how he was already redressed to go get her suitcase while she was still recovering to be certain.

"Relax, Princess." Ian bent and brushed his lips over her forehead. "Rest while I go get your things, so you're ready for your dessert when I get back."

"Yes, Sir Ian." Charlotte smiled at him and continued to float as he walked away from the bed.

By the time he returned to the room with her suitcase in hand, she'd fully recovered and sat up in bed as soon as he walked in the door. "You must not have fully undressed before." She waved her hand in his direction, referring to the fact that he'd only removed his jacket and tie since dinner.

"No, I couldn't wait that long to be inside you," Ian chuckled as he placed her suitcase on the dresser beside his. "But I'm getting completely undressed now, so we can play with our cake."

Charlotte pictured all the places they were about to eat cake off of each other's bodies as Ian started undressing. He removed his shirt and draped it over the same chair he'd previously laid his jacket and tie on at some point while she was otherwise occupied with their sexcapades. Then he stepped out of his loafers and bent to remove his ankle holster.

She wasn't surprised to see that he still carried a weapon at all times, knowing he would probably always feel the need to have one available to protect himself and the people he cared about. In one of their discussions about the progress they were making in therapy, he'd disclosed how he'd started carrying three concealed weapons right after her kidnapping. So, she knew he'd made fabulous progress by being down to just the one in only two months.

Truth be told, knowing he had a weapon on him to be able to defend them if necessary made her feel safer. So, she didn't think it would be a problem if he never got to the point of being able to leave his house without one. That's why she didn't say a word to bring attention to his need to be able to protect them, as Ian secured his weapon in the specialty case he carried in his suitcase before he finished undressing.

Charlotte got out of bed and walked over to the table, opening the cake box to figure out how best to apply the contents to Ian's body for her to eat it off of him. She was surprised to see that the confection was deconstructed, with an ice pack under the container of ice cream to prevent it from melting while in the box with three more individual containers for the cake, hot fudge, and crumbled toppings.

"Should we put this together the way they had it at the restaurant? Or leave it deconstructed and just use the ice cream and hot fudge for play time?" Char motioned to the four containers in the box as Ian walked over to the table.

Now that they were both nude, she took a moment to appreciate the contours of his body. He was lean, but not bulky, obviously fit with just the right amount of muscle mass for Charlotte's taste. *Especially that six-pack I can't wait to run my tongue over to remove the chocolate sauce.*

The hair on his chest and down his happy trail was even lighter than the hair on his head, though not quite as blond as the hair on his arms and legs. While her sister, cousins, and friends seemed to appreciate the way the wrestlers they knew waxed or had their body hair lasered off to look good on television, Charlotte preferred a man who kept the more manly look of body hair. Though she did appreciate how Ian kept his pubic region trimmed, so she didn't have to worry about accidentally swallowing a long hair while giving him a blow job. A hair tickling her throat was a worse trigger for her gag reflex than his cock pushing in too far.

"I say we leave it deconstructed, so we don't have to worry about getting a crumble of toffee, chocolate, or cake stuck in an orifice where it shouldn't be." Ian's reply brought her out of her mental musings of where she planned to lick the ice cream and hot fudge from his body. "Though I suppose, to eat the cake, you'll want to dip it in the ice cream and fudge. But I don't think they have to stay in the containers for you to dip the cake in."

"Oh, they won't be staying in the containers," Char cooed, grinning as she lifted the fudge container out of the box. "But we might want to move all this to the bathtub, so we don't end up with a mess we can't clean up out here."

"As you wish, Princess." Ian grinned at her as he picked up the box in one hand and took her free hand in the other. He led her to the restroom and helped her step into the tub built for two. Once he joined her, he placed the box on the side of the tub beside her and laid down on the other side of the large, jetted tub. "Since this is your dessert, I'll let you have control of our play time for now. But you'd better save me a little bit of the fudge and ice cream to eat off your nipples before we fill this tub up and wash it all off."

"Yes, Sir Ian." Charlotte gave him a silly salute before opening the container of fudge she'd been warming in her hand and drizzling half of it over his abs and cock.

"Fuck," Ian groaned, closing his eyes as his dick twitched in response to the feel of the fudge. "I wasn't expecting it to still be warm after being in the container with that ice pack."

Charlotte didn't mention how she'd been holding it to use her body heat to stave off any chill it might have from the ice pack on the opposite side of the box. She just smiled as she opened the ice cream container, leaving it on the ice pack to keep the portion she didn't scoop out with her fingers cold.

Since she'd drizzled the chocolate on the ridges of his abs, she smeared the ice cream on the V of his obliques. Ian cursed again at the cold contact, biting his bottom lip when she hooked the pointer finger on her clean hand under his piercings to lift his cock, so she could spread the remainder of the ice cream on her fingers down the opposite side of his shaft from where she'd drizzled the fudge.

Once his parts were properly coated for her licking pleasure, Char pinched off a piece of cake and trailed it through the chocolate and ice cream on one side of his torso before popping it in her mouth. She repeated the process, alternating between the places on his abs and obliques where she dipped the cake until she'd consumed approximately half of the decadent dessert.

Ian remained mostly stoic throughout the whole process, though the way his dick twitched every time she came close to touching it made it clear he was more than ready for her to take him in her mouth. Being in control of their playtime made it clear to Charlotte what Ian got out of being dominant in their sexual activities most of the time. While it was a truly heady feeling to know she had that power over his pleasure, she didn't feel comfortable being in control for very long. She just had a harder time getting her mind to shut off and let her enjoy the time with Ian, when she had to think of what she needed to do next.

Being ready for him to take over, she rushed through licking the remainder of the fudge and ice cream from Ian's abs and obliques. *Is it wrong that I think this would have been better if he was directing me where and when to lick it all off of him?*

Once the sticky goo was off of his torso, she slid over a little in the tub to focus on licking his cock clean. *I wonder how long I can lick his dick before he takes control and commands me to suck his cock?*

She swirled her tongue around his engorged head a few times before going back to licking his shaft like an ice cream cone. She'd only teased him for a minute or so before he groaned, "Fuck, I can't take it anymore," and grabbed her hair to guide her mouth back to the tip.

Charlotte couldn't stop the giggle that escaped as he pushed into her mouth, giddy that she'd been correct in what it would take for him to wrest control from her for the rest of the night.

"Suck me, Princess." Ian lightly pressed her head down as he lifted his hips to fuck up into her mouth. "Swallow my cock until my cum mixes with the ice cream and chocolate you're licking off me."

Charlotte relaxed as Ian fucked her mouth, reveling in his dominance and forgetting all her worries about the future.

"Use your hands, Princess," Ian commanded. "Use one to jack off what you can't take in your mouth and the other to cup my balls."

Char followed Ian's instructions to the letter, squeezing lightly with the hand holding his testicles while roughly handling the base of his shaft. Her nipples hardened almost to the point of being painful and her clit throbbed with her own arousal from being so turned on by his demanding directions.

"Fuck, yeah, just like that," Ian moaned.

Charlotte bobbed her head at the pace Ian set with his hand in her hair and constant bucking of his hips. She sucked hard as he pulled back, knowing he loved the way it felt when she wouldn't let him leave her mouth. Then she relaxed her throat to allow him to push as far back as she could handle when he bucked back up.

"Time to finish your dessert, Princess," Ian warned as she felt his balls tighten up in her hand. Ian chanted her name as he started to spurt, holding her still with the head of his cock so far back in her throat she didn't even taste his cum.

Charlotte relaxed her throat, knowing closing it off to actively swallow would be counterproductive. She continued to breathe through her nose, focusing on holding back her own orgasm as Ian filled her belly with his release.

When the final jet of his cum had exited his body, Ian pulled Charlotte off his cock and lifted her up into his arms. He kissed her passionately, delving deep into the recesses of her mouth with his tongue, as if he was trying to find any place his cum might still be present. She returned the kiss with equal ardor, wrapping her arms around his neck as she clung to him.

"Time for my turn with dessert, Princess." Ian wagged his eyebrows suggestively as he broke the kiss. "I hope you left me some."

"I left half of everything for you, Sir Ian." Charlotte smiled as he shifted their position, sitting up and sliding over to the other side of the tub, so he could reach the box that was holding what was left of the treat.

"Such a good girl," Ian praised her as he took the fudge container and poured it over the tops of her breasts.

Charlotte basked in the delectation, invigorated and eager to spend the rest of the night pleasing and being pleasured by the man she loved.

While she didn't actively think about the trial she'd face going to volunteer at the shelter the next day, she knew she could get through it and anything else that came her way with Ian by her side.

Chapter Twenty-Five

Charlotte felt like she was sitting on a chair made of pins and needles as she sat in the waiting room at the Heart's Destiny Clinic first thing Thursday morning. Her period was late. Not just a day or two late the way she'd thought it might be from stressing out at the possibility of being pregnant. But three days late, without even a slight twinge of cramping or any of her normal PMS symptoms.

Could I have possibly psyched myself out so much that I've fooled my body into skipping it this month? That's possible, right?

She was so worked up that she'd contemplated buying a home pregnancy test, as soon as she'd woken up on Monday morning with no sign of even minimal spotting. But after the fiasco at Thanksgiving over a home pregnancy test, she decided it wasn't worth the risk of her family speculation to even have the box for one anywhere near the Burleson Ranch.

So, she'd spent some extra time volunteering at the youth center in town, the shelter in San Antonio, and helping Brooklyn get the south bunkhouse set up to be the Madeline Ashbury Foundation's first group home in Texas, trying to ease her stress through serving others. While she felt fulfilled by giving so much of her time to such worthy causes, none of those volunteer opportunities took her potential pregnancy completely off her mind.

Maybe my pregnancy thoughts are why I didn't have any flashbacks, or an anxiety attack, the first time I went back to volunteer at the shelter last weekend? Or the extra times we went back earlier this week? I mean, it's kind of hard to worry about a dead man, when all my synapses are firing with "Baby, Baby, Baby," constantly on repeat.

Having Ian and Brody tagging along for some of that volunteer time certainly eased any anxiety she might have had about flashbacks to her time at the shelter with Roberto in residence. She loved having them there to help her through, even though their outings together probably didn't help her efforts to keep from thinking about possibly having a family with the two of them in the future.

Her time with the Campbells felt more like family time than the friend dates Ian claimed they were on, especially when they took Brody to SeaWorld for the first time after volunteering at the shelter on Tuesday. Ian had soothed any residual anxiety Charlotte had about volunteering at the shelter, both her first time back when it was just the two of them, and then the extra time she'd spent there with both Ian and Brody. He'd made her feel like they were there as a family unit, not just as friends spending a day with his child.

As they sat watching the orca shows at SeaWorld, Charlotte could easily picture them going back multiple times over the years, pushing strollers throughout the park as their family grew. She'd always imagined having a large family like the one she'd grown up in, and the more time she spent with Ian and Brody, the more she pictured them as the beginning of that large family.

She hadn't mentioned it to Ian yet, but if they ever got married, she wanted to adopt Brody, so he would know that she loved him as much as she would love any other children she and Ian might have together. She wasn't sure how Ian would feel about that, though. While they had declared their love for one another and expressed their wishes to grow as a couple, they hadn't really discussed their plans for the future. At least, not as more than the way they were already spending time together.

Her biggest fear was that while she was dreaming of a wedding and babies and building a bigger home on the ranch, he was only thinking of hot sex when they could sneak it in between friendly outings with their separate families. *What am I going to do if I find out I'm pregnant today, and he doesn't want more than the friends-with-benefits relationship we've been having for the past couple of months?*

I know he said he wanted to step up and be a father to our baby when we thought it was a possibility three months ago. But being a father to the baby doesn't mean anything has to change between us.

And after the tragic way he lost his wife, he might not feel like he ever wants to get married again.

If I'm pregnant, I don't want to stick with the status quo. I want to be married before I have a baby. Preferably to my baby's father. But I don't want him to marry me just because I'm pregnant either.

Damn, I wish we'd have talked a little more about what we both want for the future before I came here for this appointment.

Charlotte was fighting not to break down in tears when Arden finally called her back for her doctor's visit.

How soon do pregnancy hormones cause mood swings?

Charlotte's mind whirled as Arden went through the standard procedures. She didn't register half of what the woman was saying while her body reacted to Arden's directions as if on auto-pilot.

Shit! Is the weepiness I'm feeling my first pregnancy symptom? Surely, if my hormone levels are elevated enough to register as pregnant on a test, then there's enough flowing through my system to be the cause of my crazy crybaby feelings. Right?

Being lost in her own thoughts, she didn't comprehend what Arden said about a blood test and was confused when she handed her a urine specimen cup.

"Wait!" Charlotte held up her free hand in the universal symbol for stop while holding the cup in the other. "Are we doing a urine test or a blood test?"

"Sorry, I know I say the same thing so many times a week that I speed through it a little too fast sometimes," Arden apologized with a smile. "We're doing a urine test first. If it comes back negative, then we'll skip the blood test. If it comes back positive, then we'll do a blood test to check your hCG levels to verify the approximate date of conception."

"Oh, um, okay." Charlotte stood from where she'd been seated in the exam room while Arden took her vitals and walked to the restroom down the hall to pee in the cup.

If it comes back positive, I'm pretty sure I can narrow down the date of conception to either the twenty-fifth or twenty-sixth of May. Though if our child ever asks, I'll claim the twenty-sixth. In a Sunday school classroom without a condom is a much better story to tell our child about their conception than in the storeroom of a bar with a broken condom. And probably the closest to immaculate conception that anyone I know can get. Charlotte found herself giggling at her own thoughts as she followed the directions on the signs posted in the restroom for preparing and giving her urine sample.

Yep, this test is definitely going to come back positive. If not, then I might need to be committed for these rapid-fire mood swings.

After depositing the full specimen cup in the cubby in the wall for whoever tested it to remove it from the other side in the next room, Charlotte finished her business in the restroom and washed her hands before returning to the exam room, where she waited for either Dr. Magnum or Arden to come in and give her the results.

While it probably wasn't more than five minutes, the time she sat waiting for either Dr. Magnum or Arden to give her the results of the test felt more like five hours. She kept going over the possibilities in her head, trying to decide her course of action once the test results came back, telling her whether she was pregnant or not.

If it's positive, then I need to go talk to Ian and start making plans for how we'll raise the baby together. I need to know if he wants to combine our households, or plan a schedule where the baby spends time with both of us.

If he wants us to move in together, then we'll have to figure out where on the ranch we want to build a house. We could move into the empty house beside Mom and Dad, but if Cait moves to the ranch full-time, too, then it won't be enough space for all of us for very long. But maybe that could be an option while our house is under construction.

But how long is it going to take to get a house built? After hearing Justin and Amy talking about picking a spot to build next, I'm sure they've already talked to the Walkers to be next in line for new construction. So, it'll probably be a while before they can free up a crew to build us a house. But, maybe Cait could move into the house I'm living in now, so we can have a little more space next door to my parents, if they can't get to our build before the baby is born.

Realizing her thoughts were veering strictly toward a positive pregnancy test, Charlotte switched mental gears, trying to be prepared, so she didn't look like an idiot without a plan if the doctor asked her which method of birth control she wanted to start. *If it's negative, then I think I want to go with one of the pill options. They seem like they're easier to stop whenever we decide we're ready for kids.*

While the shot would be more convenient, so I don't slip up and forget to take a pill once in a while, I'm not sure I like the idea of having to wait twelve weeks for it to wear off. What if Ian and I talk and decide we're ready to try for babies sooner than that?

Not being sure of how soon we might want to have kids rules out the long-term methods of birth control like the I.U.D. and implant, too.

She had already ruled out the birth control patch on the first day she looked at the pamphlets because of how anything stuck to her skin made her itchy. She'd also decided against the vaginal ring, internal condom, and diaphragm because she didn't want to have to insert them herself.

Even if remembering to use them every time wasn't an issue like with condoms, I'd be afraid I wouldn't get them inserted properly, so they wouldn't be as effective as they claim. And I don't see the point of using sponges and spermicides that aren't at least ninety percent effective. So, yeah, I definitely want to go with one of the pill options.

But even if I get started on that today, I should probably plan to talk to Ian as soon as I leave here. I know he's expecting me to come over this morning to plan the writing workshop that we want to do at the youth center this summer. But maybe he can send Brody to work with Cait, so we can have a more serious discussion about the future of our relationship, too.

Whether we're pregnant or not, I don't want to keep feeling like we're friends with benefits instead of a real couple. I know that means we'll have to start telling people we're dating. But that needs to happen, so we can have more overnight dates like we did last week. And maybe some sleepovers at each of our houses, so I'm not the only one picturing us as a family unit.

She was finally brought out of her mental rabbit hole by a knock on the door before Dr. Magnum opened it and stepped inside. Charlotte couldn't tell from the look on the doctor's face if her test was positive or negative, but she didn't get the chance to ask when Arden followed the doctor into the room, pushing a phlebotomy cart.

"I'm pregnant," Char blurted, knowing Arden had said they'd only do a blood test if the urine test came back positive.

"Ya, yes," Dr. Magnum stuttered, looking surprised that Charlotte announced it instead of waiting to be told her test results.

My family is never going to let me live it down that I was wrong about our dreams. Charlotte was glad she was already sitting down as she felt the room spin at the realization that Memmaw Judy's predictions for her future were already starting to come true. *Hope you're happy in Heaven, Memmaw, celebrating the pending birth of your namesake.*

"There are options if you're not ready…" Dr. Magnum started.

But Charlotte quickly cut her off. "Oh, no, I don't need any options. I'm having and keeping my baby. I already have a first name picked out, whether it's a girl or a boy, though I'm pretty sure it's going to be a girl."

"Oh, well, good," the doctor sputtered before composing herself at the sudden change in direction of the conversation. "I hope you get the girl you want, though it's way too early to tell the sex of the baby at this point. Based on your last period, I'm estimating your date of conception as the twenty-seventh, but we'll verify that with the blood test. That puts your baby due on February seventeenth."

Arden set everything up and drew Charlotte's blood while Dr. Magnum reviewed the things that Charlotte needed to limit or eliminate during her pregnancy, went over a timeline of the various doctor's visits and tests they'd be doing in the next few months, and answered any questions Char had about her pregnancy and prenatal care.

Once the initial prenatal measurements and exam were done, Charlotte was given an expectant parent's bag containing a few baby items, her prescription for prenatal vitamins, and more pamphlets about the various stages of pregnancy and baby growth. She scheduled her next two prenatal appointments for July eighth and August fifth, with her first ultrasound slated for the same time as her monthly appointment in August.

Now to go break the news to Ian.

Ian paced his living room, nervously awaiting Charlotte's arrival for their workshop planning session. He wasn't nervous about the writing workshop Charlotte asked him to collaborate on for the youth center.

He already had several ideas for things they could do with the teens they'd be working with during the week-long program they'd be offering in August. He also knew when combined with Charlotte's ideas, their program would help all the kids participating feel better prepared for any composition classes they'd be taking in the fall when school was back in session.

No, Ian was nervous because he thought he'd screwed up the night before when he scheduled a playdate for Brody with Charlotte's youngest brother's kids. He knew she wasn't ready for her family to know they were dating, and he might have let it slip when he was talking with Anthony about the schedule for the day.

But, fuck, I miss our time alone every morning at school, so I had to come up with a way for us to have the morning alone. And with three kids and a fourth on the way, I'm sure Anthony wants some alone time with his wife, too. So it seemed like the perfect solution for Brody to go to work with Cait this morning and hang out with them at their house until lunch time while Charlotte and I have some time together, and for us to take all the kids on a trail ride this afternoon while Anthony and Kay have some time alone.

Ian knew he should have talked to Charlotte about his idea before volunteering her to help him watch her nieces and nephew for the afternoon. But after Anthony had pulled him aside to give him the brother speech about dating his sister, Ian hadn't had the chance to figure out how to apologize to Charlotte for informing another of her brothers of their status as a couple.

Hell, I don't think I ever apologized for making my feelings for her clear to her other brothers and Avington cousins back in April. But with everything else going on back then, I'm not sure she realizes they all know how and when we met, much less that they knew we were together before we officially started dating.

Since they had to know everything to help me protect her and rescue her from the cartel, I can't really apologize for telling them about our relationship before she was ready to even admit to us being in one. So it seems pointless to apologize for something I wouldn't go back and change.

No, I'll keep my apology to just this most recent reveal of our relationship, Ian decided as he heard Charlotte's Equinox pulling into his driveway, wishing he'd had time to go buy her a bouquet of flowers to go with the apology before she arrived. He went to the door, opening it before she even had a chance to walk up on the porch, much less ring the doorbell.

Upon seeing him standing in the doorway, Charlotte started speaking as she was halfway up the walkway. "Has Cait already left for the ranch?"

"Yes," Ian answered automatically.

"Darn, I was hoping she could take Brody with her, so we can talk this morning." Charlotte looked dejected as she walked up the stairs.

"Well, then you'll be happy to hear that Brody went with her to have a playdate with your nieces and nephew." Ian wasn't sure if he should be relieved that telling Charlotte about the childcare plans for the day was going so well, or worried about whatever she wanted to talk about that originally put that troublesome look on her face. "And we're going to take all the kids on a trail ride this afternoon. I worked it out with Anthony last night, so we can have some time alone this morning and he and Kay can have some time alone for the afternoon."

"Oh, perfect." Charlotte sounded relieved as she walked by him into the house without so much as a peck of a kiss in greeting. "Though we'll probably have to come up with some inside activities to do with the kids, since it looks like it'll be a stormy afternoon."

Ian didn't get a chance to elaborate on his talk with Anthony as Charlotte breezed into his dining room, where he had his laptop set up with his outline of ideas for the writing workshop already pulled up for them to go over. She sat down at the table, but didn't pull her own laptop out of the bag she laid on the table before blurting, "Where do you see our relationship going in the next few months?"

"Um, what?" Ian sputtered, confused by her sudden topic change as he took a seat beside her.

"I mean, what are we doing? Are we dating? Or are we just friends with benefits? And do you see our status changing over the next few months?"

Ian took a moment to really look at Charlotte, trying to figure out the cause of her frantic questioning. She was nervously fidgeting in her seat with her gaze bouncing around the room, not landing anywhere for more than a second and not making eye contact with him at all.

"I thought we made all that clear last week when we declared our love for the first time," Ian started, reaching over to take her hands in his, and hopefully getting her to focus on him instead of looking around the room. "We are definitely dating. Exclusively. And hopefully, in the next few months, we'll be making our status as a couple known publicly."

Ian stopped short of telling her that he wanted them to move in together and start planning their wedding, afraid she was having second thoughts about being in a relationship with him at all. When Charlotte finally settled her gaze on his, some of that fear dissipated at seeing her starting to relax as she comprehended his reply.

"Now, what's got you so worked up this morning that you're questioning us?" Ian prayed they were still on the same page when it came to where they thought they were in their relationship.

Charlotte bit her lip, her nerves obviously coming back as she squeezed his hands. *Fuck! She's having second thoughts and is starting to think she doesn't really love me. But I can't let her end things between us without fighting for our love.*

"Please tell me you haven't changed your mind about us," Ian demanded, needing to find a way to stop her from rejecting him. "I love you, Charlotte. I don't want to spend a day of my life without you. Please tell me you still feel the same."

"Yes, Ian," Charlotte whimpered, a single tear slipping from her eye. "I love you and still want us to be a couple. I just needed to know for sure that's how you feel before I tell you about my doctor's appointment this morning."

"Doctor's appointment? What's wrong?" Ian shook his head, releasing one of her hands to reach up and wipe away her tears that were starting to flow freely down her beautiful face. He fought to keep the tears from his own eyes as he worried about what kind of medical battle she might be facing. He wanted to be her rock to lean on, no matter what diagnosis she might have gotten that morning. *Fuck! I bet she found some kind of cancer.* "Whatever it is, we'll fight it together, Princess."

"You'd better not fight it!" Charlotte slapped his chest with her free hand, starting to laugh through her tears and completely confusing Ian. "And you'll have to wait a few years before you can start teaching her how to fight for self-defense."

Charlotte needs me to teach her to fight for self-defense? She's not making any sense. Fuck! Does that mean it's a brain tumor?

"You're going to have to start from the beginning, Princess. Why did you go to the doctor this morning? And what did the doctor diagnose you with?"

"I went to the doctor last week to get started on birth control," Charlotte explained through her giggles. "But I had to go back this morning for some tests before she could start me on the pill. And apparently, we both need to stick to teaching English because we suck at remembering the sex-ed portion of sixth-grade health class and were way off on our estimate of ovulation dates. I can't start on birth control because I got pregnant the weekend the condom broke, and we thought it was still safe to go without the next day at church."

"You're pregnant?" Ian was in shock at the revelation.

"Yes." Charlotte nodded.

"Holy shit!" Ian jumped up from his chair, scooping Charlotte up in his arms as he stood and knocking both of their chairs over. "We're gonna have a baby!" He couldn't stop shouting with excitement as he bounced around the room, holding her tight against him the whole time.

"Put me down, you loon, or Judy's gonna be born with shaken baby syndrome!" Charlotte's roaring laughter wiped away the rest of her tears, even as she clung to him to keep him from actually releasing his hold on her.

"Judy? You already have a name picked out?" Ian stopped bouncing, setting her down on the table since both of the closest chairs were laying on their sides on the floor.

"Yes, Judy, after my memmaw. Jude, if it's a boy." Charlotte blushed lightly as she explained where she came up with the baby's name. "But I'm almost positive we're having a girl."

"Oh, and what makes you so positive?" Ian arched an eyebrow, surprised his practical girlfriend would admit to a gut feeling. He wondered if admitting to the hunch was what caused her to blush.

"You're going to think I'm crazy." Charlotte shook her head.

"Never," Ian disagreed.

"You should. I certainly thought my family was crazy when they started talking about believing things they dreamed were actually going to happen. And now I'm starting to believe they were right."

"So, you dreamed about having a little girl?" Ian didn't think it was crazy at all to hope a dream about having children came true.

"No, not exactly," Charlotte chuckled. "But for the past couple of months, my nightmares have been replaced by dreams of Memmaw Judy visiting me from Heaven to tell me about my future. And she told me I'd be heavily pregnant with a little girl by Christmas this year. And if what she said about her having thirteen great-grandbabies by Christmas next year is true, I won't be the only Burleson of this generation expecting on New Year's."

"And you think thirteen is possible by Christmas of next year?" Ian wasn't so sure of that number being very likely, even with there being so many Burlesons starting relationships recently.

"Well, when I first started having these dreams about Memmaw's predictions back in March, I didn't," Charlotte admitted, grinning. "But that was when I only thought four was a possibility this year. But now, Anthony and Kay will have four once baby Sam is born and Antonio's adoption is final. Josh apparently has a baby we haven't met yet. Bobby and Brooklyn's little girl will bring the family total to six instead of the four I originally thought."

Charlotte counted them off by holding up a finger for each child, as Ian recalled hearing how Bobby and Brooklyn found out they were expecting a little girl via the ultrasound they had the previous week. "Our little one will be lucky number seven, which puts the family more than halfway there by February. Oh, and I saw Justin and Amy at the OB-GYN last week, so if they aren't already expecting, I'm betting they will be soon. And with her being a twin, they could add numbers eight and nine to the family total. So, yeah, with five of my siblings and cousins left to pitch in a kid or two, and only needing four or five more, I definitely think we could easily make it to Memmaw's lucky thirteen by Christmas of next year."

Ian quickly checked her mental math before laughing. "With Jen and Julie also being twins, Jake, JJ, and Becky could theoretically opt out and thirteen would still be easily attainable."

"Exactly, which is why I firmly believe this baby is a little girl." Charlotte placed her hand over her still-flat stomach. "And since Memmaw told me about her, I have to name her Judy after Memmaw."

Giving in to his need to share in the moment of bonding with their child, Ian covered Charlotte's hand with his. "Have you thought of a middle name yet?"

"Not really." Charlotte shook her head slightly without breaking eye contact with Ian. "But since I picked the first name, I figured you might want to pick the middle name."

Ian shuffled through a few ideas in his head, trying to find a middle name that would be as meaningful as the first name Charlotte had already decided on and that also sounded nice rolling off the tongue when combined with Judy. "We could go with Judy Anne, so she'd share your middle name. Or Judy Carol, so she's named after each of our grandmothers."

"Anne was actually Memmaw's middle name," Charlotte chuckled. "So, maybe we should skip it, so our daughter can be the third generation to name her daughter after Memmaw. Besides, I think I like Judy Carol better."

"Whatever you want, Princess." Ian leaned down and pecked her lips with his. "And we have a few months to decide, so if you change your mind and decide you prefer a different name, we have plenty of time."

"We actually have a lot of things we need to decide on pretty soon, though," Charlotte sighed, her shoulders slumping. "I don't want to tell anyone else about the baby until we're out of the first trimester, but we should probably start admitting we're dating. I don't want to make a big announcement like Justin and Amy did at Justin's birthday party to let them know we're dating, but I don't want anyone to be completely shocked by our baby announcement, either. So we have to let them know we're dating if anyone asks, like now, so it won't be a huge surprise when the thirteenth week rolls around, and we announce that we're expecting."

"If you're on board with finally admitting we're dating, then you won't be mad at me for my conversation with Anthony about us last night." Ian grinned at the incredulous look Charlotte gave him, holding his hands up in surrender as he explained. "I didn't outright admit we're dating, but when I suggested the childcare swap today and volunteered you to help me watch his kids, he figured it out. And gave me quite the brother speech about treating his sister right."

"Oh, I figured Bobby would have already had the honor of giving you that speech back in April," Charlotte chortled, grinning.

"Oh, he did," Ian laughed along with her, nodding his head. "So did Jake and Josh. But apparently, none of them said anything to Anthony about what was going on between us."

Realizing he had to be completely honest with her, he took a deep breath and stopped laughing. "But those conversations were all in February and March, when I had to fill them in on meeting and falling for you in December while looping them in on the case and my suspicions that I'd inadvertently put you in danger."

"Oh, wow." Charlotte looked shocked as she stared at him for a moment. "I'm surprised none of them mentioned any of this to me. Or warned me away from you to try to keep me safe."

"I'd like to say that's because I got their seal of approval," Ian quipped with a self-deprecating shrug. "But I'm sure they were afraid warning you off of me would only make me more appealing to you, so they opted to not mention me at all to keep from making the situation worse."

"No, they know I'm not rebellious like that." Charlotte rolled her eyes at him.

"Rebellious or not, all brothers worry that reverse psychology will bite them in the ass when trying to safeguard their sisters," Ian disagreed, shaking his head. "That's why I haven't said anything to Cait about staying away from the Walkers."

"What's wrong with the Walkers?" Charlotte looked at him with confusion once again. "They're all nice, hardworking guys that any mother in town would be proud to have their daughter dating."

"Oh, I'm sure," Ian chuckled, feeling the urge to roll his eyes now. "Your mother has probably drilled that message home to you and Becky for years now. But none of them are mature enough to be what Cait needs in a boyfriend."

"Well, luckily for Cait, this is a free country, and you don't get a say in what she needs in a boyfriend," Charlotte retorted. "And we don't have time for me to argue her side to keep you from overstepping in her life, when we only have a couple of hours to figure out a few changes we're going to need to make to our lives."

"Oh? What kind of changes?" Ian hoped she was referring to a bigger change to their relationship status than just letting people know they were dating. While he hadn't gone ring shopping yet, he could definitely see proposing in the near future. *And hopefully, this conversation will let me know if she's far enough along in accepting our relationship to be ready to say "yes" when I do.*

"Well, first of all, are we going to work out a visitation schedule for the baby and keep maintaining two households? Or are you going to move to the ranch to raise the baby with me?"

"We're moving in together," Ian adamantly declared. "But it'll be easier if you move in here."

"Easier?" Charlotte screeched, pushing him back so she could hop off the table and pace around the room. "Seriously? That's your argument for why we should move in together?"

"It's one of them," Ian tried to explain, confused about what set her off. "There's also the fact that your house is too small for all of us. Plus, I'm locked into a lease here until the end of the year. And this house is too much for Cait to afford on her own, so I can't just move in with you and let her take over the lease."

"Yeah, my house is too small, but the house next door to my parents isn't," Charlotte argued, slamming her fists on her hips as she turned to glare at him. "Especially if Cait moves into my house, which she could do rent free. And the Walkers will let you out of the lease without a problem when we give them the contract to build us a bigger house on the ranch."

"We can't build a house on your family ranch." Ian groaned in frustration at how their exciting news about being pregnant was being followed with an argument about where they'd live as a family. "Even if what's left of my savings after moving here would be enough for a down payment, I don't have enough time on the job here to qualify for a loan to build a house."

"Well, luckily for you, I'm a Burleson, so we won't need a loan to build a house. I have plenty in savings from my dividends and salary as a board member at Burleson Incorporated to cover the down payment. And I'll be thirty in seven months, which is about when I'm guessing the Walkers will be able to start construction on our house, so I'll have access to my trust fund to pay for all of it."

Ian knew the Burlesons were wealthy, but before that moment, he hadn't thought of their wealth or how it might cause a rift between him and Charlotte. The whole family was so down to earth that he never realized just how many socioeconomic levels separated his family from hers.

He stood there stunned speechless, not sure how to respond to her emasculating statement. *"Fuck, no, I'm not going to be a kept man" is probably not the best response right now. But damn, if that's not the only thing I can think of to respond to her saying she'll pay for our house to be built.*

Apparently, Charlotte realized what he was thinking as she cringed when their eyes met. "I'm sorry. I know you're not interested in me for my family's money, and what I just said made it sound like I'm trying to buy you off to do things my way."

"Uh, yeah," Ian huffed, still unsure how to respond.

"And I realize you're just old-fashioned enough to feel like you have to be the sole provider for your family," Charlotte continued until Ian interrupted.

"No, I don't have to be the sole provider," Ian interjected. "But I want to be an equal partner, not made to feel like I'm mooching off my baby momma."

"Ugh! Don't call me that!" Charlotte cringed, her whole body shuddering with disgust.

"Sorry. I knew better the instant it left my mouth."

"I'm sorry, too," Charlotte apologized once more, her posture relaxing as she walked back over to where Ian was standing. She reached up and placed a hand on his jaw before continuing. "I didn't mean to make you feel that way. But if we decide to combine households, then we're going to have to deal with combining our bank accounts, too. So, maybe we need to table that discussion for a little while to give you time to decide if that's something you can live with or not. Like you said about the baby's name, we've got time to think about everything and make the best decisions for all of us."

"Yeah, I think you're right about needing some time to think before deciding anything." Ian let out a breath he hadn't realized he'd been holding, and pulled Charlotte into his arms. He needed to feel his connection with her to know they could get through anything as long as they made the decisions together. "And I have a much better idea for what we can do until it's time to go pick up the kids from your brother."

"Oh, yeah? What's that?" Charlotte grinned up at him, wrapping her arms around his neck as she snuggled in closer to him.

"I thought maybe I could demonstrate some of the benefits of living together to motivate us both to want to work out the little details to make that happen." Ian wagged his eyebrows suggestively as he picked Charlotte up and started heading for the stairs leading to his bedroom.

"But what about planning our writing workshop?" Charlotte playfully protested, arching her back but not really trying to get out of his embrace.

"Maybe we can consider this research for our first book collaboration?" Ian suggested with a grin as he took the stairs two at a time. "I'll happily be your muse for writing all the sex scenes."

"Then I really should have brought my computer up here with us, so I could take notes of how to describe your dick and any unusual positions we try out." Charlotte gave him a mischievous smile.

Ian groaned at the thought of how she might describe his cock in her portions of their future books just to mess with him. "I'm sure you can remember what my cock looks like when it comes time to write those scenes." He shook his head at her reference to needing her computer. "And if not, then I'll gladly give you a live demonstration while you're writing, so you don't need to make notes now. Though I think you can remember to call it a long, thick cock instead of describing it as a throbbing, purple member, like in the books I remember my mom and grandma reading when I was a kid."

"Oh, yeah, we're definitely writing contemporary romance," Charlotte laughed. "I couldn't even keep from laughing at those descriptions when I read a few of the bodice rippers we cleaned out of Memmaw and Pappaw's house before my sister and cousins moved in there."

"Good," Ian grinned, dropping Charlotte in the middle of his king-sized bed. "Now how about we enjoy a few of those unusual positions we'll have to practice a few times for you to be able to describe them properly, so our readers don't get hurt trying them out at home."

Chapter Twenty-Six

Ian had mixed feelings about going with Charlotte to meet her newest nephew in the birthing center attached to the Heart's Destiny Clinic. On one hand, he was excited to see the facility where she would most likely deliver their child in February, wanting to be well prepared for where to go when the time came. He had thought he'd ask to see the facility on Monday when he went with her for her next prenatal appointment, so he could ask any questions he might have in preparation for their baby's birthday. Now that he was getting an early glimpse at the facility with all of Charlotte's family present, however, he didn't feel like he could ask any of the questions he already had for the doctor, nurses, and facility staff, which was causing some serious trepidation about making a misstep on this visit.

Since Charlotte didn't want to tell anyone about the baby until after the first trimester, he knew he had to limit his outward show of interest in all things baby related with her whole family around. It was hard enough that she hadn't wanted to make any kind of announcement that they were dating, but not broadcasting to the world that the woman he loved was carrying his baby was starting to seem like an impossible task for Ian.

Oh, she was okay for them to admit they were dating if someone outright asked about their relationship. But she didn't want him to do anything "showy" to make their love evident to the world because she knew it would cause her mother to gloat even more than she already was about being right in trying to push them together.

Yeah, it's going to be monumentally hard not to make our baby announcement this evening with everyone talking about the other babies being born in the Burleson family over the next few months.

Ian just hoped he could keep his elation at being the father of one of those babies from showing on his face as they walked down the hall to where everyone was gathering outside Kay's hospital room.

"What's going on? Why is everyone in the hallway?" Charlotte looked around between her family members and friends who were standing in the hallway.

"The doctor's in with Anthony, Kay, and Sam right now," Hazel explained as more of Charlotte's family arrived behind them.

There were a couple of conversations going on as the information was relayed to each new person who arrived, but most of the people in the hallway kept the noise down so as not to disturb any of the other patients there at the time. Brody released Ian's hand to go sit and quietly play with Antonio, Maria, Tia, and Britney. Britney was Rick's daughter and would be walking back up the aisle with Charlotte at Rick and Fiona's wedding, since she was her father's best girl instead of Rick having a best man.

Maybe Brody can be my best man if I can convince Charlotte to marry me. Then Rick won't have any reason to want to kick my ass if Charlotte picks Fiona as her matron of honor.

After they'd had a couple of arguments over the whole living together situation, Ian was starting to realize that he was going to have to bite the bullet and agree to move onto the ranch if he ever wanted her to say yes to his proposal. Since he finally decided to give up his prideful way of thinking that he had to be the sole provider for their family, it was just a matter of figuring out how to pop the question that was preventing them from beginning their move.

He didn't have long to ponder the possibilities that he'd been coming up with recently, though, as the doctor opened the door and invited them all back into the room.

"Wow, ya'll weren't joking when you said only half of your family was in the room earlier," the doctor chuckled as she walked through the crowd in the hallway.

"At least we're mostly quiet and respectful of sleeping newborns," Bobby shrugged, grinning at the doctor as she walked past him wend Brooklyn.

"And I texted the rowdy GWA crew to tell them to wait until they're home with the baby to visit, so you won't be overrun with twice as many friends popping up here tonight," Rick added.

Ian didn't hear the doctor's reply as he was carried away by the herd of Burlesons starting to push forward to enter Kay's room. Once inside, Ian stepped over to the side of the room, trying to stay out of the way as the women of the family crowded around Kay's bed to see the baby.

He hadn't been wrong when he thought the conversation would turn to the other babies being born into Charlotte's family in the near future. With Amy starting to show early, she and Justin had announced to their family that they were expecting twins at the beginning of December. They'd shared their joyous news the weekend after Charlotte and Ian found out they were expecting, which he thought was part of what prompted Charlotte to want to wait to make their announcement.

After filling in the family members and friends who hadn't been there earlier to hear the discussion about baby Sam's name, Kay warned Amy to ask Justin's motivations while picking baby names.

"I don't think we have to worry about that," Amy laughed, shaking her head at Kay's warning to make sure Justin didn't pick a name after a musician or video game designer without telling Amy. "We're naming our children after family members."

"Oh, you already have names picked out?" Susan beamed at her son and future daughter-in-law.

"Yeah, if we have boys, they'll be Jerry Thomas and Jonah David," Justin replied to his mother.

"And if we have girls, they'll be Judy Shanae and Mary Renee," Amy added.

"Oh, ya'll weren't there when Char claimed the name Judy for her daughter!" Becky exclaimed, shaking her head at the names Amy and Justin picked for their children if they had daughters.

Shit! Has she already told her sister about our baby? Ian darted his eyes over at Charlotte, trying to figure out from her panicked expression if he should step up and tell everyone about the baby or not.

"When did Char claim a baby name?" Hazel questioned her daughters, looking back and forth between Becky and Charlotte.

"Back when we helped Anthony and Kay move." Becky waved her mom's question off as if it didn't matter. "It was first thing that morning, when we were packing the kitchen. So Justin was upstairs with the guys breaking down the beds, and Amy hadn't arrived yet. That's why ya'll missed it."

Wait! She wasn't even pregnant when they moved, so why would she claim the name then?

"She said Memmaw came to her in a dream and told her about her first born being a girl," Becky explained as if she'd heard Ian's mental question, chuckling. "So if the dream comes true, then she's gonna name the baby Judy for Memmaw proving her wrong about prophetic dreams."

"Oh." Amy turned to look at Justin. With her head turned, Ian couldn't see her expression, but he could hear the slight quiver in her voice that indicated she was worried about upsetting Charlotte with her choice of baby names. "Do we need to pick a different girl's name?"

"No, don't do that," Charlotte objected, her slightly higher voice the only indication she was uncomfortable with the conversation. "Obviously, you're going to have babies before me, so if you have girls, by all means name one of them Judy. I have plenty of time to pick something else."

"Are you sure?" Amy looked skeptical as she glanced back and forth between Charlotte and Justin.

"Yes, I'm positive." Charlotte gave Amy a reassuring smile. "Besides, I can always give my future daughter the middle name that Memmaw and I share."

Yeah, Carol Anne sounds just as good to me as Judy Carol. Ian smiled reassuringly at Charlotte, wondering if she was thinking of the same possible baby name.

"Who knows?" Justin filled the silence that suddenly surrounded them. "Maybe we'll find out we're having boys at the next ultrasound, and us having similar name ideas for girls won't matter."

"Let's hope so, Cuz." Bobby slapped a hand on Justin's shoulder. "Since Mary is one of our top name picks since we found out we're having a girl. And since our baby is due before yours…"

"Don't listen to him," Brooklyn cut him off, pointing at Bobby with her thumb. "He ruled out Mary Madeline because he doesn't want our daughter to be picked on in school for such a biblical-sounding name. So, we're going with Madeline Hazel and calling her Maddie."

Thankfully, Bobby and Brooklyn took the spotlight off of Charlotte with their announcement. Hazel couldn't take the conversation back to the prospect of Charlotte expecting to have a daughter, when she was too busy beaming about having a granddaughter named after her.

Ian, however, couldn't stop thinking about Charlotte having their child already growing inside her. When she took her turn holding baby Sam, Ian could only stare in awe, imagining the day he'd see her holding their newborn for the first time.

Fuck! I can't wait that long for us to move in together and start living as a family. I have to come up with a perfect proposal idea ASAP.

When Brody and Antonio stood on either side of Charlotte looking down at baby Sam in her arms, Ian suddenly had an epiphany of how he should propose.

Surely we can sit off away from the rest of her family for the fireworks on Thursday, especially if some of them are occupied with the new baby in the family and stay on the ranch instead of going to the town celebration. And I have plenty of time to talk to Brody between now and then, so he can ask her to be his mom at the same time I ask her to be my wife.

Damn, I can't wait to marry my sweet Charlotte and fill our house with the love and laughter of a few little Burleson-Campbells.

~~~

Thursday, July 4, 2019

Charlotte wasn't sure why Ian thought they needed to move to the other side of City Hall from where their families had gathered for the Independence Day picnic to have a better view of the fireworks display. With the town's fireworks show being shot off the top of the tallest building in town by the licensed pyrotechnics who worked for the fire department, the large aerial explosions could be seen from as far away as the main cluster of houses on the Burleson Ranch. So, she didn't see any reason to go to the side of the building with the fewest people to be able to see it. But when Brody insisted he wanted to go sit where he could see the fire trucks, which were parked at the back of the building in case they were needed for the fireworks, she couldn't disappoint him by refusing to move with him and Ian.
~~~

"Is this good?" Char pointed to a grassy spot away from the crowd and as close to the barricade nearest the fire trucks as she felt comfortable sitting.

"Perfect!" Ian announced, setting down the cooler and spreading out the quilt he'd carried around from where they'd been seated on the other side of the building.

"Hey, Char," Ridge Deere hollered from his post by one of the fire trucks. As a fireman with the Heart's Destiny Fire Department, he was one of the crew on standby, in case there was a fireworks mishap during the show. Ridge was a year younger than his brother Ryder, the middle school physical education teacher, and the same age as Charlotte. She'd had a little bit of a crush on him in high school, but he'd never shown an interest in her because her brothers and cousins had made it known that all the Burleson girls were off-limits to all their friends. "Whatcha doin' over here instead of at the cookout?"

"Brody wants to be able to see ya'll in action, if your coworkers set City Hall on fire by screwing up the fireworks," Charlotte yelled back, pointing at Brody beside her on the blanket as she joked with Ridge.

"Sorry, little man, we've got the chief up there this year, so I don't think we'll have to do much more than sit back and watch the show." Ridge waved at Brody without leaving his post. "But if you want to see the trucks up close, have Char and your dad bring you to the station when I'm on duty, and I'll let you help me wash 'em."

"Cool!" Brody bounced with excitement at the prospective activity. "Can we, Dad?"

"Sure," Ian agreed with a chuckle. "But we've got a lot going on this weekend, so we'll have to get with Ridge later to plan when we can go to the station."

They didn't have much of a chance to continue talking as the fireworks display started. They ended up laying down, with Charlotte and Brody both using Ian's arms as pillows, so they could see the fireworks without straining their necks.

They "oohed" and "aahed" at the display, pointing out each of their favorite colors and styles of the mortars being shot off from the top of the building. It was another of those times when Charlotte felt like they were spending time together as a family, and could really picture repeating the experiences for years to come with at least four more children in their expanding family.

Leah Mae Wright

If I ever want to actually have that big family with Ian, maybe I should quit being so stubborn and agree to move off the ranch to live with him in town. I guess it's not that big a deal to have to drive a few miles to spend time with our extended family or go for a horseback ride.

She didn't have enough time to devise a way to tell Ian that she'd be willing to move into his rental before the fireworks ended. Char sat up, thinking it was time to pick everything up and head home. But apparently, Ian and Brody had other ideas.

When they sat up, the two of them turned to her as they each went up on one knee. Charlotte was really confused when they each took one of her hands, Ian her left and Brody her right. "What are ya'll doin'?"

Ian grinned at the way her Texan accent overrode her English teacher enunciation, but he didn't point it out the way he had several times over the last six months. "We have a couple of questions for you before we take you home tonight."

"Oh?" Charlotte wasn't sure what Ian might ask with Brody as a witness. *If the look on Brody's face is any indication, they're probably going to ask if I can sweet-talk Nana Marie into opening up the Creamarie for a late-night ice cream cone before we go home.*

"You have to go first, Dad," Brody prodded, reaching over with his free hand to poke his father in the side.

"Sorry, I just got excited and forgot the whole speech I had prepared," Ian chuckled self-deprecatingly.

"Yeah, you really shouldn't give up your day job to be an actor," Charlotte quipped, thinking back to their semi-failed attempt at role-play the month before. "Remembering your lines is kind of vital, so you wouldn't even make it past the initial audition for one of Becky's productions."

"Good thing I have no intention of auditioning for one of Becky's productions, either at the local theater or for the movies," Ian laughed, smiling, and wagging his eyebrows to show he recognized her reference to their previous conversation about his acting ability. "Although, if you want to consider the last few months as my audition for the role I really want for the rest of my life, then I hope I've lived up to your standards."

What role is he talking about?

Charlotte didn't get a chance to figure it out as Ian went on. "I love you. I fell head over heels for you the night we met, and just keep falling more and more each day. I want to spend the rest of my life in the role of your husband and the father of your children. Charlotte Anne Burleson, will you do me the honor of becoming my wife? Will you marry me?"

"Oh, Ian," Char choked out the words, happy tears filling her eyes.

"And will you adopt me and be my mom?" Brody added before Charlotte could get the "yes" to pass her lips.

"Yes!" Charlotte squealed, the happy tears pouring down her face. "Yes, to both of you." She turned to look at Ian first. "I'll marry you." She then turned her head to look at her soon-to-be son. "And yes, I'll adopt you and be your mom."

She was engulfed in the four arms of the Campbells, whose name she would soon share. As her arms went around both Ian and Brody, she turned her head to meet Ian's lips, kissing her fiancé to seal their engagement.

She was lost in the kiss until Brody pulled out of the hug. "Wait, Dad! You forgot the ring!"

Charlotte chuckled as they pulled back from their embrace, so Ian could stick his hand in his pocket. "Brody, I'm officially putting you in charge of making sure your dad shows up for the wedding, since he's getting so forgetful in his old age."

"Don't worry, Princess," Ian retorted, grinning as he pulled a box from his pocket. "I'll remember to show up for the wedding. But we should probably stick to traditional vows instead of writing our own, unless you're okay with me reading them from a cheat sheet during the ceremony."

"I'm cool with traditional," Charlotte grinned back. "But you might want to practice saying *'I do'* for the next couple of months, so you don't forget what to say in that traditional ceremony."

"I think I can handle *'I do'*," Ian winked as he opened the box in his hand to reveal a princess cut solitaire on a gold band. "But don't make me wait too long to say it."

"Yeah, about that." Charlotte held out her hand for Ian to put the ring on her finger. "I'm going to have to check with Fiona this weekend to find out the exact dates she'll be home for their next holiday break, so we can plan all our wedding festivities then. That's why I said you have a couple of months, because I know it will be around Labor Day."

And hopefully, I'll still be able to fit into the style of dress I want by then.

"Around Labor Day sounds perfect to me," Ian agreed, giving her another peck of a kiss before they all stood to pack up, since the rest of the crowd already seemed to have dispersed.

"Wait! This is why you wanted to sit on this side of the building." Charlotte grabbed Ian's arm as he picked up the cooler, causing the melted ice and cans of soda inside to slosh. "Because you knew I wouldn't want a big production in front of my family."

"Of course, Princess." Ian grinned, draping the quilt over the cooler. "Although, I do think we should invite your parents out to dinner to tell them. We need to take them someplace fancy, and I need to be the one to pay for it, so they know I'm not after your money when we move onto the ranch."

"They won't think that," Charlotte started, then realized how he'd finished his statement. "Wait! You're moving onto the ranch?"

"Yeah," Ian nodded and shrugged. "That is where you want to live. And I intend to live with my wife and family, so we're moving onto the ranch just as soon as you can get me out of my lease with the Walkers."

"Oh, I see how you are," Charlotte playfully teased Ian. "You don't want my money, but you want my ability to sweet talk the Walkers into letting you out of your lease."

"What can I say?" Ian shrugged with a little half-grin. "They like you better than they like me. So, if you ask, I'll be able to move before January."

"Fine, but you get to tell my parents that you asked me to marry you without asking for my hand first."

"I can do that," Ian agreed confidently.

Yeah, I should probably warn him about how Daddy scares off any guys who dare to step foot on the ranch with the intention of dating me or Becky with his shotgun. But what fun would that be?

~ ~ ~

Ian wasn't sure why Charlotte vetoed his idea to take her parents out for a fancy dinner to tell them about their engagement. *Yeah, they'd figure out something was up when we showed up in our Sunday best to take them to dinner on a Friday night, but they're still going to know something's up when it's just the four of us eating dinner at her house, too.*

But Ian didn't want to start off his engagement by arguing with his fiancée, so he went along with her plan to dress casually and let her cook their meal. Remembering back to the conversation he'd had with Charlotte's parents the night his house was broken into by the cartel, Ian realized he'd probably made a misstep by not telling Bob his intentions before proposing.

Fuck! Hopefully, the fact that I told him I love her back in March will be an acceptable declaration of my intentions, so he won't be too upset by the fact that I didn't ask for her hand.

Not that his realization would do him any good when he hadn't thought about how old-fashioned her parents were until he was driving to the ranch for dinner with them the day after he proposed to their daughter.

Fuck! And with Charlotte not wanting to tell anyone about the baby until after the first trimester, I can't even use the news of another grandchild to soften the blow.

Ian nervously punched in the code to the gate to get onto the ranch, and drove over to park in Charlotte's driveway. He got out of his Range Rover just as her parents walked up from the direction of the hay barn.

Maybe this conversation won't be so bad if they're nice and relaxed after getting frisky in the loft the way Charlotte and I did a couple of weeks ago. Ian smiled at the memory, hoping it looked friendly and not as lascivious as his mental vision of Charlotte laid out on a horse blanket in the hay loft.

"Oh, Ian," Hazel greeted him with a one-armed hug. "Char didn't tell us you'd be comin' for dinner."

"Yeah…" Ian returned her embrace, pulling back quickly to shake Bob's hand before they all walked toward the house. "I'm looking forward to learning how much of your culinary talent Charlotte inherited."

"She's a fair hand in the kitchen." Hazel smiled as they walked into the house without knocking. "But I don't know how much of it is inherited, so much as a learned trait, since I actually learned to cook from Bob's mom."

"Memmaw taught me how to cook, too." Charlotte joined their conversation, even though he didn't think she'd heard his portion of it when they were still outside.

"Yep, just like I'll teach your young'uns to cook one of these days." Hazel smiled as she hugged Charlotte in greeting.

Ian wished he could get in on the affectionate greetings with Charlotte, yearning to kiss her even if he had to keep it chaste with her parents as an audience. But with Bob and Hazel standing in between them, and Charlotte turning to pull a pan from the stove, he didn't get a chance for even a half-hug, much less the kiss he wanted to lay on her.

"The table's already set, if ya'll want to wash up and have a seat," Charlotte called out as she straightened to lift a roast out of the oven.

"Can I help you carry anything to the table?" Ian hoped offering to help her would give him a moment alone with her while her parents took their seats at the dining room table.

"No, I've got it." Charlotte smiled as she passed him, carrying the large pan full of roast, potatoes, and carrots into the dining room.

Her parents excused themselves to go wash up after feeding the horses, giving Ian the opportunity to swoop in for that kiss as soon as she sat the pan down on the table.

As soon as their lips touched, he almost forgot why they were there from being so lost in her taste and the feel of her in his arms. Bob clearing his throat as he and Hazel stepped back into the room was the only reason Ian finally stopped kissing Charlotte.

Ian quickly washed his hands in the kitchen sink before they took their seats. Bob said grace, and they started dishing up their plates before an awkward silence settled over the room. Ian wasn't sure what to say to lighten the mood in the room and get the conversation off on the right foot.

"Should I have brought my shotgun to this dinner?" Bob finally broke the silence for him, arching an eyebrow as he looked back and forth between Ian and Charlotte.

Remembering the stories Charlotte's brothers had told him about Bob sitting on the front porch cleaning his gun every time a boy came to pick up Charlotte or Becky for a date when they were teenagers, Ian grinned as he bent to remove his thirty-eight from his ankle holster. "I've got us covered for weaponry," Ian quipped as he placed the gun down on the table beside his plate, making sure it was aimed away from everyone seated at the table.

"Damn, boys are gettin' too smart. Using my own tactics against me," Bob chuckled as the ladies both laughed. "I suppose this means ya'll've got somethin' to tell us?"

"Yes, sir," Ian smiled, reaching over to take Charlotte's hand, and realizing she wasn't wearing her engagement ring. *Probably to keep anyone from guessing before we could tell them.* "We're getting married."

"Oh, goodness!" Hazel gushed, covering her mouth with both hands.

"Nice touch with having your gun to ensure you get my blessing," Bob chuckled again. "Congratulations. Though I'll feel more comfortable welcoming you to the family once you put your peashooter away."

"This is not how I expected this conversation to go," Charlotte laughed as Ian put his gun back in the holster.

"Do you have a date picked out? Oh, and let me see the ring. Or do you even have a ring since this was such a surprise?" Hazel babbled excitedly, not giving them a chance to respond to the first question before she continued.

"We're thinking the week of Labor Day, so Fiona can be my matron of honor." Charlotte covered the first of Hazel's questions, while Ian addressed the second.

"Yes, I gave her a ring last night." Ian looked pointedly at Charlotte's bare left hand. "But I'm not sure why she's not wearing it now."

"I put it in my jewelry box this morning after searching for fifteen minutes to find it in my bed where it slipped off in the middle of the night," Charlotte explained as she stood to go get the ring. "I'm going to have to take it to be resized before I can wear it."

"The week of Labor Day, I can work with that." Hazel pulled her phone out of her back pocket and pulled up her calendar app while Charlotte walked to her room to bring the ring back to show them. "Labor Day is the second of September, so we can do your wedding shower on the first. Do you want to get married the following Saturday or Sunday?"

"Saturday," Charlotte answered as she walked back into the room and held the ring out to her mother. "So we aren't having to rush to get ready between services at church, the way we're going to be this weekend for Fiona's wedding."

"Oh, how beautiful," Hazel fawned over the ring for a moment before handing it back to Charlotte and looking at the calendar again. "So, we'll do the wedding on the seventh, with the rehearsal and rehearsal dinner on the sixth. Who all do I need to get measurements from for the wedding party?"

"I'm thinking Fiona and Becky." Charlotte took her seat and placed the ring on the table between her plate and Ian's. He picked it up and turned to unclasp her necklace, sliding the ring on the chain so she could wear it without losing it until she could get it resized. "Oh, and Maria as our flower girl, with Brody as our ring bearer."

"Oh, I guess that means I can't make him my best man." Ian wasn't sure if Rick would be okay with Fiona walking back down the aisle with any of the other groomsmen he was planning on having in the wedding. "Rick won't want to pull Trent or Jake into the ring for walking Fiona back up the aisle, will he?"

"Depends on how flirty your friend Trent gets," Charlotte teased, grinning at him, and adjusting her necklace, so the ring hung in the center.

"We'll pair her with Jake, so we know he won't be too flirty," Hazel decided, making notes on her phone. "I'll need Trent's contact information to get his measurements for the tuxes. Are they the only two groomsmen you had in mind?"

"I was actually thinking Trent, Jake, and Josh," Ian admitted. "But that was when I thought Charlotte would pick out at least four bridesmaids and Brody would be my best man."

"And I thought you'd only pick Trent and Cait to stand up with you, so I narrowed it down to two." Charlotte rolled her eyes. "Guess we should have discussed it a little more last night."

Damn, I probably should have thought of asking Cait. Ian cringed, feeling guilty for not thinking outside the typical gender lines for wedding attendants and excluding his sister. "Could we have Cait as your third bridesmaid to even things up?" *And maybe pair her up with Josh, so she doesn't want to kick my ass for not including her?*

"Perfect!" Hazel exclaimed, not giving Charlotte a chance to state her opinion. "We'll pair Cait with Josh and Becky with Trent, so we don't have brother and sister walking down the aisle together."

And so Hazel can get in some more matchmaking. Ian looked at Charlotte, waiting for her to decide who would actually be her third bridesmaid.

"Sounds good to me," Charlotte nodded after swallowing a bite of her food. She looked directly at her mother and smiled mischievously. "Now we just need to know how far along you've gotten in finding everything from my wedding book, so I can pick out other options if those aren't still available."

"Oh, it's all still available." Hazel waved a hand through the air as if she was circling everything in Charlotte's wedding book. "The dresses might not be exactly like the ones you originally picked out, but they're extremely close. So close that I don't think you'll change your mind about them once you see them. And now that we have a date set, I just need everyone's measurements to order everything."

They continued chatting while they finished eating, moving on to discuss their living arrangements before going back to wedding planning, so Charlotte didn't have to get up again to go get her wedding book. Ian was surprised at how amenable the Burlesons were to his sister moving into the house that Charlotte was currently living in, with Charlotte, Ian, and Brody moving into the house next door to theirs, until a bigger house could be built on the ranch for their family.

Now I just have to convince Caitir that she's ready to live by herself again. Hopefully, it won't be too difficult since she'll be surrounded by the whole Burleson family and won't really be alone.

~~~
~~~

Sunday, July 7, 2019

Char wasn't sure what Fiona and Rick were thinking when they opted to have their parents sit at the head table with them instead of their wedding party, but she was glad to be able to join Ian at one of the cluster of tables where their families were seated for the majority of the wedding reception. She only had to get up and go to the microphone stand being used by the band when it was time for her to give her toast to the newlyweds.

Ian leaned over and kissed her cheek when she returned to the table, whispering in her ear. "Are we going to release our wedding party to sit with the other guests, too, so Rick and Fiona can sit together at our wedding reception?"

"Oh, geez, I didn't even think of that being the reason they chose to have their families up there instead." Charlotte stopped herself short from announcing that her pregnancy brain was to blame for her lack of mental clarity, not wanting to explain her reason for choosing the sparkling grape juice for all the toasts to the three of her brothers at her table or the rest of her family at the tables around them. "Yeah, we probably should, but I think I'd rather it just be you, me, and Brody at the head table, instead of having my parents up there with us."

"We can do that," Ian agreed, grinning. "But it'll most likely just be the two of us, since Brody will probably ditch us to go sit with his cousins like he did tonight."

Char laughed when she realized Brody's seat was already vacant. She looked around, and sure enough, Brody was sitting at the table to their left with his four cousins, Anthony, Kay, Memmaw Hazel, and Pappaw Bob.

Look at me thinking like a mom already and referring to my parents as Memmaw and Pappaw for my kids. That transition happened faster than I expected.

"I can't believe Kay feels up to being out and about like this so soon after having a C-section," Brooklyn sighed when she noticed Charlotte looking at the table where Kay was sitting. "I'm exhausted just carrying Maddie around, and she's not even born yet."

"Don't worry, Brie-Baby, you'll bounce back just as quick. That's one of the benefits of being a Burleson," Bobby chuckled as he leaned over and kissed his wife's temple, leaving his arm around her shoulders as he pulled back. "Once the baby's born, you can focus on recovering 'cause there's always a half dozen of us around to carry the baby while you get your energy back."

"And even when some of us have to head back out of town for work, Mom will always be there to babysit whenever you need a break," Jake added, nodding his head at Hazel holding baby Sam, so Anthony and Kay could have time to eat their dinner. "And if ya'll can get in there with Anthony and Kay to keep her distracted with grandkids at events like this, maybe she'll be too busy to pull any matchmaking mischief on the rest of us."

"Is that how ya'll got to sit here with us instead of being paired up with a couple of the single ladies in town?" Bobby arched an inquisitive eyebrow at the twins.

"Yep," Jake replied at the same time Josh shook his head in the negative.

"Cait's one of the single ladies in town," Josh pointed out, tilting his head in Cait's direction, where she was seated beside him.

"Yeah, but Cait's on the ranch all the time now, so she's like another sister," Jake disagreed with Josh.

"You realize having Brie on the ranch all the time was the ploy Ma used to match us up, right?" Bobby looked at Jake like he couldn't believe his lack of common sense to see the repeat of the same matchmaking scheme. Charlotte had to agree with Bobby. While Jake was academically brilliant, their family often joked that Josh stole all his common sense in utero because of missing things like that. "And if she could get one of ya'll to move home and stay in the same house with Cait, she'd do it in a heartbeat."

"Maybe I should move into the spare room with Jen, Julie, and Becky, instead of moving into your house, Char," Cait piped up, looking nervously at Josh and Jake.

"If that's where you'd feel most comfortable, then I'm sure the girls would be glad to have you." Char smiled reassuringly at Cait, hoping her future sister-in-law didn't feel pressured by her mom to date one of her brothers.

"I'm surprised Ma hasn't already tried to talk you into moving into my old room at her house, so these two'll be right across the hall whenever they're home on leave." Bobby nodded his head at the twins while grinning at Cait.

"Oh, she's mentioned the abundance of empty bedrooms at her house," Cait giggled, relaxing a little at being included in the conversation about Hazel's conniving way of matchmaking. "But I pointed out how she needs to keep those bedrooms available for out-of-town guests whenever the GWA rents out the whole B and B."

"Smart thinking." Josh grinned, holding his hand up for a fist bump with Cait. "Way to keep Ma from matchmaking."

Cait giggled as she bumped her fist with Josh.

Huh? Maybe I was wrong about there not being any chemistry between Cait and one of my brothers.

Charlotte didn't have much time to ponder the potential for her mother and her matchmaking minions to capitalize on what she was seeing between Cait and Josh, as her thoughts and the conversation around the table were both cut short when the emcee called all the single ladies to the dance floor for the bouquet toss.

"Hey, where are you going?" Ian grabbed Charlotte's hand when she stood to participate. "You're not single anymore. You're engaged, so you don't need to try to catch the bouquet this time."

"Exactly, I'm engaged," Charlotte retorted, pulling her hand free while grinning mischievously at her fiancé. "Not married yet, so I still have time for another do-over before getting hitched."

Ian made a face as Charlotte smiled at him and sauntered off to join the group of ladies gathering on the dance floor. She inwardly giggled at teasing him by pretending to want to catch the bouquet, knowing she had no intention whatsoever of actually catching it.

"Let's show everyone how the heel women of the GWA fight dirty for what we want, even if it's just a bouquet." Charlotte couldn't remember the individual names of the women who wrestled with the team name of the Precious Stones to know who was speaking, but she recognized Allissa Walters, whom the Precious Stones dragged into the group, from the last wedding they'd attended in town, when she was one of Randi's bridesmaids.

"Yeah, I'm moving away from the two of you," Allissa laughed, stepping away from her friends to the side of the crowd. "I don't need an accidental elbow giving me a black eye before TV in two days!"

"Oh, I'm sticking with you," Charlotte chuckled, moving closer to Allissa and away from the fray. *Not only will being away from the ladies fighting for the bouquet be physically safer, but it'll also be less likely that I'll be close enough to catch it.* "Black eyes don't work for teaching middle school either."

Allissa nodded her agreement, while making faces at her friends a few feet away. They were all so busy making faces at one another, or in Char's case laughing at the silly antics of the women wrestlers, that they didn't see the actual bouquet toss until it almost struck Allissa in the face. Charlotte didn't think Allissa meant to catch it, but she kind of had to with it being thrown right at her.

"Guess you really are trying to avoid a black eye," Charlotte laughed.

"Yeah, I just didn't think it would be Fiona trying to give it to me," Allissa chuckled with her, as the ladies dispersed, so the single men could take their place on the dance floor.

When Charlotte got back to the table, Ian pulled her into his lap, wrapping her in his muscular arms, regardless of their audience. She slipped her arms around his broad shoulders, returning his public display of affection.

"We aren't going to any more weddings before ours," he grumbled before planting a claiming kiss on her lips.

Charlotte was definitely not disappointed that Ian missed out on the garter toss as their tongues tangled. She quickly got lost in the ardent exploration of one another's mouths, forgetting for a moment that they were surrounded by her family. Though her family was obviously surprised by their PDA, since it was more than she'd ever allowed before.

"Dude, I know ya'll are in love and all," Bobby groaned, tossing a balled-up napkin at them to break their kiss. "But I don't need to see you playing tonsil hockey with my sister."

"You guys have some weird sayings in Texas," Cait laughed, shaking her head at Bobby.

Char and Ian just looked at each other and shrugged, smiling at one another as Charlotte moved back to her own seat to watch as the bouquet and garter pictures were set up and taken.

Leah Mae Wright

"Hey, Darlin', you need to come back up for pictures," Dean hollered across the room, twirling the pink garter on his finger, and grinning at Allissa, as the crowd of men shuffled off the dance floor.

Allissa seemed to be reluctant to go back out on the dance floor for pictures, but she took the seat Philippe directed her toward. There were numerous catcalls from around the room, as Dean got down on one knee in front of Allissa at the direction of the photographer. He then placed the garter on Allissa's leg before turning and responding to the comments about when the two of them were getting married from a few of the guys.

"Yeah, well, if this means we're the next to get married, then ya'll can all plan to come back here for our wedding on our Labor Day break in September."

"Sorry, Dean. That week is already spoken for, so Fiona can be here as my matron of honor!" Charlotte shouted, unintentionally announcing her and Ian's engagement to the whole town. Though her family all knew, they hadn't intended to announce it to everyone else in town until after Rick and Fiona's big day, so as not to steal the spotlight at their wedding.

Though I don't really think a couple of boring school teachers can really steal the spotlight from the over-the-top showmanship of the GWA.

"Guess that means we'll have to plan a Thanksgiving wedding, Darlin'." Dean wagged his eyebrows suggestively at Allissa.

"I still don't understand why ya'll are in such a rush to get married that you can't schedule it for when we've already put in for leave time this year," Jake grumbled. "It's gonna be hard to get the extra time off with only two months' notice to our commanding officers, especially since we're both already planning to be off the last week of September to be here for the board meeting."

"Can't you just swap the last week of September for the first week?" Charlotte beseeched her brothers, worried that her dream wedding would be marred by one or both of them being absent. "You can always Skype in for the board meeting, but you can't Skype in for my wedding."

"Yeah, possibly," Josh smiled at Char. "As long as I'm not spun up for a short mission that week."

"Sorry, Sis, but we don't really have a choice about when we have to run an op," Jake apologized with a half-shrug. "But if you move the wedding to the end of September or the end of December, you know we'll both most likely be here since we put in for those leaves last year."

"But Justin and Amy are already planning their wedding for the end of December," Josh pointed out, shaking his head at Jake.

Charlotte could feel herself tearing up at the thought of her brothers not being able to be at her wedding, tuning out the conversation at the table about their schedules. It wasn't just because they were her brothers that she wanted them there. Ian also wanted the two of them to stand up with him as his groomsmen. Char had no clue whom he might substitute in their place if Jake or Josh couldn't make it.

But I'll already be at the end of the first trimester the first week of September. I can't push it back further than that or I'll risk not being able to fit in my dream wedding dress. I mean, I could get lucky and not really show until the fourth or fifth month like Brooklyn. But since I'm female, and twins are hereditary only in women, and Mom had twins, there's a pretty good chance that we could have twins. And if that's the case, then I'm more likely to show early like Amy.

"What's the matter, Princess?" Ian reached over and brushed a tear from Char's cheek that she hadn't even realized had slipped from her watery eyes.

"We can't wait any longer than the first week of September to have the wedding," Charlotte sobbed, leaning over into her fiancé's warm chest. "Or I might not fit in my wedding gown."

"Oh, sweet Charlotte, don't worry about that." Ian pulled her into his arms as she cried on his shoulder. "I'm sure the gown can be tailored to fit, even if you gain a few pounds between now and then."

"Not with the corset-style bodice on my dream wedding dress," Char wailed, lifting her head to look into Ian's azure blue eyes as her tears continued to flow uncontrollably. "I can't squeeze a baby bump into a corset, so we have to get married before I start showing."

"Okay, well, then we won't move the wedding date," Ian reassured her. "And if Jake and Josh can't be here, then I'll pick some different groomsmen."

"Did you say something about a baby bump?" Hazel appeared out of nowhere, hovering over Charlotte and Ian's chairs and still cradling baby Sam in her arms. "Are you gonna give me another grandbaby soon?"

Shit! Charlotte hadn't realized how loudly she'd spoken. "So much for not telling anyone until after the first trimester."

"I'm just glad it was you who spilled the beans and not me," Ian chuckled, grinning to try and get her to smile.

"It's still your fault for choosing my brothers as your groomsmen," Char quipped as she pulled back slightly to wipe her tears, resolving to laugh instead of cry about her inadvertent baby reveal.

"I'll make it up to you later, Princess," Ian promised, wagging his eyebrows as he released Charlotte, so she could turn and confirm what her mother clearly overheard.

"Yes, Mom, we're adding to the family in February."

"Oh my goodness!" Hazel squealed, drawing the attention of everyone in the room. "Did you hear that, Sammy? You're gonna have another cousin in February!"

"Geez, Ma, chill," Anthony chuckled, taking his son from Hazel's arms. "You're gonna bust Sam's eardrums, tryin' to announce your next grandbaby to the whole state of Texas."

Charlotte could only laugh as the rest of her family surrounded them to offer their congratulations. They were soon joined by more friends than Charlotte could believe she'd been blessed with, all to share in the joy of both of their unintentional announcements.

Guess Memmaw was right. I am actually going to get my happily ever after with Ian.

Epilogue

Charlotte couldn't believe the day had finally come when she would live out all her teenaged dreams for her wedding. She wasn't sure how her mother and the various merchants around town had managed to find current versions of the styles she'd picked fourteen years earlier as a high school freshman. But even if they weren't by the exact same designers whose photographs Charlotte had clipped from magazines to put in her wedding book back then, they were close enough to the originals that even she couldn't tell they were updated versions.

The whole day, she felt like Ian's Princess being pampered and primped by her friends, who she lovingly called the Glam Squad. They had arrived early that morning, kicking Ian and Brody out of the house they now shared next door to her parents and sending him across the driveway on the ranch to the house his sister was now occupying to get ready for the day, even though Cait left them there to join the other ladies for the Glam Squad's services. Though Lexi, Kayla, and Cassidy were all three providing nail, hair, and makeup services to the wedding party and the women of Charlotte's family, she made sure to sit in each of their chairs for the specialty service they each practiced daily.

First, Lexi had picked the perfect pearl nail polish for Charlotte's wedding day. Then Kayla had curled and pinned Charlotte's hair back in what she called a relaxed down-do instead of a traditional updo. Charlotte opted not to wear a veil, so she used bobby pins with little white flowers on the ends to accent the style. Finally, Cassidy had finished off Char's wedding day look with the perfect makeup job that looked natural but also wouldn't make her look washed out in any of the photos.

Leah Mae Wright

By the time everyone was through with the Glam Squad, Charlotte barely had time to peek into the chapel to see that all the decorations were perfectly in place before she had to go to the bride's room behind the baptismal to change into her wedding dress. She enjoyed a moment alone with Fiona, Becky, and Cait as they helped one another with fastening their dresses before her parents arrived with Maria, who was already wearing her flower girl dress and carrying the basket of flower petals.

Just as they were going through the final checklist to make sure everything was in place, and she had all her good luck tokens on her, Charlotte's phone buzzed with an incoming text from Ian.

Ian: Where are you? You're supposed to be at the church, but your tracker shows you still on the ranch.

Char: I left it at home because it didn't match the earrings I'm wearing today. But I'm here. All dressed up & ready to walk down the aisle. {Bride Emoji} {Groom Emoji}

Charlotte knew Ian would probably always need to know where she was after everything they'd been through earlier in the year, but she hoped he realized there were certain situations in life when she wouldn't be wearing the charm necklace he'd bought her and hidden a tracker inside. *And not always because it clashes with what I'm wearing. I'm pretty sure I'm not going to be allowed to wear it while giving birth, either. Or if I ever have to go into the hospital for surgery of any kind.*

Ian: After the baby is born, we're getting you a VCH piercing, so I can put a tracker in the jewelry nobody but me will ever see.

Charlotte burst out laughing at his silly plan, quickly typing out a reply.

**Char: Only if you get another piercing that also has a
tracker. {Eggplant Emoji}**

**Ian: Deal. Figured I need to add the one your dildo has,
so you don't ever have to choose between the 2.**

**Char: Wonder if the piercer can add to the dildo at the
same time? It might be nice to have it match you.**

**Ian: You need the dildo to match me, so you can take me
in your pussy & ass at the same time? If that's what
you want, then I'll gladly ask about piercing your dildo
to match me.**

"Are ya'll tryin' to get started on the honeymoon before the wedding?" Becky teased her sister, pointing to the phone in Char's hands.

"Something like that," Charlotte admitted, typing a quick message back before putting her phone in her purse.

**Char: Maybe? We'll have to talk more about that later,
though. I've got to go get married now. See you at the
end of the aisle. Love you! {Kiss Emoji}**

Ian: Can't wait. Love you, too, Princess! {Kiss Emoji}

Her mother gave her another quick hug and blubbered once more about what a beautiful bride she was before rushing out to take her seat, so they could get the wedding started. She walked out of the bridal suite on her father's arm, following Kathy Harrison and the rest of the ladies in the wedding party down the hallway to the vestibule, so she could line them up to enter the chapel.

"Don't be nervous, Sweetheart." Her father, Bob, patted her hand reassuringly as Maria stepped through the door to enter the chapel first. "Ian might not be much of a rancher, but he's a good man who'll do right by you and your babies."

"Thanks, Daddy." Charlotte leaned her head over to rest her cheek on her dad's bicep for a moment, appreciating the man who spent her whole life showing her what to look for in a partner and potential spouse, as they watched Cait take her turn stepping into the chapel. "And these jitters aren't nerves. More like excitement for starting the next stage of my life."

"That's good," Bob choked out. "But as your dad, I don't need to know about how Ian excites you."

Becky giggled in front of them as Fiona stepped through the door into the chapel. Charlotte stifled her own chuckles, though she couldn't suppress the smile that spread across her face as she caught a glimpse of Ian at the end of the aisle when the door opened for Becky to step through.

When the music changed to Richard Wagner's **Bridal Chorus** and the doors opened for Charlotte to walk down the aisle on her father's arm, she barely registered most of her surroundings. Her focus narrowed down to Ian standing at the end of the aisle with Brody by his side. If asked about it later, she'd have to refer to the photographs Philippe was taking to remember the positions of the bridesmaids and groomsmen. She only had eyes for the love of her life and the little boy who would legally be her son when they signed the adoption papers along with the certificate of marriage after the ceremony.

"Dearly beloved, we're gathered here today to join Michael Ian Campbell and Charlotte Anne Burleson in holy matrimony," Pastor Harrison began. "Who gives this woman to be married to this man?"

"Her mother and I." Bob leaned down and kissed Charlotte's cheek before shaking Ian's hand. He then placed Charlotte's hand in Ian's before stepping back to take his seat in the front row of the church.

"I love you," Ian mouthed as Pastor Harrison gave a speech about love and the sanctity of marriage.

"I love you," Char mouthed back, smiling at the love of her life as she eagerly awaited the point in the ceremony when she could say "I do" and become Mrs. Charlotte Anne Burleson-Campbell.

~~~
~~~

Man, wedding receptions are a lot more fun on this side of the ballroom, Ian thought as he sat through dinner and the various toasts given by the wedding party. *And now that she's the one tossing the bouquet, I won't have to hold Charlotte back to keep her from another do-over of catching one when the rest of our family and friends eventually get married.*

As they stood from the table to step over to the middle of the dance floor for the bouquet and garter toss, Hazel approached with a mischievous gleam in her eyes. "I just wanted to offer you a few suggestions of who to aim for," she started as she pulled them into a simultaneous hug. "I'm thinking either Cait and Josh, Jake and Kara, Jen and Liam, or Julie and Dion."

"Mom, I'm not going to aim for anyone," Charlotte protested, even as she returned her mother's one-armed hug.

"And I know that the secret to a happy life is a happy wife, so I'm going to follow my bride's lead on this one." Ian grinned and winked at Charlotte before leaning down to hug her mother and whisper, "But I'll keep your pairings in mind when I toss the garter after seeing who catches the bouquet."

Charlotte shook her head and rolled her eyes, obviously hearing his whispered words to Hazel. "You're not really going to throw the garter at Mom's pick for whoever catches the bouquet, are you?"

Ian waited until Hazel was far enough away that she couldn't hear him before replying. "With those four couples as options, sure. Since none of them are in the same town long enough to actually date, much less get married, I don't think it will matter to any of them. Besides, I want to be a good son-in-law. And what better way to do that than to let your mom think I'm helping her with her matchmaking plans?"

"I'm not sure if you're just sucking up to her to keep getting extra desserts at Sunday supper, or if you've secretly joined her matchmakers' club," Charlotte chuckled as they made their way across the dance floor to where the emcee was standing to direct them for tossing the bouquet and garter.

As the single ladies spread out between the newlyweds and the reception tables, Charlotte turned her back to them, looking up at Ian and grinning. "Just because I'm married and a momma now, doesn't mean I have to join the Matchmaking Mommas. So, I'm going to make sure nobody can accuse me of targeting them by looking at my hubby instead of where I'm tossing the bouquet."

Charlotte pushed up on her tiptoes and pecked her lips on Ian's. Then, without warning, she took a step back from him to make sure she had room for her straight arms to swing without hitting him, and tossed the bouquet backwards over her head.

Ian had to chuckle at her mischievous grin, watching his beautiful bride's face instead of looking to see who caught the bouquet, though he knew it was his sister from the shouting of the crowd. "I suppose you want me to toss the garter the same way. Huh, Princess?" Ian arched an eyebrow at Charlotte, who nodded her head in agreement.

"Yeah, I've got a better idea." Ian grinned at her before turning and calling Brody over to help him. Brody ran over from the table where he was sitting as Charlotte sat down in the chair that suddenly appeared on the dance floor. "Want to help me toss the garter?"

"Yeah!" Brody bounced with excitement, slipping on the dance floor in the shoes he wore with his tuxedo to match his father.

"Okay, yeah, you do have a better idea." Charlotte grinned as Ian went down on one knee in front of her and lifted the hem of her wedding gown up to just above her knees, so he could see to remove the garter.

"Oh, I like the way Ian does this," someone shouted from the group of guys gathering on the dance floor. "It's way better with a little leg showing."

"Hey, those are my sister's legs," Josh barked toward where the Walkers were congregated on the dance floor. "And you'd better not be looking at them."

"Dude, it's not a big deal." Aiden held up his hands in surrender toward Josh. "All the girls show off more leg than that every summer in their short shorts."

"Doesn't matter if a girl is wearing short shorts that show off her legs or not," Jake interjected. "You don't get to look unless a lady asks you to, so avert your eyes."

"How about you hurry this up, hubby?" Charlotte suggested, "so we don't have a riot on our hands before you can toss the garter."

"As you wish, wifey." Ian winked at Charlotte as he removed the azure blue garter from just above her knee and lowered her dress back to the floor. He gave her a quick peck as he stood back up. Then turned and picked Brody up, handing him the garter.

"How am I supposed to throw it? And who am I throwing it to?"

"Shoot it like a rubber band," Ian suggested.

"No, you throw it like a baseball," Charlotte protested, jumping up out of the chair, and stopping Brody from looping it around one finger the way Ian had taught him to shoot Cait with the hair bands she left laying everywhere. "I can't believe you taught him to shoot people with rubber bands." Charlotte shook her head and glared at Ian. "That's going to get him in trouble in school next year."

"No, Mom, we only shoot rubber bands at Aunt Cait when she doesn't put them back in the bathroom," Brody informed her.

"That'll still get you on Santa's naughty list," Charlotte warned Brody. "You should pick them up and put them away for her instead."

"Okay," Brody shrugged, not seeming to care for the life lesson. "Who am I throwing the garter to?"

"Uncle Josh," Ian suggested, grinning at Charlotte.

"Just close your eyes and throw it," Charlotte countered. "That way it'll be a surprise to see who catches it."

Ian turned his back to the group of guys gathered to catch the garter, watching Brody's face as he closed his eyes. Ian couldn't stop the chuckle when his son partially opened his eyes to look around before he actually threw the garter toward the crowd.

"Oh, aren't you a cutie," Philippe gushed as Ian turned around to see that his son had tossed the garter to a kid he didn't recognize, who was standing at the edge of the group. "Come on up here for the pictures and bring your dad to be in it with you."

"I'm, uh, here to meet my dad." The little boy, who looked to be about eight or nine years old, tentatively stepped forward, looking around like he wasn't sure where his parents were in the room.

"What's your name?" Ian knelt down, placing Brody on the floor beside him, and hoping having his son by his side would help ease the child's obvious anxiety.

"His name's Josh," Brody answered for the kid. "We were playing before, while ya'll were taking pictures. You said to throw the garter to Josh, so I threw it to him."

"I said to throw it to Uncle Josh," Ian explained. "I didn't know you knew anyone else named Josh."

"Is your uncle's name Josh Burleson?" The kid's eyes widened as he looked at Brody expectantly.

"Yeah," Brody nodded, turning to point at Charlotte's brother, Josh. "He's right over there."

"Oh my goodness! He looks just like our Josh when he was a little boy." Hazel squealed and covered her mouth with her hand, as the little boy turned and walked up to Josh.

"I'm Joshua Jacob Jones."

Triple J! Ian seemed to realize whom the little boy was at the same time Charlotte and Josh came to the same conclusion. Charlotte squeezed his shoulder, placing her hand on him as if she needed him to hold her up for a moment. He took her hand in his, standing to take her in his arms as they watched the moment unfold when Josh met his son for the first time.

The child extended his hand to Josh to shake. "And I think you're my dad."

Next in Heart's Destiny

Joshin' Around

Heart's Destiny Book 6

Lt. Josh Burleson was known as the jokester of his family due to his penchant for finding the humor in life to help him deal with the darker aspects he saw in his job. Raised on the family ranch, he'd been taught to work hard and play harder. And his playtime wasn't limited to just joshin' around with his family and friends.

As a Navy SEAL, he wasn't lacking when it came to available women to spend his nights with when he wasn't off on a mission. With him also being one of the Burleson bachelors, it wasn't just the frog hogs who chased after him. As a single guy, he'd had more than his fair share of one-night stands, starting with the buckle bunnies who offered themselves up back when he was a teenager competing in the team roping competitions of the rodeo with his twin, and ending when he met the woman that he fell in instalove with at Christmas.

As soon as Josh saw Cait walk into his childhood home for a late Christmas celebration, he fell head over heels for her. But after seeing the toll of military life paid by the relationships of his fellow SEALs, Josh knew he couldn't pursue anything with her until after his minimum service requirement was over. So Josh did the only thing he could do — he started a long-distance and leave-time friendship with Cait while making plans to get out of the Navy to move home and marry her.

Leah Mae Wright

While home during one of his leave times, Josh sent in a DNA sample to an online family tree site like the rest of his family. When the results came in, he saw an extra person listed as sharing fifty percent of his DNA in the Parent-Child section of his DNA match list on the site. Floored by the realization that he was a father, Josh had to put his plans to build a relationship with Cait on hold. He needed to settle the situation with his child, and his child's mother, before he could commit to moving home to pursue the lovely Cait.

Cait Campbell wasn't sure she'd ever feel comfortable going out and dating again after the trauma her family had endured over the past few years. Not only had her brother lost his first wife, but both he and Cait had been injured in the drive-by shooting that ended Mari's life. While her physical scars had long since healed, Cait wasn't so sure the internal ones that kept her trapped in her brother's house ever would.

When her brother had the idea of moving their family from San Diego to Texas, she developed high hopes of moving on with her life. Getting away from the cartel hub of the city and learning about life in a rural area seemed like just what she needed to move past her agoraphobia and start feeling social again. She even felt an instant attraction to one of the men she met during her first week in Heart's Destiny, Texas.

Then she found out their move was her brother's way of hunting down the head of the cartel, who had targeted them back in San Diego, and her fear of leaving the house came back tenfold. And even though the one man she'd been attracted to in the last two-and-a-half years was the same man who ultimately killed the leader of the cartel to set her free of her fear of another attack on her family, she still didn't think she could have more than a little light flirtation with Josh because of his dangerous career as a Navy SEAL.

When Josh's son showed up at the wedding reception for his sister and Cait's brother, they faced even more barriers to the relationship they both secretly craved. Could they come together to form an unconventional family? Or would all that joshin' around just lead to trouble and more heartbreak for Cait?

DISCLAIMER: This surprise Navy SEAL dad, friend's sister, instalove, alpha male, scared woman, cowboy romance book contains references to past gun violence, profanity, and graphic sex scenes, as well as multiple scenes with the hero rescuing kidnapping and rape victims alongside his fellow SEALs and family members. It is intended for adult readers (18+) who are not easily offended.

Next in the Galactic Wrestling Association

<u>*Dean's Darlin'*</u>

Galactic Wrestling Association Book 2

Dean Hunter enjoyed his life, living like a rock star while traveling the world, as one of the top stars of the Galactic Wrestling Association, after growing up with wealth and privilege in Heart's Destiny, Texas. He didn't have relationships with women because he was literally in a different city at least three-hundred days a year. But after his best friend lifted the ban on dating his sister, Dean was starting to wonder if he should act on the crush he'd had on her in high school.

He contemplated how to make a long-distance relationship with his best friend's sister work, until a week after the ban had been lifted. Then, when he saw the newest addition to the women's division of the GWA roster for the first time, Dean felt like he'd been struck by lightning. For the first time in his life, he understood what everyone in his hometown was talking about when they discussed instalove, and knew he didn't feel it for his high school crush because he fell instantly for the newest woman to join the GWA roster.

Allissa Walters grew up in a trailer park about an hour outside of Las Vegas. Raised by a single mom and surrounded by the other women who worked in the brothel across the road, she learned young not to trust men. With limited resources, she had to use her physical attributes to earn a living. But instead of stripping, or becoming a prostitute, like many of the women she knew growing up, Allissa took every modeling or acting gig she could find. She got lucky when one of her first gigs turned out to be as a ring girl for a mixed martial arts fight, and she caught the eye of a local fight promoter, who was looking for women to work in his independent wrestling promotion.

It took almost a year to save up the money from her modeling gigs to pay him to train her to become a professional wrestler. But from the first moment she stepped inside a squared circle, Allissa was hooked on the adrenaline of performing. She soaked up every lesson in the ring like a sponge, dreaming of the day she'd be good enough to work on bigger shows with a worldwide promotion.

She finally achieved her dream when she got a try-out match with the Galactic Wrestling Association. She signed a contract with them that night and took off traveling with the GWA the next day.

Unfortunately, dreams sometimes come true with a side dish of nightmares. She could handle the flirty, male wrestlers hitting on her. If she ignored them, they eventually backed off. She could even handle the booker who tried to get a little handsy. She was a trained fighter, after all, so spraining his wrist, as she got away from his hands, was simple. And more than enough to teach him to keep his hands to himself. But she wasn't sure what to do when she found herself the target of a stalker.

Dean was confused by what he'd done wrong to cause the woman of his dreams to hate him. But months after Allissa had come to work with the GWA, she was still doing everything she could to avoid him. None of his typical flirting techniques had worked. Neither had enlisting the help of the matchmaking women, who had recently paired off with his twin brother and best friend and now worked with Allissa closely enough to become her best friends. Even contriving situations to spend time with her had backfired.

But when Dean found out Allissa was in danger from a stalker, he was determined to protect her, whether she liked it or not. He just hoped there really was a fine line between love and hate, so maybe he could convince Allissa to cross it with him.

Leah Mae Wright
DISCLAIMER: This opposites attract, instalove, suspenseful, sports romance book contains threats from a stalker, gun violence during a kidnapping attempt, profanity, and graphic sex scenes. It is intended for adult readers (18+) who are not easily offended.

Books by Leah Mae Wright

Heart's Destiny Series

A Brief History of the Founding Families of the Fictional Small Town of Heart's Destiny, Texas – Free on Book Funnel
Courting Kay – Anthony Burleson and Kay Lee
Courting Kay Bonus Scenes
Wrestling with Randi – James Hunter and Randi Lee
Bobby's Bride – Bobby Burleson and Brooklyn Barns
Adoring Amy – Justin Burleson and Amy Lawton
Charlotte's Wedding – Ian Campbell and Charlotte Burleson
Joshin' Around – Josh Burleson and Cait Campbell
Dion's Dream Girl – Dion Davis and Julie Burleson
Destined for Deanna – JJ Burleson and Deanna Wolfe (Coming Soon)
Lights, Camera, Ashlyn – Darius Davis, Ashlyn Lawton, and Cade Starling (Coming Soon)

Galactic Wrestling Association Series

About The Author

Leah Mae Wright lives in Florida with her husband and fur babies. Her head has been filled with romantic stories for as long as she can remember, beginning with fairy tales as a small child growing up in Oklahoma and carrying through to countless ideas of her own throughout the years, as she has moved around to live in several different states. Now that her children are grown and life has slowed down, she's letting them out of her head, so they can join the libraries of her fellow fans of romance. Leah's literary world is a wonderful place that has no Covid, no real politicians, and a few unreal towns. Her favorite part about her characters living in her literary world is knowing that they are guaranteed a happily ever after.

You can keep up to date with Leah's future book plans at:
www.leahmaewright.com – Be sure to sign up for the Newsletter to receive emails about new releases, sales, and freebies.
www.facebook.com/LeahWrightAuthor
www.amazon.com/author/leah_wright
https://www.instagram.com/leahmaewrightauthor/
https://www.pinterest.com/LeahMaeWrightAuthor/

Leah Mae Wright

Provide your feedback to the author at:
Leah's Literary World Facebook Group
LeahWrightAuthor@gmail.com
Leah@LeahMaeWright.com

You can also review Leah's books on Amazon, Goodreads, Bookbub,
and Fictiondb.